T. E. (Thomas Edward) Bridgett

Our Lady's Dowry

T. E. (Thomas Edward) Bridgett

Our Lady's Dowry

ISBN/EAN: 9783741129995

Manufactured in Europe, USA, Canada, Australia, Japa

Cover: Foto ©Andreas Hilbeck / pixelio.de

Manufactured and distributed by brebook publishing software
(www.brebook.com)

T. E. (Thomas Edward) Bridgett

Our Lady's Dowry

OUR LADY'S DOWRY;

OR

How England gained and lost that Title.

A COMPILATION

BY THE

REV. T. E. BRIDGETT,

OF THE CONGREGATION OF THE MOST HOLY REDEEMER.

Permissu Superiorum.

LONDON: BURNS AND OATES,
Portman Street and Paternoster Row.
1875.

LONDON :
ROBSON AND SONS, PRINTERS, PANCRAS ROAD, N.W.

CONTENTS.

Contents.

PART III. DISLOYALTY.

OUR LADY'S DOWRY;

OR

How England gained and lost that Title.

INTRODUCTION.

'THE contemplation of the great mystery of the Incarnation,' wrote Thomas Arundel, Archbishop of Canterbury, in 1399, 'has drawn all Christian nations to venerate her from whom come the first beginnings of our redemption. But we English, being the servants of her special inheritance and her own Dowry, as we are commonly called, ought to surpass others in the fervour of our praises and devotions.'[1]

We learn, then, from the testimony of the highest ecclesiastical authority in England, making public appeal to well-known fact, that in the fourteenth century England was commonly called throughout Europe OUR LADY'S DOWRY.

There are some who think that this title is one of England's greatest glories. There are others who reckon it to her disgrace. To both the work I have undertaken to write ought to be of interest. It is not a work of controversy; it is not an apology. It is an historical investigation. I do not of course in any way disguise my own judgment on the matter. It has been a work of pride for me to bring to light so many proofs, as will be found in the following pages, of our forefathers' wisdom and

---

[1] Wilkins, *Concilia*, tom. iii. p. 246.

B

piety. It is also a tribute of devotion that I offer to the Mother of my Redeemer and my Creator. Yet I can say boldly that it is an impartial statement of facts. I began and continued my researches with the words of St. Bernard sounding in my ears : 'Virgo regia falso non eget honore, veris cumulata honorum titulis.' This royal Virgin stands in no need of spurious honours, loaded as she is with true titles to our veneration. I have therefore simply stated what I have found, and kept back nothing that could influence my reader's judgment as to the nature of the devotion which won for England the name of our Lady's Dowry.

I believe that a great part of what I have collected will be entirely new to most even of my Catholic readers. Our old writers are but little known, and in many cases such of their works as have been printed are rarely to be met with. They certainly do not deserve the oblivion into which they have fallen.

I have besides collected, from a large number of old volumes, illustrations of the various forms which devotion assumed in Catholic times. When these are brought together they become full of interest, and give a vivid picture of the modes of thought and manner of life of our ancestors. But it is evident that they must in a great measure be unknown to all but such as, like myself, have gone in search of them ; and I am not acquainted with any one who has hitherto taken this trouble, or, at least, has given his researches to the world.[2]

How far different would have been the case had the Virgin Mary been a pagan fiction instead of the Mother of the living God ! Then a hundred pens would have been occupied about her. No pains would have been deemed too great, no researches

[2] I do not forget *The Church of our Fathers*, by Dr. Rock, or *The Celebrated Sanctuaries of the Madonna*, by Dr. Northcote. Both these works supply many very interesting facts. But Dr. Rock treats of the devotion to the Blessed Virgin incidentally, and Dr. Northcote only of one feature of it. I have endeavoured, even when treating of the same subjects, not to go over the same ground. While these pages are passing through the press, I observe in the *Month* the first part of some records of English devotion to the Blessed Virgin, compiled by Mr. Waterton.

too minute, which could illustrate the origin and character and results of her worship. But we have yet to wait for the Protestant historian who will investigate the religion of his Catholic ancestors with the caution and impartiality manifested in the study of heathen mythology. I recognise indeed with joy that juster views are beginning to prevail. The labours of Mr. Maitland have done him honour, and have awakened a desire to know the truth about those dark ages which Hume and Robertson and so many others had calumniated. Hence the careful publications of the Surtees, the Camden, the Early English Text Societies, and of the Master of the Rolls. Yet it must be admitted that our best writers, such as Thorpe, and Kemble, and Hallam, have been guided by prejudice rather than by impartial love of truth whenever they have touched upon the Catholic religion.

We have a curious example of this in the otherwise able work of Mr. Kemble on the Saxons in England. This writer having recorded some of the visions of hell related by Venerable Bede, continues : 'No doubt the distempered ravings of monks, made half mad by inhuman austerities, unnatural restriction, and wretched themes of contemplation, would in themselves be of little worth. We can comprehend the visions of a St. Francis of Sales, an Ignatius Loyola, a Peter the Hermit, a Santa Theresa, or, even more readily, those of a Drithelm or a Madame Guyon ; but how shall we understand the record of them by a Beda or a Fénélon?'[3]

This passage occurs in a chapter devoted to a very patient and ingenious discussion of the religion of the pagan Saxons. Mr. Kemble gathers and compares every fragment of Saxon literature in which is found the name of a mythical deity or hero ; and he has taken much pains to arrive at the spirit of those bygone days. Yet he has bestowed so little attention on the actual religion of the majority of Christians, upon which he pretends nevertheless to pass judgment as a master, that he makes both here and elsewhere the most pitiable blunders. 'We can understand the visions of a St. Francis of Sales,' he

* *The Saxons in England*, vol. i. chap. xii. p. 386.

says. Where had he read them? and how then could he understand them? He evidently intended to give St. Francis— the polished nobleman, the refined and highly educated student, the saintly man of the world, so to speak—as a specimen of the 'monk made half mad by inhuman austerities' and the rest. Yet St. Francis lived less than three centuries ago. His position in Europe was very prominent; his action on his times very considerable. His writings are numerous and classical in their kind. It would not be allowed to a historian and a scholar like Mr. Kemble to write so recklessly on any subject but that of the Catholic religion. He would have been deterred by self-respect, if not by fear of exposure, from rounding off a period with illustrations from heathen mythology made in sheer ignorance of the names which he quoted. There must then be a serious deficiency in English education, which encourages writers thus to rely on the ignorance of their readers, and to string together at random a number of Catholic saints in the full assurance that their respective characteristics will be utterly unknown.

I am not here noting an accidental mistake on an unimportant subject, but a style of writing. I am complaining that, while almost superfluous care is taken to be well informed in other matters, there is one subject alone on which the grossest ignorance prevails, and no serious attempt has been made by our most famous historians to dispel it. That subject is the religion of their own Christian ancestors. What, for example, is more deserving of conscientious study than the devotion to the Blessed Virgin, which fills so large a place in the history of the human mind? Whether beneficial or pernicious, it is a very important fact, and merits patient and minute attention, and a cautious and philosophical consideration. Yet it has been treated with a levity and impertinence which are a disgrace to our literature. I will justify the severity of this censure, not by quotations from a Hume or a Robertson, but from one whose name ranks deservedly far higher.

Mr. Hallam has written as follows :[4]

[4] *View of the State of Europe during the Middle Ages*, chap. ix.

'That the exclusive worship of saints, under the guidance of an artful though illiterate priesthood, degraded the understanding and begot a stupid credulity and fanaticism, is sufficiently evident. But it was also so managed as to loosen the bonds of religion and pervert the standard of morality. If these inhabitants of heaven had been represented as stern avengers, accepting no slight atonement for heavy offences, and prompt to interpose their control over natural events for the detection and punishment of guilt, the creed, however impossible to be reconciled with experience, might have proved a salutary check upon a rude people, and would at least have had the only palliation that can be offered for a religious imposture—its political expediency. In the legends of those times, on the contrary, they appeared only as perpetual intercessors, so good-natured and so powerful that a sinner was more emphatically foolish than he is usually represented if he failed to secure himself against any bad consequences. For a little attention to the saints, and especially to the Virgin, with due liberality to their servants, had saved, he would be told, so many of the most atrocious delinquents, that he might equitably presume upon a similar luck in his own case.

'This monstrous superstition grew to its height in the twelfth century. For the advance that learning then made was by no means sufficient to counteract the vast increase of monasteries, and the opportunities which the greater cultivation of modern languages afforded for the diffusion of legendary tales. It was now, too, that the veneration paid to the Virgin, in early times very great, rose to an almost exclusive idolatry. It is difficult to conceive the stupid absurdity and disgusting profaneness of these stories, which were invented by the monks to do her honour.

'Whether the superstition of these dark ages had actually passed that point when it becomes more injurious to public morals and the welfare of society than the entire absence of all religious notions, is a very complex question, upon which I would by no means pronounce an affirmative decision.'[5]

[5] It is fair to Mr. Hallam to state that, in a supplementary volume,

I do not think it an exaggeration to say that this page of Mr. Hallam has formed the judgments of educated Englishmen during the last half century on the subject of Catholic devotion to the Blessed Virgin.

Conscious that his assertions might probably shock some of his readers, he attempts to justify them by a long note, in which he relates four or five of the miracles attributed to the Blessed Virgin's intercession.

'Le Grand d'Aussy,' he writes, 'has given us several of the religious tales by which the monks endeavoured to withdraw the people from romances of chivalry. The following specimens will abundantly confirm my assertions, which may perhaps appear harsh and extravagant to the reader:

'There was a man whose occupation was highway robbery; but whenever he set out on any such expedition he was careful to address a prayer to the Virgin. Taken at last, he was sentenced to be hanged. While the cord was round his neck, he made his usual prayer; nor was it ineffectual. The Virgin supported his feet "with her white hands," and thus kept him alive two days, to the no small surprise of the executioner, who attempted to complete his work with strokes of a sword. But the same invisible hand turned aside the weapon, and the executioner was compelled to release his victim, acknowledging the miracle. The thief retired into a monastery, which is always the termination of these deliverances.

'At the monastery of St. Peter, near Cologne, lived a monk perfectly dissolute and irreligious, but very devout towards the Apostle. Unluckily he died suddenly without confession. The fiends came as usual to seize his soul. St. Peter, vexed at

published thirty years later, he somewhat modified his early strictures, and expressed a more favourable judgment on the religion of the Middle Ages. But he did so only when he had been convicted of gross errors by the writings of Lingard, Maitland, and Digby. Besides, his retractation, if such it may be called, which is rather a pleading of self-defence, is very little known, while his first accusations have been repeated in every subsequent edition of his book. With regard, indeed, to the subject with which I am here concerned—the devotion of the Middle Ages to the Blessed Virgin—I am not aware that he ever withdrew any accusation he had made.

losing so faithful a votary, besought God to admit the monk into Paradise. His prayer was refused, and though the whole body of saints, apostles, angels, and martyrs joined, at his request, to make interest, it was of no avail. In this extremity he had recourse to the Mother of God. "Fair Lady," he said, "my monk is lost if you do not interfere for him ; but what is impossible for us will be but sport to you, if you please to assist us. Your Son, if you but speak a word, must yield, since it is in your power to command Him." The Queen Mother assented, and followed by all the virgins moved towards her Son. He who had Himself given the precept, Honour thy father and thy mother, no sooner saw His own parent approach than He ran to receive her, and taking her by the hand inquired her wishes. The rest may be easily conjectured. Compare the gross stupidity, the atrocious impiety of this tale, with the pure theism of the *Arabian Nights*, and judge whether the Deity was better worshipped at Cologne or at Bagdad.'

Before I conclude the extract, Mr. Hallam's invitation to compare Mahometanism with mediæval Christianity compels me to make the remark that the *dissoluteness* of the monk, had he lived at Bagdad, would not have been thought to expose him to any danger or need of help at God's tribunal. To what does the expression ' pure theism' refer ? Surely not to the purity of morals of the *Arabian Nights* ! If not, then it must be intended to contrast the Mahometan idea of God with the Christian idea of the Incarnation. This certainly betrays the animus of Mr. Hallam, but it relieves me from answering the objection made by others, that it is the Blessed Virgin who obscures the idea of the Incarnate God.

Mr. Hallam continues : ' It is unnecessary to multiply instances of this kind. In one tale the Virgin takes the shape of a nun, who had eloped from the convent, and performs her duties ten years, till, tired of a libertine life, she returns unsuspected. This was in consideration of her having never omitted to say an *Ave* as she passed the Virgin's image.[6] In another,

* I invite the reader to see how the purified imagination of Miss Adelaide Proctor treated this legend.

a gentleman in love with a handsome widow consents, at the instigation of a sorcerer, to renounce God and the saints, but cannot be persuaded to give up the Virgin, well knowing that, if he kept her his friend, he should obtain pardon through her. Accordingly, she inspired his mistress with so much passion that he married her within a few days.'[7]

This note contains the whole of Mr. Hallam's evidence on the subject of devotion to the Blessed Virgin. I have no care to examine or defend the stories here given, but I shall make some reflections on this whole passage which will explain my purpose in this long quotation.

1. First, then, Mr. Hallam's authority is Le Grand d'Aussy, a French writer of some reputation towards the end of the eighteenth century. The histories referred to will be found in the fifth volume of his *Fabliaux ou Contes*. Knowing how grievously Mr. Hallam had been misled on another occasion when he quoted the words of St. Eligius on the authority of Robertson and Mosheim,[8] I have taken the precaution to read carefully the volume of Le Grand d'Aussy which treats on the poetical legends of our Lady. I do not say that Mr. Hallam has misquoted, nor that he has been misled by his authority. But he has quoted him very insufficiently, and made a very strange use of his materials.

Mr. Hallam says that the stories that he repeats from Le Grand 'will abundantly confirm his assertions' as to the immoral tendency of the religion of the Middle Ages. Would it not have been fair if he had added that the stories which he himself gives as specimens illustrative of popular teaching were chosen by D'Aussy as being 'the most absurd of all that I have read'?

And when giving them Le Grand adds cautiously, that they

---

[7] This finale should at least have made Mr. Hallam modify his assertion, that retirement into a monastery is always the termination of miraculous deliverances.

[8] This famous blunder was exposed by Dr. Lingard, and afterwards by Dr. Newman. It is acknowledged by Mr. Hallam in a note to subsequent editions, though he says 'no one is to blame,' whereas every one was to blame.

are not to be taken as specimens : ' Ought we to judge of a century by its legends ?' he asks ; ' and among these ought we to
choose the most foolish and stupid ?' He has even left us what
I may consider a prophetic warning. 'A writer,' he says, ' turning over old books, comes by chance on a passage or anecdote
or pretended historical fact, curious by its very silliness. He
takes note of it and records it in some work that he writes,
hoping that it may amuse his readers. After him comes a compiler of anecdotes, *even a historian*, and struck with the singu-
larity of the passage, and thinking that he sees in it the spirit
of the century when it was written, makes use of it also, *and
pronounces judgment on the century itself on such grounds.*'[9]

I cannot help thinking that Mr. Hallam must have skipped
this page of his author, or he would scarcely have ventured to
accomplish his prophecy so minutely.

It is not, however, only Mr. Hallam who has done this. I
have quoted him because he is one of the best informed and
most cautious and impartial of our historians. I trust that there
are exceptions unknown to myself ; but so far as I can discover,
all our English Protestant historians, when alluding to this
subject of devotion to the saints and the Blessed Virgin, write
with the same ignorance, the same indecent boldness, and the
same flippant disregard of calumny.

I feel confident that any one who shall have the patience to
read and to weigh the evidence I have accumulated in this
volume, as to the nature of mediæval devotion to our Lady, will
agree that I am not using language in any way exaggerated or
unbecoming when I speak of the ignorance and flippancy displayed by Mr. Hallam on this subject. I know his merits, and
the authority he justly possesses. Indeed it is merely on account of that authority that I dwell so much on his words.
The same things have been said by thousands of others ; but
coming from his pen they are accepted as the convictions of
one who had read and reflected much, and who has been praised
for ' the fearless honesty of his judgments.'[10]

---

[9] *Discours Préliminaire*, tom. vme.
[10] His epitaph in St. Paul's Cathedral.

I doubt not that where religious prejudice did not interfere, his judgments were formed with caution and expressed with moderation. But he had imbibed in his education a contempt for the Catholic Church which utterly warped his mind. I know nothing more startling than the candour (shall I say ?) or effrontery with which, when about to pass judgment on the religious and literary ignorance of the seventh, eighth, ninth, and tenth centuries, he acknowledges ' that he hardly pretends to any direct acquaintance with the principal writers, such as Bede, Alcuin, Hincmar and Raban.'[11] It is evident that a man of his immense reading could only have passed over such authors from deliberate and preconceived contempt. It is clear also that he must have been still less acquainted with minor writers. I confess my inability to understand how, without violating all rules of propriety, he should write and publish any judgment whatsoever on matters of which he was wilfully ignorant ; but that that judgment should be expressed in terms of the direst censure on mere partial and secondhand testimony seems to me a crime of the most enormous magnitude, affecting as it does not only the character of millions in past centuries, but that of the majority of Christians of his own day.

2. But besides the unfair choice and still more unfair conclusion which Mr. Hallam has made, I find that he has slipped into his censure an accusation for which his authority gives him no pretext whatever. ' A little attention to the saints,' he writes, ' and *especially to their servants*, had saved, he would be told, so many atrocious sinners,' &c. I have read through the collection of *Contes Dévots* of Le Grand d'Aussy with the view of testing this accusation. They are not edifying. I willingly admit that many of them are scandalous, and as such they have been condemned by Catholics ; but in the whole collection there is absolutely not one in which there is the most distant allusion to liberality to priests or monks as being either the cause or the effect of a miracle. Among the acts thus rewarded we find frequently charity to the poor, but never gifts to churches or monasteries. Far from this, one miracle saves a monk when

[11] P. 597 of ed. of 1869.

robbing a monastery from which he is flying; and another story tells how the monks were 'ravished with delight' when they heard how a poor gentleman had been relieved at their own expense.[12] There is therefore no ground for Mr. Hallam's accusation that monks invented such stories in order to draw gifts to their abbeys and shrines.

I go much farther. No one can read attentively these tales without noticing that most of them are satires on the monks and hermits. I do not mean that they were intended to decry religion or the monastic state, as if they had been written by or for modern enemies of the Catholic Church. It seems that their authors were monks, and they were written in French verse, not for the uneducated people, but for the amusement of the clergy, and of knights and ladies in their castles. They are dramatic and amusing, sometimes too licentious in detail; and above all they are satirical. Holy monks and hermits are shown to be frail. Spiritual pride is chastised by grievous falls; and it is only when the poor monk has been brought by his presumption to ruin and shame that the author seems to take pity on him, and calls in the Blessed Virgin to his rescue. The form of this expedient savours of the Middle Ages and the times of faith, but surely the expedient itself, of good-humouredly setting all right before the story ends, is not unknown to modern literature. Indeed, nothing but prejudice could have prevented Mr. Hallam from seeing that many of these stories must have been regarded by their authors and by their readers or hearers as religious fables, and that it is simply ridiculous to take them *au grand sérieux*.

Of course I am speaking now not of all miraculous histories, but of the rhymed legends from which Mr. Hallam quotes. He has himself noticed their character. 'These tales, it may be said, were the product of ignorant men, and circulated among the populace. Certainly they would have excited contempt and indignation in the more enlightened clergy. But I am concerned with the general character of religious notions among

---

[12] See *Du Sacristan*, p. 86, and *Du Prud'homme qui avait été Marchand*, p. 159.

the people ; and for this it is better to take such popular com-
positions, adapted to what the laity already believed, than the
writings of comparatively learned and reflecting men.   However, stories of the same cast are frequent in the monkish
historians.'

Let us look more closely into facts. The legends from which
he has quoted certainly did not circulate among the populace.
They were the novels, the fashionable literature of the day,
differing from our own only in that they were tinged with
religious notions.   But there were other stories in circulation
recorded by grave authors and preached to the people.

Mr. Hallam has introduced his observations by saying, ' that
no one can take a philosophical view of the Middle Ages without
attending more than is at present fashionable to their ecclesiastical history.'   Now a philosophical view presupposes a careful
attention to all facts.   One important fact at least has been
passed over by Mr. Hallam.   The great promoters of the devotion to the saints and the Blessed Virgin were not ignorant or
avaricious monks.   The most learned, the most enlightened, the
most disinterested and austere, the most saintly in their own
lives, and the sternest opponents of popular vice, the most zealous and successful reformers of morals, were exactly those who
did most to encourage both clergy and people in devotion to the
saints and especially to the Queen of saints.   The names of St.
Dominic, St. Peter Damian, St. Bernard, St. Anselm, occur
at once to the mind.   If I mentioned St. Bernardine of Sienna
and St. Alphonsus in later times I should seem to Catholics to
be needlessly singling out names from the multitude of saintly
missionaries who have looked on increased devotion to the
Blessed Virgin as a great instrument in the reformation of
morals.

Had Mr. Hallam, then, drawn attention to the fact that collections of our Lady's miracles of mercy were made by such fearless denouncers of iniquity as St. Peter Damian and such
unworldly men as St. Peter Celestine, and had he then tried to
solve the problem how such men could encourage a superstition which ' loosened the bonds of religion and perverted the

standard of morality,' he would have written more philosophically, and probably have obtained a juster 'view of Europe during the Middle Ages,' than by attributing, as he does, the invention and propagation of miracles to artful and avaricious cunning playing on ' stupid credulity and fanaticism.'

3. The phrase ' exclusive worship of saints' suggests a state of things which has no reality in history whatsoever.

If the Church has ever given the fullest encouragement to the popular devotion towards the ' saints and servants of God,' it is because by no other means can the exclusive claims of God to supreme adoration and undivided allegiance be so powerfully impressed on the soul, as by the honour given to those who made the service of God the whole object of their lives.

When God worked a miracle to vindicate the integrity of His servant Samuel, ' all the people greatly feared the Lord and Samuel. And all the people said to Samuel : Pray for thy servants to the Lord thy God, that we may not die. . . . And Samuel said : Fear not : you have done all this evil ; but yet depart not from following the Lord, but serve the Lord with all your heart, and turn not aside after vain things, which shall never profit you, nor deliver you, because they are vain. And the Lord will not forsake His people for His great name's sake. . . . . And far from me be this sin against the Lord that I should cease to pray for you, and I will teach you the good and right way. Therefore fear the Lord, and serve Him in truth and with your whole heart, for you have seen the great works which He hath done among you. But if you still do wickedly, you shall perish' (1 Kings xii.).

This passage contains all the principles on which the cultus of the saints is founded. God glorified His faithful servant by a miracle, to teach the Israelites that the one thing great is submission to Himself. Those who witnessed the power of the saint with God ' greatly feared the Lord and Samuel ;' and the immediate result was consciousness of sin and fear of its chastisements. This was taken advantage of to bring about reformation of life, by the promise of pardon, conditional on two things, the intercession of the saint and fidelity in God's service.

There is, then, no such thing as the 'exclusive worship of saints.' The worship of the saints neither excludes nor encroaches on the worship of God. It is part of it, and a very important part. The people who 'greatly feared the Lord and Samuel,' and who asked Samuel 'to pray for them to the Lord his God,' practised the only kind of worship of the saints which ever found encouragement in the Catholic Church. And Samuel at least saw no contradiction between such worship and 'serving God in truth and with the whole heart.'

4. I must demur also to the description of Catholic legends as 'representing the saints *only* as perpetual good-natured intercessors.' I have probably a larger acquaintance with this class of literature than had Mr. Hallam, and I could easily gather a long list of examples of the special intervention of the saints to punish obstinate sinners. I do not deny, however, that these are exceptional instances. The saints were generally invoked as intercessors for repentant sinners, or as being powerful to obtain temporal or spiritual benefit from the bounty of God for their clients. Mr. Hallam thinks that the Catholic view tends to encourage immorality and presumption. He would rather see the saints as 'stern avengers,' prompt to interpose their control over natural events for the detection and punishment of guilt.'

Mr. Hallam was no doubt a great man ; yet he reminds me of the words of Isabella in Shakespeare's play of *Measure for Measure :*[13]

> 'Could great men thunder
> As Jove himself does, Jove would ne'er be quiet ;
> For every pelting, petty officer
> Would use his heaven for thunder, nothing but thunder.'

Such seems to be Mr. Hallam's notion of a moral religion ; 'thunder, nothing but thunder.' I am inclined to think that the Catholic view, which represents Almighty God as generally reserving to Himself the punishment of guilt, while He makes many saints the channel of His mercies, should be more acceptable to the humble consciousness of our own frailty, and is

[13] Act ii. sc. 2.

more in harmony with the words of Holy Scripture. Certainly the Bible tells us that God has the prerogative of vengeance, and that He has but few ministers to execute wrath; while He wishes the great multitude rather to imitate the Father in heaven, who maketh His sun to rise upon the good and the bad, and raineth upon the just and the unjust.[14]

5. The intercession of the saints is a part of God's plan of mercy, and since presumption in the mercy of God is one form of human vice, it would be strange indeed if the perversity of the human heart had never sought to wrest the power and goodness of the saints to its own ends. Yet I am convinced that such abuse of devotion is of rare occurrence. Hope in the prayers of Mary retained in the midst of sin, and in spite of sin, is a very different thing from presumption prompting to sin with greater boldness. Most of the stories which were current of sinners who were rescued by Mary's intercession, on account of acts of devotion continued even during a sinful life, refer to those who hoped, not to those who presumed. They sinned through weakness, but still clung to the hope of repentance and forgiveness. It may be said that the propagation of such stories would encourage presumption. I do not deny that such might be accidentally the result. The same, however, may be said of preaching the mercy of God. Has the clemency of Jesus Christ to 'the good thief' never been abused? The question should be, Did the writers and preachers who spoke of Mary's miracles of mercy utter no warnings against presumption? On this point I challenge impartial investigation. It will be found that the universal teaching is like that of our own St. Aelred, in that very twelfth century which Mr. Hallam describes as given up to an 'almost exclusive idolatry.' 'But how are we to serve Mary? Brethren, no service pleases her so much as this—that with all love and affection we humble ourselves before her Son; for all the praise and service we give her Son she counts it as her own. Let no one say, "Though I should do this or that against the Lord, I do not care much, I will serve holy Mary, and be safe." It is not so. But if, *after* our sins, we wish to

[14] Rom. xii. xiii.; St. Matt. v. 45.

be reconciled with our Lord, then we must needs have recourse
to her and commit our cause to her.'[15]

This is the language of one of those monks who, according
to Mr. Hallam's reading of history, counteracted the beneficial
effects of increased learning, and were the great promoters of
corruption and monstrous superstition.

6. With the charge of credulity I will not deal. By those
who believe that miracles and supernatural interventions are
impossible, or who absurdly relegate them to one epoch, of course
the accusations of knavery and credulity will be freely used.
By such convenient generalisation much trouble is avoided in
the investigation of facts. But charges of this kind are as
easily despised as made. A multitude of subjects connected
with the Middle Ages have been examined with the utmost diligence and most scrupulous caution. Perhaps some one will
give a similar attention to the subject of miracles and appari-
tions. When this shall have been seriously done by a man
anxious to discover truth, if such a man shall still bring charges
of imposture and fanatical stupidity against Catholics, it will
then be our duty to reply seriously to the accusation or to plead
guilty. But as yet I am not aware of any opponent of the
Church who has dared to look into facts, or who, having met
them on his path, has invented even a plausible theory to get
rid of them.

In the mean time it is easy to perceive the uncomfortable
feelings produced by the evidence for Catholic miracles, by the
eagerness with which every unauthenticated story is selected
for exposure.

It remains for me to explain in a few words what the reader
may expect in the following pages. The book will be divided

[15] St. Aelred, Serm. 20, Migne, *Patrologia*, tom. 195, col. 553. The
reader who wishes to pursue this subject may consult Segneri, *Il Devoto di
Maria*, introduzione; also the Ven. Grignon de Montfort, *Traité de la
vraie Dévotion*, who distinguishes seven classes of false devotees of Mary,
whom he calls—1, critical; 2, scrupulous; 3, exterior; 4, presumptuous;
5, inconstant; 6, hypocritical; 7, interested. See also P. D'Argentan,
Conférences sur les Grandeurs de la très-sainte Vierge, Conf. 15.

into Three Parts. In the First will be found the doctrine that was current in England about our Lady. I have selected for translation passages which are valuable for their intrinsic excellence, and which, taken together, will both give a pretty complete body of doctrine regarding the Blessed Virgin, and serve as specimens of many of our native writers. In the Second Part I have arranged in different chapters illustrations of the various methods in which our forefathers strove to show their love and veneration for the Mother of their God and their Redeemer.

The illustrations in the Second Part range through the whole of the nine centuries between the conversion of England and the Reformation; whereas in the First Part I have quoted few writers later than the twelfth century. That is the period fixed by Mr. Hallam when devotion to the Blessed Virgin reached its climax and, in his opinion, its most monstrous degradation. It is also a period regarding which we have abundant materials for forming a judgment. In my own opinion its writers are superior not only to those who preceded, but to those who followed them.

I shall be rewarded for my toil if I should excite an interest in our old English writers, so little known even to Englishmen. I hope the day is not distant when an effort will be made by Catholics to rescue from oblivion the treasures of theology which are still in the manuscripts of our great libraries. While much has been done in England to illustrate our history and our literature by the editing of our old writers, pure theology has been passed over with contempt; and we are indebted for what is known to us almost exclusively to continental scholars. This is a reproach to England which it is time for Catholics to efface.

I must express my regret not to have been able to include Ireland within the scope of my inquiries. But the subject demands a knowledge of the Irish language and Irish archæology, in which I am deficient. One circumstance, however, I may mention, to show that in spite of many points of difference, and even in the midst of political strife, the English and Irish were united in faith and devotion.

c

The Annals of the Four Masters inform us that the Irish parliament, before the Reformation, voted a sum of money that a certain number of wax candles should be kept perpetually burning before the image of our Lady of Trim in county Meath. Also, that during the wars continually waged between the native Celts and the Norman invaders, it was agreed on both sides that no one of either race should be molested while on a journey to visit our Lady of Trim.

It is a sad thing that men having the same faith and the same devotion to the gentle, sweet, and peaceful Mother of our Blessed Redeemer should have been thus engaged in making and repelling war. But the agreement just mentioned is not only a proof of the unity of faith, which not even deadly hatred could divide, but it is also a proof of the humanising influence of devotion to the Blessed Virgin, which to some extent mitigated even the horrors of war.

From the intimate ecclesiastical relations between England and Scotland in the eleventh and twelfth centuries there seemed no reason why the latter country should not be included in the limits of our Lady's Dowry. I have therefore not hesitated to make use of Scottish writers and Scottish illustrations of my subject.

I regret that I have to exclude one of the most important Scottish writers, Richard of St. Victor. But having admitted St. Anselm and Peter of Blois, because, though born on the Continent, they taught in England, in pursuance of my plan I had to omit such as, though born in England or Scotland, taught or wrote only on the Continent.

In the Third Part of my book I inquire how our Lady lost her English Dowry, and trace out a phase of the Reformation which has not perhaps hitherto received sufficient attention.

I conclude this Introduction, and enter on the subject of my studies, with the following apology of our old Norman poet, Walter Mapes :

> ' Pone scribentium tot esse millia
> Quot habent nemora frondes et folia,
> Quot cœli sidera et guttas maria,
> Indigne Virginis scribent præconia.

Cum laudes Virginis promere studeo,
Penso materiæ pondus et paveo,
Quæ huic congruant verba, non habeo;
Vincor, et fateor me vinci gaudio.'[16]

To which I add the beautiful invocation which Chaucer puts into the mouth of the prioress:[17]

'O Mother Maid! O Maid and Mother free!
   O bush unburnt, burning in Moses' sight!
That down didst ravish from the Deity,
   Through humbleness, the spirit that did alight
   Upon thy heart, whence, through that glory's might,
Conceived was the Father's sapience,
Help me to tell it in thy reverence!

Lady, thy goodness, thy magnificence,
   Thy virtue, and thy great humility,
Surpass all science and all utterance;
   For sometimes, Lady, ere men pray to thee,
   Thou go'st before in thy benignity,
The light to us vouchsafing of thy prayer,
To be our guide unto thy Son so dear.

My knowledge is so weak, O blissful Queen,
   To tell abroad thy mighty worthiness,
That I the weight of it may not sustain;
   But as a child of twelve months old, or less,
   That laboureth his language to express,
Even so fare I; and therefore, I thee pray,
Guide thou my song, which I of thee shall say.'

PROLOGUE TO FABIAN'S CHRONICLE (fifteenth century).

'Wherfore, to the lorde that is Celestyall,
   I wyll nowe crye, that of his Influence,
Of grace and mercy, he wyll a droppe let fall,
   And sharpe my wytte with suche experyence,
   That this may fynysshe with his Assystence,
With fauour of the virgyn his Moder moste excellent,
To whom I thus praye with mynde and hole entent:

    Adsit principio Sancta Maria meo.

Moste blyssed Lady comforte to such as calle
   To the for helpe in eche necessyte,

---

[16] Published by Mr. Wright, for the Camden Society.
[17] Wordsworth's version.

And what thou aydest may in no wyse Apalle
  But to the best is formyd in ylke degre :
  Wherfore good Lady I praye it may please the,
At my begynnynge my penne so to lede,
That, by thyne ayde, this werke may hanc good spede.'

PART I.

DOCTRINE.

CHAPTER I.

THE IMMACULATE VIRGIN.

THE earliest Christian writers in England exhausted every epithet and title they could find to express the immaculate purity and perfect sanctity of the Blessed Mother of God. Venerable Bede quotes the words of the Irish poet Sedulius :

> ' To her we sing
> Who bore in time the world's eternal King,
> And peerless in the human race has found
> A mother's joys by virgin honours crown'd.'

To Bede she is the Genitrix incorrupta, the Virgo incomparabiliter benedicta—the Mother undefiled, the Virgin blessed beyond compare. We shall see in his discourse on the Visitation what idea he had conceived of her sublime sanctity.

St. Aldhelm calls her ' the garden enclosed,' ' the fountain sealed up,' ' the one dove amid the threescore queens,' and many other titles culled from the mystic Canticle of Canticles.

The grave Alcuin writes verses in which he names her ' his sweet love, his honour, the great hope of his salvation, the Queen of Heaven, the flower of the field, the lily of the world, the fountain of life.'[1]

A MS. now in the University Library at Cambridge, called the Book of Cerne, and which belonged to Ethelwald, Bishop of Sherbourne in 760, contains the following prayer to the Blessed Virgin, a clear monument both of the faith and devotion of the

---

[1] ' Tu mihi dulcis amor, decus, et spes magna salutis
Auxiliare tuum servum, clarissima virgo . . . .
Tu regina poli, campi flos, lilia mundi,
Hortus conclusus, vitæ fons, vena salutis,' &c.
Alcuini Op. t. ii. p. 223, ed. Frob.

Anglo-Saxons in the time of Venerable Bede:[2] 'Holy Mother of God, Virgin ever blest, glorious and noble, chaste and inviolate, O Mary Immaculate, chosen and beloved of God, endowed with singular sanctity, worthy of all praise, thou who art the advocate for the sins (peril) of the whole world ; O listen, listen, listen to us, O holy Mary. Pray for us, intercede for us, disdain not to help us. For we are confident and know for certain that thou canst obtain all thou willest from thy Son, our Lord Jesus Christ, God Almighty, the King of Ages, who liveth with the Father and the Holy Ghost, for ever and ever. Amen.'

This and much more we find in the writers of the Anglo-Saxon Church ; and thus they tried to express the idea of absolute sinlessness and perfect excellence which had been impressed on their minds by their first teachers in the faith, and which was developed by their constant study of Holy Scripture and their meditation on the mysteries of Redemption.

There were among them no native heresies to be refuted, no tongues pretending to honour the Incarnate Son of God by slighting and depreciating His chosen Mother. They read, indeed, in the writings of St. Jerome of the monstrous errors of Helvidius and Jovinian, and they sometimes record with horror the blasphemies of those heretics ; but many ages were to pass before such words would be spoken by English tongues or written by English pens.

Having, therefore, no controversy to sustain, our Anglo-Saxon writers do not refute opinions which it did not occur to them to imagine, nor make assertions where there was no denial. They neither assert, nor much less deny, the exemption of our Lady from the stain of original sin. They speak of her immaculate purity in terms which may well include that grace ; but not until it had been denied were English writers zealous in its defence. Then, indeed, Alexander Hales, Thomas Hales,

---

[2] Published in *Home and Foreign Review*, October 1862, p. 481: ' Sancta Dei genitrix, semper Virgo beata, benedicta, gloriosa, et generosa, intacta et intemerata, casta et incontaminata, Maria immaculata, electa et a Deo dilecta, singulari sanctitate prædita, atque omni laude digna, quæ es interpellatrix pro totius mundi discrimine, exaudi, exaudi, exaudi nos, sancta Maria,' &c. The ms. is marked Ll. i. 10.

Richard Middleton, Robert Cowton, John Marchely,[3] and others wrote learned dissertations against the opponents of Mary's singular privilege, and none were more zealous than the English in celebrating the feast of the Conception.

Indeed, as we shall see in the Second Part, it was from England that this feast spread through Europe. Its first originator was one who linked together the Anglo-Saxon and Anglo-Norman Churches, Abbot Helsin; and it was in the great abbeys filled with Saxon monks and ruled by Norman abbots that it met at once a unanimous reception. Nothing could better prove the unity of faith of the two races.

Matthew Paris relates that Geoffry, who was elected Abbot of St. Albans in 1119, just ten years after the death of St. Anselm, and who died in 1146, caused the feast of our Lady's Conception to be celebrated with increased pomp.[4] It must therefore have been already established some years in the abbey, during or before the time of St. Anselm.

But at the beginning of the second half of the twelfth century, the news reached England that the famous Abbot of Clairvaux, St. Bernard, had opposed the celebration of this feast in the Church of Lyons (in 1140). As was natural, his opinion would be embraced by many of the Cistercians, who were now just making their first foundations in England; and this would arouse the zeal, if not the indignation, of the great Benedictine abbeys, which shared the reproach of innovation addressed by St. Bernard to the Church of Lyons.

Among those who took up the pen in defence of the feast, and of the doctrine it involved, was Nicholas, Prior of St. Albans in Hertfordshire, or, as Tanner thinks, of Wallingford, a cell dependent on St. Albans. His original treatise or letter is lost, but we have part of a correspondence to which it gave rise between him and Peter, Abbot of St. Remi, and afterwards Bishop of Chartres, more commonly known as Peter of Celles. This correspondence or controversy is worthy of being better

---

[3] Franciscan writers mentioned in the *Collectanea Anglo-Minoritica.*

[4] 'Conceptionem B. Virginis . . . in cappis festive celebrari.' *Vita Abb.* p. 62, ed. Wats.

known than by the passing allusions given to it in treatises on
the Immaculate Conception. It shows what were the true
grounds of the opposition to the feast in the twelfth century,
and that it was not until a later period that the opposition took
the form of a dogmatic denial of Mary's singular privilege.

As I have said, the first letter of the English prior to the Norman abbot is lost, but we may judge of its contents from the reply.

Peter of Celles begins by the remark that, however beautiful
and seductive the things which Nicholas had written about the
Blessed Virgin, they were wanting in the solid foundation of
authority. He then draws a contrast which will surprise us at
the present day. 'English levity must not be indignant if
French maturity is more solid. England is an island surrounded
by water, whence it happens that its inhabitants are affected by
the qualities of this element, and are frequently tossed about
by too great fickleness into vain and fanciful speculations,
whence they come to compare or even to prefer their dreams to
visions. The fault is not so much theirs as that of their climate.
In any case, my experience is that the English are greater
dreamers than the French.'[5] The good abbot seems to allude to
the vision of Helsin. St. Bernard had also treated this vision
with little respect in his letter to the canons of Lyons. But to
continue. After developing at some length his own immov-
ableness from the ancient ways, Peter declares his entire devotion to the Mother of God, and his conviction that the Blessed
Trinity never brought from the divine treasure house anything
so excellent, except the humanity of the Word Incarnate. 'This,'
he says, 'I confess in my heart and profess with my lips. You
profess the same, though with more vehemence, perhaps with
too great vehemence. You pour yourself out in praise of the

---

[5] As this character of the English is little known, it may be well to
give the original: 'Nec indignetur Anglica levitas si ea solidior sit Gallica
maturitas. Insula enim est circumfusa aqua, unde hujus elementi pro-
pria qualitate ejus incolæ non immerito afficiuntur, et nimia mobilitate in
tenuissimas et subtiles phantasias frequenter transferuntur, somnia sua
visionibus comparantes, ne dicam præferentes. Et quæ culpa naturæ, si
talis est natura terræ? Certe expertus sum somniatores plus esse Anglicos
quam Gallos.' Petri Cellensis, *Epist.* lib. vi. ep. 23.

Blessed Virgin. Well, so do I, and even to overflowing. You wish to honour her Conception, and I even her Predestination. You honour the rose, I even the stalk that bears it. You praise the flower and the fruit, I even the leaves and the bark, &c. If to honour her it were necessary to make a long journey, I would gladly travel not only as far as the shrine of St. Thomas in England, but to the shrine of St. Thomas in India. I will ever take part in all assemblies in which our Lady is worthily honoured, whether the commemoration is termed Conception, or Nativity, or Assumption, or called by any other name.'

He then explains that his only objection is the novelty of the feast now introduced. 'But perhaps you will say: "Do you, a mere abbot, dare to fill up the wells of ever-springing devotion, or forbid them to be dug deeper? Do not the moderns drink of the same Holy Spirit as the ancients? Does not St. Jerome say, that in the temple of God every one may bring his offering, whether gold, or silver, or precious stones, or other poorer gifts—goat-skins, or aught else? The Nativity of the Blessed Virgin was not solemnised at the beginning of the Church; but as the devotion of the faithful increased, it was added to the other solemn festivals. Why then should not the zeal of Christian devotion now add the day of her Conception?"

'To this I reply : I would far more willingly open the cataracts of heaven and the fountains of the deep in honour of the Virgin than close them. Nay, if her own Son Jesus—were such a thing possible—had left undone anything for the exaltation of His Mother, I, her servant and her slave, would try to make it up, if not in effect, at least in affection. I would rather have no tongue than use it against our Lady. I would rather have no soul than diminish anything of the glory of hers. No doubt it ever was lawful and ever will be lawful for the Church, the Spouse of Christ, during her sojourn in this world, according to the changes of times and of persons and of things, to vary her decrees, and to find new remedies for new diseases, and to appoint new festivals for her saints. But gold and silver have a mint in which they must be coined—the seat of Peter and the court of Rome, which holds the principality and the keys of heaven. It belongs to her to open to us, in the dispensation of God, the secrets of God's counsels, and the oil of grace runs down from the head (Aaron) to the borders of his vestment.

'This seat of Peter, in which Moses sits, that is in which resides "the immaculate law which converts the soul," this is the Rock which falls and crushes the gatherings of the heretics, which stops all profane novelties of word, which cuts off what is superfluous and fills up whatever is incomplete. I should then be glad indeed if this Mistress and Directress of Christendom, with the authority of truth, had weighed in the scales of a general consultation[6] and had approved (this festival of) our Lady's Conception, and had propagated it from sea to sea. If the sun, that is the Pope, and the moon, that is the Roman Church, had gone before, then no less quickly than securely would I have walked in their light, without fear of slipping or of stumbling.'

He then goes on to criticise some parts of the letter he had received from Nicholas. He says that he has been scandalised by his language about St. Bernard, whose virtues he relates, especially his eminent devotion to the Blessed Virgin, which had caused him to dedicate not one church but all the churches of the Cistercians in her honour. 'If then,' he concludes, 'you wish to wound the pupil of our Lady's eye, write against her Bernard.' Nicholas seems also to have spoken slightingly of the Cistercians, for the holy Abbot of St. Remi enters into a very warm and generous defence of them.[7]

The rest of the letter is taken up in the discussion of a saying of Nicholas—that 'the Blessed Virgin overcame all sin, not by fighting against it, but by never experiencing any attack.' Peter, on the contrary, contends that though she never consented

---

[6] Lance communis consilii. This is exactly what the Holy See has done in our own days. From the above we may judge how gladly the holy abbot would have welcomed the definitions of the Immaculate Conception, and of the infallibility of the Pope, made by Pius IX. with the applause of the whole Church.

[7] Hi sunt qui monetam nostri jam in agonia positi ordinis reformaverunt. Hi sunt qui regulam beati Benedicti pene combustam, sicut Esdras veterem legem, restauraverunt, &c.

in any way to sin, yet, at least before the Incarnation, she may not have been free from every attack of temptation, which, without inflicting the slightest stain, would have increased her grace, her merit, and her glory. It was only like treading scorpions under her feet without being stung by them; and this in no way derogates from her glory.[8]

He concludes playfully by saying that he shall hide himself in a cavern, expecting that a very storm of thunder and lightning will now burst upon him from Nicholas.[9]

He was not mistaken. What he had said about the Blessed Virgin being tempted, excited the indignation of her English client.

He first defends himself from the charge of having forgotten what was due to St. Bernard, who had just been canonised.[10] St. Augustin, he says, did not doubt of the sanctity or glory of St. Cyprian, though he combated his opinion and proved it erroneous. 'Do not think,' he continues, 'that I combat St. Bernard out of obstinacy. I do it with a pure conscience. Let me tell you what I have heard from some Cistercians, who were truly religious men and true lovers of the Blessed Virgin. I keep back their names, lest I stir up ill feeling against them among their brethren. A certain lay brother then at Clairvaux, of holy life, in a vision of the night saw Abbot Bernard clad in snow-white garments, but having a brown stain on his breast. Surprised and sad he asked the meaning of this. The saint replied, "Because I wrote what I ought not on the Conception of our Lady I bear this spot upon my breast, the sign of my purgation." The brother related what he had seen, and one of the brethren committed it to writing. It was brought before a general chapter of the order, and by common consent

[8] Tolle pugnam, tolles et victoriam. Tolle victoriam, tolles et coronam. Tolle coronam, tolles et gloriam. The question of concupiscence is quite distinct from that of original sin. See Suarez.

[9] *Epistolæ Petri Cellensis*, lib. vi. no. 28.

[10] Nuper est in Ecclesia canonizatus, et ab humano judicio exemptus. St. Bernard was canonised in 1174, twenty years after his death. The correspondence must therefore have taken place between this date and the year 1180, when Peter became Bishop of Chartres.

the writing was burnt, since all the abbots preferred rather to endanger the glory of the Blessed Virgin than the good fame of St. Bernard. It was not thus that St. Paul acted, who accuses himself of being a blasphemer, that he may more exalt the glory of his Redeemer. And indeed I believe that St. Bernard appeared to a simple lay brother, who knew nothing about this controversy, and made known to him his fault, for the very purpose that the sagacity of the general chapter might perceive how much he wished his mistake to be condemned and the glory of the Virgin's Conception to be published. If then I make known what he wished to be known, this is not to injure his fame or deny her glory.'

He then proceeds to defend his proposition that the Blessed Virgin never felt the assault of sin, and to refute Peter's reasoning about the necessity of combat for merit. She had abundant occasions of advancing in grace and merit, he argues, without being tempted. 'She felt hunger, thirst, and cold, and was tried by many tribulations and calamities, and daily advanced in patience. And not only did she merit by the occasions from without, but by her continually increasing interior love of every virtue—her contemplation of God, her incomparable charity, her absolute and perfect purity.'

He replies to the charge that he had advanced some things in his former letter which he could not prove by authority, in this manner : ' If I have written anything of the Blessed Virgin which I have not read in canonical Scripture, still it redounds to the praise of the Virgin and to the praise of her Son ; and being deduced from Holy Scripture, I have either written what was true though hidden, or what was probable and Catholic. Many things are conjectured about the Virgin which are nowhere read, and we may keep to our conjectures until proof is brought of the contrary.'

Abbot Peter had drawn a distinction between the two periods of our Lady's life, before and after she became the Mother of God, and had admitted that all concupiscence was utterly extinguished in her from the time that she was ineffably overshadowed by the Holy Ghost, though he had not granted this privilege for the first part of her life. Prior Nicholas, with more justice, denies that she ever experienced the assaults of temptation from within, though he gladly allows a distinction between the two epochs, which he thus draws out :

' Even when not yet a mother, Mary was alone amongst all virgins saluted by the angel as full of grace, and afterwards alone amongst all mothers was the sanctuary of the Holy Ghost. Before her maternity she was as the fleece of whitest wool, unstained by any touch of sin ; as mother she was penetrated with the Holy Ghost, and, like the fleece, dyed in richest purple and set apart for the use of the King of Kings. But the fleece, though belonging to the body, as St. Jerome remarks, has none of the passions of the body; and Mary, though in the flesh, knew none of the concupiscences of the flesh.'[11]

To this letter Peter replies that he has been misunderstood. ' I believe, I say, I maintain, and I swear that the most Blessed Virgin was endowed with special privilege in her eternal predestination, nor from the moment of her conception did she suffer the slightest stain, but remained ever and persevered to the end in spotless integrity; and as she was blessed beyond human nature, so are her perfections sublime and hidden beyond human thought. Like two rams, we have been trying our horns one against the other, and may have used diversity of words ; but the pure eye of our intention, by which we both sought only the honour of our Lady, has never been dimmed, and, by God's help, never will be dimmed.' He then recalls the contest between St. Augustin and St. Jerome regarding the conduct of St. Peter at Antioch. ' Behold how the cedars of Libanus bend their heads before the wind in different directions, though both remain firmly rooted in charity. Each one abounds in his own sense. There was 'no error in articles of faith, endangering the salvation of either ; for they were like two olive-trees, or two candlesticks burning in God's presence (Apoc. xi. 4). What wonder, then, if the wind toss us in different directions, who are like dry chaff before it ?'

He then explains in what sense he had said that Mary was

[11] *Inter Epist. Petri Cellensis*, lib ix. ep. 9.

tempted. 'She was tempted not to her injury, but to her probation; not so as to yield, but so as to conquer; not from within, but from without. She was tempted in this, that the enemy could cast in the suggestion, but not that either the inferior part of her soul felt delectation or her will gave consent. The Holy Scripture says, "To him that shall overcome I will give to sit with Me in My throne, as I also have overcome and am set down with My Father in His throne" (Apoc. iii. 21). So then the Blessed Virgin, seated by the throne of Him who sits upon the throne of grace, her Son Jesus, tells now of all the victories she gained, not by sleep but by watchfulness, not by repose but by combat, not by flight but by resistance. Was the Mother happier or holier than her Son ? Was she stronger or more full of grace? Yet Jesus was led into the desert, to be tempted by the devil; and the Apostle says that He was tempted in all things to be like us, yet without sin. And he who is tempted, does he not feel the temptation?'

After this explanation he might well conclude that there was little real difference between his sentiments and those of his friendly opponent.   •

'You praise the Blessed Virgin; so do I. You say that she was holy; so do I. You exalt her above the choirs of angels; so do I. You assert that she was free from every sin; so do I. You maintain that she is the Mother of God and our advocate with God; so do I. Turn hither or thither as you will in your veneration and glorification of Mary, I go with you. But if you wish to strike a new coin different from what is in common circulation, and without the approval of the See of Peter, to whom it belongs to approve or disapprove the order of the universal Church, then I hold back, nor will I pass the bounds marked out. I believe and confess that there are more things unknown about this most holy Virgin than are known, for her grace and glory are high above our reach. Still I believe in the Gospel, not in dreams; and "if in anything I be otherwise minded, that also will God reveal" (Phil. iii. 15) when and how He may please. . . . And now, if my axe has slipped from its handle and inflicted any wound, forgive me, as I also forgive you. Pray for me, dearest friend, and may I one day see you face to face, whose voice I have more than once listened to in your well-penned letters.'

Such was the matter and manner of the famous controversy about the Immaculate Conception in its outset. Would that it had remained as calm and charitable to the end! Had the principles laid down by St. Bernard in his letter to the canons of Lyons, and by Peter of Celles in the above letters, on the judgment of the Holy See, been always borne in mind, the matter would have been quickly settled.

When the feast of our Lady's Immaculate Conception next returns, let us think with gratitude on the Englishman of the twelfth century who defended so warmly her singular privilege, and on the Frenchman who, with no less devotion to Mary, upheld so clearly the prerogatives and the infallibility of the Apostolic See.

PETER OF BLOIS (twelfth century).

The following extract is from Peter of Blois, who, though a native of France, resided in England, and was Archdeacon of Bath and finally of London. He died about 1200.

'An evil tree had brought forth evil fruits—the concupiscence of the flesh, original sin, the germ of all evils, the leaven of universal corruption, and the common beginning of our ruin. Therefore, in order that a remedy for original evil might be found in original good, the flesh of Mary, though springing from that evil tree of perdition, was yet exempted and sanctified. And though she received the fulness of grace and sanctity from her mother's womb, yet when the Holy Ghost descended on her in the conception of the Word of God, He poured out on her more exuberantly the fulness of heavenly grace. This may be understood from the words of the angel. "Hail," he says, "Mary, full of grace." See here the fulness of grace; yet he adds, "The Holy Ghost shall come upon thee." Here the measure is filled up and flowing over.

'Since, then, the flesh of Mary was freed from sin, and since she received grace according to a certain measure, she is called

D

blessed, but not absolutely so, but blessed amongst women. But since Christ received grace not according to measure, and since He was altogether free and exempt from sin, He is pronounced absolutely blessed. "Blessed is the fruit of thy womb." Mary's flesh was sanctified ; the flesh of Christ was not sanctified, but was holy and sanctifying.

'This diversity of sanctification was prefigured in the twofold tithes of the Old Testament. The children of Israel paid tithes of all their goods to the Levites. But the Levites paid tithes of their best to the high-priest. So from the mass of humanity the flesh of Mary was exempted and sanctified, as a kind of tithe and first-fruit ; and then from that most holy flesh a still nobler and holier portion was chosen, which the Word of God assumed and united to Himself (Numbers xviii. 26-28).'[12]

St. Aelred (twelfth century).

I add two passages from the sermons of an English Cistercian abbot, contemporary of St. Bernard :

' Ezechiel says, " He brought me to the gate which looks towards the East, and it was shut" (Ezech. xliv. 1). The most holy Mary is this Eastern gate. For a gate which looks towards the East is the first to receive the rays of the sun. So the most Blessed Mary, who always looked towards the East, that is, towards the Brightness of God, received the first rays, or rather the whole blaze of light of that true Sun, of which the prophet Zachary sang : "The Orient from on high hath visited us" (Luke i. 78). This gate was shut and well guarded. The enemy could find no entrance, no little hole whatever (nullum omnino foramen). It was shut and sealed with the seal of chastity, which, by the entrance of the Lord, was not broken, but rather made more firm and sure.'[13]

And again :

' Mary, the sister of Aaron, went out before the children of Israel when they passed over the Red Sea, and she led the way

---

[12] Peter of Blois, Serm. 38, *Bib. Max.* tom. xxiv. p. 1116.
[13] Seventeenth Sermon, col. 305, vol. cxcv. of Migne's *Patrologia.*

with her timbrel (Exod. xv. 20). In this she was a type of the true Mary, who leads the way to all who have passed through the sea of this present life. · She goes before them in dignity, she goes before them in sanctity, she goes before them in purity and mortification. But she goes before them also in this, that she was the first of all to pass. She was the first of the whole human race who escaped the curse of our first parents. Therefore was it said to her by the angel, "Blessed art thou amongst women;" that is, while all other women are under a curse, thou alone amongst them deservest this wondrous blessing.'[14]

As England has the honour of having first celebrated the festival of our Lady's Conception, so have her schools the credit of being the first to defend it scientifically. England, Ireland, and Scotland have each claimed to be the birthplace of Duns Scot, the famous Doctor Subtilis. Luke Wadding advances strong, though not conclusive, arguments in favour of Ireland. But it is certain that it was in Oxford that Duns Scot was educated and lectured, and he there composed his best works. In his third book on the Sentences (distinct. 3, qu. 1), he defends the Immaculate Conception as the more probable opinion; but in distinct. 18 he asserts it more emphatically.

His fame, however, and his influence on the controversy which followed are due not so much to his writings, as to the tradition of his wonderful success in an oral discussion. It is said that he was summoned from Oxford to Paris in 1305, in order to be the champion of our Lady's privilege, against many opponents, and that his triumph was so remarkable as to have exerted a lasting influence, not only on the Franciscan order, to which he belonged, but on the University of Paris. Alexander Natalis, indeed, treats the whole of this Parisian episode as a fable; but his objections have been solidly refuted by John de Luca, the continuator of Wadding.[15]

As some of the Dominicans are known to have contested the privilege of the Immaculate Conception, I am glad to give

[14] Nineteenth Sermon, col. 319.
[15] See Wadding, *Annales Minorum,* t. vi. 40-52; Natalis, ad sæc. xiii. cap. v. art. 1; Joannes de Luca, pp. 134-36.

here the words of an English Dominican, Father Bromyard, who wrote at the beginning of the fifteenth century a *Summa Prædicantium*, or Suggestions and Materials for Preachers.

Under the word Maria he writes : 'The feast (of the 8th of December) would have been better called Sanctification than Conception, because Mary was conceived in original sin, and the solemnity must be referred to the point of her sanctification, not to that of her conception' (n. 33). This would seem a clear denial of Mary's privilege, but in reality it is not, for (n. 10) after quoting St. Thomas, the great doctor of the Dominican order, he says, that ' Mary was sanctified in her " animation," that is, in the union of her soul with her body, and not before, because sanctification and purification are the work of grace, and the soul alone is the subject of grace or capable of receiving it.' It might still be thought that he admitted the presence of original sin at least in the first moment, had he not explicitly denied this. His words are as follow : ' A merchant who has no land on which to build goes seeking a site, and after much search and disappointment at last finds what he wants, and exclaims with joy, " This is my place of rest at last." So acted the Son of God. He wished to assume human nature of some woman, in order to dwell with us ; but seeking from the beginning of the world He found none worthy to be His dwelling-place, since all were infected with original sin or actual sin, or with both. At last at the end of the world He found this most pure Virgin, in whom was no sin, original or actual; and rejoicing in His good fortune, He exclaimed, " This is My rest for ever and ever ; here will I dwell, for I have chosen it" (Ps. cxxxi. 14).'[16]

From this it will be seen how carefully our old writers must be read, with some knowledge of the controversies of the day, and the distinctions invented by theologians, lest they be misunderstood, and quoted in favour of doctrines or denials which they would have repudiated.

In connection with Mary's Immaculate Conception and pleni-

[16] *Summa Prædicantium*, auctore Joanne Bromyard, parte ii. cap. iii. p. 12, ed. Antverpiana, 1614.

tude of grace is her position as the second Eve, undoing the work of the first :

VENERABLE BEDE (eighth century).

Contrast between Eve and Mary.

'It was indeed a fit beginning of our restoration, that the angel of God should be sent to a Virgin about to be overshadowed by the Divine Spirit, since the serpent was sent by the devil to a woman about to be seduced by the spirit of pride; or rather the devil himself came in the serpent, and by the deception of our first parents robbed the human race of the glory of immortality. Therefore, since death entered by means of a woman, life also fitly came back by means of a woman. The one was seduced by the serpent, and offered man the fruit of death; the other was taught by God through the angel, and brought to the world the Author of salvation.'[17]

ŒLFRIC (tenth century).

'Let us also be mindful of how great dignity is the holy maiden Mary, the Mother of Christ. She is blessed above all women; she is the heavenly Queen, and the comfort and support of all Christian men. Our old mother Eve shut to us the gate of heaven's kingdom; and the holy Mary opened it again to us, if we ourselves by evil works shut it not against us. Much may she obtain of her Child, if she be fervently thereof reminded. Let us therefore, with great fervour, pray to her that she mediate for us to her own Child, who is both her Creator and her Son, true God and true man, one Christ, who liveth and reigneth with Father and with Holy Ghost, those Three, one God, to all eternity. Amen.'[18]

PRAYER OF EVE.

In the Blickling Homilies, written in Anglo-Saxon in the tenth century, the article of the Creed, 'He descended into hell,' is

[17] Beda, Hom. 47, ed. Giles.
[18] Œlfric, Hom. vol. ii. p. 23, ed. Thorpe.

developed ; and Eve is introduced making the following prayer
to our Lord :

' Thou, O Lord, art just, and Thy judgments are right ; therefore deservedly I suffer these torments.   In Paradise I was in
honour, and I did not perceive it ; I became perverse and like to
foolish brutes.   But Thou, Lord, shield of my youth and of me,
be not mindful of my folly, nor turn from me Thy presence nor
Thy mercy, and turn not in anger from Thy servant.   Hear, O
gracious God, my voice, with which I, poor one, cry unto Thee,
for my life and my years have been consumed in sorrow and
lamentation.   Thou knowest my fashioning, that I am dust and
ashes, if Thou beholdest my unrighteousness.   I entreat Thee
now, Lord, for the sake of Thy servant, St. Mary, whom Thou
hast honoured with heavenly glory.   Thou didst fill her womb
for nine months with the prize of all the world.   Thou knowest
that Thou, O Lord, didst spring from my daughter, and that
her flesh is of my flesh, and her bone of my bones. Have mercy
upon me now, O Lord, for the honour of her glory.'[19]

[19] Blickling Homilies, p. 88 (Early English Text Society, ed. 1874)

CHAPTER II.

THE VIRGIN MOTHER OF GOD.

AT the Council of Hatfield, held in A.D. 680, the Anglo-Saxon Church received and published the decrees of the Council of Lateran, A.D. 649. One of these decrees runs as follows :

'If any one shall not confess, in accordance with the teaching of the holy Fathers, that the holy and ever-virgin and immaculate Mary is properly and truly the Mother of God, since at the end of ages, without union with man, but of the Holy Ghost, she conceived God Himself the Word, specially and truly, who before all ages was born of God the Father, and brought Him forth without corruption, retaining indissolubly her virginity even after the birth ; let him be condemned.'[1]

It would be superfluous to multiply quotations from our ancient writers regarding either of these dogmas—the perpetual virginity of our Lady, or her real divine maternity. The expression 'ever-virgin Mother of God' occurs in almost every page of their writings. I shall therefore be content with two extracts from the Anglo-Saxon homilist, Œlfric.

ŒLFRIC (tenth century).

On Mary's Perpetual Virginity.

'Also Ezechiel the prophet saw in his prophecy a closed gate in the house of God, and an angel said to him, "This gate shall be opened to no man, for the Lord only will go in by that gate, and again go out, and it shall be shut for ever." That closed gate in the house of God betokened the holy maidenhood of the blessed Mary. The Lord, of all lords Lord, that is Christ, entered her womb, and through her was brought forth in human

[1] Wilkins, Con. i. 53; Haddan and Stubbs, vol. iii. p. 146.

nature, and that gate is shut for ever; that is, Mary was a Virgin
before the birth, and a Virgin at the birth, and a Virgin after
the birth.'[2]

'The maidenhood of Mary was manifoldly betokened in the
old law. God bade Moses the leader take twelve dry rods from
the twelve tribes of the people of Israel, and lay them before
the holy ark within the great tabernacle; and He would by those
rods declare whom He had chosen for bishop. Then, on the
second day, Aaron's rod was found growing with boughs, and
blowing, and bearing nuts. Verily the dry rod, which was not
planted in the earth, nor clothed with any rind, nor with sap
quickened, and yet grew, and blew, and bare nuts, betokened
the blessed Mary, who had no society of man, and yet bare the
Living Fruit, who is the true Bishop and the Redeemer of our
souls.'[3]

OLD ENGLISH CAROL (fifteenth century).[4]

> 'I sing of a Maiden
>   That is matchless;
> King of all kings
>   To her Son she ches.[5]
>
> He came all so still
>   To His Mother's bower,
> As dew in April
>   That falleth on the flower.
>
> Mother and maiden
>   Was never none but she;
> Well might such a lady
>   God's Mother be.'

ALMA REDEMPTORIS MATER.[6]

> 'As I lay upon a night,
> My thought was on a Lady bright

[2] Thorpe's translation, vol. i. p. 195.   [3] Ibid. vol. ii. p. 9.
[4] From Wright's *Songs and Carols*, p. 30. I have modernised the
spelling.   [5] Chose.
[6] Wright's *Songs and Carols*, p. 88.

That men callen Mary of might,
    Redemptoris Mater.

To her came Gabriel so bright
And said, " Hail, Mary, full of might,
To be called thou art adight ;"
    Redemptoris Mater.

Right as the sun shineth in glass,
So Jesus in His Mother was,
And thereby wit men that she was
    Redemptoris Mater.

Now is born that Babe of bliss,
And Queen of heaven His Mother is,
And therefore think me that she is
    Redemptoris Mater.

After to heaven He took His flight,
And there He sits with His Father of might,
With Him is crowned that Lady bright,
    Redemptoris Mater.'

Such were the songs of the fifteenth century. They differ
in language, but not in doctrine or in sentiment, from the songs
of the Anglo-Saxons.

An old manuscript presented to his cathedral library by
Leofric, Saxon Bishop of Exeter, in 1046, contains a collection
of Anglo-Saxon poetry by anonymous writers, probably of the
ninth or tenth century. The translator, Mr. Thorpe, thinks that
the religious pieces ' possess little attraction for any class of
readers' except the philologist. Certainly the Catholic reader
will be of a different opinion. I give Mr. Thorpe's translation
of a part of a hymn on our Lord's Nativity. The translation
follows the original, word by word.

ANGLO-SAXON HYMN.

' O thou Mary, of this midworld the purest woman upon
earth of those who have been throughout all ages ; how thee
with right all with speech endowed name and say, men over

earth, blithe of mood, that thou art Bride of the most excellent
Lord of heaven.   So also the highest in the heavens, also Christ's
disciples, say and sing that thou Lady art, with holy virtues, of
the glory host, and of mundane natures under the heavens, and
of hell's inmates.   For that thou, alone of all mankind, nobly
didst resolve, boldly devising, that thou thy maidenhood to the
Lord wouldst bring and give without sins. . . . Therefore the
Lord of triumph bade His high messenger hither fly from His
majesty, and to thee His might's efficacy quickly made known,
that thou the Son of the Lord in pure nativity shouldest bring
forth, in mercy to mankind, and thyself, Mary, undefiled ever
preserve. . . . Manifest to us now the honour that to thee the
angel, God's messenger, Gabriel brought.   At least this beseech
we dwellers on earth, that thou the comfort make known to
people, thine own Son, that we may afterwards with one accord
all exult.   Now we before that Child gaze in our thoughts ; intercede for us now with bold words, that He let us not any
longer in this vale of death error obey, but that He us convey
into His Father's kingdom, where we sorrowless may after
dwell in glory with the God of hosts.'[7]

   In the Blickling Homilies, lately published in Anglo-Saxon
with English translation, are sermons on the Annunciation ;
but in reading them I was reminded of some Latin sermons attributed to St. Augustin, though thrown by the Benedictine
editors into the list of doubtful or spurious works.   On comparison I found that the Anglo-Saxon homilist evidently worked
with these before him, although he exercised some skill in selection and development.   However, I think it better to omit these,
and to give in preference two very original and beautiful meditations on the Annunciation by Anglo-Norman writers of the
twelfth century.
   The first extract is from

ST. AELRED (twelfth century).

On the Annunciation.

' It may be said of Mary as of Rachel : she was well favoured,

---

[7] *Codex Exoniensis*, translated by B. Thorpe, pp. 17-19.

and of a beautiful countenance (Gen. xxix. 17). Though of the most blessed Mary it is sweet to think that she was most beautiful even in corporal beauty, yet now I apply these words to the interior beauty of her soul. But ah, who can worthily speak of her beauty whom He, who is "beautiful above the sons of men" (Ps. xliv.), loved so far above all other creatures as not only to dwell within her soul, but to prepare for Himself a holy dwelling in her body? "While the King was at His repose, my spikenard sent forth its odour" (Cant. i. 11). Yes, when He was in the bosom of His Father, He smelt the perfume of her virginity, and gazed on the beauty of her soul. And therefore is the angel sent to announce His coming, not only into her heart but into her flesh.

'O, what heavenly nuptials, in which God is the Bridegroom, a Virgin is the bride, and an angel is the witness and negotiator! Nuptials in which the Virgin loses not her virginity, nor God His Divinity, nor the angel his dignity. Nuptials in which is a greater marvel yet; for the Bridegroom becomes the Son, the bride becomes the mother, since the Son in taking flesh to become man wedded, so to say, the soul of that most holy Virgin to His Divinity. Well might the angel salute her: "Hail, full of grace, the Lord is with thee; blessed art thou amongst women."

'And now consider the wedding-presents which the Son of God made to His spouse. Call to mind the presents which Abraham's son sent by his father's servant to Rebecca; for she also, like Rachel, was a beautiful and pure virgin. The servant of Abraham found her near the water, and there addressed her, and gave her the presents (Gen. xxiv. 15). And our most beautiful Virgin Mary was also wont to stay near those spiritual waters, the Holy Scriptures. She could say with the prophet: "He hath brought me up on the waters of refreshment" (Ps. xxii. 2). The angel found her there. "Entering in," says the evangelist, "the angel said: Hail, full of grace, the Lord is with thee." Where did he enter in? Doubtless where she had hidden herself from the vanities of the world and its cares; where she had entered her chamber and closed the door, and prayed in secret to her Heavenly Father. Was she not drawing waters with joy from the fountains of the Saviour? (Is. xii. 3) that is from the Holy Scriptures, where she had read of a virgin giving birth, and of the advent of the Saviour. Perhaps at that very time when the angel came to her she held Isaias in her hands. Perhaps she was then meditating on that prophecy: "Behold, a Virgin shall conceive, and bear a Son, and His name shall be called Emmanuel" (Is. vii. 14). Methinks that in that very hour that prophecy had caused a most lovely contest in her heart. I fancy that when she read that a virgin should one day give birth to the Son of God, a secret and timid wish rose in her heart that she might be that favoured one; and then again she thought that she was altogether unworthy of so great a boon. So charity struggled with fear, and devotion with humility. Now she almost despaired in her great fear, and then, out of the abundance of her great desire, she could not but hope. Devotion urged her to aspire; but at once her great humility bade her check her aspirations. And in the midst of this hesitation, this fluctuation, this desire, the angel enters in and says: "Hail, full of grace."

'The servant of Abraham gave Rebecca golden earrings and bracelets. So, too, did the angel Gabriel adorn the ears of Mary by his salutation. With what beautiful bracelets did he adorn her arms when he announced to her the Son whom she should carry in her arms! It is said in the Book of Canticles, "Pulchra es et decora, castissima in deliciis — How beautiful art thou, and most chaste in thy delights!" (Cant. vii. 6.) There are two kinds of chastity—that of the flesh and that of the spirit. The chastity of the spirit is humility. Now it is no great thing to preserve the chastity of the body among hardships, nor the chastity of the soul in the absence of temptation. Carnal pride, indeed, a carnal man may feel; but the spiritual pride that tempts the perfect can hardly exist in those who are destitute of virtue. But as it is a great thing in the midst of riches and luxury to preserve the chastity of the body, so is it the height of virtue to be free from pride in the abundance of divine favours. And such was the chastity of Mary's soul. Favoured in every spi-

ritual grace above the rest of human beings, she still calls herself the handmaid of the Lord ; and the Evangelist tells us she
went to minister to Elizabeth, and then to obey the summons
of the Roman Emperor. She, full of God, greater than the
world, higher than the heavens, the honour of virgins, the glory
of women, the praise of men, the joy of angels ; she, whom the
Son of God has chosen for His Mother, calls herself the handmaid ; she, who was so nobly saluted by an angel, lives in
humble obedience to a carpenter ; she, the Queen of heaven, who
carries God within her, pays deference to age, and humbly salutes her kinswoman. Well do the words apply to her, " Pulchra
es et decora, castissima in deliciis (Cant. vii. 6)—How beautiful art thou, and how comely, My dearest, in delights !" [8]

We shall see in the Second Part that one of the favourite
devotions in England was the repetition of the ' Hail Mary,' or
Angelic Salutation. I therefore give a meditation of

ARCHBISHOP BALDWIN (twelfth century).

On the Angelic Salutation (abridged).

' Cogitabat virgo qualis esset ista salutatio. Mary thought
and reflected what was the nature and meaning of the angel's
salutation. Let us reflect, too, as far as we may.

' *Ave*,—Hail !

' This is not one of those salutations by the road-side which
our Lord forbade to His messengers—Neminem per viam salu-
taveritis (Luc. x. 4)—nor one of those salutations in the market-
place which He bade His disciples despise (Matt. xxiii. 7). It
was no word of flattery, of insincerity, of treachery, of self-in-
terest. Whether it is a prayer for grace or a declaration of
grace already given, it expresses neither false praise nor pretended benevolence. It was thus spoken by the angel to be
repeated by ourselves, a jubilation to the heart that conceives it
and a sweetness to the mouth that speaks it.

---

[8] St. Aelred, Serm. viii., Migne, *Patrol. Lat.* tom. cxcv. col. 253.

'*Ave gratia plena*,—Hail, full of grace !

'Who can understand with what or how great grace she was filled who brought forth the "only-begotten Son of God, *full of grace and of truth*"? We read, indeed, of Stephen that he was *full* of grace and of strength (Acts vi. 8). But Mary was so much more full than Stephen, as she had more capacity for grace, she who conceived the Author of grace, whom the world cannot contain. Elizabeth, too, was *filled* with the Holy Ghost. But the Holy Ghost taught her to admire the greater plenitude of Mary. "Whence is this to me, that the Mother of my Lord should visit me?" Her fulness was that of the good measure, "pressed down, shaken together, flowing over," that through her the grace of God might abound in us.

'We may say that she had a threefold grace—the grace of beauty, the grace of favour, the grace of honour.

'The *grace of beauty* consists in well-proportioned features, good complexion, and sweet expression.

'I speak of the beauty of Mary's soul rather than of her body ; although the beauty of the soul often radiates from the body. The psalm does not say, all the beauty of the King's daughter is within, but from within (*ab intus*) (Ps. xliv. 14).

'The exquisite harmony of the interior features of Mary is seen, if we consider how her humility was equal to her honours, her condescension to her dignity. The more she was magnified by God, the more did she magnify God—Magnificat anima mea Dominum, quia fecit mihi magna. The more she was magnified, the more did she dwell on her own lowliness—Respexit humilitatem ancillæ suæ. Well, therefore, did Elizabeth admire her majesty and her condescension.

'The beauty of complexion is in the mixture of white and of red—of the purity which loves what is fair, of the modesty that blushes at what is foul. Yes ; Mary was full of grace, since gratia super gratiam mulier sancta et pudorata" (Eccli. xxvi. 19) —"A holy and shame-faced woman is grace upon grace."

'But that beauty may be perfect, the face must be anointed with the oil of gladness. How well was Mary thus anointed when her soul exulted in God her Saviour!—Tota pulchra es, amica mea, et macula non est in te (Cant. iv.).

'Nor has she only the grace of beauty, but that of *favour* also. Is she not loved by all, praised by all, honoured by all first after God? Is she not the very love and praise and glory of angels and of men? Viderunt filiæ Sion et beatissimam prædicaverunt (Cant. vi. 8). As she herself foretold, Beatam me dicent omnes generationes — "All generations shall call me blessed."

'And thirdly, she has the *grace of honour;* but of what honour, it is beyond my power to say. In her everything is worthy of honour—what she has in common with others, and what belongs specially to herself. For even what she shares with others she has in a singular manner and more eminent degree (Communia enim singulariter habet, quia superexcellenter præ cæteris habet, quæ cum cæteris habet). She is chaste and humble, gentle and benign. Other virgins possess these virtues, but not like her. She surpasses all, she, the Queen of the world, the Mistress of heaven, the Mother, Daughter, Sister, Spouse of God.

'*Dominus tecum,*—The Lord is with thee.

'But was it not said also to Gedeon: "The Lord is with thee, most valiant of men"? (Judg. vi. 12.) And the Psalmist says: "Dominus virtutum nobiscum" (Ps. xlv. 12). And Christ also says to us: "Behold, I am with you all days to the consummation of the world" (Matt. xxviii. 20). And of Christ Isaias says: "He shall be called Emmanuel, that is, the Lord with us" (Isai. vii. 14). All this is true; but the same prophet had just said: "Behold, a Virgin shall conceive, and shall bear a Son, and His name shall be called Emmanuel."

'How, then, would He have ever been with us, if He had not first been with Mary? He came to her, to be with her, and in her, and from her, that through her He might also be with us.

'He says: "His delights are to be with the sons of men" (Prov. viii. 31). What, then, were His delights to be with that one whom He had chosen from amongst all to be the minister of these delights ?

If, therefore, He is with us, sharing our nature, communicating His grace, that we may be children and heirs of God, brethren and coheirs of Jesus Christ, we owe this great gift to her to whom in a singular way it was said, " The Lord is with thee." Thus is she the coöperatrix in the salvation of the world. Alone she could not procure it, but she gave her ministry ; with the affection of a mediatress, she brought to us the Mediator who could do all.

' The Lord is with thee, Mary ! The work to which thou art chosen is beyond all human power or wisdom ; but the Lord is with thee, to whom " no word is impossible."

' When Gedeon was chosen to free the children of Israel from Madian, it was said : " The Lord be with thee, most valiant of men ;" valour was commemorated because valour was needed, and the God of strength supplied the strength. So, too, in the work of our salvation the fulness of grace is commemorated, since it is a work begun in grace and ended in grace, and all the praise is ascribed to Him, the Author of grace, who did the work with Mary's coöperation.

' *Benedicta tu in mulieribus,*—Blessed art thou amongst women.

' Eve by pride and disobedience merited the sentence of malediction. " God resists the proud" (1 Pet. v. 5) ; but "pride is the beginning of every sin, and he that holdeth it shall be filled with malediction" (Ecclus. x. 15). But Mary humbled herself, and merited a blessing. As her Son humbled Himself to be accursed for us, so also Mary humbled herself to a state which was esteemed unblest. She chose perpetual virginity, and renounced the blessing of fecundity.

' Whether she had read in Scripture the promise of God, " Behold, a Virgin shall conceive," and thus understood how pleasing to God must be the state to which so great a grace was promised, or whether the same Holy Spirit taught her who taught the prophet, most certainly she chose and loved virginity,

and despised the opprobrium of men. And thus she received
the very blessing of fruitfulness which she had renounced, and
received it without the curses which accompany it in other
women. Without sin she conceived and without pain brought
forth Him who takes away the curse. No longer can men reproach women with being the cause of all misery. It is to a woman we owe Him in whom we are blessed with every blessing.'[9]

The following explanation of the 'Hail Mary' is from a book
called *The Mirror of our Lady.* It was written for the Sisters
of Sion, a religious community of royal foundation at Isleworth,
on the banks of the Thames. It was printed in 1530, but the
date of its composition was between 1415 and 1450. It has
been edited for the Early English Text Society by the Rev.
J. H. Blunt, who attributes the authorship to Dr. Thomas Gas-
coign, who was Vice-Chancellor and Chancellor of Oxford.

THE HAIL MARY.

'*Ave Maria.* This salutation is taken of the Gospel of the
greeting of the angel Gabriel and of Elizabeth, and it was the
beginning of our health. And therefore this word Ave, spelled
backward, is Eva : for like as Eve's talking with the fiend was
the beginning of our perdition, so our Lady's talking with the
angel, when he greet her with this Ave, was the entry of our
redemption. And so Eva is turned into Ave, for our sorrow is
turned into joy, by mean of our Lady. For Eva is as much to
say as woe, and Ave is as much to say as joy, or without woe.
Therefore, meekly and reverently thanking this glorious Queen
of heaven and Mother of our Saviour for our deliverance, say we
devoutly to her, Ave Maria, Hail Mary.

'*Mary* is as much to say as sterne (star) of the sea, or light-
ened, or lady. For all that are here in the sea of bitterness
by penance for their sins she leadeth to the haven of health.
Them that are rightful she lighteneth by increasing of grace.
And she sheweth herself lady and empress of power, above all
evil spirits, in helping us against them, both in our life and in

* Published in Migne's *Patrologia Latina*, tom. cciv. p. 467.

E

our death and after. Therefore we ought often, and in all our needs, call busily upon this reverent name of Mary. For as the same merciful Lady saith to St. Bridget, when angels hear that glorious name they joye, and they that are in purgatory hearing that name are comforted and gladded. Rightful men are strengthened the more by more near assistance of angels to them, by naming of that holy name. Fiends tremble for fear when they hear this dreadful name. And there is no sinner on earth so cold from the love of God, but that if he call upon this most helpy name Mary, with that intent that he will turn no more again to his sin, the fiend flieth away from him, or never dare come again to him but if he fall again in will of deadly sin. Therefore, both for love and worship of our most reverend Lady, and for our own profit, say we often and devoutly Ave Maria, Hail Mary. Some use, when they hear the fiend named in play or in wrath, to say Ave Maria; that like as he joyeth in the vicious naming of his own name, so is he rebuked by naming of this holy name Maria.

'*Gratia plena,*—Full of grace. Diverse saints had divers gifts of grace, but never creature had the fulness of all graces but our Lady alone. For she was filled in body and soul with the Lord and Giver of all graces, and therefore it followeth: *Dominus tecum,*—The Lord is with thee. For with her He was in her heart by excellence of grace, and in her reverend womb, taking there a body of our kind.

'*Benedicta tu in mulieribus,*—Blessed be thou in all women. For by thee both men and women are restored to bliss everlasting.

'*Et benedictus fructus ventris tui Jesus,*—and blessed be Jesus, the fruit of thy womb. Blessed be the womb, and blessed be the fruit thereof, which is life and food to angels in heaven, and to men in earth; that is Jesu, that is to say Saviour. For He hath saved us from sin and from hell, He saveth us daily from the malice of the fiend, and from perils, and He hath opened to us the way of endless salvation; therefore endlessly be that sweet fruit blessed. Amen. So be it.'

The rest of the dialogue between Gabriel and Mary, and the

work of the Incarnation, is thus commented on by the Venerable Bede, whose words I am obliged to shorten :

VENERABLE BEDE (eighth century).

After explaining the angel's announcement about the dignity of the Son of God, who was to be born of Mary, he thus develops Mary's words in reply, ' " How shall this be done, because I know not man ?"—*i. e.* How can I, who have resolved to spend my life in virginity and chastity, conceive and give birth to a son ? She is not incredulous to the angel's words, she does not ask how they can be fulfilled ; but while she is certain that what she now hears from the angel, and had before learnt from the prophet, must be fulfilled, she asks in what order it is to be accomplished : for the prophet, who had foretold the event, had not foretold its mode, but had left that to be unfolded by the angel.

' *The angel answering said to her : The Holy Ghost shall come upon thee, and the power of the Most High shall overshadow thee.* The Holy Ghost came upon that Virgin in two ways, and showed in her the extent of His power. First, He purified her soul, as far as human frailty will permit, from all stain, that she might be worthy of the heavenly birth ; and secondly, by His sole operation, He created in her womb the holy and venerable body of the Redeemer. The power of the Most High overshadowed her, for the Holy Ghost filled her heart, calming all concupiscence, freeing from all earthly desires, and filling soul and body with heavenly gifts. . . . He *overshadowed,* as when between ourselves and the midday sun we place the foliage of a tree or other shade, to render the light and heat supportable. Our Redeemer is indeed like the sun in brightness and in power, enlightening us by the knowledge of truth and inflaming us with His love ; and the full rays of this Sun the Blessed Virgin received. But the sun, that is, the divinity of our Redeemer, veiled Himself beneath our human nature, so that His Virgin Mother might sustain His presence.

' *But Mary replies : Behold the handmaid of the Lord ; be it done to me according to thy word.*

' Certainly she is greatly founded in humility who can thus

call herself the handmaid of her Maker when she is chosen to
be His Mother.   She is pronounced blessed among women by
an angel's words, and taught mysteries of redemption as yet
unknown to other mortals ; and yet she is not elated by the
singular excellence of her deserts, but, thinking only of her own
natural condition and of the Divine condescension, she humbly
joins herself to the company of Christ's servants, and prepares
herself devoutly to fulfil her service.'

Bede concludes his homily with a beautiful exhortation to
humility.[10]

This seems the place to give the commentary of the same
saint on some words of our Lord often misunderstood.   In this
case the words of Bede have been adopted by the Church, and
are read (somewhat abridged) in the office of the Blessed Virgin.

VENERABLE BEDE.

On Mary's Blessedness.

' And it came to pass, as He spoke those things, a certain
woman from the crowd, lifting up her voice, said to Him :
Blessed is the womb that bore Thee, and the breasts that gave
Thee suck (Luke xi. 27).

'This woman gives proof of great faith and great devotion,
who, while scribes and Pharisees are tempting and blaspheming
the Lord, recognises His Incarnation with such sincerity beyond
others, and confesses it with such confidence, as to put to shame
both the calumnies of the great men who were then present and
the perfidy of all future heretics.   For as the Jews, blaspheming
the works of the Holy Ghost, were then refusing to believe that
Jesus was the true Son of God, consubstantial with the Father ;
so also later on did heretics, by their denials that the ever-virgin
Mary, through the operation of the Holy Ghost, had ministered
the substance of her own flesh to the only-begotten Son of God,
maintain that He ought not to be acknowledged as true Son of
man and consubstantial with His Mother.   Now if the flesh of
the Son of God (born according to the flesh, Rom. i. 3) is
declared foreign to the flesh of the Virgin Mother, then there

[10] Hom. 47, ed. Giles.

would be no reason why the womb that bore Him and the breasts which nourished Him should be blessed. . . . Yet the Apostle says that God sent His Son, made of a woman, made under the law (Gal. iv. 4). Nor are those to be heeded who would read " born of a woman, made under the law," but " made of a woman ;" for when He was conceived in the Virgin's womb, He did not derive His flesh from nothing, nor from elsewhere, but from His Mother's flesh. Otherwise He could not truly be called the Son of man, if He had not His origin from man.

' Therefore, having said thus much against Eutyches, let us also raise our voice together with the Catholic Church, of whom this woman was the figure, and let us raise, too, our souls out of the midst of the crowd, and let us say to our Saviour : Blessed is the womb that bore Thee, and the breasts that gave Thee suck. . . .

' *But He said : Yea, rather, blessed are they who hear the word of God, and keep it.* Our Saviour beautifully assents to this testimony of the woman, and asserts that not she only who merited to bear corporally the Word of God is blessed, but all those also who, by the hearing of faith, conceive spiritually the same Word, and by the observance of good works strive to give birth to Him or to nourish Him in their own hearts or in the hearts of others. And, besides, the Mother of God is indeed blessed in that she was the temporal minister of the Incarnation ; but she is far more blessed, because she remains for ever the guardian of His love.'[11]

Another passage of the Gospels frequently misinterpreted, and which bears on our Lady's maternity, is the answer given by our Divine Redeemer to His Blessed Mother at the marriage feast of Cana. I give the interpretation of the Venerable Bede as the one commonly accepted in England.

Venerable Bede.

On the Words of Jesus Christ.

' *What is to Me and thee, O woman ? My time is not yet come* (John ii. 4). Certainly He who commands us to honour father

---

[11] Beda, Hom. 19, ed. Giles.

and mother would not dishonour His own Mother; nor would He deny her to be His Mother from whose virgin flesh He did not disdain to take flesh. The Apostle says, ' Who was made to Him of the seed of David, according to the flesh" (Rom. i. 3). But how was He of the seed of David according to the flesh, if He was not of the body of Mary according to the flesh, which came down from David ?

'But being about to work a miracle, He says, "What is there between thee and Me, O woman ?" To signify that not from His Mother did He receive in time the beginning of that divinity by which the miracle was to be worked, but that He had it eternally from His Father. What, then, is there between Me and thee, since the divinity, which I have from My Father, has nothing in common with thy flesh, from which My flesh is taken ?

' *My hour is not yet come i.e.* to prove by My death the weakness of the humanity derived from thee. I have first to manifest, by working miracles, the power of My eternal Godhead. But the hour would come when He would show what there was in common between Himself and His Mother, when dying on the Cross He was careful to commend His Virgin Mother to His virgin disciple.'[12]

AVE REGINA CELORUM.

[From a small 4to volume of the fifteenth century, preserved in the Advocates' Library, Edinburgh (Jac. v. 7, 27). It was first printed by the late Mr. W. B. D. D. Turnbull in a scarce volume, *The Visions of Tundale*, &c., published by him at Edinburgh in 1843.]

> 'Heyle be thou Mary tho moder of Cryste
> Heyle be tho bleste that euer bare chylde
> Heyle be thou conseyude all by lyste
> Thi son Jesus bothe meke and mylde
> Heyle meydon swete that neuer was fylde
> Heyle weyle and wytte of all wysdum
> Heyle feyrer then tho floure unfylde
> *Ave Regina Celorum.*

> Heyle comly qwene comforth of care
> Heyle godly lady bothe feyr and bryght

[12] Beda, Hom. 18, ed. Giles.

Heyle tho socur of all owre sare
Heyle tho lampe that lenys hus lyght
Heyle godly lady in the was plyght
Tho joy of man bothe all and sum
Heyle tabarnakull hee on heyght
    Mater Regys Angelorum.

Heyle cumly qwene tho fayrest of all
Heyle in the oure blys is bredde
Heyle on the all wemen wyl call
When thei with chylde ben by stedde
Heyle that all fyndes wyll drydde
And schall do to the day of dom
With meydens mylke thi chylde thou fydde
    O Maria flos Virginum.

Heyle tho fayrest of all gud fame
Heyle that God schase to his boure
Heyle tho lampe that euer is lyghtand
To hye and lowe to ryche and pore
Heyle swetur than ony savour
Heyle that all oure joy of come
Heyle of all women frute and floure
    Velud rosa vel lillium.

Heyle gudly grounder of all grace
Heyle blestefull starne of tho see
Heyle tho saluer of oure solace
Heyle tho chefe of chastite
Heyle tho well of all mercy
Heyle that bare God of heyvon
Heyle tho tempull of the trinite
    Funde preces ad filium.

Heyle blestfull virgyn of all virgyns
Heyle medyn modur and blestfull mey
Heyle the norse of swete Jesus
Heyle gudly qwene as thou well mey

Heyle he lady to thi son thou prey
That we mey cum to his kingdome
For hus and for all oder thou prey
            Et pro salute fidelium.'[13]

ECCE ANCILLA DOMINI.

[From the same manuscript and work.]

'Seyde tho virgyn withowttyn vice
Whom Gabriell hur gret graciously
That holy pynakell perued of price
Of the schall sprynge a full swete spice
Then seyde tho meydon full myldely
And sythen I am so lytull of price
            Ecce Ancilla Domini.

Heyle be thow gracious withowthon gilte
Maydon borne alderblest
Wythin thi body schall be fulfyllyd
That all these prophetes have preched so preste
God will be borne within thi brest
Then seyde tho meydon full myldely
To me he schall be a welcome geste
            Ecce Ancilla Domini.

But when sche sawe an angell bryght
Sche was aferde in all her thoght
And of his speche elles wonder sche myght
Then seyde the angell drede the noght
A blestfull tythyne I have the broght
Then seyde tho meydon full myldely
Os God will so be it wroght
            Ecce Ancilla Domini.

That angell seyde conceyve thou schalt
Within thi body bryght

---

[13] *The Visions of Tundale*, together with Metrical Moralisations and
other Fragments of Early Poetry, hitherto inedited, p. 145.   Edin 1843.

A childe that Jesus schall be called
That is grace Goddis son of myght
Thou art his tabernakull I-dyght
Then seyde tho meydon full myldely
Sethen he seyde neuer ageyn ryght
    Ecce Ancilla Domini.

Call hym Jesus of Nazareth
God and mon in on degre
Ryght os mon schall suffer dethe
And regne in David dignite
A blestfull worde he send to the
Then seyde tho meydon full myldely
He schall be dere welcum to me
    Ecce Ancilla Domini.

Bot with mannis mode neuer I mette
Now lorde how schall I go with chylde
Then seyde the angell that her grett
With non suche thou schalt be fylde
The holy goste will in tho byldon
Then seyde tho meydon full myldely
Os God will so be it done
    Ecce Ancilla Domini.

When the angell was vanesched awey
Sche stode in stody all in hur thoght
And to herselfe sche can sey
All Goddis wille schall be wroght
For he is well of all witte
As wyttnesse well his story
At that worde knot was knytte
    Ecce Ancilla Domini.[14]

[14] *The Visions of Tundale*, &c., Edinburgh, 1843, p. 142.

CHAPTER III.

OUR LADY'S JOYS.

FROM the two preceding chapters it will have been seen how sublime was the idea entertained concerning the sanctity of her for whom 'He had done great things, who is Almighty, and whose name is Holy.'

Immaculate in her conception, filled with grace before the Annunciation, what must she have become after the overshadowing of the Holy Ghost, and the accomplishment of the Incarnation? To what degree of sanctity must she have arrived after bearing the Son of God in her womb, giving birth to Him, living with Him in the intimate familiarity of a mother? I must now let our old English writers tell us what they thought of these things. The first extract is from the sermons of Adam Scot, a Premonstratentian Abbot in Scotland.

ADAM SCOT (twelfth century).

On the Mother and the Child.

'O what humility, that God should be born of a Virgin, the Son of God be wrapped in swaddling clothes ! O what meekness, to be laid in a manger ! Is not a manger the place for oxen and for asses? And that Child is God, the Wisdom of His Father ! Who would not wonder at seeing the Wisdom of God laid before an ass, the Divinity before an ox? Yet so was it right it should be ; for how otherwise would " the ox have known his Master, the ass his Master's crib"?

'O Child, Creator of all things, how humbly Thou liest in the manger, though Thou rulest in the heaven ! There the heaven of heavens cannot contain Thee, and here Thou art enclosed in a narrow crib. In the beginning of the world Thou didst clothe the earth with herbs and trees, springing up and bearing fruit; Thou didst adorn the firmament with sun and moon and stars, and didst fill the air with birds, the waters with fish, the earth with reptiles and with beasts. And now at the end of the world Thou art wrapped in swaddling clothes! O majesty, O humility; O height, O depth; O immense, eternal, O Ancient of days; yet, O little One, O Infant not yet a day old upon the earth!

'Rejoice and be glad, O Virgin. Thou embracest Him whom the innumerable choirs of heavenly spirits cannot comprehend as He lies in the bosom of His Father. Now thou bowest down before Him as thy Creator, then thou liftest Him up as an Infant; now thou salutest Him as thy Lord, then thou embracest Him as thy Child; now thou liest prostrate in soul before Him as the Most High, and then thou smilest on Him as a little one. O, rejoice and exult to-day in Him to whom thou hast given birth. O sweet Virgin, O gentle Virgin, assist us and protect us in the terrible day of judgment, that as we have rejoiced in His coming as our Redeemer, we may not tremble when we see Him coming to be our judge.'[1]

Such maternal relations, such ineffable joys as are touched on in the above passage, suppose the soul of Mary filled by divine grace with a purity and sanctity unknown to any other creature. This conclusion has been drawn by

St. Anselm (eleventh century).
On the Sanctity of the Mother of God.

'It was fitting that that Virgin should be resplendent with such a purity, that under God a greater could not be imagined; to whom God the Father disposed to give His one and only Son (whom, as born from His heart and equal to Himself, He loved as Himself) in such a manner that He might be by nature one and the same Son in common of God the Father and of the Virgin. Her the Son Himself did choose to make substantially a Mother for Himself. And from her the Holy Spirit willed, and was about to accomplish in act, that That should be con-

---

[1] Adami Scoti, Serm. 25; Migne, *Patrol. Lat.* tom. cxcviii. col. 244.

ceived and born from which He (the Holy Ghost) Himself proceeded.'[2]

This reasoning of St. Anselm, that from Mary's relations with the three Persons of the ever-blessed Trinity she must have been endowed with the greatest conceivable purity, has been justly adduced as a proof of the belief of our great Doctor in the Immaculate Conception. Though he does not state this conclusion explicitly, yet neither does he anywhere contradict it, and there are good grounds for believing that he established (I do not say originated) in England the feast of our Lady's Conception.[3]

The union between the Virgin Mother and the Divine Child has been beautifully developed by the intimate companion of St. Anselm,

EADMER (eleventh century).

On Mary's Love for Jesus.

'Though the love which was interchanged between such a Mother and such a Son was both wonderful and ineffable, yet if there is some mother who loves her good and only son with an ardent love, if there is some good son who with· a similar love repays his good and gentle mother, they may make some attempt to contemplate the affection between that Son who alone is good, and that Mother who is gentle and tender beyond all women.

'Other sons divide their love between two parents; other parents share between them the possession of their child. But this Virgin Mother, happiest of parents, alone possesses all right to her Son; this Son owes all His filial affection to none besides His Virgin Mother.

'And again, other mothers first love their children, as yet unconscious of their love and unable to return it; but Mary's Son is eternal—not only her Son but her Creator. He first loved her with surpassing love and chose her for His Mother. And in His love and choice of her He gave to her those two gifts in which her heart delighted. He confirmed in her the

---

[2] *De Conc. Virgin.* c. 18, Op. t. i. p. 152, ed. Gerberon.
[3] On this subject see the *Treatise on the Immaculate Conception,* by the Right Rev. Dr. Ullathorne, pp. 127-29 ; and App. B, p. 228.

virginity she had embraced, and conferred on her the fecundity
she had renounced. And what fecundity? She received it from
that Holy Spirit who alone gives fruitfulness and life, and without whom fruitfulness becomes barren, and is cut down and
cast into the fire. And indeed it was fitting that only by the
overshadowing of the Spirit of God should that Virgin be
rendered fruitful who was destined to bear the God and Saviour
of the world.

'What, then, shall we say? Is any mind of man able to conceive the measure of the love which God bore towards this holy
Virgin, any more than the height of honour He conferred upon
her? And thou, O most blessed amongst women, what love
didst thou bear to Him who worked such mighty things in thee,
which indeed have caused all generations to call thee blessed?
In truth thy soul did magnify the Lord, and thy spirit did exult
in God thy salvation. O wondrous salvation! which not only
raised thee, O Lady, to an inestimable height of glory, but healed
a world hideous from the wounds of sin.

'O Jesus our God, Son of this most happy Mother, Power and
Wisdom of Thy Heavenly Father, we pray Thee, by the mercy
which made Thee become man for us, enlighten our hearts that
we may understand the thoughts and feelings of Thy sweetest
Mother. What was her exultation and her joy when she clasped
Thee in her arms, at once so little and so great! How did she
imprint her sweet and frequent kisses on Thy infant face!
What caresses did she invent to soothe Thy tears as Thou didst
lie in her lap! O, teach us but a little to penetrate the affections of her heart, that, though the weight of our sins prevents
us from knowing these things as they were, yet may we draw
some consolation from them in our pains.

'No one who understands the love of Mary for her Son can
be a stranger altogether to its sweetness; and no one who tastes
its sweetness need despair of having a share in its reward. What
has been the reward of Mary's love all Christians know, since
they most certainly believe that she had been exalted into
heaven and raised above all the angelic choirs.'[4]

[4] *De Excellentia B.V.M.* cap. 4; in App. ad Op. S. Ansel, tom. ii. p. 167.

As the Purification of Mary may perhaps be considered by some an objection to what has been said, I will quote two passages to show what was thought by our fathers on that mystery:

VENERABLE BEDE.

On Mary's Purification.[5]

'The Gospel read on the feast of the Purification shows us that it is principally remarkable for the humility of our Lord and Saviour, as well as of His most pure Mother; since they who owed nothing to the law yet subjected themselves to the law's decrees. . . As the Lord who issued the law of His divine will chose when He appeared on earth as man to be under the law, that He might redeem those who were under the law, and that we might receive the adoption of sons, so also His Blessed Mother, who by a singular privilege was above the law, yet to give an example of humility would not be exempt from its enactments, according to the word of the Wise Man: "The greater thou art, the more must thou humble thyself in all things" (Ecclus. iii. 20).'

PETER OF BLOIS.

On Mary's Purification.

'How is it that the holy and immaculate one, as though she had been like other women in the conception and birth of her Son, has recourse to the Purification prescribed to women by the law? The Son answers for His Mother: "Thus," He says, "it befits us to fulfil all justice" (Matt. iii. 15). The first woman, the mother of all, and of our sins, seeking to excuse herself in her sins, cast her guilt upon another; but the Mother of God, the Mother of mercy, like her Son, paid what she did not owe. . . .

'Might not that most holy Virgin have said: What need have I of purification for such a birth as this? Why need I enter the Temple, when God has made me His sanctuary? What need have I or has my Son of these oblations, since He will offer Himself on the altar of the Cross to redeem all? But ah, Lady! speak not thus; be amongst the rest of women like one of them.

[5] Beda, Hom. 24, ed. Giles.

Remember how thy Son, though without sin, deigned to be circumcised. Enter the Temple, O Blessed Virgin, offer the Blessed Fruit of thy womb. A day will come when He will not be offered in the Temple, or in Jerusalem, but outside the city, not in the arms of Simeon, but on those of the Cross. A day will come when He will not be redeemed by birds as He is to-day, but will redeem us in His Blood, since God has sent Him to be the redemption of His people. That will be the evening sacrifice, as this is the morning one. Rejoice, O Mother, in the morning sacrifice; for in the evening one thou wilt grieve, and a sword will pierce thy soul. Rejoice, O Mother, and exult, O daughter of Sion, rejoice and sing the song of thy virginity. Or, rather, listen, O Virgin, for Anna and Simeon are singing with thee. The holy Simeon sings the canticle of justice, and Anna that of continence. Sing thou also the canticle of chastity, the new and hitherto unheard canticle of virginity and fruitfulness, of humility, glory, and beatitude. "Behold," she says, "from henceforth all generations shall call me blessed." [6]

The above extracts will have shown the depth and sweetness with which Englishmen in the rude times of William Rufus and of Henry II. meditated or discoursed on the Gospel narrative. The next passage is from a beautiful treatise on ' Jesus twelve years old,' which St. Aelred, one of the first of our Cistercian abbots in the twelfth century, wrote at the request of a devout friend. I am sorry that I have only space for a short extract.

ST. AELRED.
On the Finding of the Child Jesus.

'Tell me, O most sweet Lady, Mother of my Lord, what were your feelings, your surprise and joy, when you found your most sweet Son, the Boy Jesus, not amongst boys, but in the midst of the doctors; when you saw all eyes bent upon Him, all ears attentive to Him; when small and great, learned and unlearned, were speaking of His prudence and His answers? "I have found," she says, "Him whom my soul loves, I hold Him;

---

[6] Petr. Bles. Serm. 11 and 12; Bib. Max. Lugd., tom. xxiv. See also Sermon by St. Anselm, Hom. 6; Op. tom. i. p. 242, ed. Gerberon.

and I will not let Him go" (Cant. iii. 4). Yes; hold Him, O
sweet Lady, hold fast Him whom thou lovest, cast thyself upon
His neck, embrace Him, kiss Him, and make up for His three
days' absence by multiplying thy delights.

'"My Son," she says, "why hast Thou done so to us? Behold
Thy father and I have sought Thee sorrowing" (Luke ii. 48).
Again I ask thee, O Lady, why didst thou grieve? Thou didst
not, I am well convinced, fear hunger or thirst for the Boy, whom
thou knewest to be God; but thou complainedst that the ineffable delight of His presence had been withdrawn from thee
even for a little. For so sweet is the Lord Jesus to those who
taste Him, so beauteous to those who see Him, so tender to those
who embrace Him, that the shortest absence is matter for the
greatest grief.

'"How is it," He asks, "that you sought Me? Did you not
know that I must be about My Father's business?" Even now
He begins to open the secret of those heavenly mysteries in
which for three days He had been busy. . . .

'But how shall we understand what the Evangelist says:
"They understood not the word that He spoke unto them"? I
do not think that this is said of Mary, who from the moment
when the Holy Ghost came upon her, and the power of the
Most High overshadowed her, could not be ignorant of any of
the counsels of her Son. No, when the others understood not
what He said, Mary, knowing and understanding, "kept all
these words, pondering them in her heart" (Luke ii. 19). She retained them in her memory, ruminated on them in meditation, and
compared them with whatever else she had seen or heard of Him.

'Thus that most Blessed Virgin even then was mercifully
caring for us, lest such sweet and necessary things should by
any negligence be forgotten, and so neither written nor preached,
and so posterity be deprived of the delights of this spiritual
manna. Therefore this most prudent Virgin faithfully preserved
all things, modestly kept silence about them, and then at the
proper time brought them forward and committed them to the
holy Apostles and disciples, to be preached to the world.'[7]

---

[7] Bib. Max. Lugd., tom. xxiii. p. 154.

In the meditations which I have been quoting on our Lord's Incarnation and relations with His Virgin Mother, it may have been noticed how each writer dwells with evident delight on the joy and exultation which must have filled Mary's heart.

The English had always a very marked devotion to our Lady's joys. As any one familiar with modern books of piety, modern confraternities, or churches will notice a special devotion to the Mother of Sorrow ; so any one who has turned over our earlier literature must have met with frequent evidence that to our forefathers Mary appeared especially as the 'Blissful Maiden.' I shall show elsewhere that the title of our Lady of Pity, so often met with in the Middle Ages, is not to be understood as equivalent to our Lady of Dolours, but to our Lady of Mercy ; and five candles, symbolic of her five joys, were set to burn before statues called by that or other names.

' I gif half an acr of lond,' says an old yeoman in his will,[8] ' to find yerely evermore, v. gaudyes brennyng before our Lady, in the chancel of St. John Baptist, at every antiphon of our Lady, and at every feste of our Lady, at macsse of the same feste, evermore.'

Etymologists are not agreed as to the origin of the word 'gaud;' but it would seem from the above and many similar expressions, that not only is it derived from the Latin *gaudium*, but that it is connected with the joys of our Lady. Candles, which were often decorated with flowers, and burnt to tell ot her joys, and beads for counting the joyful salutations, may first have been called gauds, and then the word may have been transferred to anything nicely decorated or used for joyous purposes ; until at last, by a modification and restriction of meaning, it has come to designate what is bright and showy (gaudy). We shall see in another chapter a similar transformation of the meaning of the word 'bead.'

I think that the prevalence of devotion to our Lady's joys in England was due, in great measure, to the tradition that this was the favourite devotion of the martyr of whom all England

* Blomefield's *Norfolk*, i. 278.

F

was so proud, St. Thomas of Canterbury. A Latin hymn was commonly attributed to him.

MARY'S SEVEN JOYS.

'Gaude virgo, mater Christi,
Quem per aurem concepisti
 Gabriele nuntio :
Gaude, quia Deo plena
Peperisti sine pœna
 Cum pudoris lilio :
Gaude, quia Magi dona
Tuo nato ferunt bona,
 Quem tenes in gremio :
Gaude, quia reperisti
Tuum natum, quem quæsisti
 In doctorum medio :
Gaude, quia tui nati
Quem dolebas morte pati
 Fulget resurrectio :
Gaude, Christo ascendente
Et in cœlum te tuente
 Cum sanctorum nubilo
Gaude, quæ post Christum scandis,
Et est tibi honor grandis
 In cœli palatio.'

The tradition was that St. Thomas used to repeat these verses very frequently, and that our Lady appeared to him and revealed also seven heavenly joys.

However, the number five prevailed over that of seven. The joys from the visit of the Magi and from the finding of the Divine Child in the Temple, mentioned by St. Thomas, were omitted, and the five joys commonly recorded in prayers and songs were these—the Annunciation, the Birth, the Resurrection, the Ascension, and the Assumption.

The number was thus made to correspond with that of our Lord's wounds, which were often commemorated at the same time. Thus John Baret of Bury, in his will, says: 'I wille have at myn interment at my diryge and messe v. men clade in blak in wurshippe of J'hus v. woundys, and v. women clad in whitte in wurshippe of oure Ladye's fyve joyes, eche of them holdyng a torche of clene vexe;' and John Gosselyn says: 'I wyl and bequethe to the fyndyng of v. lights to brenne in the honour of the v. wounds of our Lord God and the v. joies of our Lady St. Mary, to brenne upon my grave every holyday in tyme of dyvyne service,' &c.[9]

Sometimes, however, the number of joys commemorated was fifteen. John of Gaunt left fifteen marks of silver to the high altar of the Carmelites in London, in honour of our Lady's fifteen joys.[10]

I give a specimen of English devotion just before the Reformation.

THE FIVE CORPORAL JOYS.[11]

'Rejoice, o virgin, Christ's mother dear,
Which hast conceived, by hearing with ear
Of Gabriel's salutation.
Rejoice, because to God thou art lefe
And barest Him, without pain or grief,
In chaste conversation.
Rejoice, because thy most dear Son,
Whom thou didst see through the heart run,
Rose with manifestation.
Rejoice, because He ascended plain
Before thy face into heaven again,
By His proper excitation.
Rejoice, because thou followest Him,
And great honours to' thee is given
In the heavenly habitation :

---

* *Wills of Bury St. Edmunds*, p. 17 (Camd. Soc.), and Blomefield's *Norfolk*, v. p. 446. For other examples see Dr. Rock, *Church of our Fathers*, vol. iii. p. 291. [10] *Test. Eborac.* p. 228.

[11] From a Prymer of 1538; Maskell, *Monum. Rit.* ii. p. 74. Another hymn may be found in the *Month* for May 1873, borrowed from the *Old English Miscellany* (Early English Text Society, 1872).

Where the fruit of thy womb everlasting
We may behold through thy deserving
In joy without mutation.'

PRAYERS ON THE FIVE JOYS OF OUR LADY.

[From the *Ancren Riwle*, written in semi-Saxon in the thirteenth century.]

I.

'Sweet Lady, St. Mary, for that same great delight which thou hadst within thee at the very time when Jesus, God, the Son of God, after the salutation of the angel, took flesh and blood in thee and of thee, receive my salutation with the same Ave, and make me to think little of every outward delight, and comfort me within, and by thy merits procure for me the joy of heaven. And as certainly as in the same flesh that He took of thee there was never sin, nor in thine, as I believe, after the same conception, whatever may have been before,[12] cleanse my soul from fleshly sins.

'*Hail Mary*, &c. to *The Lord is with thee.*

'The *Magnificat*, standing.

'Hail Mary, to the end, five times.

II.

'Sweet Lady, St. Mary, for the same great joy that thou hadst when thou sawest that blissful Child, born of thy pure body for the salvation of mankind, with whole virginity and maiden's honour, heal one who through will am stained as I fear, whatever I may be as to deed, and grant that I may in heaven behold thy joyful countenance, and behold thee, and thy maiden's honour, if I am not worthy to be blessed in thy fellowship.

'Hail, Mary, full of grace, the Lord is with thee. Ad Dominum cum tribularer (Ps. cxix.). Five Hail Marys.

III.

'Sweet Lady, St. Mary, for the same great joy which thou

[12] This does not imply doubt as to Mary's actual sinlessness or immaculate conception. The expression refers to a controversy then existing as to the freedom from concupiscence before the overshadowing of the Holy Ghost. On this subject see pp. 29, 31.

hadst when thou sawest thy dear Son, after His sweet precious
death, arise to joyful life, His body sevenfold brighter than the
sun, grant me that I may die with Him and rise in Him ; die to
the world, and live spiritually ; share in His sufferings as His
follower on earth, that I may be His companion in blessedness
in heaven. For the great joy which thou hadst, Lady, of His
joyful resurrection, after thy great sorrow, after my great sorrow
in which I ever am here, lead me to thy joy.

‘Hail, Mary, full of grace, the Lord is with thee. Retribue
servo tuo (Ps. cxviii.). Five Hail Marys.

IV.

‘Sweet Lady, St. Mary, for the great joy which thou hadst
when thou sawest thy bright blissful Son, whom the Jews
thought to imprison in the stifling tomb, as another mortal man,
without hope of rising again ; sawest Him so gloriously and
graciously, on Holy Thursday, ascend up to His joy into His
kingdom of heaven ; grant to me that I may with Him cast all
the world under my feet, and ascend up now in heart and mind ;
and when I die that I may ascend spiritually, and at the judgment day all bodily, into the blessedness of heaven.

‘Hail, Mary, full of grace, the Lord is with thee. In con-
vertendo (Ps. cxxv.). Hail Mary five times.

V.

‘Sweet Lady, St. Mary, for the same great joy that filled all
the earth when thy sweet blissful Son received thee into His
infinite bliss, and with His blissful arms placed thee on the
throne, and a queenly crown on thy head brighter than the sun ;
O high heavenly Queen, so receive these salutations from me
on earth, that I may blissfully salute thee in heaven.

‘Hail, Mary, full of grace, the Lord is with thee. Ad te
levavi (Ps. cxxii.). Five Hail Marys.

‘V. The Holy Ghost shall come upon thee.

‘R. And the power of the Most High shall overshadow thee.

Let us pray.

‘Pour forth, we beseech Thee, O Lord, Thy grace into our
hearts, that we, to whom the Incarnation of Christ Thy Son

was made known by the message of an angel, may, by His Passion and Cross, be brought to the glory of His resurrection; through the same Christ our Lord. Amen.

The Antiphon.

' Ave regina cœlorum,
Ave domina angelorum ;
Salve radix, sancta porta
Ex qua mundo lux est orta.
Ave virgo gloriosa
Super omnes speciosa.
Vale, o valde decora,
Et pro nobis semper Christum exora.

' *V.* Egredietur virga de radice Jesse.
' *R.* Et flos de radice ejus ascendet.

Oremus.

'Deus qui virginalem aulam, &c.

' Gaude Dei genitrix, virgo immaculata. Gaude quod gaudium ab angelo suscepisti. Gaude quod genuisti æterni luminis claritatem. Gaude mater, gaude sancta Dei genitrix. Virgo tu sola mater innupta. Te laudat omnis Filii creatura genetricem lucis, sis pro nobis pia interventrix.

' *V.* Ecce Virgo concipiet.
' *R.* Et pariet Filium.

Oremus.

'Deus, qui salutis æternæ, &c.

' The Antiphon *Alma Redemptoris*, with prayer. Then say fifty or a hundred Aves, more or less, as you have leisure. Then the versicle, " Behold the handmaid of the Lord, be it done to me according to thy word." . . . Whoso pays attention to the word Maria may find in it the first letters of the five psalms aforesaid.'

One more specimen I give of these old devotions, which will illustrate both the language and the piety of the thirteenth century.

THE FIVE JOYS OF THE BLESSED VIRGIN.[13]

[From a ms. in the library of Trin. Coll. Cam. (B 14, 39) of the first half
of the thirteenth century.]

I.

' Seinte Marie, lovedi brist,
Moder thou art of muchel mist,
Quene in hevene of feire ble ;
Gabriel to the he liste,
The he brouste al wid riste
Then holi gost to listen in the.
Godes word ful wel thou cnewe ;
Ful mildeliche therto thou bewe,
Ant saidest, " So it mote be !"
Thi thonc was studevast ant trewe ;
For the joye that to was newe,
    Levedi, thou haue merci of me !

II.

Seinte Marie, moder milde,
Thi fader bicome to one childe,
Suc joyc ne scal never eft be.
The stronge fend that was so wilde,
Godes hondiwerc he spilde,
For on appel of the tre.
Levedi, mon thou broutest bote,
The stronge fend an under fote,
Tho thi sone was boren of the :
For the joye that tho was swote,
Levedi, yemme grace that I mote
Wid al mine miste lovien tho.

III.

Seinte Marie, quene in londe,
Godes moder ant Godes sonde,
That te sculde been so wo ;
Jewes hiden thi sone an honde,
Judas soldin him to honde,
On the rode heo gonnen him slo ;

[13] Published in the *Reliquiæ Antiquæ.*

The thridde dai he ros to live ;
Levedi, afte were thou blive,
Ac never so thou were tho.
Levedi, for then ilke sive
That tou were of thi sone blive,
Al mi sunnes thou do me fro !

IV.

Seinte Marie, maydan ant mere,
So lengore o so betere thou were,
Thou here him alle that clepet the to :
In muchele blisse that tou were,
Tho thinne swete sone i-bere
I-siu him in to hevene sten.
E sit arist as ure drist,
And weldet al as hit is rist,
We mowen i-heren ant i-sen.
Levedi, for thi muchele miste,
The swete blisse of hevene briste,
Seinte Marie, herude me.

V.

The fifte joie is feirest in wede,
Tho thou in to hevene trede,
To him that was of the i-born.
Nou thou art in hevene quene,
Mit tine sone, brist ant scene ;
Al folc the heret therfore.
There is joie ant eke blisse
That ever last, wid-oute misse
Ant ther thou art quene i-corn,
Levedi, tuct thou me mi bene,
For the joie that ever is newe,
Thou let me never be furlorn.'

So famous was this devotion to our Lady's joys, that when the good citizen Fabian, in the time of Henry VII., wrote his Chronicle, and divided it into seven books, he was not satisfied with invoking our Lady's help at the beginning, but he dedicated each book to one of her seven joys, concluding each with some English verses in her honour.

I give as specimens the first two joys :

FABIAN'S CHRONICLE.

I.

'Thus here endeth the first part of this work, containing or divided in seven parts, as before is showed. And in the way of a thank to be given to our most blessed advocate and helper of all wretches that to her list to call, I mean that most blessed Virgin our Lady St. Mary, Mother of Christ; for that of her grace hath furthered this work hitherto ; and for to impetre of her grace the grace and aid of her most merciful countenance to accomplish this work, begun, as before is showed, under support of her most bounteous grace, here will I with humble mind salute her with the first joy of the seven joys which begin

Gaude flore virginali, &c.

'Most virginal flour, of all most excillent,
Piercing of angels the highest hierarchy,
Joy and be glad, for God omnipotent
Hath thee lift up and set most worthily
Above the number and glorious company
Of His blessed saints, with most high dignity
Next after Him most honoured to be.

II.

' And here I make an end of the second part of this work ; and in yielding graces to our most consolatrice, that most blessed Virgin, our Lady St. Mary the Virgin, her I again salute with the second of the foresaid seven joys which beginneth

Gaude sponsa cara Dei, &c.

'Be joyous, the spouse of God most dear,
Which, like to the sun, most clearest of light,
When in the day he shineth most clear
The world illuminest by means full right,
And through the virtue of thy full might
Causest the world to be resplendissant,
By mean of the peace which is full abundant,' &c.

CHAPTER IV.

OUR LADY'S WORDS.

THE *Little Children's Little Book*, written in the fifteenth century to teach the rules of courtesy and good manners to the young, proposes to them the example of our Blessed Lady:

> 'Little children, here ye may lere
> Much courtesy that is written here;
> For clerks that the seven arts cunne
> Seyn that courtesy from heaven come,
> When Gabriel our Lady grette,
> And Elizabeth with Mary mette.'[1]

Many other virtues besides courtesy are to be learnt from our Lady's Visitation to St. Elizabeth, and in the present chapter I give a translation of a homily of Venerable Bede on this mystery, adding some other fragments on the sublime lessons conveyed by our Lady's words and by her silence.

OUR LADY'S WORDS.

[*Ancren Riwle* (thirteenth century).]

'Our dear Lady St. Mary, who ought to be an example to all women, was of so little speech, that we do not find anywhere in Holy Writ that she spake more than four times. But, in compensation for her seldom speaking, her words were weighty, and had much force. Her first words that we read of were when she answered the angel Gabriel; and they were so powerful that as soon as she said, "Behold the handmaid of the Lord, be it done to me according to thy word," at this word, the Son of God and very God became man; and the Lord, whom the whole world could not contain, enclosed Himself within the womb of the maiden Mary. Her next words were spoken when she came and saluted Elizabeth, her kinswoman. And what power,

---

[1] Published by Early English Text Society, 1868.

thinkest thou, was manifiested in those words? What! That a child, which was St. John, began to leap in his mother's womb when they were spoken. The third time that she spoke was at the wedding; and there, through her prayer, was water changed into wine. The fourth time was when she had missed her Son and afterwards found Him. And how great a miracle followed those words! That God Almighty bowed Himself to a man, to a carpenter, and to a woman, and followed them, as subject to them, whithersoever they would! Take heed now, and learn diligently from this, how great efficacy there is in speaking seldom.'[2]

The longest discourse of our Blessed Lady, and that which most reveals to us the secrets of her immaculate heart, is her song of praise, the *Magnificat.* The reader will perhaps be glad to see an old English version of this canticle, which has been ever so familiar and so dear to Christian lips.

OLD ENGLISH VERSION OF THE MAGNIFICAT[3] (about 1400).

'Mi soule magnifieth the lorde : and my spirit fulout ioiede in god myn heethe.

'For he bihelde the mekenesse of his handmaide : lo forsothe of this alle kynredis shulen seie me blessid.

'For he that is miȝti hath don to me grete thingis : and his name is Hooli.

'And his merci is fro kynrede in to kynredis : to men that dreden him.

'He made myȝt in his arm : he scatride proude men with the thouȝt of his herte.

'He sette doun myȝti men fro ceete : and enhauncide meke men.

'He hath fulfillid hungri men with goodis : and he hath lefte riche men voide.

'He havynge mynde of his merci : took up Israel his child.

'As he hath spokun to oure fadris : to abraham and to his seed in to worldis.'

[2] *Ancren Riwle*, p. 77 (Camden Society's edition).
[3] Maskell, *Monumenta Ritualia*, vol. ii. p. 62.

VENERABLE BEDE (eighth century).

Homily on the Visitation.

'Since the human race had perished by the contagion of the pestilence of pride, it was fitting that, at the very first outset of the time of salvation, some manifestation should take place of the humility by which we are healed. And since by the rashness of woman death entered the world, it was also fitting that, as a sign of returning life, devout women should strive to outdo each other in services of humility and piety. First of all, therefore, did the Blessed Mother of God, venerable no less from her virginal purity than from her piety, show how the road of humility leads to the heights of the heavenly country. The citizens of that country are as the angels of God, who neither marry nor are given in marriage. Who, then, so well as that unsullied Virgin could teach us the glory of that heavenly life, and the virtues by which we may attain to it?

' No sooner, therefore, had she enjoyed the angelic vision and annunciation, no sooner did she know what heavenly Child she should bring forth, than, instead of being elated by these heavenly favours as if they were her due, to fit herself still more for the gifts of God she fixed her every thought on the preservation of humility, and answered the archangel : " Behold the handmaid of the Lord, be it done to me according to thy word." And not to angels only but to men also does she show humility ; and such is her height of virtue, she humbles herself even to her inferiors. Who is ignorant that a virgin consecrated to God holds a higher rank than a devout married woman? Who can doubt that the Mother of the eternal King is rightly preferred to the mother of a soldier in His army? Yet Mary remembered how Holy Scripture says : " The greater thou art, the more humble thyself in all things" (Ecclus. iii. 20). And when the angel had returned to heaven, she arose and went into the hill-country. Though she carries her God in her womb, she seeks the home and the familiar intercourse of God's servants. She enters the house of Zachary and salutes Elizabeth, whom she knows to be the mother of the servant and forerunner of our

Lord. She journeys not in doubt of the announcement that had been made to her, nor to test the angel's word by a woman's evidence ; no, she goes to congratulate her fellow-servant on the gift of God, and to give to her aged kinswoman such careful service as a youthful maiden could bestow.

' *And it came to pass that when Elizabeth heard the salutation of Mary, the infant leaped in her womb, and Elizabeth was filled with the Holy Ghost* (Luke i. 41).

' When the Blessed Virgin opens her lips to salute, immediately both Elizabeth and John are filled with the Holy Ghost. Both are taught by the same Spirit. Elizabeth understands the dignity of her who salutes, and blesses and venerates her as the Mother of her Lord. John understands that his Lord is carried in the Virgin's womb. His tongue cannot speak, but he salutes Him by the exultation of his soul ; and even before his birth shows by such signs as are in his power how gladly and how devoutly he will undertake in his youth the office of Precursor. Then was accomplished what the angel had foretold : "He shall be filled with the Holy Ghost from his mother's womb."

' *And Elizabeth cried out with a loud voice.*

' Well does she utter a great cry, when she recognises gifts so great. Well does she recognise with a loud voice the bodily presence of Him who is present everywhere. It is a loud voice, not lifted high in clamour, but filled with devotion. It was impossible for her to praise God in low tones, who was herself lifted up by the fulness of the gifts of the Holy Spirit ; who bore him in her womb than whom none is greater among the sons of women ; and who rejoiced in His coming who was conceived by a Virgin, and who should be called and should be the Son of the Most High.

' *And she said : Blessed art thou among women, and blessed is the fruit of thy womb.*

' Not only blessed among women, but with an eminent blessing among all blessed women. Nor is he the fruit of her womb blessed after the manner of the saints, but, as the Apostle says : " Of whom is Christ according to the flesh, who is over all things, God blessed for ever" (Rom. ix. 5). Of the origin of

this fruit the Psalmist speaks in mystic words, when he says :
"The Lord will give goodness, and our earth shall yield her
fruit" (Ps. lxxxiv. 13). The Lord "gave goodness" when He
decreed to save the human race from guilt by His only-begotten
Son ; He "gave goodness" when, by the grace of the Holy Ghost,
he consecrated to Himself a temple in the Virgin's womb. And
"our earth gave its fruit" when the same Virgin, whose body
was of our earth, gave birth to a Son co-equal to His Father in
His divinity, though consubstantial with His Mother in the
truth of His humanity.

'Isaias also, looking forward to the time of man's redemption, says : "In that day the bud of the Lord shall be in
magnificence and glory, and the fruit of the earth shall be high"
(Isaias iv. 2). The bud of the Lord was indeed in glory when
the everlasting Son of God appeared in time in the flesh, and
by the greatness of His heavenly virtues shone before the world.
The fruit of the earth was high when, in the power of His
resurrection, God raised to the highest heaven in immortal glory
the flesh which He had taken from our nature in its mortality.
Truly, then, is it said : "Blessed art thou among women, and
blessed is the fruit of thy womb." Incomparably blessed is she
who received the glory of that divine Bud, yet preserved the
crown of her integrity. Blessed among women, by whose virginal
childbirth the malediction of the first mother is turned aside
from the sons of women. Blessed is the fruit of her womb, by
whom we have received both the seed of incorruption and the
fruit of the heavenly inheritance which we had lost in Adam.
Truly and singularly blessed, who did not after His birth receive
grace from the Lord of blessings as we may, but who to save the
world Himself came blessed in the name of the Lord.

' *And whence is this to me, that the Mother of my Lord should
come to me ?*

'O, what great humility in the soul of this prophetess !
How true is that word of the Lord : "To whom shall I have
respect, but to him that is poor and little and of a contrite
spirit, and that trembleth at My words?" (Isaias lxvi. 2.)
Elizabeth recognised her visitor as the Mother of God as soon

as she beheld her. But she finds in herself no such merit as to entitle her to a visit from so great a guest. The Spirit who had bestowed on her the gift of prophecy conferred on her also that of humility.

' *For behold, as soon as the voice of thy salutation sounded in my ears, the infant in my womb leaped for joy.*

' By the revelation of the same Spirit, Elizabeth understood that leaping of her infant to mean that the Mother had come of Him whose forerunner he should ·be. How wondrous, how quick is the operation of the Holy Ghost ! There is no delay in learning where the Holy Ghost is teacher. In one and the same moment with the voice of the salutation arises the joy of the infant ; for when the voice reached the ears of the body the power of the Spirit entered the heart of the listener, and set on fire not only the mother but her child also with the love of the Lord who had come to them. Wherefore also this mother of our Lord's Precursor announces publicly to those who are present what she had learned in secret. For she adds :

' *Blessed art thou that hast believed, because those things shall be accomplished that were spoken to thee by the Lord.*

' In a wondrous way the Spirit with whom Elizabeth was filled gave her the knowledge of things present, things past, and things future. She shows that she has learnt things present, when she calls the Blessed Virgin the Mother of her Lord, and calls the fruit of her womb blessed. She proves her knowledge of the past, when she alludes to the words of the angel to Mary, and to Mary's faith. And she intimates her knowledge of the future, when she declares that the things that have been foretold will be certainly fulfilled.

The Magnificat.

' But if such, as we have seen, was the light which shone in the mind of the mother of the Precursor, who can tell, who can conjecture the greatness of the grace which filled the Blessed Mother of God ? Let us listen to her words, if perchance by means of them we may in some slight degree discover what passed within her soul.

' When, then, she heard the answer of Elizabeth, who called her blessed among women, named her the Mother of her Lord, praised her faith, and showed how she and her son had been filled with the Holy Ghost at the voice of her salutation, Mary could no longer keep silence on the gifts she had received. As befitted her maiden modesty she had hitherto kept silence about the heavenly oracle, and venerated in the secrecy of her own heart the hidden mystery of God. She awaited reverently the moment when it should please Him who is the Dispenser of gifts to manifest what special gift He had bestowed on her, what special secret He had revealed to her. But now that she finds that the Holy Spirit has made known to others what graces He had given her, she opens the heavenly treasure which her heart contained.

' *My soul doth magnify the Lord, and my spirit hath exulted in God my Saviour.*

' In this canticle Mary first acknowledges the gifts specially conferred on herself, and then enumerates the general benefits which God never ceases to bestow on the human race.

' A soul " magnifies the Lord" which dedicates to the praise and service of God all its affections, and proves its sense of the Divine Majesty by the observance of God's precepts. A spirit " exults in God its Saviour" which takes no thought of earthly pleasures, and is neither softened by prosperity nor crushed by adversity, but which delights only in the remembrance of its Creator, from whom it expects eternal salvation. But though these words are adapted to all the perfect, yet they could be uttered by none so fitly as by the Blessed Mother of God, who, by a special privilege, was both inflamed with a spiritual love of God, and rejoiced in having conceived Him corporally. She had a special right above other saints to rejoice in her Jesus, that is in her Saviour, since she knew that He would derive His temporal birth from her, who was to be the eternal Saviour of the world, and who in one and the same Person was her Son and her Lord.

' In the words which follow she teaches us how meanly she thought of herself, and that all her merits were due to divine grace.

'*Because He hath regarded the humility of His handmaid; for behold, from henceforth all generations shall call me blessed.*

'She shows that she is indeed the humble servant of Christ in her own judgment, but at the same time declares that she has been suddenly raised by heavenly grace, and glorified to so high a degree, that her eminent blessedness shall be rightly the wonder and the praise of all nations.

'She then goes on to tell of the gifts of God's love to her, and with due thanksgiving acknowledges the wonderful things she has received:

'*For He that is mighty hath done great things for me, and holy is His name.*

'She therefore attributes nothing to her own deserts, but refers all her greatness to the gift of Him, who being Himself by His nature mighty and great, makes His little ones great and His weak ones strong. She appropriately adds, "His name is holy," that she might admonish and instruct her hearers, and all those to whom her words should come, to believe in that name, and diligently to invoke it, that they also may be partakers of eternal holiness and true salvation, according to the prophet's words: " It shall come to pass, that whosoever shall call upon the name of the Lord shall be saved" (Joel ii). For that is the name of which she had said: " My spirit has exulted in God my Saviour." She continues still more clearly:

'*And His mercy is from generation to generations, unto them that fear Him.*

'By "generation and generations" she means either the two races of Jew and Gentile, or all nations throughout the world, foreknowing that they would believe in Christ; for, as St.'Peter says, " God is not a respecter of persons; but in every nation, he that feareth Him and worketh justice is acceptable to Him" (Acts x. 35). In perfect agreement with these words of Mary is the word of our Lord, when He declared that not only is His Mother blessed, who merited to bear Him corporally, but all those who observe His precepts. For when He was once teaching the people and working miracles, and all wondered at His wisdom and power, a certain woman lifted up her voice from the

G

crowd and said to Him, "Blessed is the womb that bare Thee, and the breasts that gave Thee suck" (Luke xi. 27). But He gladly received this witness to the truth, and immediately added : " Blessed are they that hear the word of God and keep it," in order that the woman and all who heard Him might hope for blessedness if they were willing to obey His commands. It was as though He had said : " Although it is a singular privilege of my Mother to be judged worthy to conceive as a virgin and bear in her womb the Incarnate Son of God, to bring Him forth and nourish Him, yet they also will have a high place in that life of perpetual' beatitude, who conceive in a chaste heart His faith and love, who bear in their minds a diligent memory of His precepts, and by zealous exhortations try to nourish the same faith and love in the hearts of their neighbours."

' But now that the venerable Mother of God has taught that His mercy will be with all who fear Him, it remains for her to indicate what those deserve who proudly resist the truth.

' *He hath showed*, she says, *might in His arm ; He hath scattered the proud in the conceit of their heart.*

' By " His arm" she signifies the operation of His own power. For He requires the help of none, but He has power when He has will. This she says in contradistinction from our good works, since we are strong, not in the strength of our own liberty, but in God, as it is written : " Neither did their own arm save them, but by Thy right hand and Thy arm and the light of Thy countenance" (Ps. xliii. 4).

' " He hath scattered the proud in the conceit of their heart," because pride is the beginning of every sin (Eccl. x. 15); and on account of it the Lord cast the human race forth from secure possession of a heavenly country, and scattered them far and wide in the wanderings of this exile ; yea, and He has reserved a more terrible dispersion still for those who fear not to be obstinate in sin.

' *He hath put down the mighty from their seat.*

' She calls those now the mighty whom she just before called the proud. They are called proud because they exalt themselves beyond the measure of their condition. They are called mighty, not as really being such, but as trusting in their strength, and refusing to seek the help of their Creator. They alone, however, are truly mighty who know how to say with the Apostle : " We can do all things in Him who strengthens us" (Phil. iv. 13). Of such it is written : " God doth not cast away the mighty, whereas He Himself also is mighty" (Job xxxvi. 5). He hath therefore put down the mighty from their seat, *and hath exalted the humble ;* for every one that exalteth himself shall be humbled, and every one that humbleth himself shall be exalted ;" although the words may also be rightly understood to mean that sometimes even those who have been cast down by the Lord on account of their pride, at last, through His mercy, return to the grace of humility, and thus by the merit of devout humility are raised up to honour. Thus Saul for his pride was cast down from the seat of legal doctrine, but afterwards, on account of the submission of his humility, was raised to evangelise the faith of Christ.

' *He hath filled the hungry with good things, and the rich He hath sent empty away.*

' Those who now hunger after eternal things with ardent desires, and who cease not to strive after their possession by unwearied perseverance in good works, will be satisfied when the glory of their Redeemer, which alone they have desired, shall at length appear ; whereas those who prefer earthly to heavenly riches, in the day of the last judgment shall be cast away from God, emptied of every blessedness, and shall therefore be punished with the devil in the pain of endless misery. We see these things in no small part fulfilled even in this life ; for the humble are filled with the alms of God's bounty, and grow rich with the abundance of heavenly virtues ; while those who proudly boast of their earthly riches, or who exalt themselves on account of the abundance of their good works, as if these were done by their own strength, are inwardly deprived of the light of truth.

' *He hath received Israel His servant, being mindful of His mercy.*

' *Israel* is interpreted to mean a man who sees God. By this name, then, the whole body of the redeemed is designated, for whom God appeared as a visible man among men, that they might be able to see God.

'He hath *received* Israel, as a physician does a sick man to cure, as a king does his people to defend them from the inroads of the enemy; or rather that He might overthrow the enemy, make His people free, and grant them to reign with Him for ever.

'*His servant*—puerum, His child—noting his obedience and humility, for only by humility can we reach the possession of our redemption. "Unless you become as little children you shall not enter the kingdom of heaven."

'"Being mindful of His mercy." Yea, for if God has taken our human nature to redeem mankind, this is not from any human merit, but from the free gift of divine clemency. For what could we merit after sin but the just chastisement of our Maker? Wherefore, whoever are destined to salvation and eternal life must attribute this, not to themselves, but to His grace, who in the midst of anger is mindful of mercy (Habac. iii. 2).

'*As He spoke to our fathers, to Abraham, and to his seed for ever.*

'The Blessed Virgin makes special mention of Abraham, because, though many fathers and saints gave mystical testimony to the Incarnation, to him first were the secrets of the Incarnation and of our Redemption clearly predicted. To him specially it was said: "In thee shall all the nations of the earth be blessed." '

After some further developments, Ven. Bede concludes thus:

'By the grace of God, if we always keep in mind the acts and words of the Blessed Mary, we shall always persevere in the observance of the works of a pure and virtuous life. It is a most excellent and useful custom that has grown up in the Holy Church, that Mary's hymn is sung by all daily at Vespers —cum psalmodia Vespertinæ laudis. Thus the minds of the faithful are stirred, by a more frequent memory of our Lord's Incarnation, to a greater devotion, and confirmed in solid virtue by the frequent thought of the example of His Mother.'[4]

[4] Beda, Hom. 40, ed. Giles.

To this beautiful homily of one of our first Catholic writers in England I add, as an appendix, a fragment from one of our last before the Reformation—Sir Thomas More. It occurs in one of his devotional treatises on Holy Communion, and applies the lesson of the Visitation to the reception of the Holy Eucharist.

SIR THOMAS MORE.

A Lesson drawn from the Visitation.

'St. Elizabeth, at the visitation and salutation of our Blessed Lady, having by revelation the sure inward knowledge that our Lady was conceived with our Lord, albeit that she was herself such as else, for the diversity between their ages, she well might and would have thought it but convenient and meet that her young cousin should come visit her, yet now, because she was Mother to our Lord, she was sore marvelled of her visitation, and thought herself far unworthy thereto, and therefore said unto her : " Unde hoc, ut veniat Mater Domini mei ad me ?—Whereof is this, that the Mother of our Lord should come to me ?" But yet for all the abasement of her own unworthiness she conceived thoroughly such a glad blessed comfort, that her holy child St. John the Baptist leaped in her womb for joy; whereof she said : " Ut facta est vox salutationis tuæ in auribus meis, exultavit gaudio infans in utero meo,—As soon as the voice of thy salutation was in mine ears, the infant in my womb leaped for joy."

'Now like as St. Elizabeth, by the Spirit of God, had those holy affections, both of reverence considering her own unworthiness in the visitation of the Mother of God, and yet for all that so great inward gladness therewith, let us at this great high visitation, in which not the Mother of God, as came to St. Elizabeth, but one incomparably more excelling the Mother of God than the Mother of God passed St. Elizabeth, doth so vouchsafe to come and visit each of us with His most blessed presence, that He cometh not into our house but into ourself,—let us, I say, call for the help of the same Holy Spirit that then inspired her ; and pray Him at this high and holy visitation so to inspire us that we may both be abashed with the reverent

dread of our own unworthiness, and yet therewith conceive a
joyful consolation and comfort in the consideration of God's inestimable goodness. And that each of us, like as we may well
say with great reverent dread and admiration, " Unde hoc, ut
veniat Dominus meus ad me?—Whereof is this, that my Lord
should come unto me?" and not only unto me, but also into me,
so we may with glad heart truly say at the sight of His blessed
presence, " Exultavit gaudio infans in utero meo,—The child
within me, that is to wit, the soul in my body (that should be
then such a child in innocence as was that innocent infant St.
John), leapeth, good Lord, for joy." '

It will be a fitting complement to what has been said of our
Lady's words, if I add a few passages on her spirit of meditation
and reserve.

VENERABLE BEDE.

On our Lady's Meditations.

' His Mother Mary kept all these words, pondering them in
her heart (Luke ii. 19).

' Everything which the Virgin Mother knew to be said or
done, either concerning the Lord or by the Lord, she kept deli-
gently in her heart, committing it carefully to her memory, in
order that when the time for preaching or writing of the Incarnation should arrive, she might be able to explain completely
the whole order of things as they occurred.'[5]

' Observing the laws of maidenly reserve, Mary had no wish
to reveal to any one the secrets of Christ which she knew; but
waited with reverence for Him to reveal them when and as He
might please. She, however, with vigilant heart investigated
everything, as the Gospel says: she pondered things in her
heart,—conferens in corde suo; *i.e.* comparing things together.
She compared what she saw done with what she had read as
predicted. She saw that she who was of the family of David
and born in Nazareth had conceived of the Holy Ghost the Son
of God; and she reflected how she had read in the prophet

[5] Hom. 17, ed. Giles.

Isaias : " There shall come forth a rod out of the root of Jesse, and a flower shall rise up out of his root, and the Spirit of the Lord shall rest upon Him" (Isai. xi. 1). She had read : "Thou Bethlehem Ephrata art a little one among the thousands of Juda ; out of thee shall He come forth unto me that is to be the Ruler in Israel, and His going forth is from the beginning, from the days of eternity" (Mich. v. 2). And now she saw that she had given birth in Bethlehem to the Ruler of Israel, who was born eternally before all ages from His Father. She saw that she a Virgin had conceived, and brought forth a Son, and called His name Jesus ; and she had read in the prophet : " Behold, a Virgin shall conceive, and bear a Son, and His name shall be called Emmanuel." Again she had read : " The ox knoweth his owner, and the ass his master's crib" (Isa. i. 3), and she beholds the Lord laid in a crib, in which ox and ass are wont to feed. She remembers how it had been said to her by the angel : " The Holy Ghost shall come upon thee, and the power of the Most High shall overshadow thee, and therefore the Holy which shall be born of thee shall be called the Son of God ;" and she remembered that she had read how the mode of His birth could not be known except by revelation : " Who shall declare His generation," ' &c.[6]

Somewhat similar to the reflections of St. Bede are those of

St. Aelred.

On Mary's Prudence.

' " The heart of her husband trusteth in her" (Prov. xxxi. 11). Who is the husband of the soul is easily known from the words of the Apostle : " I have espoused you to one husband, that I may present you as a chaste virgin to Christ" (2 Cor. xi. 2). A husband who trusts in his wife securely trusts his property with her, either to spend or preserve. Let the soul, then, see whether it is worthy of this confidence. If she has science, if she has wisdom, and knowledge of the Scriptures, she has received these things from her husband, not only to be kept,

[6] Hom. 45, ed. Giles.

but also to be distributed. If she receives grace in labour, in fasts, in vigils, in psalmody, these things also are for distributing to others. If she receives grace in compunction, in prayer, in spiritual affection, in contemplation, these are to be kept, and not to be distributed. The faithful spouse must not be proud and call her husband's property her own. What she has received for distribution she must neither enviously hoard up nor arrogantly distribute ; nor must she imprudently spend what she received to keep.

'Observe, then, how well God's heart might trust in Mary. That she attributed nothing to herself is evident from her humble answer to the angel : " Behold the handmaid of the Lord." That she did not prefer herself to others is clear from the visit she made to salute God's servant Elizabeth, at the very time that she herself bore God within her womb. How carefully she preserved her spouse's good, is proved by the Evangelist : " Mary kept all these words, pondering them in her heart." How faithfully she distributed them when the time came, her hymn of praise will show : " My soul does magnify the Lord." '[7]

Moral Conclusion (for Nuns) on Talkativeness.

'When a priest comes to visit you, hear his words and sit quite still, that, when he parteth from you, he may not know either good or evil of you, nor know anything either to praise or blame in you. Some one is so learned and of such wise speech, that she would have him to know it ; who sits and talks to him and gives him word for word, and becomes a preceptor who should be a nun, and teaches him who is come to teach her ; and would, by her own account, soon be celebrated and known among the wise. Known she is well ; for, from the very circumstance that she thinketh herself to be reputed wise, he understands that she is a fool ; for she hunteth after praise and catcheth reproach. For at last, when he is gone away, he will say : " This nun is a great talker."

'Eve in paradise held a long conversation with the serpent,

---

[7] Twenty-fifth Sermon, col. 857, Migne, *Patrol.*

and told him all the lesson that God had taught her and Adam
concerning the apple; and thus the fiend, by her talk, understood at once her weakness, and found out the way to ruin her.
Our Lady St. Mary acted in a quite different manner. She
told the angel no tale, but asked him briefly that which she
wanted to know. Do you, my dear sisters, imitate our Lady,
and not the cackling Eve.

‘Wherefore let a nun, whatsoever she be, keep silence as
much as ever she can and may. Let her not have the hen's
nature. When the hen has laid she needs must cackle. And
what does she get by it? Straightway comes the ‘chough and
robs her of her eggs, and devours all that of which she should
have brought forth her live birds. The poor pedlar makes more
noise to cry his soap than a rich mercer all his valuable wares.’[8]

[8] The *Ancren Riwle*, p. 67 (Camden Society's edition).

CHAPTER V.

OUR LADY'S DOLOURS.

I HAVE already said that the special devotion in old England was to our Lady's joys. Yet of course they would be no Christian hearts that could forget her dolours. Nor were our ancestors insensible to the deep and terrible anguish which has found sympathy among all the sorrowing children of Eve. They knew how to weep with those that weep, as well as to rejoice with those who rejoice.

They received also from their teachers exhortations not to forget her whose image they saw in every church, on the rood beam, standing in tears at the right side of the crucifix.

ÆLFRIC (tenth century).

On Simeon's Prophecy.

'Then said the old Simeon to the Blessed Mary, "His sword shall pierce through thy soul." The sword betokens Christ's passion. The Blessed Mary was not slain nor martyred bodily, but spiritually. When she saw her Child taken, and iron nails driven through His hands and through His feet, and His side afterwards wounded with a spear, then was His suffering her suffering; and she was then more than a martyr, for her mind's suffering was greater than her body's would have been had she been martyred. The old Simeon said not that Christ's sword should pierce through Mary's body, but her soul. Christ's sword is here set, as we said, for His passion. Though Mary believed that Christ would arise from death, her Child's suffering went, nevertheless, very deeply into her heart.'[1]

[1] *Homilies of Ælfric*, translated by B. Thorpe, vol. i. p. 147.

St. Edmund (thirteenth century).

On our Lady's Dolours.

' You ought also to meditate on the most sweet Virgin Mary, with what anguish she was filled when she stood at the right hand of her most sweet Son, and received the disciple in the place of the Master ; and how great was her grief when she received the servant for the Lord, and the son of a sinner for the Son of God. She might, indeed, apply to herself the words of the prophet : " Call me not beautiful, but rather call me bitter ; for the Lord Almighty has filled me with bitterness and with great grief" (Ruth i. 20). So also might she say that word of the canticle of love : " Wonder not if I am brown, for the sun has altered my colour." Hence some one moved with piety thus addressed her : " O beautiful Lady, now of a truth have you felt that most sharp piercing of the sword, of which spoke Simeon on the day of thy Purification ; now hast thou received what was promised thee by Anna the prophetess." '[2]

As in the previous chapters I have given many specimens of the contemplations of saints and learned men, I will give here in preference some extracts from the popular dramas by which the mysteries of the faith were brought to the hearts of the people perhaps more effectually than by sermons. Three sets of old mysteries are still preserved, and have been printed : the Coventry, Chester, and Towneley (or Wakefield) plays. They are of different degrees of merit, and do not always come up to the height of their argument (as in the case of St. Joseph's character). Still of our Lady they treat not only very reverently but with great propriety. It is not, however, from these that I have taken my specimen of the treatment of this subject.

The following lines are part of a sacred drama, and intended to be represented on the afternoons of Good Friday and Holy Saturday. The ms. from which it was printed[3] is of the first years in the sixteenth century.

[2] *Speculum Ecclesiæ*, cap. xxii. ; *Bib. Max.* tom. xxv. p. 825.
[3] In the *Reliquiæ Antiquæ*, vol. ii. p. 124.

'SCENE—THE FOOT OF THE CROSS.

Joseph of Arimathea and Mary Magdalen, and other Maries.

*   *   *   *

Joseph.

I hear thee, Magdalen, bitterly complain;
What good creature may himself refrain?

Magdalen.

O friend Joseph, this Prince had never peer,
The well of mercy that made me clear!
Now, good Joseph, come near and behold.
O, had you seen His pains manifold!
Joseph, look better, behold and see
In how little space how many wounds be.
Here was no mercy, here was no pity!
O good Joseph, I am all dismayed
To see His tender flesh thus ruefully arrayed,
    Wounded with nail and spear.
O dear Joseph, I feel my heart wax cold,
These blessed feet thus bloody to behold,
Whom I washed with tears manifold,
    And wiped with my hair.
O, how rueful a spectacle it is!
Never has been seen, nor shall be after this,
Such cruel rigour to the King of bliss,
    The Lord that made all
Thus to suffer in His humanity!
O Maker of man, what love and pity
    Hadst Thou for us so thrall?

Joseph.

Alas, Magdalen, you make my heart to relent,
Beholding His body thus torn and rent
    That inwardly I weep;
But, good Magd'len, show unto me
Where is Mary, His Mother, so free,
    Who hath that Maid to keep?

Magdalen.

Ah, Joseph, from this place is she gone.
To have seen her a heart of stone
   For ruth would have relent.
Many men speak of lamentation
Of mothers, and of their great desolation
When that their children die and pass ;
But of His piteous tender Mother, alas !
The woe and pain passes all other ;
Was there never so sorrowful a mother.
When she heard Him for His enemies pray,
And promised the thief the blisses aye,
And to herself no word would say,
   She sighed, be ye sure ;
The Son hung and the Mother stood,
And ever she kissed the drops of blood
   That so fast ran down ;
She extended her arms Him to embrace,
But she might not touch Him, so high was the place,
   And then she fell in swoon.

Joseph.

Ah, good Magdalen, who can her blame
To see her own Son in so great a shame ?
But, Magd'len, had He of her thought in His passion ?

Magdalen.

Yes, yes, Joseph, of her He had great compassion,
For, hanging on the Cross most pitifully,
He looked on that Maid, His Mother, ruefully,
As who say, ' Mother, the sorrow of your heart
Makes my passion more bitter and more smart
Dear Mother, because I depart now,
John, my cousin, shall wait on you,
   Your comfort for to be.'
Lo, He had her in His gracious mind,
To teach all children to be kind
   To father and mother of duty.

Joseph.

Ah, good Lady, full woe was she !
But can you tell what words said He
    There in that great distress ?

Magdalen.

O Joseph, this Lamb so meek
In this cruel torment and painful eke
    But few words He had ;
Save that in great agony
He said these words : ' I am thirsty !'
    With cheer demure and sad.

Joseph.

Magd'len, suppose ye His desire was to drink ?

Magdalen.

Nay, verily, friend Joseph, I think
    He thirsted for no liquor.
He thirsted water of charity
For our faith and fidelity.
    He pondered the rigour
Of His passion done so cruelly :
For the health of man's soul chiefly
    He thirsted and desired ;
And then, after torments long,
And after pains fell and strong,
    This meekest Lamb expired.
O, what displeasure is in my mind,
Remembering that I was so unkind
    To Him that hangs here,
That hangs here so piteously,
For my sins done so outrageously!
O meekest Lamb, hanging here on high,
Was there none other mean, but Thou must needs die,
    Sinners to reconcile ?
O, where shall any comfort come to me
And to His Mother, that Maid so free ?
    Would God I might here die !

Come hither, Joseph, behold and look
How many bloody letters be written in this book,
   Small margin here is.

Joseph.

Yea, this parchment is stretched out of size!
Remember, man, remember well, and see
How liberal a man this Lord was and free;
   Which, to save mankind,
One drop of blood has not kept or spared.

   *   *   *   *

O Lord, by Thy death we are preserved,
   By death Thou hast slain death.
Was never no love like unto Thine,
That to this meekness Thyself would incline,
   And for us to yield Thy breath.
Thou knew there was no remedy to redeem sin
But a bath of Thy blood to bathe men's souls in;
   And Thou wert well content
To let it run out most plenteously.
   Where was ever such love?

   *   *   *   *

Magdalen.

O ye wells of mercy, digged so deep,
Who may refrain, who may not weep?

Other Mary.

Magd'len, your mourning avails nothing;
Let us speak to Joseph, him heartily desiring
For to find some good way
   The crucified body down to take
And bring it to sepulchre, and so let make
   End of this woful day.

Enter NICODEMUS.

Nicodemus.

O worthy Lord, who made all things of naught,
With most bitter pain to death art Thou brought,
   Thy name blessed be!

O, how pitiful a sight it is
To see the Prince of everlasting bliss
   To hang on this tree !

    *   *   *   *

Joseph.

Good brother, of your complaint cease ;
You renew again great heaviness
   Now in these women here.

Nicodemus.

Great comfort we may have all,
For by His godly power arise He shall,
   And the third day appear.
For once He gave me leave with Him to reason,
And He showed of this death and of this treason,
   And of this cruelty ;
And how for mankind He came to die,
And that He should arise so gloriously
   By His mighty majesty,
And with our flesh in heaven to ascend.
Many sweet words it pleased Him to spend
   Then speaking unto me ;
That no man to heaven might climb,
But if it were by grace of Him
   Which came down to make us free.

Joseph.

To take down this body let us essay ;
Brother Nicodemus, help, I you pray,
To knock out these nails so sturdy and great ;
O Saviour, they spared not Your body to beat !

Magdalen.

Good Joseph, handle Him tenderly.

Joseph.

Stand near, Nicodemus, receive Him softly ;
   Magdalen, hold His feet.

Magdalen.

Haste now, good Joseph, haste you quickly,
For Mary, His Mother, will come, fear I,
　Ah, ah ! that Virgin so sweet !

Nicodemus.

I saw her beneath on the other side
With John ; I am sure she will not abide
　Long from this place.

Magdalen.

Alas, she comes !　Ah, what remedy !
Good Joseph, comfort her steadfastly,
　That Virgin so full of woe.

Enter the BLESSED VIRGIN *with* ST. JOHN.

Mary.

Stand still, friends ; haste ye not so ;
　Have no fear of me.
Let me help to take my dear Son down.
　　*　　　*　　　*　　　*

Joseph.

Take comfort, Mary ; this wailing helps nothing.
Your dear Son we will to His sepulchre bring,
　As it is all our duty.

Mary.

God reward you of your tenderness !
I shall assist you with all humbleness.
　But yet, ere He depart,
Suffer me my mind for to break ;
Howbeit full scantily may I speak
　For faint and feeble heart.
O Gabriel, Gabriel !
Of great joy did you tell
　In your first salutation ;
You said the Holy Ghost should come in me,
And I should conceive a Child in virginity,
　For mankind's salvation !

H

That you said truth right well know I ;
But you told me not that my Son should die,
   Nor yet the thought and care
Of His bitter passion which He suffered now.
O old Simeon, full soothly said you
   To speak you would not spare !
You said the sword of sorrow should enter my heart ;
Yea, yea, just Simeon, now I feel it smart
   With most deadly pain.
      *   *   *   *

St. John.

You should leave off your painful affliction,
Calling to your mind His resurrection:
   This know you and that best.

Mary.

I know it well, or else in rest
   My heart should never be ;
I might not live nor. endure
One minute, but I am sure
   The third day rise shall He.
      *   *   *   *

O Judas, why didst thou betray
My Son, thy Master ?   What canst thou say
   Thyself for to excuse ?
Of His tender merciful charity
Chose He not thee one of His twelve to be ?
   He would not thee refuse.
Gave He not thee His body in memorial,
And also in remembrance perpetual,
   At His supper there ?
He that was so comely and fair to behold,
How durst thou, cruel heart, to be so bold
   To cause Him die thus here ?
By thy treason my Son here is slain,
My sweet, sweet Son ; how should I refrain
   This bloody body to behold ?'

The lamentation continues at great length and with much pathos, but perhaps scarcely with sufficient dignity for the Mother of God.

The following lines were first printed by Mr. Wright in his edition of the Chester Plays:

THE LAMENTATION OF MARY.

'Of all women that ever were born
    That bare childer, abide and see
How my Son lieth me beforn,
    Upon my skirt, taken fro the tree.
Your children ye dance upon your knee
    With laughing, kissing, and merry cheer;
Behold my Child, behold well me,
    For now lieth dead my dear Son dear.

O woman, woman, well is thee;
    Thy child's cap thou castest upon;
Thou pickest his hair, beholdest his ble,
    Thou wottest not well when thou hast done.
But ever, alas! I make my moan
    To see my Son's head as it is here;
I pick out thorns by one and one,
    For now lieth dead my dear Son dear.

O woman, a chaplet chosen thou has,
    Thy child to wear it doth thee liking;
Thou pinnest it on, great joy thou mas,
    And I sit with my Son sore weeping.
His chaplet is thorns sore pricking;
    His mouth I kiss with a careful cheer;
I sit weeping and then singing;
    For now lieth dead my dear Son dear,' &c.[4]

THE MOTHER OF SORROWS (fifteenth century).

'Mary Mother, come and see,
    Thy Son is nailed on a tree

---

[4] Chester Plays, vol. ii. p. 204.

Hand and foot, He may not go,
His body is wounded all in woe.

Thy sweet Son that thou hast borne,
To save mankind that was forlorn,
His head is wreathed in a thorn,
His blissful body is all torn.

When he[5] this tale began to tell,
Mary would not longer dwell,
But hyed her fast to that hill
There Jesu His blood began to spill.

" My sweet Son, that art me dear,
Why have men hanged Thee here ?
Thy head is wreathed in a brere .[6]
My lovely Son, where is Thy cheer ?

Thy sweet body that in me rest,
Thy comely mouth that I have kissed,
Now on rood is made thy nest ;
Leve Child, what is me best ?"

" Woman, to John I thee betake ;—
John, keep this woman for My sake ;
For sinful souls My death I take,
On rood I hang for man's sake.

This game alone Me must play,
For sinful souls I die to-day ;
There is no wight that goeth by the way
Of My pains can well say." [7]

I conclude my extracts by a prayer taken from an old English ms. called ' The Wooing of our Lord,' and published by the Early English Text Society.

---

[5] Probably St. John.   [6] Briar.
[7] Wright's *Songs and Carols of the Fifteenth Century*, p. 65.

THE WOOING OF OUR LORD.

'Jesu, sweet Jesu, my love, my darling, my Lord, my Saviour, my honey-drop (nectar), my balm, sweeter is the remembrance of Thee than honey in the mouth. Who is there that may not love Thy lovely face? What heart is there so hard that it may not melt at the remembrance of Thee? Ah, who may not love Thee, lovely Jesu? For within Thee alone are all things united that ever may make any man worthy of love to another.   *   *   *

'Ah, whom may he love truly who loveth not his brother? Then whosoever loveth not Thee is a most wicked man. Now, my sweet Jesu, I have left for Thy love flesh's kinship, and yet born-brothers have cast me aside; but I reck of nothing whilst I hold Thee, for in Thee alone may I find all friends. Thou art to me more than father, more than mother. Brothers, sisters, or friends, none are to be esteemed as anything in comparison with Thee. Ah, Jesu, sweet Jesu, grant that love of Thee be all my delight.   *   *   *

'They lead forth Longinus with the broad sharp spear. He pierces His side, cleaves the heart, and there comes flowing out of the wide wound the blood that redeemed [us], and the water that washed the world from guilt and from sin. Ah, sweet Jesus, Thou openest for me Thy heart, that I may know [Thee] truly and read therein true love-letters, for there I may openly see how much Thou lovedest me. With wrong should I refuse Thee my heart, since Thou hast bought heart for heart. Lady, mother and maiden, thou didst stand here full nigh, and sawest all this sorrow upon thy precious Son. Thou wast inwardly martyred within thy motherly heart, when thou sawest His heart cloven asunder with the spear's point. But, Lady, for the joy that thou hadst of His resurrection the third day thereafter, grant me to understand thy sorrow, and heartily to feel somewhat of the sorrow that thou then hadst; and that I may help thee to weep because He so bitterly redeemed me with His blood, so that I, with Him and with thee, may rejoice in my resurrection at doomsday, and be with thee in bliss.'

CHAPTER VI.

OUR LADY'S GLORY.

In the acts of the canonisation of St. Thomas of Cantalupe, Bishop of Hereford, who died in 1282, and was canonised in 1330, a witness who had spoken of invoking 'our Lady' was asked by the Italian commissioner what Lady she meant. She answered that of course she meant the Lady of heaven, and that such was the common mode in her country of calling on the Blessed Virgin.[1]

Mrs. Jameson is mistaken in supposing that this title first became appropriated to the Blessed Virgin in the ages of chivalry, meaning by chivalry the positive institution of later mediæval times. Ure Lavedi was the familiar designation of the Anglo-Saxon, as Notre Dame Sainte Marie was of the Anglo-Norman, and Our Lady St. Mary of the English. In the Anglo-Saxon charters of the ninth century, signed by kings and bishops, she is always spoken of as Dei Genitrix, domina nostra,[2] or Sancta Maria regina gloriosa Dei Genitrix.[3]

All believed that the Virgin Mary, having most humbled herself on earth, was now most highly exalted in heaven. I will, however, let them give their own explanation of their belief.

ÆLFRIC.

Mary the Queen of all Saints.

'O thou blessed Parent of God, ever maiden Mary, temple of the Holy Ghost, maiden before conception, maiden in concep-

---

[1] 'Requisita, de qua domina intelligebat dicendo : Dulcis domina adjuva me ? respondit, quod de domina cœli, et quod erat talis modus et communis in patria per talia verba invocare auxilium B. Mariæ.' *Acta SS.* vol. xlix. ad Oct. 2.

[2] Deed of Cænwulf, A.D. 821 ; Cod. Dip. ed. Kemble, i. 270.

[3] Deed of Æthelwulf, A.D. 844 ; ib. v. 94.

tion, maiden after conception, great is thy glory on this festival [All Saints] among the beforesaid saints ; because through thy pure childbirth holiness and heavenly honours came to them all. We speak of the heavenly Queen, as is usual, according to her womanhood; yet all the faithful Church confidently sing of her, that she is exalted and raised above the hosts of angels to the glorious throne. Of no other saints is it said, that any of them is raised above the hosts of angels, but of Mary alone. She manifested by her example the heavenly life on earth; for maidenhood is of all virtues queen, and the associate of the heavenly angels. The example and footsteps of this Maiden were followed by an innumerable body of persons in maidenhood, living in purity, renouncing marriage, attaching themselves to the heavenly Bridegroom Christ with steadfast mind and holy converse, and with white garments, to that degree, that very many of them suffered martyrdom for maidenhood, and so with twofold victory went glorious to the heavenly dwelling-places.'[4]

'We read here and there in books that very often angels came at the departure of good men, and with ghostly hymns led their souls to heaven, and what is yet more certain, men at their departure have heard the song of men and women with a great light and sweet odour; by which it is known, that those holy men who through good deserts come to God's kingdom, at the departure of other men receive their souls, and with great joy lead them to rest.

'Now if Jesus has often showed such honour at the death of His saints, and has commanded their souls to be conducted to Him with heavenly hymn, how much rather, thinkest thou, He would now to-day [the Assumption] send the heavenly host to meet His own Mother, that they, with light immense and unutterable hymns, might lead her to the throne which was prepared for her from the beginning of the world.

'This festival excels incomparably all other saints' massdays, as much as this holy Maiden, the Mother of God, is incomparable with all other maidens. This feast-day to us is yearly, but to heaven's inmates perpetual.'[5]

[4] Œlfric's Homilies, vol. i. p. 547.   [5] Ibid. p. 441.

On our Lady's Assumption.

'The angels rejoice, because to-day the Mother of Christ is assumed into heaven. Since men rejoice who are ever sad and sorrowful, how should not the angels rejoice, whose nature it is to be glad, and whose state admits no sadness? How should not they rejoice over the Mother of God ascending into heaven, who rejoice over one sinner doing penance? Or how should not the angels rejoice, when the Lord of the angels rejoices? Yea, Christ rejoices, and with festive pomp goes to meet His Mother. He disdains not to fulfil His own law enjoining that honour be paid to parents. David, who was a figure of Christ, rejoiced and sung hymns before the ark of the Old Testament. Think you, then, that Christ does not rejoice before the ark of the New Testament, before the Propitiatory, before the Sanctuary of the Holy Ghost? Let, then, the angels rejoice and go to meet their Lady, the Queen of angels, the Mediatress between God and men. Let them mark what the Baptist did while still in his mother's womb. Did he not leap for joy at the coming of Mary? The infant's soul was melted when Mary spoke. Let, then, the angels also melt with joy, now that they will both hear the voice and possess the presence of Mary.

'Let no one be surprised if I call Mary the Queen of angels and their Mistress. They are proud to call her their Lady whom the Lord of the angels chose to be His Mother. Inasmuch as she most gloriously and ineffably brought forth the Son and Heir of God, she has thereby inherited a more glorious name than that of angels. It is great and glorious for the angels that they have been made the ministers of God. But beyond all doubt it is both greater and more glorious for Mary that she has been made God's Mother. The Apostle says that eye hath not seen, nor ear heard, nor has it entered the heart of man, how great things God has prepared for those who love Him. What, then, has He prepared for her who bore Him? To which of the angels has it been said: "The Holy Ghost shall come upon thee"?

To which of the angels has that wondrous loving and familiar word been spoken : " Come, My chosen one, and I will place in thee My throne"? Come, He says, My chosen one, come. He calls her to the sublimest height of glory. Many are called, few are chosen. She is both called and chosen, nay, preëminently chosen. "Blessed, O Lord, is she whom Thou hast chosen; she shall dwell in Thy courts" (Ps. lxiv. 5) ; nay, rather, He shall dwell in her, and place His throne in her, since He has chosen her as a dwelling-place for Himself. "This is My rest from generation to generation. Here will I dwell, since I have chosen it" (Ps. cxxxi. 14).

'Other holy souls are indeed also thrones of God, but not like Mary. She is the throne on which rests the Spirit of God ; a throne indeed, but not one from which He casts forth His thunderbolts, and promulgates sentences of death and decrees of eternal reprobation; not that of which it is written : "From the throne proceeded lightnings and voices and thunders" (Apoc. iv. 5). From this throne Christ rules with peaceful jurisdiction. Through the presence, the prayers, the merits of His Mother, the Son of God distributes freedom to the captives, light to the blind, rest to the weary, health to the sick, plenty to the poor, security to the timid. From this throne He grants fidelity between friends, reconciliation between enemies, certainty in doubt, guidance in error, solace in tribulation, defence in war, home in exile, a safe port in shipwreck. From this He gives wisdom to the ignorant, exaltation to those who have been cast down, consolation to widows and orphans, grace to beginners and to those who advance, and a crown of glory to the perfect and triumphant.

'Let the sun be taken from the universe, and there will be night. Let Mary be taken from heaven, there will be amongst men only darkness and confusion.

'Christ had left His Mother for a time on earth, till she should have communicated to His disciples all that she had witnessed in her familiar intercourse with her Son and had laid up in her heart. He left her that she might, according to the ancient prophecy, bruise the serpent's head, and plant the faith an'l love of Christ more firmly in the hearts of believers, and present to her Son without spot or wrinkle the Church which, on His ascension, he left to her instruction.   Yet it seemed to Christ that He had not wholly ascended into heaven until He had drawn her thither to Himself, from whose flesh and blood He had derived His own humanity. With a great desire, therefore, He desired to have with Him that vessel of election, that virginal body, in which He delighted, and in which He found nothing displeasing to His divine purity ; that vessel which He had filled with the fragrance of all heavenly odours, with the abundance of all virtues, with the fulness of all graces.

' It was in Mary's womb that the power of the Holy Ghost wondrously and ineffably compounded, from the Godhead, flesh and soul, that incense which Christ the High Priest of the good things to come (Heb. ix. 11) offered on the altar of the Cross to His Father as the evening sacrifice. By reason of the indwelling of this incense the holy Mother of God became odoriferous and sweet in her delights. She ascended, therefore, as "a pillar of smoke of aromatical spices, of myrrh and frankincense, and of all the powders of the perfumer" (Cant. iii. 6).   Hence some of the angelic spirits were not present among the others who assisted at the passage of the Blessed Virgin out of the desert of this world.   Perhaps they had been sent out to minister to the heirs of salvation.   These, wondering at the sweetness of so much fragrance, exclaimed, " Who is this that cometh up from the desert flowing with delights ?" (Cant. viii. 5.) As if they had said, How can such abundance of heavenly delights be found in the desert of mortal life, where there is nothing but sorrow and toil and affliction of spirit ? Even we, who feed on the good things of the Lord, who are gladdened by the rushing of the river in the city of God (Ps. xlv. 5), in the torrent of pleasure, in the glory of His countenance, enjoy not such delights.   But ah! let the angelic powers cease to marvel at the delights of this desert ; for what was formerly a desert has now become a garden of delights, as the prophet says : " He will make her desert as a place of pleasure, and her wilderness as the garden of the Lord" (Isai. li. 3).

'What are these delights in this Blessed Virgin? They are
such as these—that she was chosen by the Lord, announced by
the prophets, longed after by the patriarchs, saluted by the
angel, rendered fruitful by the Holy Ghost; that she was prefigured in the rod of Aaron, in the fleece of Gedeon, in the gate
of Ezechiel, in the bush of Moses; that without corruption she
conceived, without weariness was pregnant, and without pain
gave birth; that she is the gate of life, the first-fruits of virgins,
the beloved one of the eternal God. Let not the angels wonder
if she is assumed into splendour and glory, who was at once the
mother and the handmaid of God, His sister and His spouse,
His mother and His daughter. The Mother of God once laid
her Son in an humble crib: to-day she is placed by her Son on
a lofty throne. She laid her Son between two animals; she is
placed by her Son above His holy angels. She carried her
Child into Egypt; she is now herself transported from this
world's desert into heaven. She clothed her Babe with poor
swaddling clothes; she is clothed by Him in a robe of everlasting brightness. Her Son pours out on her His humanity and
His divinity, His eternity, His splendour, and His joy; so that
He is seen, embraced, and possessed by His Mother as the only-
begotten of the Father, to whom be all honour and glory for
ever and ever. Amen.'[6]

In the above beautiful sermon Peter of Blois, who, though
Archdeacon of Bath, was by birth a Frenchman, may have been
somewhat inspired by St. Bernard's eloquence; but one who
had received all his education in England and in Scotland, and
who was a contemporary of St. Bernard, has written of our
Lady's glory with equal eloquence, and perhaps with still greater
penetration and spiritual insight. I allude to

St. Aelred.

On Mary's Assumption.

'We ought at all times to praise and honour Mary, and with
all devotion to meditate on her sweetness; but to-day, on the

[6] Petri. Bles. Serm. 33; Bib. Max. Lug. tom. xxiv.

feast of her Assumption, we should especially rejoice with her, for to-day was her joy made full. Great was her joy when the angel saluted her. Great was her joy when she experienced the coming of the Holy Ghost, and that wonderful union took place within her womb between the Son of God and her flesh, so that He who was the Son of God became her Son also. Great was her joy when she held that Son within her arms, kissed Him, ministered unto Him ; and when she heard His discourses, and beheld His miracles. And because she had been greatly saddened in His passion, she had marvellous joy in His resurrection, and still more in His ascension. But all these joys were surpassed by the joy which she received to-day.

'You know well, my brethren, that in our Lord Jesus there are two natures, the divine and the human. Those two natures are so perfect in Him that the divine nature was not changed by its union with the human, nor was the human nature absorbed by the divine. Therefore is He both equal to the Father and less than the Father; equal on account of His divinity, less on account of His humanity. Now, my brethren, it is certainly a great good and a great joy to know our Lord Jesus Christ according to His humanity, and so to love Him and to think of Him ; to witness, as it were, in one's heart His birth, His passion, His wounds, His death, His resurrection. But he has far greater joy who can say with the Apostle, "If we have known Christ according to the flesh, yet now we know Him so no longer" (2 Cor. v. 16). It is a great thing to see Him lying in the manger, but far greater to see Him reigning in heaven. It is a great joy to see Him fed at the breast, but still greater to see how He feeds all things. It is a great joy to see Him in a Maiden's arms, but a greater joy to see how He embraces and supports the heavens and the earth.

'Now, up to this day, the Blessed Virgin knew her Son according to the flesh; for though after His ascension all her desires and love were with Him in heaven, yet, so long as she remained in the flesh, the memory of what He was in the flesh could not leave her. His words, His deeds, and the image of the beauty of His face were ever in her mind. But to-day she

passed away from this world, and went to the heavenly kingdom, and began to contemplate His glory and the divinity of
His Father; and her joy was made full and her desire was
accomplished. "I have found," she says, "Him whom my
soul loveth" (Cant. iii. 4).

'Up to that day she might have said, " I have sought Him,
and have not found Him" (Cant. iii. 1); but now she adds, " I
will arise and will go about the city. In the streets and the
broad ways I will seek Him whom my soul loveth" (Cant.
iii. 2).

'By this city I understand the heavenly Jerusalem, whose
streets are paved with pure gold, and ever resound with alle-
luias. "I will arise," she says. Did I dare, I would say that
the Blessed Mother of God first laid down her body, and then
rose again in it to everlasting life. But though I do not dare
to affirm this, since I cannot prove it if any one should gainsay
it, yet I dare to think it. But one thing I dare most surely
affirm, that to-day the Blessed Virgin—"whether in the body
or out of the body I know not, God knoweth"—ascended into
heaven, and in the eagerness of her soul went round the whole
of that heavenly city.

'She saw the white robes of the virgins, the rosy crowns of
the martyrs, the thrones of the apostles, and in them all she
beheld the reign of her Son. And now she finds Him so perfectly, so blissfully, that up to that day she seems never to have
found Him. Beyond the reach of all the saints to such a knowledge of the Divinity does she come, that now she cries that she
has indeed found Him whom her soul loveth.

'"The watchmen who guard the city found me" (Cant. iii. 3).
These watchmen are the angels who guard the city of God, that
is, the holy Church, and protect it from the attacks and am-
bushes of the devil. Most certainly the whole host of angels
went out to-day to meet the Blessed Mary. They found her in
the world, and bore her from the world. But though she beheld the brightness of the angels, their glory and beatitude, this
did not satisfy her; but all the more she longed to gaze on Him,
whom above all she loved. Therefore she asks : "Have you

seen Him whom my soul loveth ?" And adds : " When I had
passed them a little I found Him whom my soul loveth" (Cant.
iii. 4). O blessed soul, which passed beyond, not only the
patriarchs and prophets, the apostles, martyrs, confessors, and
virgins, but the angels also, the thrones and dominations, the
cherubim and seraphim, and all the host of heaven, and so at
length reached its beloved One.   Then it found Him and embraced Him : " I hold Him," she says, " and will not let Him go"
(Cant. iii. 4).   Yes, she holds Him in the embrace of perfect
charity, and can never let Him go, because she can never love
Him less.

' Let us lift up our hearts, then, to this our Lady and our
Advocate. Let us consider how great a hope we possess in her.
As she is more excellent than every creature, so she is more
merciful and benign. Let us, then, pray to her with confidence,
who both can help us by her excellence and will help us by
her mercy. Let us pray her to intercede for us with her Son,
that as He deigned to be born of her for us, through her He will
have mercy on us ; who, with the Father and the Holy Ghost,
liveth and reigneth, world without end. Amen.'[7]

ST. ANSELM (eleventh century).

On the Gospel of the Assumption.

The Church has chosen for the feast of the Assumption
the history of the two sisters, Mary and Martha, and of the
defence made by our Lord of the former against the complaints
of the latter (Luke x. 38, &c.). St. Anselm having explained
in a sermon in what sense this Gospel is applied to Mary, he was
urged to write what he had said. I give some portions of the
homily :

' " *Intravit Jesus in quoddam castellum,*—Jesus went into a
certain town" (castle). By a castle is understood a tower and
the outer wall which surrounds it. These defend each other.
By means of the wall the enemy is kept away from the citadel,
and by means of the citadel he is driven from the wall. Mary,

<hr>

[7] S. Aelred. Serm. 18 ; Migne, *Patrol.*

then, may well be compared to such a castle. The perfect purity of her soul and body so surrounded her, that no temptation of the flesh could ever approach her. And since pride often subdues those whom sensuality cannot overcome, she was also protected by the citadel of humility. In her was neither proud virginity nor soiled humility, but virgin humility and humble virginity.

'O sublime Virgin, who was Mother of God; O humble Mother, who was handmaid of God !

'Into this castle, then, Jesus entered. The door by which He entered was her faith. "Blessed was she who believed; for those things were accomplished which were told to her by the Lord."

'"And a certain woman named Martha received Him into her house; and she had a sister called Mary."

'These two sisters, according to the interpretation of the Fathers, signify the two kinds of lives in the Church; Martha the active, Mary the contemplative. Now as the Mother of God is singular and preëminent in all things, so is she in the union of those two lives. Never was Martha so active, never Mary so contemplative, as in her.

'Others may receive a guest into their houses; she received as guest the only Son of God, who had not where to lay His head; and not only into her house, but into her womb.

'Others may clothe the naked with a changeable and perishable garment; she clothed the Word of God with the garment of her own flesh, a garment which He will never put off, and which will never perish.

'Others may feed the hungry and the thirsty with food and drink; she fed the Man-God in His need, not only with food, but with food of her own substance. Yes, she performed towards the Son of God all those six works of mercy, which He will take as done to Himself even when they are done to the least of His. Besides giving Him hospitality, clothing and feeding Him, when He was infirm in His infancy, she not only visited Him, but bathed and soothed and nursed and tended Him. "Martha, indeed, was busy about much serving." And when He was arrested and crucified, she was with Him in His imprisonment : "There stood by the cross of Jesus, Mary His Mother."

'She was indeed solicitous and troubled when He fled into Egypt from the face of Herod, who persecuted Him, and slew so many children. She was troubled when she saw the Jews plotting His death. She was troubled, and a sword pierced her soul, when she saw her Son seized, bound, scourged, spit upon, crowned with thorns, scoffed at, buffeted, crucified, dead, and buried. The words may well be applied to her : "Martha, Martha, thou art careful and troubled about many things."

'But no one can doubt that Mary would have wished her Son to be delivered from all tribulation, and herself to be assisted in her trouble by the Divinity, which she knew to belong to Him by that contemplation which is the part of Mary. In this sense, therefore, Martha complains that her sister has left her alone to serve, and asks for her help.

'But now as to the part of Mary, who shall tell how perfect it was in the Blessed Virgin ? If the part of Martha was so perfect beyond conception, what is that part which is praised as the best part, and which shall not be taken away? O, how great was the sweetness of God in the soul of the Blessed Virgin, when the Holy Ghost came upon her, and the power of the Most High overshadowed her, and she conceived of the Holy Ghost ! What ineffable sentiments must she have had about God, when the Wisdom of God lay hid within her, and fitted to Himself a body in her womb? "Christ is the power of God and the wisdom of God, and in Him are hid all the treasures of wisdom and of knowledge." But Christ Himself was in Mary ; therefore in Mary were the power of God and the wisdom of God, and all the treasures of wisdom and of knowledge. She sat not merely at the feet of the Lord, but at His head, and listened to the Word speaking by His mouth. She laid up all the words of the angels, of the shepherds, of the Magi, and of her Son, and pondered them in her heart. No one ever tasted how sweet the Lord is as did Mary. She was inebriated of the fulness of the house of God, and drank of the torrent of His delights. With her, nay, within her, was the Fount of Life, from which flowed all the perfection of both lives. If she was busy about many things with Martha, she found her delight in one thing only with Mary; for one thing only is necessary; the many things have passed away, the one thing remains for ever.

'No longer now is she solicitous how to serve Him as a Child, for all the hierarchies of angels serve Him as their Lord. No longer is she troubled, flying with Him into Egypt from the face of Herod; for He has ascended into heaven, and Herod has gone down into hell from before His face. No longer is she disturbed on account of the many things that the Jews did against Him; for all things now are subject unto Him. And now Mary herself is exalted above the choirs of angels; now all her desire is fulfilled, she sees God face to face as He is, and rejoices with her Son for ever.

'This is the best part which shall not be taken from her; may we be partakers in it by her merits and her prayers, through her Son Jesus Christ, who liveth and reigneth with God the Father, in the unity of the Holy Ghost, for ever and ever. Amen.'[8]

OUR LADY CROWNED.

The following are two stanzas of a poem taken from a MS. of the early part of the fifteenth century, though the poem itself is older:[9]

'Veni, electa mea, meekly chosen
Holy mother and maiden queen,
On sege[10] to sit seemly by Him on high,
Thy Son and eke Thy Child.
Here, Mother, with Me to dwell,
With thy sweet Babe that sitteth in bliss,
Here in joy and bliss that shall never miss,
Veni, coronaberis.
For macula, Mother, was never in thee;

[8] S. Anselmi, Hom. 9, Op. t. i. p. 253, ed. Gerberon.
[9] Published by Early English Text Society, 1867, p. 2.
[10] Seat.

I

Filia Sion, thou art the flower ;
Full sweetly shalt thou sit by Me,
And bear a crown with Me in tower;
And all My saints to thine honour
Shall honour thee, Mother, in My bliss,
That blessed body that bare Me in bower ;
Veni, coronaberis.'

In the foregoing chapters I have, as much as possible, let
our fathers speak for themselves.   Though the extracts I have
given have been purposely taken from many writers, living under different civilisations and using different tongues, yet their
conception of her of whom they write is identical.   I have not
had to choose, here a bit and there a bit, to form an ideal of my
own.   There is an ideal in the mind and traditions of the
Church, which is objective and gazed upon by all alike.   Those
who have lived in active communion with the Church, in any
country and in any age, have felt the presence of this ideal of
the Immaculate Mother of God.   They were like students copying from one original.   As we look on their canvas we see that
they vary in their perceptions of beauty, and in their skill in
depicting it ; yet we know at a glance that they have been
studying the same masterpiece.   And because that original is
before our eyes also, we pass judgment on the copies, and praise
them as they seem to us to reproduce more or less perfectly that
which none can render adequately, and which we, perhaps, who
pass judgment, could not depict at all.

The ideal of the Blessed Virgin lives in the traditions of the
Church, and is handed on from age to age.   The outlines are
contained in the Church's dogmas—the Immaculate Conception,
the perpetual virginity, the absolute sinlessness of Mary ; the
virginal conception, divine maternity, and in all the different
events of her life as related in the Gospels.   The colours are
gathered from the books of the Old and the New Testaments,
and in the selection and mingling of these colours, and in the
vigour or delicacy with which they are used, is seen the talent
and the skill of each artist.

Let it not, however, be supposed that because they aim at an ideal they are not copying a reality. The Mother of God is a reality which surpasses our sublimest conceptions. She was the very incarnation, so to say, of divine grace. It is only when this principle is assumed, and taken as a key to the holy Gospels, that they give up all their depths of meaning and hidden beauties.

Our modern artists in search of realism travel to Palestine, and study landscape and atmosphere, architecture and costume, and then, in the midst of the most faultless surroundings, give us a mere human peasant girl, whom they call the Virgin Mary. The masters of art in better days cared little for such trivialities, but threw their whole souls into their endeavour to embody the ideal which they venerated and loved. So at the present day we have pretended Lives of the Blessed Virgin, filled with details of Oriental manners, which, whether correct or not, are utterly misplaced when the soul has other and better matter for its meditation. It is indeed refreshing to turn from such sentimental prettiness to the sublime contemplations of our ancestors, and to see in their glowing words the reflection of their profound and constant meditation on Holy Scripture, and of their tender and practical devotion.

In the study of the devotion of Englishmen to the Blessed Virgin Mary, which will form the Second Part of this work, our attention will not be confined, as it has been hitherto, to the few who were the lights of Holy Church, but will include the whole body of the faithful—men, women, and children, bishops and kings, knights and merchants and serfs, nuns and matrons, even saints and sinners. It was indeed the fervour and extent of their devotion, far more than their doctrine, which gained for their country the title of Our Lady's Dowry.

PART II.

DEVOTION.

THE STONEBOW, LINCOLN,
With Statues of the Blessed Virgin and St. Gabriel.

CHAPTER I.

THE HONOURS PAID TO OUR LADY.

It has been my wish to be the historian rather than the apologist of our forefathers. Yet I feel that I cannot enter upon the detail of the honours paid by them to the Blessed Virgin without some few words of explanation and defence.

1. Collier says : 'The practice of immediate address to the saints, as far as we can discover, did not prevail in England till the tenth century. At this time, in the homily of the Assumption of the Blessed Virgin, there is a direct prayer to the Blessed Virgin to intercede for them.'[1] Collier would not, I think, have made an assertion which he did not believe to be true. Yet his statement is a striking example of the power of prejudice to keep people from looking into facts. He found himself as an Anglican committed to the position that 'invocation of saints is a fond thing vainly invented,'[2] and he liked to fix the time of its invention as late as possible. He did not feel the absurdity of supposing that a practice like that of invoking saints was suddenly adopted without opposition, nay, without consciousness of innovation, by Christians whose vital principle was to make no change in the traditions of their fathers. He did not see the utter impossibility that the Saxons, ever travelling to Rome and back, should have differed in faith or practice from the nations of the Continent. He had a controversial position to maintain, and he seems to have turned his eyes from evidence, or else to have persuaded himself that the writings of St. Aldhelm and of Alcuin, though admitted to be genuine by all scholars, were really forgeries of a later age.

[1] Collier, *Eccl. Hist.* book iii. vol. i. p. 515; similarly Soame's Bampton Lectures, pp. 216-18.　　[2] Article xxii. of Church of England.

However this may be, much more evidence than was possessed in the time of Collier has been brought to light, and it is placed beyond all question that the direct invocation of saints was practised by our ancestors from the first preaching of St. Augustin till the Reformation of Edward VI. Then, indeed, it was ordered 'that no man should maintain purgatory, invocation of saints, the six articles, beadrolls, images, relics, lights, holy bells, holy bread, holy water, &c., or any other such abuse and superstition contrary to the King's Majesty's proceedings.'[3]

In the time of Elizabeth the madness went so far, that they not merely declared it unlawful to ask the saints to pray, but were afraid lest the saints should pray without being asked; and tried to persuade themselves that this last chance of their salvation had no foundation. 'Thou wilt object further,' says the Anglican Homily on Prayer,[4] 'that the saints in heaven do pray for us, and that this prayer proceedeth of an earnest charity that they have towards their brethren on earth. Whereto it may be well answered, first, that no man knoweth whether they do pray for us or no. And if they will go about to prove it by the nature of charity, concluding that because they did pray for men on earth, therefore they do much more the same now in heaven,—then may it be said by the same reason, that as oft as we do weep on earth they do also weep in heaven, because while they lived in this world it is most certain and sure they did so.'

Alas, could the saints have wept in heaven, they would have shed tears abundantly at seeing men thus perversely rejecting the mercies of God for their salvation, and heaping up sophisms to deprive themselves of Christian hope and consolation.

At the present day, after three centuries of religious frenzy, during which men have gone on to defend those sad negations, for no other reason than because it pleased the Cranmers, Ridleys, and Hoopers of Edward VI. to advance them, many are returning to better thoughts, and even those who cling to the

---

[3] Burnet, *Reform.* vol. ii. part ii. p. 230 (anno 1549).
[4] Part ii.

Elizabethan traditions are seeking new ground for their defence.

2. The controversy, however, did not begin with the Protestant Reformation; I may indeed say with truth that it had been exhausted before that time.

Wickliffe had said as much against the invocation of saints as has been said in the last three centuries, and our best Catholic controversialists in modern times have been able to add little to the answers given to Wickliffe in the fifteenth century.

The chief Catholic writer in England, at that time, was Thomas Netter, a Carmelite, more commonly called Waldensis, from the village of Walden where he was born. His discussion of this subject is very full. I will give the substance of his arguments rather than his language.[5]

It is a wondrous thing, he says, how it could ever enter the mind of a Christian man that to pray to a creature, however holy, is idolatry. Have not holy men prayed to sinners, begging them to keep the law of God? And if they could pray so humbly and earnestly as they did—'For Christ we are ambassadors; we beseech you be reconciled to God' (2 Cor. v. 20)—why cannot we also earnestly and humbly ask these very saints now to intercede for us, that we may do what they desired?

But, said Wickliffe, Christ is ever living with the Father to intercede for us, and is ever most ready to pour Himself into the soul that loves Him; what need, then, to enjoy His conversation, to make saints our mediators, since He is more merciful and more prone to hear than any of them?

To this Thomas retorts, by asking Wickliffe how he dares to send out his preachers, that people, as he declares, may draw from them the waters of life, since the Fount of life must be more accessible than such muddy brooks as these. And why should it be more absurd for men to draw near to God by mediators than for God thus to draw near to us?

But he replies more directly that, as God is not absent because He comes through His preachers, neither is the Fount of grace far off because it is opened to us by the prayers of saints.

---

[5] Thomas Waldensis, *Doctrinale Fidei*, t. iii.

God is near to us, objected Wickliffe; nearer than the saints.
No, answered Netter; 'our iniquities have divided between
us and God.' He is near by nature, but His grace is far from
us. To the arguments by which Wickliffe contended that from
the nature, the presence, the mercy of God there could be no
need of saints, Netter replied, very truly, that such arguments,
if valid, would prove there was no need of Jesus Christ. In
fact, the theories of Wickliffe would prove the redemption unnecessary and impossible.

'Who would have recourse to a king's jester,' said the heresi-
arch, 'when he could have easy access to the king himself? And
though the saints are not jesters, yet there is far more distance
between God and His saints than between any earthly king and
his jesters.' But so, also, said Thomas Netter, the humanity of
Christ is as nothing in comparison with the Divinity. Therefore
your argument would prove it foolish to approach the throne of
God through our Lord's humanity, when the God of infinite
clemency is so near and so ready to receive us.

Wickliffe argued against the invocation of saints, not only
from the nature of God, but from that of man. Your powers
are but finite, he said; they are little enough for God. Do not
squander them by your devotion to saints. Give the whole attention of your mind and vigour of your soul to God.

But Thomas reminds him that our power of loving is also
finite. Hence it must be unsafe to squander it on creatures; and
so by enforcing the first great commandment he would destroy
the second. And again, our power of honouring is limited.
Must we therefore refuse any honour to parents in order to give
it all to God? Moreover, the Incarnation itself must be injurious to God's glory and to our souls, since by means of it
our love, our honour, our devotion, flow on to the humanity of
Christ, and must therefore, according to Wickliffe, be diverted
from His Godhead.

And, indeed, some of Wickliffe's followers did not hesitate
to draw the conclusion, and would not allow that Christ as
man could be either adored or prayed to. Thus the objections
which had been levelled against the saints, under pretext of

honouring Jesus Christ, ended by insulting Him, and reducing Him to the state of His dishonoured servants.

3. In our own days these theories are again brought up. Bishop Colenso thinks prayer to Jesus Christ unscriptural ; and Dean Stanley agrees with him, but thinks it may be justified in certain circumstances.

Speaking of the Litany of his Church, he admits that the direct invocation of Jesus Christ ' is a deviation from the precepts of Scripture and from the practice of ancient Christendom ;' yet it is, so he thinks, a remarkable exception in favour of our Lord as against the invocations of saints, which may be explained by its historical origin, and justified, ' if we remember that it is an exception.' The historical explanation which he gives is, that in times of overwhelming distress (at the invasion of the barbarians in the fifth century) men's feelings became so impassioned and vehement that they used unwonted language, and instead of addressing their prayers merely to their Heavenly Father, they began to invoke Jesus Christ directly. Later on, saints also were invoked from the same intense feelings, though without the same justification. ' It was in the Litanies of the Middle Ages,' he says, ' that we first find the invocations, not only of Christ our Saviour, but of those earthly saints who have departed with Him into that other world. These we have now, with a wise caution, ceased to address. But the feeling which induced men to call upon them is the same in kind as that which runs through this exceptional service [the Anglican Litany], namely, the endeavour, under the pressure of strong emotion and heavy calamity, to bring ourselves more nearly into the presence of the Invisible. Christ and the saints at such times seemed to come out like stars, which in the daylight cannot be seen, but in the darkness of the night were visible. The saints, like falling stars or passing meteors, have again receded into the darkness. We, by increased reflection, have been brought to feel that of them and of their state we know not enough to justify this invocation of their help. But Christ, the Lord and King of the saints, still remains—the Bright and Morning Star, more visible than all the rest, more bright and more cheering, as the darkness of the night becomes deeper, as the cold becomes more and more chill.'

This singular passage has been examined from a theological point of view, and in relation to the teaching of his own Church, by the Rev. Canon Liddon.[6] I must confess that to me it is utterly unintelligible in whatever way it is regarded. How can prayer offered to Jesus Christ as God-Man be explained by the Rogation Litanies of the fifth century? What connection is there between strong emotions and forms of prayer drawn up deliberately and adopted by countless nations for more than a thousand years? Strong emotion, Tertullian tells us, made the pagans forget their fictitious deities, and invoke the true God in their distress. That is intelligible enough; for fear awoke earnestness, and then the voice of conscience spoke clearly and was listened to. But, according to Dean Stanley, fear and distress made Christians innovate on scriptural and primitive precedent, instead of calling their attention to what they had always known though disregarded. Can such strong emotions be taken as safe guides? Evidently not, for the very same feeling, as Dean Stanley thinks, made Christians also invoke the saints; and yet 'increased reflection' has made Protestants abandon that practice. Dean Stanley is well aware that increased reflection is making them everywhere abandon many other practices, and amongst others the very one that he is defending. Could he really hope to convince them that they are wrong by the mere use of a rather puzzling metaphor? If the Blessed Virgin is a 'falling star' in the judgment of Anglicans, is not her Divine Son a 'meteor' which has passed away, in the opinion of other followers of the Reformation? Dean Stanley indeed thinks that the *morning* star is becoming more visible as the *night* is advancing! But others tell us that the day is breaking when the morning star will vanish altogether.

My only purpose in dwelling on this theory is, that it illustrates one of the effects of abandoning the invocation of the saints. That invocation, among other lessons, teaches all Catholics most practically the infinite distance between our Lord

* In a note to his Bampton Lectures.

Jesus Christ, true God though true man, and the saints, who are but His creatures, though He deigns to call them His friends. With many Protestants, on the contrary, our Divine Lord is regarded as little more than a saint, and some are finding fault with their own sects for retaining this last fragment of mediæval worship.

4. And yet, with the evidence of this decline before his eyes, and in the very process of opposing it, Canon Liddon has not feared to assert that ' one effect of the expulsion of antiphons and hymns addressed to the Blessed Virgin and other saints from the liturgy of the Church of England has been to throw the praises, prayers, and adorations which the Church of England publicly addresses to our Lord Jesus Christ into a sharper prominence than belonged to such prayers in pre-Reformation times, or than belongs to them now in the Church of Rome.'[7]

There are three centuries of history by which to try a theory like the above; there are also many learned and candid men who have had personal experience of the two systems; had Canon Liddon applied either of these tests, he would scarcely have advanced so bold a proposition. The 'sharp prominence' is not a question of grammatical forms, but of the impression in the minds of those who use them. It is no doubt true that language is addressed to our Lady often very similar in certain expressions to that which is used in praying to her Divine Son; but it is simply notorious, amongst all candid and well-informed persons, that the ideas which underlie this language are in the two cases absolutely different; nor is there any possibility of confounding the idea of a saint with that of the Divinity.

Dr. Newman on the point of becoming a Catholic made an observation which, in the thirty years which have since elapsed, has become far more evidently true. 'If,' he wrote, 'we take a survey of Europe at least, we shall find that those religious communions which are characterised by the observance of St. Mary are not the Churches which have ceased to adore her Eternal Son, but such as have renounced that observance. The regard for His glory, which was professed in that keen jealousy

[7] Note to his Bampton Lectures.

of her exaltation, has not been supported by the event. They who were accused of worshipping a creature in His stead still worship Him; their accusers, who hoped to worship Him so purely, where obstacles to the development of their principles have been removed, have ceased to worship Him altogether.'⁸

These facts, which are too uniform and too universal to be accidental, are to be explained by the very nature of the veneration paid to our Lady. It is technically called *hyperdulia*, as being greater in degree than the honour given to other saints or to angels (*dulia*), and as distinguished from the worship given exclusively to God (*latria*). Many Protestants seem to suspect that these are distinctions invented by Catholics in self-defence; and especially that hyperdulia must be, even in the Catholic view, a veneration but one step removed from divine. It is, of course, the highest veneration after that of God. And yet so far is it from encroaching on divine worship, that I may truly say that, though all the honours paid to the saints tend to God's glory, yet hyperdulia gives to God incomparably more glory than simple dulia, for the reason that it exalts the Majesty of God in a more striking manner. I will try to explain this by examining its nature.

The Blessed Virgin Mary is venerated from a double point of view—in her relations as a saint to the God who is her beginning and her end; and in her special relations to the Incarnation, and through the Incarnation to each of the three divine Persons. I may say she is venerated as the Queen of the saints and as Mother of God. It is as the Queen of saints I will now consider her and the honour we pay to her. Let us first get an accurate notion of sanctity, and then we shall comprehend what is meant by *dulia* and by *hyperdulia*.

There are many attributes of God which we are bound to imitate: 'Be ye imitators of God, as most dear children.' There are some which we are forbidden to copy: 'Revenge not yourselves, for it is written: Vengeance is Mine.' Now that which is above all inimitable and incommunicable is the independence of God. God is His own beginning, His own end, His own

* *Essay on Development*, chap. viii. sec. 2.

rule. Yet this is the very attribute of God which we are tempted to imitate; and sin is nothing else but this imitation, man taking himself and his inclinations for his rule, and making himself his end. 'You shall be as gods, knowing good and evil' (Gen. iii. 5).

On the other hand, the renunciation of this spurious imitating of God, the refusal to live for self, the constant taking of the mind and will of God for the rule of thought and will and act, the living for God only—this is sanctity.

What, then, is the divine excellence which is the object of supreme worship? It is an infinite excellence, which is independent, and existing for itself.

What is the excellence called sanctity, which is the object of inferior worship? It is especially dependence, submission.

Though the saint is like God, yet the distinctive character of his sanctity is unlikeness to God in that of which God is jealous; and the more perfect he is in sanctity, the more perfect is this opposition, as I have just explained.

What, then, is hyperdulia? It is the recognition that the Blessed Virgin, just because she copied God most perfectly, usurped nothing of His incommunicable prerogative of independence; that she is highest because lowliest; that she is deserving of the highest honour after what is divine because she was most perfectly what a creature should be.

There is no paradox in all this. When a servant is praised in his quality of servant, it is for virtues the very opposite to those praised in the master in his quality of master. There may be many points of likeness between them as men, but the ideas of master and of servant exclude each other.

But in the saints this opposition which I have pointed out, this quality of dependence as opposed to God's independence, does not merely affect some part of their lives; it enters into every act. It is the very character of Christian virtue that it is done for God. Humility is not merely one virtue among many; it is of the essence of every virtue. If we praise the faith of a saint, we indicate the humility of his mind, captivating every thought into submission to the revealed mind of God. If we praise his hope, we mean that his heart was lowly, not trusting in itself, but in the strength of Him in whom it could do all things. His love is the humility of his will, subject in all things to the will of God, and making the infinite perfection of God all its good. And so with other virtues.

The theory of dulia and hyperdulia and latria may be somewhat subtle ; but so is the theory of walking, while the practice is most simple.

Listen to a simple Englishwoman, writing five hundred years ago. Mother Juliana was an anchorite of Norwich, who lived in the reign of Edward III. She has left a book of Revelations, in one of which she writes : ' Wisdom and truth made our Lady Mary to behold her God so great, so high, so mighty, and so good. This greatness and this nobility of her beholding of God fulfilled her of reverend dread, and with this she saw herself so little and so low, so simple and so poor, in regard of her God, that this reverend dread fulfilled her of meekness. And thus by this ground she was fulfilled of grace and all manner of virtues, *and passeth all creatures.*'[9]

With Protestants, then, who know nothing practically of the invocation of saints, and who approach the subject with their minds warped by false representations, or at least with the vague idea of finding something like what is familiar to them in heathen worship—the greater and the lesser gods—it is a natural error to suppose that the abolition of prayer to the saints would throw into ' sharper prominence' the prayers addressed to God. In their minds the saints are like so many hills which rear their heads around the mountain of God. To exalt the hill is to make a rival to the mountain, and to obscure the view of it. But with Catholics, if God in His infinite, uncreated, independent excellence is a mountain, the saints are valleys at its foot ; and the deepest of these valleys, and that which by its very depth exalts the height of the mountain, is the Blessed Virgin Mary.

St. John saw in his vision ' a throne set in heaven, and upon the throne One sitting' (Apoc. iv.). But also round about the throne were four-and-twenty seats, and upon the seats four-and-

* First Revelation, chap. vii.

twenty ancients sitting, clothed in white garments, and on their heads were crowns of gold.'.

Now according to the Protestant plan it would have brought the throne of the Eternal into ' sharper prominence' if the seats of the ancients had been removed, and the golden crowns hidden away. But God had a far different plan of bringing His own throne into prominence. 'The four-and-twenty ancients fell down before Him that sitteth on the throne, and adored Him that liveth for ever and ever, and cast their crowns before the throne, saying: Thou art worthy, O Lord our God, to receive glory and honour and power; because Thou hast created all things, and for Thy will they were and have been created' (v. 11).

So acts the Catholic Church in her Litany, which gave so much offence to Protestants. Her saints are crowned indeed, and sit on thrones around the throne of God; but the Church, after imploring mercy from each of the Persons of the ever-blessed Trinity, turns to the saints, and with her *Ora pro nobis* begs them to fall before the throne of God, and casting their crowns at His feet, help her to obtain mercy from Him who liveth for ever and ever.

5. I must take notice of another view which has been recently invented to defend the old antagonism. When Dr. Pusey wrote his *Eirenicon*, filled with criticism of the language used by Catholics to the Blessed Virgin, he elicited the following letter from a clergyman of his own communion:[10]

' Under cover of a protest against Roman excesses Dr. Pusey accepts the *Ora pro nobis*; and in so doing he accepts all. For secondary worship is not rejected by the Anglican Church, as he maintains, because it has a tendency to become primary, but for a diametrically contrary reason, because it never can be primary; because it never can involve the entire surrender of body, soul, and spirit; because it necessarily makes a fatal separation between the devotional faculty and the principle of moral obedience. We may have no object of worship to which obedience is not due. " See thou do it not; I am of thy brethren; wor-

[10] Rev. Arthur Gurney (chaplain to the English church, Paris), letter to the *Morning Post*, dated December 4, 1865.

K

ship God." No Christian ever yet worshipped the Virgin, whatever expressions he might use, as a separate goddess, but only as one endowed with certain powers by God. And this is precisely the essence of creature-worship : that it creates secondary objects of devotion, which can be served, and are served, as by the brigands and harlots of Italy, without any aim after moral obedience.'

It is rather bold in Mr. Gurney to put out his brand-new theory as that held from the beginning by the Anglican Church. But let that pass. It is curious that just about the same period a critic in the *Times* found fault with Dr. Newman's statement (which he probably misunderstood), 'that Catholic devotion to the Blessed Virgin has far more connection with . . . . . the festive aspect of Christianity . . . . . than with what is strictly personal and primary in religion.' The critic reminded him of 'the exercises of the Mois de Marie in French churches,' and asked if he had never 'heard a fervid and earnest preacher at the end of them urge on a church full of young people, fresh from Confirmation and first Communion, a special and personal self-dedication to the great patroness for protection amid the daily trials of life, as in an English church they might be exhorted to commit themselves to the Redeemer of mankind? Right or wrong,' continues the critic, 'such devotion is not a matter of the " festive aspect" of religion, but most eminently of what is personal and primary in it ; and surely of such a character is a vast proportion of the popular devotion.'[11]

The facts are certainly as here stated ; and these facts were within Mr. Gurney's reach. He need not have wandered in his imagination to the 'brigands and harlots of Italy.' He had but to step into a church in Paris, or open the first book of devotion, to find that though moral obedience is not due to our Lady in the same sense as it is due to God, yet there is no 'fatal separation between the devotional faculty and the principle of moral obedience,' since the great and constant object of devotion to our Lady and the saints is to obtain the grace by which to bring the soul into obedience to God.

[11] *Times*, March 31st, 1866.

I am glad here to quote the testimony of Mr. Furnivall, the editor of many of the publications of the Early English Text Society. This gentleman writes in the preface to a volume of 1867, called *Hymns to the Virgin and Christ*: 'A survey of our early religious poetry will, I believe—and so far as I may speak from some work at it—result in a verdict favourable to the plain good sense and practical going straight to the main point, which Englishmen pride themselves on. ... The burden of the early songs (as I read them) is a prayer for forgiveness of sins, a desire to get out of the filth of the flesh, and rise, as well here as hereafter, into the purer and higher life which to the believer union with his Saviour implied and implies.'

As to 'the brigands and harlots of Italy,' who cause such distress to Mr. Gurney—if such they be as he describes—I have treated of their case in the Introduction to this volume. I confess, however, I am rather sceptical on this matter. It is on record how the Pharisees once thought that the 'publicans and harlots' were 'without any aim at moral obedience.' But our Lord thought otherwise, and even promised that their efforts would be effectual.

Perhaps it may be the same still. 'Misled by calumnious representations,' says Mr. Digby,[12] 'the modern traveller, a purblind Argus, all eyes and no sight, when he hears of crimes in Catholic countries, immediately concludes that the same men whom he sees in the morning kneeling in the churches are employed at night in conspiracies against thrones, or breaking into houses, and robbing on the highways; but the union of devotion with crime is nowhere the general order, as he supposes. Who turn their backs to altars with such scorn as the wretches in Spain and Italy who are now the enemies of all virtue and of all honour? Where is there less external worship, less symbolic observance, than with that population boasting of its Protestantism, and left by hirelings to wander over every waste, till, forgetful of all lofty aim, it produces animals sensual and often savage, as the records of tribunals can attest, worthier of acorns than of other food created for man's use? Or where is

[12] *Compitum*, book ii. chap. ix.

there less than with the factions of that capital, only of late years perverse, which now employs the names of the days of the month to designate its insurrections ?'

6. To sum up, then, what has been said : It would appear from the reasons, the facts, and the testimonies here adduced, that the devotion to the Blessed Virgin, instead of being either idolatrous, superstitious, or immoral, is on the contrary most salutary in all its influences. Besides being a debt due to our Lady, and which we cannot withhold without ingratitude and injustice, it brings before the soul in the most effectual manner the supremacy of God, the divinity of Jesus Christ, the true dignity and end of a creature. It presents to the soul a vision of moral and spiritual beauty of the most exalted and at the same time the most attractive nature. God has given us the Blessed Virgin, His own Mother, to be on earth the model of all the perfections to which we can aspire ; and in heaven our perpetual help in all the weaknesses to which we are subject and the temptations to which we are exposed.·

The Apostle had said to his disciples : 'Whatsoever things are true, whatsoever modest, whatsoever just, whatsoever holy, whatsoever lovely, whatsoever of good fame, . . . think of these things' (Phil. iv. 8) ; and Christian hearts have felt that when they thought of Mary they thought of all these things in their most winning shape ; and Christian poets in their hymns, Christian artists on their canvas, Christian doctors in their writings, Christian saints in their contemplations, and Christian people in their prayers, have found in Mary a sweetness which has made temptation less powerful, vice less seductive, virtue more easy, life less miserable, and death less terrible.

This was partially recognised by Wordsworth when, struggling between his better instincts and the prejudices of his sect, he wrote his sonnet on the overthrow of our Lady's worship in England :

> ' Mother ! whose virgin bosom was uncrost
> With the least shade of thought to sin allied ;
> Woman ! above all women glorified,
> Our tainted nature's solitary.boast ;
> Purer than foam on central ocean tost,

> Brighter than eastern skies, at daybreak strewn
> With fancied roses, than the unblemished moon
> Before her wane begins on heaven's blue coast,—
> Thy image falls to earth. Yet some, I ween,
> Not unforgiven, the suppliant knee might bend,
> As to a visible power, in which did blend
> All that was mix'd and reconciled in thee
> Of mother's love with maiden purity,
> Of high with low, celestial with terrene.'

These beautiful lines were kindly meant towards Catholics. Yet we do not need and cannot accept such an apology for our forefathers or for ourselves. An excuse for erroneous worship may, perhaps, be sometimes found in ignorance, as St. Paul pleaded in mitigation of the sensual yet beautiful polytheism of the Athenians (Acts xvii. 30). But those whose hearts were purified and elevated enough to *invent* the Blessed Virgin—as the poet seems to insinuate—must have known well the worship due to God and the worship forbidden by Him ; nay, must have known it far better than the rude and violent men who rose up against their worship, and branded it as superstition and idolatry. Catholics used to call the Blessed Virgin Speculum Justitiæ—the mirror of all that is right in virtue and perfect in grace. If, looking into that mirror as they did, they had forgotten the first principles of true religion, they were certainly without excuse. Dr. Trench, now Protestant Archbishop of Dublin, gazing on a picture of the Assumption by Murillo, could not help thus addressing the artist :

> ' What innocence, what love, what loveliness,
> What purity must have familiar been
> Unto thy soul before it could express
> The holy beauty in that visage seen !'

He must be indeed blind who does not see the ' holy beauty' of the character of our Lady, as portrayed in all the writings and prayers I have quoted in the preceding chapters. Every thoughtful and candid man must therefore admit that, whether that character, that ideal, was invented or merely recognised and portrayed, love, loveliness, purity, must have been familiar to the souls of such writers.

Is it, then, possible that such men were, each and all, taking for their model the very mistress of true spiritual worship, and at the same time offering to herself a veneration which she would reject with horror? nay more; that the very reason they offered her this false homage was the enthusiastic admiration they entertained for the true worship she had herself given to their common Creator? Surely this is too strange a paradox to be seriously held.

CHAPTER II.

LET us now see how our forefathers understood both the theory and the practice of the veneration of our Lady.

My first extracts shall be from sermons of the saintly Abbot of Rievaux. He will explain what we owe to Mary, and the need men have of her intercession.

St. Aelred.

What we owe to Mary.

'Our great care should be, that we so conduct ourselves towards the Blessed Virgin as that she may be willing to undertake our cause with God. What, then, shall we do? What offerings shall we present to her? O, that we could only pay her at least what we strictly owe! We owe her 'honour; we owe her service; we owe her love; and we owe her praise.

'First, then, we owe her *honour*, since she is the Mother of our Lord. For he who does not honour the Mother, without any doubt dishonours the Son.

'Again, the Scripture says: "Honour thy father and thy mother." And is not Mary our Mother? Certainly she is most truly such. Through her we have been born, through her we. are fed, through her we grow. Through her, I say, we have been born, not to the world, but to God; through her we are fed, not with natural milk, but with that of which the Apostle says: "I have given you milk, not strong food" (1 Cor. iii. 2). Through her we grow, not in size of body, but in strength of soul. Let me explain this birth, this milk, this growth.

'We were once—as you believe and know—in death, in decay, in darkness, in misery. But through the Blessed Mary, much better than through Eve, we have been born, because from her Christ was born. She is the Mother to us of life, of incorruption, and of light. Does not the Apostle say that Christ is "made to us by God wisdom and justice, sanctification and redemption"? (1 Cor. i. 30.) She, then, being Mother of Christ, must be Mother of our wisdom, of our justice, of our sanctification, of our redemption. Is she not, then, more our Mother than the mother of our bodies?

'And does she not also feed us with milk? The Word of God, the Son of God, the Wisdom of God, is bread; He is solid food. Only strong ones like the angels could eat of that food. We, who were little ones, could not partake of food so solid; we were on earth, and could not ascend to eat on that heavenly bread. What, then, has been done? That Bread descended into the womb of the Blessed Virgin, and there was, made milk, such milk as we could drink. Think of the Son of God in Mary's lap, in Mary's arms, at Mary's breast; and He has become milk to you. And this our good Mother provides for us.

'Again, think of Mary's chastity, her charity, her humility; and, after her example, grow in chastity, in charity, in humility. So imitate your Mother.

'2. But, secondly, we owe Mary *service*, since she is our Lady. The Spouse of our Lord is surely our Lady; the Spouse of our King is surely our Queen. Therefore let us serve her; for the Apostle commands : "Servants, be subject to your lords in all fear" (1 Pet. ii. 18). And if he disobeys God's precepts who does not serve his carnal masters, without doubt they also deserve blame who do not serve this spiritual Mistress.

'But how must we serve her? Brethren, no service pleases her so much as this—that with all love and affection we humble ourselves before her Son; for all the praise and service we give her Son she counts it as her own. Let no one say : "Though I should do this or that against the Lord, I do not care much; I will serve holy Mary, and be safe." It is not so. When a man offends a son, he thereby offends the mother. But if *after* our sins we wish to be reconciled with our Lord, then we must needs have recourse to her and commit our cause to her.

' 3. Thirdly, we owe her love. She is our own flesh, she is our sister. Do I seem presumptuous? Nay; the Son of God, because He is the Son of man, is our Brother. Let us love her, since she loves us. Indeed we ought to love that sister, whose sanctity, whose benignity, whose purity have profited not her only, but all of us.

' 4. Lastly, we owe her *praise*. Scripture bids us praise God in His saints (Ps. cl. 1). If the Lord is to be praised in those saints by whom He works miracles, how much more is He to be praised in her in whom He—the Wonder of wonders —was made flesh! If they are to be praised who keep their chastity, how much more she who chose virginity, and received fruitfulness as its reward! If they are to be praised by whom God raised the dead, how much more she by whose sanctity the whole world has been raised from death eternal! Let us, then, praise her with our mouths, and beware lest we insult her by our acts. He gives but feigned praise who cares not to imitate what he praises. He truly praises Mary's humility who strives himself to be humble. He truly praises her chastity who execrates and scorns all impurity and lust. He truly praises her charity whose whole desires and efforts are to love both God and his neighbour with a perfect love.'[1]

In this passage St. Aelred does not speak of asking our Lady's intercession in our needs. I add, therefore, another extract from the same sermon :

St. Aelred.

On Mary's Intercession.

' "Cum jucunditate nativitatem Beatæ Mariæ celebremus, ut ipsa pro nobis intercedat ad Dominum Jesum Christum,—With gladness let us celebrate the nativity of the Blessed Virgin Mary, that she may intercede for us to our Lord Jesus Christ."

'Wonderful is the mercy of our Lord Jesus Christ. He is our Judge, and He knows that we are wretched, and of ourselves can bring no good cause before His tribunal. He is indeed merciful, and wishes to show us mercy. Yet He cannot

[1] Serm. 20; Migne, *Patrologia*, tom. cxcv. col. 522-24.

but judge justly. How, then, does He provide for us? He
teaches us to live well, yet we live badly. In our baptism He
forgave all our sins, yet we fell from that first grace. Often
have we promised amendment, yet we always continue to sin.
He gives us room for repentance, yet we neglect it. And yet
after all this He still spares us; and because we have become
unworthy to be heard by Him, He gives us His own friends,
that we may ask their help, and through them draw near to
Him and be reconciled.

'Thus it happens also among men. When their lord is
angry with them, they have recourse to his familiar friends, or
perhaps to his wife. Then, if they are not really guilty, their
lord listens more willingly to their defence when undertaken
by those or by her whom he dearly loves. If they are guilty,
then, at the petition of his friends, he pardons. We have
found[2] this in a certain holy king, who used to be delighted
when any one interceded for a criminal whom by the laws he
was constrained to punish, since thus he found a just excuse for
granting pardon. The king no doubt imitated our Lord, who,
that He may be able to pardon us even with justice, wills that
His friends intercede for us.

'Now let each one of us look to himself, and consider how
his own case stands with the Lord. How have we lived in His
sight? We are but men, and He is God; we are servants, and
He is our Master; we are creatures, and He is our Creator. Yet
we have not worshipped our God as we ought; we have not
obeyed our Master as we should; we have not loved our Creator
as was His due. Therefore, if we know ourselves well, we shall
see that we cannot answer Him one in a thousand, as Holy
Scripture says (Job ix. 3). What, then, shall we do? We can
hide nothing from Him. " All things are naked and open to

[2] *Invenimus.* St. Aelred had been brought up in the court of David,
King of Scotland, a holy king, son of St. Margaret. He has also written
the Life of St. Edward. It is not evident whether he refers to what he
had seen or to what he had read. Kings had then more power to punish
and to pardon than now. St. Thomas à Becket, a contemporary of St.
Aelred, when chancellor to Henry II., frequently obtained pardon for others
by his influence.

His eyes" (Heb. iv. 13). Let us offer Him our prayers. Let us beseech Him : " Enter not into judgment with Thy servants" (Ps. cxlii. 2). But it is not enough to offer Him our own prayers only. Let us seek her help, whose prayers He will never despise. Let us go to His Spouse, to His Mother, to His perfect Handmaid. The Blessed Mary is all this. Therefore " with joy let us celebrate her festival, that she may intercede for us with our Lord." If by the grace of God we have done anything good, if she present it to her Son, He will not despise it. And for the evil we have done without doubt she will obtain pardon.'[3] 'The greatness of Mary's love for men is proved by the many miracles and many visions by which the Lord deigns to show that she especially intercedes with her Son for the whole human race. It is in vain for me even to attempt to show how great is her charity; no human mind is able to conceive it.'[4]

The Premonstratensian abbot, Adam Scot, who wrote about 1180, speaks in the most glowing language of the honour due to the Mother of God.

ADAM SCOT.

On the Worship of Mary.

' Mary is our mistress, our advocate, our sweetness and our life, our hope and our mediatress. She is the Mother of God, the Queen of angels, the conqueror of the devils, the refuge of the miserable, the solace of orphans, the help of the weak, the strength of the just, &c. &c. But these are words which will sooner be exhausted than her prerogatives will be explained, so great is the fulness of her grace.

' Mary is the temple of the Lord. Like Anna in the temple of Jerusalem, let us not depart from it day or night. Let us venerate this temple, let us rejoice and exult in it ; let us pray in it and hope in it ; and praying, praising, and trusting, let us not depart from it. The humanity of Christ is a holy temple, nay the holy of holies, in which dwells all the fulness of the Divinity corporally (Col. ii. 9). But that temple also is holy,

[3] Serm 20.   [4] Serm. 17.

His blessed and glorious Mother, in whom He was conceived by
the Holy Ghost and dwelt for nine months.

'O most glorious, most beauteous temple of the only-begotten
Son of God, open to us the door of thy mercy and clemency;
permit us to enter thee, and receive the prayers we offer in thee.
We raise our voices to the Lord in thee, that He may hear our
voice from His holy temple, and our cry may enter into His ears.

'O my brethren, never depart from this temple; pour out
your prayer and declare your tribulation within it. Mary is the
Mother of Christ, and the prayer you present through her will
be listened to by God, who, born for us, yet yielded to be hers
(qui pro nobis natus, tulit esse tuus).'[5]

With a similar fervour spoke the Archdeacon of Bath in the
next century.

PETER OF BLOIS.

On our Lady's Praises.

'O Mary, who shall speak thy praises? Who shall tell of
thy power? Though the daughters of Sion exalt thee, though
queens praise thee, and all the assembly of the saints proclaim
thy glory, yet are all honours and all praise, compared with thy
blessedness, but as a torch compared with the sun, or a drop with
the vastness of the ocean. In our miseries and our distress thou art
ever prompt and powerful to help. Thou art sweet in the mouth
of those who praise thee, sweet in the hearts of those who love
thee, sweet in the memory of those who invoke thee. Every sex
and age and condition, all tribes and peoples and tongues, magnify thee. Thou art the chosen myrrh, the column of aromatical
smoke, the bundle of myrrh on the Spouse's breast, the pine-
tree outstretching its branches of grace and salvation. Amongst
all and above all art thou blessed and most blessed; the most
beauteous, most gracious, most glorious Mother of Him who
grants grace and glory, honour and everlasting life; to whom be
all honour and glory, for ever and ever. Amen.'[6]

[5] Serm. 40, Adami Scoti; Migne, *Patr.* tom. cxcviii. col. 357.
[6] Serm. 38; Bib. Max. t. xxiv. p. 1117.

Instead of the absurd fear felt by some moderns of giving to
our Lady, by word or deed, more honour than she deserves, our
forefathers were conscious that they would fall short of her due,
and that they were unworthy to speak her praises at all.

ANONYMOUS WRITER (fifteenth century).

'Forasmuch as neither ye nor any other creature on earth
is sufficient or worthy duly to praise the glorious Queen of
heaven—that is the reverend Mother of God and Lady of angels
—therefore first at the beginning ask her leave to praise her,
and say, *Dignare me laudare,* &c.; *i.e.* " Holy Virgin, vouchsafe
that I praise thee."'

' And for [*i.e.* because] the fiends are ever busy to let [*i.e.*
hinder] her praising, as thing that turneth them to their great
shame and reprief, by cause that the meekness of that clean
Virgin overcame them in all their pride, therefore ye ask help
against them when ye say, *Da mihi virtutem,* &c.; *i.e.* " Give
me strength against thine enemies." '[7]

I conclude this chapter with some specimens of the language
used in addressing our Lady. Many other examples will be given
in subsequent chapters.

The following are two prayers to the Blessed Virgin from a
MS. written either just before or soon after the Conquest, in
Latin, but in Saxon characters.[8]

SAXON PRAYERS.

' Mother 'of God and my Lady, O blessed Mary, I implore
thee, through our Lord Jesus Christ,[9] to have mercy on me a
sinner, but thy servant N.; for my sins are multiplied above the

[7] *The Mirror of our Lady,* part ii. (Early English Text ed.) p. 80.
[8] Univ. Lib. Camb. Ff. i. 23, published in *Home and Foreign Review,*
October 1862, p. 497.
[9] This manner of invoking our Lady—'through our Lord Jesus Christ'
—is a proof of the belief that our Lord is not only Mediator between God
and man, but also between man and man. He is the link of charity between us and the saints. So St. Paul: ' I beseech you, brethren, through
our Lord Jesus Christ, and by the charity of the Holy Ghost, that you help
me in your prayers for me to God' (Rom. xv. 30).

sands of the sea, and I have no refuge but in thee, O my Lady, O holy Mary; therefore on my knees I beg that thou wilt intercede for me with our Lord God, that by thy holy prayers He may deign to forgive me all my sins.'

'Holy Mary, glorious Mother of God and ever Virgin, who didst merit to give birth to the Salvation of the world, and didst bring the Light of the world and the Glory of heaven to those who sat in darkness and in the shadow of death; be my merciful mistress, the enlightener of my heart, my helper with God the Father Almighty, that I may deserve to receive the pardon of my sins, and to escape the darkness of hell, and to come to life eternal. Through our Lord,' &c.[9]

ST. GODRIC'S HYMN.

In the Life of St. Godric, written by Reginald, his intimate friend, in the twelfth century, a vision is related which was granted to the saintly hermit, while 'before the altar of Mary, the holy Mother of the Lord, he was calling on her only Son, the Lord Jesus.' He saw two young ladies standing at each end of the altar. His joy was so great that he felt sure the vision was from God. After a time they moved towards him, and the one on the right hand said : 'Godric, do you know me ?' and when he replied that he did not, she told him that she was the Mother of mercy and the Mother of Christ, the Virgin Mary; and that the other figure was that of Mary Magdalen. The Blessed Virgin promised her constant patronage. Godric fell at her feet, and said : 'To thee, O Lady, my most pious advocate, I commit myself ; O, forget not in thy pity to direct, protect, and keep me.' Then they both placed their hands on his head, smoothed his hair, and the whole place was filled with the odours of paradise.

Then the Mother of mercy sang to him a canticle, which he had to repeat after her several times, as a boy learns his lessons ; and he remembered both the words and the music till the end of his life. The words were in English (*i.e.* Semi-Saxon). The Blessed Virgin then told him that whenever he should be

* See note 9 on previous page.

wearied with pain, or temptation, or spiritual dryness, he should sing this canticle and he would be consoled. Then she made on his head the sign of the Cross, and this was frequently repeated by St. Mary Magdalen, and the vision departed. The words of the song have been preserved :

> ' Seinte Marie, clane virgine,
> Moder Jesu Christ Nazarene,
> Onfo, scild, help thin Godrich,
> Onfang, bring heali widh the in Godes rich.
> Seinte Marie, Christes bour,
> Meidenes clenhed, moderers flour,
> Delivere mine sennen, regne in min mod,
> Bring me to blisse wit thi selfe God.'[10]

A Good Orison of our Lady.

(Early English modernised.)

' Christ's meek Mother, St. Mary,
My life's light, my beloved Lady,
To thee I bow and my knees I bend,
And all my heart's blood to thee I offer.
Thou art my soul's light and my heart's bliss,
My life and my hope, my safety therewith indeed !
I ought to honour thee with all my might,
And sing thee the song of praise by day and by night,
For thou hast holpen me in many ways,
And brought me out of hell into paradise.
I thank thee for it, my beloved Lady,
And will thank thee while I live.
All Christian men ought to worship thee,
And sing thee a song of praise with exceeding great joy,
For thou hast delivered them out of the devil's hand,
And sent them in bliss to angels' land.
Well ought we to love thee, my sweet Lady ;
Well ought we for thy love to bow down our hearts.
Thou art bright and blissful above all women,
And good thou art, and to God dear above all men.
All the company of maidens honour thee alone,

[10] *Libellus de Vita S. Godrici* (Surtees Society, 1845), pp. 117-19.

For thou art the flower of them all before God's throne.
There is no woman born that is like to thee,
Nor is any thy equal within heaven's kingdom.
High is thy royal seat above cherubim,
Before thy dear Son among seraphim.
Merry sing the angels before thy face,
Playing, carolling, and singing between.
Full well it pleaseth them to be before thee,
For they are never·tired of beholding thy fairness.
Thy bliss may no one understand,
For all God's kingdom is under thy hand.
All thy friends thou makest rich kings ;
Thou givest them royal robes, bracelets, and gold rings.
Thou givest eternal rest full of sweet bliss,
Where that death never comes, nor harm, nor sorrow.
There bloom in bliss blossoms white and red,
Where never snow nor frost may hurt them ;
There may none fade, for there is eternal summer.
No living thing there is weak or sorrowful.
There they shall·rest who here do honour thee,
If they keep their life clean from all evil ;
There they shall never sorrow nor toil,
Nor weep nor mourn, nor hell-stinks smell.
There shall they be presented with golden cups,
And have poured out to them eternal life with angels' joy.
No heart may think nor aught reach,
Nor no mouth utter, nor tongue teach,
How much good thou preparest within paradise
For them that work day and night in thy service.
All thy household is clothed with white ciclaton,
And they all are crowned with golden crowns ;
They are as red as the rose, as white as the lily,
And evermore they shall be glad, and sing throughout merrily.
With bright gem stones their crown is all bedecked,
And they all do what pleaseth them, so that nothing thwarts
        them ;
Thy dear Son is their King, and thou art their Queen.

They are never annoyed by wind nor by rain,
With them is evermore day without night,
Song without sorrow and peace without fight.
With them is mirth manifold, without trouble or annoy;
Music and games, abundance of life's pleasure, and eternal
        play.
Therefore, dear Lady, long will it appear to us wretches
Until thou from this poor life to thyself us fetch.
We may never have perfect joy
Ere we to thyself come unto thy high honour.
Sweet Mother of God, gentle maiden and well-beloved,
Thine equal was never born, nor ever more shall be.
Mother thou art, and Virgin void of all vice;
Throughout high and holy in angels' rest,
All the host of angels and all holy things
Say and sing that thou art of life the well-spring;
And they all say that thou art never wanting in mercy,
Nor shall any man that worships thee ever be lost.
Thou art my soul's [light] without leasing,
After thy dear Son most beloved of all things.
All heaven is full of thy bliss,
And so is all this earth of thy mercy.
So great is thy mercy and gentleness,
That no man earnestly prayeth thee may lack [miss] thy help.
Each man that looketh to thee thou givest mercy and grace,
Though he may have much offended and grieved thee sorely;
Therefore I entreat thee, holy Queen of heaven,
That thou, if it be thy will, hear my petition.
I entreat thee, Lady, for the greeting
That Gabriel brought thee from our heavenly King;
And also I beseech thee for Jesus Christ's blood,
Which for our benefit was shed upon the cross,
For the great sorrow that was in thy mind
When thou at His death before Him stoodest,
That thou make me clean outwardly and inwardly,
So that not any kind of sin may ruin me.
The loathsome devil and errors of all kinds

L

Banish from me far away, along with their foul filth.
My dear life [love], from thy love shall nothing separate me,
For on thee depends my life, and my salvation also.
For thy love I toil and sigh very often;
For thy love I am brought into bondage;
For thy love I forsook all that was dear to me,
And gave thee all myself.   Dear life, think thou of that;
That I have at times made thee angry, I am truly sorry.
For Christ's five wounds do thou give me mercy and grace.
If thou hast no mercy upon me, I know full well
That in hell-pain I shall swelter and burn.
Full well thou sawest me, though thou wert silent,
Where I was, and what I did, yet thou didst bear with me.
If thou hadst taken vengeance upon my wickedness,
Truly I had wholly lost the bliss of paradise.
Thou hast yet borne with me for thy goodness.
And now I hope to have full forgiveness;
And now I hope never to fall into hell-pain,
Since I have come to thee and am thine own servant.
Thine I am, and will be now and evermore,
For on thee and on God's mercy depends all my life.
My dear sweet Lady, for thee I long exceedingly;
Unless I have thy help I shall never be joyful.
I thee entreat that thou come to my death,
And chiefly then manifest thy love.
Receive my soul when I depart from this life,
And shield me from sorrow and everlasting death's care.
If thou wilt that I thrive, take good heed to me,
For I shall never prosper unless it be through thee.
With very evil vices my soul is fast bound;
Nothing so well as thou can heal my wounds.
To thee alone is all my trust, after thy dear Son;
For His holy name, of my life grant me the loan.
Suffer not the devil [enemy] to touch me,
Nor to draw me into hell-pain.
Take heed to me, so that be what may, it will ever be best
       for me;

For thine is the worship, if I, wretch, may well thrive.
Thou forsakest no man for his wickedness,
If he is ready to repent and prayeth thee for forgiveness.
Thou canst easily, if thou wilt, all my sorrow allay,
And much better see [what is needful] for me than I can
      say.
Thou canst easily requite my greeting,
And all my labour, and my sorrow, and my kneeling.
In me there is nothing fair to be seen,
Nor anything that is worthy to be before thee;
Therefore I pray thee that thou wash me and clothe,
Through thy great mercy that spreadeth so very wide.
It is not to thy honour that the devil should entice me;
If thou wilt permit it, truly he will greatly rejoice,
For he would never that thou shouldst have honour,
Nor that any man that honoured thee should have gladness.
Thou knowest full well that the devil hateth me,
And chiefly because I worship thee;
Therefore I entreat thee to guard and protect me,
So that the devil may not trouble me, nor error harm me.
So thou dost and so thou shalt for thy mercy,
Thou shalt give me a fair portion of heavenly bliss.
If I have sinned much, much will I repent,
And perform my shrift and fair thee pray.
The while I have my life and health,
From thy service shall nothing separate me;
Before thy feet I will lie and cry,
Until I have forgiveness of my misdeeds.
My life is thine, my love is thine, my heart's blood is thine,
And if I dare say it, my dear Lady, thou art mine.
All honour have thou in heaven and also on earth,
And all joy have thou as much as thou deservest.
Now I beseech thee, by Christ's charity,
That thou thy blessing and thy love give to me;
Preserve my body in purity.
God Almighty grant me for His mercy,
That I may see thee in thy exalted bliss,

And that all my friends may be the better now to-day
That I have sung thee this English lay.
And now I beseech thee, for thy holiness,
That thou bring the monk to thy joy
That made this song of thee, my dear Lady,
Christ's meek Mother St. Mary!   Amen.'

PRAYER TO THE BLESSED VIRGIN (fifteenth century).

'Mary, Mother, well thou be;
Mary, Maiden, think on me;
Maiden and mother was never none
To thee, Lady, but thou alone.
Sweet Mary, Maiden clean,
Shield me from all shame and tene;
And out of sin, Lady, shield thou me,
And out of debt, for charity.
Lady, for thy joyes five
Give me grace in this life
To know and keep over all thing
Christ's faith and God's bidding;
And truly win all that is need
For me and mine, both clothes and feed.
Help me, Lady, and all mine;
Shield me, Lady, from hell-pine.
Shield me, Lady, from villany
And from all wicked company.
Shield me, Lady, from evil shame,
And from all wicked fame.
Sweet Mary, Maiden mild,
From the fiend thou me shield;
That the fiend me not dere,
Sweet Lady, thou me were.
Both by day and by night
Help me, Lady, with all thy might.
For my friends, Lady, I pray thee,
That they may saved be

To their souls and their life,
Lady, for thy joyës five.
For mine enemies I pray also,
That they may here so do
That they nor I in wrath die.
Sweet Lady, I thee pray,
That they that be in deadly sin,
Let them never die therein ;
But, sweet Lady, thou them rede
For to amend their misdeed.
Sweet Lady, for me thou pray to heaven's King,
To grant me housel, Christ, and good ending.
Jesu, for Thy holy grace
In heaven's bliss to have a place.
Lady, as I trust in thee,
These prayers that thou grant me ;
And I shall, Lady, here belive
Greet thee with Aves five,
A Paternoster and a Creed,
To help me, Lady, at my need.
Sweet Lady, full of win,
Full of grace and good within,
As thou art flower of all thy kin,
Do my sins for to blin,
And keep me out of deadly sin,
That I be never take therein.'

VERSES OF THE FOURTEENTH CENTURY.

(Spelling modernised where possible.)

'Thou, woman, boute vere
Thine own father bere ;
Great wonder this was
That one woman was mother
To father and eke her brother,
So never no other has.

Thou my sister and my mother,
And thy Son is my brother;
   Who should then dread?
Who so hath the king to brother,
And eke the queen to mother,
   Well ought now to speed.

Dame, sister, and mother,
Say thy Son my brother
   That is doomsman,
That for thee that Him bare
To me be debonnair
   My robe He hath on.

Sithey He my robe took,
Also I find in book
   He is to me y-bound;
And help He will, I wot,
For love the charter wrote
   And the ink-horn of His wound.

I take to witnessing
The spere and the crowning,
   The nails and the rood;
That He that is so kind
This ever hath in mind,
   That bought us with His blood.

When thou gave Him my weed,
Dame, help me at the need,
   I wot thou might full well;
That for no wretched guilt
I be to hell y-pult,
   To thee I make appeal.

Now, Dame, I thee beseech,
At thilk day of wrech
   Hoe by thy Son's throne,

When sin shall be sought
In work, in word, in thought,
   And speak for me thou one.

When I must needs appear
For my guilts here
   Tofore the doomsman,
Sister, be there my vere,
And make Him debonnair
   That thy robe hath upon.

For have I thee and Him,
That marks bore with Him,
   That charité Him took,
The wounds all bloody,
The tokens of mercy,
   As teacheth holy book.'

PRAYERS OF ST. ANSELM.

The lines just given are evidently founded on a reminiscence of the prayers of St. Anselm. These prayers and meditations were a favourite manual of devotion among English
Catholics. St. Thomas of Canterbury used them to prepare
for Mass. There are several addressed to the Blessed Virgin.
The following is a specimen :

'Well does the world know, nor can we sinners ever forget
it; well, O Lady, do we know who was that Son of man who
came to seek and to save that which was lost; nor do we forget
that if He was the Son of man, it was because He was thy Son.
Wilt thou then, O Lady and the Mother of my hope, wilt thou
forget that truth which was so mercifully revealed to the world,
so gladly published, and so lovingly received? That good Son
of man came to save what was lost, and came without being
asked; and will His Mother despise that lost one even when
she is asked? That good Son of man came to call the sinner
to repentance; and will His good Mother despise the sinner
even when he repents? That good God, I say—that meek and

lowly Man, that merciful Son of God, that compassionate Son
of man—came to seek the sinner wandering far away; and wilt
thou, His good Mother and powerful Mother of God, wilt
thou repel the wanderer when he returns and prays ?

'As the Son of God is the bliss of the Saints, so is thy Son
the salvation of sinners.   There is no hope of pardon but in
Him who was conceived of thee; no justification but in Him
who was borne by thee; no salvation but in Him who was
born of thee.   Therefore, O Lady, thou art the Mother of Him
who pardons and of those who are pardoned—of Him who jus-
tifies and of those who are justified—of Him who saves and of
those who are saved.   O blessed confidence! O safe refuge!
The Mother of God is our Mother; the Mother of Him in whom
alone we hope and whom alone we fear is our Mother; the
Mother of Him who alone can save or destroy is our Mother.'

CHAPTER III.

In the present chapter I will give some account of certain public forms of devotion to our Lady, such as the votive Mass, the Little Office, litanies, hymns, and antiphons, reserving the Angelic Salutation and the Rosary for separate chapters.

By Acts of Parliament of Edward, Elizabeth, and James, which were rigidly enforced, Catholic books of devotion, such as Missals, Breviaries, and Primers, were ordered to be burnt. Still the scanty materials that remain are sufficient to give some notion of the prayers which were formerly addressed in this island to her whom all generations shall call blessed.

Votive Mass.

The holy Sacrifice of the Mass can be offered to God alone. The words of St. Augustin are well known : ' We do not make temples, priesthoods, sacred rites, and sacrifices to the martyrs ; but their God is our God. We honour, indeed, the places dedicated in memory of them, as of holy men of God. But who ever heard any priest of the faithful when standing at the altar, even built over the holy body of a martyr, to the honour and worship of God, say in the prayers, " I offer to thee sacrifice, Peter or Paul or Cyprian" ? Whereas in those places dedicated to their memories oblation is made to God, who made them both men and martyrs, and has associated them in heavenly honour with His holy angels.'[1]

A Mass 'of the Blessed Virgin' is therefore merely a Mass in which the Blessed Virgin is commemorated; in which thanksgiving is made for her graces, and the benefit of her prayers is

[1] S. Aug. De Civ. Dei, l. viii. c. xxvii.

asked from God. Such Masses are appointed in the Missal for each of our Lady's festivals. A votive Mass is one which does not correspond with the office of the day, but is chosen and said, when the Church allows, in order to satisfy the votum or special devotion of the priest who celebrates or of the faithful who have asked it.

The origin of the votive Masses of the Blessed Virgin is generally attributed to an Englishman, Alcuin. Froben, his editor, remarks, however, that Alcuin, according to his own assertion, merely extracted them from the Missal of his monastery at Tours. This is true. Yet Alcuin does not say that he had not been their first author, and certainly he composed one in honour of St. Boniface, whose martyrdom had lately taken place. In any case it was Alcuin who propagated them throughout Europe. 'I send you,' he writes,[2] 'a missal chart, that you may be able on different days to direct your prayers to God, according to your devotion ; sometimes in honour of the Holy Trinity, sometimes in earnest desire of wisdom, sometimes for the tears of penance, sometimes for perfect charity ; or, again, if you wish to secure the prayers of the angels or of all saints. Also, should any one wish to pray for his own sins, or for a loving friend, or for several friends, or for his brethren who are departing from this world; or when any one wishes specially to implore the intercession of the Blessed Virgin Mary, Mother of God, or to invoke the merciful assistance of your most holy father Boniface.'

The two Masses of our Lady in the 'Book of Sacraments' of Alcuin are as follows :

Mass of the Blessed Virgin for Saturday.

'*Coll.* Grant, O Lord, we beseech Thee, that we Thy servants may enjoy constant health of body and mind, and by the glorious intercession of Blessed Mary ever Virgin, be delivered from all temporal afflictions, and come to those joys that are eternal. Through our Lord Jesus Christ, &c.

'*Lesson* of Ecclus. (xxiv. 14-16). From the beginning, &c.

[2] Ep. 192, ad Fuldenses ; conf. Ep. 46.

' *Gospel.* St. Luke (x. 38-42). At that time Jesus entered a certain town, and a woman named Martha received Him, &c.

' *Secret.* May, O Lord, by Thy own mercy and the intercession of Blessed Mary ever Virgin, this oblation procure us peace and happiness, both in this life and in that which is to come. Through, &c.

' *Postcom.* Having received, O Lord, what is to advance our salvation, grant we may always be protected by the patronage of Blessed Mary ever Virgin, in whose honour we have offered this sacrifice to thy Majesty. Through, &c.

' *Super populum.* O Almighty God, defend by the right hand of Thy power Thy servants from all perils, and by the intercession of Blessed Mary ever Virgin make us enjoy both present and everlasting happiness. Through, &c.'

Mass for the Commemoration of St. Mary.

' *Coll.* Pardon, Lord, the sins of Thy servants ; and though by our own acts we are unable to please Thee, yet by the intercession of the Mother of Thy Son our Lord Jesus Christ may we always think on what is pleasing to Thee, and execute it with pure hearts, words, and deeds. Through, &c.

' *Secret.* Receive, O Lord, our oblations and prayers, and by the intercession of Blessed Mary ever Virgin may our sins be cleansed away, and bend to Thyself our rebellious wills, and grant us life eternal. Through, &c.

' *Com.* Grant, O Lord God, that the holy mysteries which Thou hast granted for our reparation may be to us a remedy both present and future.

' *Another Com.* Purify, O Lord, by the intercession of Blessed Mary ever Virgin, Thy faithful, both in body and mind, that being touched by Thy inspiration they may be able to avoid hurtful pleasures ; and that we may not be enticed by their seductions, may we ever feed on Thy sweetness. Through, &c.'

The votive Mass of the Blessed Virgin was not merely said occasionally, as now, when feasts of double rite, as they are called, and which exclude votive Masses, are greatly multiplied.

It was said almost daily, and commonly known to the people as the Mary Mass.

It was generally said at early dawn. Indeed the Mary bell which rang for this Mass was the well-known sound which told the sleeping world that day was come. Those who had work or business before them hastened to be present at the Mary Mass, for there is abundant evidence that there were but few in those days who did not hear Mass daily.

I have gathered several documents regarding this Mass in England, by which the frequency of its celebration in every kind of church will be evident.

In *cathedrals*. In the *Valor Ecclesiasticus* there is mention of the sum of money paid ' to the clerics and choristers who sang daily the Mass of the Blessed Virgin in the chapel called Salve in the cathedral church of Salisbury, according to the ordinance and foundation of Richard Pore, formerly Bishop.'³

At St. Paul's, London, Eustace de Fauconbrigge, Bishop of London, A.D. 1215, assigned lands for the behalf of poor clerks frequenting the choir, and celebrating the holy Office of our Lady; so that six clerks should be made choice of every day, with one priest of the choir, by turns, to be at the celebration of the Mass of our Lady, and also to say Matins and all other canonical hours at her altar. This foundation was increased by the prior and convent of Thetford in 1299. The executors of Hugh de Pourte in 1318 gave a yearly rent to maintain one taper of three pounds' weight, to burn before our Lady's altar every day while her Mass should be celebrated, and at every procession before her altar.⁴ Of course similar customs prevailed in every cathedral.

In *abbey churches* the Mary Mass was solemnised with much pomp. Matthew Paris tells us that Abbot William of St. Alban's, in 1214, seeing that in all the noble churches in England the Mass of the Blessed Virgin was every day solemnly sung to music (ad notam), ordained with the consent of the whole convent that for the future this should also be done at

³ *Valor Ecclus.* ii. 85; apud Rock, *Church of our Fathers*, iii. p. 261.
⁴ Dugdale's *St. Paul's*.

St. Alban's. Six monks were assigned to minister at this Mass, and a beautifully-sounding bell was cast and blessed by the Bishop, and called by Mary's name, to be thrice rung to call the faithful to assist. Sir Richard de Clohale gave a gold chalice for this Mass.[5] The historian of Glastonbury also informs us that in 1322 eight priests were appointed for singing of our Lady's Mass daily ' with melodious chant.'[6] At the celebration of the Mary Mass in the crypt at Evesham, twenty-four wax lights were burnt every day, and thirty-three lamps were lighted.[7]

Nor was this the only Mary Mass at Evesham, for in 1360 a new chapel was built in the cemetery near the abbey gate to receive a statue, before which, as the abbot who builds the chapel asserts, ' to the honour of the Blessed Virgin and His own glory, God works great and innumerable miracles.' To this chapel two secular priests were assigned yearly. One had to say Mass of the Blessed Virgin at daybreak, and the other a Requiem Mass at nine o'clock. Each celebrated the early Mass on alternate days, and both had to assist at the Blessed Virgin's Mass in the crypt.[8]

Collegiate churches followed the example of the abbeys and cathedrals, as the college of St. Elizabeth at Winchester, founded by Bishop John de Pontys in 1300; and others.[9] Even many *parochial churches* had not only an altar of our Lady, but a priest whose daily duty it was to say Mass there. In many wills small sums are left for the maintenance of the ' St. Mary priest.' ' The guilds in the parish,' says Dr. Rock, ' often helped to keep up the Mary Mass, as we learn from accounts of churchwardens.' He adds that in all the great families of England there was a priest who said daily in the private chapel our Lady's Mass.

Any one who looks through the various collections of old wills that have been made will find this same devotion manifested. Land, cattle, small sums of money, are left to provide lights during our Lady's Mass, or gold and silver vessels for her

---

[5] *Lives of the Abbots of St. Alban's,* pp. 80, 81, ed. Wats.
[6] Joannes Glaston. p. 268, apud Rock.
[7] Stevens, Appendix to Dugdale, p. 146 ; Tindall's *History of Evesham,* p. 103.   [8] Tindall, pp. 222, 194.   [9] Dr. Rock, ubi supra.

altar, or rich vestments ; and, above all, in the Masses left for
the repose of the soul almost always our Lady's Mass is asked,
at least for the Saturday.[10]

The Little Office and Primers.

In the modern Roman Breviary are three forms of Office of
the Blessed Virgin ; one for feasts, one for Saturdays, and one
called the Little Office.   The last is said to have been used in
the sixth century ; but it was revived, as well as revised, in the
eleventh by St. Peter Damian.   Pope Urban II., in the Council
of Claremont, in 1096, made it of universal obligation for priests
and religious ; but the obligation was again restricted by St.
Pius V.

As the Little Office was both short and devout, many pious
laymen joined with the clergy in saying it, not merely in public,
but also in private.   It became one of the principal devotions of
the educated classes.   It was written in MS., sometimes of a
very splendid kind, and was one of the earliest books printed.

But both written and printed books, though called from
this office the Horæ Beatæ Virginis, or Hours of the Blessed
Virgin, contained also several other forms of' devotion, just
like our own prayer-books.   Such prayer-books, in one or other
form, have existed for the use of the laity from very early
times, and were commonly called Primers, as containing among
other things elementary instructions and prayers, as the Creed,
Lord's Prayer, Angelic Salutation, and Ten Commandments.

In the miscellaneous records of the Tower of London an
ancient roll has been preserved, belonging to the thirteenth
century.   'It is written on both sides of a narrow slip of vellum (or rather three pieces sewed together) about three inches
wide and three feet long, and, when rolled up, about half an
inch diameter, so that it was well calculated for carrying
about the person.'   It contains the first fourteen verses of St.

---

[10] See examples quoted by Dr. Rock, vol. iii. p. 264, to which I may
add a curious entry from the churchwardens' accounts of St. Mary Hill,
London : 'A.D. 1531. Three gallons and six pynts of malvesay for a yere
for Lady's masse, 3s. 9d.'

John's Gospel in Latin, then an exhortation in French to say five Paters and five Aves in honour of our Lord's five wounds. Then some French verses for the adoration of the Blessed Sacrament. Then a beautiful method of hearing Mass, viz. sixty-five verses in French, forming a kind of litany of supplication to our Lord, with Latin prayers. Then follows a method of assisting at the seven canonical hours, which I will give presently. Afterwards Latin prayers, and an indication of the Psalms recommended for various occasions; and, lastly, a long and beautiful prayer in Latin. This prayer-roll has been published at length in Bentley's *Excerpta Historica.*

A Primer, all in English, belonging to the end of the fourteenth or first years of the fifteenth century, has also been published in full, with dissertations and notes, in the second volume of Mr. Maskell's *Monumenta Ritualia Ecclesiæ Anglicanæ.*

From the frequent mention of handsomely-bound primers in old wills it is evident that, during the fourteenth and fifteenth and sixteenth centuries, the recitation of our Lady's Hours was a favourite devotion of the noble and the educated. In 1391, Margaret, Countess of Devon, leaves two primers to her daughter; in 1399, Eleanor, Duchess of Gloucester, leaves her daughter ' a book with the psalter, prymer, and other devotions, with two clasps of gold, enamelled with my arms, which book I have often used.' In 1415, Michael, Earl of Suffolk, leaves his ' little prymer which belonged to John de la Pole, my brother.'[11]

'There is a beautiful vellum illuminated MS. at Stonyhurst College,' says Miss Strickland, 'which has either belonged to Elizabeth of York' (wife of Henry VII.) ' or her mother' (Elizabeth Woodville, queen of Edward IV.). ' It is the Offices of the Virgin. Every margin is highly wrought by the art of the illuminator, and each hour of the Office of the Virgin is headed with a painting of some incident in her life or scriptural illustration. . . . On the last fly-leaf but one there is written the name " Elizabeth Plantagenet, the Queen." '[12]

[11] *Testamenta Vetusta,* by Sir Harris Nicolas.
[12] *Lives of the Queens of England,* vol. ii. p. 443, ed. 1851.

'Books which had in them the canonical hours were sometimes left by will, to be fastened to a desk or reading-stand
nigh some altar, that those who wished might say or sing their
Matins and Evensong out of them; for such an end did John
Norys bequeath "his portous of paper rial to be chayned in
the chapel of our Lady" in the church of South Lynn, where
he had been vicar.'[13]

But it was not only rich and noble lords and ladies who had
primers, and who said the Office of our Lady. It seems to have
been the favourite devotion of all who could read. There exists
an old poem written by a pupil of Dan Lydgate, towards the
end of the fourteenth or beginning of the fifteenth century, as
an instruction in manners to a little boy, a gentleman's son.
The following lines occur :[14]

> ' Afore all things, first and principally
> In the morrowe when yᵉ shall up rise,
> To worship God have in your memory,
> With Christ's cross look yᵉ bless you thrice,
> Your Pater Noster sayeth in devout wyse,
> Ave Maria, with the holy Crede,
> Then all the day the better may ye spede ;
> And while ye be abouten honestly
> To dress yourself and don on your array,
> With your fellow, well and treatably,
> Our Lady's matins aviseth that ye say,
> And this observance useth every day,
> With prime and hours ; and withouten dread
> The blessed Lady will grant you your meed.'

It may be observed here that the Office is said with a companion ('with your fellow'). This seems to have been the ordinary method of reciting it.

In a report on the state of England made by the secretary to
the Venetian Embassy in 1496-97 occurs the following picture
of our forefathers : 'They all hear Mass every day, and say many
Paternosters [Rosaries] in public, the women carrying long
strings of beads in their hands, and whoever is at all able to
read carries with him the Office of our Lady ; and they recite it

[13] Dr. Rock, *Church of our Fathers*, vol. iv. p. 144.
[14] Published by the Early English Text Society.

in church with some companion in a low voice, verse by verse, after the manner of religious.'[15]

Our holy martyr Fisher has left us a beautiful picture of the devotions of a noble lady of the same period, in his funeral sermon of the Lady Margaret, Countess of Richmond and mother of Henry VII. 'Right studious she was in books, which she had in great number, both in English, Latin, and in French, and for her exercise and for the profit of other she did translate divers matters of devotion out of French into English.[16] ... Every day at her uprising, which commonly was not long after five of the clock, she began certain devotions, and so after them, with one of her gentlewomen, the Matins of our Lady, which kept her to then she came into her closet; where then with her chaplain she said also Matins of the day; and after that, daily heard four or five Masses upon her knees, so continuing in her prayers and devotions unto the hour of dinner, which, of the eating day, was ten of the clock, and upon the fasting day, eleven. After dinner full truely she would go her stations to the altars daily; daily her Dirges and Commendations she would say, and her Evensong before supper, both of the day and of our Lady, beside many other prayers and psalters of David throughout the year; and at night before she went to bed she failed not to resort unto her chapel, and there a large quarter of an hour to occupy her devotions. No marvel though all this long time her kneeling was to her painful, and so painful that many a time it caused her back pain and disease. And yet nevertheless daily, when she was in health, she failed not to say the Crown of our Lady, which, after the manner of Rome, containeth sixty-and-three Aves, and at every Ave to make a kneeling,' &c.[17]

The Lady Margaret in these devotions followed in the footsteps of her patroness St. Margaret, Queen of Scotland, of whom

[15] *A Relation of the Island of England*, &c., printed for the Camden Society.

[16] Among other treatises, the fourth book of the *Imitation of Christ.*

[17] *A Mornynge Remembrance had at the Month's Mind of the noble Princess Margaret*, &c., by the Right Rev. Father in God John Fisher, Bishop of Rochester.

M

her biographer tells us that, 'during Advent and Lent, after a short sleep she would rise at midnight, and going to the church, she would say alone Matins of the most Holy Trinity, Matins of the holy Cross, and lastly Matins of our Lady. Then when the clergy came at the early hour to recite the Matins of the day, she would continue her prayers until she had finished the whole Psalter.'[18]

This was about the year 1093; whence we learn that the movement made in the south of Europe some years earlier to revive the Office of our Lady had extended before the end of the eleventh century into Scotland.

In these early devotions these pious ladies believed that they were imitating the example set by our Lady herself in the Temple; for the preacher told them that 'every day, from morrow to underen' (*i.e.* from the early morning until Tierce or nine o'clock), 'she was in her prayers.'[19]

. Even when tyrannous laws had forbidden in England all invocation of our Blessed Lady, devout Catholics would sometimes meet together in secret to recite the Office of the Blessed Virgin. Of this we have a proof in the register of criminal proceedings taken against all who were suspected of leanings to the old faith, after the second unsuccessful rising in the northern counties in 1569. Thomas Wright, vicar of Seaham, confesses[20] that he says daily in his house with certain others the Office of the Blessed Virgin. This poor priest had evidently conformed to the new order out of fear, and was probably hoping for better times, should Elizabeth die.

Besides the 'Little Office,' which was the authorised form of devotion, we find in old books another shorter office called 'Of the Compassion of our Lady;' and as we see in the account given above of the prayer-roll of the thirteenth century, there was then a method used by the laity of participating to some degree in the canonical hours, by saying instead of each hour five Our Fathers and Hail Marys and an appropriate prayer.

---

[18] *Bol. Acta SS.* Jun. x. 828.   [19] *Liber Festivalis,* p. 143.
[20] Depositions, &c. p. 199, published by the Surtees Society in 1845.

These prayers could easily be learnt by heart, as they were in Anglo-Norman verse. The following is a translation:

Lay Method of Joining in the Divine Office (thirteenth century).

'For Matins say five Pater Noster and five Ave Maria, and this

Prayer.

'Lord Jesu, who at the hour of Matins didst, by Thy sweet pleasure, willingly suffer Thyself to be smitten on the face, to be mocked, spit upon, and buffeted, and at the same hour didst raise Thyself from the dead and deliver Thy own from purgatory; grant me pardon of my sins and patience in tribulation.

'For Prime say five Pater Noster and five Ave Maria; and then,

'Lord Jesu, who at the hour of Prime wast through envy charged by the Jews before Pilate, in their shameless folly, with much perfidious crime, and at the same hour didst show Thyself to the Magdalen, who loved Thee much; show me, Lord, Thy face, and give me grace to do well.

'For Tierce say five Pater Noster and five Ave Maria; and then,

'Lord Jesu, I cry to Thee for mercy, who at the hour of Tierce wast reviled by the Jews, tied to a pillar, and all Thy body scourged, and at the same hour didst enlighten Thy Apostles with the Holy Spirit; enlighten my heart with Thy love, that I may serve Thee day and night.

'For midday (Sext) say five Pater Noster and five Ave Maria; and then,

'Lord Jesu, who at the hour of noon wast fastened to the cross with nails, amidst sinners and wicked persons, by the perfidious and wretched Jews, and at the same hour didst take flesh of a true Virgin the holy Mary; for that annunciation give me pardon of my sins.

'For None (three o'clock) say five Pater Noster and five Ave Maria; and then,

'Lord Jesu, who at the hour of None didst pray for us and deliver up Thy soul to Thy Father, who is always in every place as it pleaseth Him, and at that same hour didst ascend into heaven and confirm our faith; bring me to heaven, that I may there enjoy Thee!

'For Vespers say five Pater Noster and five Ave Maria; and then,

'Lord Jesu, who at the hour of Vespers wast with love and reverence taken down from the cross by Joseph of Arimathea, and at that same hour didst give Thy flesh in the sacrament at Thy supper; for that holy sacrament deliver me from the incumbrance of sin.

'For Complin say five Pater Noster and five Ave Maria; and then,

'Lord Jesu, who at the hour of Complin didst, when Thou prayedst, sweat drops of blood, and didst awaken Thy disciples and tell them of the treason of Judas and the wicked host who horribly fixed a price for Thee, and at that same hour wast devoutly laid in the sepulchre; for that holy sepulture defend me from purgatory.

'A hundred days' indulgence is given to those who say these hours with good faith.' Some words are here illegible.

Several other methods of recalling, at the different hours of the day when the Office of our Lady was said, the various stages of our Lord's Passion or the joyful and sorrowful events of our Lady's life are given in the printed editions of the Horæ, both in Latin and in English. They were written in verse, so as to be easily committed to memory.

A writer of the fifteenth century gives some very quaint yet pious reasons

Why our Lady is praised at the Seven Hours.

'At Matins time there appeareth a star in the firmament, whereby shipmen are ruled in the sea, and bring themselves to right haven; and for [*i.e.* because] our merciful Lady is that star that succoureth mankind in the troublous sea of this world, and bringeth her lovers to the haven of health, therefore it is worthy that she be served and praised at Matins time.

'At Prime time [*i.e.* six o'clock] there appeareth a star before the sun, as if it were the leader or bringer forth of the sun. And our Lady came before, and brought forth to mankind that Sun of righteousness that is our Lord Jesus Christ.

' At hour of Tierce [*i.e.* nine o'clock] labourers desire to have their dinner ; and our Lady hath brought forth to us Him that is food and bread of life, our Lord Jesus Christ—comfort and refection to all that labour in His service.

' At hour of Sext [*i.e.* noon] the sun waxeth more hot; and by means of our Lady the everlasting Sun hath showed the heat of His charity more largely to mankind.

' At hour of None [*i.e.* three o'clock] the sun is highest ; and the highest grace and mercy that ever was done to man in earth was brought in by means of our Lady.

' At evening time the day faileth much ; and when all other succour faileth our Lady's grace helpeth.

' Complin is the end of the day ; and in the end of our life we have most need of our Lady's help.

' And therefore in all these hours we ought to do her worship and praising.'[21]

My next extracts will illustrate our Lady's Office.

Ave Maris Stella,
With English version of the fourteenth century.[22]

' Heyl, levedy, se-stoerre bryht
Godes moder, edy wyht,
Mayden ever vurst and late ;
Of heveneriche sely gate.

Thylk Ave thai thow vonge in spel,
Of the aungeles mouheth kald Gabriel,
In gryht ous sette and shyld vrom shome,
That turnst abakward Eves nome.

Gulty monnes bond unbynd,
Bryng lyht tyl hoem that boeth blynd ;
Put vrom ous oure sunne
And ern ous elle wynne.

Shou that thou art moder one
And he vor the take oure bone ;

' Ave maris stella,
Dei Mater alma,
Atque semper Virgo,
Felix cœli porta.

Sumens illud Ave
Gabrielis ore,
Funda nos in pace,
Mutans Evœ nomen.

Solve vincla reis,
Profer lumen cæcis,
Mala nostra pelle,
Bona cuncta posce.

Monstra te esse matrem,
Sumat per te preces, .

---

[21] From the *Mirror of our Lady*, written about 1430 (Early English Text Society, 1873).   [22] From the *Reliquiæ Antiquæ*, vol. ii. p. 228.

That vor ous thy chyld by-com	Qui pro nobis natus,
And of the oure keinde nom.	Tulit esse tuus.
Mayde one thou were myd chylde	Virgo singularis,
Among alle so mylde,	Inter omnes mitis,
Of sunne ous quite on haste,	Nos culpis solutos,
And make ous meoke and chaste.	Mites fac et castos.
Lyf thou gyf ous clene	Vitam præsta puram,
Wey syker ous garke and lene,	Iter para tutum,
That we Jesus y-soe	Ut videntes Jesum,
And ever blythe boe.	Semper collætemur.'

To the Vader, Chryst, and to the Holy Gost beo thonk and heryinge,
To threo persones and o God, o menske and worshypinge.'

*Lessons of the Little Office of the Blessed Virgin in an old
English Translation of about* 1400.[23]

'I. St. Mary, Maid of maidens, Mother and Daughter of
the King of Kings ; solace us that we moun [may] have by thee
the mede of heavenly kingdom, and with the chosen of God
reign without end.

'II. St. Mary, most piteous of all piteous women, holiest
of all holy women ; pray for us that by thee maiden He take
our sins, that for us was born and reigneth above heavens ;
that by His charity our sins be forgiven to us.

'III. Holy Mother of God, that deservedst werthily to conceive Him that all the world might not hold ; with thy meek
beseeching wash away our guilt, that we again bought [redeemed]
by thee may stize up to the seat of endless bliss ; there thou
dwellest with thy Son without time.'

The Hymn Quem terra, pontus, sidera[24] (sixteenth century).

'The Governour of the triple engine,
Whom the earth, the sea, and the heavens doth honour,
Conceived is in the womb of a Virgin,
Whose name is Mary, by God's high power.
A Maiden's womb, immaculate and pure,
Him hath conceived, without spot or crime ;

---

[23] Maskell, *Monumenta Ritualia*, vol. ii. p. 10. I have modernised the
spelling, but not changed the words.
[24] From the Prymer, ed. 1538; Maskell, vol. ii. p. 5.

To whom the sun and moon and every creature
Do serve alway in their course and time.
Blessed is that Mother replenished with grace,
In whose womb the Creator immortal
Hath not disdained to take His place,
Holding in His hand the world over all.
Of the heavenly messenger blessed is she
Through the grace of the Holy Ghost inspired,
For out of her womb proceeded He
Whom all the nations of the world desired.'

Litany.

When St. Augustine advanced with his monks to meet
King Ethelred, they sang a litany. It has been disputed whether
this was like the present Roman Litany of the Saints, in which
the name of the Blessed Virgin comes before all others, after
that of her Divine Son. It is, however, admitted that this was
in use in the eighth century. In one Anglo-Saxon litany published by Mabillon, the words *Sancta Maria, ora pro nobis,* are
repeated three times. I am not aware when litanies were first
composed of titles and invocations of our Lady, nor have I seen
any printed specimen. The following has been copied by a
friend from a ms. in the British Museum.[25] It is of the early
part of the thirteenth century.

It begins as usual with the Kyrie eleyson and the invocations of the Blessed Trinity, and then continues :

'   Sancta Maria, ora pro nobis.
    Sancta Maria, Mater Christi sanctissima, o.p.n.
    Sancta Maria, Dei Genitrix, o.p.n.
    Sancta Maria, Mater innupta, o.p.n.
    Sancta Maria, Mater intacta, o.p.n.
    Sancta Maria, Mater inviolata, o.p.n.
    Sancta Maria, Virgo virginum, o.p.n.
    Sancta Maria, Virgo perpetua, o.p.n.
    Sancta Maria, gratia Dei plena, o.p.n.
    Sancta Maria, æterni Regis Filia, o.p.n.

        [25] Cotton ms., Titus A. xxi. Mariale.

Sancta Maria, Christi Mater et Sponsa, o.p.n.
Sancta Maria, Templum Spiritus Sancti, o.p.n.
Sancta Maria, cœlorum Regina, o.p.n.
Sancta Maria, angelorum Domina, o.p.n.
Sancta Maria, Scala cœli, o.p.n.
Sancta Maria, paradisi Porta, o.p.n.
Sancta Maria, Fons caritatis, o.p.n.
Sancta Maria, Mater misericordiæ, o.p.n.'

And so continues at great length.

Antiphons.

Another favourite devotion of our forefathers was the singing of antiphons in honour of our Lady.

An antiphon or anthem derives its name from the custom of singing in alternate choirs; but the name is also given to certain short hymns, metrical or not, even when sung by one choir only. In the present Roman Breviary are four antiphons in honour of the Blessed Virgin, to be said at the different seasons of the year, at the conclusion of certain parts of the office. They begin respectively with the words, 'Alma Redemptoris Mater,' 'Ave Regina cœlorum,' ' Regina cœli lætare,' and 'Salve Regina.' They were first introduced into the Roman Breviary in 1520, but were used by the Franciscans from the year 1249.[26] Antiphons in honour of the Blessed Virgin were ordered to be sung at the end of Complin by a general chapter of the Benedictines held at Northampton in 1444, 'in order before sleep to implore her help by whom the serpent's head was crushed.' This was only a renewal of a more ancient decree.

The singing of antiphons soon became a favourite devotion with priests and people, even apart from the office, and foundations were made and even confraternities instituted for this purpose. The music seems to have been sometimes very elaborate, since we find such notices as the following. At the abbey of Evesham chaplains are to be assigned to our Lady's altar skilled in her antiphons.[27] John Barnet, Bishop of Bath and

[26] *Merati in Gavantum.* tom. iii. p. 215.   [27] Tindall's *Evesham*, p. 112.

Wells, founded in 1365 a lamp to burn day and night before
the statue of our Lady in St. Paul's, London; and also that
after Matins an anthem of our Lady, sc. 'Nesciens Mater,' or
some other solemn one suitable to the time, should be sung
before the image with a versicle, which being performed, the
person highest in dignity present to say a collect of the Blessed
Virgin, followed by the 'De Profundis.'[28]

Henry VI., the founder of King's College, Cambridge, and
of Eton, prescribes in the statutes, 'That every day of the
year, at a fitting hour of the evening, all the choristers of our
royal college, together with the master in chant, shall enter the
church at the sound of a bell, which shall be always rung except on Holy Thursday or Good Friday; and these wearing surplices and ranged around a statue of the Blessed Virgin, with
the candles lighted, shall sing solemnly and to the very best of
their skill an antiphon of the Blessed Virgin, with the verse
Ave Maria, &c. and the prayer Meritis et precibus,' &c.

This pious king did not, however, originate the custom of
students saluting our Lady by an evening hymn. It was already
in use in other colleges. Indeed the evening antiphon seems
to have occupied with our Catholic forefathers almost the same
place that is now filled by the evening Benediction of the Blessed
Sacrament—a form of devotion not then established. The following extracts will justify this assertion.

In the statutes of St. Mary Magdalen College, Oxford,
Bishop Wayneflete says: 'Our pleasure is that on every Saturday throughout the year, and on all the eves of the feasts of
the Blessed Virgin, after Complin, all and each of the fellows
and scholars and ministers of our chapel do devoutly perform
among themselves in the common hall, by note, an antiphon in
honour of the glorious Virgin.' By the statutes for the collegiate church of Whittington College, London, it is ordained
that even on ferial days, throughout the year, about or after
sunset, when the poor labourers and those who live near the
church are giving up work and business, when there is no reasonable hindrance, the chaplains, clerks, and choristers of the

[28] Dugdale's *St. Paul's.*

college who are at home, after the ringing of a small bell set apart for that office, shall meet in the chapel of St. Mary, in the said church, and there sing to the honour of our Saviour and His Mother an antiphon with versicles and prayer.[29]   To keep up this custom many guilds were established.   Stow[30] tells us of one such called the ' Salve,' in St. Magnus' Church, near London Bridge, which was flourishing in A.D. 1343.   Certain citizens, ' of their great devotion to the honour of God and His glorious Mother, our Lady Mary the Virgin, began and caused to be made a chauntry to sing an anthem to our Lady called "Salve Regina" every evening ; and thereon ordained five burning wax lights at the time of the said anthem, in the honour of the five principal joys of our Lady aforesaid ; . . . and thereupon many other good people of the parish. . . proffered to be aiders to support the said lights, and the said anthem to be continually sung, paying every person every week a halfpenny ; and so that hereafter with the gifts a chaplain to say Mass for all benefactors.'   This of course is only one specimen of a beautiful devotion practised throughout England.   To many of my readers will have already occurred the memory of Chaucer's beautiful picture of the village school and of the boys learning to sing our Lady's antiphon.   It is too faithful a picture of Catholic England in the fourteenth century to be omitted ; but before giving it, I will translate from the works of St. Peter Celestine the original tale which Chaucer has developed.

St. Peter Celestine's Tale.

' There was a widow in England who had an only son, a little boy learning letters, who, amongst other things, learnt the responsory of the Blessed Virgin, "Gaude Maria Virgo," which he used to sing devoutly as he went through the streets.   But as he came one day into the Jews' quarter he sang his antiphon as usual, saying, "Let the wretched Jew blush."   Then a certain Jew, calling him secretly into his house, slew him, and cast him into a ditch near the threshold.   The mother sought

---

[29] Quoted by Dr. Rock, vol. iii. p. 278.
[30] *Survey of London*, vol. i. p. 495.

her child for many days, and not finding him was very sad. But at length she came to the Jews' quarter, and ran up and down, when the child began to sing "Gaude Maria." When the mother heard it she and many others ran and found him; and when they asked what had happened, he replied, "When I entered this house I fell fast asleep, and while I slept the Blessed Virgin came and said, 'How long will you sleep? rise up and sing;' and I rose and began to sing her antiphon." [31]

Mr. Tyrwhitt writes in his Introduction to Chaucer, that he has not been able to discover from what legend of the miracles of our Lady the Prioress's Tale is taken. Nor do I know whence St. Peter derived her history. Chaucer, however, writes:

> ' There was in Asia, in a great city,
> Amongës Christian folk a Jewery,
> Sustained by a lord of that country
> For foul usure and lucre of villainy,
> Hateful to Christ and to his company.'

It is sufficiently curious that by an Italian the scene of the story should be laid in England, and by an Englishman in Asia. However, as St. Peter Celestine's version is at least a century older than that of Chaucer, it more probably coincides with the original. Hence Mr. Tyrwhitt is not well grounded when he writes: 'From the scene being laid in Asia, it should seem that this was one of the oldest of the many stories which have been propagated at different times to excite or justify several merciless persecutions of the Jews upon the charge of murdering Christian children.'

It is true that in Chaucer the 'provost' puts to death all the Jews who were cognisant of the crime, but this is only ' poetical justice;' the legend in the earlier form says nothing whatever of this. And here, without in any way excusing the many acts of regal or popular barbarity committed against the Jews in England, I would remark, that as yet the whole truth has not been told. Compare with the opinion now generally entertained, that any one in the twelfth century could kill a Jew with impunity, the following passage from a treatise of Peter of Blois,

[31] St. Peter Celestine, *Op.* vi. cap. xvii.; Bib. Max. t. xxv. p. 815.

Archdeacon of Bath : ' The unsubstantial (umbratilem) nature of the justice of our days is seen in this fact, that if a bishop or priest is killed, the punishment of such a crime is passed over on some empty pretence ; while for the murder of a Jew the utmost rigour of the law is enacted. Of the whole multitude who gave either counsel or assistance towards the slaughter of the blessed Archbishop Thomas not even one lost an ear. But when the wife of the Jew Aaron was killed the whole country shuddered at the horrible kinds of tortures inflicted on the actors and abettors of the crime.'[32] But this is a digression. To return to our story. Chaucer's picture of the little school was no doubt drawn from life, not in Asia but in England.

' A little school of Christian folk there stood
Down at the farther end, in which there were
Children a heapë come of Christian blood,
That learnéd in that schoolë year by year,
Such manner doctrine as men used there :
That is to say, to singen and to read,
As smallë children do in their childhede.

Among these children was a widow's son,
A little clergion,[33] seven year of age,
That day by day to schoolë was his won,[34]
And eke also, whereas he saw th' image
Of Christë's mother, had he in uságe
As him was taught, to kneel adown, and say
Ave Maria, as he go'th by the way.

This little child his little book learning,
As he sat in the school at his priméře,
He *Alma Redemptoris* heardë sing,
As children learnéd their antiphonere :
And as he durst, he drew him near and near,
And hearken'd aye the wordës and the note,
Till he the firstë verse couldë[35] all by rote.

Nought wist he what this Latin was to say,
For he so young and tender was of age ;
But on a day his fellow 'gan he pray
T' expounden him this song in his languáge,
Or tell him why this song was in uságe :
This pray'd he him to construe and declare,
Full often time upon his kneës bare.

[32] Petrus Bles. Canon Episc. ; Bib. Max. t. xxiv. p. 1180.
[33] Young clerk.   [34] Custom.   [35] Knew.

His fellow, which that elder was than he,
Answér'd him thus: " This song, I have heard say,
Was maked of our blissful Lady free,
Her to salute, and eke her for to pray
To be our help, and succour when we dey.
I can no more expound in this mattére:
I learnë song, I can[34] but small grammére."

" And is this song maked in reverence
Of Christë' mother?" said this innocent;
" Now certes I will do my diligence
To conne[35] it all, ere Christëmas be went,
Though that I for my primer shall be shent,[36]
And shall be beaten thriës in an hour,
I will it conne, our Lady for t' honóur." '

One more illustration of the popular use of antiphons I may mention; for though insignificant in itself, it is associated with an honoured name. It seems that the street-singers appealed to Christian piety and charity by these popular hymns. In allusion to this custom, Sir Thomas More, after resigning the chancellorship, called together his family, and telling them that they would still live together, though they would have to reduce their expenditure, added merrily, that if it came to the worst, ' may we yet with bags and wallets go a-begging together, and, hoping that for pity some good folks will give us their charity, at every man's door to sing *Salve Regina*, and so still keep company and be merry together.'[37]

But the time was now come when the religion of Sir Thomas More, of Cardinal Fisher, of Lady Margaret, and of Henry VI. was to be called superstition and idolatry; when those who clung to the old faith could no longer be ' merry together,' and the hymns and antiphons of our Lady would strengthen the hearts of confessors in filthy dungeons, but would no longer gladden the hearts of the people from the lips of the trained choristers after the toil of daily labour.

I conclude this chapter with an

Old English Version of the Salve Regina (about 1400).

' Heil, queene, modir of merci, heil liif, swetnesse and oure hope. To thee we crien, outlawed sones of eve, to thee we

[34] Know.   [36] Disgraced.   [37] Roper's *Life of More*.

siȝyen wethmentynge and wepynge in this valei of teeris. Hiȝe therfore thou oure avocat, turne to us tho thi merciful yȝen, and shewe thou to us iesu the blessid fruyt of thi wombe aftir this exilyng.

'*Vers.* Virgyn modir of the chirche, everlastynge ȝate of glorie, be thou to us refuyt anentis the fadir and the sone.

'*Resp.* O merciful.

'*Vers.* Virgyn, merciful virgyn, piteuous, o marie swete virgyn, here the preieris of meek men to thee piteuously criyng.

'*Resp.* O piteuous.

'*Vers.* ȝete out preieris to thi sone fiechid to the cross, ful of woundis: and for us al for scourgid: with thornes prickid: ȝouun [given] gal to drynke.

'*Resp.* O swete.

'*Vers.* Gloriouse modir of god, of whom the sone was fadir: prei for us alle, that of thee maken mynde.

'*Resp.* O meek.

'*Vers.* Do awey blamys of wrecchidnesse: clense the filthe of synneris: ȝyne to us thurȝ thi preieris liif of blessid men.

'*Resp.* O celi [*i.e.* happy].

'*Vers.* Reiside above hevenes: and crowned of thi child, in this wrecchid vale to giltie be lady of forȝivenes.

'*Resp.* O hooly.

'*Vers.* That he lose us for synnes for the love of his modir: and to the kyngdom of clernesse lede us the kyng of pitee.

'*Resp.* O merciful, o piteuouse, o hooli, o meek, o seli, o swete marie, heil.

'*Vers.* Heil ful of grace, the lord is with thee.

'*Resp.* Blessid be thou among alle wymmen, and blessid be the fruyt of thi wombe.'[38]

[38] Maskell, *Monum. Ritual.* vol. ii. p. 71.

CHAPTER IV.

THE ANGELIC SALUTATION.

THERE is no devotion to the Blessed Virgin in such esteem or such frequent use among Christians as the Angelic Salutation, since by means of it we repeat words taught by God'Himself to the angel Gabriel and to St. Elizabeth, and a beautiful prayer approved by the Holy Church. It can scarcely be uninteresting to study the history of this prayer in England.

The learned and pious antiquarian, Canon Rock, asserts that the latter part of this formula—viz. 'Holy Mary, Mother of God, pray for us sinners, now and at the hour of our death. Amen,'—was 'unknown to, and therefore never said by, our countrymen when England was Catholic;' while the first part, or what is properly called the salutation—viz. 'Hail, Mary, full of grace, the Lord is with thee; blessed art thou amongst women, and blessed is the fruit of thy womb, Jesus'—'was never used in England in public or private prayer, except indeed once a year in the offertory of the Mass of the fourth Sunday in Advent,' until the thirteenth century.   Dr. Rock adds, that the Anglo-Saxons and Anglo-Normans 'would have been as glad as we are to say, had it been known, the beautiful prayer as we now have it.'[1]   Questions of date therefore, as between Catholics, are purely antiquarian, or devotional only in so far that we like to associate our prayers with the memory of those who have used them before us.   Yet I am convinced that Dr. Rock is incorrect in both his assertions; and that we must assign a much earlier date than the thirteenth century to the use of the 'Hail Mary,' and an earlier date than the sixteenth to the *popular* use of the 'Holy Mary,' &c.

[1] *Church of our Fathers*, vol. iii. pp. 315-19,

The arguments by which Dr. Rock seeks to prove that the 'Hail Mary' was unknown in Saxon times are two : first, that it is not mentioned in any extant document ; and secondly, that where instructions are given about teaching the people the Lord's Prayer, nothing whatever is said of the Angelic Salutation. That it was not known for more than a century after the Norman Conquest, he proves from a similar silence of documents. 'Had such a form of prayer been known, either in England or elsewhere, up to A.D. 1172, St. Godric, who died in that year in his hermitage at Finchale, Durham, and whose heart had ever glowed with such a very warm love for

> " Seinte Marie, Christes bour,
> Meidenes clenhed, moderes flour,"

would have assuredly been but too glad to have said it along with the Our Father and the Belief, which it was his wont, while yet a youth in the world, to repeat often to himself as he went along the road,' as we learn from his biographer.

These arguments are very far from conclusive. They suppose that if the 'Hail Mary' had been in common use, it would necessarily have been mentioned in connection with the Our Father. But a prayer might be very popular and yet not have acquired such liturgical and authoritative recognition as to be classed with the Apostles' Creed, or the prayer appointed by our Lord Himself. Even at the present day, though the Angelic Salutation frequently accompanies the Lord's Prayer both in liturgical and popular use, and though we associate the two forms of prayer in our minds, yet they neither hold the same rank, nor is the knowledge of them imposed on the laity under the same obligation.

So far as we can learn, the 'Hail Mary' was not adopted into the Church's liturgy (with the exception already made) before the thirteenth century. But we have proofs, both direct and indirect, that long before that time it was in popular use both in England and in the rest of Europe.

First, then, what are the probabilities of the case ? Could men have the practice of congratulating and praising Mary, as

they certainly had at all times, and not use the inspired words
with which God Himself had congratulated and praised her?
It has been truly said that 'all devotion to the Mother of God
springs from the "Hail Mary," as all harmony springs from the
octave. A few notes are all the elements of song, as the four
words, "Hail, full of grace!" are the elements of all the love and
veneration, the devotion and worship of the Church for our
Blessed Mother.'[2]

Can any one conceive that when Bede wrote the homily on
the Visitation, or Baldwin the meditation on the Annunciation,
which I have given in the First Part of this work, those holy
men did not raise their souls to heaven, and repeat to Mary the
words on which they were commenting? This is not a mere
conjecture. There is a meditation sometimes attributed to St.
Anselm, and more probably composed by St. Aelred for his
sister.[3] He tells her to enter in spirit the room where Mary received the angel's message, and when the angel descends from
heaven, to salute Mary with him, exclaiming: 'Hail, full of
grace,' &c. Then often repeating these words—hoc crebrius
repetens—to consider the magnitude of that grace, &c. Could
Dr. Rock think that St. Godric did not meditate in the same
way? In what sense was the formula unknown? Surely it was
known by heart to every man and woman tolerably instructed
in the Gospel history. At least when recalling the Annunciation they would have repeated the angelic words. The words
are, by their nature, made for repetition. When God revealed
to St. Elizabeth what had passed at Nazareth, she could not but
repeat the heavenly greeting : 'Blessed art thou among women.'
In a life of St. Ildephonsus brought from Spain into France in
the ninth century,[4] it is said that the saint, having a vision of
our Lady, drew near to her, repeating over and over again the
words : 'Ave Maria, gratia plena, Dominus tecum ; benedicta tu
in mulieribus, et benedictus fructus ventris tui.' It matters not,
as the Bollandists justly remark, whether this vision is true or
the life authentic. The life, which was undoubtedly written

[2] The Archbishop of Westminster.
[3] Med. 15, inter Op. S. Anselm.   [4] *Acta SS.* vol. lv. p. 1108.

before the ninth century, testifies either to what happened or to what its writer conceived natural and probable.

Such isolated examples might be multiplied. But it may be asked : What record have we of the use of the Angelic Salutation ás a popular devotion ?

Let us first examine Dr. Rock's statement as to other countries. St. Peter Celestine, before his elevation to the papacy in 1294, composed several opuscula, which have been printed from his original manuscripts. Among these is a collection of miracles of the Blessed Virgin. No date is assigned to any of these, but several, if not all, were collected from books. They therefore may be taken to illustrate the devotions of previous centuries no less than of the thirteenth. Nor is there the least appearance that St. Peter Celestine thought that the forms of devotion which he records were of recent introduction in the Church. Many of these stories relate to the Angelic Salutation. In one he tells of a cleric who was accustomed to salute our Lady by the 'Hail Mary,' and the 'Beatus venter,' &c., and who was cured of wounds inflicted on his lips ; in another, of a simple layman who repelled an assault of evil spirits by the 'Hail Mary ;' in a third, of a monk who used to sing the five Psalms[5] beginning with the letters of Mary's name, 'together with the antiphon Ave Maria.' Another story is the following : 'In a certain town of the kingdom of Hungary was a virgin of the utmost simplicity, but very devout to God and to Mary. She knew no other prayer but half of the Angelic Salutation, viz. "Hail, Mary, full of grace, the Lord is with thee." But as she used to repeat these words continually and most devoutly, a ray of sunshine was seen by all over her head at all times and wherever she was. When the bishop heard of this, he taught her the rest of the words, viz. "blessed art thou amongst women," &c. But when the maiden frequently repeated these words every day, the ray of sunshine left her. The bishop was greatly astonished, and prayed our Lord to show him what this meant ; to whom the Lord made answer : "Where divine grace abounds human

[5] These Psalms are given in the *Ancren Riwle*, written in England early in the thirteenth century. Vide antes, p. 70.

teaching is superfluous." Then the bishop forbade the maiden to say in future any other words than those to which she had first been accustomed by the inspiration of divine grace; and doing this she recovered the former favour.'[6]

In the time, then, of which St. Peter Celestine writes—evidently long before his own, for he is telling of what happened in another country, and had probably been recorded in some book—the Angelic Salutation was so authorised a form of prayer that the bishop did not consider it right that it should be mutilated, and St. Peter thinks it necessary to explain that the maiden was very simple (simplicissima) who thus pronounced it imperfectly. Now St. Peter Celestine was born in 1215. How, then, can it be maintained by Dr. Rock that in 1174 the Angelic Salutation was not popularly recited, 'either in England or elsewhere'?[7] It may be observed that the above history also furnishes us an example of the frequent repetition of the 'Hail Mary.' This is also illustrated by another story of the same collection, where an abbot persuades a soldier, in order that he may obtain a great favour from our Lady, to keep himself pure for a year, and to repeat every day of that period the Angelic Salutation a hundred times.

But—to go back to a century earlier than that of St. Peter Celestine—Arnold of Chartres, the intimate friend of St. Bernard, writing in the first half of the twelfth century, and commenting on the salutation of Mary by the Angel Gabriel, remarks that 'the Church saved by Christ, and ever exulting in the remembrance of its joy, keeps up the custom of repeating this salutation.'[8] To repeat the 'Hail Mary' was, then, at this period, not merely a practice known to a few, not a custom belonging to a religious order, not a custom of some one nation, but a

---

[6] *Bib. Max.* tom. xxv. p. 816.

[7] Similar legends are related by Cæsar of Heisterbach, and by writers of the twelfth century.

[8] *De Laudibus Mariæ*, Bib. Max. Lug. tom. xxii. p. 1282. As this passage seems to have escaped the notice of Mabillon, or those who have written on the 'Hail Mary,' I give the original: 'Hunc salutandi morem salvata per Christum, semper gaudia sua commemorans, exultans servat Ecclesia.'

custom of the Church. And no intimation is given us by
Arnold that it had been recently introduced. It is 'a custom
kept up by the Church,' an immemorial custom.

To the same period belongs the history related by Heriman,
and which Mabillon considers the first origin of the Rosary.
This author tells of a lady in Belgium named Ada, who used
to say sixty 'Hail Marys,' twenty prostrate, twenty kneeling,
and twenty standing.[9] This act of devotion, on account of a
miracle which it was believed to have wrought, obtained a great
celebrity ; and a certain Count Gosceguin induced his soldiers
to practise it. We find, then, at the beginning of the twelfth
century, the words of the Angelic Salutation so familiarly known
to a multitude of common soldiers, that their leader is able to
induce them to adopt the recitation of it after a particular
fashion. It is placed, therefore, beyond doubt, that the simple
people at this time universally learnt this salutation of the
Blessed Virgin as it is learnt now, from priests and schoolmasters and parents. This carries us back into the eleventh
century, in which we have the testimony of St. Peter Damian,
who was born in the tenth, and may be considered a witness
for both. He tells us of a cleric who, though only half-witted,
'among the cinders of his useless life retained one little spark
of sense and devotion, so that every day before the altar of the
Mother of God, inclining his head, he would sing the words,
"Ave Maria, gratia plena, Dominus tecum ; benedicta tu in
mulieribus." '[10] Whence could a half-witted man have picked
up this scrap of prayer but from frequently hearing it ? I confess
my inability to trace back the use of this formula as a popular
devotion to an earlier period.[11] But in this mention of it in the

---

[9] See Mabillon, *Præf. ad sæc. 5um Act. SS. Bened.* § 127. The exact
words are given : 'Ave Maria, gratia plena, Dominus tecum; benedicta
tu in mulieribus, et benedictus fructus ventris tui.'

[10] S. Petri Dam. Opusc. xxxiii. cap. iii. tom. iii. p. 577, ed. Bassan.
1783.

[11] In a list of errors charged against the Vaudois in a MS. of the fourteenth century, given in the *Reliquiæ Antiquæ* of Messrs. Wright and
Halliwell, p. 247, is the following : 'That the "Hail Mary" is not to be
said, because its author is unknown.'

eleventh century there is nothing to indicate its recent introduction, while there is everything to lead us to suppose a much
higher antiquity.

It seems, then, to be generally admitted by the learned, as
by Mabillon, Benedict XIV., Trombelli, Grancolas, and the
recent continuators of the Bollandists,[12] that the recitation of
the 'Hail Mary' cannot be traced back *as a public or popular
devotion* beyond the eleventh century, at least by the evidence
of any documents now known to exist. As, however, such a
devotion does not suddenly spring up and become popular, it
is almost certain that it was gradually spreading throughout
Europe during the preceding centuries.

The use of this formula in the East was probably still more
ancient. At the end of a baptismal and penitential ritual of
the Syrian Church is a collection of the prayers in use among
the people. After the Lord's Prayer occurs the Angelic Salutation, in the following form: 'Peace to thee, Mary, full of grace,
our Lord is with thee; blessed art thou amongst women, and
blessed is the fruit who was in thy womb, Jesus Christ. Holy
Mary, Mother of God, pray for us sinners. Amen.' The ritual
in which this prayer is contained is attributed to Severus, Patriarch of Antioch in the year 513, by the Bollandists, who
defend its authenticity against the objections of Grancolas.
Whether of this date or somewhat later, it is curious as containing the germ of what we call the third part of the 'Hail
Mary.'

One thing, then, all must admit. Whether the devotion of
the Angelic Salutation were ancient and universal, or only introduced amongst the people in the eleventh and twelfth centuries, at least by the end of that period it was so thoroughly
rooted in the hearts of Catholics that it was looked on as an
imperfection, if not a sin, to be ignorant of it. It was henceforth classed with the Lord's Prayer, not indeed as imposed
under the same obligation, but as belonging to the elements of

[12] Mabillon, *Præf. ad sæc, 5um Act. SS. Bened.;* Benedict XIV., *De
Festis B. Mariæ Virginis, De Festo Rosarii;* Trombelli, Dissert. ix.;
Grancolas, *Comment. in Brev. Rom.* l. i. cap. xv. p. 73; Bolland. *Acta SS.*
vol. lv. tom. vii. Oct. p. 1108.

Christian instruction. The Venerable Bede had urged Egbert, Archbishop of York, to see that the priests taught the people the Creed and Lord's Prayer, and this had been done by the Council of Clovesho in A.D. 747. Similarly the statutes of Theodulf, Bishop of Orleans in the eighth century, which were translated into Anglo-Saxon by Bishop Œlfric in 994, speak only of the Paternoster and the Creed. Such laws, I repeat, in no way prove that the custom of saying the ' Hail Mary' was then either unknown or little popular ; yet they may be fairly cited in proof that the Angelic Salutation had not then attained the position which it holds in later legislation.[13]

In 1196, Odo, Bishop of Paris, tells priests to exhort the people to say the Creed, Lord's Prayer, and the Salutation of the Blessed Virgin ; and in that century the union between England and France in language and ecclesiastical customs was so close that they might almost be considered one nation.

But let me come to direct English evidence.

In the Constitutions of Alexander, Bishop of Coventry in 1237, all Christians are exhorted to say daily seven Paters, seven Ave Marias, and two Credos.

By the statutes of St. Richard of Chichester, A.D. 1246, all the laity are to be taught the Creed, the 'Our Father,' and 'Hail Mary.'

In those of the Bishop of Durham, A.D. 1255, a similar provision is made.

Lastly, in the Constitutions of Walter and Simon, Bishops of Norwich, it is ordered that children be taught the Creed, the Lord's Prayer, and the 'Hail Mary ;' complaint is made that even some adults do not know these, and they are therefore to be examined and instructed when they come to confession.

It will be seen that these four dioceses do not lie together, but in the extreme north and south, in the east and in the west, so that we may judge from them what was the universal practice and discipline in England. There is not the slightest appearance in these decrees that any new prayer is being intro-

[13] In later times ' the Paternoster and Creed' was an expression which included the ' Hail Mary,' as I shall show presently.

duced. In none of them is the 'Hail Mary' given at length or explained, any more than the 'Our Father' or the Creed. The three prayers are supposed to be familiarly known to all the clergy. For anything we can discover to the contrary from these decrees, the 'Hail Mary' may have been as long in popular use as the Lord's Prayer or the Creed of the Apostles. I do not say that this is the case; but that the legislation of the thirteenth century, far from indicating, as Dr. Rock supposes, the period of the first promulgation of the Angelic Salutation, indicates, on the contrary, a long-established and universal custom of using it in public and in private prayer.

The thirteenth century was a great period of legislative reform in the Church in England, when abuses were corrected and good customs confirmed. When Alexander Stavenby drew up his Constitutions in A.D. 1237, he found the 'Hail Mary' as familiarly known to his diocesans as the 'Our Father.' He instructs his clergy, therefore, not to promulgate or teach a new form of prayer, but to exhort the people to be faithful in their daily use of what they knew. The other bishops either regret or provide against ignorance, but not more of the Angelic Salutation than of the Lord's Prayer. They consider that ignorance of either prayer is a serious evil and scandal. Since, then, no period can be assigned of legislative introduction of this prayer amongst the people, and since no special or combined effort to promulgate it is recorded in history, it must have either been introduced into England with Christianity itself and spread with its spread; or if this is denied, and it is supposed to have crept in gradually and established itself by the mere strength of popular devotion, then centuries would be required to elapse before it could have become familiar to every peasant man and woman from Chichester to Durham. Yet Dr. Rock supposes it unknown 'in England or elsewhere' in 1172, about half a century before the promulgation of the above decrees. How, we may ask, had it been introduced and spread in the mean time, and where is the record of this remarkable movement?

I have certainly not made these remarks in disparagement of

our excellent Catholic antiquarian, but for fear that his great authority should gain credit for an error both of fact and of principle. It is one of the most fruitful sources of mistakes to suppose that the earliest known documentary mention of a practice coincides with the period of its introduction. This would only be the case if everything were immediately consigned to writing, if all that has been written had come down to our own days, and if all that has been preserved had been carefully examined—three conditions, not one of which has been fulfilled.

M. Lecoy de la Marche informs us that there is manuscript evidence to prove that the custom of saying the ' Hail Mary' at the end of the exord of the sermon—a custom still observed on the Continent—dates back to the thirteenth century. This is found, for example, in the sermons of Pierre de Limoges, who was in England in 1262. As in the twelfth and thirteenth centuries Englishmen preached in France, and Frenchmen in England, the same customs probably obtained in English pulpits as in French.[14]

An English document of the thirteenth century, and probably of the earlier part, shows to what extent the recitation of the ' Hail Mary' then prevailed. This is the Rule for Female Hermits, or the *Ancren Riwle*.[15] It supposes throughout that both the nuns and their maid-servants know well the Angelic Salutation, which is consequently not written in full, but generally spoken of as the ' Ave' or the ' Ave Maria.' The nuns are told to say five 'Aves' before our Lady's statue when they rise, to say the ' Paternoster' and ' Ave Maria' both before and after each of the seven hours of the Office of our Lady, to say five 'Ave Marias' with a prayer in honour of each of our Lady's five joys, to say at a certain time of the day fifty or a hundred ' Aves ;' and ' they who either cannot or may not say Matins may say instead thirty "Paternosters," and "Hail Mary" after each " Paternoster," and " Glory be to the Father" after each " Hail Mary ;" for Evensong twenty, and for every other hour fifteen.'

[14] See *La Chaire Française au Moyen Age*, pp. 271 and 99.
[15] Published in 1853 by the Camden Society.

The maid-servants who cannot read the hours are to say ' Paternosters' and ' Ave Marias,' as also before and after meat, if they do not know the proper prayers. The author concludes his book with these words : ' As often as ye read anything in this book, greet the Lady with an " Ave Maria" for him who made this Rule and for him who wrote it, and took pains about it. Moderate enough I am who ask so little.' Who can persuade himself that the recitation of the Angelic Salutation was of recent introduction into England, when thus practised and thus alluded to in the thirteenth century?

In 1351 Thomas, thirtieth Abbot of St. Alban's, decrees that a pause should be observed between the ' Kyrie eleyson,' and also in the middle of each verse of the Psalms, of the duration at least that is required to say slowly and distinctly, ' Ave Maria, gratia plena, Dominus tecum.'[16]

In the foundation statutes of the Priory of Maxstoke, in the middle of the fourteenth century, occurs the following : ' Moved by zeal of pious devotion, like the rest of Christ's faithful, towards the Mother of grace, the glorious Virgin Mary, and for her sake towards her blessed mother St. Anne, I will and ordain, that when the office of Matins of the Blessed Virgin Mary is finished in choir, and also at the end of her Mass and after each of her hours, the priest who has celebrated Mass, or the president at the office, in the same tone in which he has ended the office shall say the Angelic Salutation and the commendation of her mother—this ordinance to be observed for ever in this manner : " Ave Maria, gratia plena, Dominus tecum ; benedicta tu in mulieribus, et benedictus fructus ventris tui, Jesus. Amen. Et benedicta sit venerabilis mater tua Anna, ex qua tua caro virginea et immaculata processit." And the choir will answer, " Amen." '[17]

I may here mention some indulgences recorded by a Scotch writer as having been granted by Pope John XXII. (A.D. 1372).

1. He renewed the indulgence granted by Urban IV. to those who add the name of Jesus at the end of the Hail Mary.

---

[16] *Gesta Abbatum*, vol. ii. p. 420 (ed. Master of Rolls).
[17] Dugdale, *Monast.* vol. vi. p. 525.

2. Also to those who kneel or bow at the name of Jesus.

3. An indulgence to all those who say the Psalter of the Blessed Virgin, composed by Stephen Langton, Archbishop of Canterbury.

4. To those who say three times the Angelic Salutation kneeling, while the bell is rung after Complin.

5. For saying the Magnificat at Vespers.

6. For saying at the end of any work, 'The sweet name of Jesus Christ, and the name of His glorious Mother the Virgin Mary, be blessed for ever. Amen.'

7. For saying these words, 'Nos cum prole pia benedicat Virgo Maria.'[18]

The historian of the Reformation, Bishop Burnet, asserts that while Popery prevailed in England, 'the teaching of children by their parents the Lord's Prayer, the ten Commandments, and the Creed in the vulgar tongue was crime enough to bring them to the stake,' and this monstrous assertion has been repeated and defended by others.[19] It scarcely deserves attention ; yet an interesting refutation has been lately brought to light.   This is an *Instruction for Parish Priests*, written in verse by John Myrc at the beginning of the fifteenth century.[20]

In explaining what questions the confessor is to put to his penitent, he says :

> 'Canst thou thy Pater, and thine Ave,
> And thy Creed now tell to me ?
> Gif he saith he can it not,
> Take his penance then he mot.
> To such penance then thou him turn
> That will make him it to learn.'

The next lines are under the following Latin heading :

> 'Quod sufficit scire in lingua materna'—

'It is enough if he knows them in his mother tongue.'

> 'Gif he can it in his tongue,
> To give him penance it is wrong.'[21]

[18] Fordun, *Scotichronicon*, lib. x. ch. xiii.
[19] By the Rev. J. Lewis, in the *Collectanea Curiosa*, vol. ii. p. 187.
[20] Edited for the Early English Text Society (1868) by Mr. E. Peacock.
[21] ll. 917-924.

Again, in the instructions to the parish priest :

> ' The Paternoster and the Creed
> Preach thy parish thou must need,
> Twice or thrice in the year,
> To thy parish whole and fere [*i.e.* boldly].
> Teach them thus and bid them say
> With good intent every day :
> " Father our, that art in heaven,
> Hallowed be Thy name with meke stevene [*i.e.* voice];
> Thy kingdom be for to come
> In us sinful all and some ;
> Thy will be do in earth here
> As it is in heaven clear ;
> Our each day's bread, we Thee pray,
> That Thou give us this same day ;
> And forgive us our trespass,
> As we done them that guilt us has ;
> And lead us into no fonding,
> But shield us all from evil thinge.   Amen." '

And immediately afterwards :

> ' Hail be thou, Mary, full of grace ;
> God is with thee in every place ;
> I-blessed be thou of all women,
> And the fruit of the womb Jesus.   Amen.'

Then follows a curious version of the Creed, which I am sure will be interesting to my readers. In this and the above I modernise the spelling without changing the words.

> ' I believe in our holy dryght
> Father of heaven, God Almight,
> That all things has wrought,
> Heaven and earth, and all of nought.
> On Jesu Christ I believe also
> His only Son, and no mo [*i.e.* more],
> That was conceived of the Holy Sprite
> And of a maid I-born quite ;
> And afterwards under Pounce Pilate
> Was I-take for envy and hate,
> And suffered pain and passion,
> And on the Cross was I-done.
> Dead and buried He was also,
> And went to hell to spoil our foe ;
> And rose to life the third day,
> And stegh [*i.e.* ascended] to heaven the fortieth day.
> Yet He shall come with wounds red
> To doom [*i.e.* judge] the quick and the dead.

In the Holy Ghost I believe well;
In holy Church and her spell [*i.e.* word].
In God's body I believe now
Among His saints to give me row [*i.e.* place],
And of my sins that I have done
To have plenere remission.
And when my body from death shall rise
I leve to be with God and His,
And have the joy that lasteth aye;
God grant Himself that I so may. Amen.'[22]

I may note here that the parish priest is only told to teach his people the Paternoster and Creed. The same is said to the godparents:

'Hast thou been slow and taken not heed
To teach thy godchilder Paternoster and Creed?'[23]

And yet in the explanation the 'Hail Mary' is given. From this it appears that the 'Hail Mary' was looked on as a kind of appendage to the Lord's Prayer.[24]

Messrs. Wright and Halliwell, among the various scraps of antiquity called *Reliquiæ Antiquæ*, have given many specimens of 'Paternosters' and 'Ave Marias.' I give some of the latter. The first example is said by the editors to be from a MS. of the earlier part of the thirteenth century. This is a further proof of what has been said above against the date assigned by Dr. Rock, since already early in the thirteenth century the Angelic Salutation is versified, as was also the Lord's Prayer.

Ave Maria of thirteenth century.

'Marie ful off grace, weel de be,
Godd of hevene be with thee,
Oure alle wimmen bliscedd tu be,
So be the bern datt is boren of thee.'

Of same date.

'Hayl Marie, fol of milce [*i.e.* mercy or grace], God is mit the,

[22] ll. 422-453. The ten Commandments are also explained very fully;
l. 961 sq.   [23] l. 1161.
[24] On a font at Bradley, co. Lincoln, of the date A.D. 1500, are these words: 'Pater Noster, Ave Maria, and Criede, leren ye chyld yt is nede.' Note by Mr. Peacock, p. 72.

thu blessede among wymmen, i-blessed be frut of thine wumbe
So be it.'

Also thirteenth century.

' Heyl Marie, of grace i-fild,
And of God himself i-tild,
Blisceth be thu among wimmen,
For thu art of Davi kinges kin,
Blesced be the frut of thi wombe,
For it is Goddes owene lombe.'

Fourteenth century.

' Heyl Marie, ful of grace, God is whit thee, and blessyd be
thou among alle wymmen, and blessed the fruyt of thi wombe
Jhesus. Amen.'[25]

One more example from a collection of early English prayers
of the middle of the thirteenth century :

' Heil Marie, ful of grace,
The lauird thich the in hevirilk place,
Blisced be thu mang alle wimmein
And blisced be the blosmo of thi wambe. Amen.

Moder of milce and maidin Mari,
Help us at ure hending, for thi merci,
That suete Jhesu that born was of the,
Thu give us, in is godhed him to se.
Jhesu for the moder luve and for thin hali wondis,
Thu leise us of the sinnes that we are inne bunde.'

In the *Mirror of our Lady*, of the fifteenth century, the form
is thus given : ' Hail Mary, full of grace, the Lord is with thee ;
blessed be thou in all women and above all women; and blessed
be Jesu, the fruit of thy womb. Amen.' In another place the
words 'Dominus tecum' are translated, ' *Our* Lord is with thee.'

It will have been remarked that to none of these formulæ are
the words added which we now invariably join to the Angelic
Salutation, viz. ' Holy Mary, Mother of God, pray for us sinners,

[25] Pope Urban IV., A.D. 1261, added to the Angelic Salutation as hitherto
said the words ' Jesus. Amen.'

now and at the hour of our death. Amen.' It seems indeed to be now admitted by the learned that this addition, as regards the Liturgy, is scarcely older than the sixteenth century.

Mabillon declares[26] that he has not found the words in any printed book or MS. before the year 1500; and this of course is not a mere negative argument, since the MS. and books abound where the Salutation (strictly so called) is given alone. In the year 1514, it is given as we now say it in the Breviary of the Order of the Redemption of Captives. In a Breviary of 1521, the last part occurs without the words, 'now and at the hour of our death;' but these are added in a Franciscan Breviary of the year 1525.[27] The invocation, as now used, was added to the Roman Breviary by St. Pius V. in 1568. However, it should be borne in mind that the liturgical books did not in this case originate a prayer which was afterwards adopted by popular devotion; but on the contrary, popular devotion, dissatisfied with the simple salutation of our Lady, and feeling the need of grace, had added prayers, first in one form and then in another, until they had at last almost settled into that which we have at present, which, by being taken into the Breviary, has received liturgical sanction, and is henceforth the Church's authorised prayer.

That this was the case may be gathered from Mone's *Hymni Latini*, where many metrical glosses on the 'Ave Maria' are given. Most of these conclude with the words, 'ventris tui, Jesus;' but one from a MS. of the fifteenth century adds, 'Sancta Maria, ora pro nobis;'[28] another of the same century, 'Mater Dei, ora pro nobis peccatoribus;'[29] while a little Italian hymn of the fourteenth century has the words, 'Sancta Maria, ora pro nobis, nunc et in hora mortis.'[30] Each of these is imperfect

[26] Mabillon, *Præf. in sæc. 5um Act. SS. Bened.* § 122-124.

[27] These researches of Mabillon seem to have been confirmed by those of modern antiquarians, among whom I may mention Trombelli in Italy, Binterim in Germany, Dom Guéranger in France, Dr. Rock in England.

[28] Mone, vol. ii. No. 392.

[29] Ibid. No. 400, though one MS. of the hymn does not contain these verses.

[30] Ibid. p. 94. The Latin words are mixed up with the Italian, and begin the verses.

alone as compared with our present form, which unites them all.

Many other examples are given by Trombelli[31] from Italian poetry of the fifteenth century. The sermons also of St. Bernardin of Siena distinctly mention the prayer, 'Sancta Maria, Mater Dei, ora pro nobis peccatoribus. Amen,' as a common addition to the Angelic Salutation.[32] St. Bernardin died in 1444. The addition has been attributed to St. Vincent Ferrer, who died in 1419. Pelbart, who wrote towards the end of the same century, recommends the addition of these words : ' Sancta Maria, Mater Dei et Domini nostri Jesu, ora pro me et pro omnibus peccatoribus.'[33] Trombelli also bears witness to a MS. Breviary of the beginning of the fifteenth century, which, among several prayers to be said after Complin, gives the Angelic Salutation almost as we now have it. The word ' Christus' is added after ' Jesus,' and the word ' peccatoribus' is omitted.

It is evident, then, that during the fifteenth century prayer to the Mother of God, as an addition to her salutation, was gradually spreading throughout Europe.

Navarrus testifies that in Spain it had long been the custom, before the change made by St. Pius V., to add the words : ' Sancta Maria, Mater Dei, ora pro nobis peccatoribus. Amen.'[34]

As to England, we have the explicit statement of the author of the *Mirror of our Lady*, printed in 1530, though written about a century earlier. ' Some say, at the beginning of this salutation, "Ave benigne Jesu ;" and some say after, "Maria, Mater Dei," with other such additions at the end also. And such things may be said when folk say their Aves of their own devotion. But in the service of the Church, I trow, it be most sure and most meedful to obey to the common use of saying as the Church hath set, without all such additions.'[35]

In the second chapter of the First Part of this work I have

---

[31] Trombelli, *De Cultu publico &c., Disquisitio*, Dissert. 4a, qu. 3.

[32] Sermo 6 in Annunt. B.V.; Sermo de Passione.

[33] *Pomœrium seu Stell. Cor B.M.V.* l. i. pt. iv. art. iii. cap. iv.

[34] De Orat. cap. xix.

[35] Reprinted by the Early English Text Society.

given a commentary on the ' Hail Mary' by Baldwin, Archbishop
of Canterbury in the twelfth century.   About the beginning of
the sixteenth century many commentaries were published in English, some by private authors, some by authority.   There is one
published by Henry VIII., and drawn up by his bishops, which
is very beautiful and quite Catholic, and I regret that I have
not space for it.   I would gladly also have added the paraphrase
given in the *Mirror of our Lady*, and the long treatise contained
in the *Pilgrymage of Perfecyon*, printed in 1531 by Wynkin
de Worde ;[36] but I have room only for a short extract from this
last.

As may be seen from the forms above given, the Angelic
Salutation was first said as it appears in the Gospel, without
the addition of the Name of Jesus.   This was ordered to be said
by Pope Urban IV. in A.D. 1261.   On this subject the author of
the *Pilgrimage of Perfection* writes : ' But the devotion of the
faithful people cannot be contented only to hear of her purity
and graces, and of her benedictions and bounteousness toward
her servants, and the blessed Fruit of her virginal womb; but
they would have also the said blessed Fruit expressed.   And
therefore of their devotions they have added this holy Name
Jesus ; and that much conveniently, forasmuch as this holy
Name Jesus was showed by the angel to the Blessed Virgin before she conceived Him, and also to that other holy virgin Joseph,
her spouse, the witness of her pure virginity.   And therefore
He was so named in His circumcision.   Yea, and above all this,
it was decreed in the high consistory of the Trinity, before the
world was create and made, that Jesus should be the Name of
the Son of God in earth.   And that not without great mystery;
for Jesus is as much to say as a Saviour, whose property is to
save His people from their sins, as the Gospel recordeth.   And
therefore in us that be His servants this holy Name should be
alway in our memory sweeter than balm, in our lips sweeter
than sugar, in our tongues sweeter than honey, in our mouth
all melody, and in our hearts all solace, joy, and jubilation.
For there is none other Name under heaven, as Scripture saith,

[36] A copy is in the University Library, Cambridge.

whereby we may be saved, but only this Name Jesus. Which holy Name, devoutly expressed and spoken to the Mother of God, most highly pleaseth her, and is best accepted. For why, it is the Fruit of her womb, the fruit of life, the fruit of health, the fruit of grace and glory, her sweet Son Jesus, which above all other things most inclineth her ear to hear our requests and to pray to God for us. And not only it moveth her so to do, but also all the other saints and angels to pray with her for us, to the great confusion of the fiends of hell. For, as St. Paul saith, in the Name of Jesus all knees do bow, both in heaven, earth, and also in hell, and all tongues do confess that our Lord Jesus sitteth in heaven on the right hand of His Father; to whom be all glory and praising, honour and laud, world without end. Amen.'[37]

The holy Name of Jesus was struck out of the formula by Henry VIII., no doubt because it had been added by order of a Pope.

Of the recitation of the ' Hail Mary' in England, or of the graces obtained by it, of course no record has been kept except in the Book of God.

In the Third Part of this work I shall relate in detail the history of its gradual disuse, together with that of all other devotions to our Lady. It will be sufficient to say here a few words on the subject. The ' Hail Mary' had been attacked by the Lollards, and was neglected by Tyndall and some of the first reformers of the sixteenth century. But others, as Latimer, when accused of speaking against it, either retracted their words or explained them away, and it continued to be taught by royal authority during the reign of Henry.

In 1535 a primer was published *cum privilegio regali*, in which many of the antiphons are attacked in the most violent language. The Introduction says of the ' Salve Regina,' ' than the which, what antichrist, yea, what devil in hell, could devise anything more pestilent, heretical, or more to the diminishing, reproach, subversion, and villanous treading under foot and trampling out of the most holy and blessed blood of our sweet Saviour,'

[37] *The Pilgrymage of Perfecyon*, ch. xxiii. '

o

&c. Yet the author (Marshall, I believe) has an instruction for children, in which he tells them to begin and end the day by saying the 'Paternoster,' 'Ave Maria,' and Creed. In this instruction the Angelic Salutation is given in the following words, which are the first instance I have met *in a prayer-book* of the new rendering :

'Heyle Marie, *greatly in Godiles favour,* the Lord is with the, blessed arte thou amonge wimen, and blessed be the frute of thy wombe, Jesu Christe. So be it.'

In another part of the book there is a commentary on the 'Hail Mary,' where the old version, 'Hail, Mary, full of grace,' is retained. The commentary is very Lutheran in tone, and intended to diminish as much as possible the force of the words. The author also insists very emphatically, 'that in these words no petition but pure praises and honours are contained.' And in conclusion he adds, that after saying the 'Hail Mary,' 'here may be added a petition and desire that we may pray for them which say evil of this Fruit and Mother. But who are they that say evil of them ? Truly they which persecute and curse His word (which is the Gospel) and the faith of Christ, as nowadays do the Jews and Papists.' This and a great deal more in the same work indicate clearly enough the spite of Tyndall and his friends, who were now endeavouring through prayer-books, as they had just before done by their controversial writings, to introduce Lutheranism into England.

This book was, however, soon suppressed by royal authority, and the 'Hail Mary' was taught in the Prymer and Instructions published by the king and his bishops. It was also contained in the Prymer of the first year of Edward VI., A.D. 1547, but omitted in subsequent editions, as well as in the Common Prayer-book of A.D. 1549.

It was restored by Mary, but again abolished by Elizabeth ; and thenceforward it was considered a crime to repeat it, though no formal declaration had been made to that effect.

I gladly conclude this chapter with a few examples of its public use by the victims of Elizabeth and James.

Robert Johnson, a priest, on a false charge of taking part in

an imaginary conspiracy, after being cruelly racked and imprisoned, was executed at Tyburn on 28th May 1582. 'The
rope was put about his neck, and he was willed to pray, which
he did in Latin. They willed him to pray in English, that they
might witness with him; he said, "I pray that prayer which
Christ taught in a tongue I well understand." A minister cried
out : "Pray as Christ taught ;" to whom Mr. Johnson replied :
"What! do you think Christ taught in English?" He went
on saying in Latin his Pater, Ave, and Creed, and "In manus
tuas," &c.; and so the cart was drawn away, and he finished this
life as the rest did. They all hanged until they were dead, and
so were cut down and quartered.'

John Body, a native of Wells, a learned man and convert to
the faith, though a layman, was condemned to death for no
other crime but that of denying the Queen's spiritual supremacy
and maintaining that of the Pope. He was executed at Andover,
November 2d, 1583. When called upon at the gallows to confess his crime, he said to the people : 'Be it known to all you
that are here present, that I suffer death this day because I
deny the Queen to be the supreme head of the Church of Christ
in England. I never committed any other treason, unless they
will have hearing Mass or saying the "Hail Mary" to be treason.' His mother hearing afterwards of her son's happy death
made a great feast upon that occasion, to which she invited her
neighbours, rejoicing at his death as his marriage, by which his
soul was happily and eternally espoused to the Lamb.

Another convert, George Swallowell, publicly retracted his
heresy in the pulpit, for he was a Protestant minister, and was
immediately cast into prison, where he remained for a year.
Though he quailed for a moment at his trial, a single word from
a priest who was condemned with him restored his courage,
and he suffered one of the most brutal butcheries of those cruel
times with heroic constancy. His last words were to request
that all Catholics present would say three Paters, three Aves,
and the Creed for him. He suffered at Darlington, July 26th,
1594.

The same devotion to the 'Ave Maria' is related of other of

our martyrs.[38]   May they now in their glory ask our Lady to look with pity on her ancient Dowry !

As an appendix to this chapter, I give one of those poems which were our forefathers' delight, in which each word of some favourite prayer forms the beginning of the successive strophes. Of course no real poetry is to be sought in such puzzles.   The following example, published by Mone, is from the pen of the famous Robert Grosstest, who died Bishop of Lincoln in 1253, and who has been foolishly claimed as a precursor of the Reformation.   He had at least inherited from St. Hugh, his predecessor, his devotion to our Lady of Lincoln, before whose image he probably composed the following lines :

Ave Maria.

' *Ave* Dei genitrix et immaculata
Virgo, cœli gaudium, toti mundo nata
ad salutem, hominum in exemplum data,
dignare me laudare te, virgo sacrata.

Maria, miseria per te terminatur
et misericordia per te revocatur,
per te navigantibus stella maris datur,
lumen viæ panditur, portus demonstratur.

Gratia te reddidit, virgo, gratiosam,
te vestivit lilio, sparsit in te rosam,
te virtutum floribus fecit speciosam,
intus et exterius totam luminosam.

Plena medicamine, abundans unguentis,
audi preces pauperis coram te plangentis,
respice in faciem lacrimas fundentis   ·
et livoris vulnera sana, plagas mentis.

Dominus rex omnium ex te nobis fecit
cellam pigmentariam, et in te confecit
medicinam omnium, quæ sibi subjecit,
morbos ægrotantium saluti refecit.

[38] See Challoner's *Memoirs of Missionary Priests, &c.*

Tecum tota trinitas fecit mansionem,
plenitudo, sanctitas tecum stationem
elegerunt intra te, ad perfectionem
præbendo te omnibus vitæ lectionem.

Benedicta benedic te benedicentes,
ut in tuis laudibus semper sint ferventes ;
infunde dulcedinem in eorum mentes
ut in sanctis moribus sint proficientes.

Tu in mulieribus optima figura
angelorum omnium regem paritura,
a creante omnia singulari curâ
dignior es condita omni creaturâ.

Et benedictus Deus, qui cuncta creavit
et in matris utero te sanctificavit,
et beatus genitor, qui te generavit,
et beata ubera matris, quæ lactavit.

Fructus tuus, domina, fructus angelorum,
quo fruuntur, cibus est omnium sanctorum,
ipsa delectatio, dulcedo eorum,
qui suorum ambulant viam mandatorum.

Ventris habitaculum rex regum intravit,
quasi tabernaculum hoc inhabitavit,
pugnaturus propter nos ibi se armavit
armis condecentibus, quibus hostem stravit.

Tui ergo filii redempti cruore,
quem in crucis prælio fudit cum liquore,
hac peruncti gratia te laudamus ore,
ut in tuis laudibus simus et amore.'[39]

[39] Mone, *Hymni Latini*, tom. ii. p. 100.

Translation of the above.[40]

' *Hail*, O Maid immaculate ; hail, predestinated
Virgin Mother of our God, through whom regenerated
Earth salvation finds, heaven joy, best model contemplated ;
Make my lays thy fitting praise, O Virgin consecrated.

Mary, all our misery, our woe, through thee have ended,
And forgiveness from on high hath through thee descended ;
'Tis through thee that o'er the sea shines out hope's star so
          splendid,
And the light is on the waves, the sheltering port extended.

Full of every saving cure, in heavenly gardens growing,
Hear my sad plaints, weak and poor, all thy aid bestowing ;
Look upon this face, whose tears are ever overflowing,
Heal the pain of heart and brain which I to thee am showing.

Grace it is, O Virgin, that such charms in thee discloses,
Clothing thee with lilies, scattering o'er thee roses ;
All the flowers that virtue showers round thee it disposes,
And the light within, without, sweetly it exposes.

The Lord, the King of all things, hath made for our refection,
In thee, His chosen Daughter, His vessel of election,
A storehouse of all healing things that owe to Him subjection,
That they may cure our sickly souls and lighten our dejection.

Is with thee the Trinity, as within a dwelling,
Plenitude and sanctity over thee outwelling,
Making thy perfection far beyond the telling,
Type to all of highest life and crown of all excelling.

Blessed art thou ; do thou bless those who thee are blessing,
Make them praise thee fervently, all thy worth confessing ;
Pour out all thy sweetness, thy seal their souls impressing,
That each day in holiness they may be progressing.

[40] I am indebted for this translation to Denis Florence McCarthy, Esq.
The fidelity to the original and the double rhymes twice repeated make it
indeed a literary feat.

Amongst women beautiful, fairest thy formation,
Thou broughtest forth the angels' King for our adoration ;
Sacred from aught of sinfulness by special dispensation,
Thou wert made the worthiest of all God's creation.

And blessed is that God who all things hath created,
Who within thy mother's womb thee hath consecrated ;
And blessed be the father who thee hath generated,
And blessed be thy mother's breasts, and bless'd the thirst
      they sated.

The fruit of thine, O Lady, is the angels' fruit untainted,
The fruit which they enjoy is the fruit of all the sainted ;
The sweetness and delight, which the prophet's pen hath
      painted,
Of those who walk'd the ways of God, and never wholly
      fainted.

Thy Son's blood, O Lady, on the hard cross streaming,
Mix'd with water, saved us, through the darkness gleaming :
For a grace so mighty, partly from thee beaming,
Let us raise our songs of praise, our eyes with glad tears
      teeming.

Womb the great King enter'd as a habitation,
Tabernacle rather for His adoration,
Where He learn'd to battle for the world's salvation,
Bless'd for aye be it we pray through every generation.'

The following are verses from a MS. of the early part of the
fifteenth century :[41]

' Hail be thou, Mary, Christ's Mother dear,
    That art Queen of heaven, fair and sweet of cheer,
    That art Star of heaven shining bright and clear ;
    Help me, Lady, full of might, and hear my prayer :
                          Ave Maria.

[41] Published by Early Text Soc. 1867, p. 6.

Hail be thou, Mary, that high sittest in throne !
I beseech thee, sweet Lady, grant me my boon :
Jesu to love and dread, and my life to amend soon,
And bring me to that bliss that never shall be done :

> Ave Maria.

Hail be thou, Mary, glorious Mother hende ![42]
Meekness and honesty, with abstinence, me send,
With chastity and charity into my life's end,
And that through this prayer, Lady, I mote to heaven's
  bliss wend :

> Ave Maria.'

Lines by Walter Mapes.

' Hanc voce non timida
  Quilibet salutet ;
  Non est enim tumida
  Ut non resalutet ;
  Et si semel humili
  Vel affectu facili
  Te resalutaverit,
  Ne sis unquam dubius
  Quin maternas Filius
  Preces exaudierit.'[43]

[42] Gentle.   [43] Poems of Walter Mapes (Camden Society, 1841).

CHAPTER V.

BEADS AND BELLS.

THE word 'bead' has undergone in English a curious transformation of meaning.

It is the past participle of the Saxon verb *biddan*, to bid, to invite, to *pray*. Thus in early English it is often used simply for *prayers*, without any reference whatever to their nature or the mode of reciting them.[1] To 'bid the beads' is merely to say one's prayers. 'Bidding the beads' also meant a formal enumeration of the objects of prayer, or persons to be prayed for. A bead-roll is a list of persons to be prayed for. Beadsmen or beads-women are not necessarily persons who say the Rosary, but simply those who pray for others, especially for their benefactors.

But as a custom was introduced in very early times of counting prayers said by the use of little grains or pebbles strung together, the name of prayer got attached to the instrument used for saying prayers; and in this sense the word 'beads' is commonly used by Catholics at the present day.

Lastly, the idea of prayer was dropped out altogether in Protestant times, and the name of 'beads' was left attached to any little perforated balls which could be strung together merely for personal adornment, without any reference to devotion.

But although in our old English documents 'the bidding of beads' does not necessarily imply the use of the Rosary, nor indeed any devotion whatever to the Blessed Virgin, yet from the thirteenth century this was very commonly the sense. I say

[1] See examples quoted by Richardson in his Dictionary, *e.g.* in Holland's translation of Livy : ' The senate, now destitute of all helpe of man, moved the people to devotion, to their beads, and praiers unto the gods.'

from the thirteenth century, because it is at least proved beyond contradiction, as we have seen in the last chapter, that
from that time the Rosary, almost as we now have it, was in
popular use. And it should be remarked that the old writers
did not attribute to St. Dominic either the first suggestion of
honouring our Lady by the Angelic Salutation, or the frequent
repetition of this formula, or the use of beads to count these
repetitions. All these things he found already in common use.
He arranged and remodelled them, dividing the Aves into decades, or sets of ten, preceded by the Pater, and attaching a
meditation to each decade; and propagated this devotion by
himself and his children far and wide.

The Bollandists have indeed thrown doubt on the connection
of St. Dominic with the Rosary. But without attaching any
authority to the revelations of Alain de la Roche, I cannot understand how they should have been accepted so easily, had not
a living tradition subsisted among the Dominicans in the fifteenth
century attributing the Rosary to their great founder. I may
observe also, that quite lately a confirmation of this tradition
has been brought to light. M. Lecoy de la Marche tells us that,
in a manuscript sermon by Etienne de Bourbon, a Dominican
preacher, born in 1193, and who consequently may have known
St. Dominic himself, the devotion of saying the fifty 'Hail
Marys' is recommended, though no mention is made of St. Dominic.[2] The question may probably be settled by a further
examination of the manuscript sermons of the thirteenth century.

It is not, however, necessary for me to enter upon the origin
of the Rosary, beyond what I have said about it in the last
chapter. I confine my remarks to England; and I need scarcely
say that I do not admit the statement of Alanus, that St. Dominic himself preached the Rosary in England, any more than
his derivation of the word 'Bead' from the Venerable Bede,
whom he claims, without any foundation, as one of its early
propagators. Alanus says that in his own day (he died in 1475)
large Rosaries were still to be seen hanging in churches in England for public use. But to come to something more certain.

---

[2] *La Chaire Française au Moyen Age*, p. 345.

William of Malmesbury tells us of the Lady Godiva, wife to Count Leofric, 'that she bequeathed a circle of threaded jewels, upon which she was wont to number her prayers, to be hung about the neck of the Blessed Virgin's image in a church at Coventry.'[3] Dr. Rock, who quotes this passage, would not, in accordance with his theory of the very late introduction of the use of the Angelic Salutation, allow that this circle of gems had been used for counting anything but Paters or Creeds, or perhaps Psalms. To me it appears much more probable that Lady Godiva, though she lived in Saxon times, and two centuries before St. Dominic, yet counted her Aves on her beads, and bequeathed at death to our Blessed Lady the jewels which had served during lifetime for her honour.

It is not necessary to explain here the method of saying the Rosary, which must be familiar to all my readers;[4] but to understand the documents I am about to quote in proof of the love of our ancestors for this form of prayer, it must be remarked that though the devotion of the fifty 'Hail Marys' was called the Rosary, being as it were a chaplet of roses placed on the brows of the Mother of God, yet the beads had never this name as they have now. They were called 'a pair of beads,' or 'a pair of Paternosters,' or 'Ave beads,' or simply a 'Paternoster.' The string of beads did not always consist of the same number; sometimes it was only a decade, which would be counted over and over again. It was generally attached to a ring which could be worn on the little finger, and the beads were not gathered into a circle, but fell in a straight line. This is sometimes represented on effigies still to be seen. The longer beads were often worn publicly as a pious ornament or profession of devotion. Chaucer says of his prioress :

> ' Of small coral about her arm she bare
> A pair of bedes, gauded all with green,
> And thereon hung a broch of gold full shene.'

Even merchants did not disdain thus to appear. In the church

---

[3] De gestis Pontif. l. iv. fol. 165.
[4] It is beautifully explained by Cardinal Wiseman in his essay on *Minor Rites and Offices*.

of All Hallows, near the Tower of London, may still be seen tho
effigy of John Rulche, carrying a rosary on his arm.

Indeed at the end of the fifteenth century it had become almost a matter of fashion to carry the rosary publicly. A Venetian account of England of the year 1500 says: 'In publico dichino
molti Pater noster [*i.e.* rosaries] de i quali le donne portano
lunghe filze in mano.' The *Monumenta Vetusta*[5] give a plate of
the effigy of Richard Patten, father of Bishop Wainflete, which
was in the south aisle of Wainflete church. He carries hanging from his girdle three things—a purse, a dagger, and a rosary
—being thus, it would seem, provided for every emergency. On
a brass in Lambeth church (A.D. 1520) a lady of the Howard
family has a rosary of ten decades suspended from the waist.
Besides the brass of John Rulche already mentioned, in the
church of All Hallows, Barking, there is a brass of Andrew
Evyngar and his wife, who has a long rosary with tassel suspended from the girdle. The date is 1536. In St. Helen's,
Bishopsgate, is a brass of John Williams and wife. The husband has a short rosary at his waist; the date 1490. In the
same church is the brass of a merchant, of which the inscription
is lost. The rosary has a tassel at each end, and is suspended
from the waist. In St. Albans, Hertfordshire, are two brasses
of merchants, of about 1450. Both wear short rosaries.

These examples are sufficient to show the universality of the
devotion of the Rosary at the beginning of the sixteenth century,
when the beads were thus publicly carried, not only by priests
and nuns, but by men and women of all classes.

It is principally owing to the fact that beads were used in
this form of devotion, that we can glean, at the present day,
any information concerning a matter too minute and too commonplace to have been recorded in formal history. As beads
were often materially valuable, their existence and nature are
frequently mentioned in old documents. Thus, in the account
presented by the chamberlain to King Henry VI. of the various
jewels which had been delivered to his majesty to make his New-
Year's gifts in 1437, occurs the following: 'Item, delivered by

[5] Vol. iii. pl. 6.

your said commandment to Robert Rolleston your wardrober, one pair of beads of chalcidony garnished with gold, the which was some time given the king by my Lord of Gloucester, the which contains twelve gauds and three little.'[6]

We find, then, that a handsome set of rosary-beads was considered a fitting present to be offered to a king, and to be given by him again to an honoured subject.[7]

In the churchwardens' accounts of St. Mary Hill, London, there is an entry which tells us even the weight and price of a rosary. The date is 1524, and the words are as follows: 'two pair of beads of silver gilt, 13 oz. at 3*s.* 4*d.*=2*l.* 3*s.* 4*d.* Item, a pair of coral beads gauded with gaudys of silver and gilt, 10 oz. at 3*s.* 4*d.*=1*l.* 13*s.* 4*d.*' As these prices represent much larger sums at the present day, we easily understand that a handsome rosary would be a fair legacy. It is often the only precious article bequeathed in a will, having been perhaps a present. Thus in the will of Richard Towgall, chantry priest in Gateshead (A.D. 1541), occur the following legacies: 'a pair of aumer beyds gardit with silver gardis,' and 'a pair of beyds of white bone.' Again, William Salvayne, Knight (A.D. 1440), leaves to his brother John, 'par magnum precularum de gagate [agate] et aliud par Custanciæ consanguineæ meæ. Sibillæ sorori meæ unum par precularum de corall cum gaudiis de gagate.'[8] The gaud was a large bead on which the Paternoster was said. It was usually richer than the rest.[9]

John Petty, Lord Mayor of York, by his will (A.D. 1508) bequeaths: 'To my daughter Anne a pare corall beides y[t] was hir moder's w[t] rynges and jewels at thame;' also 'to Sir William Spenser a sarssynett tippitt and a pare of bedes of ten.'[10]

John Crofts of Hedon, in 1504, leaves his beads to ornament

---

[6] Bentley's *Excerpta Historica*, p. 150.

[7] The beads were sometimes large and clumsy. 'His confessor shook his great pair of beads upon him almost as big as bowls,' says Sir Thomas More in his amusing apologue of the wolf who went to confession to the hypocritical fox. *Dialogue of Comfort*, ch. xiv.

[8] *Wills of the Northern Counties* (Surtees), pp. 117, 87.

[9] See on this word, p. 65.

[10] *Testamenta Eboracensia*, vol. iv. p. 334 (Surtees, 1868).

the feretry of the Blessed Sacrament: ' Lego capsulæ pertinenti festo Corporis Christi unum par precoms (*sic*) de cristall, pro ornamento ejusdem.'[11]

John Roncliff, rector of the church of Shelford Magna (1492), leaves to his sister-in-law, Catherine, his ' preculas de jasper ;' and to the Master of Peterhouse, Cambridge, ' preculas meas de aumber.'[12]

Isabel Wilton (1486) leaves to her daughter, Marion, ' 1 payr of·bedis of corall conteignyng thre tymes 50, with all the gaudis of silver and gilt, and of every side of gaudis a bede of silver.'[13]

Anne, Lady Scrope, widow of John, Lord Scrope of Bolton, leaves by her will (A.D. 1498), ' to the rood of North door' (*i.e.* the famous Rood at St. Paul's, London) ' my heart of gold with diamond in the midst. To our Lady of Walsingham 10 of my great beads of gold laced with silk, crimson and gold, with a great button of gold, and tasselled with the same. To our Lady of Peue' (Westminster) ' 10 of the same beads. To St. Edmund of Bury 10 of the same beads. To St. Thomas of Canterbury 10 of the same beads. To my Lord Cardinal 10 aves with 2 paternosters of the same beads. To Thomas Fincham 10 aves and 2 paternosters of the same beads.'[14]

This magnificent rosary, like that of Lady Margaret, mentioned by Cardinal Fisher, consisted of sixty or sixty-three aves.

There occurs frequent mention of precious rosaries in the wills of great people. Humphrey de Bohun, Earl of Hereford (A.D. 1361), leaves to his nephew 'a nouche of gold surrounded with large pearls, with a ruby between four pearls, three diamonds, and a pair of gold paternosters of fifty pieces with ornaments, together with a cross of gold, in which is a piece of the true cross of our Lord.'[15] Thomas Beauchamp, Earl of Warwick (A.D. 1369), bequeaths 'a set of gold beads with buckles, which the queen gave me ;' also another 'set of beads of gold and a ring.'[16] John of Gaunt, Duke of Lancaster (A.D. 1397), leaves

[11] *Testamenta Eboracensia*, vol. iv. p. 231 (Surtees, 1868).
[12] Ib. p. 107. [13] Ib. p. 17. [14] Ib. p. 153.
[15] *Testamenta Vetusta*, by Sir H. Nicolas, p. 67. [16] Ib. p. 80.

'a chain of gold of the old manner, with the name of God in each part, which my most honoured lady and mother the queen, whom God pardon, gave me, commanding me to preserve it, with her blessing; and I desire that he' (his son Henry, Duke of Hereford, Earl of Derby and afterwards King Henry IV.) 'will keep it, with the blessing of God and mine.'[17]

Eleanor, Duchess of Gloucester (A.D. 1399), leaves to her mother, the Countess of Hereford, 'a pair of paternosters of coral.'[18] So does Richard Scrope, Lord of Bolton, leave 'a pair of paternosters of coral' to his son (A.D. 1401); and Thomas Beauchamp, Earl of Warwick (A.D. 1400), 'a pair of paternosters of coral with buckles of gold' to his cousin.[19] That these were precious heirlooms is evident, for Roger, Lord Scrope (A.D. 1403), leaves to his son and heir 'my pair of paternosters of coral with a jewel of gold which belonged to my lord my father; also a cross of gold, which I usually carry about me.'[20]

The Rosary was therefore clearly a favourite devotion with the great and noble. It was no less so with the learned and the saintly. William of Wykeham, the famous Bishop of Winchester, who died A.D. 1404, bequeaths to the Archbishop of Canterbury, Thomas Fitzalan, 'a pair of beads of gold appended from a bracelet of gold, having these words engraved on them : "*J.H.S. est amor meus.*"'[21] Of the holy Archbishop of Canterbury, Robert of Winchelsey, we are told that 'he loved the Blessed Virgin with a most spiritual love, and honoured her above all other saints and next after God. Hence no sooner was he free from business than he used at once, wherever he might be, to begin counting the Angelic Salutation on his fingers.'[22]

The Rosary was also a devotion enjoined on the students of colleges. In the statutes of Eton, Henry VI. orders that before the High Mass, either in the church, the cemetery, or the cloister, they shall say, for the remission of the sins committed

[17] *Testamenta Vetusta*, by Sir H. Nicolas, p. 141.
[18] Ib. p. 147.   [19] Ib. p. 155.
[20] Ib. p. 160.   [21] Ib. p. 767.
[22] Stephen Birchington in his Life, apud Wharton, i. 13.

by the five senses, five decades of the beads with the Creed ;
thus making up, with what had been said during Matins and
the other hours, the whole fifteen decades.[23]

So also Bishop Wainflete, in the statutes of Magdalen
College, Oxford, obliges the president and fellows to say each
day the five decades.[24]   A century earlier, Archbishop Islip, in
the statutes of Canterbury Hall (A.D. 1362), ordered that those
who did not say Mass 'should recite fifty " Hail Marys," with
" Our Father" and Creed, as is the custom.'[25]

It is almost needless to say that if the Rosary was said on
beads of gold by kings and nobles, or on beads of coral by
bishops and prioresses, it was said no less devoutly by the poor
on beads of wood or bone.

'I desire,' said John, Lord Scrope, in his will, A.D. 1451,
'that at my funeral my corpse be carried by my sons and servants to the chapel of St. Stephen, commonly called Scrope's
Chapel, within the cathedral church of York, twenty-four poor
men clothed in white gowns and hoods, each of them having a
new set of wooden beads, walking before it ; and I will that
these poor men stand, sit, or kneel in the aisle before the entrance to that chapel, saying their prayers as well at the Dirge
as at the Mass,' &c.[26]

Walter, Lord Montjoy, by his will, A.D. 1474, endows a
hospital where seven old serving-men or tenants of his estates
are to be maintained.   'I will that every of them be obliged
to say daily our Lady's Psalter twice, within the chapel of the
said hospital.'[27]

Thomas Wyndesor, among many other pious bequests to
the honour of the Blessed Sacrament and of our Lady, wills
'that there be one hundred children, each within the age of
sixteen years, at my mouth's mind, to say our Lady's Psalter
for my soul in the church of Stanwell, each of them having
four pence for his labour.'[28]

But the will of Lord Marney is still more interesting, both

---

[23] Apud Dr. Rock.
[24] Life of Wainflete.
[25] Wilkins, *Conc.* t. iii. p. 56.

[26] *Testam. Vetust.* p. 271.
[27] Ib. p. 335.
[28] Ib. p. 353.

for its details and because it was drawn up shortly before the Reformation, A.D. 1523. Leaving directions for the founding of an almshouse, he says : ' I will that every of the said five poor men shall be such as shall say at least their Paternoster, Ave, and Creed in Latin. . . . At their uprising they shall say, for the souls of Sir Robert Marney [and others enumerated] five Paternosters, five Aves, and one Creed; and every day go to the church of Leyr. Marney, and there hear Mass in the new chapel. Moreover, I will that at their first coming into the church, every of them shall kneel down before the Sacrament and say a Paternoster and an Ave; and then go to my tomb, and there kneeling down, say for my soul and for the other souls above named three Paternosters, three Aves, and one Creed, in worship of the Trinity; and then go down into the church, and there, in the time of Mass or Masses, or else before their departure from the said church, say for the above-named souls our Lady's Psalter ; and at night, before their going to bed, every one of them to say, kneeling on their knees, five Paternosters, five Aves, and the Creed for the souls aforesaid.' He then allows the 'De Profundis' to be said in lieu of the five Paters and Aves, and the ' Dirige' instead of our Lady's Psalter, by those who can read Latin.[29]

In the above list of Englishmen who loved the devotion of the Rosary perhaps I might have included the brave and famous Sir William de Walworth, Lord Mayor of London, whose sword struck down Wat Tyler in 1380, and whose statue now adorns the Holborn Viaduct, near which place this event occurred. There is indeed in his will a legacy of 'unum rosarium,' which the editor of the *Excerpta Historica*[30] takes to be ' a rosary.' But I hesitate to adopt this interpretation, both because beads seem to come out of place in the midst of a number of lawbooks ; and still more because, so far as I can discover, the beads were not at that period known by the name of rosary, though the prayer itself was so called. On the other hand, I do not know of any law-book which even in irony was called

[29] *Testam. Vetust.* pp. 610, 611.
[30] Bentley's *Excerpta Historica*, pp. 137, 140.

P

by so sweet a title. There is certainly no improbability in supposing that the famous citizen of London was as well acquainted with the use of the beads as with that of the sword, and his devotion to our Lady is evident from other parts of his will. He bequeaths 'his soul to Almighty God, to the glorious and Blessed Virgin Mary, to St. Michael and all saints; and his body to be buried in the chapel of the Blessed Virgin Mary in the church of St. Michael, in Crooked-lane, at the corner of the altar.' He was a member of a religious confraternity, which is mentioned in his will, and to which he leaves money for Masses. In fact, the books, the good works, the charities, and deeds of devotion mentioned in his will show him to have been a man of whom English Catholics may be proud.

But I think we may fairly conclude, from the evidence before us, that in the fourteenth and fifteenth centuries the use of the beads in England was universal; it was common to kings and nobles, to churchmen and to soldiers, to the most learned and most ignorant, to old age and to youth. It long survived the Reformation, and was with the greatest difficulty at length abolished. The attachment of the people to the use of the beads appears in the articles exhibited against Ferrar, Bishop of St. David's. This man, who suffered as a Protestant under Mary, was accused as a favourer of superstition under Edward. Amongst other charges, 'Whereas superstitious praying upon beads is not only ungodly, but reproved in the king's majesty's injunctions, the said bishop, meeting many with beads in their hands, never rebuked any of them.' To which he answered: 'That in the time of the rebellion in Devonshire and Cornwall threatening to come into Wales, he teaching the people the true form of prayer according to God's holy Word, and declaring the prayer upon beads to be vain and superstitious, yet durst not, for fear of tumult, forcibly take from any man his beads without authority. And touching the not reproving such as he should meet wearing beads, he remembereth not that he hath so done, unless it were in the rebellion-time, at which time he durst not rebuke such offenders.'[31]

[31] Foxe, *Acts and Monuments*, vol. vii. pp. 6, 13.

It would seem that the beads became so offensive to our reforming monarchs more because of the blessing attached to them than because of the prayers said upon them. The following is a translation of the prayer with which the English Church used formerly to bless the beads. It is from the Sarum Pontifical.[32]

' O only ineffable and incomprehensible Creator, Almighty God, by whose word and power all things are created, by whose gift we have received whatever we possess for our life's health ; we earnestly beseech Thee, that from the seat of Thy Majesty Thou wouldst deign to pour forth Thy blessing and heavenly sanctification on these instruments of prayer [oracula sive precaria] of Thy faithful servants. May these instruments be received in the sight of Thy clemency, as the gifts of Abel Thy servant and of Melchisedech were pleasing to Thee. And whoever endeavours by means of these to honour by holy service the most Blessed Mary, Mother of God, may her Son our Lord Jesus Christ return him great things for small ; may He accept his devotion, forgive his sins, fill him with faith, indulgently succour him, mercifully protect him, destroy whatever is adverse to him, and grant him what is prosperous. May he have in this life the merit of holy actions, the zeal of charity, the affection of holy love ; and in the next may he obtain eternal glory with the holy angels. Through our Lord Jesus Christ.'

It seems scarcely credible that a blessing such as this should have caused the possession of the beads to be reputed felonious in the time of Elizabeth, yet such was the case.

When the Catholic religion had been restored for a few days in the churches of Durham in the year 1569, by the Earls of Northumberland and Westmoreland, proceedings of the most barbarous character were instituted against even the simple people, who had taken no further part than to join in the reinstated worship. The details of these prosecutions have been published by the Surtees Society. The form of accusation was as follows (omitting only some of the verbiage) :

' That by the laws of England, not only Mass, Matins, Even-

---

[32] Given by Mr. Maskell, *Monum. Ritualia*, vol. i. p. 151.

song, private confession, procession, hallowing of water, bread, and other superstitious Latin services, &c. devised *of late years*(!) by the Bishop of Rome, *ancient* (!) enemy to the crown of England, with all his usurped authority, for most just cause is utterly abolished, but also all books and ornaments belonging to the same service is or ought to be defaced and rent, and especially all altar, holy-water stones, *and beads*, as monuments of idolatry and superstition, so that no memory of the same do remain in walls, pavements, or elsewhere, within any church or house within this realm;'

Yet, notwithstanding this, 'by the instigation of the devil and open contempt of the queen's majesty's godly proceedings, divers evil-disposed persons did unlawfully erect an altar and holy-water stone, and came to Mass, Matins, Evensong, procession, and like idolatrous service, thereat kneeling, bowing, knocking, and showing suchlike reverent gesture, *used praying on beads*, confession or shriving to a priest, took holy water and holy bread, &c. &c., to the peril and damnation of their own souls and slander of God and Christian people : therefore by reason of these premises A. B. is a stubborn and rebellious hinderer of God's word and Christ's religion and the queen's proceedings, and a notorious favourer of idolatry, superstition, and popish Latin service.'[33]

From the deposition of various witnesses it appears that immense crowds flocked to the Mass, delighting to sign themselves with holy water once more, to taste blessed bread, and to be reconciled with the Church. One poor woman acknowledges that 'she occupied her gauds [*i.e.* said her beads], as many thousands did.'[34]

But the laws then in force were not considered stringent enough. Two years later by statute (13 Eliz. c. 2) the pains of *præmunire* were extended to all who should import or receive any Agnus Dei, crosses, or beads, &c. blessed by the Pope or by any one holding authority from him—these penalties being, that after conviction the defendant should be out of the sovereign's protection, and his lands and tenements, goods and chattels,

[33] Surtees Society Public. for 1845, p. 131.   [34] Ib. p. 164.

forfeited to the sovereign, and his body remain in prison at the sovereign's pleasure. Nor was the statute left as a dead letter. In 1577, Mr. Tregian was condemned to perpetual imprisonment for having received an Agnus Dei from the martyred priest, Cuthbert Maine. Lastly, in 1616, Thomas Atkinson was convicted of being a priest, on no other evidence than that of beads found in his possession, and executed at York. This venerable man was more than seventy years old when he was hung, disembowelled, and quartered. Challoner adduces contemporary evidence that God glorified His confessor by visible miracles during his imprisonment, and also that our Blessed Lady appeared to him, and revealed to him the death by which he should glorify her Son; as he made known to some fellow-prisoners.

Notwithstanding all this, the Rosary continued a favourite devotion during the penal times, and even Confraternities of the Rosary were founded and maintained.

Having given this sketch of the history of the Rosary in England, I will now add a few details regarding its various forms.

An approved form of this devotion was, and still is, to say sixty or sixty-three 'Hail Marys,' with six 'Our Fathers.' This number was adopted under the idea that the years of our Lady's life were sixty or sixty-three. This is called our Lady's Crown. When Bishop Fisher mentions this devotion of Lady Margaret, he adds that it was 'after the usage of Rome,' as if it were not very common in England.

In the answer of John Lambert, who was put to death by Henry VIII. in 1538, he speaks of 'saying our Lady's Psalter upon the ten beads that come from the Crossed Friars, or upon the five beads hallowed at the Charter House.'[35]

It is not ascertained when the name of Rosary was first given to this prayer. Monelia quotes from the life of Blessed Clare of Gambacourt, born in 1362, that when twelve years old she used to sing the praises of God, and to say the Rosary and other prayers. The Confraternity of the Rosary was approved

[35] Foxe, v. p. 211.

in 1475.   The word ' Psalterium Beatæ Virginis' seems to be the older designation.

It may perhaps be necessary here to clear away an equivocal word.   The word 'Psalter of Mary' has been applied to the Rosary or to the repetition of 150 Angelic Salutations; but it has also another and an earlier meaning.   The learned Mone has published several psalters, and given details of many more. He says that Mary Psalters were composed for private devotion and used in the eleventh century.   St. Anselm composed one, which may be found in his works ; and he had many imitators, amongst others St. Edmund of Canterbury and Stephen Langton. Now as these psalters consist generally of 150 strophes, and each strophe begins with the word 'Ave,' we have in reality a devotion which, in a casual mention of a chronicler, might easily be mistaken for the Rosary, though in reality different.   The prologue of St. Edmund's Psalter is as follows :

' O Maria, Mater pia,	Me dignare te laudare
O benigna, laude digna,	Verbis dignis, sanctis hymnis,
Plena Dei lumine,	Et psalmorum carmine.'

Then each verse begins with ' Ave.'[36]

I have not been able to find in the authors who have treated of the Rosary any ancient documents showing the nature of the meditations attached to the decades from the thirteenth to the sixteenth century, though they assert that such meditations were in use.   I have gleaned, however, some evidence that, at least in the sixteenth century, the 'mysteries' were not precisely those now universally adopted.   Stapleton, a famous English theologian, writing in Louvain in 1589, happens to mention those in use in his time.   The five joyful mysteries were : 1. the Annunciation ; 2. the Visitation ; 3. the Nativity ; 4. the Adoration of the Magi ; 5. the Confession of Simeon and Anna. The five sorrowful mysteries were : 1. the Circumcision ; 2. the Flight into Egypt ; .3. the Loss of our Lord when twelve years old ; 4. the Crucifixion ; and 5. the Burial.   The five glorious were the same as at present.[37]

[36] Mone, *Hymni Latini*, vol. ii. pp. 245, 254.
[37] Stapleton, *Promptuarium Catholicum*, Op. tom. iv. p. 838.

A Spanish writer, Father Arias, S.J., writing towards the end of the sixteenth century, alludes to the ordinary Rosary as containing the following mysteries. The five joyful are: 1. the Annunciation; 2. the Incarnation; 3. the Visitation; 4. the Birth; 5. the Presentation. The sorrowful and the glorious are the same as those we now select.[38]

It would appear from this that the usage was not uniform.

I have already remarked that the word Rosary was seldom if ever used before the sixteenth century to designate the beads themselves. It was not even restricted to the form of prayer said upon the beads. I have seen a small volume in English, though printed in Antwerp, by Martin Emprourer in 1543. It is called: ' The mystic sweet Rosary of the faithful Soul, garnished round about as it were with fresh fragrant Flowers, according to the Truth of the Gospel, with fifty Pagens [*i.e.* Pictures] of the Holy Life and Passion of our Lord Jesu Christ, with certain Places of Holy Scripture, corresponding every Pagen,' &c.

The first picture represents our Lady with the Divine Child in her arms. Under her feet is the crescent, and also the serpent twining round it. The figure of our Lady is surrounded by a rosary of five decades. Instead of the great beads or paternosters are flowers, containing within them representations of our Lord's feet and hands wounded, and His wounded Heart. At foot are the Pope, cardinals, bishops, knights, &c. After this picture is a prayer in honour of one of our Lord's wounds, followed by the ' Our Father;' then ten pictures, each with an appropriate prayer, followed by the ' Hail Mary.'

The second decade begins with a picture of our Lady. Angels are holding a crown over her head. Beads also surround this picture, with a medal attached. Holy women are kneeling at our Lady's feet.

The pictures represent principally the mysteries of our Lord's life as follow: 1. The Creation of Eve; 2. the Birth of Mary;

---

[38] Aria's work was translated into Latin by Dulcken, a Carthusian, and published in 1608. It is given in the *Summa Aurea*, published by Migne, tom. v.

3. Mary's Presentation in the Temple ; 4. her Marriage ; 5. the Annunciation ; 6. the Visitation ; 7. the Birth of our Lord ; 8. the Visit of the Shepherds ; 9. the Circumcision ; 10. the Adoration of the Magi.

The second decade contains : 1. the Purification ; 2. the Flight into Egypt ; 3. the Finding in the Temple ; 4. the Interior of the Workshop of Nazareth ; 5. our Lord's Baptism ; 6. His Temptation ; 7. His Curing of the Sick; 8. the Wedding Feast of Cana; 9. the Pardon of Magdalen ; 10. the Entry into Jerusalem. Then, in the three next decades, follow the Passion and Death, the Resurrection, Ascension, and final Judgment.

I have found the same mysteries recommended for meditation by the celebrated Lansperg, and I have no doubt that this is an English version of his ' Rosary,' though his name does not occur. The same Lansperg gives a still shorter form, in which each mystery begins, 'Ave benignissime Jesu, qui,' &c., and then continues : ' Ave et tu, O gloriosissima Dei Mater, Virgo Maria, gratia plena,' &c. This seems to be the form alluded to by the author of *Our Lady's Mirror*, when he says that such additions may be made in private devotion, but not when the ' Hail Marys' are said publicly.

Louis Blosius has also a similar form of meditations, which he calls a Rosary. Perhaps the *Rosarium* mentioned among the books of Sir William de Walworth was a book of meditations, though I know of nothing of the sort of so early a date.[30]

The annexed engraving is from a piece of stained glass, once in Whitby Abbey, and now preserved in Raby Castle. It is very interesting, not only for the Rosary, but for the representation of our Lord's Sacred Heart surrounded by thorns.

The Gabriel Bell.

After the Rosary, the most popular usage of the ' Hail Mary' was that which we now call the Angelus.

It had for centuries been the custom to ring a bell called the curfew (or cover fire) at sunset, when Pope John XXII. in 1327 granted an indulgence to all who should say, during the

[30] See before, p. 209.

ROSARY, WITH FIVE WOUNDS, SACRED HEART, ETC.
Subject from stained glass formerly in Whitby Abbey, now in Raby Castle.

Inscription.

Ave piissima Virgo Maria, quæ es rubens rosa et super omr.em creaturam indumento divini amoris induta.

Translation.

Hail, most pious Virgin Mary, who art a red rose, and clothed with a vestment of divine love above every creature.

ringing of this bell, three 'Hail Marys.'[40]   This evening salutation of Mary soon became popular throughout Europe.   In
England, not three but five 'Hail Marys' were said, together
with the Lord's Prayer.   This we learn from a constitution of
Archbishop Arundel in 1399, in which the same form of devotion is extended to the morning.   He informs us that he does
this at the request of King Henry IV.   This is the same prince
to whom, as we have seen above, his father, John of Gaunt, left
a golden rosary, which he had himself received from his mother,
Queen Philippa.

The Archbishop of Canterbury writes to the Bishop of London
and the rest of his suffragan bishops, that 'the contemplation of
the great mystery of the Incarnation, in which the Eternal Word
chose the holy and immaculate Virgin, that from her womb He
should clothe Himself with flesh, has drawn all Christian nations
to venerate her from whom come the first beginnings of our
redemption;' but that 'we English being the servants of her
special inheritance, and her own Dowry, as we are commonly
called, ought to surpass others in the fervour of our praises and
devotions.'   He then describes how the power of England has
increased, and ascribes these successes and prosperity to the
intercession of the Blessed Virgin.   Therefore, that this protection may be continued, at the special desire of the king,
Henry IV. (just come to the throne), he enjoins that as hitherto the devotion of the faithful has been accustomed to honour
Mary at the ringing of the curfew, by saying the Lord's Prayer
once and the Angelic Salutation five times, so also the bell
should be rung early in the morning in all cathedral, collegiate,
monastic, and parish churches, and the same prayers be said.
To those who perform this devotion he grants forty days' indulgence.[41]

In an edition of the *Horæ Beatæ Virginis ad Usum Sarum,*
printed in Paris in 1526, it is said that Pope Sixtus granted
indulgences at the request of Elizabeth, wife of Henry VII., to

[40] Gregory IX. had already a century before ordered the bell to be
rung in the evening, that the people might pray for the Crusades; and
St. Bonaventure in 1269 had exhorted the Friars Minor to propagate the
evening Ave.   [41] Wilkins, tom. iii. p. 246.

those who said the 'Ave Maria' three times at 6 A.M., three times at noon, and three times at 6 P.M.; and that the Archbishops of Canterbury and York, with nine other bishops, on the 26th March 1492, also granted forty days' indulgence for the same. The 'Ave Maria' was preceded by the prayer 'Suscipe,' &c., 'Receive the word, O Virgin Mary, which was sent to thee from the Lord by an angel.' The Angelus, as we now have it, is of a date subsequent to the Reformation. In 1536, by an injunction of Thomas Cromwell, acting as vicar-general of Henry VIII., this beautiful devotion was forbidden, not from any scruple about the 'Hail Marys,' but, as it was expressly declared, out of hatred to the Pope. 'That the knolling of the Aves, which hath been brought in and begun by the pretence of the Bishop of Rome's pardon, henceforth be omitted, lest the people do hereafter trust to have pardon,' &c.[42]

Bells.

The devotion just mentioned suggests a few words more on the subject of bells in connection with devotion to our Lady.

A special bell was frequently set apart for the morning and evening Aves, and this was called the Gabriel Bell. But in almost every peal of bells there was one dedicated to the Blessed Virgin, and called by her name. Prior to the Reformation inscriptions on church bells were nearly always of a religious character, and if the bells were still in existence no doubt an interesting collection of epigrammatic devotion to the Blessed Virgin might be made. But few of the present bells are of ancient date. Church bells were part of the plunder of Henry, Edward, and Elizabeth. 'When any sacred building,' says the Rev. Mr. Haweis, 'was, in the pithy phrase of Henry's commissioners, "deemed superfluous," the next thing was to ascertain the collective weight of the bells, and estimate the lead on the nave, aisles, and cloister, that the king might know how much they would represent in a wager or a gift.'[43]

[42] Wilkins, tom. iii. p. 817. On the subject of the Angelus, see the Bollandists, vol. lv. p. 1109; but they make no mention whatever of England, or of any of the facts above narrated.

[43] *Sketches of the Reformation*, by the Rev. J. O. W. Haweis, p. 110. See also *Letters relating to the Suppression of Monasteries*, letter 142.

Nor did his majesty restrict his wager to the bells of suppressed monasteries. Dugdale informs us how the king staked the bells of St. Paul's Cathedral, London, and by one cast of the dice lost them to Sir Amyas Paulet.

When the Lord Protector Somerset had brought the country to the lowest state of misery, he melted down the bells to make cannon, or sold them for money.

Yet there remain still a few of the ancient bells, and the following epigraphs may serve as specimens of those that are now lost. The *Monumenta Vetusta*[44] give a drawing of a bell cast in 1366, belonging to a nunnery in Essex, with the inscription:

> 'O Mater Dei, memento mei,'

which was also a favourite device on tombs and brasses.

The naming of bells seems to have been an ancient custom. Abbot Adam of Evesham, in 1160, had two large bells made, called Jesus and Gloriosa. William Boys, abbot in 1345, made two other great bells, called Mary and Egwin.

On Mary was written:

> 'Me sonante pia succurre virgo Maria.'

On Gloriosa was the inscription:

> 'Ave gloriosa virginum regina,
> Vitis generosa, vitæ medicina.'[45]

A not unfrequent inscription both on bells and over doors[46] was the following:

> 'Hac non vade via, nisi dicas Ave Maria:
> Hail Mary say, when you pass this way.'

In the cathedral of Oxford a bell bears the words,

> 'Stella Maria maris, succurre piissima nobis;'

which I may translate:

> 'O Mary, Star of the sea,
> In pity our succour be.'

In the cathedral of Gloucester the following inscription is found:

> 'Sum rosa pulsata mundi Maria vocata;'

[44] Vol, ii. plate 17.

[45] *Chronic. Evesh.* p. 100, 297 (ed. Master of Rolls).

[46] *E.g.* on a bell in Norfolk, and over a porch in the cathedral of Aberdeen.

which, though rather obscure, was probably intended to convey some such ideas as the following :

> ' The rose when shaken fragrance sheds around,
> The bell when struck pours forth melodious sound ;
> The heart of Mary moved by earnest prayer
> Will scatter grace and sweetness everywhere.'

A very common inscription on bells is the Angelic Salutation :

> ' Ave Maria, gratia plena, Dominus tecum ;'

or shorter,

> ' Ave Maria, gratia plena ;'

or simply,

> ' Gratia.'

Prayers were inscribed on bells, sometimes for the preservation of the bell itself, sometimes for the hearers, and sometimes for the givers.

An example of the first :

> ' Serva campanam Sancta Maria sanam :
> Holy Mary, keep this bell
> Safe and sound thy praise to tell.'

A prayer for the hearers is conveyed in the words,

> ' Protege pura via quos convoco Virgo Maria :
> Mary, let thy blessing fall
> Upon those who hear my call.'

A bell at Alkborough in Lincolnshire has the following English inscription :

> ' Jesu for yi modir sake
> Save al the sauls that me gart make.'[47]

Such inscriptions surely sound better than those invented since the change of religion, generally merely the names of givers, churchwardens, or founders, or rhymes like the following at Calne in Wiltshire :

> ' Robert Forman collected the money for casting this bell
> Of well-disposed persons, as I do you tell.'

Or this at Alderton in the same county :

> ' I'm given here to make a peal
> And sound the praise of Mary Neale.'[48]

---

[47] Gart make, *i.e.* caused to be made.

[48] See paper on Church Bells, by Rev. W. C. Lukis, in Wiltshire *Arch. Mag.* vol. ii.

Weever[40] has preserved for us a long list of inscriptions formerly on the walls, under the pictures and statues, and near the altars of the Blessed Virgin in England. They are nearly always in rhyme. I give a few:

> ' Nos rege, summe Pater; nos integra protege mater.
> Nos ope conforta cœlorum fulgida porta.
> Ad fontem veniæ ducat nos dextra Mariæ.
> Sit nobis portus ad vitam virginis ortus.
> Virgo salutata juvet omnes prole beata.
> Sede locata pia nostri memor esto Maria.
> Quæ super astra manet lapsorum vulnera sanet.
> Quæ cœlo floret pro nobis omnibus oret.
> Mater virtutis det nobis dona salutis.
> Virgo Maria tuos serva sine crimine servos.
> Virginis auxilium foveat nos nunc et in ævum.'

These are but a few out of a long list. These inscriptions, says Weever, ' being holden to be superstitious, were defaced, erased, washed over, or obliterated' by the commissioners in the first year of Queen Elizabeth.

Postscript. It may be of use to those who wish to inquire into the controversies concerning the origin of the custom of reciting the ' Hail Mary,' and the institution of the Rosary, to remark that Cardinal Lambertini (afterwards Benedict XIV.), besides his remarks in his treatise *De Canon. Sanct.* (l. iv.), and in his treatise *De Festo Ros.*, wrote a learned Discursus in 1726, which is to be found in the *Analecta Juris Pontif.* 4ᵉ série, 31ᵉ livr. (tom. ii. p. 1380), published in 1860. This treatise was not known to the Bollandists when they published their remarks on the life of St. Dominic in 1733. Those remarks did not, however, change Lambertini's judgment; for he wrote his work *De Festo* after reading their objections.

I gather from many authorities that the use of the Rosary had, in a great measure, died out in the fourteenth century in the rest of Europe, while it certainly flourished during that time in England.

[40] *Discourse on Funeral Monuments*, p. cxvi.

CHAPTER VI.

·Having now to give an account of our Lady's Feasts, let me begin by explaining in what sense a feast or fast can be said to belong or be dedicated to a saint.

A festival is indeed a day set apart immediately to the worship of God. The great act of worship on each feast-day, the Holy Sacrifice of the Mass, is offered to God alone. The prayers of the Divine Office are addressed almost exclusively to Him. It is God's word that is preached; and His grace is sought in the reception of the Sacraments. Yet these things may be done secondarily or indirectly in honour of a creature eminent in sanctity. The day may be selected to commemorate what God did for that saint, and what that saint did for God. This may form the subject of the lessons of the Divine Office, or of the instruction and exhortation of the preacher. The Holy Sacrifice may be offered in commemoration and thanksgiving for the saint, to implore the benefit of his intercession or the grace to imitate his example. As a saint is most honoured by the effort made to reproduce his sanctity, the conscience will be purified by confession and the soul strengthened by Holy Communion under his invocation and for his glory; and in this sense the celebration of a festival, which is an act of supreme worship (latria) offered to God, is also an act of inferior honour (dulia) offered to God's saints.

The festivals of the Blessed Virgin were therefore the days when God was worshipped by a special and solemn commemoration of His ever-blessed Mother.

The number of such days varied from four to seven between the first arrangement of the ritual of the Saxon Church by St. Augustin, and the new order of things introduced under Edward VI. I shall first give a few details on the origin of the various festivals, and then add some remarks on the mode of celebration common to them all.

Origin of our Lady's Festivals.

In endeavouring to ascertain the origin of a festival there frequently arises no little embarrassment from the apparently contradictory statements of ancient writers. Of course the assertion of an old liturgical writer may really be erroneous and misleading ; but besides this, a festival may have been celebrated even for centuries in one country before it was introduced into another. Again, a commemoration may have been made in the churches of a religious order long before it was accepted by those of another, or by the secular clergy. Or the celebration may have been at first confined to the clergy, and at a later period have been extended to the laity also, or made 'of obligation,' as it is called. If, however, these variations of discipline are kept in mind, we shall be able to come to some safe conclusions regarding the dates of our English festivals.

In Anglo-Saxon times but four feasts of our Lady were observed in England, which I may mention according to their order in the year.

The Purification.

This festival was and is still celebrated on the 2d February. There is no doubt that the Roman missionaries established its celebration in England, for it was already kept in Rome in the sixth or even in the fifth century. Venerable Bede, having alluded to the processions made in heathen Rome in the month of February, thus describes the Christian festival which gave them a new form and object : 'The Christian religion has changed these customs; for in the same month on St. Mary's day all the people, with priests and ministers, go forth with hymns through the churches and the chosen places of the city; and all carry in their hands the lighted tapers they have received from the bishop. And not on this day alone, but the good custom has spread ; and on the other feasts also of the blessed and ever-virgin Mother the people have learnt to do the same.

And this is no longer done, as in pagan times, for the purification of an earthly kingdom, but for the commemoration of that
heavenly one, in which, according to the parable of the prudent
virgins, all the elect, with the lamps of good works burning, will
go to meet the Spouse their King, and enter with Him into the
nuptials of the heavenly city.'[1]

From the procession here alluded to, the feast was commonly
called Candlemas ; and the external emblem of the lighted wax
tapers became a fruitful theme for the exhortations addressed
on that day to the people.   Besides the memory of our Lord's
parable alluded to by St. Bede, other moralities were gathered
from the candle, as in the following old English homily of the
twelfth century:

' As our Lady St. Mary bare her holy royal Child spiritually in her heart and bodily in her hands, so ought we to obey
our Lord Jesus Christ in our hearts—fide et dilectione—through
a right faith and true love to God and to man, and to bear in
our hands burning candles.   In Christo enim corpus et anima
et divinitas, et in candela cera exterius, luminulum interius,
ignis in ambobus,—In our Saviour there was seen outwardly
His body, and the holy soul was within unseen, and the great
Wisdom existed in each of them.   So is the wax of the candle
visible and the wick within invisible, and the fire is in both.
And therefore every Christian man ought to have in his hand
to-day in church a light burning, as our Lady St. Mary and her
holy company had.'[2]

The Anglo-Saxon Œlfric says in one of his homilies :

' It is appointed in the ecclesiastical observances that we
on this day bear our lights to church, and *let them there be
blessed;* and that we should go afterwards with the light among
God's houses, and sing the hymn that is thereto appointed.
Though some men cannot sing, they can, nevertheless, bear the
light in their hands; for on this day was Christ, the true Light,
borne to the temple, who redeemed us from darkness, and

---

[1] Beda, *De Temporum Ratione*, cap. xii. ed. Giles.
[2] *Old English Homilies of the Twelfth Century*, p. 46; Early Engl.
Text Society for 1873.

bringeth us to the Eternal Light, who liveth and ruleth for ever.'[3]

A prayer was appointed for the blessing of the candles in Leofric's Missal. According to Dr. Rock, there used to be two distinct blessings; one over the unlighted wax tapers, the other over the fire (very likely a burning candle) from which they were afterwards all lit.

The procession took place before Mass, and on getting back again to their church the people stopped for the offering up of the Holy Sacrifice.[4]

Lanfranc, in his Directory for the abbey of Bec, which afterwards became the rule in our great English abbeys, writes :

'At Tierce all are clothed in albs ; after Tierce a carpet is spread before the altar and the candles laid upon the carpet. The priest in alb and stole blesses them, sprinkling them with holy water and incensing them. Then they are distributed by the *custos*. When they are being lighted, the cantor sings the antiphon "Lumen ad revelationem," and then the hymn "Nunc dimittis." Then, as they go forth in procession, the cantor begins the antiphon " Ave gratia," and others if necessary. They pass through the great gates of the monastery and make a station before the crucifix ; then singing the antiphon " Cum inducerent," they reënter the choir, the bells are rung, and the Mass is celebrated.'[5]

It will be seen from this account that the ceremonial of this festival in the Anglo-Norman Church differed little from that of the Anglo-Saxon and from what we observe at the present day.

Osbern, a precentor of Canterbury in the time of Lanfranc, and who, at his desire, wrote the life of St. Dunstan, gives us the following story, which illustrates the usages of the times: ' On the feast of the Purification,' he says, ' the people went with great devotion to the church of our Lady at Glastonbury; amongst others, Herstan, the father of St. Dunstan, and Kinedrida, his mother, who was then with child of him. All held

[3] Ælfric's *Hom.* ed. Thorpe, t. i. p. 151.
[4] Rock's *Church of our Fathers*, vol. iv. p. 60.
[5] *Op. D. Lanfranci*, tom. i. p. 96, ed. Giles.

Q

candles in their hands and were assisting at the solemn Mass, when, while the Gospel was being read, how the parents brought the Child Jesus to the temple, suddenly all lights in the church were extinguished, and thick darkness filled the temple. The people stood in fear and amazement, when suddenly the candle which Dunstan's mother held appeared alight, and from it all relit their candles. This showed how her child would one day be a light to dispel the darkness of his nation.'[6]

An omen very different is noticed by Roger of Wendover of King Stephen. While he was besieged in Lincoln by the Empress Matilda, he went on Candlemas-day to the cathedral to hear Mass. His candle broke and was extinguished in his hand while he offered it, and the pyx fell down upon the altar with the Body of Christ.

The candles which had been carried in procession were usually offered to the church, to be used during the year. Indeed the laws of the Anglo-Saxon and Danish kings ordered this tribute. King Ethelred decreed, 'Let light-scot be paid at Candlemas; let him do it oftener who will;' and those of Cnut, 'Light-scot thrice in the year: first, on Easter-eve, a halfpenny-worth for every hide [of land]; and again on Allhallows' Mass as much; and again on the Purification of St. Mary the like.'[7]

Newcourt, writing of the church of Layton, in Essex, says: 'This church being dedicated to the B. V. Mary, her five holy days were solemnly kept in it; and for oil and tapers to be set upon those festivals, and for providing frankincense on all the holy days, the abbot of Stratford—Langthorn, who had the patronage and rectory of this church—was to take care, the providing of which he laid on the tenants of the said church; and in 35 Hen. VI., as appears by the Year-Book of Reports of that time, the said abbot, called parson of the church Beatæ Mariæ de Leyton, did sue an assize and set forth, "That he and his predecessors were to have half an ounce of cotton-wick and three pound of wax to make a candle or taper to burn in the said church, before the image of the B. Mary yearly on five

---

[6] *Acta SS. Bol.* t. xvi. p. 359.
[7] *Ancient Laws,* Thorpe, pp. 343, 367.

festival days, viz. her Annunciation, Conception, Purification, Assumption, and Nativity; and to have a glass lamp and a gallon of oil to burn in the lamp within the said church, before the crucifix or rood there; and also one pound of frankincense yearly to the praise of God and all saints, there in the same church on festival days to incense throughout the year." [8]

I may mention here that the pious ceremony called 'churching,' or blessing of women after childbirth, was instituted in memory of our Lady's purification and presentation of her Divine Child in the Temple, and was therefore accompanied by the ceremonial of bearing a lighted taper. [9]

The Annunciation.

It is admitted by all that this feast has been celebrated at least since the fifth century. Both the Greek and Latin Churches kept it on the 25th March; though, because of its falling in Lent, the Church of Toledo for a time kept it eight days before Christmas, as it is also marked in a Roman *Ordo.* In England it was certainly celebrated in March.

Though the great event celebrated on this festival is the Incarnation of the Son of God, and this day has been sometimes called the feast of the Conception, yet since the visible circumstances of the Incarnation consisted in the angelic message and our Lady's reply, this has been always reckoned among the feasts of the Blessed Virgin. An old German almanac calls it 'Our Lady in Lent;' [10] a Council of Toledo, 'the Festival of the Mother of God;' and the English, 'Lady-day.' [11]

Yet in the Directory of Lanfranc it is not reckoned among the festivals of the first class. These were five only, Christmas, Easter, Pentecost, the Assumption, and the feast of the church. It was probably celebrated less solemnly, because of its falling in Lent. If it fell on a Sunday in Lent, its celebration was deferred to the next day, lest the Sunday office should

---

[8] *Repertorium*, vol. ii. p. 380.

[9] This is mentioned in Thorpe's edition of the Penitential of St. Theodore, but not in the more genuine one of Haddan and Stubbs. But it is known to have been a most ancient rite.

[10] Dictionary of De Wetzer. [11] See Butler.

be omitted; if on the Thursday, Friday, or Saturday of Holy
Week, or on Easter Sunday, it was celebrated on the Thursday
in Easter week.[12]

The Assumption.

The feast of the Assumption of our Lady was reckoned by
Lanfranc, as we have just seen, among the five principal festivals of the year.   It was our Lady's greatest feast.   Alban
Butler proves the celebration of this feast in East and West in
the sixth century.   It was appointed to be kept as a strict holiday by the laws of Alfred, whereas it was not till the reign of
Edgar that the three other festivals of our Lady then celebrated
were raised to this rank.[13]

The death of our Lady had been celebrated in some churches
on the 18th January, but the 15th of August was the day generally appointed to celebrate our Lady's Assumption, and no other
day was ever known in England.

The reader may see in the First Part of this work what was
the doctrine preached on this festival.   It was that of our Lady's
glory; and our ancestors did not hesitate in their belief that
this glory included her uncorrupted body as well as her soul.
Nor did this belief depend upon the apocryphal history of the
fifth century, rejected by Pope Gelasius.   The incidents of this
history were often, indeed, recorded in painting and employed
by poets ; but I do not find them referred to by preachers, certainly not as the basis of the feast.

The Nativity.

The fourth feast celebrated by the Anglo-Saxons was that of
our Lady's Nativity.

Mr. Procter, in his history of the Anglican Prayer-book,
while admitting that this festival was kept in the East in the
seventh century, asserts that it was not observed in the West
till long after that date.   I cannot explain this statement in a
writer generally careful.   One of the poems of St. Aldhelm, who

[12] *Pro Ordine S. Benedicti*, Op. Lanf. tom. i. p. 132, ed. Giles.
[13] Lingard's *Anglo-Saxon Church*, vol. i. p. 427.

wrote in the seventh century in England, distinctly states that
the feast of the dedication of the church built by the Princess
Bugge was the Nativity of our Lady:

> ‘ Istam nempe diem qua templi festa coruscant
> Nativitate sua sacravit Virgo Maria.’

The festival is also mentioned by Venerable Bede, who died
in 735. Butler gives us authorities which prove its celebration
in Rome in the sixth century. It is true that it was not made
obligatory till a later period, and is therefore omitted in the lists
of ecclesiastical solemnities by the Council of Mayence in 813.
But in the ninth and tenth centuries it was celebrated in many
places with great pomp, and ranked as one of the principal festivals of the Church. Pope Innocent IV., in 1243, at the desire
of the Sacred College of Cardinals, and in fulfilment of a vow
they had made, ordered that an octave should be kept of our
Lady's Nativity. St. Anselm[14] had already in the eleventh
century given leave for this octave to the Prior of Canterbury,
because this custom prevailed in other churches. Some churches
for a time did not celebrate this feast on the 8th of September,
which was the day assigned to it in the Roman Church, but they
afterwards conformed. In England, however, the Council of
Clovesho, in 747, had decided that the English Church should,
in all matters of ritual, be guided by the books which had been
received from Rome.

The festival of our Lady's Nativity is connected with the
memory of the last days of St. Hugh of Lincoln, of whom a
Protestant writer has said, that ‘in the whole range of English
worthies, few men, indeed, deserve a higher and holier niche.’[15]

When the saint was returning to England to die in the year
1200, he reached St. Omer's on September 5th. Fearing that
he might not reach England by the 8th, and might thus be prevented from celebrating our Lady's festival by offering the Holy
Sacrifice, he determined to remain for a few days at St. Omer's.

---

[14] *S. Ansel. Ep.* lib. iv. 40 (ed. Gerberon), also lib. iii. 52.
[15] Rev. J. P. Dimock, in the Preface to his edition of the *Magna Vita
S. Hugonis*, for the Master of the Rolls, p. xxxi.

Though very unwell, he went to the Cistercian monastery of Clermaretz on the vigil, and passed the night in the infirmary, and next morning celebrated with much devotion the last Mass but two that he was ever to offer. His biographer, Adam, who was eye-witness of what he records, thus continues :[16] ' By the help of the Mother of Mercy, her most devout servant and vicar (St. Hugh), after celebrating Mass in her honour, felt a great relief in his sickness. Having passed thus the day of her festival with joy and exultation of soul, next day he proceeded with his company to Wissan, and at daybreak of the 10th he embarked. Having invoked the mother of the great Mother of God, namely St. Anne, the breeze, which till then had languished, suddenly filled the sails. All those who pass the sea are accustomed to look to Mary as to the star of the sea to direct their course, and to call on Mary's mother by prayers, and to make offerings to her to obtain a favourable breeze. To St. Anne, next after her daughter, St. Hugh nourished a most familiar and special devotion ; and she in turn repaid him by speedy help in all his necessities and dangers. On this occasion also she answered as soon as she was invoked, and cheered him with a calm and quick passage ; so that as soon as he landed (at Dover) he hastened to the church to celebrate the Mass of her child-birth.'

By this last expression Adam probably means the Mass of our Lady's Nativity, which, as we have just seen, was kept with an octave in many churches in England.

Having made mention of St. Hugh, I may as well add in this place another trait of his devotion to our Lady. Adam, his biographer, relates that ' to the honour of the ever-virgin Mary, Mother of the true Light, St. Hugh had greatly increased the luminary of the church of Lincoln, and assigned to its treasury such ample revenues, that the vast space of the cathedral was almost as brilliantly lighted during the night offices by the multitude of tapers as it was during day by the rays of the sun.'[17]

[16] *Magna Vita*, p. 328.   [17] Ib. p. 366.

The Conception.

In the Provincial Council of Canterbury, held under Archbishop Simon Mepham in St. Paul's, London, A.D. 1328, it was decreed :

' Among all the saints the memory of the Blessed Virgin and Mother of our Lord is celebrated more frequently and more solemnly, since she is believed to have found greater grace with God, who ordained beforehand her conception for the temporal origin of His only-begotten Son, and for our salvation. Therefore that the consideration of these first beginnings of our redemption, in which devout minds find matter of spiritual joy, may increase devotion and salvation in all ; following in the footsteps of the Venerable Anselm, our predecessor, who, in addition to the more ancient festivals of the Blessed Virgin, instituted the solemnity of her Conception, we decree and command that the feast of the Conception be celebrated with festive solemnity in all the churches of our province of Canterbury.'[18]

As the institution of the festival of Mary's Conception by St. Anselm has been called in question, it may be interesting to give a few historical details about this feast. It is certain that a feast in honour of Mary's Conception was celebrated in the Eastern Church long before the time of St. Anselm. Passaglia also claims precedency over England for Naples and for Spain. However this may be, there is no doubt that the propagation of the feast through Europe took place especially from the eleventh century, and that the origin of the movement was in England. Nor can there be any question that it was generally attributed to St. Anselm. The Benedictine editor of the works of St. Anselm, Dom Gerberon, denies the holy doctor to be the author of the treatise commonly attributed to him on Mary's Conception. This he does, not on extrinsic, but intrinsic grounds. He thinks the historical narrative of the revelation made to Abbot Helsin is apocryphal.

One thing at least is beyond doubt, that the history in question was in circulation at, if not before, St. Anselm's time. In

---

[18] Wilkins, *Con.* tom. ii. p. 552.

an old Danish Breviary were read the following lessons for the feast of the Conception of the Blessed Virgin :[10]

Lectio V. 'At the time when William, the most powerful duke of the Normans, having overthrown Harold, king of the English, had subdued England, it happened that the king of the Danes, having heard of the death of his relative Harold, was preparing to enter England, both to revenge his death and to conquer the land which he said belonged to him. When the news reached him, William fortified all the castles of England with soldiers and provisions, and prepared himself to resist the Danes. But having consulted with his nobles, he sent Abbot Helsin, a prudent man and most devout to God and the Blessed Virgin, into Denmark, both to find out the intentions of the king, and to endeavour, as far as possible, to obtain peace.'

Lectio VI. 'The venerable abbot, having set sail, arrived safely in Denmark, and presenting himself to the king, offered gifts and friendship on the part of William, the new king of England, and paid honour to the nobles of the land by his gifts. Being therefore honourably received and treated by the king of the Danes, he remained with him a considerable time. At last, when he had brought to a successful issue the business on which he had been sent, and had obtained permission from the king to return, he again set sail with his companions. But when they were far from land a fierce tempest and contrary wind arose, which threatened his destruction, especially as they were being driven headlong on some rocks. In great fear, and with no hope of safety, they began to weep and to call on the merciful Lord and His most holy Mother, that they would deign to help them in that great danger of death.'

Lectio VII. 'While, therefore, they thus humbly and devoutly prayed to God, behold the angel of the Lord, clad in pontifical robes, appeared near the ship, and calling the abbot by name, said, "Abbot Helsin, come near and speak with me ; I am an angel sent to you to announce the Conception of the Blessed Virgin." While all were in astonishment, and the abbot

---

[10] Published from an ancient MS. by James Langebek, at p. 253 of the third volume of his *Scriptores Rerum Danicarum.*

rose up, he who appeared to them said, "If you wish to avoid this danger, promise the most gracious Mother of God that you will celebrate the feast of her Conception, the day on which this incomparable Virgin, destined to be the Mother of God, was conceived in her mother's womb, and teach others, as many as you can, to keep the same solemnity." '

Lectio VIII. 'Then the prudent abbot said: "How can I keep the feast, when I know not the day of her conception?" The heavenly messenger replied: "On the sixth of the Ides of December is the day of her revered conception; and the same office which is said on her Nativity will be said on her Conception, the word *Nativitas* being changed, wherever it occurs, into *Conceptio*." Having said this, the heavenly messenger disappeared. Then the venerable abbot, on his knees, made a vow to the Blessed Virgin to celebrate the feast of her Conception. And immediately the sky became serene and the tempest ceased; and with a prosperous wind the devout abbot returned to England, and narrated to all the wonders that had occurred in the voyage. And while he lived he solemnly celebrated the above feast, and appointed it to be kept in his monastery, and invited many in England to celebrate it; and in course of time, not only in England, but in many other provinces, to the honour of the Mother of God this feast is solemnised, although some doubt whether it ought to be kept. But be it far from the hearts of the devout to entertain such scruples, since the festival of Mary's Conception redounds to the glory of her Creator.' The date of this event would be 1067.

The history here given is related in almost the same terms in the two documents attributed to St. Anselm. The Anglo-Norman poet Wace, or Eustacius, who wrote from about 1150 to 1170, has left a poem on the conception and life of the Blessed Virgin. He begins by saying 'that it was never heard that any one celebrated the feast of the Conception till the time of King William,'[20] and then relates the history of its institution almost word for word as in the lessons of the Danish Breviary.

[20] ' N'en fu onques parole oïe,
Qu'à nul tans ainçois feïst on

The same history is given in English verse of the fourteenth century, in North English dialect,[21] which, with a little change of the spelling, is easily intelligible :

> ' On Jesus Christ they cry and call,
> And on Mary that helps all.
> " Lady," they said, " that art so mild,
> Pray for us to thy sweet Child ;
> All must we drown so, welaway !
> Lady, now help, for well thou may," ' &c.

Now, whatever opinion may be entertained of the vision or revelation, the history is not open to the objection made by Gerberon, that there was no such abbot as Helsin at the time named, and no such voyage into Denmark. Notices in the *Ramsey Register* and in the *Domesday Survey* prove that Helsin, or Elsi, was abbot both in the reigns of Edward and of William, and incidentally mention his ' absence in Denmark.' Hence Sir H. Ellis says of the preceding history, that the historical portion of it must have had some foundation in truth, though the miraculous conclusion of the story gives the whole the appearance of a fable.[22] The mission to Denmark is also defended against the criticisms of Gerberon by the learned Langebek.

Again, we have positive proof that if St. Anselm, as is probable, extended the feast to the whole of England, it was already kept before his time in the great Benedictine abbeys.[23]

The Presentation.

The feast of our Lady's Presentation as a child in the temple

---

Feste de sa Conception,
Dessi c'au tans le roi Guillaume.'
The poem has been published by MM. Mancel and Tributien of Caen : *L'Etablissement de la Fête de la Conception Notre-Dame*, par Wace.

[21] Published by Sir H. Ellis in his *Introduction to Domesday Book*, vol. ii. p. 99.

[22] Ib. p. 104. Does the vision of St. Paul give the history of his shipwreck the appearance of a fable ?

[23] On this subject see *antea*, p. 25. The reader is referred on the whole subject of the doctrine and feast of the Immaculate Conception to the learned treatise of Dr. Ullathorne, Bishop of Birmingham.

was not established in the West until the fourteenth century; and it was only in 1460 that Pius II. extended its celebration outside France. The fact, however, which it commemorates was by no means unknown to our Saxon forefathers, as is proved by the following lines, which occur in a poem of the Exeter MS., belonging to the ninth, or perhaps to an earlier, century.

St. Joseph is introduced as debating in his perplexity the pregnancy of the Blessed Virgin, before the mystery was revealed to him by the angel. He exclaims, 'It is widely known that I, from the bright temple of the Lord, received joyfully a damsel pure, spotless. And all now is changed, through I know not what.'[24] This festival was celebrated on 21st November.

Visitation.

The feast of our Lady's Visitation was instituted by Urban VI. in the fourteenth century, in the hope that the prayers of the Blessed Virgin would put an end to the great schism which was troubling the Church.

The office of the festival was drawn up by an Englishman, Cardinal Adam Eston. He was born at Hereford, and was a Benedictine monk, and afterwards Bishop of London.[25] This was in 1389. In 1441 the feast was confirmed by the Council of Basle, and fixed for the 2d July. In some churches, however, another day was observed. In York the feast was celebrated in April, as appears from the Calendar of the York Missal, published for the Surtees Society in 1874. It was, in fact, only added to the Calendar by Convocation of York in the year 1526.

Obligation of the Festivals.

The obligation of celebrating a festival may be local or universal. It may belong only to the clergy or to a religious order, or it may be extended to the laity also. It may require only assistance at the Holy Sacrifice or the sacred offices, or it may include the cessation from all servile work as well.

[24] *Codex Exoniensis*, p. 12.
[25] Artaud de Mentor, *Lives of Roman Pontiffs*, vol. i. p. 540 (Eng. tr.).

By the laws of King Alfred *freemen* were exempted from servile work for twelve days at Christmas, seven days before and seven days after Easter, and the whole week before St. Mary-Mass in harvest (the Assumption), besides some other days.[26]

Towards the end of the tenth century we find, by the Canons of Œlfric, ' that all the nation should fast before the Mass-days of St. Mary and the Mass-days of the holy Apostles.'[27]

The laws of King Ethelred (A.D. 1008) decree : ' Let all St. Mary's feast-tides be strictly honoured, first with fasting, and afterwards with feasting.'[28]

The feasts here alluded to were the Purification, Annunciation, Assumption, and Nativity.

The Synod of Exeter (A.D. 1287) extended the obligation to the feast of our Lady's Conception ;[29] as did a Provincial Council of Canterbury in 1328.[30]

There was, of course, no obligation to receive Communion on any of these days, yet there is no doubt that they were the favourite seasons for performing that great act. The *Ancren Riwle*, or directions for female recluses, written in the thirteenth century, assigns fifteen days in the year for Communion, and states this to be the number given to lay brethren in the religious orders. The days were the following : ' Midwinter ; *Candlemas*, Twelfth-day ; on Sunday half-way between that and Easter ; *Lady-day*, if it is near the Sunday, because of its being a holiday ; Easter-day ; the third Sunday thereafter ; Holy Thursday (*i.e.* Ascension) ; Whitsunday ; Midsummer-day (probably St. John Baptist, 24th June) ; St. Mary Magdalen (22d July) ; the *Assumption ;* the *Nativity* of the Blessed Virgin ; St. Michael's-day (29th September) ; All Saints' (November 1st) ; and St. Andrew's (November 30th).'[31] It will be seen from this list that the four feasts of our Lady which were then days of obligation were selected as days of Communion. To what extent the practice of communicating on these feasts prevailed among the laity, we have now no means of determining.

---

[26] *Ancient Laws*, &c. (ed, by B. Thorpe, 1840).   [27] Ib. vol. ii. p. 363.
[28] Ib. vol. i. p. 309.   [29] Wilkins, *Con.* ii. 145.   [30] Ib. p. 552.
[31] *Ancren Riwle*, p. 413 (ed. Camden Society).

It may be asked, in what spirit were the festivals observed, and how did they benefit the morality of the people? Judging from what we see everywhere, holidays will have been, like many other divine institutions—indeed, like our Lord Himself —an occasion of sin to the ill-disposed, and a means of grace to men of good will. And this seems, indeed, to be the testimony of history. Archbishop Peckham complains of their inobservance in 1291, Archbishop Mepham in 1330, and Archbishop Islip in 1359.[32]

The principal abuses seem to have arisen from the holding of fairs and markets on the holidays, and from the frequentation of taverns. A constitution of the Bishop of Lincoln in 1418 speaks of an early Mass, which used to be celebrated on the feasts of the Blessed Virgin, which was popularly nicknamed the 'Glutton-Mass,' because many persons assisted at this in order to be free to spend the rest of the day drinking and amusing themselves. The bishop takes measures to prevent such abuses, and to oblige the people to assist at the High Mass and to hear the sermon.

Father Bromyard, writing at the end of the fourteenth century, complains that many people treat their souls as the bear-leaders treat the bears: 'On a festival the bear is brought out and baited by dogs, so that "the better the day, the worse for the bear." So do some treat their souls on the feasts, exposing it to be baited by the devils, and offending God by their evil works more than during the whole preceding week;' and he quotes the words of divine anger: 'Odi et projeci festivitates vestras—I hate and have rejected your festivities' (Amos v. 21). 'When festivals are thus kept,' continues the zealous friar, ' neither will God hear us, nor His saints befriend us;' and he tells how a saint once appeared to such a client, and asked why he was invoking him so much. 'Because,' replied the man, ' among all the saints thou art my special friend, and after God and His Blessed Mother I trust most in thee, and call upon thee in my need.' But the saint replied, 'How can I be a friend of

[32] Wilkins.

my Lord's enemies? If you wish me to hear you and befriend
you, make yourself the friend of God.'[33]

Notwithstanding all this, and whatever other evidence of
abuses may be on record, no reasonable doubt can be entertained
of the immensely beneficial moral results of the celebration of
our Lady's feasts. We do not judge of a country solely by the
denunciation of a preacher against an abuse, nor by the decrees
of councils. Evil is ever more apparent than good, and viola-
tions of good order attract attention and may be chronicled for
ever, while wide-spread observance neither draws commendation at the time nor remains on record, except in the Book of
Life.

In spite, then, of the fairs, which sometimes made thrifty
and avaricious people neglect their souls—in spite of the taverns,
which attracted the idle and disorderly—the great multitude
joined in the divine offices, listened to the sermon, followed the
procession, said our Lady's Hours, or the Rosary, perhaps received holy Communion, renewed their resolutions of a Christian
life, and engaged, for our Lady's love, in some of those good
works of charity, which certainly flourished in mediæval England. We shall see something of this when we come to the
history of our Lady's guilds, which held their meetings, said their
prayers, made their processions, and did their good works on her
various festivals.

I ought not to pass over altogether the pageants and miracle-
plays, which were closely connected with the celebration of
festivals from the thirteenth to the sixteenth century.

Long before that time St. Gregory the Great, whom England
looked up to as her doctor and apostle, had sanctioned the principle on which these amusements were tolerated or encouraged.
Writing to St. Mellitus in 601, he tells him that, ' as the Saxons
had been used to feast in honour of their idols, the temples must
be changed into churches, and tents of branches be erected round

---

[33] *Summa Prædicantium*, p. 292. It will be seen that all the popular
legends or parables (for, of course, a story like this is meant for nothing
else) were not, as Mr. Hallam would represent, intended to favour laxity
and presumption.

them on the feast of the dedication, or of the martyrs whose
relics they contain, and then a religious banquet is to be held.
They will then no longer immolate animals to the devil, but eat
them to the glory of God, and give thanks for their feast to the
Giver of all good things. They will thus be more easily led
from external enjoyments to those of the soul. For there is no
doubt that it is not possible to retrench at once from rude people all their pleasures; and he who strives to ascend to a lofty
summit must do it by steps, not by leaps.'

How long these public feasts lasted, or whether the advice
of St. Gregory was ever carried out, we have no record. The
feast provided for the people in the middle ages was one of the
mind, not of the body, and a religious instruction as well as a
popular amusement.

Mr. Morley, in his *First Sketch of English Literature*, after
giving an account of the invention and progress of the mysteries
and miracle-plays until about the middle of the fourteenth century, when they were acted especially by the inferior clergy,
writes as follows: ' In the hands of the English guilds—which
stood for the rising middle classes of the people—miracle-plays
received a development peculiar to this country. Instead of
short sequences of three or four plays, complete sets were produced, and they told what were held to be the essential parts of
the Scripture story from the creation of man to the day of judgment. . . . . Each guild was intrusted permanently with the due
mounting and acting of one play in the set. Thus, at Chester,
the tanners played the *Fall of Lucifer;* the drapers played the
Creation and Fall and the *Death of Abel;* the story of *Noah's
Flood* was played by the water-leaders and the drawers of Dee.
Among the possessions of each guild were the properties for its
miracle-play, carefully to be kept in repair, and renewed when
necessary. . . . . The stage-furniture was as handsome in thrones
and other properties as each company could make it.

' In this country,' continues Mr. Morley, ' the taste for miracle-plays was blended with the old desire to diffuse, as far as
possible, a knowledge of religious truth; and therefore the sets
of miracle-plays acted by our town-guilds placed in the streets,

as completely as might be, a living picture-Bible before the eyes of all the people.'[34]

Pageants similar to those of the great towns of England were the delight of the Scotch also. The Council Register of the Burgh of Aberdeen[35] contains many entries regarding the religious processions of Corpus Christi and Candlemas, from 1442 till 1533. I give one as a specimen, and it must be remarked that the ordinance is entirely civil, not ecclesiastical. I must somewhat modify the old Scotch spelling.

'The said day (30th January 1505) it was fundin by the old lovable consuetude and right of the burgh, that in honour of God and the Blessed Virgin Mary the craftsmen of the same, in their best array, kepit and decorit the procession on Candlemas-day yearly; which old and lovable consuetude the provost, baillies, ripely avised, satisfied and approved the said right, and atour statued and ordained that the said craftsmen and their successors shall perpetually, in time to come, observe and keep the said procession as honourably as they can. And they shall, in order to the offering of the play, pass two and two together socially; in the first the fleshers, barbers, banturs, cordinaris, skinners, coopers, wrights, hat-makers and bonnet-makers together, walcaris (*i.e.* fullers), litstaris (*i.e.* dyers), woolsters, tailors, goldsmiths, blacksmiths, and hammermen; and the craftsmen shall furnish the pageants—the cordwainers, the Messing; websters and woolsters, Simeon; the smiths and goldsmiths, the three kings of Cologne; the litsters (*i.e.* dyers), the emperor; the masons, the three knights; the tailors, our Lady, St. Bride, and St. Helen; and the skinners, the two bishops. And two of each craft to pass with the pageant that they furnish to keep their gear; and if any person or persons happens to fail and break any point before written, and be convict thereof, he shall pay forty shillings to St. Nicolas work, and the baillie's unlaw unforgiven; and to the observing and keeping of the same, all the said craftsmen was obliged by their hands upholden.'

---

[34] *A First Sketch of Eng. Lit.* by H. Morley, p. 101. I must refer the reader to Mr. Morley's very interesting account for further details.
[35] Published by the Spalding Club.

On the 22d May 1531, the pageant mentioned (for Corpus Christi) is different : 'The fleshers represent St. Bestian and his tormentors ; the barbers, St. Lawrence and his tormentors ; the skinners, St. Stephen and his tormentors ; the cordwainers, St. Martin ; the tailors, the coronation of our Lady ; the dyers, St. Nicolas,' &c.

There are no doubt some, both in Scotland and in England, who will exclaim against all this ; and it is perhaps useless to discuss the matter. There are others, however, who think that the drunkenness and ignorance of the multitudes in Scotch and English towns would be much lessened by reviving—though perhaps under other forms—the innocent and religious amusements of our ancestors ; and who, even while they admit that some incidents of the mysteries may have been apocryphal, esteem them far less apocryphal, and certainly far less hurtful, than the doctrines which Knox and his fellow revolutionists substituted in their place.

The devotion to our Blessed Lady was not merely festal. The vigils of her feasts were kept as *fasts*.

Fasting and Almsgiving.

John of Peckham, Archbishop of Canterbury, granted the following indulgence in A.D. 1283 :

'To all the faithful of Christ, to whose knowledge the following page may come, brother John, by divine permission humble minister of the Church of Canterbury, health and true charity in the Lord. No mortal is able worthily to honour the glorious Virgin Mother of God, whose empire extends over heaven and earth, and whose power is in Jerusalem, above all other creatures. Nothing under God is more useful to us than her patronage. Wherefore we consult not only for our own misery, but for the salvation of all the faithful, when we stir them up to the honour of this holy Mother.

'Since, then, the whole life of Mary was a fast, and she made use of food to sustain life, not to minister to the palate, and her continual abstinence had made her like a column of incense ascending upwards, to honour her and to imitate her example our

R

holy father St. Francis used to keep a perpetual fast from the feast of the holy Apostles (St. Peter and St. Paul) to the feast of her Assumption. We therefore, applauding the example of our pious father, to the honour of this great Empress, and trusting in her overflowing merits, grant to all Christ's faithful, being truly penitent, who shall fast the whole of the forty days preceding the feast of the Assumption, which begin on the octave of the Apostles, ten days' indulgence for each day. But to such as are hindered by weak health from fasting continuously, yet undertake to fast on occasional days, we grant the same number of days' indulgence. And to all who reverently and devoutly publish this indulgence to an assembly of the people we also grant a similar indulgence, each time they do this to the honour of the Blessed Virgin.'[36]

It is clear that the archbishop would never have hoped to find souls devout and zealous enough to undertake the fast he thus recommends, had not the practice of voluntary fasting been already a well-established custom. And this is known to have been the case. To take but one meal and to drink only water, on Saturday, was a frequent vow.

Alms, which naturally accompanied fasting, were also given in our Lady's honour. Indeed this was so constant a practice, that it acquired a peculiar name as Lady's meat or Lady's loaf. A pretty devotion is recorded of the mother of St. Thomas of Canterbury. She used to weigh her little child and give to the poor, in our Lady's honour, his weight in clothes or food. In this connection I may mention what Osbern, in his Life of St. Dunstan, relates of the noble lady Elgiva or Ethelfleda. To be under the direction of St. Dunstan, then a monk at Glastonbury, she had built herself a cell near the abbey church. 'There she would pray and listen to the word of God, and feed the hungry, and clothe the naked, and engage in every kind of good work. So great was her veneration for the Blessed Virgin, that she maintained at her own expense several priests to sing her praises, and she was sure to obtain from our Lady anything she asked.' Osbern goes on to tell how when once her nephew King Ethel-

[36] Wilkins, *Con.* tom. ii. p. 94.

stan, with a large company, had come to visit her, and the mead was not sufficient for their entertainment, Elgiva went with great confidence to our Lady, and by her prayers obtained a repetition of the miracle of Cana in a multiplication of the beverage.[37]

It is related in the life of St. Godric, who died in the twelfth century, and whose virtues and miracles were recorded by an eye-witness, Reginald of Durham, that every Saturday he was wont to distribute alms to the poor, for the love of the Mother of God. One Friday evening it happened that he had nothing left in his hermitage, and he bade his servant go and spread a net in the pond, saying that God would send them something during the night, that they need not send the poor away empty on the morrow. The servant reminded him that the pond was nearly dried up with the heat, and that it was a folly to spread the net on the sand. 'Do it, nevertheless,' replied the saint. On the morrow they found that a badger (?) had been caught in the net; and the servant carried it to Durham, sold its skin for seventeen pence and bought bread with the money; and though more poor people than usual came that day they all received abundantly. Hence St. Godric used to say that where the heart is rich, the hand will always find something to give.[38]

Another example of almsgiving in honour of our Lady is found in the will of John Stockdale, Alderman of York, who died A.D. 1506. ' To my wiff Ellen my new house in Petergait, as long as she keepeth her soul and unmarried' (in the Middle Ages a widow frequently made a public vow of chastity in the hands of the bishop, and was called an advowess), 'so yᵗ she yerly on Candilmesse day mayk a dyner to thirteen men and a woman, in the honour of Christ and His twelve apostells, and yᵉ woman in yᵉ worshipe of oure Ladye, and to kepe our Lady Masse wekely on yᵉ Saturday.'[39]

It may be noticed that in the last two examples mention is made of the Saturday, as a day on which to offer special acts of

[37] *Acta Sanctorum*, tom. xvi. ad 19 Maii.
[38] *Libellus de Vita S. Godrici*, p. 358 (Surtees Society, 1845).
[39] *Testam. Ebor.* vol. iv. p. 257 (Surtees Society, 1868).

homage to our Lady. I may conclude the chapter with a few words on this subject.

The Saturday.

It is needless to enter upon the history of the early observance of the Saturday as a kind of festival in the East and as a fast in the West, and the reasons of this variation, since they in no way concerned devotion to the Blessed Virgin.[40]

An argument in favour of the dedication of the Saturday to our Lady in the eighth century has been drawn from the fact that the votive Mass of the Blessed Virgin is assigned by Alcuin to the Saturday. There is, however, no proof that this arrangement was made in the time of Alcuin, who in his letters says nothing of a fixed day, but rather supposes the contrary.[41]

It is at least beyond doubt that before the eleventh century the Saturday was considered as peculiarly dedicated to the Mother of God. 'A beautiful custom,' writes St. Peter Damian, 'has grown up in some churches, that on every Saturday in Mary's honour Mass is celebrated, unless some feast or ferial in Lent prevent it.' St. Peter greatly promoted this devotion as well as the recitation of the Little Office, and the fast of Saturday.[42] Pope Urban II., in the Council of Claremont in 1096, made the Office of the Blessed Virgin on Saturday of obligation. The same Pope introduced the Preface of the Blessed Virgin in the Missal.

It was, of course, natural that the fast or abstinence of Saturday, though not originally instituted in our Lady's honour, should be kept in her honour when the day had come to be dedicated to her.

A Scotch writer of the fourteenth century, either Fordun, or his continuator Bower, says : 'In the days of our fathers the Sabbath [*i.e.* Saturday] was held in great veneration, in honour of the Blessed Virgin, principally by the devotion of women,

---

[40] See Alban Butler, *Feasts and Fasts,* part i. ch. ii. in fin.

[41] 'Sanctæ Dei Genetricis . . . Missam superaddimus perdies aliquot, si cui placuerit, decantandam.' Ep. 46. See the *Monitum Prævium* of Froben. in t. ii. Op. Alcuin.

[42] Pet. Dam. Opusc. xxxiii. cap. iii. and iv.

who every Saturday, with great piety, restricted themselves to one meal, and that merely of bread and water.'[43] He tells how the Sovereign Pontiff set apart the whole Office of the Saturday to our Lady. 'Therefore the faithful on this day, inflamed with zeal for Mary, to please her Son, keep a solemn Office to His most gracious Mother. They sing also her solemn Mass with the "Gloria in excelsis." '[44]

'Let each of us,' he continues, 'see whether he has the affection of a good son towards this Mother, rejoicing more in her honour than in his own, and feeling her dishonour more than his own shame. But if a sinner can thus love Mary, how much more does her innocent Son Jesus, the God of charity ! In this confidence many churches, as they cannot set apart all days to her, have chosen at least one day in each week.'[45] He then complains that the old customs are no longer strictly observed. 'Prelates are very culpable in allowing the people to vary the days of fasting in honour of Mary, since, for reasons already stated, the Saturday is dedicated to her. But now you will find both men and women take good suppers, even eating eggs on Saturday, who on Tuesday or Thursday would not touch a crust of bread, lest they should break our Lady's fast. Thus the fasts appointed by the Church, either in the Ember days or vigils of Apostles, they transgress without fear, while neither for God nor man would they violate a fast which they have undertaken of their own accord on days when meat is allowed. O self-will, enemy of the soul, opposed to God and pleasing to the devil !'

Of course, these reproaches were only meant to fall on those who did works of counsel while neglecting those of precept.

[43] *Scotichronicon*, lib. vii. ch. xlii.
[44] Ibid. ch. xliv.   [45] Ibid. ch. xlviii.

CHAPTER VII.

IN modern times the custom prevails of calling a multitude of objects—streets, squares, institutions, inventions, articles of dress, and the rest—by the name of the popular sovereign, statesman, hero, heroine, or dancer of the day. Among our ancestors it was our Blessed Lady who gave her name to many things, from the great ships of war of Henry V., with her effigy on the prow, to the little maidenhead-spoons, often mentioned in old wills, and so called because our Lady's head formed the termination of the handle.

I may notice, however, a remarkable exception. In England, until the fifteenth century, very few women bore the name of Mary. I do not say that it was never given in baptism. There is a Mary, Abbess of Romsey and daughter of King Stephen ; a Mary, daughter of Henry II., also a nun ; a daughter of St. Margaret of Scotland also bears this name, and a sister of St. Thomas of Canterbury; and a Mary, Queen of Man, does homage to an English king. But such exceptions are very rare. In the long lists of names signed to Saxon charters, or mentioned in Norman chronicles or English wills, Mary very seldom occurs. This omission can scarcely be attributed to accident, and certainly not to want of devotion. It seems to me that a feeling of intense reverence might, at the same time, suggest a kind of consecration of sweet and sinless things to our Lady by calling them after her, and yet forbid the appropriation of the sublime name to personal beings, who, though immeasurably superior in nature, were yet subject to positive imperfection and to sin. This view seems to be confirmed by a fact mentioned in the Life of St. Godric. Reginald of Durham tells us that a girl named Juliana,

having been miraculously cured at the tomb of the saint, had
her name thenceforth changed to that of Mary, as if she were
now less unworthy to bear so great an honour.[1]

I do not in the least suggest that the contrary custom which
now exists indicates less humility or less reverence for the
Mother of God. Devotion expresses itself in various forms. St.
Augustin remarks that the centurion, who deemed himself unworthy that our Lord should enter under his roof, would not
have found fault with Zaccheus, who made haste to welcome
Jesus as his guest. St. Peter at one time, on witnessing the
miraculous draught of fishes, falls at Jesus' feet, saying, ' Depart
from me, for I am a sinful man, O Lord ;' but at another time,
moved by a similar miracle, he casts himself into the sea in his
eagerness to get more quickly to his Lord. St. Lewis, King of
France, was once told of the devotion of a holy friar, who always
tasted of the first fruits of the season in gratitude to the Giver
of all good things, and thenceforth abstained from their use in
a spirit of mortification. The saintly king, seeing that his position did not allow an exact imitation of this example, caught up
nevertheless its spirit, by doing the very reverse. He denied
himself the taste of the first fruits, but after that ate what were
set before him. Thus in one epoch Christians might refrain
from giving the name of Mary out of veneration, while at another,
from a similar veneration, they might delight in giving or in
taking it.

Among the objects called after Mary the noblest were

The Churches.

At the Reformation some of our churches changed their
designation. That which is now called St. Saviour's, near
London Bridge, was formerly St. Mary Overies. Innumerable
churches were pulled down. Yet even to this day there are very
few towns which have not a St. Mary's Church, the dedication,
if not the fabric, dating from Catholic times. This custom of
dedicating churches to God in honour of our Lady did not begin
in England in the twelfth century. It was as common among

---

[1] *Vita S. Godrici,* p. 435 (Surtees Society, 1845).

the Saxons as the Normans; and the Saxons themselves believed that they derived it from the Britons. It is not necessary to engage in the controversy concerning the introduction of Christianity into England by St. Joseph of Arimathea.[2] Even though this be rejected, there remains the fact, proved by primitive traditions and by existing charters, that at Glastonbury, before the Saxon invasion, there had been a church dedicated to our Lady. In 704, Ina, King of the West Saxons, writes concerning the church of the ever-virgin Mary as being the first in the kingdom of Britain, and the fountain of all the Christianity of the island.[3]

William of Malmesbury, in the twelfth century, gave the story as he had read it in old records: 'Now Joseph of Arimathea came with twelve companions to Britain, and had assigned to them by the pagan king, Arviragus, a kind of island in the swamps not far from Wells, in Somersetshire. The island was called Innis Withrin, and afterwards Avalon and Glastonbury.

'Soon after these holy men,' says Malmesbury, 'had commenced their common life in this desert island, they were admonished by a vision from the Angel Gabriel that they should build there, on a spot designated from on high, a church in honour of the Blessed and Holy Virgin Mother of God. A prompt obedience was given to this command. Walls were erected of wattled osiers, and a small chapel completed by them in the thirty-first year from the Passion and the fifteenth after the Assumption of the ever-glorious Virgin. Poor, indeed, it was in appearance; but it was richly adorned with divine benedictions; and as it was the first church which had ever been built in this land, so did the Son of God distinguish it, as of greater dignity than the rest, by directing that it should be dedicated in honour of the Virgin Mother. . . . . In course of time all of them were taken away from this earthly prison, and then the spot which had been the dwelling of saints became the haunt of wild animals, till at length it pleased the Blessed Virgin

[2] The authorities and arguments on both sides may be found in the *Dublin Review* for July 1868.　　　　[3] Ib. p. 91.

to bring the remembrance of her oratory back to the minds of the faithful.'[4]

It is said that St. David had erected another church on this spot; but it is certain that King Ina, at the beginning of the eighth century, built an entirely new church, and contributed to it many precious ornaments. 'He gave,' says Mr. Stevens, quoting ancient authorities, ' 2640 lb. weight of silver for the chapel, 264 lb. of gold for the altar ; the chalice and paten had 10 lb. of gold, the censer 8 lb. and 20 mancs of gold, the candlesticks 12 lb. of silver, altar vessels 17 lb. of gold, the basins 8 lb. of gold, the vessel for the holy water 20 lb. of silver, the images of our Lord and St. Mary and the twelve Apostles 175 lb. of silver and 38 lb. of gold ; the altar and priestly vestments all interwoven with gold and precious stones.'[5]

Our Lady's Abbey of Glastonbury took the precedency of all others, until in the twelfth century this was given to St. Alban's. It remained famous until the Reformation, when its last saintly abbot, Richard Whiting, who had refused to surrender to Henry, was barbarously hung without trial.

A century before Ina rebuilt our Lady's church at Glastonbury, St. Augustin, England's Apostle (A.D. 607), built a church in honour of the ever-virgin Mary at Ely.[6] This church, having been destroyed by Penda, was rebuilt and rededicated to our Lady by St. Etheldreda about fifty years later, and became famous for miracles.[7]

St. Lawrence, Archbishop of Canterbury, companion and successor of St. Augustin (A.D. 619), built a church of the Holy Mother of God in the monastery of St. Peter's at Canterbury. This church was consecrated by St. Mellitus.[8]

Venerable Bede tells us how St. Cedd, Bishop of London, who died in 664, was buried in the stone church of the monastery of Lestringham, dedicated to the Blessed Virgin.

William Thorn relates how St. Mildred built a monastery

[4] W. Malm. *Antiq. Glast.* vol. iii. p. 292, ed. Gale.
[5] Stevens' *Monas.* vol. i. p. 422.
[6] Dugdale, Bolland. *Acta SS.* ad Mai. 26.
[7] *Acta SS.* vol. xxv. ad 23 Junii.   [8] Beda, *Hist.* l. i. cap. xxix.

and church (A.D. circ. 700), which were dedicated in honour of the Blessed Virgin by the Archbishop St. Theodore.

These examples are sufficient to show the special devotion to our Lady learnt by the Anglo-Saxons from their first Christian teachers. We find also from St. Aldhelm,[9] who wrote in the seventh century, that these churches were farther intended to recall some special mystery of our Lady. Thus the festival of the magnificent church built by the Saxon Princess Bugge was our Lady's Nativity.

In the twelfth century arose the orders of Citeaux and of Sempringham, in both of which it was a rule that all their churches should be dedicated to the Blessed Virgin.

In course of time there was scarcely a town in England without its church of St. Mary, and in large cities were two or three and even more.

From Arnold's *Chronicle*, written about the year 1500, we learn that there were then in London 118 parish churches, besides 36 non-parochial. The churches named after our Lady are 18, perhaps more, for he does not give the titles of some of the churches of the regulars. They were dedicated in honour of the Assumption, of the Salutation, of our Lady of Bethlehem, of Grace, of Pity, &c., but were popularly called from some object in the neighbourhood—Mary-at-the-Hill, Mary Woolchurch, Mary-at-the-Bowe, Mary Avery, or Overies, and the rest.[10]

Lady Chapels.

Many large churches, whether dedicated to our Lady or to some other saint, had a portion set apart called the Lady Chapel. St. Bennet Biscop, who made five journeys to Rome and back out of love and veneration for the Prince of the Apostles, built in the year 674 a monastery and church on the river Were, and dedicated them to St. Peter. Afterwards he built a second monastery and church, which he dedicated to St. Paul. Yet his great devotion to the Apostles, at whose tombs he had so often prayed, could not make him forget the Queen of the Apostles ;

[9] See previously, p. 229.
[10] See complete list in *Month*, March 1871, p. 328.

and he built another church or chapel in or by the church of St. Peter, which, as Bede tells us, he dedicated 'to the Blessed Mother of God and ever-virgin Mary.'[11]

In the Life of St. Adrian, whom St. Bennet Biscop had conducted from Rome to England, and who had been buried in Canterbury, it is related that when the church was burnt in which his body lay, he appeared to a certain man and said, 'Go and tell Bishop Dunstan, Adrian, the servant of God, has sent you this message : "You repose in a well-covered house, while the Mother of our Lord and we her servants are exposed to the inclemency of the air." Therefore St. Dunstan repaired this church of the Blessed Virgin, and used to frequent it at night with great devotion. One night, when he entered the church, he saw St. Adrian among the choirs of the blessed with the Queen of the World praising the Lord.'[12]

The biographer of St. Dunstan[13] also relates this or a similar event, but with detail which makes us know the position of the chapel : 'One night he visited the church of St. Augustine, and prayed much there, and then went on to the church of the Mother of God at the east end to pray there. When he came near to it singing psalms, he heard voices inside, and looking through a crack, he saw the church filled with choirs of virgins moving in procession and singing the hymn of Sedulius :

> " Cantemus socii Domino, cantemus honorem,
> Dulcis amor Christi personet ore pio," &c.'

This indication of the Lady Chapel as at the east end of the abbey church seems to show that Dean Stanley is incorrect in attributing the origin of this site to the thirteenth century. ' This notion,' he writes (*i.e.* the peculiar holiness of the east), ' happened to coincide in point of time with the burst of devotion towards the Virgin Mary which took place under the pontificate of Innocent III. during the first years of the thirteenth century ; and therefore, in all cases where there was no special local saint, this eastern end was dedicated to " our Lady," and the

[11] Beda, *Vita Beatorum Abbatum*, ed. Gale, tom. iv. p. 390.
[12] Bolland. *Acta Sanct.* t. i. p. 597, ad Jan. 9.
[13] *Acta Sanct.* tom. xvi. p. 357, ad Maii 19.

chapel thus formed was called the "Lady Chapel." Such was the case in the cathedrals of Salisbury, Norwich, Hereford, Wells, Gloucester, and Chester.'[14]

The matter is of little importance, except that the expression used about the 'burst of devotion' in the thirteenth century might perhaps mislead some to suppose that the Blessed Virgin was not esteemed and honoured before that time as she now is. Devotion may of course become more intense, or take new forms, and the propagation of the Rosary in the thirteenth century no doubt greatly deepened the feelings already existing; but the writings quoted in the First Part of this work—nearly all of them of the twelfth or earlier centuries—are alone enough to show that no change of principle took place in the thirteenth or later centuries.

Altars.

In the poem already alluded to, St. Aldhelm thus describes the interior of a Saxon church in the seventh century:

'During the reign of Ina (685-726), Bugge, the servant of Christ, built a new church of great size, with fourteen altars; besides which she consecrated an apse for the Virgin's altar. . . . The building was well lighted by glazed windows, and well supplied with costly ornaments. The altar hangings were wrought of gold thread; the chalice also was of gold set with precious stones, with a broad paten of silver to hold the divine medicine of our souls, the Body and Blood of Christ. The cross also was of gold set with gems. The thurible hanging from the roof sent forth its fumes, and breathed sweet odours when the priests offered the holy Masses.'

From the constant mention in documents of altars of the Blessed Virgin, we should imagine that there were very few churches indeed that did not possess one, and many had two, and even more.

By the decree of a Provincial Council under Archbishop Wulfred in A.D. 816, it was ordered 'that the bishop should have

[14] *Historical Memorials of Canterbury*, by Dean Stanley, p. 205. I should add that it is not quite clear whether the chapel mentioned in St. Dunstan's Life was not detached from St. Augustine's church, and at the east end of the monastery.

painted on the wall of the oratory, or on a tablet, or on the altars, to what saints they were dedicated.'[15]

This, however, had long been the custom, for more than a hundred years before the date of this decree St. Aldhelm had exercised his ingenuity in composing poetical inscriptions for churches and altars. His example had been followed by Alcuin and others. Many of these inscriptions have been preserved, and are interesting and valuable monuments of the faith and devotion of the times, though they betray unskilful hands.

I venture a translation of one specimen of each of the above. St. Aldhelm writes:

> ' Let Mary's prayer this house of God protect,
> Which to her name and triumph we erect.
> The Word of God, Light of the Father's light,
> Our nature took of her, a Virgin bright.
> O gentle Lady, thou wilt not despise
> Our bended knees, pale cheeks, and weeping eyes,' &c. [16]

Our English Alcuin, educated by Archbishop Egbert, the friend of Venerable Bede, and himself the teacher and adviser of Charlemagne, and the light and glory of Europe in the eighth century, was tenderly devoted to the Blessed Virgin. He has composed several inscriptions for her altars. Here is one:

> ' O Virgin Mother of our God, O Star
> Of life's dark sea, we hail thee from afar ;.
> O, by thy merits keep in spotless fame
> This altar sacred to thy glorious name.'[17]

[15] Haddan and Stubbs, vol. iii.

[16]   ' Hanc aulam Domini servat tutela Mariæ,
        Cui veneranda rudis sacrantur culmina templi,
        Et nova consurgunt sacris vexilla triumphis.
        Hac celebratur honor sacræ Genetricis in aula,
        Quæ verum genuit lumen de lumine Patris.
        Quem clamant Titan almo spiramine vates,
        Fœmina præpollens, et sacra puerpera virgo.
        Audi clementer populorum vota precantum,
        Marcida qui riguis humectant imbribus ora,
        Ac genibus tundunt curvato poplite terram,' &c.
These lines have been sometimes attributed to Alcuin, but have been vindicated to St. Aldhelm, on the faith of ms., by Dr. Giles. S. Aldhelmi Opera, p. 118.

[17]   ' Virgo Maria, Dei Genitrix, castissima Virgo,
        Lux et stella maris, nostræ Regina salutis:

What were the thoughts and feelings of our Saxon fore-fathers as they prayed before the altars of the Blessed Virgin, and what were the graces which they attributed to her inter-cession, we may learn from Alcuin's own pen. At the end of his long poem on the holy kings and bishops of his native pro-vince of York, he relates the following history :[18]

'There was a youth brought up in the city of York, of simple mind but very fervent life. He was the guide of my boyhood by his counsels. One night he was intent on his usual prayers in the church of the Mother of Christ, when suddenly a soft light filled the whole place, and there appeared a man of ma-jestic stature and brilliant aspect, clad in white robes. The youth had fallen at his feet in terror, but he raised him up with gentle words, and showed him an open book.

'When the youth had read what was written in it, the heavenly visitor closed the book, and said : "You shall know and see greater things still;" and with these words he disap-peared. After a few months the young man was struck down by a pestilence, and remained long between life and death, scarcely able to draw breath. While he lay in my arms, sud-denly the soul was caught away, and the lifeless body remained. But after a time, returning to himself, he again moved his limbs, and told me that a certain man had led him into beautiful re-gions, where he saw many persons filled with joy. Some were unknown to him, and others known, but especially he recognised those who had belonged to that holy church. They embraced him, and seemed as if they would have kept him with them altogether; but his guide quickly brought him back into his

---

Hanc aram meritis semper vivacibus ornet,
Quae sacrata suo condigno constat honore.'
Alcuini Op. ed. Froben. t. ii. p. 225.

Again at p. 223 :
'Perpetuam mundo genuisti Virgo salutem,
Quapropter mundus totus te laudat ubique ;
En ego quippe tuus famulus te laudo camœnis,
Tu mihi dulcis amor, decus et spes magna salutis ;
Auxiliare tuum servum, clarissima Virgo.'
[18] Ibid. p. 257.

body, saying, "You will be better at sunset, but another of your brethren will die to-day; for him you saw the seat prepared." The word proved true. He grew better as the sun was setting, but the other died before noon. But again, the same year, after a short time, this youth was struck by the pestilence, and immediately foretold to me, "I shall die of this disease; I shall soon leave the prison of my body." Thus it happened; for the force of the sickness soon brought him to extremity. When he fell into his agony, one of the brethren was watching, an upright and truthful man; and he saw descend from the high roof a man of bright aspect and dress, who placed his mouth on the mouth of the dying youth, and gently embraced him as he lay. Then returning, after releasing the soul from the prison of the flesh, he carried it with him beyond the stars.'

More famous among the Saxons, as an example of the power of prayers addressed to Mary, was a history that is related by Eddi, Bede, and Alcuin. I refer to the cure of St. Wilfrid in A.D. 704. As the account of Alcuin is less known, I will give it here. The event happened at Meaux in France, when the saint was returning to England from Rome. 'He was struck down by a severe illness, and brought to the last extremity, and lay for four days as if dead, speechless, and only proving that he lived by a faint breathing. His disciples stood around him weeping, when suddenly on the fifth day the father sat up, and opening his eyes, told them how God had sent to him an angel in white vestments and bright face, who said, "I am Michael. The Lord has sent me from heaven to tell you that you will recover from this sickness, on account of the merits and prayers of His holy Mother Mary, who, on her heavenly throne, has opened her ears to the sighs and tears and prayers of your companions, and has obtained for you life and health. But be ready for the fourth year. I will then again visit you, for you shall die in peace in your own country."' All which happened as it had been foretold.[19]

[19] ' Me pius altithronus Michaelem misit olympo
Dicere, quod morbo nunc confortaberis isto,
Pro meritis sanctæ Matris precibusque Mariæ

Alcuin is not quite correct in saying that St. Wilfrid related his vision to his companions. Both Bede and Eddi declare that he told it only to one, with strict injunctions of secrecy for a time. Yet no doubt whatever can be cast on the vision, or at least on the belief of St. Wilfrid. The first Life of St. Wilfrid was written by Eddi, a companion of the saint. It was written, as he tells us in his prologue, at the request of Acca, Bishop of Hexham. Now, this Acca is the intimate friend to whom St. Wilfrid related what had occurred, and no one did or could suspect him of falsehood. The words of Eddi are as follows. After relating the illness as above, he continues : ' On the fifth day, at dawn, behold the angel of the Lord, clad in white array, appeared to our holy pontiff, saying, " I am Michael, the messenger of the Most High God, who has sent me to announce to you that some years of life are added to you, on account of the intercession of St. Mary, ever Virgin Mother of God, and on account of the tears and prayers of your subjects, which have reached the ears of God. And this shall be a sign to you, that you shall at once get better and recover your health, and reach your country ; and the principal part of your property shall be restored to you, and you shall end your life in peace. Be prepared ; for after four years I will again visit you. And now, remember, that you have built houses in honour of St. Peter and St. Andrew, the Apostles, but you have built none to St. Mary ever Virgin, who has interceded for you. You must supply this omission, and dedicate a house in her honour."

' After these words the angel of God disappeared. But our holy pontiff, as if roused from sleep, sat up amidst his attendants, who were singing and weeping, and he said : " Where is Acca the priest ?" Acca drew near with joy, thanking God, with them all, that they saw him sitting up and speaking. Then having sent away the brethren from the place, he revealed the whole vision (as above related) to his most faithful priest Acca

---

Quæ gemitus, lachrymas, sociorum et vota tuorum
Auribus e solio cœlesti audivit apertis
Deposcens tibimet vitam simul atque salutem.'

Alcuini Op. t. ii. p. 248.

alone, who is now, by the grace of God, bishop of holy fame ; and immediately the above-named holy priest, being of quick intelligence, understood the matter, and thanked God, who, at the intercession of the holy Virgin Mary, Mother of the Lord, and the prayers of the subjects (of the holy bishop), had added years to his life, just as He added fifteen years to the life of King Ezechias ; namely, five because of the choice he had made of his father David ; five more on account of the intercession of the prophet Isaias in the temple of God ; and lastly, five on account of the virtues of the king himself, and his weeping as he turned his face to the wall.'[20]

The learned Benedictine editor, Mabillon, remarks that St. Wilfrid is not mentioned to have built a church to the Blessed Virgin ; but Montalembert quotes authority to the contrary. In fact, ' on his return to Hexham, St. Wilfrid caused the church of St. Mary to be erected, of which some remains may be seen near the church of the ancient priory. It was of a form quite new in England, built round, with four porticoes towards the four regions of the world.'[21]

I have given this history at such length, both as illustrating the immediate subject of churches, and also because we have here unexceptionable evidence of the belief of our Saxon forefathers in the seventh and eighth centuries.

After St. Aldhelm, Eddi is our earliest Saxon writer. We see that the same devotion to the Blessed Virgin, and precisely similar belief in the supernatural intervention of the Queen of heaven, as men loved to call her, gave rise to the first comparatively rude structures of the seventh century, and inspired the erection of the magnificent abbeys and cathedrals of the thirteenth.

I will add one more illustration from the life of St. Wilfrid. When he felt his end was near, he had his treasures divided into four portions, and said to the abbots and monks who accompanied him, ' My dearest brothers, I have thought for some time of returning yet once more to that See of Peter from which I

[20] *Acta SS. Ord. Bened.* App. ad vol. v.
[21] Montalembert, *Monks of the West*, vol. iv. p. 330, Eng. trans.

received justice and freedom, to end my life there. I shall take with me the chief of these four portions for an offering to the basilicas of St. Mary[22] and St. Paul the Apostle. But if, as often happens to the old, I should die before accomplishing my wishes, I enjoin you, my faithful friends, to send these gifts to the churches I mention.'[23]

It seems that almost the last act of St. Wilfrid was to consecrate the church built by Egwin at Evesham, and which became so famous in later times. There is a vision of the Blessed Virgin connected with the origin of this church also; but since it has been the subject of controversy, I will not dwell on it, further than to remark that what has been related of St. Wilfrid proves that there is at least no anachronism in attributing such a vision to Egwin in 708.[24]

Bridges.

The subject of churches of our Lady which became famous sanctuaries and objects of pilgrimage will require a chapter to itself. I will conclude the present one by a few words on the chapels which stood on or by the side of bridges. Very many such were built in England; so that on entering or leaving a town it was the custom to pause in prayer in these little sanctuaries. In most of them Masses were said at a very early hour, especially for the benefit of travellers. The chapel on London Bridge, dedicated to St. Thomas, is famous. Such chapels were erected on bridges in York, Sheffield, Lincoln, Leeds, Wakefield, Durham, Rochester, Salisbury, Rotherham, Droitwich, Bradford, Derby, and many other places.

[22] S. Maria Maggiore, in Rome, founded about the middle of the fourth century, also in obedience to a vision of the Blessed Virgin. See Northcote's *Sanctuaries of the Madonna.*

[23] Montalembert, Eddi, ubi supra.

[24] For the history see Montalembert, *Monks of the West*, vol. iv. p. 348; Northcote's *Sanctuaries*, p. 236; Caswall's *May Pageant;* and for what can be said against it, Haddan and Stubbs, *Councils*, vol. iii. p. 279; and on the forgeries Papebroch, Bolland. vol. ii. April, pp. 30, 31. But former writers have made mistakes, which have been cleared up by the Rev. W. Macray, in his edition of the *Chronicon Abbatiæ de Evesham* for the Master of the Rolls. If I understand him, he seems to accept the charter of Egwin given by Dominic, which is different from that published by Kemble.

Mr. Frost, in his continuation to his History of Bradford, conjectures that the present Ive Bridge may have been originally Ave Bridge, and have derived its name from the custom of saluting some statue of the Blessed Virgin, though the chapel itself was dedicated to St. Osith or Sitha. A chapel dedicated to St. Mary the Virgin was built together with the bridge at Leeds in 1376. It stood at the north-east end. At the dissolution of chantries under Edward VI. it was made into a school, and subsequently into a warehouse. The historian of Leeds, far from regretting this change, makes some very curious reflections. 'Strange,' he writes, 'must be the difference between the aspect of Leeds bridge now, and that which it presented shortly after its erection (in the 14th century): then witnessing the occasional transition of a haughty nobleman and his mailed retainers proceeding upon some expedition of rapine and revenge, or of cowled monks engaged on the business of their convents, or mendicant friars imposing on the credulity and fleecing the pocket of the poor, or of miserable serfs, ignorant as brutes, and degraded to the lowest stage of humanity; with no indications of commerce, with no appearance of opulence, with little to animate or to interest the feelings of the observer: now from morning to night reverberating with the wheels of countless carriages, crowded with passengers and the means of conveying the rich manufactures of one of the most important and industrious regions of the kingdom to the remotest countries of the globe.'[25] This outburst of vulgar pride has been caused by the mention of the Masses said in St. Mary's chapel. There was an occasion when our Lord's Apostles called His attention to the great stones of which the Temple was constructed, and when He answered by foretelling its utter destruction. There was another when they gazed with pride at the riches of those who cast large sums into the treasury, and when He bade them take notice of the mites of the poor widow.[26] Perhaps if we try to look at things with our Lord's eyes, without begrudging Leeds its present riches, we shall be less dazzled by them, and wonder

---

[25] Parsons, *History of Leeds*, vol. i. p. 104.
[26] St. Mark ch. xii. ver. 42 ; ch. xiii. ver. 1.

whether many of the artisans or even the merchants who throng its bridge are before God as exalted as the poor serfs of the fourteenth century, who, at least, knew how to hear Mass and to say their beads in our Lady's Chapel.

A more intelligent historian would rather have remarked how the faith and piety of our forefathers laid the foundations even of material prosperity.

Ancient histories tell us that it was often monks and priests who built the bridges,[27] or how they exhorted the rich to this good work. St. Dunstan's Penitential mentions road-mending and bridge-building among the good works incumbent on the rich. Leland, in his *Itinerary*, tells us of many bridges built out of piety. Here is an instance : ' The bridge at Bedford-upon-Turege is a very notable work, and hath twenty-four arches of stone. A poor priest began this bridge, and, as it is said, he was animated so to do by a vision. Then all the country about set their hands unto the performing of it, and since lands hath been given to the maintenance of it. There standeth a fair chapel of our Lady *trans pontem* at the very end of it, and there is a fraternity in the town for the preservation of this bridge, and one waiteth continually to keep the bridge clean from all ordure.'[28]

Sir Richard Hoare, in his History of Wiltshire, gives a detailed account of the bridge and chapel built over the Avon at Salisbury. Mass was said at dawn every morning. To this chapel a hospital for old people was attached. ' The mastership before the Reformation was as profitable as it was honourable, from the vast sums they had daily given for oblations, obventions, &c., in the chapel, wherewith divers lands were purchased.'[29] This source of revenue, by which bridges were built and repaired and hospitals maintained, was of course entirely cut off by the Reformation, when, as we know, they went to such a pitch of impiety and madness as to take the very altar-stones and put them in the bridges, to be trodden under the feet

---

[27] In London the first wooden bridge was built by monks, the first stone bridge by a secular priest.   [28] Leland, *Itin.* ii. p. 76.
[29] Sir Richard Hoare's *Wiltshire*, pp. 46, 99, and 763.

of men and cattle.[30] After this barriers had to be substituted on our bridges in the place of open chapels, and forced tolls instead of voluntary offerings.

[30] The churchwardens of Kilbie in Lincolnshire report in 1566: 'Item, ij altar stones, which is defacid and laid in high waies and serveth as bridges for sheepe and cattall to go on, so that ther now remaineth no trash nor trumpery of popish peltrie in our said church.' Peacock's *Church Furniture*, p. 110.

CHAPTER VIII.

IMAGES OF OUR LADY.

THE most popular and explicit memorials of our Lady were her images or representations; and as these have certainly had a very important influence on millions of souls, and have given rise to probably the fiercest and bitterest attacks that have ever been made on Catholic practice, I must devote some space to an account of this practice and controversy. Happily calmer and more reasonable feelings prevail at the present day on the subject of images than in the sixteenth century, and we can tell or read of past controversies without renewing their heat.

Historical Sketch.

When St. Augustin and his companions advanced in procession to meet King Ethelbert, they carried aloft a cross and a board or tablet on which was painted an image of our Saviour. Thus the first appearance of Christianity to our Saxon forefathers was connected with the use of external representations of the objects of faith.[1]

St. Bennet Biscop, who died in 690, and had made several pilgrimages to Rome, brought back with him a variety of pictures on panels, which he placed round the walls of the church which he had built at Wearmouth and dedicated to St. Peter. Venerable Bede tells us what these were. The eastern end or apse had representations of 'the Blessed Mother of God and ever-Virgin Mary' and of the twelve Apostles. The Gospel history was pictured on the southern wall, and the visions of St. John in the Apocalypse on the northern wall.[2]

This use of images continued uninterrupted until the Reformation. Some persons, indeed, have made much of the dis-

---

[1] Beda, *Hist. Eccl.* l. i. cap. xxv.　　[2] Beda, *Life of St. Benedict.*

tinction between flat pictures and sculptured figures or statues.[3] It may be that the use of the former is more ancient,[4] but certainly our Saxon ancestors were not aware of any difference in principle between the two, and used both as soon as native skill was equal to the production of works of art.

A Council of Exeter A.D. 1287 orders that in every parish church shall stand an image of the Blessed Virgin, besides the statue of the patron saint of the church.[5]

In many churches there were two, three, and even more statues of our Lady. Thus in the church of St. John Baptist, Perth, when Knox began his work of demolition, there were thirty-nine altars, of which five were dedicated to the Blessed Virgin. They are described as : 1. the Altar of the Blessed Virgin (simply) ; 2. Altar of the Presentation ; 3. St. Mary of Consolation ; 4. Salutation or Annunciation ; 5. Visitation.

There can be no doubt that each of these was distinguished by a statue or a picture of the mystery whence it was named.

Various Forms.

In some pictures our Lady was represented in historical aspects—at the visit of the Wise Mén, or at the foot of the Cross, or with the dead body of her Son on her lap. In others, and more commonly, she was carrying in her arms the Divine Child, yet not as she appeared on earth, but in her glorified character, transfigured, so to say, by the veneration of Christians. Sometimes she was crowned and seated on a throne, sometimes assumed into heaven.

An entry in the churchwardens' accounts of St. Margaret's, Westminster, of 1545, runs : ' Paid to Mr. Barnard for the table of the Conception[6] now standing at the high altar 16*l.* 10*s.*' I am not aware how this mystery was represented by English art. Three years after the above date the picture must have been

[3] Angl. Homily on the Peril of Idolatry.
[4] Mabillon, *Acta SS. Ord. Bened.* sæc. iv. Introd.
[5] Wilkins, *Con.* ii. 139.
[6] Considering the date, I take this to be a representation of our Lady, considered immaculate in her conception, rather than a picture of the Annunciation.

destroyed, according to the injunctions of Edward VI., with all other pictures throughout England.

In All Saints' church, York, and at West Wickham, Kent, our Lady may still be seen in the stained glass as a little girl taught by St. Anne.

Representations of the Annunciation and of the Visitation were very common.

In West Wickham is a picture in the glass of our Lady offering flowers to the Divine Child, who stands at her feet and lifts up both hands to receive them.

In Winchester Cathedral she is pictured in the stained glass as seated on a throne, crowned, without the Divine Infant, and with both hands joined in prayer.

Under the screen of York Cathedral is still to be seen an image in relief which has escaped all the iconoclastic furies of the Reformation. The Blessed Virgin is as a young maiden, crowned with flowers, surrounded with rays of light and angels. The hands are crossed on the bosom. This might represent the Immaculate Conception or the Assumption.

All these varied forms gave rise to corresponding titles, as our Lady of Grace, of Consolation, of Pity.

Amid our scanty records it is not easy to discover the various types thus designated. One of the commonest titles is that of our Lady of Pity, both in England and in Scotland. In Latin it is written 'de Pietate ;' but as piety and pity have sometimes the same meaning in old English, I do not think that by our Lady of Pity our ancestors meant our Lady of Compassion, in reference to her dolours, but simply our Lady of Clemency or Mercy. There are indeed examples of this title given to statues where our Lady is represented at the foot of the Cross ; but it is also unmistakably given to her when she bears in her arms the Infant Jesus, or is represented alone. Thus on a brass in the church of Forant in Wiltshire, she is kneeling in prayer, her head crowned with flowers, and on one side is an angel saluting her with the words, 'Ave Maria, gratia plena ;' on the other is the parish priest, with the scroll, 'Moder of Pity, pray for me.' The date is 1504.

But the most curious account that I have met with is that of our Lady of Bolton. The image so called stood over the second altar in the south aisle of Durham Cathedral. It was a very beautiful image, but its peculiarity was that it contained other images inside it. 'It was made to open with gimmers, from the breast downwards, and within was painted the image of our Saviour, finely gilt, holding up His hands, and betwixt His hands a fair and large crucifix, all of gold; which crucifix was to be taken out every Good Friday, and every man crept unto it that was then in the church; after which it was hung up again within the said image. And every principal day the said image was opened, that every man might see pictured within the Father and the Son and the Holy Ghost, most curiously and finely gilt; and both the sides within very finely varnished with green varnish, and flowers of gold, an elegant sight for all beholders.'[7] In the same church was another altar of our Lady of Pity.

Materials.

Statues of our Lady were sometimes made of pure gold; more frequently of silver or silver gilt.

In the preceding chapter I have mentioned the gifts of King Ina to Glastonbury, among which was a statue of silver of St. Mary. This was in the seventh century. In Lincoln in 1536 were several silver statues of our Lady. The principal one is thus described in the Inventory: 'A great image of our Lady, sitting in a chair, silver and gilt with four polls, two of them having arms in the top thereof; having upon her head a crown silver and gilt, set with stones and pearls, and one bee with stones and pearls about her neck, and an ouche depending thereby; having in her hand a sceptre with one flower, set with stones and pearls, and one bird in the top thereof; and her Child sitting upon her knee, with one crown upon His head with a diadem set with stones and pearls; having a ball with a cross, silver and gilt, in His left hand, and at either of His feet a scutcheon of arms.'[8]

In York Cathedral in 1510 was a silver-gilt image of the

---

[7] *Antiquities of Durham*, p. 33.   [8] Dugdale, vol. viii. p. 1279.

Blessed Virgin, seated on a throne, weighing nineteen pounds;
and another, silver gilt, carrying the Divine Child, with a sap-
phire in His hand.   This the hebdomadarius carried every day
to Mass at the high altar.   Its weight was five pounds eleven
ounces.   Also an image of our Lady, of gold, weighing three
and a half ounces.   Also a great image of the Blessed Virgin of
silver gilt, with the Divine Child in her right hand and lilies in
her left.[9]

In Lincoln was also a tabernacle of ivory standing upon four
feet, with two leaves, with an image of our Lady in the middle,
and the Salutation of our Lady in one leaf and the Nativity of
our Lady in the other.   Henry III. left by his will a silver image
of our Lady to the abbey of Westminster, and a gold image to
his son Edward I.[10]

We learn from the Acts of St. Etheldreda, written by a monk
of Ely in 1163, that Abbot Brithnod in the year 970 had made
images of the Blessed Virgin, and had covered them with gold
and silver and precious stones, and that at the coronation of
William the Conqueror these were sacrilegiously stript, and only
the images of bare wood left.

Among the treasures of the shrine of St. Edward at Westminster was an image of the Blessed Virgin in ivory, of precious
workmanship, given by St. Thomas, who had zealously promoted the Confessor's canonisation.   In the churchwardens'
accounts of St. Mary Hill, London, mention is made of 'an
image of our Lady of mother of pearl.'   Most of the statues
were, however, made of alabaster, marble, stone, or wood; and
these were almost invariably, when inside the churches, painted
and gilt, as appears from many legacies in wills and churchwardens' accounts.

Dr. Milman tells us, in his History of the Jews, that 'while
the chancellor and the whole body of the University [of Oxford]
were in solemn procession to the relics of St. Frideswide, they
were horror-struck by beholding a Jew rush forth, seize the
cross which was borne before them, dash it to the ground, and

---

[9] Dugdale, vol. viii. p. 1204.
[10] *Collection of Royal Wills*, by J. Nichols, p. 16.

trample upon it with the most furious contempt. The offender seems to have made his escape in the tumult, but his brethren suffered for his crime. Prince Edward was then at Oxford, and by the royal decree the Jews were imprisoned, and forced, notwithstanding much artful delay on their part, to erect a beautiful cross of white marble, with an image of the Virgin and Child, gilt all over, in the area of Merton College, and to present to the proctors another cross of silver, to be borne in all future processions of the university.'

The images in the churches frequently stood under handsome canopies or tabernacles. In the churchwardens' accounts of Walberswick, co. Suffolk, A.D. 1474, is the following extract from a will: 'I will that my executors do peynte and gylde the tabernakyll of our Lady of Pity at my cost, according to the forme of the image of Seynt Mary of Pity of Southwold;' and again another in 1503: 'I will that my executors doo peynte and gylde the tabernkyll of our Lady of Pity at my cost.' Many such entries occur.

Decorations.

It is certain that the custom prevailed in England, not only of painting but of dressing statues. I have not to discuss questions of taste, but to be a faithful historian. I do not know the antiquity of this custom; but William of Malmesbury, who wrote early in the twelfth century, and who is speaking of former times, says in his History of Glastonbury: 'There is an image of the Blessed Virgin there which remained untouched when a great fire formerly surrounded it and consumed the palls and all the ornaments of the altar, *neither was the veil touched that hung from her head.* But on the face of the statue blisters arose from the heat of the flames, as on the face of a living man, and remained there long, proving to the beholders the divine protection [by which the statue and veil were unconsumed].'

The Anglican Homily on the Peril of Idolatry, which may at least be trusted as a witness, says: 'Our[11] churches stand full of such great puppets, wondrously decked and adorned, garlands

---

[11] By 'our' the writer means Christian. When he wrote all such statues had been destroyed in England.

and coronets be set on their heads, precious pearls hanging about
their necks; their fingers shine with rings set with precious
stones; their dead and stiff bodies are clothed with garments
stiff with gold. You would believe that the images of our men
saints were some princes of Persialand with their proud ap-
parel,' &c.

In a list of ornaments belonging to the church of Holy
Trinity, Milford, occur the following items: 'Coats belonging
to our Lady: A coat for the good days of cloth of tissue bordered with white, and for her Son another of the same in like
case. A coat of crimson velvet, and another for her Son in like
case. A coat of white damask, and another for her Son in like
case, bordered about with green velvet.'[12]

Dr. John London, Cromwell's agent in the suppression of
monasteries in 1538, writes: 'I have pulled down the image of
our Lady at Caversham, whereunto was great pilgrimage. The
image is plated over with silver, and I have put it in a chest
fast locked and nailed up. . . . All these, with the coats of this
image, her cap and hair, my servant shall bring.'[13]

Blomefield, in his History of Norfolk, quotes the following legacy to St. Stephen's, Norwich, in 1509: 'I, Beatrix Kril-
kemer, bequeath to our Lady in the same church my best beads,
to hang about her neck on good days.' Similarly in 1523 Alice
Carre 'gave her coral beads to the beautifying of our Lady in
the feastful days.'[14]

King Henry III.[15] had an emerald and a ruby taken out of
rings left him by the Bishop of Chichester as a legacy, and hung
upon the forehead of a silver statue of our Lady, which Queen
Eleanor his wife had set up in the feretry of St. Edward at
Westminster.

John Carr, of York, in his will (A.D. 1487) says: 'I bewit
my gold ryng with the diamond to hyng aboute the nek of the
ymage of oure Lady yᵗ standes abowne oure Lady altar in the

---

[12] *Notes and Queries*, third series, iii. 179.
[13] *Letters on Suppr. of Mon.* p. 221 (Camden Society).
[14] Vol. iv. pp. 153-4.
[15] Dart's *Antiquities of Westminster*, vol. i. pp. 26-7.

Mynster, where they sing oure Lady Messe. Also I bewit another ryng w^t a ruby and one torcos to hynge aboute oure Lord's nek that is in the armis of the same ymage of oure Lady.'[16]

Agnes Hilyard, widow, by her will (A.D. 1497) leaves ' one old "noble" to be offered for the image of the Blessed Virgin Mary at Beverly, to hang round the neck ; and to the Blessed Virgin at Fisholine 3s. 4d., to buy a mantle for the image ; to the image of the Blessed Virgin at Mollescroft 3s. 4d. in gold, to hang round the neck.'[17]

William Brokshaw, of East Retforth, by his will (1499) leaves a ' serkelett' (circlet ?) gilt and adorned with stones for the image of the Blessed Virgin, in the procession on the feast of Corpus Christi, and on the feast of All Saints, and in the play called *Mankind* (in ludo de Mankynd) and other plays.'[18]

Dame Catherine Hastings leaves (A.D. 1506) 'to our Lady of Walsingham my velvet gown ; to our Lady of Doncaster my tawny camlet gown ; to our Lady of Belcrosse my black camlet ; to our Lady of Himmingburgh a pece of cremell and a lace of gold of Venys sett w^t perle.'[19]

But this devotion was much more ancient than the fifteenth century, since Lady Godiva, before the Conquest, left her circlet of jewels on which she was wont to count her prayers to be hung round the neck of our Lady in Coventry.[20]

Veneration.

Bede speaks of *venerandas imagines.* The very making and. adorning of the images with such care was no doubt a species of veneration. This was testified in other ways also. Sometimes the images were carried in procession. At others our Lady's clients bowed towards her image or knelt before it.

Another practice of veneration was to hang near the statue or to place before it on feast days what were called ex-votos, which were of many kinds.

Henry VII., as we learn from his will, had a silver statue made of himself in a kneeling posture, to be offered to our Lady

---

[16] *Testamenta Eboracensia*, vol. iv. p. 27 (Surtees Society, 1868).
[17] Ib. p. 133.   [18] Ib. p. 164.   [19] Ib. p. 257.
[20] William of Malmesbury.

of Walsingham. Crutches were left hanging up by those who
had recovered the use of their limbs; or representations in wax
of cures effected or desired. Many other examples will be
mentioned in subsequent chapters. But perhaps the principal,
the oldest, and most universal method of testifying veneration
to our Lady was by burning wax tapers or lamps before her images.

One or two examples will suffice to illustrate this subject.

Stevens in his Appendix to Dugdale tells us that at Evesham
' before the altar of St. Mary in the crypt, according to ancient
custom, one lamp ought to burn by day and one cresset by night;
and at every Mass of St. Mary two wax lights to be lighted up.
At the celebration of the Mass of St. Mary [in the church]
twenty-four wax lights ought every day to burn. Of these the
sacrist finds six, the seneschal one, and the altar-keeper all the
rest. At the same Mass there ought also thirty-three lamps to
be lighted up, which lamps the altar-keeper is to supply.'

The keeper of our Lady's chapel in Westminster Abbey, says
Dart, was to see that on the Assumption and Purification of
the Virgin Mary twenty lamps and fifty tapers should be placed
in the hands of statues of saints. In this chapel hung a lamp
night and day; and afterwards Ralph de Gloucester hung two
there upon an iron rod, which Henry III. removed, and ordered
a wax taper to burn instead of them.[21] Such details could easily
be multiplied from the chronicles of all the great churches. And
the smaller ones followed humbly their example.

By the churchwardens' accounts of St. Mary Hill, London,
we learn that in 1353 John Causton, mercer, left the rents of
certain tenements for ' one priest and five tapers before the
image of our Lady at the high altar of the Salutation,' &c.

Agnes Complyn, of Wyke, near Winchester, by her will,
1503, bequeathed ' to the light before the crucifix in that church
twenty pence, to the light of the Blessed Mary three ewe sheep,
and to St. Christopher's light six ewe sheep.'[22]

Cattle were often thus left, and the churchwardens fed and
sold them to maintain the luminary of the church.

---

[21] Dart's *Antiquities of Westminster*, vol. ii. pp. 4, 5.
[22] *Journal Brit. Arch. Assoc.* 1863, p. 200.

William de Chepmanslade, Vicar of Wells, in his will, A.D. 1311, leaves 'to his brother Geoffry his tenement in Wells, he to maintain two wax torches at the elevation of the Body of Christ at the great altar in the church, and forty pence for the light of the Blessed Mary, where "Salve Sancta Parens" is sung, behind the great altar.'[23]

Matthew Paris relates of William, twenty-second abbot of St. Alban's, many acts of devotion to our Lady. I will give them in his own words: 'In his time provision was made by Walter of Ramsey, that two wax candles should burn every day while the Mass of the Blessed Virgin is sung without music—viz. for the Church.[24] And that Mass is sung always with the golden chalice and its own vestment, and four lighted tapers, two of which—viz. those toward the east—were acquired by Adam the Cellarer.

'This abbot also, seeing that in all the great churches of England the Mass of the Blessed Virgin is daily sung solemnly with music (*ad notam*)—though in our church, what is not done in others, every Saturday, unless there is a reasonable obstacle, there is a solemn commemoration of the Blessed Virgin through the whole day and night in white vestments—he decreed, with the consent of the whole convent, that in future every day the Mass of the Blessed Virgin should be sung solemnly to music, six monks every day being appointed to minister; and he appointed a monk as guardian of the altar and all belonging to it.

'Also a special and beautiful bell was appointed for calling to the Mass at this altar. Also he presented a new image of Mary (*Mariola*) to the church, and had the old one placed over the altar where the Mass of the Blessed Virgin is sung to music.

'He also appointed that the taper, which we are accustomed to wreathe about with flowers, should be burnt before the beautiful image (*nobilem Mariolam*) both day and night on the principal feasts, and during the procession which takes place on the commemoration of our Lady.

'He also had a Psalter splendidly bound and fixed to a read-

---

[23] *App. to Third Report of Historical* MS. *Commission*, p. 361.
[24] 'Decantatur sine nota, videlicet pro Ecclesia.'

ing-desk before this altar and image, for the constant use of the brethren praying there.'

The same Matthew Paris relates the following history, which illustrates the devotion on which I am writing : ' In the year 1225, Count William of Salisbury,[25] who had fought beyond the seas, entered ship to return to England. After having tossed about for many days and nights, when all despaired of life, he cast into the waves his precious rings and gold and silver and rich dresses, that he might pass into his heavenly country as poor as he had entered his earthly country. And when all seemed desperate, a large taper shining brilliantly was beheld by all at the top of the mast, and a most beautiful Lady standing beside it protected the light from wind and rain. At this they all took courage ; but while the rest did not understand what the vision portended, Count William assigned the grace to the Blessed Virgin Mary ; for from the day when he first put on the military belt he had maintained a taper before the altar of the Blessed Mother of God, that it might burn continually at the Mass which every day is sung together with the canonical hours in honour of the Blessed Virgin. Next day they were driven on an island, and after some time reached England.'[26]

Many critics will be filled with scorn at him who wrote and him who practised such things. I will merely remark that when such scorners shall have attained to the veneration for the majesty of God and the sense of earthly nothingness which made William Longespée cast away all worldly goods that he might go more humbly into the presence of his Judge, then they will probably think differently on such matters, and, instead of passing censure, they will be more inclined to light a taper themselves before our Lady's statue for having obtained for them such precious graces from her Son.

Controversies.

In the fourteenth century the followers of Wickliffe accused

---

[25] This was William Longsword, or Longespée, natural son of Henry II. by Rosamond Clifford, a knight equally brave and devout. His son too inherited both his valour and his piety. See Bentley's *Excerpta Historica*, pp. 341, 671.   [26] Mat. Paris, *Hist. Major.* p. 325, ed. Wats.

the Catholic multitude, and even the Catholic Church herself, of the grossest idolatry, principally on account of the veneration shown to images. The accusation was renewed in, if possible, more unmeasured language by the Reformers of the sixteenth century, and even to the present day is repeated in books and sermons. Catholics, however, are not easily terrified at such clamour. Our Lord prepared them to expect reproach and calumny. He committed His doctrine and discipline to His Church, with which He promised to be present till the end of time; and His Apostle warns us not to be moved from our allegiance to that doctrine thus received from lawful pastors, though an angel from heaven should teach differently. But, said very truly our old English theologian, Thomas Netter, in this case our faith is not tried by an angel from heaven. If we distrust the Catholic Church on account of her veneration of sacred images, it will be necessary to believe that the truth of doctrine and the purity of worship, which were unknown to her, were the common possession of God-forsaken Jews, of the impious and sensual followers of Mahomet, of the obscene and furious Greek Iconoclasts, and of the obscure and fanatical sects of Cathari, Albigenses, Waldenses, and Lollards.[27] This argument has lost nothing of its force since. A Catholic has not to do violence to his own feelings in order to decide that in such a matter William of Wickham and John Fisher were more likely to be right than Hugh Latimer and Thomas Cranmer; Sir Thomas More than Thomas Cromwell; St. Francis of Sales, the author of *L'Etendard de la Croix*, than Bishop Jewel, the reputed author of the Homily on Peril of Idolatry.

The veneration of images in the Catholic Church is a matter so perfectly harmless in practice, and so extremely simple in theory, that nothing but heated passions could have succeeded in making it into the monstrous thing which it is sometimes represented. What those passions were we may read in the history of the Greek Iconoclasts and of the Protestant Reformation. At the outbreak of this last movement, when the Duke of Somerset ordered the removal of all images from churches

[27] Thomas Waldensis, *Doctrinale Fidei*, cap. cl.

T

in the first year of Edward VI., Gardiner, Bishop of Winchester,
who had gone along with the Reformation hitherto, denying
the Pope's supremacy under Henry, and even yielding in many
other points, began now at last to recoil from the work of destruction. He wrote several letters to the Protector Somerset,
and to others, which are given in Foxe. Though he advances
many able arguments for the use of images, I here allude to
him only for the honest defence he makes of the simple Catholic
people.

'There is forbidden,' he writes to Ridley, 'by the second
Council of Nice *cultus divinus*, and agreeth with our aforesaid
doctrine, by which we may creep before the cross on Good
Friday, wherein we have the crucifix in honour, and use it in a
worshipful place, and so earnestly look on it, and conceive that
(which) it signifieth as we kneel and creep before it whilst it
lieth there, and whilst that remembrance is in exercise. With
which cross, nevertheless, the sexton, when he goeth for a
corpse, will not be afraid to be homely, and hold it under his
gown while he drinketh a pot of ale—a point of homeliness
which might be left; but yet it declareth that he esteemed no
divinity in the image. But ever since I was born, a poor parish-
ioner, a layman, durst be so bold, at a shift (if he were also
churchwarden), to sell to the use of the church at length, and
his own in the mean time, the silver cross on Easter Monday
that was creeped unto on Good Friday. In specialities there
have been special abuses; but generally images have been taken
for images, with an office to signify a holy remembrance of
Christ and His saints. ... An image hath no worship of itself,
but remaineth in its nature of stone or timber, silver, copper, or
gold; but when it is in office, and worketh a godly remembrance in us by representation of the thing signified unto us, then
we use it worshipfully and honourably. ... And if we may not
contemn the images of Christ and His saints when we have
them (for that were villany), nor neglect them (for that were
to have them without use, which were inconvenient), we must
have them in estimation and reputation, which is not without
some honour and worship, and at the least in the place where

we conveniently use them, as in the church, as where they serve us rather than we them.'

To a Captain Vaughan, who, as a justice of the peace, had lent his sanction to a riot in which images had been destroyed at Portsmouth, Gardiner writes : ' I would use preaching ; but to a multitude persuaded in the opinion of destruction of images I would never preach. For (as Scripture willeth us) we should • cast no precious stones before hogs. Such as be infected with that opinion, they be hogs, and worse than hogs (if there be any grosser beasts than hogs be), and have ever been so taken. . . . It is a terrible matter to think that this false opinion conceived against images should trouble any man's head ; and such as I have known vexed with that devil (as I have known some), be nevertheless wonderfully obstinate in it ; and if they can find one that can spell Latin to help forth their madness, they be more obdurate than ever were the Jews, and slander whatsoever is said to them for their relief.'

Gardiner's testimony to the innocent nature of the venera-tion of images by the Catholic multitude may be suspected by some, and his account of the destroyers of images may seem exaggerated ; but it must be remembered that he was an eye-witness of the conduct of both, and he occupied that position between the two which left him quite free to judge and to side with either. He calls the iconoclasts ' hogs,' and he testifies that they were such in the rest of their conduct. ' The pretence is of the spirit, but all is for the flesh—women and meat—with liberty of hand and tongue, a dissolution and dissipation of all estates.'[28] And it will hardly be contended that they were spiritual men, or that it required any spiritual insight to under-stand the Reformers' declamations against images. They were just such sophisms as are fitted to the capacity of the most brutal and ignorant men. The mobs of Constantinople in the eighth century, who wreaked their fury on images ; the mobs of London in the sixteenth, or those of Paris in the eighteenth ; were these animated by zeal against superstition and idolatry ? or were they not, as Gardiner says, the victims of a species of blind madness and diabolical possession ?

[28] Gardiner to Somerset, May 21, 1547.

They were goaded to their deeds of violence by misapplied texts of Scripture. The principal of these was the command, ' Thou shalt not make to thyself any graven image,' &c. But here let me remark, that Wickliffe and the Lollards did not accuse Catholics, as so many Protestants do, of omitting this command from the Decalogue. One of the first who invented this calumny was Sir Henry Spelman, in his notes to some Anglo-Saxon canons. He pretends that these words were purposely omitted by the clergy, because they were conscious that they were violating them by the worship of images, which they encouraged. This accusation has since become one of the commonplaces of controversy. As the matter regards our English forefathers, and touches their character not only for religion but for veracity, I may be allowed a few words of explanation and defence.

The ' ten words' of the Law are given both in Exodus and Deuteronomy; but we are left to our own conjectures on the subject of their division. The method of division which has prevailed in the Catholic Church is that adopted by St. Augustin and St. Thomas, and it seems best to suit the subject-matter. The first commandment forbids us to have any God but the one true God. The words which follow, ' Thou shalt not make to thyself any graven image,' &c., are by English Protestants accepted as a distinct commandment, but by us are understood to be merely a development and explanation of what has preceded; because the violation of them would involve a sin against the first commandment, and not a sin of a different species.

But· if all these words are united in one precept, how are there ten commandments, and not rather nine? In this way: as Protestants divide the first commandment of Catholics into two, so also Catholics divide into two the Protestant tenth commandment. To covet a man's wife is an utterly different *kind* of sin from that of coveting his house or his cattle. Hence ' Thou shalt not covet thy neighbour's wife' is with Catholics the ninth commandment, and ' Thou shalt not covet thy neighbour's goods' is the tenth. This arrangement changes the order assigned to the intermediate commands; so that what is the third to Protestants is the second to Catholics, and so on for the rest. The Catholic arrangement, besides that it divides the words according to the subject-matter, has in its favour the fact, that in this way the ninth commandment ('Thou shalt not covet thy neighbour's wife') corresponds with the sixth ('Thou shalt not commit adultery'); and the tenth ('Thou shalt not covet thy neighbour's goods') with the seventh ('Thou shalt not steal'); and there seems to be equal reason for distinguishing interior sins as external acts.

Thus far no sensible Protestant would blame us, even if he differed in opinion. Let me now go a step farther.

It has been a common custom in all times and nations to abridge the commandments, in order to facilitate their committal to memory. For this purpose verses or rhymes have been often introduced. Catholics then, thinking as they do that the words 'Thou shalt not make to thyself any graven image,' &c. are merely an explanation of the words that have gone before, and that such development was rendered especially necessary only to the Jews, who lived amidst idolatrous nations, have frequently omitted these altogether when the Decalogue has been given in abridgment.

If, now, our opponents had accused our forefathers of indiscretion in omitting what was very important for Christians as well as for Jews, a controversy would have arisen on a fair ground; but to accuse them of deliberately omitting a whole commandment, in the consciousness that they were themselves violating it, and because they wished to make others violate it, is to be guilty of 'bearing false witness.' To make clear the full malice of this accusation, I will give some examples of the abridgments of the Decalogue of which I have spoken.

Robert of Sorbonne, a Catholic theologian of the thirteenth century, has left the following lines in a treatise on confession:

'Sperne deos, fugito perjuria, sabbata serva,
Sit tibi patris honor, sit tibi matris amor.
Non sis occisor, fur, mœchus, testis iniquus,
Vicinique thorum, resque caveto suas.'[29]

Here the whole of the first commandment (or the first and

[29] Bib. Max. Patr. (Lug.), tom. xxv. p. 351.

second of Protestants) is reduced to the words 'sperne deos,' 'despise gods.' It is quite open to Protestants to find fault with these verses, or to complain of their too great conciseness. Taken literally, Robert would teach us to despise *all*, gods; but it is evident he was composing a 'memoria technica,' and supposes that ample information is possessed by his Christian readers, both with regard to the true God, whom they are to worship, and as to the false gods, or idols, which they are to despise. Yet, for making such an abridgment as this, the crime has been imputed of tampering with God's Word.

Let me now give a Protestant compendium. I find one to my hand, composed by Dr. Watts, a Nonconformist divine of some renown. He writes as follows:

> 'Adore no god beside Me, to provoke Mine eyes,
> Nor worship Me in shapes and forms that men devise.
> With reverence use My name, nor turn My word to jest;
> Observe My Sabbath well, nor dare profane My rest.
> Honour and due obedience to thy parents give,
> Nor spill the guiltless blood, nor let the guilty live;
> Preserve thy body chaste, and flee th' unlawful bed;
> Nor steal thy neighbour's gold, his garment, or his bread;
> Forbear to blast his name with falsehood or deceit;
> Nor let thy wishes loose upon his large estate.'

In these lines there is much that is open to fair criticism. It was bold of the doctor to interpolate the words, 'nor let the guilty live,' which are assuredly a very wide paraphrase of the words 'Thou shalt not kill.' But that which a Catholic would still more object to is his rendering of the words of Deuteronomy, 'Thou shalt not covet thy neighbour's wife, nor his house, nor his field, nor his man-servant, nor his maid-servant, nor his ox, nor his ass, nor anything that is his.' All this Dr. Watts calls simply 'his large estate.' There seems, indeed, no reason why field and house, ox and ass, and even man-servant and maid-servant, should not be called estate, since it is the service, not the person, of the servants which is in question. But is the wife also a chattel? Does the large estate include her also?

These are fair questions to put to Dr. Watts, or to all Protestants who class the wife with ox and ass. But to act towards Protestants as they have acted towards Catholics, I should accuse Dr. Watts of deliberately suppressing one of the commandments—of deliberately crushing two commandments into one, in order that, by afterwards pretending to make an abridgment, he might leave out the word ' wife' altogether. I should accuse him of this, and I should impute to him the motive that he was living in habitual adultery, and that he was anxious to encourage his Nonconformist brethren to commit adultery, and that therefore he consciously tampered with the Word of God, which forbade the crime.

This would be precisely a parallel charge to the one invented by Sir Henry Spelman, copied by Wilkins and Burnet, and repeated in ten thousand books up to the present day. Would Protestants like us to treat them as they habitually treat us?

And yet this is not all. Several twelfth-century writers, such as Hoveden, Simeon. of Durham, Wendover, and others, in almost identical words tell us that, in 792, Charlemagne sent to the English bishops the decrees of the second Council of Nice, in which, say these writers, ' many things unseemly, and, alas, contrary to the true faith, were found ; especially since it was decreed by the unanimous consent of all the Oriental doctors, being not less than three hundred bishops, that images ought to be adored, a thing which the Church of God altogether execrates.'

Mr. Soames and others have caught eagerly at this testimony. They have drawn from it the most fantastic conclusions—viz. that the Anglo-Saxon bishops of the eighth century ' set at open defiance the Pope's authority,' and that they repudiated the image-worship which in later times defiled the English Church.

Into the controversy itself about the deutero-Nicene decrees, and their temporary rejection in the West, I need not enter. It is sufficient to remark that the writers of the twelfth century—whether mistaken or not as to the fact they report[30]—all declare that the Church of their own day execrated image-worship, and they all believed that in this the Church of the twelfth century was in perfect agreement with that of the eighth. They knew

[30] On this question Dr. Lingard's *Anglo-Saxon Church*, vol. ii. p. 115, and note G in Appendix, should be consulted.

nothing of any change of practice since the days of their forefathers.

Now no one can doubt that, in the twelfth century, image-
worship had attained all the development it ever received in
England. The fair conclusion would therefore be, that those
who thus wrote lived in the sincerest persuasion that their
veneration of images was both innocent and primitive, and that
it never even occurred to them that it was the worship forbidden
by the first (or second) commandment. And yet these men,
who tell us how their Church altogether execrates the worship
of images, are the very men who are accused by Protestants of
suppressing a commandment with a guilty conscience.

One more specimen I may give of rancorous malignity (it
can be called by no milder name) in these accusations against
our Catholic forefathers. There was a book called *Liber Festivalis*, used by Catholics before the Reformation. It contained
sermons for festivals, and was written for the use of priests, as
a manual from which they might teach their people. In one of
these sermons the writer says : ' Men should learn by images,
whom they should worship and follow in living. To do God's
worship to images every man is forbidden. Therefore, when
thou comest to the church, first behold God's Body under the
form of bread upon the altar ; and thank Him that He vouchsafe to come from the holy heaven above, for the health of thy
soul. Look thou upon the cross, and thereby have mind of the
passion He suffered for thee. Then on the images of the holy
saints ; not believing on them, but that by the sight of them
thou mayest have mind on them that be in heaven, and so to
follow their life as much as thou mayest.'[31] Who would not

---

[31] In the *Book of Curtesy*, published by the Early English Text Society, is the following instruction for children :

    ' When ye come to the church, my little child,
    Holy water ye shall upon you cast ;
    Before the cross with cheer both meek and mild
    Then kneeleth down, and knocketh on your breast ;
    Thanking the Lord that on the cross did rest,
    And there for you suffered His heart to bleed ;
    Seyth or ye rise Pater, Ave, and a Crede.'

have thought that a Protestant would have rejoiced to find so clear a testimony that the proper use of images was well understood before the Reformation, and that the accusations he had heard were not to be trusted? Yet Strype, after quoting the above passage from the *Liber Festivalis*, can only make the following commentary: 'Here we may observe with some wonder, how no countenance is here given to worship images, the great practice of the Popish Church; but the clear evidence of the second commandment struck some awe on the writer's mind, that he dared not, in the face of the commandment, exhort to that which was so plain a breach of it.'[32]

'He dared not'! Mark the malice of the words, meaning he would gladly have done it, had he had the courage. Strype at least is more bold, for he dares, in the face of evidence to the contrary, to renew the old calumny. Pipe to these men and they will not dance, mourn to them and they will not weep. Their minds are made up. Catholics shall be foul idolaters, whatever books or facts may say.

From these specimens of controversial unfairness it will be seen that Bishop Gardiner did not exaggerate when he said: 'Such as are vexed with that devil' (the image-hating devil) 'be nevertheless wonderfully obstinate, . . . and slander whatsoever is said to them for their relief.'

On the scriptural arguments against the use or veneration of images I will here say nothing. Those who wish to know the answers given by Catholics to such texts of Scripture and passages of the Fathers as are usually quoted may consult our theological treatises and books of controversy.[33] I have said enough to

---

A Greek of the thirteenth century thus accuses the Latins: 'When they enter the holy temples they fall prostrate on their faces, and first murmur something; then rising on one finger they kiss the cross, and having finished their prayers then rise, and do not kiss the sacred images. They call the holy Mother of God only Holy Mary' (Bib. Max. tom. xxvii. p. 608). Poor Catholics! accused by Greeks of insufficient devotion to our Lady and her images, accused by Protestants of too much!

[32] Strype, *Eccles. Mem.* vol. i. p. 221.

[33] No one has written more profoundly than our English theologian Thomas Waldensis, in his treatise, *De Cultu Imaginum*, against the Lollards.

explain the practices of our forefathers, and enough, I trust, to justify them to men of good-will. I will add one more extract to show the doctrine taught in England previous to the Reformation.

In the book called *Dives and Pauper*, printed in 1493, occurs the following passage : ' On this manner, I pray thee, read thy book,[34] and fall down to ground, and thank thy God that would do so much for thee, and worship Him above all thing ; not the image, not the stock, stone, nor tree, but Him that died on the tree for thy sin and thy sake. So that thou kneel, if thou wilt, before the image, not to the image. Do thy worship afore the image, not to the image. Make thy prayer before the image, not to the image. For it seeth thee not, heareth thee not, understandeth thee not. Make thine offering if thou wilt before the image, but not to the image. Make thy pilgrimage not to the image nor for the image (for it may not help thee), but to him that the image representeth to thee. For if thou do it for the image, or to the image, thou doest idolatry.

' *Dives.* Methinketh that when men kneel before the image, pray and look on the image with weeping tears or knock their breasts, with other such countenance, they do all this to the image, and so weeneth much people.

' *Pauper.* If they do it to the image, they sin greatly in idolatry, against reason and kind [*i.e.* nature]. But as I said before, they may do all this before the image and not to the image.

' *Dives.* How might they do all this before the image and not worship the image ?

' *Pauper.* Oft thou seest that the priest in the church hath his book before him. He kneeleth, he stareth [*i.e.* looks fixedly], he looketh on his book, he holdeth up his hands, and for devotion, in case [*i.e.* it may be], he weepeth and maketh devout prayers. To whom, weenest thou, the priest doth all this worship ?

' *Dives.* To God, and not to the book.

' *Pauper.* On the same manner should the lewd man [*i.e.* the

[34] *i.e.* the crucifix, which he had just called the layman's book.

ignorant] use his book, that is imagery and painture, not to worship the image, but God in heaven, and saints in their degree.

'*Dives.* This example is good, but knowest thou any better?

'*Pauper.* When the priest saith his Mass at the altar, commonly there is an image before him, and commonly it is a crucifix, stone, or tree portrayed.

'*Dives.* Why more a crucifix than any other image?

'*Pauper.* For every Mass-singing is a special mind-making of Christ's passion. And therefore he hath before him a crucifix to do him have the more fresh mind, as he oweth to have, of Christ's passion.

'*Dives.* The skill is good; say forth.

'*Pauper.* Before this image the priest sayeth his Mass, and maketh the highest prayers that holy Church can devise, for salutation of the which and of the deed he holdeth up his hands, he louteth, he kneeleth in case, and all the worship that he can do he doth. Overmore, he offereth up the highest sacrifice and the best offering that any heart can devise, that is Christ, God's Son of heaven, under form of bread and wine. All this worship doth the priest at the Mass before the image, and yet I hope that there is no man nor woman so lewd [*i.e.* ignorant] that he would say that the priest singeth his Mass, nor maketh his prayer, nor doth his worship, nor offereth up God's Son Christ Himself to the image.

'*Dives.* God forbid that any man or woman should say so or believe. That were error most of all errors.

'*Pauper.* On the same manner should the lewd man do his worship before the image,' &c.

CHAPTER IX.

PILGRIMAGES AND MIRACLES.

PERHAPS no Catholic practice excited more opposition among the Reformers of the sixteenth century than that of making pilgrimages to sanctuaries. The outcry arose principally from certain preachers, such as Latimer, who had no objection to behold a great confluence of people towards their own pulpits, even to the neglect of neighbouring churches, but who pined with envy if they saw their own parishioners or auditors go away to offer prayers at a sanctuary of our Lady. The cry of 'superstition' was gladly caught up by the courtiers of Henry VIII. and Edward VI., who grew rich on the plunder of those famous shrines. Then, to justify the spoliations, arguments were eagerly collected against the veneration of one place above another, and the whole subject of sanctuaries and pilgrimages has long since become one of the battle-fields of controversy.

In this controversy I have no wish to engage, except as an historian. I will give a slight sketch of English pilgrimage, with some account of the objections urged by the Lollards of the fourteenth and fifteenth centuries, and the answers they then received.

History of Pilgrimage.

No one can have the most limited acquaintance with the writings of the Fathers of the fourth century without having observed the peculiar reverence then paid by Christians to the memorials or sanctuaries of the martyrs. The writings of St. Jerome, St. Augustin, St. Ambrose, St. Chrysostom abound with illustrations and commendations of this spirit. ' Do you wish to know, O Paula and Eustochium,' writes St. Jerome to those ladies, ' how the Apostle describes the peculiarities of each province, and how even to our own day the vestiges remain of those virtues or errors remarked by him? The faith of the Roman people was the theme of his praise ("I give God thanks," writes St. Paul, "... because your faith is spoken of in the whole world"—Rom. i. 8). And now in what other place is there such an eager concourse to the churches and to the tombs of the martyrs? Where else does the Amen so resound like the thunder of heaven, till the empty temples of the idols are shaken by the sound from the neighbouring Christian churches? Not that the Romans have a different faith from that of all the churches of Christ; but among them devotion is greater and simplicity of faith more perfect.'[1]

After quoting this and other passages of the Fathers, an English writer of the fifteenth century, Thomas Netter, or Waldensis, exclaims: 'What wonder, then, if the Romans drew to themselves pilgrims from the whole world, to be strengthened by witnessing their faith and zeal?'[2] On few countries was this influence exercised more powerfully than on England. The spirit of pilgrimage in England is coeval with Christianity. St. Jerome and St. Chrysostom in the fourth century, Palladius and Theodoret in the fifth, testify to the pilgrimages made by the Britons to Rome and to Jerusalem.[3]

No sooner had St. Alban shed his blood for the faith than his tomb became a British pilgrimage. Constantius, writing in the fifth century, tells how St. Germanus, having suppressed the Pelagian heresy in Britain, A.D. 429, 'hastened to blessed Alban to return thanks *through the martyr* to God, the author of their victory; and Germanus, who carried with him relics of all the Apostles and of various martyrs, having made his prayer, commanded the tomb to be opened, and laid up in it these precious gifts, taking with him, however, in exchange earth stained with the martyr's blood.'[4]

The Anglo-Saxons were still more remarkable for their love

---

[1] S. Jerome, in *Ep. ad Gal.* l. ii. in prolog.
[2] Thomas Wald. *Doctrinale Fidei*, l. iii. p. 818.
[3] See the passages quoted by Haddan and Stubbs, *Councils*, vol. i. pp. 10-14.   [4] *Vita Germ.* i. 25.

of pilgrimage. The road between England and Rome became thronged.[5] But their veneration for the tomb of our Lord in Jerusalem, or the tombs of the holy Apostles in Rome, did not make them neglect the sanctuaries bequeathed to them by the British Church, as St. Alban's and our Lady's Church at Glastonbury, nor the places which now became famous amongst themselves by the belief that Mary had chosen them in preference to others.

Writers who wish to justify their own dissensions by imagining similar jealousies in former times have pretended that the Norman conquerors slighted the Saxon saints. The charge is utterly without foundation. It was at the request of Lanfranc that the lives of his predecessors, St. Odo and St. Dunstan, were written; and the Anglo-Saxon sanctuaries of the Blessed Virgin continued famous until the Reformation, notwithstanding that many more grew up to share their honours between the twelfth and sixteenth centuries.

It is impossible to give any account of the degree to which the custom of making pilgrimages prevailed in the four centuries before the Reformation in England. Some notion of it may be formed from the account which will be given in the next chapter of our Lady's sanctuaries; though it must be remembered that these only made a part of the places of pilgrimage in England.

I will give one fact. The Consuetudines of Hereford Cathedral, drawn up in 1250, make provision for pilgrimage just as we do for excursions and visits to the seaside in the summer. If a canon began residence at the beginning of the year he might make one pilgrimage that year, but not so if he only began residence at Easter.

The periods of absence allowed were as follows: for a pilgrimage in England, three weeks; to St. Denis at Paris, seven weeks; to Rome or to St. James at Compostella in Spain, sixteen weeks; to St. Edmund's in Pontigny, eight weeks; to Jerusalem, one year.

[5] It is enough to allude to the lives of St. Bennet Biscop, St. Wilfrid, St. Aldhelm, St. Boniface.

Any canon who has kept residence continually 'may every year have one pilgrimage in England, according to the custom of the Church; but he shall make but one pilgrimage beyond the seas in the whole of his life.'[6]

Theory of Pilgrimage.

Netter, in his defence of pilgrimages against the objections of Wickliffe and his followers, adduces nine reasons why God glorifies one place above another, and thereby draws to it a concourse of suppliants. First, we are vividly reminded of the saint whose bones repose there, or to whom the church is dedicated, and so led to the imitation of his virtues; secondly, our devotion is stimulated to greater fervour; thirdly, we by our congratulations and rejoicing become partakers in the merit of their good works; fourthly, we ask more earnestly, and therefore receive more abundantly, the help of their prayers; fifthly, our charity is inflamed towards the martyrs of God and the God of the martyrs, and our spirit of religion and of zeal increases; sixthly, we endeavour even on earth to make them some compensation for their toils and ignominies; seventhly, we acquire true honour ourselves by our association with these friends of God; eighthly, great graces and even miracles are often obtained in such pilgrimages; and ninthly, the very remembrance afterwards of our visit to a holy place renews our devotion and becomes a lifelong gain.[7] For each of these reasons he adduces testimonies of the early Fathers of the Church. But as the Lollards despised authority and relied on popular objections, Netter examines these one by one.

A priest named Denerose had complained that pilgrimages rob the parish churches to enrich a few famous sanctuaries; and yet, said he, if miracles make these places famous, there is certainly no greater miracle than takes place in every Christian church; 'for the transubstantiation of bread into the Body of Christ, which takes place in parish churches, is a greater miracle than the raising of the dead to life.'

[6] Consuetudines, published in *Archæologia*, vol. xxxi. p. 251.
[7] Thomas Waldensis, *Doctr. Fidei*, tit. xv. cap. cxxxvi. (tom. iii. p. 824).

Let me remark, before giving Netter's answer, that the saints have used a similar argument—not to deter people from pilgrimages, but to induce them to love their own churches. St. Alphonsus writes, in his twenty-second visit : 'The venerable Avila used to say that amongst all sanctuaries he could neither find nor desire a more delightful one than a church in which the most Blessed Sacrament is reserved.' And in the twenty-third visit he says : 'Many Christians submit to great fatigue, and expose themselves to many dangers, to visit the places in the Holy Land where our most loving Saviour was born, suffered, and died. We need not undertake so long a journey, or expose ourselves to so many dangers ; the same Lord is near us, and dwells in the church only a few steps distant from our houses.' But while saying these things, the saint had no thought of decrying pilgrimages ; and his own devotion when visiting Loretto confirms the truth of what our English theologian replies to the objection of Denerose.

Netter answered that miracles may be considered in two ways—either as they are in themselves, or as they affect those who behold them. When our Lord strengthened the limbs of the palsied man, the people 'were astonished, and they glorified God and were filled with fear, saying, We have seen wonderful things to-day' (Luke v. 26) ; and again, when He cast out the devil from the dumb man, 'the multitudes wondered, saying, Never was the like seen in Israel' (Mat. ix. 33). And yet in the presence of Israel the Red Sea had dried up, the manna rained from heaven, God had come down on Sinai, the prophets had raised the dead and cleansed the lepers ; and even at that very time the angel descended yearly into the pool, and cured the sick man who first stepped in from whatever disease affected him. Still this one deed of our Lord caused more stupor to the people, and seemed to them greater. Similarly the multiplication of the loaves to feed the five thousand was in appearance and relatively a greater miracle than the constant and daily feeding of the whole world on the fruits of the earth, springing so wonderfully from their seeds. In this sense also, and in condescension to our weakness, our Saviour said : 'You shall do greater miracles than these that I have done' (John xiv. 12). Yet was any of His followers born of a virgin, or transfigured, or did he rise from the dead? But some of them have done what seemed greater miracles than their Master's; for from their visible nature or unusual appearance they caused greater surprise, more devotion, more faith, and in that sense were greater.[8]

Certainly this first objection was not a very formidable one, though probably enough it was preached and made impression. So, too, Luther began his preaching by very pitiable yet captious sophisms. 'If bells,' he said, 'were rung and candles lighted for the publication of an indulgence, what ought to be done when the Gospel is read?' As if our astonishment on the one hand, or our external honours on the other, are proportioned to the intrinsic excellence of a thing, and not rather to its rarity.

'But,' continued Denerose, 'if this is so, then the smaller churches will be despised and abandoned by the people; and so it may come that Canterbury alone will be the accepted place of God, like the Temple of Jerusalem, and all our small churches must be removed, like the high places of the Jews; and yet by the providence of God the Jewish Temple was destroyed when the Gospel was preached, in order that in all places men might worship God in spirit and in truth.'

Netter replied that there could be no comparison between the 'high places' and our parish churches. If there was any similarity between the Jewish dispensation and that of the Christian Church, then the Temple might represent the cathedrals, the synagogues the parish churches, the gatherings of the prophets and sons of the prophets the monasteries; and then the high places would correspond to the conventicles of the heretics. But in truth sacrifice was forbidden among the Jews, except in the one place selected by God; whereas the Holy Sacrifice and sacraments and all that is most holy in Christianity are to be found in the very humblest of Christian churches equally with the greatest, and such churches may be built everywhere.

[8] Thomas Waldensis, *Doctr. Fidei*, cap. cxxxv.

U

Nor is there any danger of such churches being neglected or despised because of pilgrimages to more famous ones. Did St. Paul despise all the churches which he had visited with Barnabas because he went up to Jerusalem to see Peter? Were the synagogues all forsaken because the people went up to Jerusalem? Did the people of the churches of Ephesus complain because the elders of their churches went to meet St. Paul at Miletus? (Acts xx.) Or the people of Crete because the Apostle summoned their bishop, St. Titus, to come to him at Nicopolis (Tit. iii. 12.) 'Surely,' concluded Netter, 'such subtilties as these you object are like the complaints of jealous women.'

Let me add that, according to the testimony of Foxe, it was the Lollards themselves who derided the parish churches. After railing against the sanctuaries for being preferred to the smaller churches, they began to rail against all churches, as the Albigenses and other sects had done before.

The objections of Wickliffe were of a more subtil nature. They were drawn from the conduct of God rather than that of men. 'It is a heresy of Antichrist,' he said, 'to pretend that Christ is an acceptor of persons or of places as regards the influence of grace.' And again : 'The power of God will not suffer itself to be shut up in such narrow space.'

Netter asked whether it was Antichrist who said to the Apostles, 'Stay you in the city till you be endued with power from on high' (Luke xxiv. 49), or whether the power of God was shut up in the cœnaculum because He chose there to manifest it? God neither shuts up His power in a corner, nor does He shut up His power from a corner, so that it may not there appear and thence diffuse itself. Yet it is free to Him to choose any corner, just as virtue went out from the fringe of Christ's robe to the woman who touched it with faith, while it would not go out from His whole dress to the crowds who pressed upon Him.

As to accepting of places, Christ worked miracles at Capharnaum which He did not work at Nazareth. He does not accept persons, for ' in every nation he that feareth God and worketh justice is acceptable to Him' (Acts x. 25). Yet on the other hand, He does not treat all men in the same way : 'there are diversities of graces, but the same Spirit' (1 Cor. xii. 4). He does not accept places; for 'in every place where men pray, lifting up pure hands' (1 Tim. ii. 8), their worship is acceptable; yet sometimes He bestows graces more liberally in one place than another.

Netter confirms all this by many passages from the Fathers and examples taken from Scripture and the lives of the Saints. But I have abridged, and merely given the substance of this controversy as it stood in the fourteenth and fifteenth centuries.

Let me observe how time has vindicated the spirituality of our forefathers. What derision was poured out on them by the bitter railings of the Lollards and the sarcasms of the Protestant Reformers! Yet 'Wisdom was justified of her children.' When the famous sanctuaries had been levelled with the ground, when Catholics had been driven even from the humble parish churches, when Elizabeth refused, even at the pleading of the French king, to allow them to erect some few chapels in which to worship according to the ancient rites, they did not think themselves unable to worship God or to obtain His graces. They met in private houses to take part, at the risk of fine and imprisonment, in the Holy Sacrifice and to receive the Bread of Life; and when the banished priest had returned and been condemned to death, they purchased the connivance of the jailer, and the squalid dungeon in which the holy confessors were awaiting death became a sanctuary, where Mass was said and heard with a devotion unsurpassed at Canterbury or Walsingham, and where our Lady is reported more than once to have visited and consoled her faithful children.

Practice of Pilgrimage.

But if the theory of pilgrimages can be justified by the theologian, what must the historian say of the practice? On this subject modern English notions are derived almost exclusively from Erasmus and from Chaucer.

Erasmus, in his *Colloquies*, seems to deride pilgrimages, and is often quoted to that purpose. But he has explained himself as only finding fault with their abuse. 'The Colloquy on visit-

ing sacred places,' he writes, ' checks the superstitious and extravagant fancy of certain people, who imagine it the height of
piety to have seen Jerusalem, whither, over such wide distances
of sea and land, run old bishops, leaving their flocks, which
ought to be tended ; thither go men of rank, deserting their
families and their estates ; thither go husbands, whose children
and wives require some guardian of their education and their
modesty ; thither young men and women, not without great
danger to their morals and chastity. Some even go again and
again, and, indeed, do nothing else all their lives ; and all along
the name of religion is given to superstition, love of change,
folly, and rashness.'[9]

Certainly against such abuse of pilgrimages the Saints
would speak much more strongly than Erasmus. St. Boniface,
the Apostle of Germany, who himself made more than one pilgrimage to the tombs of the Apostles, writes to Cuthbert, Archbishop of Canterbury, urging him not to allow women, and
especially nuns, to make pilgrimages to Rome, because of the
dangers which then existed on the road, and of which he had
witnessed many sad examples.

However, as pilgrimages, when Erasmus wrote his *Colloquies* (A.D. 1524), were, as he tells us, greatly fallen into dis-
repute, it would have been better to have exhorted his readers
to behave with prudence and piety than to have kept them
away altogether by ridicule and sarcasm. He certainly forgot,
when he was so zealous that others should stay at home and do
their duty, that he was himself a wanderer from the monastery
where he had made profession ; and that even if this could be
justified by any dispensation, yet his peregrinations about
Europe were assuredly undertaken from no higher motives than
those of the pilgrims.

But it is to Chaucer's *Canterbury Tales* that we must attribute the antipathy (in a religious point of view) entertained
towards the pilgrimages of our forefathers. And indeed, if the

---

[9] From his defence, called *De Utilitate Colloquiorum,* translated by
Mr. Nichols, in his edition of the *Pilgrimages to Walsingham and Canterbury,* Introd. p. xx.

generality of pilgrims were like most of those depicted by Chaucer, and if they spent their time on the road in no more profitable manner than in relating obscene stories such as Chaucer puts into the mouths of some of them, then there was good call for the lash of the satirist as well as for the exhortations of the pulpit and the warnings of the confessional. But is there really any ground for thinking that Chaucer's picture represents the real state of things? It will be answered that he cannot be supposed to have greatly violated probabilities, since this would have been a literary as well as moral fault. But to this it may be objected that Chaucer is a satirist, and that it is quite sufficient for a satirist to have some ground on which to stand, that his representations may not be altogether devoid of reality; but it would be a violation of common sense to conclude that the types which he selects are of common occurrence. Molière may have copied Tartuffe from real life, but is Tartuffe therefore the representative of French piety in the days of Louis XIV.? Yet this is the mode of reasoning frequently adopted with regard to Chaucer. Each of his characters is erected into a class, and the fictions of a freethinking and licentious poet have more weight than would be granted to the records of a great and impartial historian.

Chaucer, wishing to find a motley group of men and women taken from all classes of society, in order that he might give variety as well as unity to his collection of tales, must have noticed that religion alone could bring together such a group. But it is almost as unreasonable to conclude that the pilgrims in general beguiled the weariness of the road by telling obscene stories, because Chaucer's Miller does this, as it would be to argue that in modern England Protestant pedlars talk metaphysics and pure religion, because Wordsworth in his *Excursion* has chosen to put such discourses in the mouth of his pedlar; or that Eastern sultans invariably lie a-bed in the mornings, listening to stories of fairies and genii, because the compiler of the *Arabian Nights* has adopted this device of stringing tales together. Perhaps Chaucer has observed the probability of things better than the writers just mentioned; but our judgment on that point must be formed from other sources, not from the mere fact of his choice.

If we judge of pilgrimages in England in the olden times by what we read of or see in other countries, we shall conclude that the practice was of immense general benefit, though easily liable to be abused. It is of course impossible to prevent the frivolous, the eccentric, the superstitious, the worldly, the lovers of change and adventure and amusement, from joining themselves to the humble, devout, and sincere in such excursions; and if unable to corrupt the good by their example, they could at least bring discredit on their devotion. It appears even that the numbers of such imperfect pilgrims have sometimes so increased, that the good have been deterred from joining in their company, and at last a pilgrimage has become a disorderly assembly, and has been suppressed by public authority. St. Alphonsus, writing in Italy in the last century, relates the punishment divinely inflicted on an immense concourse of people, who had assembled at a celebrated sanctuary of Mary, but had profaned the feast with dances, excesses, and immodest conduct; and he then 'entreats the clients of Mary to keep away as much as possible from such sanctuaries during festivals, and also, as far as they can, to prevent others from going there; for, on such occasions, the devil gains more profit than the Blessed Virgin derives honour by it. Let those who have this devotion,' he says, 'go at a time when there is no concourse of people.'[10]

So also St. John of the Cross, a century earlier, wrote in Spain in the following terms: ' Very often our Lord grants His graces by means of images in remote and solitary places. In remote places, that the pilgrimage to them may stir up our devotion, and make it the more intense. In solitary places, that we may retire from the noise and concourse of men to pray in solitude, like our Lord Himself. He who goes on a pilgrimage will do well to do so when others do not, even at an unusual time. When many people make a pilgrimage I would advise staying at home, for in general men return more dissipated than they were before; and many become pilgrims for recreation more

[10] *Glories of Mary.*

than for devotion. If faith and devotion be wanting, the image will not suffice. What a perfect living·Image was our Saviour upon earth ! and yet those who had no faith, though they were constantly about Him, and saw His wonderful works, were not benefited by His presence. This is the reason why He did no miracles in His own country.'[11]

All this proves not only the possibility but the existence of abuses, and we have no reason to suppose that the English dif fered in this respect from neighbouring nations. But if they fell into error, they were not without those who rebuked them, and that roundly. A famous Dominican preacher of the fifteenth century, Father Bromyard, says : 'There are some who keep their pilgrimages and festivals not for God, but for the devil. They who sin more freely when away from home, or who go on pilgrimage to succeed in inordinate and foolish love—those who spend their time on the road in evil and uncharitable conversa-tion, may indeed say *peregrinamur a Domino*—they make their pilgrimage away from God and to the devil.'[12]

But, on the other hand, we have no reason to think that such abuses were very frequent, nor could they be any reason for abolishing pilgrimage altogether. It was not indeed on this ground they were attacked by the Reformers, but on religious pretences, as superstitious in their very nature, and when carried out as the Saints would have wished.

It would be well, then, if those who derive all their know-ledge from Chaucer, and who sneer at the profanity or super-stition or false devotion of their Catholic forefathers, would try themselves to strike the balance between the true piety and humble devotion on the one hand, and the worldly vanity and empty formality, on the other, which meet on a Sunday morning in a fashionable Protestant church at the present day. When they have seriously thought over this question, they may then ask themselves whether the amount of imperfect or false piety would justify them in recommending that all such churches should be closed or pulled down, and whether society would be

[11] *Ascent of Mount Carmel,* book iii. ch. xxxiv. Lewis's trans.
[12] *Summa Prædicantium,* Tit. Festa, n. 6.

improved by such a process. They will then know how to judge of the conduct of Henry VIII.

Miracles.

Before giving some slight account of the most famous sanctuaries of our Lady, I must touch on one other subject.

Did not our forefathers show great credulity by believing in miracles worked in these sanctuaries? Was it not indeed the report of miracles which caused the fame of a sanctuary? And did not the priests counterfeit miracles? Was it not the discovery of some shocking impostures that caused public indignation, and the destruction of the places of pilgrimage, under Henry?

No doubt that these questions represent the traditional view of Protestants. Who has not heard of the Holy Blood at Hales proved to be a duck's blood renewed every Saturday? Or of the Rood of Grace of Boxley, of which the machinery was exposed to view before it was burnt at Paul's Cross?

Yes, these things are copied by author after author, scarce one of them pausing even for a moment to weigh the evidence. I do not profess to know what documents may exist in our State Papers on these points, but I am also sure that none of our Protestant Church historians know more than myself. As they do not quote original documents, we may suppose they consulted none. They charge Catholics with imposture of the basest kind and with the grossest credulity, and certainly exhibit in their own persons at least the second of these qualities. Since Henry and Edward took the greatest pains to destroy every evidence of miracles, whether true or false, ' so that no memory of the same might remain,' it is perhaps impossible at the present day to clear up these matters and trace the histories to their sources; but it may be safely said, that any one who believes such stories as those of the Blood of Hales or the Rood of Boxley, on such evidence as is yet *in print*, exhibits a credulity *in evil* quite equal to any credulity in good which can be laid to the charge of any monk or peasant in the Middle Ages.

Let me take one of these stories as a specimen; and I do so

because it is invariably referred to by Protestant writers. Green, in his *History of Worcester*, says that ' one of the most atrocious deceptions practised in the worship of images was reserved for public exposure' at Worcester. 'A very large image of our Lady,' he continues, ' held in great reverence, was found, when stript of the veils that covered it, to be the statue of a bishop ten feet high.'[13]

Now here a question occurs at once. Supposing the truth of this story, in what did the ' deception' consist? and why was it so ' atrocious'? If a piece of wood, that has served to represent one object, can be used to represent another, I am at a loss to see the wickedness of the transformation.

But waiving this point, does the account seem probable? Our Lady ten feet high! Well, that is certainly possible, if the statue was raised high above the earth, though there is no authority for placing ' our Lady of Worcester' on the top of a column. We know it stood over the high altar. But a bishop ten feet high changed into an image of the Blessed Virgin! Had he mitre and beard? If so, did the veils conceal the face as well as the body? If he was smooth-faced and fair, like a young girl, how did they know him for a bishop? Certainly the story sounds improbable enough.

What, then, are the authorities? Green quotes three—Burnet's *History of the Reformation*, Collier's *Church History*, and Staveley's *Romish Horse Leech*. I have not thought it worth while to consult the *Horse Leech*, feeling sure he has sucked his venom out of Burnet. Burnet gives no authority, but evidently he has copied from Lord Herbert. Lord Herbert refers in general to ' our records.' Collier does indeed put down in his history what Burnet and Herbert had related, but he has the fairness to remark that the only author quoted by Herbert is untrustworthy. This author is William Thomas; but of our Lady of Worcester Thomas says nothing. Let us, then, look at ' our records.' Among the *Letters on the Suppression of the Monasteries*, published by the Camden Society, there are several which relate to Worcester, yet there is no allusion to this monstrous

[13] Vol. i. p. 96.

image. Again, in 1866, Mr. Noake published a *History of the Monastery and Cathedral of Worcester*, and he had access to all the records preserved in the cathedral, and has made diligent use of them. This historian, after relating how the image was destroyed in 1538 by Cromwell, agent of Henry VIII., says : ' Some of our local historians have handed down a record, or tradition, that this celebrated image, when stripped of the veils that covered it, was found to be a statue of a bishop ten feet high. The truth of this statement has been warmly denied ; and it is evident that the strife of parties was sufficient at that time, not only to distort real facts, but to originate statements entirely false.'[14]

Thus, then, the researches of a candid Protestant—who has carefully examined original documents, and given in his history details of all the images of our Lady in Worcester utterly inconsistent with Lord Herbert's fable—have thrown the charge of ' atrocious imposture' off the shoulders of the monks on to those of their calumniators ; and this famous oft-repeated story of the Lady-bishop, now that it is ' stript of its veils,' turns out to be a mere cock-and-bull story of the ordinary Protestant type.

One of these inventors of falsehood is William Thomas, whose work, called the *Pilgrim*, has been republished by Mr. Froude. It consists of a supposed dialogue between the author and some Italian gentlemen. The following is a specimen :

' Now, quoth I, hearken well unto me in this mine answer against miracles, and you shall hear things of another sort. In time past England hath been occupied with more pilgrimages than Italy hath now.[15] For as you have here our Lady in so many places—di Loretto, di Gracia, &c.—even so had we our Lady of Walsingham, of Penrice, of Islington, ... and so many Holy Roods, that it was a wonder. And here and there ran all the world ; yea, the king himself, till God opened his eyes, was

---

[14] *History of Monastery &c. of Worcester*, p. 534.

[15] The work was written in the time of Edward VI., and the author was clerk of the council to his Majesty, to whom he was also a kind of private tutor.

as blind and obstinate as the rest. And these roods, and these our Ladys, were all of another sort than these your saints be; for there were few of them but that, with engines that were in them, could beckon, either with their heads or hands, or move their eyes, or manage some part of their bodies, to the purpose that the friars and priests would use them.'[16]

And Mr. Froude has thought that he 'was doing useful service in bringing' this stuff 'again before the world.'

Another specimen of Mr. William Thomas's history may interest my readers, and help them to appreciate the nature of the war waged against miracles at the Reformation. It happens fortunately that there are few episodes of English history on which we have so much and such authentic information as on what passed at the death of St. Thomas of Canterbury. The account[17] Mr. William Thomas gave to his Italian friends was that, after the knights had murdered the archbishop, 'incontinently as these gentlemen were departed, the monks of that monastery locked up the church-doors, and persuaded the people that the bells fell on ringing of themselves; and there was crying of " Miracles, miracles !" so earnestly, that the devilish monks, to nourish the superstition of this new-martyred saint, having the place long time separate unto themselves, corrupted the fresh water of a well there with a certain mixture, that many times it appeared bloody, which, they persuaded, should proceed by miracle of the holy martyrdom. And this water marvellously cured all manner infirmities, insomuch that the ignorant multitude came running thither of all lands. Yea, and more; these feigned miracles had such credit at length, that the poor king himself was persuaded to believe them, and in effect came to visit the holy place, with great repentance for his passed well-doing; and for the satisfaction of his sins gave many great and fair possessions unto the monastery of the aforesaid religious. And thus finally was this holy martyr sanctified of all hands. But the king's majesty, that now is dead [Henry VIII.], finding the manner of this saint's life to agree ill with proportion to a very saint, and marvelling at the virtue of this water that healed

[16] *The Pilgrim*, p. 87.   [17] Ib. p. 36.

all diseases, as the blind world believed, determined to have
substantial proof of this thing; and in effect found these miracles to be utterly false. For when the superstition was taken
away from the ignorant multitude, then ceased also the virtue
of this water, which now remaineth plain water, as all other
waters do. So that the king, moved of necessity, could no less
do than deface the shrine that was author of so much idolatry.'

So the explanation of the miracles which were witnessed not
by hundreds, but by hundreds of thousands, from the very day
of the martyrdom till the Reformation, which were testified to
by men the most learned and acute, and which overawed even
Henry II., is that the monks put 'a certain mixture' into some
water which gave it a red colour; and the evident proof that the
bones of St. Thomas, or the water in which his blood had been
mingled, had never worked any real miracles is, that when the
saint's bones had been burnt and the people were forbidden to
mention his name, the miracles ceased! No doubt, as Mr.
Froude says, the English public 'will welcome an opportunity
of seeing the conduct of Henry VIII. as it appeared to an Englishman of more than common ability, who himself witnessed
the scenes which he describes.'[18]

It is necessary to remark that the charges of imposture were
not made until Henry had taken means to destroy all documentary evidence, and the monks who were accused had been
driven forth as wanderers, and would have risked their lives by
a reply. The words 'false miracles,' 'counterfeit miracles,' when
used before that time, did not imply imposture on the part of the
priests, but either false reports among the people, or miracles
worked by the power of the devil. This is an important consideration, and I will offer a few facts in proof.

Wickliffe was a great despiser of miracles, to which he could
lay no claim to confirm his teaching; and the evidence of miracles was strongly urged against him by the defenders of Catholic
doctrine. He did not answer by charging them with imposture;
but he said: 'There is no doubt that miracles are deceptive,
since the devil transfiguring himself into the person of a dead

[18] Mr. Froude's Preface to the *Pilgrim,* p. viii.

man' (the supposed saint), ' or into an angel of light, can work great miracles in the person of a dead man who is damned.'

His opponent, Netter, tells him he would have been a capital agent of the chief priests of the Jews; for if he had succeeded with this theory he would have brought our Lord's resurrection into doubt, and deprived the world of all the fruits of the Apostles' preaching, since the miracles by which they proved His resurrection would have been laughed at.

' You are like those obstinate Jews,' he continues, ' of whom the Psalmist complains with a sigh, "Our fathers understood not Thy wonders in Egypt, they remembered not the multitude of Thy mercies" (Ps. cv. 7). They saw them, as St. Jerome remarks, and yet did not see them. They saw them with the eyes of the flesh, and did not see them with the eyes of the spirit. They saw, but did not understand.' So also Wickliffe understood not the miracles even when he beheld them. He was blinded by his pride.[19]

Netter adds that if Wickliffe despises miracles like Mahomet, it is simply because, like Mahomet, he cannot work them; and like the ancient philosophers, that if he cannot convince others he may at least go on disputing; for, as St. Augustin says, ' All philosophers and all inventors of sects refuted each other with their disputations; yet none passed over to the other side, each persisted in his own opinion. It was an endless strife of contradictory words. Hence when God sent His Apostles to preach He confirmed their words by miracles, and the world was converted.'

When Tyndal, at the beginning of the sixteenth century, revived the errors of Wickliffe, he adopted the same principles with regard to miracles, and systematically depreciated them. Sir Thomas More had appealed to the evidence of miracles in the Catholic Church, and called on the Reformers to show miracles in defence of their innovations. To this challenge Tyndal answers: ' Your doctrine is but the opinion of faithless people, which to confirm the devil hath wrought much subtilty.' ' When we can confound your false doctrine,' he continues,

[19] Thomas Waldensis, *Doctrinale Fidei*, cap. cxxv. vol. iii. p. 773.

'with authentic and manifest Scripture, then need we to do no miracle.' And again : 'Unto them that love not the truth hath God promised, by the mouth of Paul, to send abundance and strength of false miracles to stablish them in lies, and to deceive them and lead them out of the way ; so that they can-·not but perish for their unkindness, that they loved not the truth to live thereafter, and to honour God in their members.'

In answer, Sir Thomas More says: 'God ceaseth no year to work miracles in His Catholic Church, many and wonderful, both for His holy men, quick and dead, and for the doctrine that these heretics impugn, as images, relics, and pilgrimages, and the Blessed Sacrament of the Altar ; *and these so many, and in so many places, that these heretics themselves cannot deny it ;* but are shamefully driven to say, like the Jews, that it is the devil that doeth them.'

One more proof may be given that the charge of imposture was not thought sufficient to meet the evidence in favour of miracles.   There is a kind of poem preserved by Foxe, called the *Fantassie of Idolatry.*   It was written by one of the hangers-on of Thomas Cromwell, to be sung in ale-houses, to bring contempt on the sanctuaries.   It contains the following testimony to facts and explanation of them :

> 'Yet have we thought, that these idols have wrought
> > Miracles in many a place
> Upon age and youth ; when in very truth
> > They were done by the devil's grace.
> For the cursed devil, the master of evil,
> > To get us under his wings,
> Hath such a condition, by God's permission,
> > To work right wonderful things.'

I need scarcely say that Thomas Waldensis and Sir Thomas More were not men to be silenced by such answers as these, and that they could give good rules by which to distinguish between God's miracles and those of the devil. But for this I must refer the reader to their works.   It is sufficiently evident to any one who will take the trouble to inquire, that our forefathers were not the blind fools some moderns suppose, to be juggled by any priest who pulled the strings of a puppet; nor did any one dare to accuse them of such folly while they were alive to reply.

CHAPTER X.

SANCTUARIES AND HOLY WELLS.

In the reign of Edward VI. William Thomas said to his Italian companions: 'In time past England hath been occupied with more pilgrimages than Italy hath now.' Whether there was exaggeration in this statement I cannot say. Certainly England, as it abounded in noble cathedrals, abbeys, and even parish churches, so also did it abound in famous shrines or sanctuaries. These were not all of the Blessed Virgin. St. Edmund at Bury St. Edmund's, St. Thomas at Canterbury, St. John at Beverley, St. Cuthbert at Durham, St. Anne at Buxton, St. Michael at St. Michael's Mount, were invoked by numberless pilgrims. There were also many famous Roods before which men prayed with special fervour and devotion. It is not my purpose to speak of these. The sanctuaries of our Lady St. Mary were most numerous. Of course it is not easy to say what amount of celebrity entitles a church to be called a sanctuary or place of pilgrimage. I will, however, mention several which are spoken of as famous in old documents.

Famous Sanctuaries in England.

Walsingham.

Among all the sanctuaries of our Lady in England, Walsingham seems to have been the most famous in the fourteenth, fifteenth, and sixteenth centuries.

One of our principal sources of information regarding this sanctuary is the *Colloquies* of Erasmus. It has been conjectured that while describing Walsingham he was at the same time satirising Loretto, so that he did not care for literal accuracy when an addition of his own would serve his purpose. However this may be, there are several inaccuracies in his account, so that each detail requires confirmation from other sources. Mr. Gough Nichols has been at much pains in this respect, and from him, as well as from the original authorities, I have collected the following particulars.

Walsingham Parva was a village or small town a few miles from the sea-coast in the north of Norfolk.

The priory of Walsingham was founded between 1146 and 1174, during the episcopate of William, Bishop of Norwich.

It originated with Geoffry de Favarches, who granted to Edwy, his clerk, the chapel which his mother, Richeldis, had built at Walsingham. Edwy was required to institute or bring in a religious order, and the priory was served by regular canons of St. Augustin.

The chapel which Richeldis had built was dedicated in honour of the ever-virgin Mary; but with a reference to a MS. register, Blomefield, the historian of Norfolk, asserts that she built it in obedience to a vision, or that it was intended to represent the holy house of Nazareth.[1]

The date assigned to its first construction is in the reign of St. Edward, but this is evidently erroneous, since Richeldis could not have been then born.

The priory church, constructed at a later date, was 136 paces long, but the Lady Chapel, to judge from Erasmus's account, must have been detached, and at the north side. This was called the New Work. Erasmus says the doors and windows when he visited it in 1511 were open, but whether from some peculiar construction, or because then unfinished, does not appear. This chapel was sixteen yards long and ten wide. Inside it was the wooden chapel which was the real shrine, seven yards and thirty inches long. In this was the famous statue of our Lady of Walsingham. The church or chapel was dedicated in honour of our Lady's Annunciation. The light in the shrine was almost entirely from the candles ever burning there. 'A most grateful fragrance,' says Erasmus, ' meets the nostrils; nay,

---

[1] Weever says the same, and refers to a MS. in the library of Sir Simonds D'Ewes. See *Ancient Funeral Monuments,* p. 573.

when you look in, you would say it was the mansion of the saints, so much does it glitter on all sides with jewels, gold, and silver.'

As the records of the shrine and of all the miracles worked there were destroyed by Henry, we are ignorant how Walsingham first became a place of pilgrimage. It was so at an early date after its foundation.

Among the royal pilgrims to Walsingham we hear of Henry III. in 1241, Edward I. in 1280 and again in 1296, Edward II. in 1315, Edward III. in 1361, David Bruce in 1364, Henry VI. in 1455, Edward IV. in 1469, Henry VII. with the young prince, afterwards Henry VIII. in 1505, Henry VIII. in company with Catharine of Arragon in 1510, and of Catharine in 1513, to return thanks for the victory of Flodden. Henry VII. on the insurrection in favour of Lambert Simnel in 1487 made a pilgrimage thither, and after the battle of Stoke, in gratitude for success, sent his banner to the shrine. By his will he left to it a gold statue of himself. Henry VIII. in 1510 is said to have walked barefoot the last stage of the journey, and he presented to our Lady a necklace of great value, which, alas, twenty-eight years later he sacrilegiously took back.

Though Holinshed wrote fifty years after the destruction of Walsingham, the first road set down in his English Itinerary is that from London to Walsingham, passing through Waltham, Ware, Newmarket, Brandon, and Pakenham.[2] It is still called the Palmer's way and Walsingham Green way, says Mr. Taylor.

Those who came from the North crossed the Wash near Long Sutton and went through Lynn. Another great road was from the East through Norwich and Attlebridge, by Bec hospital, where gratuitous accommodation for thirteen poor pilgrims was provided every night. In many places on the road were chapels, in which the pilgrims as they passed offered their devotions. The most remarkable was our Lady's chapel at Lynn, still in existence.

From the Paston Letters we learn that in 1471 'my lord

[2] Holinshed, p. 247 (ed. 1587).

x

of Norfolk and my lady went to Walsingham on foot.' Sir
Bartholomew Burghersh in 1369 desires that his body may
be buried in the chapel of Walsingham before the image of the
Blessed Virgin. Antony Rivers, Lord Scales, brother-in-law of
Edward IV., leaves a vestment of cloth of gold to this shrine;
and the Countess of Warwick in 1439, 'an image of our Lady
on a table covered with glass.' Lady Elizabeth Andrews sends
a diamond ring at her death in 1474; and Catharine of Arragon
in her will sends a pilgrim to Walsingham, who is to 'dole
twenty nobles on his way thither.' Other instances of devotion
will be found in the course of this work.

Erasmus in 1511 made a pilgrimage to our Lady of Walsingham, and hung up a set of Greek verses, which Mr. Gough
Nichols has translated thus:

The Vow of Erasmus.

'Hail! Jesu's Mother, blessed evermore,
Alone of women God-bearing and Virgin;
Others may offer to thee various gifts,
This man his gold, that man again his silver,
A third adorn thy shrine with precious stones;
For which some ask a guerdon of good health,
Some riches; others hope that by thy aid
They soon may bear a father's honour'd name,
Or gain the years of Pylus' reverend sage.
But the poor poet, for his well-meant song,
Bringing these verses only—all he has—
Asks in reward for his most humble gift
That greatest blessing, piety of heart,
And free remission of his many sins.'

It is to be regretted that the petition with which these
verses conclude was either not more sincere or more lasting. It
certainly appears by Erasmus's own account of his visit to Walsingham, that his intention was to make reflections on the
superstition of others, and to display his own enlightened piety;
and perhaps still more to vaunt his Greek learning, and ridicule
the supposed ignorance of the guardians of our Lady's shrine.

He went again some years later, in company with Colet, Dean of St. Paul's, and their behaviour, according to Erasmus's account, was anything but pious or edifying.

The prior of Walsingham and twenty-one canons subscribed to the king's supremacy in 1534 ; but Blomefield tells us that the sub-prior, George Aysborrow, and sixteen others in 1536 refused subscription, and were condemned and executed for treason. In this same year, 1536, Cromwell's commissioners visited Walsingham, and took possession of it. It is curious that the commissioner, Richard Southwell, was grandfather to Robert Southwell, the Jesuit Father, who in 1595, under Elizabeth, laid down his life for the faith.

The site of the priory was sold for 90*l.* to Thomas Sydney, of Walsingham. The church and priory were destroyed, and at the present day there remains only part of the east end, represented in the woodcut given later on.

As to the famous image, Latimer, who had been made Bishop of Worcester by the influence of Anne Boleyn and of Cromwell, writes to his patron (13th June 1538) from Hartleburg, ' I trust your lordship will bestow our great Sibyll[3] to some good purpose, *ut pereat memoria cum sonitu.* She hath been the devil's instrument to bring many, I fear, to eternal fire. Now she herself, with her old sister of Walsingham, her young sister of Ipswich, with their two other sisters of Doncaster and Penrice, would make a jolly muster in Smithfield.'

The image was, indeed, brought to London, and burnt at Chelsea together with that of our Lady of Ipswich.

It should not be forgotten that just at this time Latimer preached at the execution of Friar Forrest, who was guilty of no crime but refusing to acknowledge the king's supremacy, and that the flames were fed with another famous image brought from Wales for the purpose.

I conclude this account with a pleasing little elegy found in

---

[3] Latimer alludes to the image of our Lady of Worcester, of which I have spoken in chapter ix. Perhaps it was from this expression, ' great Sibyll,' that the story was got up about the giant bishop. The word ' great' evidently means ' famous.'

a MS. of the Bodleian, the author of which is unknown, though
the volume contains a poem by Philip, Earl of Arundel, who
suffered under Elizabeth.   It was first published in the *Gentleman's Magazine :*

Lament of Walsingham.

' In the wrecks of Walsingham
    Whom should I choose
But the Queen of Walsingham
    To be guide to my muse ?

Then, thou Prince of Walsingham,
    Grant me to frame
Bitter plaints to rue thy wrong,
    Bitter woe for thy name.

Bitter was it, O, to see
    The silly sheep
Murder'd by the ravening wolves
    While the shepherd did sleep.

Bitter was it, O, to view
    The sacred vine,
Whilst the gardeners play'd all close,
    Rooted up by the swine.

Bitter, bitter, O, to behold
    The grass to grow
Where the walls of Walsingham
    So stately did show.

Such were the worth of Walsingham
    While she did stand ;
Such are the wrecks as now do show
    Of that so holy land.

Level, level with the ground
    The towers do lie,
Which with their golden glittering tops
    Pierced out to the sky.

Where were gates no gates are now,—
The ways unknown
Where the press of friars did pass
While her fame far was blown.

Owls do shriek where the sweetest hymns
Lately were sung ;
Toads and serpents hold their dens
Where the palmers did throng.

Weep, weep, O Walsingham,
Whose days are nights—
Blessings turn'd to blasphemies,
Holy deeds to despites.

Sin is where our Lady sate ;
Heaven turn'd is to hell ;
Satan sits where our Lord did sway—
Walsingham, O, farewell !'

London.

In the city or neighbourhood of London were several sanctuaries of our Lady.

In his *History of St. Paul's Cathedral* Sir William Dugdale gives the following particulars regarding devotion to our Lady in that church.

Eustace de Fauconbrigge, Bishop of London, about the beginning of the reign of Henry III. (A.D. 1215) assigned lands for the behoof of poor clerks frequenting the quire and celebrating the holy Office of our Lady; so that six clerks should be made choice of every day, with one priest of the quire by turns to be at the celebration of the Mass of our Lady, and also to say Matins and all other canonical hours at her altar.

This foundation was increased by the prior and convent of Thetford in 1299.

The executors of Hugh de Pourte, in 11 Edward II. (A.D. 1317), gave a yearly rent to maintain one taper of three pounds'

weight to burn before it every day whilst her Mass should be
solemnising, and at every procession before the same altar.

This altar was in the Lady chapel.

'But in the body of the church stood the glorious image of
the Blessed Virgin, fixed to the pillar at the foot of Sir John
de Beauchamp's tomb (viz. the second pillar on the south side
from the steeple westwards), before which was a lamp burning
every night by a foundation of John Barnet, Bishop of Bath
and Wells (A.D. 1365). He appointed that after Matins an
anthem of our Lady, sc. *Nesciens Mater*, or some other solemn
one suitable to the time, should be sung before the said image
with a versicle, which being performed, the gravest person then
present to say a collect of the said Blessed Virgin, afterwards
the psalm *De Profundis* for the souls of all the faithful, with
versicle and prayer.'

The oblations of candles and money before this image were
so great, that the Archbishop of Canterbury, Thomas Arundel,
in 1411, had to arbitrate on the disposal of them.

There was another altar of our Lady in what was called the
New Work above the choir, and also an image of our Lady there.
Thomas Hatfield, Bishop of Durham, granted an indulgence of
forty days to all such as, being truly penitent and having confessed their sins, should come thither and say a Paternoster and
an Ave, or make offerings.[4]

In another part of the church our Lady was several times
represented—at our Lord's birth, carrying the Divine Child, and
seated by our Lord's side in glory.[5]

Another famous London sanctuary was the *Church of All-
Hallows, Barking*, still in existence at the east end of Thames-
street, adjoining the Tower. It was called of Barking, as being
dependent on the Benedictine monastery of St. Ethelburga, at
Barking, in Essex. Richard Cœur de Lion in 1190 had built a
fair chapel of our Lady adjoining this church. Newcourt says
it was on the north side, but in a will of the fifteenth century

---

[4] Dugdale's *St. Paul's*, pp. 13-15.
[5] See Wood's *Ecclesiastical Antiquities of London*, pp. 151-2.

I find it mentioned as at the south side.[6] The Rev. J. Maskell feels sure that it was quite detached from the church, and one hundred yards north of the chancel. King Richard's foundation was confirmed and augmented by Edward I. King Edward IV. appointed it to be called the King's chapel, or chantry.

It was most celebrated for the famous image placed in it by King Edward I. The story of this image is related in a document preserved among the archives of the Bishop of London, and has been published by Newcourt.[7] It is so curious that I give a translation :

'To all the sons of Holy Church who shall read these letters, we, Adrian, by divine mercy Bishop of the Tartars, Legate of our Lord the Pope, wish eternal salvation in the Lord.

'We have been given to understand by the illustrious King of England, Edward, son of King Henry, that the chapel in the cemetery of Barking church, London, was wonderfully founded by the mighty Richard, formerly King of England; that the Welsh invaded England, in spite of the resistance of the said Henry, and devastated the country on every side, slaying men, women, and children in their cradles, and, horrible to relate, even women lying in childbirth ; and that they penetrated even to Ely, and took and kept it with an armed force for a whole year, and at length unharmed, when it pleased themselves, they returned to Wales.

'The same Edward, at that time a youth, beholding such ruin and such shame, to the injury of his father and the destruction of the realm, wept bitterly, and conceived such anguish of heart as to cause sickness to his body, so that lying half dead on his bed he despaired of recovery. But one night, after he had devoutly implored the clemency and help of the Mother of God, that she would by some dream or vision teach him how the English might most quickly be revenged on the Welsh, it happened that, while he slept, a most beautiful Virgin, adorned with the flowers of all virtues, viz. the glorious Virgin Mother of God— by whose prayers Christians are helped in their perplexities, and

---

[6] Will of Christopher Rawson, *Test. Eborac.* vol. iv. p. 131.

[7] *Repertorium Ecclesiasticum Parochiale Londinense,* vol. i. p. 767.

who by the operation of the Holy Ghost brought forth the un-
fading and eternal Flower, our Lord Jesus Christ—appeared to
him in a vision, and thus addressed him : " Edward, friend of
God, why do you lament? I am come to your help.   Know,
then, for certain that, while your father lives, the Welsh cannot
be entirely subjugated by the English, and this on account of
your father's vile sin and his great extortions.   But do you go
on the morrow to a certain Jew named Marlibrun, the most
cunning statuary in the whole world, who lives in Billingsgate,
in London ; cause him to make you an image such as you see
me at present.   By divine guidance he shall make thee two
countenances, one resembling my Son Jesus, and the other resembling me, so that no one shall be able truly to discover any
deformity in them.   When the statue is completed, cause it to
be placed in the chapel in the cemetery of Barking church, near
the Tower of London, and cause this to be fairly decorated on
the northern side, and then greater wonders still will occur.   For
as soon as the said Marlibrun shall have looked on these faces
within the chapel, his heart will be turned to love of heavenly
things, and he will be converted, together with his wife, to the
Catholic faith, and he will reveal to you many of the Jews'
secrets, for which they must be punished.   And do you, Edward,
when you behold this miracle, make a vow to the Almighty
God, that as long as you live, and when you are in England,
you will visit five times a year this image in honour of the
Mother of Christ, and that you will keep the chapel in repair
and maintain it, for that place is indeed to be honoured.

"When you shall have made this vow on your knees, you
will be victorious and invincible, and at your father's death you
will become King of England, and conqueror of Wales and the
whole of Scotland.   And believe me, that every just King of
England, or perhaps other monarch, who makes this same vow,
and keeps it faithfully to the utmost of his power, will without
doubt be victorious over the Welsh and the Scots."

' When she had said this she disappeared. The prince awoke,
and remembering his dream, was in an ecstasy of admiration ;
but he did everything as he had been told. And moreover in

our presence, and in presence of many nobles both English and Scotch, the said Edward of his own accord made oath, that up to this time he has found everything come true as told him in his sleep.

'We therefore, wishing the said chapel should be duly honoured and frequented by the faithful, to all who are truly penitent and have made their confession, who shall go to the said chapel for the sake of devotion and prayer, and who shall contribute to the lights, ornaments, or repairs, and shall pray for the soul of the noble Richard, formerly King of England, whose heart is buried in the same chapel under the high altar, and for the souls of all the faithful departed in Christ, the Lord's Prayer and Angelic Salutation, as often as they do it, we grant, trusting in the mercy of God Almighty, and in the merits and authority of the blessed Apostles Peter and Paul, a relaxation of forty days of the penance enjoined to them, provided that the local diocesan approve this our indulgence.

'Given at Northampton,[8] the Parliament being then held there both for England and Scotland, on the 20th day of May, in the year one thousand two hundred and ninety-one.'

Whatever may be the truth about this document[9] this sanctuary was certainly a royal foundation. It was rebuilt by Richard III., and he made provision for a college of priests.

In the privy-purse expenses of Henry VII. there is an entry on the feast of the Purification, A.D. 1503, of 6*s.* 8*d.* as an offering to our Lady of Barking.

That the statue was indeed very beautiful appears from an allusion made to it by Sir Thomas More, who, speaking of the affability of Henry VIII. when young, compares him to the image of our Lady near the Tower, which the citizens' wives could fancy to smile upon them as they prayed before it.

There was, however, another shrine of the Blessed Virgin near the Tower, viz. 'Our Lady of Graces,' at Eastminster or New Abbey, founded by Edward III. in 1349, in consequence of a vow he had made during a storm at sea.

---

[8] This should be Norham, which the transcriber probably mistook for a contraction of Northampton.   [9] On this document see Appendix.

The college of priests at All Hallows was suppressed in 1548, and the ground converted into a garden.

Another London sanctuary was at Muswell-hill. Of this Newcourt says:[10] 'Within the limits of this parish of Hornsey there was in antient time a chappel, bearing the name of our Lady of Muswell, in the place wherof Alderman Roe erected a fair house. The place taketh the name of the well and of the hill —Mousewell-hill—for there is on the hill a spring of fair water, which is now within the compass of the house. Here was sometime an image of our Lady of Muswell, whereunto was a continual resort, in the way of pilgrimage, growing (as it goes by tradition, from father to son) in regard of a great cure which was performed by this water upon a king of Scots, who, being strangely diseas'd, was (by some divine intelligence) advis'd to take the water of a well in England, call'd Muswell ; and after long scrutation and inquisition, this well was found and perform'd the cure. Absolutely to deny the cure (saith Norden) I dare not, for that the High God hath given vertue to waters to heal infirmities (is evident by the Holy Scriptures), as by the cure of Naaman the leper, by washing seven times in Jordan, and by the Pool of Bethesda, which heal'd the next that stepp'd thereinto after the water was mov'd by the angel.'

Willesden and *Muswell-hill* are associated in the minds of Londoners, the one with a junction of railroads, the other with a palace for public amusements. In the minds of our ancestors these two places were famous as sanctuaries of our Lady.[11] Our Lady of Wilsdon is mentioned specially in the Anglican Homily on the Peril of Idolatry, which will probably not prevent my readers saying a 'Hail Mary' when they pass the junction, though their attention may be aroused by the scream of the railway signal, and, not as of old, by the tolling of the Gabriel bell.

Islington was also famous for a sanctuary of our Lady ; but though the name frequently occurs in documents, I have no particulars of any interest to communicate.

[10] *Repertorium Ecclesiasticum Parochiale Londinense*, vol. i. p. 653.
[11] See Northcote's *Sanctuaries of the Madonna* for further information, p. 258.

Westminster. Though there was much devotion to our Lady in the Abbey Church of Westminster, yet there was at no great distance a chapel far more famous, called 'our Lady of the Pue.' There has been much conjecture as to the origin of this title. Mr. Walcott thinks it is derived from the four wells (*les puits*) which were near it. If so, it is strange that it should be called even in French de la Pieu, and in Latin Puia.[12]

The chapel of the Pieu or Pew was on the south side of that of St. Stephen's in the royal palace of Westminster, the site of Cotton-gardens.[13]

The origin of this sanctuary is not known. It was, however, already in existence when Edward III. founded St. Stephen's chapel, to which it was annexed, and its chaplain made a canon.

Froissart, relating the history of the rebellion of Wat Tyler, tells us that 'on the Saturday morning (after Corpus Christi, 1381), the king left the Wardrobe, and went to Westminster, where he and all the lords heard Mass in the abbey. In this church there is a statue of our Lady in a small chapel, that has many virtues, and performs great miracles, in which the Kings of England have much faith. The king, having paid his devotions and made his offerings to this shrine, mounted his horse about nine o'clock.'[14] He then relates their meeting with the rebels at Smithfield, and how Wat Tyler was struck down by the brave Mayor, William Walworth, who was immediately knighted. It was easy for Froissart to make the mistake of placing this chapel in the abbey. Other authors tell us it was in the chapel of the Pew that he prayed, and it is certain that this was not in the abbey. In 1393 the chapel was robbed of its jewels by some thieves who were afterwards captured.[15] It was just at this time that Wickliffe and his followers were

---

[12] There was a famous confraternity in London called our Lady of Puy, of which the statutes have been published by Mr. Riley, in the *Liber Albus*. Is it possible that there is any connection between these names? The confraternity was in honour of our Lady of Puy in Normandy.

[13] Cotton House, the town house of Sir R. Cotton, founder of the Cotton Library, was near the west end of Westminster Hall (Walcott). Strype was misled in supposing that the chapel of Pue was beyond St. Martin's-lane. [14] Froissart, ch. lxxvi.

[15] *Historia Vitæ Rich. II.* (ed. by Hearne), p. 125.

preaching against sanctuaries and stirring up the people to many acts of sacrilege. The goods were recovered, and restored by the king to the dean and canons of St. Stephen's.

On February 14th, 1452, the chapel and its three altars were consumed by fire. From the accounts of this calamity we learn that the scholars of Westminster had the care of serving this chapel, since the fire originated in the carelessness of a scholar who was sent to extinguish the lights. Stow quotes an author named John Pigot, that the image was richly decked with jewels, precious stones, pearls, and rings, more than any jeweller could judge the price.

The chapel was rebuilt by Anthony Woodville, Earl Rivers, brother-in-law of Edward IV. He obtained for it the privileges of Scala Cœli in Rome. His will, by which he desires to be buried before the image of our Lady in this chapel, will be given in another chapter.[16]

In the privy-purse expenses of Henry VII. occur the following items :

May 1494, 'for offering at our Lady of the pewe, 2*l.*' August 1494, 'to my lady the king's mother, for the wages of Sir John Bracy, singing before our Lady of the pewe, for a quarter's wages, 2*l.*'[17]

Burnet informs us that our Lady of Pity of the Pew was taken down in October 1545, by order of Henry VIII.

The historians of Westminster say that it is not known when the chapel itself was destroyed.

From the very curious regulations for making new serjeants-at-law, in the 13th of Henry VIII. it appears that, on the Monday following their creation, 'the new serjeants were to go with their own servants in their liveries, first through the King's-street to St. Edward' (in Westminster Abbey), 'and there offer ; and then to our Lady of Pewe, and there offer ; and then into' (Westminster) 'Hall.' After dinner, 'they go in a sober manner, with their officers and servants, unto London, down the east side of Cheapside, to St. Thomas of Acres, and there they offer ; and then come down on the west side of Cheapside

---

[16] See ch. xiii.   [17] Bentley's *Excerpta Historica*, p. 98.

to St. Paul's, and there offer at the Rood of the north door and at St. Erkenwald's shrine.' They were to repeat their visit to our Lady of the Pewe on Wednesday. Even in the first year of Edward VI., though our Lady's statue had been destroyed, the visit to her chapel was continued.'[18]

Some towns had chosen our Lady for their patroness. The seal of *Stamford* represented our Lady with the Divine Child seated under a canopy, and at their feet a burgess kneeling, in prayer. Round the counterseal was the inscription : ' Stamford Burgenses Virgo fundunt tibi preces.'

Lincoln was also dedicated to our Lady. An evidence of this is still remaining. One of the old gates of the lower city, called the Stanbow, or Stonebow, crosses the High-street. In a niche on the left side of the gate as you enter the city is a large statue of our Lady. She is crowned, and her hands are crossed on her bosom, and a serpent is under her feet. At the other side of the gate is a large statue of St. Gabriel. He holds a palm-branch in his right hand, and in his left a scroll with the words, ' Ave, gratia plena, Dominus tecum.' Thus all visitors of the cathedral, dedicated to our Lady's Annunciation, were invited to salute her as they entered the city. It is singular that these images have been neither destroyed nor mutilated.[19] The same cannot be said of the decorations of the cathedral. It was begun by Bp. Remigius, who came over with the Conqueror ; but was rebuilt by St. Hugh of Burgundy (1186-1200). This great man was called by his intimate friend and biographer Adam, ' our Lady's most devout servant and vicar,' from his tender devotion towards her. The great central tower, begun by the famous Bishop Grosstête, another devout client of our Lady, was completed by Bishop d'Alberly (1300-1320). He made an especial appeal to his people to complete this work out of love and reverence of our Blessed Lady. In this tower were hung six bells, called the Lady Bells, which formed a distinct peal from those of St. Hugh in the west tower. They have since been melted down to cast the ' Great Tom.'

[18] *Origines Judiciales*, by W. Dugdale (ed. 1671), pp. 114-118.
[19] See the woodcut at the beginning of this Part.

In 1541 Lincoln had the misfortune of receiving a visit
from Henry VIII. While he was kissing the crucifix presented
to him by Bishop Longland, and walking with his new Queen
Katherine Howard under the canopy to the chapel of the Blessed
Sacrament to make his adorations, his sacrilegious eyes were
wandering avariciously over the riches of the cathedral. Shortly
after his visit all these were seized for his majesty's use. It
will perhaps be instructive to give one specimen of the documents which authorised the spoliation of our cathedrals. I
copy the following from Dugdale :

'Henry the Eighth, by the grace of God King of England
and of France, defender of the faith, lord of Ireland, and in
earth, immediately under Christ, supreme head of the Church
of England, — to our trusty and well-beloved Doctor George
Hennage, clerk, Archdeacon of Taunton, &c.

'Forasmuch as we understand that there is a certain shrine
and divers feigned relics and jewels' (he knew at least that the
jewels were not feigned) 'in the cathedral church of Lincoln,
with which all the simple people be much deceived and brought
into great superstition and idolatry, to the dishonour of God,
and great slander of this realm, and peril of their own souls, we
let you wit, that we being minded to bring our loving subjects
to the right knowledge of the truth, taking away all occasions
of idolatry and superstition, for the especial trust we have in
your fidelities, &c. appoint you, that immediately upon the
sight hereof, repairing to the said cathedral church, and declaring unto the dean, &c. the cause of your coming, is to take
down as well the said shrine and superfluous relics, as superfluous jewels, plate, copes, and other such like as you shall think
by your wisdoms not meet to continue or remain there. And
to see the said relics, jewels, and plate safely and surely to be
conveyed to our Tower of London into our jewel-house, charging the master of our jewels with the same,' &c.[20]

'By virtue of this commission,' adds Dugdale, 'there was
taken out of the said cathedral at that time, in gold 2621
ounces ; in silver, 4285 ounces ; besides a great number of pearls

[20] Dugdale, vol. viii. p. 1286.

and precious stones, which were of great value, as diamonds, sapphires, rubies, turky carbuncles, &c. There were at that time two shrines in that church, the one of pure gold, called St. Hugh's shrine; the other of pure silver, called St. John of d'Alberly's shrine.' (This is the bishop who had built our Lady's tower, and who was held in great veneration, though he has never been canonised.) The enumeration of the ornaments of this cathedral fills sixteen columns of large folio in Dugdale. I have described some of them in a previous chapter.[21]

Among the 'superfluous jewels' seized by Henry—for they do not appear in the Inventory made in the reign of Edward— were at least three of the richest chalices. One was 'a chalice of gold with pearls and divers precious stones in the foot and in the knot, with a paten of the same having graven " Cœna Domini," and the figure of our Lord with the twelve Apostles, weighing 32 ounces.' Another was 'a great chalice silver and gilt, with the paten weighing 74 ounces, of the gift of Lord William Wickham, Bishop of Winchester, some time arch-deacon of Lincoln, having in the foot the Passion, the Resurrection of our Lord, and the Salutation of our Lady, and in the paten the Coronation of our Lady.'[22]

But I must now pass on to other places, and be content with little more than a bare enumeration; for a full account of what is even now known of our old sanctuaries would require not a chapter merely, but a volume.

Kent was famous for the sanctuary of our Lady of the Crypt or Undercroft of Canterbury Cathedral, the immense riches of which were described by Erasmus shortly before it was plundered by Henry VIII. Our Lady of Chatham, of Bradstow or Broadstairs, and our Lady of Gillingham were in the same county.

Norfolk was filled with sanctuaries. Besides the 'holy

[21] See pp. 265-6.
[22] While I write, the foundations are being laid at Lincoln of a handsome Catholic church, the gift of Arthur Young, Esq., to be dedicated to our Blessed Lady of Lincoln, and intended by the pious donor as an act of reparation to her for the neglect and insults she has received at and since the Reformation.

land' of Walsingham, there was our Lady of Thetford, our Lady of Reepham, our Lady of Pity at Horstede, and our Lady of the Mount at Lynn. This last chapel is still perfect.

Mr. Taylor in his *Index Monasticus* has given many interesting details of this county. At Norwich was our Lady of the Oak in St. Martin's church, our Lady of Pity in the church of the Austin Friars, where was the famous chapel Scala Cœli; and there was a second statue of our Lady of Pity in the Franciscan convent at Norwich.

Suffolk was scarcely less famous for sanctuaries. I may mention our Lady of Stoke by Clare, and our Lady of Wulpit,[23] and of Woodbridge,[24] but especially the famous sanctuary at Ipswich.[25]

The statue of our Lady of Ipswich was of wood, and was sent up to London and publicly burnt, as a lesson against idolatry, taught by those great masters of true spiritual worship, Henry VIII. and Cromwell, his vicar-general. But Cromwell's steward, Thacker, sends up to his master an offering he had found at our Lady's shrine at Ipswich—viz. an image of our Lady, of gold, in a tabernacle silver-gilt. This was *not* burnt!

In *Berkshire* may be mentioned our Lady of Windsor and our Lady of Eton, mentioned in the will of Queen Elizabeth of York, consort of Henry VII., and to which sanctuaries she made yearly offerings.

In *Buckinghamshire*, our Lady of Caversham, near Reading, of which Dr. John London writes to Cromwell, ' I have pulled down the image of our Lady of Caversham, whereunto was great pilgrimage. The image is plated over with silver, and I have put it in a chest, fast locked and nailed up, and by the next barge that cometh from Reading to London it shall be brought to your lordship. I have also pulled down the place she stood in, with all other ceremonies—as lights, shrouds, crutches, and images of wax hanging about the chapel—and have defaced the same thoroughly, in eschewing of any farther resort thither. . . . I have made fast the doors of the chapel, which is thoroughly well covered with lead; and if it be your lordship's pleasure,

[23] Northcote, p. 259.   [24] Ib. p. 291.   [25] Ib. p. 255.

I shall see it made sure to the king's grace's use.' (A king plundering lead !) 'And if it be not so ordered, the chapel standeth so wildly that the lead will be stolen by night, as I was served at the friars ; for as soon as I had taken the friars' surrender the multitude of the poverty of the town resorted thither, and all things that might be had they stole away. . . . In this I have done as much as I could to save everything to the king's grace's use.' What a compliment to his majesty, to tell him how to get the start of the beggars ! He adds : 'At Caversham is a proper lodging, where the canon lay, with a fair garden and an orchard, meet to be bestowed upon some friend of your lordship's in these parts.'[26]

In 1446 King George of Bohemia sent an embassy to England. Accounts of this embassy were written by two members of his suite, one a Bohemian, the other a German. These accounts are both in existence, the one in the original German, the other in a Latin translation. They contain many interesting notices of things in England. On leaving London the travellers went to Windsor, and thence to Reading. The Bohemian thus writes of this sanctuary :

'*Reading* is a town in which is a vast and elegant monastery, in which are priests of the rule of the Blessed Virgin. In the church there is a tablet' (tabula) 'fixed in front of the altar, and a most elegant image of the Mother of God ; so that I think I never beheld or shall behold one to be compared with it, even though I should go to the end of the world. Nothing more beautiful and lovely could be executed.'

From Reading they go on to *Andover* in Hampshire. 'In this town,' he writes, 'I saw a most beautiful statue of the Blessed Virgin, chiselled in alabaster.'

Then they proceed to *Salisbury* in Wiltshire. 'I never saw more beautiful images than here. One group represents the Mother of God holding the Infant Christ in her arms, and the three kings bringing their gifts to Him ; another, the angel opening the sepulchre, and Christ risen from the dead and

[26] Sir Henry Ellis's *Collection of Original Letters*, vol. ii. pp. 79-81; also Wright's series on the *Suppression of the Monasteries*.

holding a banner in His hand. But these are so lifelike, that you would imagine you saw the things done rather than represented.'

He adds, that he never expects to find in his travels such churches and monasteries as he has seen in England.[26]

In *Shropshire* was our Lady of Ludlow.[27]

In *Warwickshire*, our Lady of Warwick, our Lady of Coventry, our Lady of Wroxhall.[28]

In *Oxfordshire*, our Lady of Binsey,[29] and a statue in Oxford memorable by the devotion of St. Edmund. 'When still a youth he made a vow of perpetual chastity, and commending himself to the protection of the Blessed Virgin, chose her for his spouse; and in pledge of his engagement placed on the finger of her image a ring, on which he had caused to be inscribed the Angelic Salutation. He wore another similar ring on his own hand, and was buried with it. From the time of this solemn consecration of himself, as he confessed on his death-bed, he sought her assistance in all his necessities, and never failed to find her a refuge in trouble and a deliverer in temptations. The Lady Chapel attached to St. Peter's Church was built by him, for the use of himself and his pupils, and in it he was accustomed daily to recite the canonical Hours, together with the Office of the Holy Spirit and of the Blessed Virgin.'[30]

Cambridge had also an image of our Lady, 'to which much pilgrimage was had' in the church of the Black Friars, where Emmanuel College now stands.[31]

Besides these, Durham, Northampton, Sudbury, Cockthorpe, may be mentioned, as well as Hilbury in Cheshire, Truro in Cornwall, Marychurch in Devonshire, Depedale in Derbyshire, the great Benedictine and Cistercian abbeys, such as Fountains, York, Rievaulx, Byland, Bolton, Joreval, and many more.

---

[26] The two narrations in German and in Latin were printed together in Stuttgart in 1844.

[27] 'Super unum montium juxta Pylale, ubi quædam imago B. Mariæ Virginis valde honorabatur, non longe a dicta villa de Lodlow. *Life of Richard II.* by a Monk of Evesham, Hearne's ed. p. 178.

[28] Northcote, pp. 240-277.

[29] Ib. p. 279.

[30] Ib. p. 289.

[31] Ib. p. 290.

In *Worcestershire*, the famous sanctuaries of Worcester, Tewkesbury, and Evesham, celebrated for the apparition of our Lady to Eoves the swine-herd, and Egwin the bishop, towards the close of the seventh century.

In *Somerset* was the mother church of all England, our Lady's Church at Glastonbury, of which something has been said in a previous chapter.

We have seen how Agnes Hilyard left offerings to our Lady's images at Beverley, Fisholine, Mollescroft ; and Catherine Hastings, to our Lady of Doncaster, our Lady of Belcrosse, and our Lady of Himminburgh.[32]

Our Lady of Penrice, near Swansea, in Glamorganshire, appears to have been one of the most famous in England. This image is mentioned in a letter of Latimer, already quoted, as fit to make ' a jolly muster in Smithfield,' if joined to those of our Lady of Doncaster, of Ipswich, and of Walsingham.

In the enumeration here given no attempt has been made to exhaust the list of famous sanctuaries of our Lady in England. Many other notices might no doubt be collected out of county histories or old wills.[33] But the above will be sufficient to give some idea of the extent of that devotion which gained for England the title of ' Our Lady's Dowry.'

SCOTCH SANCTUARIES.

Our information about devotion to the Blessed Virgin in the early days of Scotch ecclesiastical history is very scanty ; indeed, few records exist of any kind. Nor were many churches apparently dedicated to her before the eleventh century ; for those sometimes supposed to be hers are, according to the learned Dr. Forbes, really the churches of St. Monsey or St. Maelrubha. But in the *Inquisitio Davidis* (A.D. 1120) the foundation of the church of Glasgow is mentioned, ' in honour of God and of holy Mary, Mother of God.' When the Cistercians entered Scotland in the twelfth century, many churches were built under the invocation of the Blessed Virgin. Dr. Forbes has collected eighty

[32] See p. 269.
[33] A more complete list is being published by Mr. Waterton.

dedications to her; nor does he think that he has by any means exhausted the number.

Among the shrines of our Lady, perhaps the best known were Aberdeen, Scoon, Dundee, Paisley, Melrose, and Jedburgh. I must be contented with a few words regarding Aberdeen.

A famous image, formerly venerated in Aberdeen, is still in existence, and is called by the title of ' Notre Dame de bon Succès,' and is in the church of Finisterre, in Brussels.[34] It is of black oak, and was for several centuries (some say six) an object of devotion in a wayside chapel, placed quite close to the old bridge over the Dee, in Aberdeen. There is a well of our Lady still to be seen at the place, though the chapel was destroyed for the enlargement of the bridge. At the beginning of the sixteenth century it was removed by the holy bishop, Gavin Dunbar, to the cathedral of St. Macarius, commonly called ' Old Machar,' which is situated on the banks of the Don. Bishop Dunbar built an aisle in the cathedral, at the end of which (it is supposed) he erected the altar of our Lady, over which he placed her statue. Another account[35] says that the statue was originally venerated in the cathedral, and removed by Dunbar to the bridge, and then brought back to the cathedral. In any case, the Aberdeen Registers[36] prove abundant devotion to our Lady in the cathedral. The cathedral itself was dedicated to the Blessed Virgin Mary and St. Machar, an Irish disciple of St. Columba. The high altar was that of our Lady, at which every morning, at nine o'clock, a Mass was celebrated ' de Beata Virgine.' The city itself was under our Lady's patronage, and its arms are a pot of lilies.

In 1543 a weekly Mass, to be said on Wednesday, ' of the Compassion of our Lady,' was founded by Alexander Kyd, a precentor of the cathedral.

---

[34] I am informed that Father Victor de Buck, S.J., one of the learned contributors to the last volumes of the *Acta Sanctorum*, is preparing a ' travail' on the subject of this image. In the little pamphlet published on the subject in Brussels there are inaccuracies.

[35] *Celebrated Sanctuaries*, by Dr. Northcote, p. 294.

[36] Published by the Spalding Club. The details given in the text are gathered from the documents there published.

In 1436 a small statue of gold, or more probably of silver gilt, called our Lady of Pity,[77] was presented by John Forstare, Knight. This was placed on the silver-gilt pyx, or shrine, presented by Bishop Henry de Lychton, for carrying the Blessed Eucharist in procession.

On the feast of the Visitation of the Blessed Virgin (A.D. 1499), Andrew Lyall, treasurer of the cathedral, made a present of a large silver statue of our Lady of Pity, weighing 120 ounces, to the high altar. Thereupon William the Bishop made an ordinance that this statue should be 'carried in procession round the cathedral on all the solemn feasts of the Glorious Virgin, and granted forty days' indulgence to all who should devoutly follow in the procession.'

Before the gift of this statue there was another at the high altar, for in the register of 1436 we find that Richard Forbes, the Dean, had presented to the high altar two images, one of our Lady and the other of St. Maurice ; and that a canon named John Clatt had given a candle-holder for placing tapers near our Lady's image.

In the register of 1496 we read that another candelabrum, with twelve lights, was given by Bishop William also to burn before the high altar. Also a 'sterne' (star) of old date before our Lady in the nave, and seven sternes given by Bishop William ; and lastly of a luminare (lamp) before our Lady in the nave, given by the same Andrew Lyall who a few years later gave the large silver image.

In the register of 1518 there is mentioned a silver heart placed before our Lady's statue.

By the register of 1549 we learn that this large statue of our Lady of Pity was accompanied by the crucifix, as was also that given by Sir John Forstare.

In 1553, Alexander Kyd gave an annual sum of money to maintain two lights before the image of our Lady of Pity, which is said to stand at the south side of the altar of the Blessed Virgin in the nave.

---

[77] It is called 'jocale de auro' and 'jocale de argento.' On the representation of our Lady of Pity, see p. 264.

This is the same priest who founded the Mass of our Lady's Compassion. At his death, in 1557, he leaves a foundation for a dole to be made on his anniversary to lame, blind, or deaf poor. Alas, how short a time were such foundations destined to endure! A Protestant historian of Scotland[38] has truly said that 'the clergy provided with a liberal hand for the necessities of the poor, the orphan, the widow, and the infirm; and the extent of their benefactions was only made manifest by the magnitude of the sufferings which met the eye of the government after the monasteries were suppressed.'

It is difficult to avoid mistakes in attempting to combine casual mentions in old registers. It would, however, appear that the image at the high altar was not the same as that mentioned as in the nave. The image at the high altar was called our Lady of Pity, and was accompanied by a crucifix (imago divæ Virginis Mariæ de pietate inscripta cum imagine Filii sui crucifixi); that in the nave is not described, but is called 'our Lady in the nave' (nostra Domina in navi ecclesiæ).[39]

The register of 1464 mentions 'two crowns of silver gilt for Christ and our Lady, with precious stones.' These could not be for the crucifix and our Lady of Pity, which were not given till 1499. Besides, the register of 1518 mentions two silver crowns 'for the Blessed Virgin and Jesus *her little* Son, with precious stones.' The weight of the crowns was twenty ounces.

From this I should conclude that the image of our Lady in the nave represented her holding the Divine Child in her arms, and though also called our Lady of Pity, was more generally spoken of simply as 'our Lady,' and it was before this that there stood the candle-holder (pro cercis superponendis) given by John Clatt in 1436, or earlier. As it stood in the nave, it was accessible to the people, who could therefore perform the favourite devotion of lighting a candle before the statue.

Besides these, there was in Aberdeen (New Town) the church

---

[38] Dr. Russell's *History of the Church in Scotland*, vol. i. ch. vii.

[39] This, however, is also called our Lady of Pity, in the foundation for two lights 'ante imaginem Virginis Mariæ Pietatis ad australem partem altaris divæ Virginis infra navem ecclesiæ collocatam.'

of St. Nicolas, with thirty altars, of which two were of the Blessed Virgin, with a third of our Lady of Pity in the vault.

The vault is to this day called the Pitty Vault.

As to the statue of the bridge, the council register of Aberdeen informs us that on the 9th January 1530, Sir William Ray, formerly chaplain to our Lady's Chapel ' of the Brig of Dee,' delivered to the bailie and convent a chalice of silver and and an image of silver of our Lady, both gilt, for the utility and profit of the said chapel.' It seems probable that this was to replace that which had been removed to the cathedral.

In the year of ill-omen 1559, Knox returned to Scotland, and by his violent harangue at Perth inflamed ' the rascal multitude,' as he calls them, to deeds of violence and sacrilege ; and in the same year, the reformers, calling themselves ' the congregation of Jesus Christ,' declared to ' the generation of Antichrist, the pestilent prelates and their shavelings, in Scotland,' that they would ' begin that same war which God commanded Israel to execute against the Canaanites.'

Was it on account of these proceedings that, as we learn from an inventory, in July 1559, Bishop William Gordon delivered to the custody of the canons at Aberdeen the silver work at St. Machar, and to ' Mr. John Leslie, person of Dyn, the image of the Virgin Marie, 114 ounces' ?

At the destruction of the cathedral of course the silver statues fell a prey to the cupidity of the reformers ; but the statue that had been formerly at the Brig, being of oak, was thrown aside. It still bears marks of cuts. The statue was kept with secret veneration by some Catholics, until William Laing, a Scotch Catholic, who held some office in the Spanish court, intrusted it in 1625 to the captain of a Spanish ship to be conveyed to Flanders. Its subsequent history may be related by Father Blackhal, a Scotch priest, who wrote a very interesting narration of part of his life in A.D. 1666 or 1667 :

' I had no money,' he writes, ' but what I gotte for saying the first Messe every morning at Notre Dame *de bone successe*, a chapelle of great devotion, so called from a statue of our Ladye which was brought from Aberdein, in the north of Scot-

land, to Ostend, by a merchant of Ostend to whom it was given
in Aberdein. And that same day that the shippe in which it
was did arrive at Ostend, the Infanta did winne a battaile
against the Hollanders, the people thinking that our Lady, for
the civil reception of her statue, did obteane that victorye to
the Princesse, who did send for the statu to be brought to
Brusselle, when the Princesse, with a solemn procession, did
receave it at the porte of the toune, and place it in this chappel,
wher it is much honoured, and the chapelle dedicated to our
Lady of bonne successe, which befor was pouer and desolat, now
is riche and wel frequented. The common beleiffe of the vulgar
people ther is that this statu was throwen in the sea at Aberdein, and carried upon the waves of the sea miraculously to
Ostend. So easie a thing it is for fables to find good harbour,
wher verities would be beaten out with cudgelles.'

The infanta here mentioned was Isabella, daughter of Philip
II. of Spain. Father Blackhal seems to have been imperfectly
informed on the history of the statue ; which is minutely given
in detail by Dr. Northcote. The statue is now venerated in the
parish church of Finisterre in Brussels.

I have willingly dwelt at some length on many little details
regarding our Lady in Aberdeen, because they show the perfect
unity even in smaller matters of devotion between English and
Scotch Catholics. Yet in 1514 the citizens of New Aberdeen
were beautifying their church of St. Nicolas 'to the honour and
free loving of God Almighty, the Blessed Virgin, and their
glorious patron,' for the 'keeping of the town fra the old inne-
mies of Ingland,'[40] so powerful was the unity of the Church, in
spite of national antipathies.

Not only did devotion exist in spite of feuds, but it appears
to have been considered the best means to end them.

Sir W. Scott, in the notes to his *Minstrelsy of the Scottish
Border*, gives the following 'bond of alliance or feud-staunching
betwixt the arms of Scott and Ker on 16th March 1529 :

'The said Walter Scott of Branceholm shall gang or cause
gang at the will of the party to the four head pilgrimages of

[40] *Burgh Register*, p. 88 (Spalding Club).

Scotland, and shall say a Mass for the souls of umquhile Andrew Ker, of Cessford, and them that were slain in his company in the field of Melrose. . . . Mark Ker of Dolphinston, Andrew Ker of Grale, shall gang at the will of the party to the four head pilgrimages of Scotland, and shall gar say a Mass for the souls of umquhile James Scot of Eshrich, and other Scots their friends.'[41]

The four head pilgrimages were Scoon, Dundee, Paisley, and Melrose.

Of Paisley nothing is known but that there was once a sanctuary of the Blessed Virgin quite near to the old abbey, built on a rock on the lands of 'Lady Kirk,' as it is described in old records. But the sanctuary has disappeared, the rock on which it stood, and even the name of Lady Kirk, and the place is now a huge quarry.

On one of the corners of the abbey wall at Paisley, in the time of Grove, there was a canopied niche, containing a statue of the Blessed Virgin. The following distich was cut at the foot :

> ' Hac ne vade via nisi diceris Ave Maria
> Sit semper sine Væ, qui tibi dicet Ave.'

WELLS.

Another form of devotion known to our ancestors was that of calling fountains and springs by our Lady's name, and giving to them a popular veneration, to which the Church in many instances lent her sanction. If this devotion requires any apology or explanation, it can be given in the beautiful lines of the Rev. R. S. Hawker, an Anglican clergyman :

The Lady's Well.

' It flow'd like light from the voïce of God,
Silent and calm and fair ;
It shone where the child and the parent trod
In the soft and evening air.

" Look at that spring, my father dear,
Where the white blossoms fell ;

[41] *Minstrelsy of the Scottish Border*, Appendix No. 4.

Why is it always bright and clear?
   And why the Lady's well?"

" Once on a time, my own sweet child,
   There dwelt across the sea
A lovely Mother, meek and mild,
   From blame and blemish free.

And Mary was her blessed name,
   In every land adored :
Its very sound deep love should claim
   From all who love their Lord.

A Child was hers—a heavenly birth,
   As pure as pure could be :
He had no father of the earth,
   The Son of God was He.

He came down to her from above,
   He died upon the Cross ;
We never can do for Him, my love,
   What He hath done for us.

And so to make His praise endure,
   Because of Jesu's fame,
Our fathers call'd things bright and pure
   By His fair Mother's name.

She is the Lady of the well—
   Her memory was meant
With lily and with rose to dwell
   By waters innocent." '

I do not know whether there was anything peculiarly Celtic
in this form of devotion, but at the present day such Lady
wells are found especially in Cornwall, Wales, and the north
of Scotland. There are, however, many in England also. In
London, besides Muswell or Mousewell, famed for the cure of
a Scotch king, there was at Westminster the famous chapel of
our Lady of Pue, which, as some think, derived its name from
the wells (in French, *puits*), which are there. Erasmus speaks

of two holy wells at Walsingham. But it is unnecessary to enumerate. I will mention only one or two in Scotland, since veneration has clung round them even to the present day. 'One of the chief places of post-reformation pilgrimage,' says Mr. Chambers, 'was the Chapel of Grace, on the western bank of the Spey, near Fochabers, a mere ruin, but held in great veneration, and resorted to by devout people from all parts of the north of Scotland. We hear of Lady Aboyne' (a Catholic) 'going to the Chapel of Grace every year, being a journey of thirty Scotch miles, the two last of which she always performed on her bare feet, as we learn from Father Blackhall's narrative. About the time of the national Covenant (1638), what remained of the Chapel of Grace was thrown down, with a view to putting a stop to the practice; but this seems to have been far from an effectual measure. In a work written in 1775, the author says : "In the north end of the parish of Dundurens stood the Chapel of Grace, and near to it the well of that name, to which multitudes from the Western Isles do still resort, and nothing short of violence can restrain their superstition." [42]

A gentleman informs me that Chapel Well on Speyside is still frequented (in 1874), and as much by Protestants as by Catholics. This takes place on Sundays in May, and in a less degree on those in August. Indeed throughout the north of Scotland there is scarcely a ruin or a memory of an old church without a well close to the spot; and many of these are held in veneration.

The General Assembly that met at Linlithgow in 1608 recommends 'that order be taken with the pilgrimages,' especially to the above-mentioned chapel and well, and to a miraculous well of our Lady at Ordiquhill in Banffshire; the Provincial Assembly of Aberdeen in 1652 is equally zealous against the well of Seggett.

A specimen of the tender mercies of these Presbyterian synagogues is very curious. On 26th Nov. 1630, at Aberdeen, Margaret Davidson was fined five pounds for sending her nurse with her child to St. Fiache's well for the recovery of its health,

---

[a] *Domestic Annals of Scotland*, by R. Chambers, vol. i. p. 324.

and Margaret and the nurse were ordered to acknowledge their offence before the session.

The same day it was ordained by the whole session with one voice, that any future pilgrim to a well 'shall be answered in penalty and repentance *in such degree as fornicators are.*'[43] As a contrast to this bit of devilish bigotry it will be pleasant to read the lines of the gentle Mrs. Hemans :

> ' Fount of the vale ! thou art sought no more
> By the pilgrim's foot, as in time of yore,
> When he came from afar his beads to tell
> And to chant his hymn at our Lady's Well.
> There is heard no Ave through thy bowers,
> Thou art gleaming lone midst thy water-flowers ;
> But the herd may drink from thy gushing wave,
> And there may the reaper his forehead lave,
> And the woodman seeks thee not in vain ;
> Bright fount ! thou art nature's own again !
>
> Fount of the chapel, with ages gray,
> Thou art springing freshly amidst decay ;
> Thy rites are closed, and thy cross lies low,
> And the changeful hours breathe o'er thee now.
> Yet if at thine altar one holy thought
> In man's deep spirit of old hath wrought ;
> If peace to the mourner hath here been given,
> Or prayer from a chasten'd heart to heaven,—
> Be the spot still hallow'd while Time shall reign,
> Who hath made thee nature's own again !'[44]

[43] Selections from the *Ecclesiastical Records of Aberdeen*, Spalding Club, vol. i. p. 110.

[44] 'Lines on our Lady's Well at St. Asaph.'

CHAPTER XI.

In the present chapter I wish to gather together several tokens of ancient devotion to our Lady, on which I have not much to communicate or which are too trifling to be treated of at any length, yet interesting enough to deserve attention.

Relics.

First, then, I may mention relics once venerated in England. It is one of the arguments in favour of our Lady's bodily assumption, that no church has ever claimed to possess any part of her body inconsistent with this belief. The strength of this argument will be manifest to those who know the very great veneration in which relics were held in the early centuries, and the extreme eagerness of individuals and churches to become possessors of them. Churches have boasted of possessing portions of her clothes, of her hair, and even of her milk, but never of her bones, as if, like the Apostles Saints Peter and Paul, she had left her sacred body in the tomb.

The following royal document will show the great esteem in which relics were held. It is a donation of relics made by Henry VI. to his new foundation of Eton.[1]

'Forasmuch as our most dear and beloved uncle of renowned memory, Henry, late Cardinal of England and Bishop of Winchester, out of the fervent love which he always testified for our good pleasure, kindly gave us in his lifetime a memorial and jewel, to us most acceptable, namely, that golden tablet called the Tablet of Burboyn, containing several relics of inestimable value, especially of the precious blood of our Lord Jesus Christ,

[1] Given in Bentley's *Excerpta Historica*, p. 43.

through whom we obtain the gift of life and salvation, and a fragment of the salutiferous word of the Cross of our Lord, which leads us to a grateful remembrance of our redemption, and also of the glorious Virgin Mary His Mother, and of His most blessed Confessor Nicholas, and of Katherine the Virgin, and of other Martyrs, Confessors, and Virgins; to the intent that we should deign to give and grant the said tablet to our beloved in Christ the Provost and our Royal College of the Blessed Mary of Eton, near Windsor, founded by us in honour of the Assumption of the said most Blessed Virgin Mary,'—hence the king makes this donation.

This tablet, left by Cardinal Beaufort to Henry VI. in 1447, contains a relic of the Blessed Virgin, but its nature is not stated. It was certainly no part of her body, unless perhaps the hair.

The Bohemian nobleman who accompanied the embassy to England in 1446[2] speaks of a relic shown in Canterbury, called Redimiculum Beatæ Virginis (probably a fillet or hair-net); also ' some hair of the Mother of God and a portion of her tomb.'

When he comes to London, he says: ' In London, which is the residence of the Kings of England, our master [*i.e.* the ambassador] was taken to some elegant gardens, planted with trees and plants, such as are not found in other regions. Afterwards he was brought into some churches most elegantly built, where many golden shrines were shown to him. As I have said elsewhere, in no place have I seen so great a number of holy relics collected together as here. When I wished to make a list of them I was told it was quite impossible for me to write them all, for they were so many that they could not be catalogued by two scribes in a fortnight. Among them I saw the girdle of the Virgin Mother of God, which she is said to have made with her own hands.' This was probably in Westminster.

Girdles of our Lady were shown in many other places. Lord Herbert, in his Life of Henry VIII., says that the girdles of our Lady were shown in England in eleven different places, and her milk in eight. Though his authority on this point is

[2] See ante, p. 321.

of little weight, as I have shown elsewhere, yet it is very probable that the girdle was venerated in several churches.

In the list of relics in the cathedral church of the Holy Trinity (Christ Church), Dublin,[3] which were destroyed in the year 1538 by the English, I find 'Zona B. Mariæ Virginis ; Item, de lacte B. Mariæ Virginis, and De sepulchro B. Mariæ Virginis.'

It is probable, though I have no authority for the statement, that these girdles were really copies of the famous relic at Prato in Italy. A traveller may have brought such a fac-simile and presented it to a church, and from being called a girdle of our Lady it would easily acquire the fame of an original, without any intention of deception.[4]

In several places in England, as well as on the Continent, relics of the Blessed Virgin's milk were venerated. These had been brought from the Holy Land, and were no doubt popularly supposed to be the true milk of our Lady. Quaresimus,[5] Apostolic Commissary of the Holy Land, tells us that not far from the grotto of the Nativity and the church of the Blessed Virgin, at Bethlehem, there is another subterranean grotto, or rather three together. In the middle cave Mass has often been celebrated. It is called the chapel of St. Nicholas. An old tradition says that here the Blessed Virgin concealed herself with the Infant Jesus, and that some drops of milk falling from her breast gave miraculous virtue to the rock on which they fell. The soil of this grotto is naturally reddish ; but when it is pulverised, washed, and dried in the sun, it becomes snow white ; and when this white powder is mixed with water, it exactly resembles milk. The soil thus prepared is called 'The Virgin's Milk.' This is the relic which, in many places of pilgrimage, is shown as 'Lac Beatæ Virginis,' and which has been the occasion of so many sneers.

This exactly corresponds to the description given by Eras-

[3] Published by the Irish Archæological Society, 1844.
[4] On the relic of Prato dissertations have been written by Giuseppe Bianchini, *Notizie istoriche &c.*, and by Trombelli. The latter treats the whole subject of relics.
[5] *Historica Terræ sanctæ Elucidatio*, tom. ii. p. 678. Antwerp, 1632.

mus in his account of his pilgrimage to Walsingham. He says
that the milk was kept in crystal and placed on the high altar
at the right of the Blessed Sacrament—that it was dried up, and
looked like ground chalk mixed with white of egg. Though all
through this Colloquy he speaks in a half-bantering tone, yet the
prayer that he offered is pious : O Virgin Parent, who with
thy maiden breast hast given milk to thy Son Jesus, the Lord
of heaven and earth; we beseech thee that, being purified by
His blood, we may also attain to that happy childhood of simplicity which, guileless of malice, fraud, and deceit, earnestly
desires the true milk of the gospel, until it grows into the perfect man, to the stature of the fulness of Christ,' &c.

In 1462, William Haute writes in his will : ' I bequeath one
piece of that stone on which the Archangel Gabriel descended,
when he saluted the Blessed Virgin Mary, to the image of the
Blessed Virgin of the church of Bourne, the same to stand under
the foot of the said image.'[6]

Now what, it will be asked, can be urged in defence of relics
like the above ? I reply that there is no need to defend them.
Each one of us may exercise his own discretion as to their authenticity. It is evident that in the case just mentioned the
testator was in the most perfect good faith. He had perhaps
made a pilgrimage to the Holy Land, and this stone had
been given him ; and he believed in it, venerated it during life
by repeating often and often the Angelic Salutation, to the
great profit of his soul, and dying he bequeathed it as a precious
legacy to his parish church.

Such was probably the origin of most of the doubtful relics
of the Middle Ages. They were placed in churches by simple
faith, or credulity if you like, but not by wilful fraud. The
priests who had the charge of them were free to conceive or express their own opinion about them, but they were not free to
destroy them because they doubted their authenticity. Were
such a liberty yielded to every priest, the most real and precious
relics might easily have perished by hasty zeal. Scepticism is
often quite as rash and foolish as credulity ; but credulity pre-

* *Testamenta Vetusta*, p. 300.

serves things that may at any time be destroyed if necessary, while scepticism, if allowed to act, would produce irreparable loss.

It may be objected that at least authority should have prevented the acceptance and veneration of false or doubtful relics. Certainly it should; and that this was the judgment of the English Church appears from the following decree, which was drawn up by the Synod of Exeter, under Bishop Peter Quivil, A.D. 1287 :

'Holy Scripture relates that miracles may sometimes be worked by the bad as well as by the good (Matt. vii. 22). Therefore in case of doubt recourse should be had to the most Holy Roman Church, which, by the grace of Almighty God, having the authority of apostolical tradition, is proved never to have erred from the right path; and her decree must be awaited; lest any one, by approving what she disapproves, in the judgment of Catholics be proved a heretic.

'Hence in the General Council (of Lyons) it was prudently forbidden to all to expose to public veneration relics recently discovered, unless they should have been first approved by the Roman Pontiff. We enjoin the observance of this prohibition; and command that no one set the relics of saints for sale, or venerate as holy in any way stones, fountains, trees, wood, vestments, or other things, on account of dreams or other fictitious proofs. For to act thus would savour of heretical pravity; and it is not lawful either to teach or to hold otherwise than we see the Roman Church, the mother of all Churches, to follow and to hold. If any presume to act contrary to this decree, unless after being admonished they renounce their error, we judge them to be severely punished as heretics.'[7]

[7] Wilkins, tom. ii. p. 155. 'Idcirco ad sacrosanctam Romanam Ecclesiam, quæ per Dei omnipotentis gratiam, auctoritate apostolicæ traditionis, nunquam errasse probatur a tramite, in hoc dubio est recurrendum.' The infallibility of the Holy See is here invoked for the canonisation of saints. It is not meant that the authentication of a relic is an infallible judgment. Absolute certainty is not required for the veneration of a relic. Since all the veneration is relative, and passes to the person to whom the relic refers, there is no sin committed even if the relic is false. Yet it is right to act with caution and prudence, equally removed from credulity and scepticism.

Z

It is probable that the above decree was not always executed, and that there were many spurious relics venerated in our churches. The Council of Trent made several decrees on this subject—amongst others, that 'no one be allowed to place, or cause to be placed, any *unusual* image in any place or church, howsoever exempted, except that image have been approved of by the bishop; also, that no new miracles are to be acknowledged, or new relics recognised, unless the said bishop has taken cognisance and approved thereof.'

But before this decree had been issued (A.D. 1563), all the relics of our churches had been destroyed by Henry, Edward, and Elizabeth, in order to seize upon the shrines and rich reliquaries which contained them.

But while admitting that the simplicity of our forefathers may have led them to expose and venerate many unauthentic relics, I must remark how the credulity of Protestants has made them accept many unauthenticated tales against relics.

The commissioners sent out by Cromwell for the suppression of the monasteries were scoffers as well as rascals. For the amusement of their master they put in their letters such things as the following: 'I missed nothing here but only a piece of the holy halter Judas was hanged withal;' or 'I have Malcolm's ear that Peter struck off.'[8] Yet learned editors have taken these things as authentic records, and declaimed against the horrible impostures of the clergy. Either they were as dull to a joke as Dogberry himself, or else, which seems more probable, they were possessed by a malice which could believe anything provided it were evil.

More than a hundred years before the Reformation, Thomas Waldensis had well explained why the Church does *not* venerate whatever has come in contact with a saint. 'If we must condescend to take notice of the scoffs and blasphemies of the Wickliffites, saying that we ought, according to our principles, to venerate the lips of Judas Iscariot because they kissed those of our Saviour, we reply that it is not mere contact that sanctifies a thing. If the thing is harmless in itself, and is lovingly

_____

[8] *Letters on the Suppression of Monasteries*, ed. Wright.

touched by a saint, or has belonged to him, then it deserves honour from those who love and venerate him. The Cross, then, is worthy of love which the Lord deigned to choose, His seamless garment is worthy of love, His spear, His nails, His crown of thorns, the scourges, the column, by all who love their crucified Lord. But the lips of the traitor, which were used for treason, are execrable, as are the impious hands of those who drove the nails, and which were moved by the evil spirit who possessed their owners' souls. Those hands were hateful to Christ, and must be hateful to His lovers. . . . The two thieves were equally near to Jesus Christ; one was sanctified by his nearness, because he loved and honoured his Redeemer; the other by his very nearness was made more guilty, because he blasphemed Him.'⁹

This was the doctrine taught by our ancestors long before Erasmus had begun to sneer or Latimer to preach. But as the Greek sophists, according to Plato, talked of their heroic ancestors, as if Agamemnon did not know the number of his fingers, so do the modern writers of tracts and newspaper articles think and scribble of the founders and professors of our ancient universities.

The principles of the legitimate use and veneration of relics were certainly well understood. Let me add a few words more about the practice. It has been a common custom to make facsimiles of certain relics, which, after touching the original, are called 'sanctified relics.' They are of course given merely for what they are; but the name of the original gets attached to them, and a sacristan finding such a memorial in his church's treasures—kept there perhaps for centuries—might catalogue it erroneously. Sometimes, again, small particles of the original are enclosed in these facsimiles, and the veneration is extended to the whole by an easy error, which is of no moral importance. Dr. Rock mentions a custom of inserting a very small particle of the True Cross in a wooden cross. This may perhaps be the case with some of those large relics venerated as fragments of the True Cross. Trombelli thinks it probable that the girdle of

* *Doctrinale Fidei,* cap. cxx.

our Lady at Prato is merely a copy of the one held in veneration in early ages at Constantinople, and that it only contains a thread of the Eastern relic. The same author suggests an explanation of the many relics of our Lady's hair. It is well known that the hair was a part of the saints' bodies most frequently treasured up. It was easy to obtain and not subject to decay. But the documents or inscriptions may have been lost, or have perished by damp or fire; and thus the hair of another female saint enshrined in silver or gold may have been supposed to be that of our Lady. He does not mean to deny the authenticity of all such relics. It is very improbable that the contemporaries of our Lady should *not* have acquired and treasured up some lock of her hair, and that it should *not* afterwards have been carefully preserved. Such may have been the relic which, as Ingulf tells us, the Emperor Henry II. received from Hugh, King of France, enclosed in a golden reliquary, and presented to the monastery of Croyland.

Leigh Hunt wrote a sonnet on a lock of Milton's hair. Had he more security for its authenticity? While I am writing, the chair of John Bunyan is being exhibited and *venerated* in Bedford.[10] Human instinct is stronger than heresy. The Church has been strangely vindicated even in her enemies. Wickliffe wrote and preached against the veneration of relics, and a few years ago, when Lutterworth church was restored, the old pulpit in which he was *supposed*[11] to have there preached was cut up into crosses and other designs and sold to his admirers, and the sounding-board reverently placed in the vestry wall. In the same vestry is exhibited a case containing what are supposed to be fragments of his cope and chasuble, though they probably belonged to an altar-frontal posterior to his time.

Thus is the principle of the veneration of relics justified in the very memory of its reviler.

Not many years ago, at the centenary festival of the poet Burns, kept in the Crystal Palace, London, thousands of Pres-

[10] June 1874.

[11] Lutterworth church was rebuilt from its foundation after Wickliffe's time, and it is very unlikely that his pulpit was preserved, since no veneration then attached to his memory.

byterian Scotchmen went with enthusiasm to see his statue un-
veiled, to listen to an ode, behold a procession, and to venerate
his gauge and his snuff box. And those who did all this to
honour a licentious poet would have scoffed at the Church for
similar modes of veneration offered to a saint.

'The human race,' says a great French writer,[12] 'is essen-
tially a guardian of relics. This instinct is found among savages,
and developed by civilisation. Private houses and museums
are filled with objects, the only value of which is that they belonged to ancestors or great men. Under the name of curiosi-
ties there flourishes in Europe a trade in relics which rather
surprises one's good sense. Autographs, printed papers, delf,
pottery, trifles of every kind, are contended for at startling prices.
In France the State obliges us to pay for a guardian of the old
clothes of the first Napoleon.[13] We procure and preserve at
great expense the linen of mummies, necklaces from Ninive,
Etruscan crockery, Huron arrows, and Algonquin calabashes.
Most of these things have no beauty, are puerile and tiresome.
Why, then, are they kept? Is it from pure curiosity? No, that
would be too silly. There is a certain feeling of veneration at
the bottom of this mania. All these things came from the hand
of man, speak of man; in all these things the human race con-
templates itself, honours and worships itself; and freethinkers
extend this kind of worship to man just in proportion as they
withdraw it from God.'

In the times which we are here considering, the churches
were both art-galleries and museums. All tended to the glory
of God. Is religion to be blamed if modern criticism can cast
doubt upon a relic?

Signboards.

It is, certainly, a curious transition from relics to signboards;

[12] Louis Veuillot.

[13] In England it does worse. Not only are the old clothes of Nelson
kept and venerated in Greenwich Hospital, but the cup used by Lady
Hamilton, who has no other claim on the country than that Nelson lived
n adulterous intercourse with her. Catholic England, which venerated
elics of the Immaculate Virgin, would have execrated the relics of an
dulteress.

but it must be remembered that a signboard was not in former times confined to taverns. Each shop had its sign ; and the choice of the sign might be an act of piety, just as the choice of a motto may indicate the bent of a man's mind at the present day.

The following extracts are from the *History of Signboards*, by Jacob Larwood :[14]

'The "Virgin" was unquestionably a very common sign before the Reformation, and it may be met with even at the present day, as, for instance, at Ebury-hill, Worcester. This sign was also called " Our Lady," as New Inn (the Chancery inn attached to the Middle Temple, London) was a guest-inn, the sign whereof was the picture of our Lady, and thereupon it was also called " Our Lady's Inn," says Stow.

' "Our Lady of Pity" was the sign of Johan Redman, a bookseller in Paternoster-row, in 1542. John Byddell, also a bookseller, had introduced this sign in the beginning of that century.

' Few signs have undergone so many changes as the well-known "Salutation." Originally it represented the angel saluting the Virgin Mary, in which shape it was still occasionally seen in the seventeenth and eighteenth centuries, as appears from the tavern-token of Daniel Grey of Holborn. In the times of the Commonwealth, however—" sacrarum ut humanarum rerum, heu ! vicissitudo est"—the Puritans changed it into the " Soldier and Citizen ;" and in such a garb it continued long after, with this modification, that it was represented by two citizens politely bowing to each other. The Salutation Tavern in Billingsgate shows it thus on its trade's token, and so it was represented by the Salutation Tavern in Newgate - street (an engraving of which sign may still be seen in the parlour of that old-established house). At present it is mostly rendered by two hands conjoined, as at the Salutation Hotel, Perth, where a label is added with the words, " You're welcome to the city."

' The "Angel" was derived from the Salutation, for that it originally represented the angel appearing to the Holy Virgin

[14] Published by J. C. Hotten, London, 1866.

at the Salutation, or Annunciation, is evident from the fact that even as late as the seventeenth century, on nearly all the trades-tokens of houses with this sign, the angel is represented with a scroll in his hands; and this scroll, we know, from the evidence of paintings and prints, to contain the words addressed by the angel to the Holy Virgin: "Ave Maria, gratia plena, Dominus tecum." Probably at the Reformation it was considered too Catholic a sign; and so the Holy Virgin was left out and the angel only retained.

'From that period also dates the sign of the "Bleeding Heart," the emblematical representation of the five sorrowful mysteries of the Rosary—viz. the heart of the Holy Virgin pierced with five swords. There is still an ale-house of this name in Charles-street, Hatton-garden, and Bleeding Heart-yard, adjoin-ing the public-house, is immortalised in *Little Dorrit*. The "Wounded Heart," one of the signs in Norwich in 1750, had the same meaning. The heart was a constant emblem of the Holy Virgin in the Middle Ages. Thus, on the clog almanacs all the feasts of St. Mary were indicated by a heart. It was not an uncommon sign in former times.

'The rose, besides being the queen of flowers and the na-tional emblem, had yet another prestige, which alone would have been sufficient to make it a favourite sign in the Middle Ages: this was its religious import. On the monumental brass of Abbot Kirton, formerly in Westminster Abbey, there was a crowned rose, with I.H.S. in its heart, and round it the words:

"Sis, Rosa, Flos Florum, Morbis Medicina Meorum;"

and in Caxton's *Psalter*, above a woodcut representing an angel holding a shield with a rose on it, occur the words:

"Per te, rosa, tolluntur vitia,
Per te datur mœstis lætioia."

It was evidently an emblem of the Virgin, and may contain some allusion to the rose of Jericho, or to the Christmas rose.'

Flowers.

This mention of Mary as the rose—Rosa Mystica, as the Church calls her—brings us naturally to the subject of flowers.

'Almost every district,' says Dr. Rock, 'had and has its Lady-grove, its Mary-field, its Mary's-well, its Lady's-mead, besides patches of ground by wood and stream, with other such-like denominations. Nay, the hind also knew how to tell the feelings of his heart ; and though he owned no mead, nor field, nor grove, upon which to bestow the name of her he loved, he could and did choose the flowers that grew there for his symbols, calling one our Lady's mantle, another Mary-gold; this Virgin's bower, that Mary's fan.'[15]

The author of the *Catholic Florist* mentions other flowers, such as our Lady's seal, our Lady's laces, our Lady's slipper, our Lady's bedstraw, our Lady's fringes, our Lady's hair. Nor must we forget the little flower of which Shakespeare sings :

> ' When daisies pied and violets blue,
>   And *lady-smocks* all silver-white,
>   And cuckoo-buds of yellow hue,
>   Do paint the meadows with delight.'[16]

Dr. Prior adds several more, as—fair maids of February, or snowdrops ; Lady's bower, Lady's comb, Lady's garters, Lady's cushion, Lady's fingers, Lady's looking-glass, Lady's seal, &c.[17]

Works of Art.

With the exception of churches, few works of ancient art have survived the Reformation. It is well known that as all the art of the Middle Ages grew up under the influence of the Church, so was it all consecrated more or less directly to religion. Hence it has all perished. When I come to tell how our Lady lost her Dowry, I shall have to rehearse some of those shameful edicts which swept from churches, and even from private houses, into the fire or the melting-pot, every object on which a sacred image was traced.

A few remnants now are treasured in our museums, to excite regret for what has perished.

I copy from Dr. Waagen the description of some miniature paintings of our Blessed Lady. Speaking of a Psalter of the

---

[15] *Church of our Fathers*, vol. iii. p. 288.
[16] *Love's Labour lost*, act v. scene 2.
[17] *Popular Names of British Plants*, by R. C. A. Prior, M.D.

eleventh century, now in the British Museum, he says : ' This
contains, in a merely drawn-in style, a large number of remarkable and generally animated subjects. Especially distinguished
for the peculiar feeling of the motive is the Virgin, enthroned
in a green almond-shaped glory, supported by four angels, pressing her cheek to that of the Infant Saviour, with her right hand
placed on His head. A large bird, seated on her left arm, is
doubtless intended for the Holy Ghost. The Child is holding
the globe in His left hand, and giving the benediction with His
right. The ground-colour beyond the glory is of a very beautiful green. The proportions are very long, the forms very
meagre, but the motives frequently happy.'[16]

The same learned critic thus describes a more important
miniature painting of our Lady in the thirteenth century :

' The *History of the English Nation*, an autograph manuscript by Matthew of Paris, an English monk, known as an
author from 1241 to his death in 1259, and whose name was
probably derived from a long residence in Paris (MSS. Regia, 14
C vii.), folio, 226 leaves, written in two columns, with somewhat small minuscule letters. The first five pages contain a
map of England, with Scotland, with very clear representations
of different cities. I mention this manuscript chiefly in order
to call attention to the picture of the Virgin, enthroned as
Queen of Heaven, with the Child ; which is one of the best
miniatures of the thirteenth century known to me, and a striking proof of the excellence which the art had attained at that
time. The throne is formed of a kind of altar, with a cushion
upon it. Head, figure, and motive exhibit unusual grandeur.
She is inclining her crowned head, with her brown hair flowing
down, caressingly to the Child, pressing her cheek against His,
while with her right hand she gives Him a red fruit. The proportions are correct, the forms full and well drawn. The execution is chiefly with the pen, shadowed with lines ; the shadows
of the tunic are blue and red shot, of the mantle green, the
parchment being left for the lights. The throne is similarly
treated, as also the simple border. Below is the figure of a

[16] *Treasures of Art in Great Britain*, vol. i. p. 145.

monk, small (in pen and sepia), lying on the ground, with the inscription : " Frater Mathias Pariensis," and a prayer, which he is addressing to the Virgin. As Matthew of Paris was known also as a painter, this picture may probably proceed from his own hand.'[10]

One more extract relating to the fifteenth century :

' There is no work, however, which bears such testimony to the state of English art from about 1420-1430 as the miniatures of a religious poem in the English language (Cotton. Faustina, B vi.). This poem occupies the last twenty-two leaves of a folio volume. . . . . P. 108a is the most remarkable picture of all. Below is a young man upon his death-bed, his delicate and noble features expressing the faith and hope in which he is expiring. At the foot of the bed stands Death in the form of a skeleton, about to pierce the heart of the patient with a red spear, and a black demon with a hook in his hand reaching towards him. Nothing else but the hook and his claws are visible. The rest of the figure has been almost entirely obliterated, and obviously with design. At the head of the dying man is an angel in the act of receiving the soul, which is represented as a naked infant. Above is the Virgin in light-violet drapery of admirable arrangement, with the crown on her head, supplicating Christ, by the breast which nourished Him, and which she is baring, to have mercy on the soul of the dying man. Christ, who is represented in a bright-crimson mantle, is showing His wounds, in token of granting His Mother's request, to the First Person of the Trinity, who is raising His right hand in benediction. This last figure is enthroned, with a long beard and a blue mantle, in which some sharp breaks already occur. Each figure is accompanied by a long scroll with the words they are supposed to utter.'[20]

A subject treated much in the same manner is represented in a plate published in the third volume of the *Vetusta Monumenta.* It is the death of John Islip, Abbot of Westminster, in 1532. He is surrounded by a group of figures of saints—St. Peter, St. John Baptist, St. Katherine, St. Margaret, and others. But

---

[10] Dr. Waagen, vol. i. letter vi. p. 158.   [20] Ib. pp. 183-4.

the Blessed Virgin stands at the foot of his bed, wearing a crown, and from her mouth comes a scroll with the words, 'Islip, O Fili, veniens miserere Joanni,—O my Son, have mercy on John Islip when Thou comest to judgment.' In the upper part of the picture our Lord is seen. His feet rest on a globe. A sword, the emblem of justice, is on one side, an olive-branch, the emblem of mercy, on the other.

Dr. Rock gives a woodcut from two wall-paintings, both done in the fourteenth century, one in Islip church, the other in the neighbouring church of Beckley, Oxon. 'St. Michael the Archangel holds the sanctuary's golden balance, in one scale of which is shown the quaking soul' (as an infant with hands joined) 'with its few good deeds; within the other are all its sins, which the devil, under the shape of a horned hairy beast, strives to make heavier, as he pulls at the beam, to make it lean towards his side. At the other end we behold the Blessed Virgin Mary' (crowned and sceptered) 'befriending by her prayers to heaven the poor forlorn sinner under trial, and in whose behalf she triumphs, as she withstands the wicked one; for, by casting her rosary upon the balance, she turns it, and so wins a soul from Satan and for heaven.'[21]

Very few such wall-pictures, which were common in all churches, escaped the whitewash in the first years of Edward, or passed undaubed through the Puritan dominion of the Commonwealth. So also of the works of art in gold and silver, on very many of which our Lady was represented, there remains not one in a thousand to tell of the skill or piety of former days. The Venetian who wrote an account of his visit to England in 1500 thus tells what he saw : 'Above all are their riches displayed in the church treasures; for there is not a parish church in the kingdom so mean as not to possess crucifixes, candlesticks, censers, patens, and cups of silver; nor is there a convent of mendicant friars so poor as not to have all these same articles in silver, besides many other ornaments worthy of a cathedral church in the same metal. Your magnificence may, therefore,

[21] *Church of our Fathers*, vol. iii. p. 197.

imagine what the decorations of those enormously rich Benedictine, Carthusian, and Cistercian monasteries must be.'[22]

Similarly the Bohemian traveller in 1465 writes that in London—probably in St. Paul's or Westminster—a large golden shrine was shown to him, blazing with precious gems. 'I never saw carving elsewhere so subtle and elegant as in that church. . . . In London alone are twenty golden shrines, adorned with precious gems, and in the whole kingdom there are as many as eighty such.'[23]

But these works of art, which excited the admiration of foreigners who had travelled through Germany, Spain, and Italy, aroused the cupidity of our own kings and nobles, who cared only for the money value of the metal, and had almost as little reverence for art as for religion—'men who would cast sacred ashes to the winds for the costly reliquary containing them, and abolish the daily Sacrifice to secure the jewelled chalice in which it was offered.'

[22] *A Relation of the Island of England*, p. 29 (Camden Society).
[23] *Itineris a Leone de Rosmital &c. Commentarii*, p. 40.

CHAPTER XII.

GUILDS OF OUR LADY.

MUCH has been written on the subject of the ancient Guilds or Fraternities of England, institutions which reach back to the earliest Saxon times, and were in full force at the time of the Reformation. Not only so, but in their chief characteristics guilds remained unchanged during the whole of that period. One of the earliest records of guild statutes contains the three features that we find in almost every guild of the fourteenth century —charity, conviviality, and piety. These confraternities were organised for the performance of various works of charity and mercy; they were enlivened and kept together by occasional social gatherings of the members; and they were elevated and consecrated to God by being placed under the invocation of some saint or pious mystery, by prayer and worship, and the performance of various other acts of religion. Even when their object was mutual protection or assistance in art or trade, like our modern Trade Unions, they still retained, in nearly every case, the three features just mentioned. The statutes of the early Saxon guild of Exeter will illustrate what has just been said :

Exeter Guild (Anglo-Saxon).

'This assembly was collected in Exeter for the love of God and for our souls' need, both in regard to our health of life here and to the after-days, which we desire for ourselves by God's doom. Now we have agreed that our meeting shall be thrice in the twelve months: once at St. Michael's Mass; secondly at St. Mary's Mass, after midwinter' (Purification, 2d February); 'and thirdly at Allhallows Mass, after Easter; and let each guild-brother have two sesters of malt, and each young man one sester and a sceat of honey; and let the Mass-priest at each of our meetings sing two Masses—one for our living friends, the other for the dead; and let each brother of common condition sing two psalters of psalms, one for the living and one for the dead; and at the death of a brother, each man six Masses or six psalters of psalms; and at a death, each man fivepence; and at a houseburning, each man one penny. And if any one neglect the day, for the first time three Masses, for the second five, and for the third time let him have no favour, unless his neglect arose from sickness or his lord's need,' &c.[1]

It will be seen that a guild served the purpose both of life and fire insurance companies, that it was an association for prayer, while the malt and honey tell of the sweet ale which our Saxon forefathers loved so well.

From the immense number of guilds in England, it would seem that almost every decent man and woman must have belonged to some guild, while many belonged to two or three at once. Mr. Taylor, in his *Index Monasticus* of the county of Norfolk, gives a list of 909 guilds in that one county; and of these I have counted no less than 155 as dedicated to our Lady, under her various titles.   •

'The guilds,' says Mr. Toulmin Smith, 'were lay bodies, and existed for lay purposes, and the better to enable those who belonged to them rightly and understandingly to fulfil their neighbourly duties as freemen in a free state.'[2] Priests, however, might belong to them in their private capacities, and priests often acted as chaplains to them. But they do not seem to have had, like many modern confraternities, weekly or monthly meetings for instruction or prayer under the entire direction of the clergy. Sometimes, indeed, their purpose is purely spiritual, as for the better celebration of the festival of Corpus Christi, for keeping up the annual celebration of a religious play, or the daily singing of an antiphon of our Lady.

In all cases the religious element enters largely into them. They all make provision for the Christian burial of deceased members and their annual obits; they all have a patron saint,

---

[1] Given by Kemble, *Saxons in England*, vol. i. App. D, p. 512.
[2] *Introduction to English Guilds*, Early English Text Society.

and keep their patron's feast; they all keep lights in the churches before their altars or statues.

Women belonged to them equally, or almost equally, with men. The members generally took an oath of obedience, but only to known and approved statutes. There was no such thing as blind obedience, and the secrecy was merely as to matters of trade. They all had payments, both regular and extraordinary. They met once, twice, three, or four times a year, to elect officers, transact business, audit accounts, feast, and pray.

I have said that they have three features in common— charity, piety, and conviviality.

1. As to *charity*, they cared for the sick, the aged, the unfortunate by fire or shipwreck. They gave marriage-dowries to poor maidens, helped people in prison, sent pilgrims to shrines. They gave feasts to the poor, beds to strangers, mended highways, repaired and built bridges and walls, helped to build churches and supply chalices and vestments, supported schools and schoolmasters.

Of course I do not mean that each confraternity furthered all these works of charity; but the above are works mentioned in various statutes, or gathered from local histories.

2. As regards *piety*, the meetings always began by prayer. The following is a specimen of the prayers offered up by guilds. It is from the statutes of the Fraternity of St. Christopher, established in Norwich in 1384 :

' In the worship of Jesu Christ, and of His dear Mother, and of St. Christopher the holy martyr, and all holy hallows, devoutly we begin this fraternity by these ordinances underwritten:

' In the beginning ye shall pray devoutly for the state of holy Church, and for the peace of the land; for the Pope of Rome and his cardinals, for the patriarch of Jerusalem; for the Holy Land and the holy Cross, that God for His might and mercy bring it out of heathen power into rule of holy Church ;[1] and that God of His mercy make peace and unity in holy

---

[1] In the Homily of the Church of England on the Peril of Idolatry, Catholics are held up to ridicule for offering this prayer for the recovery of the holy Cross.

Church; and for all archbishops and bishops, and specially for our bishop of Norwich; for all parsons and priests, and all orders of holy Church, that God of His mercy save them and keep them, body and soul, and give them grace here order to keep, and so to rule holy Church and man's soul, that it be to God's worship and salvation of their souls, and to all Christian men; for our lord the king, for our lady the queen; dukes, earls, barons, and bachelors of the land, that God of His grace save them and keep them from deadly sin, and give them grace, the realm and holy Church and their own souls so to rule and keep that it be worship to God and to all Christian men salvation; for all knights, squires, citizens and burgesses, franklins and all the tillers and men of craft, widows, maidens, wives, and for all the commonalty and Christian people, that God of His mercy save them and keep them that in this world live with truth, and give them grace so to do that it be worship of God and salvation to their souls; for all true shipmen and true pilgrims, that God for His grace give them wedering [weather] and passage, that they may safely come and go; for the fruit of the land and of the sea and the wedering; for all men that be in false belief and would[4] be in good belief, God give them grace to come to their desire; for our fathers' souls and mothers, brethren and sisteren, and for all the brethren and sisteren of this guild, and for all Christian souls. Amen.

' And also it is ordained, that this bede and prayer shall be rehearsed and said at every time that the aldermen and the brethren be together.'[5]

The above enumeration was called 'bidding the bedes.' When these intentions had been read out certain prayers were said by all, generally some Paters and Aves. These are mentioned in the following statute of the Carpenters' guild, established in Norwich 1375 : ' It was begun for this intent, for to increase a light of torches at sacrament of Christ's Body at high altar.

' Then it is that all brethren and sisteren shall come together

---

[4] *i.e.* wish to be.

[5] *English Guilds*, by Toulmin Smith, p. 22 (Early English Text Society, 1870).

on the Saturday at even next after the Ascension of our Lord Christ, every year, at the place assigned by the alderman and his two fellows in Norwich, in cause of devotion, and there bid a bede before their light in honour of Trinity, and there recommend in their mind the state of holy Church, and for peace and unity in the land; and for all the brethren's souls and sisters' souls of their guild, and all their friends' souls, and all Christians. And every of them shall say with good devotion five Paternoster and five Ave Maria before the candle burning.'[6]

The guild of the Assumption in Wigendale, county Norfolk, prescribes 'In the worship of God and of His Mother, in amendment of our life and salvation of our souls, say a Paternoster and an Ave by charity;' then some Latin versicles, among which, 'Maria Virgo semper lætare; Quæ meruisti Christum portare; Cœli et terræ conditorem; Quem de utero protulisti mundi Redemptorem.' Then a bidding prayer resembling that of Norwich, given above, with some other Latin prayers.[7]

The statutes of the guild of St. Peter in the same town of Wigendale show some of the pious practices in use :[8]

'In honour and worship of Jesus Christ, and of His dear Mother St. Mary, and of all the holy fellowship of heaven, and especially of the holy Apostle St. Peter, in whose worship this fraternity is begun. . . . At the general day, that each brother be ready with others to go to the kirk with his brethren with a garland of oak-leaves. It is ordained by the assent of all the brethren and sisters of this fraternity, that every brother and sister be ready to go to the kirk when any brother or sister is dead of this fraternity; and that every brother offer a halfpenny; and that each brother give a halfpennyworth of bread for his soul, and that he have seven Masses sung for his soul.

'And also, if he die—that is to say if he be perished by water or by land—then shall the guild brethren go seek him three mile about, and bring him to Christian men's burying, if he be not in power of his own chattel ;[9] and the light be brought before

---

[6] *English Guilds*, by Toulmin Smith, p. 37 (Early English Text Society, 1870).　　[7] Ib. p. 111.　　[8] Ib. p. 117.
[9] If he did not leave property sufficient to defray the cost of his burial.

A A

him to the dirge and to the kirk ; that is for to say, a torch that shall burn at the elevation of the Mass every Sunday.

'Also when that the brethren and sistern be gathered at their general day, what good man come to our fraternity he shall have meat and drink while it will last.

'And also a taper for to burn before St. Peter, of a pound of wax.'

On the great feast-day of the fraternity, and sometimes even more than once in the year, the members, well dressed, or wearing a livery, or adorned with the garlands of flowers or oak-leaves,[10] carrying lighted wax tapers in their hands, besides the great candle wreathed with flowers to be offered at the shrine, would go through the city in procession, to hear Mass solemnly sung at their own altar. The following day they assembled again for the Dirge and Requiem for deceased members, and then adjourned to transact business. This custom seems to have been universal. But occasionally the procession to the church took the form of a religious pageant. In the statutes of the guild of St. Mary in Beverley, founded in 1355, it is provided that 'every year, on the feast of the Purification of the Blessed Mary, all the brethren and sisters shall meet together in a fit and appointed place, away from the church ; and there one of the guild shall be clad in comely fashion as a queen, like to the glorious Virgin Mary, having what may seem a son in her arms ; and two others shall be clad like to Joseph and Simeon ; and two shall go as angels, carrying a candle-bearer, on which shall be twenty-four thick wax lights. With these and other great lights borne before them, and with much music and gladness, the pageant Virgin with her Son, and Joseph and Simeon, shall go in procession to the church. And all the sisters of the guild shall follow the Virgin, and afterwards all the brethren ; and each of them shall carry a wax light weighing half a pound. And they shall go two and two, slowly pacing to the church ; and when they have got there, the pageant Virgin shall offer her Son to Simeon at the high altar ; and all the sisters and

---

[10] On the garlands worn by guilds, see *Reminiscences of City of London and its Livery Companies*, by Rev. T. Arundell, chap. xviii.

brethren shall offer their wax lights, together with a penny each. All this having been solemnly done, they shall go home again with gladness.' It is fair to give the rest of the statutes of this fraternity. 'On the same day, after dinner, the brethren and sisters shall meet together, and shall eat bread and cheese and drink ale, rejoicing in the Lord, in praise of the glorious Virgin Mary.'[11] Then they choose the officers for the ensuing year. But let it not be thought that this was a mere festive guild. After declaring that 'prayers and offerings shall be made for the dead,' the statutes continue : ' The alderman and stewards of the guild shall visit those brethren and sisters who are poor, ailing, or weak, and who have not enough of their own to live upon ; and they shall give to these as they think right out of the guild stock, viz. to each one eightpence, sixpence, or at least fourpence, every week, to help their needs. And if any of those poor brethren dies, or any other of the guild who is not well off, he shall be buried at the cost of the guild, and have all becoming services.'[12]

3. Let me, however, say a little more on the convivial character of guilds.

An example of the union of charity with innocent enjoyment, both springing out of devotion to our Lady, is seen in the statutes of the guild of the Holy Cross, in Stratford-on-Avon.[13] This was established in or before the thirteenth century. The statutes are from a MS. of 1389. Payments were to be made four times a year, and from this fund one wax taper was to be kept up, in honour of our Lord Jesus Christ, of the Blessed Virgin, and of the Holy Cross. 'And the taper shall be kept alight every day throughout the year, at every Mass in the church, before the blessed Cross; so that God and the Blessed Virgin and the venerable Cross may keep all the brethren and sisters from every ill.' Then after other statutes on the care of the dead and of strangers : 'It is further ordained by the brethren and sisters that each of them shall give twopence a year, at a meeting which shall be held once a year, viz. a feast which

[11] There is frequent mention of ale-drinking in the statutes of guilds ; in fact, few things were done in England without ale ; but good regulations were made about sobriety.

[12] *English Guilds*, p. 149.   [13] Ib. p. 215.

shall be held in Easter week, in such manner that brotherly love
shall be cherished among them, and evil speaking be driven out,
that peace shall always dwell among them, and true love be upheld.   And every sister of the guild shall bring with her to this
feast a great tankard ; and all the tankards shall be filled with
ale ; and afterwards the ale shall be given to the poor.   So likewise shall the brethren do.   But before that ale shall be given
to the poor, and before any brother or sister shall touch the
feast in the hall, all the brethren and sisters there shall put up
their prayer, that God and the Blessed Virgin, and the venerable Cross, in whose honour they have come together, will keep
them from all ills and sins.   And if any brother or sister shall,
after the bell has sounded, quarrel, or stir up a quarrel, he shall
pay a halfpenny.'

In the regulations regarding the annual festival I have found
none so detailed as the statutes of a Salisbury guild.

Confraternity of Tailors in Salisbury.

This company must have existed at an early period, and is
said to have obtained a charter from Henry VI.   Edward IV.,
however, is the sovereign to whom they owe their actual charter
of incorporation, under the title of ' Wardens and Commonalty
of the Mystery of Tailors, Brothers and Sisters of the Guild or
Confraternity of St. John the Baptist.'   Among other privileges
he granted them permission to establish a perpetual chantry of
four chaplains, to celebrate daily in the chapel of St. John the
Baptist, in the church of St. Thomas ; and to acquire lands,
tenements, and possessions for the maintenance of this charity,
and for works of charity and godliness, to the amount of twenty
pounds' yearly value.   This charter is dated at Westminster, on
the 14th of December 1461, and was subsequently confirmed by
Bishop Beauchamp and by the dean and chapter.

Their primary regulations are as follow :

' We have ordered that in every year, in the feast of the
Nativity of St. John the Baptist, a solemn obit be holden,
while the world standeth fast, for our founder William Swayne,
and Christen his wife, and all his children, and for his father's

soul and mother's soul, and for all his friends' souls, and for all
the brethren and sisters' souls of our said craft, that be out of this
world deceased, within St. Thomas' church of Salisbury, in the
chapel of St. John Baptist; that is to say, on the even the Dirige
by note, and on the morrow the Mass of Requiem by note,
which Mass to begin when Matins be done, at eleven of the
clock.

'And that our said wardens, stewards, and chamberlains, with
all our holy craft and fraternity and our servants, to be attended
upon by the mayor of the city of the time, and other worshipful with him of the same, to bring in the light of our said fraternity from the chandler's house unto the said St. Thomas'
church, unto St. John's chapel there; and there to abide at the
Mass, and offer at the same, all our craft. And which if our
craft lack, and be not at the said Mass and offering thereof, to
give to our said craft 1 lb. of wax, without a lawful excuse is
made to the wardens and to the stewards.

'That the ten stewards for the time being, every year, shall
make and set afore St. John the Baptist, upon the altar, two
tapers of 1 lb. of wax, and a garland of roses, to be set upon St.
John's head, and that the chapel be strewed with green rushes.
And when Mass is done, to go together to our place accustomed,
where our dinner shall be holden, and there to abide at dinner
and feast till we have dined; for the which dinner every master
of the said craft shall pay, for him and his wife, twelvepence,
and for their supper, if they will come thereto, the same money.
A man alone eightpence, and a woman alone sixpence; and no
dinner, neither feast, longer by us to be kept, save only the same
day, and that yearly, to be kept while the world standeth.

'And such persons of our craft as have promised our stewards
to come to dinner, and come not, they shall pay everych of them
eightpence, to the use of the stewards which merit and do the
cost of that day.

'Also we have ordained, that at the said feast and dinner
such of our servants called journeymen as be within our said
craft shall serve the masters of the craft, in the time of bringing
in our light, and at our feast and dinner; there abiding with us

at dinner, at such place as the masters and wardens will assign. At which dinner every servant to pay fourpence; and that our said stewards, when the masters be served in at the first course, they shall purvey an honest place for all such servants, to be set at a board or boards conveniently within the same place, and to be served by the apprentices, at the masters' assignment, conveniently for their degree.

'And then for the second course of the masters, by the said stewards they be warned to arise, and for to serve in likewise the said masters as they did the first course, making them as merry as they can.

'The stewards to make yearly eight torches, weighing five score lb. and seven, and also five tapers, to be brought on midsummer-day to St. Thomas' church worshipfully, after the old rule and our custom; for the which making of torches and tapers aforesaid the said chamberlains shall receive of every brother and sister that be coupled twelvepence, and for every journeyman fourpence, and hereof to make a reckoning afore our founder while he is alive.'[14]

From the old Catholic guilds sprung the modern livery companies of London. More than one of these was dedicated to our Lady, as the Skinners' Company, and the Drapers and the Leathersellers.[15]

'The religious character of these corporations,' says Mr. Arundell, 'is not only exhibited in the mode of their foundation, in appointing chaplains to pray for each member by name, to sing Mass daily, and to say grace at feasts, but also in choosing patron saints, and founding altars to such saints in the churches, the advowsons of which they held. We know of no trade company of the kind which was not at its origin ranged under the protection of some patron saint. The Drapers claimed the Virgin Mary, Mother of the "Holy Lamb," and worshipped at St. Mary Bethlem church, Bishopsgate; the Fishmongers

---

[14] The above is from Sir R. Hoare's *History of Wiltshire*, p. 192. It confirms the opinion of the editor of *English Guilds*, that the word 'potatio' in the early guilds means a banquet, and not a mere drinking.

[15] *Reminiscences of City of London and its Livery Companies*, p. 123.

adopted St. Peter (who was himself a fisherman), and attended
at St. Peter's church; the Goldsmiths' patron saint was St.
Dunstan, supposed to have been a brother of the craft. . . The
Leathersellers claimed the Holy Virgin, and the figure of the
Mother of our Lord formed the company's common seal until
the Reformation, when, the emblem being deemed too papisti-
cal, the seal was destroyed, and a new one, still in use, was
executed.' This gentleman adds, with that peculiar facility
which belongs to many Protestant clergymen of casting forth
wholesale accusations of hideous crimes: 'The veneration paid
by the early merchants to the memory of their patron saints
was not only superstitious but idolatrous.' Yet in another
place he is compelled to say : ' Our forefathers had no tendency
to that species of unbelief which so characterises the present
age—the habit of doubting and even denying the truth and
inspiration of the sacred writings, and of treating lightly the
mysteries of our holy religion. They were not merely nominal
Christians, but they had a firm faith in the Founder of Christianity, or, as He is so beautifully designated in their earliest
form of institution to office, " Him Crucified." These simple
Christians believed in the sacred books of the old dispensation,
and in those also of the new, which record the sayings and
teachings, the miracles and sufferings, of Him who was born of
the Virgin.'

It appears to me that if Mr. Arundell had paid less attention to the Book of Homilies of his Church, and more to the
sacred books, he would have been slower in making charges of
idolatry against his forefathers. He would have read in St.
John, ' He that *keepeth His word*, in him in very deed the
charity of God is perfected, and by this we know that we are in
Him' (1 John ii. 5); and again, ' God is charity, and he that
abideth in charity abideth in God and God in him' (1 John iv. 16).
Now whether the honours paid by the guilds to St. Dunstan or
St. Peter were idolatrous or not cannot be more than matter of
opinion to Mr. Arundell ; but that the ancient guilds and livery
companies abounded in works of charity is matter of fact. Even
the mottoes of the companies might have made their historian

hesitate to class them with idolaters. That of the Skinners is
'To God only be all glory;' that of the Haberdashers, 'Serve
and obey;' that of the Ironmongers, 'God is our strength.'

One of the works of charity which has sprung from these
guilds has an almost world-wide fame; though but few who
speak of *Bedlam* connect the word in their minds with anything religious. Yet the institution known now as Bedlam or
Bethlem Hospital was a fraternity in connection with the
Drapers' Company. It was established early in the reign of
Edward III. 'To the honour of our Lord Jesus Christ, and
His sweet Mother Saint Mary, our Lady of Bethlehem, in
which most holy place our said Lord Jesus Christ was chosen
to be born, in His salvation of all His people, in which place
of Bethlehem the star appeared to the shepherds, and gave and
showed light to the kings of Cologne, who offered in the same
place of Bethlehem their gifts, gold, myrrh, and incense,—our
fraternity is begun for the same honour, in amendment of their
lives, by the assent of the friar, William Tytte, friar of the
hospital of our Lady of Bethlehem,' &c.

The Sovereign Pontiff encouraged the guilds by the grant of
spiritual favours. In the days when these associations were
hated as superstitious assemblies, or when they were mocked at
for the simple pageantry in which they delighted, of course the
Popes were blamed for the encouragement they extended towards
them. 'The Pope's wares' was a favourite theme with the
Reformers. But juster views now prevail. 'The influence of
such unions,' says a writer in Knight's *London*, 'for the exercise
of benevolence and for mutual defence against oppression, animated by the mystic enthusiasm of devotional feelings, may
easily be imagined. The eagerness shown by kings and nobles
to be received into them indicates the power of the fraternities.
It was they that made the burgess feel himself a limb of the
Church, that brought the Church to sit at his fireside, and made
it a partner in all his enterprises.'[16]

'In the midst of the perplexing problems presented by
trades-unionism, and the dangers to enterprise and manly

[16] Knight's *London*, vol. iv. p. 222.

liberty threatened by its restrictive rules,' Mr. Toulmin Smith, who had made a deep study of the subject, 'saw how the ancient principle of association, more than a thousand years old, had been in use as a living practice among the common folk; that it had been a part of the essential life of England, and always worked well till forcibly meddled with;' and he believed that if the spirit of the old guilds could be revived, it would be with great advantage to modern society.[17]

Intelligent and candid writers such as these would easily appreciate the encouragement given to the spirit of association by the Popes, though the manner of this encouragement would probably be a sad puzzle to them. I quote an example.

Guild of our Lady in St. Botolph's, Boston.

According to Foxe the Popes had granted this guild many privileges.

1. Leave to the members to choose confessor.

2. Portable altar, with leave to anticipate usual time for Mass.

3. By visiting chapel of our Lady same privilege as at Rome by visiting the 'stations' or seven churches.

4. Plenary indulgence at death.

5. Leave to have Mass, &c. even during an interdict.

6. Plenary indulgence by visit to chapel on Nativity or Assumption of our Lady; or, if prevented, they visited their parish church, and said a Pater and Ave.

7. Indulgence of Scala Cœli on Fridays, by visiting chapel.

8. Dispensation for white meats in Lent.

9. Indulgences for the holy souls on certain conditions.[18]

The guilds which, under the patronage of our Lady and the saints, had for centuries been the prolific source of every kind of public and social benefit to England, were swept away by acts of servile Parliaments in the 37th of Henry VIII. and 1st of Edward VI., and their property became a prey for the greater part to the rapacity of hungry courtiers. 'The Act of Henry,' says Mr. Toulmin Smith, 'passed in 1545 put this

[17] *English Guilds*, introduction, p. xiii.   [18] Foxe, vol. v. p. 365.

wanton and wicked pillage of public property as necessary " for the maintenance of these present wars ;" but it also cleverly put into one group " colleges, free chápels, chantries, hospitals, fraternities, brotherhoods, and guilds." The Act of Edward was still more ingenious ; for it held up the dogma of purgatory to abhorrence, and began to hint at grammar schools. The object of both Acts was the same. All the possessions of all guilds, except what could creep out as being trading guilds (which saved the London guilds), became vested by these two Acts in the Crown ; and the unprincipled courtiers who had devised and helped the scheme gorged themselves out of this whole-sale plunder of what was, in every sense, public property." The same author calls it in a note 'a case of pure wholesale robbery and plunder, done by an unscrupulous faction to satisfy their personal greed, under cover of law. No more gross case of wanton plunder is to be found in the history of all Europe— no page so black in English history.'[10]

The Scapular.

In connection with guilds of our Lady I must here add a few words about the famous confraternity of the Scapular of Mount Carmel, which is of English origin.

'A prominent place,' says Mosheim, 'among the instances of the crafty arrogance [of the mendicant orders] is due to the fable circulated by the Carmelites respecting Simon Stock, a general of their order, who died near the beginning of the century. They pretended that the Virgin Mary appeared to him, and promised that no person should be eternally lost who should expire clothed in the short mantle worn on their shoulders by the Carmelites, and called the scapular. And this fiction,. equally ridiculous and impious, has found advocates even among the Pontiffs.' He adds in a note that ' even the modern Pontiff,

---

[10] *English Guilds*, introd. p. xliii. For further information on this subject, besides the works above quoted and Herbert's *History of the Twelve Companies*, the reader can consult Dr. Rock's *Church of our Fathers*, vol. ii. pp. 395-453, where most interesting details are given. I have avoided going over the same ground.

Benedict XIV., did not hesitate to give countenance to this fable, yet in his usual prudent and cautious manner.'[20]

Now let me begin by stating the Catholic doctrine according to which the scapular is to be judged, and has been judged by Sovereign Pontiffs.

We do not attribute salvation to the possession of a piece of cloth, blest or unblest, but to the possession of the grace of God at the moment of death. It will scarcely be maintained that Catholics attach more value to the Carmelite scapular than to the water of baptism instituted by Jesus Christ. Yet all Catholics believe with St. Peter, that if baptism saves, it is not by 'the putting away of the filth of the flesh,' but 'the examination of a good conscience towards God by the resurrection of Jesus Christ' (1 Peter iii. 21). The scapular is not a sacrament, nor has it the efficacy of a sacrament. If, then, a promise is thought to have been made by the Blessed Virgin, that 'those who die with this scapular shall not suffer the pains of hell,' this can only be understood, according to Catholic principles, in one of two ways. Some have taken the words absolutely, and then they maintain that those who wear the scapular out of devout affection to the Blessed Virgin will receive through her intercession the graces necessary to a good life, or to repentance after sin, and so will obtain final perseverance. On the other hand, say the advocates of this interpretation, if men, abusing their free will, reject the graces offered to them, if they harden themselves in sin, above all, if they presume on our Lady's protection to sin more confidently, they will die in their sins, and be lost; but in that case our Lady will take care that they do not die with her scapular.

Other authors adopt another method of interpreting our Lady's promise. Cardinal Lambertini may be their spokesman. (I call him Cardinal, for he was not Pope when he wrote the work which Mosheim cites as if it were an authoritative declaration of Pope Benedict XIV.; and elevation to the Papacy does not convert books previously written into teachings

[20] Mosheim, *Ecclesiastical History*, vol. ii. book ii. cent. 13, p. 529 (ed. Soames).

ex cathedrâ.) 'According to scriptural mode of speaking,' writes this learned theologian, 'eternal life is promised to things which do indeed help towards it, yet taken alone are non-sufficient to obtain it. Thus in Rom. (ch. iii. 28) "we account a man to be justified by faith," and (ch. viii. 24) "we are saved by hope;" and (Tobias xii. 9) "alms delivereth from death, and the same is that which purgeth away sins."... Besides in the vision' of St. Simon Stock 'we do not read that he will escape hell who wears the scapular and does nothing else; for other good works are also commanded, in which it is necessary to persevere. "Brethren" (such are the words of St. Simon in relating his vision), "laying up this promise in your hearts, strive to make your election sure by good works, and not to faint. Watch in thanksgiving for so great a mercy, praying without ceasing, that the word spoken to me may be glorified to the praise of the most Holy Trinity, the Father, and Jesus Christ, and the Holy Ghost, and of the ever-blessed Virgin Mary."' Lambertini then quotes two Carmelite writers who give the same interpretation. One of them writes: 'On the part of our Lady, and as far as regards the copious grace which she will obtain, in view of the scapular which she herself gave as a sign of salvation, as a pledge of peace, the wearer will be saved; unless he on his part fall on the rock of scandal, by rash transgression, of the Divine law.'

But it may be asked, even with these explanations, what can a scapular have to do with the prayers of our Lady, or the obtaining of Divine grace? A little reflection will suggest the answer. The scapular is the symbol or badge of the confraternity of our Lady. Surely nothing but religious prejudice can blind men to the meaning of words used by Catholics on this subject, when they themselves habitually use the very same forms of expression in analogous matters. If in popular language men attribute honour, distinction, the favour of the sovereign, to the conferring on a subject the Garter of St. George, and if he would be held a caviller and a fool who should misunderstand this language, and ask how honour could belong to a piece of velvet or to diamonds, must not those also be esteemed cavillers who will not understand in what sense we attach the special favour of our Lady to a piece of brown cloth ?

It may perhaps be thought by some that the explanations I have given have only been invented in modern times, in order to reply to the scorn and ridicule of Protestants, and that in the thirteenth century Catholics would have had no difficulty in expecting their salvation from the mere fact of wearing an external badge. Of course it is not easy to say to what lengths human folly may go in any age. There certainly have been Protestants who have taken the Lutheran doctrine of faith alone literally and carried it out to its worst conclusions; and there have been others who have presumed on their acceptance with God at death, from their Calvinistic fancy that they had once been elect and that election cannot be forfeited. There certainly never was even a small sect among Catholics who held that if once invested with the scapular they would be safe, whatever might be their life. And if any individuals have so presumed (for myself I never met one, nor have conversed with any who had met one), they would soon have been roused from their delusion by the language of the Catholic pulpit. As to the thirteenth century—St. Simon Stock is supposed to have had his vision about the year 1250. Exactly at the same time the new orders of Franciscans and Dominicans were overrunning Europe, preaching in every pulpit. Here is a specimen of their style. Berthold of Ratisbonne says : ' Take the cross in your hand, and traverse the ocean, and strive against the heathen, and win back to Christendom the Holy Sepulchre and smite heathendom far and near, up and down, with your courage and your sword, and let yourself be slain in the service of our Lord God Almighty, and let them put you in the Holy Sepulchre where once our Redeemer lay, and place over you the Cross on which God Himself died for the whole human race ; and if it were possible that God should stand at the head of the sepulchre, with our Lady the Holy Virgin near Him, and all God's saints on one side, and all God's angels on the other ; take even the Holy Incarnate God's Body into your mouth ; all this may be done and even more ; yet the devils would go thither, and tear your soul from your body, and drag it down into the abyss of hell, if you knowingly are in possession of ill-gotten property, and refuse to give it up.'[21]

Such was the teaching of the thirteenth century, as of every other century, in the Catholic Church. It was a fearful teaching, and, if taken by itself, capable of sinking the sinner's heart in despondency. What reason, then, has any sinner to find fault, if the Church held out to men of good-will the merciful protection of the Mother of our Saviour and our Judge, and sanctioned the confraternities in which men enrolled themselves to encourage each other in good works, and to make more sure of her intercession?

One word as to certain controversies among Catholics. There was one in Cambridge between the Dominicans and the Carmelites in 1369-1373. As related by Fuller, it seems to have been a mere party war of jealousy.[22] That between the Jesuit Papebroche and the Carmelites was rather on the origin of the order of Mount Carmel than on the scapular. Launoy, who attacked the devotion of the scapular in 1731, can scarcely be called a Catholic. He was answered by the Carmelites and by Théophile Raynaud, a Jesuit, and the controversy has been summed up by Lambertini. Alban Butler has given the facts of the life of St. Simon Stock on the 16th May. I confess to have sought in vain for traces of this confraternity in England, nor can I add anything to the facts recorded by Butler.

The Order of the Garter.

In connection with guilds and confraternities, and especially with the illustrious order of the Scapular of our Lady, it should not be forgotten that the order of the Garter had for its patron not only St. George, but, in the first place, the ever-blessed Virgin Mary.

In the statutes of the order, drawn up by Edward IV. in the

---

[21] Quoted by Dr. Alban Stolz in his *Almanac for Time and Eternity*.

[22] Fuller's *History of the University of Cambridge*, p. 81 (ed. 1840). John Stokes, a Dominican, attacked the Carmelites for calling themselves 'the brothers of the Blessed Virgin.' He was answered by John Hornby (by some called 'Hornet-bee'), a Carmelite.

beginning of his reign, it is expressly declared 'that his an-
cestor, Edward III.' (who instituted the order, as it is thought,
about 1349), ' had done so to the honour of the Blessed Virgin,
and that out of his singular affection for her he had wished her
to be honoured by his knights. Therefore, by an unanimous
vote they had resolved that on each of the five festivals of our
Lady, and on all Saturdays, as well as on the feast of St. George,
the knights should wear, during the divine offices, a peculiar
habit, having a golden figure of the Mother of God on the right
shoulder; and that on each of these days they should recite five
times the "Our Father" and five times the "Hail Mary." '[23]
From the same motive of devotion Edward III. had inaugurated
the order on the octave-day of our Lady's Purification.

What, I may ask, would the illustrious founder have thought
of the knights of his order, who scoff at the idea of invoking
the Mother of their Redeemer, or who are perhaps declared
enemies of the Christian faith?

[23] See the *Black Book, or Register of the most noble Order of the
Garter*, vol. i. p. 48 (ed. 1724).

CHAPTER XIII.

THE Blessed Virgin has in all times and countries been looked on as the patroness of a happy death. Whether Christians thought of the agonies she endured at the death of her Divine Son, or of the peace and joy of her own death, they could not but ask her to procure them a holy and happy death from the Saviour who died for them.

Our glorious doctor, St. Anselm, well expresses this confidence. He thus addresses our Blessed Lady :

'To whom shall I show my wounds when I am dying ? To whom shall I have recourse ? Before whom shall I lay my grief ? From whom shall I hope for health, if that one resting-place of God's mercy is closed against me ?

'I recall to mind with sweet consolation, O Mary, how, in order to commend thy protection to the miserable, thou didst reveal thy name to one of thy servants in his last moments. Thou didst appear to him in his distress, and ask him if he recognised thee; and when he trembling replied that he did not, thou, in thy great benignity, O Lady, thou didst gently say : "I am the Mother of mercy."

'Ah, yes, our God is a most merciful Father, and thou art a sweet and gentle Mother. O blessed one, acknowledge those as thy children whom thy beloved Son did not disdain to call His brethren. And if a sword pierced thy soul in the crucifixion of thy innocent Son, how canst thou refrain from tears at the sight of thy children dead in sins ? Alas, there is none to help, none to take our part. Arise then, O merciful one, arise ; draw near to the sanctuary of mercy, and stretch forth thy immaculate hands before the golden altar of man's redemption.'[1]

[1] S. Anselm. Op. t. i. p. 389, ed. Ben.

The same confidence which the saint expresses in the prayer, of which the above lines are a part, caused him to draw up a form for assisting the dying, especially those who, after receiving the last sacraments, are still troubled at the thought of their sins. As this form seems to have been much used by our English ancestors, as well as on the Continent, I give it at length. It is the best answer to those who imagine that prayers to the Mother of mercy were never offered till Jesus was lost sight of as a Saviour, and only remembered as a Judge.

St. Anselm's Admonition to the Dying.

' *Question.* Do you believe the articles of the Christian faith, as they have been determined by the Church?

' *Answer.* I do believe them.

' *Q.* Do you rejoice that you die in the Christian faith?

' *A.* I do.

' *Q.* Do you acknowledge that you have grievously offended God?

' *A.* I do.

' *Q.* Are you sorry that you have offended your Creator?

' *A.* I am.

' *Q.* Are you resolved that, if God should prolong your life, you will carefully avoid offending Him?

' *A.* I am.

' *Q.* Do you hope and believe that you will attain eternal salvation, not through your own merits, but through the merits of the Passion of Jesus Christ?

' *A.* Thus I hope.[2]

' *Priest.* Come, then, while life remains, place all thy confidence in this death alone. Trust in nothing else. To this death commit thy whole self, with this alone cover thyself, in this death hide thyself. And if the Lord God will enter into judgment with thee, say: " Lord, I place the death of Jesus Christ between me and Thy judgment; otherwise I cannot contend against Thee." And if He say to thee that thou art a sinner, reply: " Lord, I place the death of Jesus Christ between

---

[2] These interrogations are slightly varied for a dying monk.

B B

Thee and my sins." If He shall say to thee that thou hast
merited damnation, say : " Lord, I place the death of Jesus
Christ between Thee and my evil deserts, and I offer His merits
for those which I ought to have, but have not." If He shall
say that He is wroth with thee, answer : " Lord, I oppose the
death of Jesus Christ between Thee and Thy anger." (Let these
last words be repeated).

'Then let the sick man say three times, "Lord, into Thy
hands I commend my spirit; Thou hast redeemed me, O Lord,
the God of truth" (Ps. xxx.).

'Then the verses : " Thou hast broken my bonds. I will
sacrifice to Thee the sacrifice of praise, and I will call upon the
Name of the Lord" (Ps. cxv. 16). " Bring my soul out of prison, that I may praise Thy Name : the just wait for me, until
Thou reward me" (Ps. cxli. 8).

'Afterwards let him say :

> " Maria, Mater. gratiæ,
> Mater misericordiæ,
> Tu nos ab hoste protege,
> Et hora mortis suscipe.
>
> Mother pure of grace divine,
> Power and pity both are thine ;
> Save us now from Satan's power,
> Take us in our dying hour.

O Virgin, by thy Son, by the Father and the Holy Ghost, I
beseech thee, be present at my last moments, for they are drawing near."

'Then the priest will say for the sick man the psalms "Deus
in nomine tuo" (Ps. liii.); "Credidi" (Ps. cxv.); "Deus in
adjutorium"(Ps. lxix.); "Voce mea" (Ps. cxli.); "In te Domine
speravi" (Ps. xxx.).

'And observe well, you who wish to enter into life eternal,
think of these five following things every day of your life, and
you will never offend God. 1st, The shortness of life ; 2d, Eternity ; 3d, The uncertainty of death ; 4th, The rewards of the
just ; 5th, The punishments of the impious.'[3]

[3] S. Anselm. Op. t. i. p. 272, ed. Ben. A similar form is found in the
rhymed treatise called *Instructions for Parish Priests*, written in the
fifteenth century by John Myrc.

St. Anselm was speechless in his last moments, though quite conscious. He died on the Wednesday in Holy Week, A.D. 1109, while they were reading to him the Passion. No doubt his blessed soul was busy in forming acts like those he had taught to others.

In the year 1253 died St. Richard of Chichester. His death, as related by eye-witnesses,[4] is very beautiful, and shows the same devotion that distinguished St. Anselm to the Passion of our Lord and to His Blessed Mother. Indeed, he seems to have been familiar with the form recommended by St. Anselm.

While hearing Mass the saint fell fainting on the pavement, and was carried to his bed, from which he never again rose. He foretold the day of his death, made a general confession to brother Radulphus (a Dominican father, who wrote his life), and received the last Sacraments.

He was asked to take something for supper, and was told to eat freely, as there was but one portion prepared. He replied : ' Yes, one is enough. Do you know what that is? It is the portion of which St. Philip said : "Lord, show us the Father," and that is enough. O, may God grant me that portion for my supper!' He made also a profession of faith.

When death drew near he asked for a crucifix, and kissing the wounds, he prayed aloud: ' I thank Thee, O Lord Jesus Christ, for all Thy mercies to me, for all that Thou hast suffered for me, so that it might well be said that there was no grief like to Thine. And Thou knowest, O Lord, that if it pleased Thee, I would willingly bear for Thee torments and death. Thou knowest the truth of what I say. Have mercy upon me, for into Thy hands I commend my soul.' These words he repeated frequently; and turning to the Blessed Virgin, he repeated with heart and voice : ' Maria, Mater gratiæ, Mater misericordiæ, tu nos ab hoste protege, et hora mortis suscipe,—Mary, Mother of grace, Mother of mercy, protect us from the enemy, and receive us in the hour of death.' He told his chaplains not to cease to repeat those words in his ears. Then he died.

If, then, it be true that our ancestors before the Reformation

[4] See Boll. *Acta Sanct.* t. x. pp. 281-306.

did not generally use that special form of prayer which we are
accustomed to add to the Angelic Salutation, ' Holy Mary, Mother of God, pray for us sinners, now and at the hour of our
death. Amen,' at least it is evident that they made the same
petition in other words.   They believed what our old Anglo-
Norman poet Wace sang in the twelfth century :[5]

' Elle est roïne et mere au roi	' She is Queen, and Mother of the King,
Et Diex ses Fiuz l'a avec soi.	And God her Son has her with Him.
Virge est el ciel, virge est en gloire ;	The Virgin is in heaven, in glory.
De li doit on faire memoire	We ought ever to be mindful of her
Et li avoir ai grant fiance ;	And put in her great confidence ;
Car bien sai et croi sanz doutance	For know well and believe without doubt,
Qui l'amera et servira	Whosoever shall love and serve her
Et de bon cuer l'ennorera,	And honour her with a good heart
N'i faudra pas qu'il n'ait s'aie	Will never lack her aid
Ou a la mort, ou a la vie.'	In death or in life.'

'He who journeys by sea looks up to the stars, to a star
that never moves, and if he keeps his eye fixed on it, and steers
by it, he is not driven at hazard on the sea.   This star signifies
our Lady St. Mary, a star in goodness, in brightness, in beauty,
pure, clear, and steadfast, and tinged by no sin.   Those who
sail by night on the sea are indeed men in this world.   But
there is no sinner so great but will be helped if he calls on Mary.'

' Ele est la mere as pechéors,	' She is the Mother of sinners,
Redrescemenz, voie et secors ;	Their guide, their way, their help.
Restoré nos a et rendu	She has restored to us
Ce que nos avions perdu ;	What we had lost.
Sainte Marie nos rendi	Yes, Mary has recovered for us
Ce que Eve nos perdi.'	What Eve had forfeited.'

I am tempted to add one or two more of these beautiful
histories.   The first is the death of Lanzo, monk of the congregation of Cluny, and prior of the abbey of St. Pancras at Lewes,
in Sussex.   He was a contemporary of St. Anselm, and the account of his last moments was written by eye-witnesses, and has
been preserved by William of Malmesbury.[6]

[5] Wace was born about A.D. 1100, a few years before the death of St.
Anselm.   In the above lines we have a specimen not only of the doctrine
preached by St. Anselm, but of the language in which he spoke.
[6] *Gesta Regum Anglorum*, lib. x. § 675, alios § 443.

'The merciful Lord, who chastises every son whom He receives, and who has promised that the just shall be partakers both in His sufferings and in His consolation (2 Cor. i. 7), allowed our prior Lanzo to suffer, for three days before His Passion, such excruciating pains, that we cannot doubt that if any stain of earth still clung to his pure soul, it was cleansed away in that tribulation. For since the Apostle who rested on his Lord's bosom has said : " If we say that we have no sin we deceive ourselves, and the truth is not in us" (1 John i. 8), and since Christ must judge every sin, either here leniently, or hereafter more rigorously, He was unwilling that one who loved Him with his whole heart should meet with any evil after death, and therefore deigned to purge away in life whatever of imperfection still remained. The confidence which our father showed in death confirms this opinion. His death then occurred as follows. On the Thursday before the Passion of our Lord, he was in good health ; and having recited the Psalter, as was his daily use in Lent, at Tierce he was about to celebrate Mass, and had already put on the vestments as far as the chasuble, and had said all the preparatory prayers, when he was seized with a sudden sickness, so painful, that casting off the vestments, and not staying even to fold them, he left the oratory. The pain continued without intermission for two days, that is till Saturday ; he could find no rest either sitting or walking, lying, standing, or sleeping. Yet during the nights he never spoke, and when they asked him to break silence he would not yield, begging them not to do violence to this monastic delicacy, since from the day he had put on the monastic habit he had never spoken between the end of Compline and the Prime of the next day.

'On the Saturday, when he was so weakened that he thought he was about to die, he sent word to the brethren, who were rising for Matins, to come and anoint him ; and when after the anointing he would give them the kiss of peace, as is the custom, he loved them so tenderly that he would not do it lying down or seated, but standing sustained in their arms. When the day broke, he was carried into the chapter, and being placed in a seat he asked the brethren to come all before him, giving them his paternal benediction and absolution, and asking them to give theirs to him in return. He then told them what to do in case of his death. Having returned whence he had come, he passed the remainder of the day and the Sunday rather more quietly. But on the Monday morning the signs of approaching death were noticed; and having washed his hands and combed his hair, he entered the oratory to hear Mass, and when he had received the Body and Blood of the Lord he returned to his bed. After a little he lost his speech, but blessed the brethren as they came before him one by one, and so the whole convent; but raising his eyes to heaven he strove with both hands to bless the lord abbot with all under him. When asked by the brethren to be mindful of them before God, to whom he was going, he signified his assent most sweetly by the inclination of his head.

'Then he made signs that they should give him the Cross; and adoring it not only with his head but his whole body, he embraced it with his hands, looking upon it and kissing it with every sign of joy. Then he gave the bystanders a sign that he was departing, and being lifted in their hands he was carried still alive into the church before the altar of St. Pancras. Then his face became sweetly inflamed with joy, and at the same time of the day at which he had fallen ill, for his purification, now purified and freed for ever from every ill, he departed to Christ. . . . .

' And God granted to Lanzo, who above all men of our time observed strictly the rule of St. Benedict, and who venerated the Blessed Mother of God and her festivals with singular affection, to celebrate as usual, on the anniversary of St. Benedict (21st March), and on the feast of the Annunciation (25th March), the High Mass before the community; and falling ill on the octave of St. Benedict, he passed away to Christ on the octave of the feast of our Lady.'

Of the holy abbot of St. Alban's, Thomas de la Mare, who died in 1396 at the age of eighty-seven, it is related that in the frightful pains of his last illness he was often heard to murmur the words: 'Jesus, mercy; Mary, help;' and that not only when awake, but even when in his sleep. He had made his profession on the Nativity of the Blessed Virgin, and he often predicted that he should die during the octave of that feast; which really happened.[7]

It was but natural that those who had loved and honoured Mary during life should wish to promote her honour after their decease. It was natural also that those who feared God's justice, while they trusted in His mercy, should seek to secure after death the most powerful succour of Mary during their time of purgation. Hence we find in Catholic times many provisions made by devout clients of Mary, which taught the children the piety of their fathers and forefathers. Thus the external honours of Mary increased with each generation; until the accumulated riches of her churches and shrines excited that avarice by which, as St. Paul had foretold, many 'erred from the faith, and entangled themselves in many sorrows' (1 Tim. vi. 10).

I have already drawn largely in previous chapters from the collections of old wills, which still survive as precious memorials of the domestic manners and piety of our ancestors. I will here add some extracts from the same source, which will farther illustrate their sentiments at the approach of death, when the heart speaks its best and truest language. I have added the dates. Unfortunately there are few such documents now in existence which go back beyond the thirteenth century.

Martin, Master of the Hospital of Sherbourne (A.D. 1259), writes: 'I bequeath my silver-bound copy of the Gospels (textum meum argenteum) to the house of Sherbourne, and beg that whenever it is taken out for the ornament of the altar, and my little statues of Mary (Mariolæ) which are also there, each of the brethren and sisters may say each day for my soul the Lord's Prayer, together with the Salutation of the Blessed Virgin,' *i.e.* the 'Hail Mary.'[8]

William Menville, High Sheriff of the Palatinate of Durham

---

[7] For an account of this holy man see vols. ii. and iii. of the *Gesta Abbatum S. Albani* (ed. Master of Rolls).

[8] *Wills of the Northern Counties* (Surtees Society), p. 7.

(in 1363 and 1370), leaves by will for maintaining the lights on the altar of the Blessed Virgin in the church of Ryton 13*s.* 4*d.*; and to maintain for ever five tapers before the altar of the Blessed Virgin in the chapel of the church of Esyngton ten marks.[9]

John de Oggill (A.D. 1372) leaves to maintain the luminary of the Blessed Virgin of the church of Brauncepath four year-old calves.[10]

Sir Bartholomew Burghersh (A.D. 1369) appoints: ' My body to be buried in the chapel of Walsyngham, before the image of the Blessed Virgin.'[11]

Joan, Lady Cobham (A.D. 1369) : ' My body to be buried in the churchyard of St. Mary Overhere, in Southwark, before the church-door, where the image of the Blessed Virgin sitteth on high over that door.'[12]

William, Earl of Suffolk (A.D. 1381) : ' I will that a picture of a horse and man, armed with my arms, be made in silver, and offered to the altar of our Lady of Walsingham ; and another, the like, to be made and offered at Bromeholme.'[13]

Sir Thomas Latimer, the famous Lollard, having returned to the faith before his death, in his will (A.D. 1401) calls himself ' a false knight of God,' but writes : ' I acknowledge I am un-worthy to bequeath to God anything of my power, and therefore I pray Him meekly of His grace, that He will take so poor a present as my wretched soul is, with His mercy, through the beseeching of His Blessed Mother and His holy saints ; and my wretched body to be buried wherever I die in the next church-yard, God vouchsafe, and not in the church, but in the utter-est corner, as he is that is unworthy to lie therein, save the mercy of God.'[14]

Thomas, Earl of Arundel (A.D. 1415) : ' I will that my exe-cutors cause a chapel to be built at the gate called Mary-gate, in Arundel, in honour of the Blessed Virgin.'[15]

Richard Beauchamp, Earl of Warwick (in 1437), appoints by his will that his body be interred in the collegiate church

---

[9] *Wills of the Northern Counties* (Surtees Society), p. 82.   [10] Ib. p. 84.
[11] *Testamenta Vetusta*, collected by Sir Harris Nicolas, p. 77.
[12] Ib. p. 81.   [13] Ib. p. 115.   [14] Ib. p. 159.   [15] Ib. p. 186.

of our Lady in Warwick, 'where I will that there be made a chapel of our Lady, well, fair, and goodly built, within the middle of which chapel I will that my tomb be made.

'That there be said every day during the world, in the aforesaid chapel, three Masses. Whereof one every day of our Lady, God's Mother, with note, as the ordinal of Salisbury doth assign. The second, without note, of Requiem. The third, also without note, to be Sunday of the Trinity, Monday of the Angels, Tuesday of St. Thomas of Canterbury, Wednesday of the Holy Ghost, Thursday of Corpus Christi, Friday of the Holy Cross, and Saturday of the Annunciation of our Lady.

'Also, I will that there be in all haste after my decease, and before all things, to be said for me five thousand Masses. Also I will that, in the name of Heryott to our Lady, there be given to the church of our Lady in Warwick mine image of gold, and of our Lady there to abide for evermore. Also I will that my foresaid executors ordain four images of gold, each of them of the weight of twenty pounds of gold, to be made after my similitude with mine arms, holding an anchor between the hands, and then to be offered in my name one of them at the shrine in the church of St. Alban, to the worship of God and of our Lady and St. Alban; another at the shrine of the cathedral church of Canterbury; the third at Bridlington; and the fourth at the shrine in the church of St. Winifred in Shrewsbury.'[16]

The author of the will from which these passages are extracted was one of the bravest knights and greatest warriors in that age of chivalry. He was born in 1381. King Richard II. and Richard Scrope, Bishop of Lichfield and afterwards Archbishop of York, were his godfathers. He was famous throughout Europe and the East for his feats of arms; gained great victories in the French wars under Henry V.; was tutor of Henry VI.; was ambassador of England at the General Council of Constance. He died at Rouen, but, according to his desire, was buried at Warwick.

Of him the Emperor Sigismund said to the King of England

[16] Will published by Hearne, 1729.

that 'no Christian prince, for wisdom, nurture, and manhood had such a knight as he had of the Earl of Warwick ;' adding thereto, 'that if all courtesy were lost, yet might it be found again in him ;' and so ever after, by the emperor's authority, he was called 'the father of courtesy.'[17]

He knew how to unite great and simple piety with wisdom, courage, and statesmanship. He went on pilgrimage to Rome and to Jerusalem.

John Ross relates of his daughter Margaret, who was married to Sir John Talbot, afterwards Earl of Shrewsbury, that 'to the honour of God she made a decree in her own house, that what person blasphemed God by swearing should that day lack ale and wine, and have only bread and water.'[18] If we may judge from Chaucer, the evil custom of swearing by the names of God, our Lady, and the saints was then sadly prevalent. This must have been an effectual check, and deserves record among acts of devotion to our Lady.

The devotion which Antony Rivers, Lord Scales, showed to our Lady during life and at death was very remarkable. Before giving his will I may mention a few traits of his character. Anthony Wydeville was, according to Sir Thomas More, 'a man of whom it would be hard to say whether he was more prompt in counsel or in act.' He was born in 1442, and was eldest son of Lord Rivers, but by his marriage with the heiress of Lord Scales received that title. Edward IV. married his sister Elizabeth. He was made Knight of the Garter and Governor of the Isle of Wight. He became famous by his tournament against the Bastard of Burgundy in Smithfield in presence of the king. He succeeded his father as Earl Rivers in 1469. His eminent military exploits during the civil wars are matter of history. But his piety and virtue were equal to his knightly accomplishments. Caxton, who in 1479 printed the English translation which Earl Rivers had made of a French book called the *Cordyale*, treating on the 'four last things,' gives an account of the pilgrimages he had made to St. James in

[17] See John Ross apud Hearne, Appendix to *Vita Richardi II.* p. 367.
[18] Ib. p. 235.

Galicia, to Rome, and holy places in Naples and France ; and of
the poems he had written against the seven deadly sins. He
had rebuilt the chapel of our Lady of the Pewe at Westminster,
and obtained for it from the Pope the indulgences of the Scala
Cœli.

Having been made governor of his nephew, the young
prince Edward V., the Duke of Gloucester (afterwards Richard
III.) determined to get rid of him, and had him arrested on a
false charge of high-treason against his own life. He was beheaded at Pontefract in 1483, being only forty-one years old. A
hair shirt was found next his skin, which he had worn for some
time before his death ; and it was afterwards hung up before
the image of the Blessed Virgin in the Carmelites' church at
Doncaster, in remembrance of his devotion.

He made his will after his arrest by the Protector.

'I bequeath my soul unto the great mercy of Jesus Christ,
and to His dear Mother our Lady Saint Mary, and to the
glorious company of heaven ; and my heart to be had to our
Lady of Pewe beside Saint Stephen's College at Westminster ;
and if I die beyond Trent, then to be buried before our Lady of
Pewe aforesaid.' Then follow many bequests ; among others he
endows a hospital at Rochester for thirteen poor folk, and
leaves money to pay prisoners' fees and small debts, to visit the
prisons of London, to help to bury the dead, and other works
of mercy. He appoints many Masses to be said. 'And I will
that all mine array for my body and my horse harness be sold,
and with the money thereof be bought shirts and smocks to
poor folks ; and my gown of tawny cloth of gold I give to the
prior of Royston, my trapper of black cloth of gold I give to
our Lady of Walsingham. . . I will that Whittington College,
of London, have a sum of money to pray for my soul.'

At the end of the will, fearing that his directions about our
Lady of Pewe could not be complied with, he made this addition : 'My will is now to be buried before an image of our
Blessed Lady Mary in Pomfrete ; and Jesus have mercy on my
soul.'[19]

[19] See *Excerpta Historica*, published by Bentley.

I have given with some detail these notices regarding the Earl of Warwick and Earl Rivers, because they show that devotion to our Lady was not a superstition of the poor and ignorant, nor the poetry and sentiment of high-born ladies, nor the fruit of the asceticism of the cloister. It strengthened our noblest knights and warriors, keeping them pure and meek and charitable in prosperity, and comforting them when overtaken by adversity.

In fact they would sometimes call themselves Knights of our Lady, having dedicated themselves to her in a special manner, and for love of her loving whatever was pure and humble, gentle and sublime.

Such must have been the knight, whose French epitaph is mentioned by Weever[20] as having been still read a little before his own time, in the church of Baldock, in the diocese of London:

> ' Reginaud de Argentein ci gist,
> Que cest chappell feire fist;
> Fut chevalier sainct Mairie,
> Chescini pardon pour l'alme prie;'

which Weever translates:

> ' Reginald de Argentyne here is laid,
> That caused this chapel to be made;
> He was a knight of St. Mary the Virgin,
> Therefore pray pardon for his sin.'

Another illustrious client of our Lady was our great hero, King Henry V. Many traits of his knightly devotion are related; but I take from Fabian's *Chronicle* some curious details of his provision for his soul's help after death.[21] 'His great business in war notwithstanding,' says Fabyan, 'this most Christian prince by' (*i.e.* during) 'his life chose his place of sepulture within the aforesaid monastery' (of Westminster); 'and there ordained for him to be sung three Masses every day in the week while the world lasteth.' He then gives some Latin hexameters, which he renders into English verse for the unlettered. Omitting

---

[20] *Antient Funeral Monuments*, p. 313.

[21] *New Chronicles of England and France*, by Robert Fabyan, pp. 589-91, Ellis's edition.

his uncouth rhymes, I give the order of the Masses, which are a curious monument of the devotion of the fifteenth century.

Besides the Mass corresponding to the office of each day, two others were to be said.

On *Sunday*, of our Lady's Assumption and our Lord's Resurrection.

On *Monday*, of the Salutation of Mary (which Fabyan interprets of the Visitation) and of her Annunciation.

On *Tuesday*, of our Lord's Nativity and of the Nativity of our Lady.

On *Wednesday*, of the Holy Ghost and of our Lady's Conception.

On *Thursday*, of Corpus Christi and of our Lady's Purification.

On *Friday*, of the Holy Cross and of our Lady's Salutation.

On *Saturday*, of All Saints, and a Requiem Mass (the office of the day being of the Blessed Virgin).

Isabel, Countess of Warwick, and wife of the Earl Richard just mentioned (A.D. 1439) : ' I desire that a chalice be made of my great sharpe and offered to our Lady in the Lady Chapel at Tewkesbury ; and to our Lady of Caversham I bequeath a crown of gold, made of my chain, weighing twenty-five pounds, and other broken gold in my cabinet. . . . I will that my tablet, with the image of our Lady, having a glass for it, be offered unto our Lady of Walsingham ; as also my gown of green alyz cloth of gold with wide sleeves ; and a tabernacle of silver, like in the timber to that over our Lady of Caversham. To our Lady of Worcester my great image of wax, now in London.'[22]

Lady Elizabeth Andrews (A.D. 1474) : ' I will that of my two rings with diamonds, the one to be sent to our Lady of Walsingham, and the other to our Lady of Wolpit.'[23]

Thomas Wilmott, clerk (A.D. 1493) : ' I will that the image of St. Mary, now standing in my study, be placed at my expense in the chapel of St. Nicolas, Ashford.'[24]

Robert Fabyan, the chronicler (A.D. 1511), has in brass on his tomb graven a figure of our Lady with her Child, and

[22] *Testamenta Vetusta*, p. 240.   [23] Ib. p. 329.   [24] Ib. p. 417.

under it the figures of his eleven children, the boys holding a scroll with the words, ' Stella Maria maris ;' and the girls a scroll with the words, ' Succurre piissima nobis.'[25]

Robert Johnson, alderman of York, by his will (A.D. 1496) orders his body to be buried before our Lady's altar in St. Michael's, York. He leaves ' to the exhibition of an honest priest, to sing at the altar of our said Lady daily, by the space of seven years, 35*l.*[26] And I will that what priest that shall serve it every day, when that he hath said Mass, that he stand afore my grave in his alb, and there to say the psalm of *De Profundis*, with the Collects, and then cast holy water upon my grave.' He also leaves to his sister his beads ' of awmer' (amber), ' which bedes containeth 50.'[27]

John Bule, Rector of the Hospital of St. Michael, Pontefract (in 1507), leaves an acre of land, ' to th' intent that a serge of wax may be sett before the ymage of oure Ladye, in oure Lady queyr, and it to burne for evermore, as I have used and customed it to be lyght.'[28]

John Stockdale, alderman of York (A.D. 1506), wills ' to be beried in St. Michael's kirk of Belfray, byfor oure Lady awter, in yᵉ Ladye quere, so yᵗ yᵉ prest, when he doth Masse, then may stand upon yᵉ end of thrugh.'[29]

Nicholas Mounteney (A.D. 1499) in his will desires that his body may be buried before the image of St. Mary in the church of Ecclesfield, near Sheffield, and directs that a priest shall say Mass for his soul for one full year after his decease.[30]

George, fourth Earl of Shrewsbury (A.D. 1538), orders in his will that, besides a thousand Masses immediately after his death, three priests, for the space of twenty years after his decease, shall sing Mass for his soul, two of them at the parish church

---

[25] *Testamenta Vetusta*, p. 511.

[26] At the time of the suppression of the chantries under Edward VI., fifty years later, from 5*l.* to 6*l.* was the ordinary income of a chantry priest for his daily Mass. In 1500, Thomas Rotherham, Archbishop of York, leaves provision for one thousand Masses, fixing the honorarium at fourpence.

[27] *Testam. Eborac.* vol. iv. p. 121 (Surtees Society, 1868).

[28] Ib. p. 93.   [29] Ib. p. 256.

[30] Hunter's *Hallamshire*, p. 392.

of Sheffield, and the other in the chapel of our Blessed Lady of
the Bridge in Sheffield.[31]   Alas, before this period had elapsed,
a statute of Edward VI. had abolished all chantries, and the
revenues had been seized; and in 1572 the chapel itself was
used as a wool warehouse.[32]

Thomas Denny (A.D. 1527) orders his epitaph to be written
thus:

> ' As I am, so shall ye be;
> Now pray for me of your charity,
> With a Paternoster and an Ave,
> For the rest of the soul of Thomas Denny.'[33]

Thomas Trethurffe (A.D. 1528), after bequeathing his soul
(as was usual) 'to Almighty God, our Blessed Lady, St. Mary
Virgin, and to all the holy company of heaven,' among other
bequests says: ' To the image of our Lady, called our Lady
Portall, at Truro, to the use and intent of, and for the reparation
of the said chapel, and of and for part of the priest's wages
there singing, and of and for the name of the said Thomas, to
be put upon the beadroll of the said chapel, xx'.'[34]

Sir Gilbert Stapylton (A.D. 1490): ' To the abbess of Aston
church, in Buckinghamshire, a girdle of silver gilt, to hang at
an image of our Lady in the said church.'[35]

But among all these old wills there is none more remarkable
for the expression of devotion to Mary than that of Sir Thomas
Wyndham, grandson of the first Duke of Norfolk, and admiral
under Henry VIII.   This brave sailor thus wrote in October
1521, shortly before his death:

' First, for the recommendation of my soul into the most merciful hands of Him that redeemed me and made it, I make and
say this my accustomed prayer: " O Lord Jesus Christ, who
from nothing hast created me, formed me, redeemed me, and pre-
destined me to be what I am, Thou knowest what Thou wouldst
do with me.   Do with me then according to Thy will, in Thy
mercy.[36]   Therefore do of me Thy will, with grace, pity, and

---

[31] Hunter's *Hallamshire*, p. 74.   The chapel was not on but near the
bridge.   [32] Ib. p. 337.
   [33] *Testamenta Vetusta*, p. 629.   [34] Ib. p. 644.   [35] Ib. p. 398.
   [36] This prayer is written in Latin, the rest of the will in English.
' Domine Jesu Christe, qui me ex nihilo creasti, fecisti, redemisti, et præ-

mercy, humbly and entirely I beseech Thee; and into Thy most merciful hands my soul I commit. And howbeit, as sinful creature in sins conceived and in sin have lived, knowing perfectly that of my merits I cannot attain to the life everlasting, but only by the merits of Thy blessed Passion and of Thine infinite mercy and grace; nevertheless, my merciful Redeemer, Maker, and Saviour, I trust that by the special grace and mercy of Thy Blessed Mother, ever Virgin, our Lady Mary,—in whom, after Thee, in this mortal life, hath been my most singular trust and confidence; to whom in all my necessities I have made my continual refuge, and by whom I have hitherto ever had my special comfort and relief,—will in my most extreme need take my soul into her hands, and it present unto her most dear Son. Whereof, sweet Lady of mercy, very Mother and Virgin, well of pity, and surest refuge of all needful, most humbly, most entirely, and most heartily I beseech thee, and for my comfort in this behalf I trust.

'Also to the singular mediations and prayers of all the holy company of heaven, angels, archangels, patriarchs, prophets, apostles, evangelists, martyrs, confessors, and virgins; and specially to mine accustomed adrowries[37] I call and cry, St. John Evangelist, St. George, St. Thomas of Canterbury, St. Margaret, St. Catherine, and St. Barbara, humbly beseeching you that— not only at the hour of death so to aid, succour, and defend me, that the ancient and ghostly enemy, nor none other ill and damnable spirit, have power to invade me, nor with his terribleness to annoy me—but also with your holy prayers to be intercessors and mediators unto my Maker and Redeemer, for the remission of my sins and salvation of my soul.

'And forasmuch as I intend and purpose, to the honour of God and our Blessed Lady St. Mary the Virgin, to adorn and vault a chapel, called our Lady chapel, set and builded at the east end of the choir, within sight of the monastery of the Holy Trinity, at the city of Norwich; and also to have in the same

destinasti ad hoc quod sum, tu scis quod de me facere vis. Fac de me secundum voluntatem tuam cum misericordia.'

[37] *i.e.* advocates, patrons.

monastery, for the comfort of my soul and remission of my sins, a yearly memorial of my obit *in perpetuum;* I will and bequeath that whensoever it shall please my Saviour Jesus Christ to call me out of this transitory life, my body be buried in the midst of the same chapel of our Blessed Lady, after my poor estate and substance that God hath given me, without damnable pomp or superfluities. Where, upon my body, I will have a tomb, as shall be thought convenient to my executors, sufficiently large for me and my two wives, if my wife Elizabeth will be there buried. And as touching the funeral interment of my body and charge of my sepulture, I remit it to the discretion of my executors, desiring them that it may be convenient after my little substance. And in any wise I will have a sermon made by a doctor of divinity at the Mass of requiem.

'Also I will have immediately after my decease, as shortly as may be, a thousand Masses to be said within the city of Norwich and other places within the shire of Norfolk: whereof I will have, in the honour of the Blessed Trinity, one hundred ; in honour of the five wounds of our Saviour Jesus Christ, one hundred ; in honour of the five joys of our Blessed Lady, one hundred ; in honour of the nine orders of angels, one hundred ; in the honour of the patriarchs, one hundred ; in the honour of the twelve Apostles, one hundred ; in the honour of all saints, one hundred ; in the honour of St. John the Evangelist, thirty ; in the honour of St. George, forty ; in the honour of St. Thomas of Canterbury, thirty ; in the honour of St. Margaret, forty ; in the honour of St. Catherine, thirty ; and of St. Barbara, thirty ; which maketh the whole number of a thousand Masses.

'Also I will that all my debts, first and before all other charges, be paid by the hands of mine executors, wherewith I charge them as they will answer before God, and discharge my conscience.

'Also I will, if any man or woman cause or complain of any injuries or wrongs done by me, and so duly proved before mine executors or supervisors, that they be restored to the uttermost.

'Also I will that mine executors, as soon as it may be borne out of my goods, do cause the said chapel of our Blessed Lady

c c

to be vaulted with freestone, after the workmanship and vaulting of the church there, as well in stars and colours as in gilding with stars, as shall be devised by mine executors; and with mine arms, badges, and devices.

'Also I will have a priest, secular or religious, to sing for me, my said wives and friends, in the said chapel *in perpetuum*, with an yearly obit, to be kept with a solemn dirge and Mass of requiem, by the prior and convent and their successors, every such a day as it shall happen me to die upon, or as near as it may be conveniently; and the said prior and convent shall *distribute* yearly, as they think convenient, *in perpetuum* . . .'

Then follows the disposition of his property.

The Protestant editor of the *Testamenta Vetusta* remarks on this will, that 'even so late as in the year 1521 the superstitious feelings which are so manifested in the early testaments were as prominent as in the darkest ages of our history.'[38] Everything with these gentlemen is superstition to which they are unaccustomed. It does not seem to occur to them to ask what was the nature of that 'Reformation' which first raised the cry of superstition as a pretext for plundering all that had been offered to God by Catholic piety; but with parrot-like pertinacity and parrot-like sense the words 'superstition and idolatry,' 'idolatry and superstition,' are repeated.

A tender devotion to our Lady comforted the last hours of Katharine of Arragon. Miss Strickland, to her own honour, has done justice to this noble lady. She has truly said that, 'sustained by her own innate grandeur of soul, her piety and lofty rectitude, she passed through all her bitter trials without calumny succeeding in fixing a spot on her name.' But in her last will she wrote: 'I supplicate that my body be buried in a convent of Observant friars; that for my soul may be said five hundred Masses; that some personage go to our Lady of Walsingham in pilgrimage, and in going by the way to deal twenty nobles,' &c. The poor divorced queen thought in her last days of that pilgrimage she had made to Walsingham with her husband in 1510 to return thanks for the birth of their first child,

[38] *Testam. Vet.* p. 580.

and her heart was still at Walsingham now in 1535.   But her will was probably never carried out.   Though Walsingham was not suppressed till three years later, yet Henry contrived with the lawyers to defeat the pious intentions of Katharine, and to seize on the money she had left for payment of debts and legacies.   Horace Walpole has written the following marvellous lines to her memory :

> ' In days of old here Amphill's towers were seen,
> The mournful refuge of an injured queen ;
> Here flowed her pure but unavailing tears,
> Here *blinded zeal* (!) sustained her sinking years.
> Yet freedom hence her radiant banners waved,
> And love avenged a realm by priests enslaved ;
> From Katharine's wrongs a nation's bliss was spread,
> And Luther's light from Henry's lawless bed.'

Thus do men gather grapes off thorns and figs off thistles !

It is indeed both curious and sad to trace in the wills of dying men the variations of royal caprice and tyranny.

In the first years of Henry VIII. the universal form adopted is to leave the soul to God Almighty, the Blessed Virgin, and the saints, and to have dirge and Mass for the repose of the soul.   In 1551, Mass has been forbidden, and we find William Bee, clerk, asking 'for dirge and *Communion* with note on the day of my burial, and alms to the poor to pray for my soul.'[39]

Cuthbert Conyers, high sheriff, dies in the first year of Elizabeth.   As usual, he bequeaths his soul to ' Almighty God, to our Blessed Lady St. Mary, and to all the holy company of heaven,' but dares not leave Masses.   Only, ' I bequeath to my ghostly father at Sedgfield 5*s.* to have me in remembrance.'[40]

Poor John Hartburne, in 1560, wishes to be buried 'with laudable ceremonies as are permitted by the law,' and leaves to Sir Robert Richardson, 'mine old friend, to pray for me, 6*s.* 8*d.*'[41]

Bartholomew Lilburne, in 1561, wishes his body to be buried ' with such duties as the church is endowed with, as it pleaseth Almighty God for to provide.'[42]

---

[39] *Wills of the Northern Counties* (Surtees Society), p. 185.
[40] Ib. p. 185. Five shillings was the ordinary honorarium for ten Masses.
[41] Ib. p. 186.   [42] Ib. p. 193.

Cuthbert Richardson, of Thurle House, county Durham, dies
in 1565. This sturdy yeoman seems to care little for the new
religion. He has his will drawn up in the old fashion. 'I bequeath my soul into the hands of Almighty God, and my body
to the earth in St. Michael's the Archangel's church, with my
duties to God and holy Church, beseeching our Blessed Lady
the Virgin Mary, with all the holy company of heaven, to help
me with their holy prayers.'[43]

This is the last explicit invocation of our Lady that I have
found in the collection of wills of the northern counties. In sad
contrast with it are the remainder, which either say nothing of
the soul or make a fanatical profession that the testator is one
of 'God's elect children.' As if the hope of being one of God's
elect children dispensed us from all need of the help of God's
elect Mother !

Let me conclude this chapter with some prayers used by our
forefathers.

An Orison to our Lady.[44]

' O Mary, all virtue maketh thee fair; all saints honour thee
in the country of heaven ; they all bless thee and say praises to
thee.   Hail, full of grace ; for the wounds of Jesus Christ,
which thou weeping sawest bloody for our wretchedness, make
us worthy to see thee, and in seeing thee, to rejoice in everlasting glory. Amen.'

Prayer for a Happy Death.[45]

' O glorious Jesu, O meekest Jesu, O most sweetest Jesu,
I pray Thee that I may have true confession, contrition, and
satisfaction ere I die ; and that I may see and receive Thy holy
Body, God and man, Saviour of all mankind, Christ Jesu, without sin ; and that Thou wilt, my Lord God, forgive me all my
sins for Thy glorious wounds ; and that I may end my life in
the true faith of holy Church, and in perfect love and charity
with my even Christian, as Thy creature ; and I commend my

[43] *Wills of the Northern Counties* (Surtees Society), p. 243.
[44] Primer of 1400 circ., apud Maskell, *Monum. Rit.* vol. ii. p. 78.
[45] From the *Horæ ad Usum Sarum*, 1508, ib. p. 262.

soul into Thy holy hands, through the glorious help of Thy Blessed Mother of mercy, our Lady St. Mary, and all the holy company of heaven. Amen.'

Another Prayer.

' O Lord God Almighty, all seeing, all things knowing; wisdom and sapience of all things; I, poor sinner, make this day, in despite of the fiend of hell, protestation, that if per-adventure, by any temptation, deception, or variation coming by sorrow or pain or sickness, or by any feebleness of body, or by any other occasion, whatsoever it be, that I fall or decline in peril of my soul, or prejudice of my health, or in error of the holy faith Catholic, in the which I was regenerate in the holy font of baptism,—Lord God, in good mind, in which I hold me now by Thy grace (whereof with all my heart I thank Thee), that error with my power I resist, and here renounce, and of the same me confess, in protesting that I will live and die in the faith of holy Church, our mother and Thy spouse. And in witness of this confession and protestation, and in despite of the fiend of hell, I offer to Thee the Credo, in which all verity and truth is contained. And to Thee I recommend my soul, my faith, my life, and my death. Amen.

' Credo in Deum.'

In illustration of this prayer I subjoin extracts from two wills conceived in the same spirit.

Thomas Pereson, Sub-dean of York (A.D. 1490), says : ' I protest to Almighty God, to Blessed Mary, and to all saints, that whatever infirmity of weakness of brain may happen to me in this sickness or any other, it is not my intention in anything to recede from the Catholic faith, but I firmly and faithfully believe in all its articles, and in all the sacraments of the Church ; and that the Church with her sacraments is sufficient for any man, however criminal, to his salvation.'[40]

Will of Thomas Rotherham, Archbishop of York (1500). The editor of the *Testamenta Eboracensia* calls it 'the most noble and striking will of an English mediæval bishop in exist-

[40] *Testamenta Eboracensia*, vol. iv. p. 53 (Surtees, 1867).

ence.'[47] Among many other things, he writes (in Latin): ' It is my wish and prayer that my executors, according to the trust which I repose in them, and as they will answer to Christ, shall use the utmost diligence that a thousand Masses be celebrated immediately, as soon as it can be done, after my death, that by so many sacrifices, and so many commemorations of the Passion of Christ, it may fare more leniently with my soul. I know that my many sins ask and deserve a great and long punishment, indeed an infinite one, since they were committed against an infinite God. Yet with St. Augustin I firmly believe and profess that my sins cannot frighten me when the death of my Lord comes into my mind ; for in the wounds of His body I desire to hide them, and to wash them, through the grace of our blessed Lord Jesus, in the sacraments of the Church which flow from His wounds. May He grant this who deigned for me to die so shameful a death, and to endure such wounds.

' I will that each priest thus celebrating have at least 4*d.* of my goods. . . .

' And I protest that in the Passion of Christ, and in the sacraments of the Church which received from that Passion their power, I place the hope of my salvation ; and that in no article of the faith do I hesitate, or have I ever hesitated ; and if perchance—which may God avert !—from sickness or other cause, in my extremity I should say otherwise, I deny it now for then, and then as now, renouncing and detesting now and ever whatever is repugnant to the spouse of Christ, His holy Church ; for as a true Christian I wish and desire to die, and I pray again and again that thus I may die. Amen, amen, amen.'

[47] *Testamenta Eboracensia,* vol. iv. p. 147 (Surtees, 1867).

PART III.
DISLOYALTY.

RUINS OF WALSINGHAM PRIORY.

CHAPTER I.

I HAVE looked in vain in our historians for a full account of the
various proceedings in the reigns of Henry, Edward, and Elizabeth with regard to the *cultus* of the Blessed Virgin. They are
so much occupied in relating the disputes and legislation concerning the supremacy of the Pope, the Real Presence, Justification, and Church government, that they have given only slight
attention to changes which, if less fundamental, nevertheless
transformed the face of the country. Legislative acts are indeed
recorded, and acts of regal plunder or of popular violence are
to be met with under their respective dates. But this is not
enough. To understand so important a chapter of the variations
of Protestantism (a chapter omitted by Bossuet), declarations
of doctrine, legislative enactments, royal proclamations and commissions, and popular movements have to be brought together
in historical sequence.

Mr. Hallam, in his summary of the English Reformation,
has written as follows : ' No part of exterior religion was more
prominent, or more offensive to those who had imbibed a Protestant spirit, than the worship, or at least veneration, of images.
. . . The populace in towns where the reformed tenets prevailed began to pull them down in the very first days of Edward's reign ; and after a little pretence at distinguishing those
which had not been abused, orders were given that all images
should be taken away from churches.' Then, after relating and
deploring acts of vandalism, he concludes : ' The whole surface of
religious ordinances, all that is palpable to common minds, underwent a surprising transformation. But this change in ceremonial observances and outward show was trifling when compared to that in the objects of worship and in the purposes for
which they were addressed. Those who have visited some Ca-

tholic temples, and attended to the current language of devotion, must have perceived, what the writings of apologists or decrees of councils will never enable them to discover, that the saints, but more especially the Virgin, are almost exclusively the " popular" deities of that religion. All this polytheism was swept away by the Reformers ; and in this may be deemed to consist the most specific difference of the two systems.'

I will not dwell here on the offensive terms 'deities' and 'polytheism,' of which I have taken some notice in the Introduction, and to which my whole book is a sufficient reply. I draw attention to this passage for other reasons. It contains almost as much information as is generally possessed by educated Englishmen on the subject. Yet if it is true that the changes introduced at the Reformation involved at the same time ' all that is palpable to common minds,' and moral results, which, though generally held by theologians to be of minor importance, are of sufficient magnitude to appear to an intelligent observer like Mr. Hallam really to constitute ' the most specific difference' between Catholicity and Protestantism, then certainly the subject deserves a more detailed study than it has hitherto received.

To justify this statement, Mr. Hallam observes that the writings of apologists and decrees of councils ought to be supplemented by personal observation of the Catholic multitude in their devotions, and the current language of priests and people. I have not refused this test. On the contrary, I have quoted throughout this volume few writings of apologists. I have recorded but few authoritative decrees of councils. I have used my best endeavours to awaken once more the ' current language' of our Catholic ancestors, and to visit them in their temples when no fear of future Protestant criticism could check the ' popular' manifestation of their feelings.

But now it is right that the same test should be applied to the Protestant Reformation. The writings of apologists and the godly exhortations of reforming monarchs require a supplement. We must try to discover in history the motives that prompted each successive step of reform. If those motives shall appear as pure and disinterested, when judged by acts, as they do in the preambles of royal proclamations and prefaces to royal Primers, if the light shall be found steadily to increase in splendour from deeper and calmer study of the Word of God, then indeed the Spirit of God may be presumed to have guided the Reformation, and to have transformed a practical polytheism and gross superstition into the worship of the one true God in spirit and in truth ; and then, however lovers of art may lament the destruction of ancient monuments, lovers of God and man must rejoice in the destruction of ' Our Lady's Dowry.'

On the other hand, if there shall appear to be no coherence of doctrine, but the most manifest contradictions, each succeeding proclamation condemning and abrogating what the preceding one had extolled as pure and excellent ; if the new lights only break on the royal guides of the nation as new motives for plundering are required ; if the houses of convocation and episcopal counsellors instead of consistency in faith show time-serving sycophancy, and are always ready to find plausible and sanctimonious justification for each act of royal caprice or tyranny ; if the houses of parliament show the most degrading servility on every occasion, and the nobility and gentry for the most part seem to care for nothing but to enrich themselves on the Church's plunder ; if the people are stirred up to the destruction of what they hear called superstition and idolatry, not by solid instruction and moral improvement, but by fiery harangues, empty sophisms, ribald jokes, scurrilous ballads, alehouse farces, and petty plunder ; and if the whole results by the confession of friends in increase of profligacy, fanaticism and infidelity,—then certainly are Catholics justified in denying the action of the Spirit of God in the process of the Reformation, whatever opinion may be entertained as to its results.

Lollardism.

The first revolt against the teaching and practice of the Catholic Church as regards devotion to the Blessed Virgin Mary was that of the Lollards in the fourteenth century. ' At this time' (A.D. 1389), says the historian of Richard II., ' the heretics used to preach against making pilgrimages, and especially to Walsingham, and to the cross of north door in the church of St. Paul's, London, saying that there is no divinity in such things, but that they are rotten posts, filled with insects, by which the innocent crowd is seduced into manifest idolatry. Alas! the chief pastors heard and saw and fostered all this, and went their ways, "one to his farm, another to his merchandise." They left their sheep exposed to the jaws of the wolves, and no one raised his staff to drive them off . . . except the Bishop of Norwich.'[1]

It is affirmed by some that Wickliffe opposed the invocation of saints.[2] Evidence to the contrary is adduced by others.[3] But it is vain to look for consistency in men like Wickliffe urged on by passion. It is certain that his followers not only inveighed against images and pilgrimages, but spoke contemptuously of the saints themselves and of their intercession, and stirred up the people to many acts of impiety and sacrilege.

Still the great mass of the people were unaffected by Lollardism; and where it maintained itself it was rather as a smouldering disaffection than a consuming flame until fanned by the harangues of the disciples of Calvin, and the proclamations of Henry, in the sixteenth century. Foxe has recorded with approbation several blasphemies which were either recanted or punished in 1521 and the following years. 'Some of these confessors of Foxe,' says Collier, 'held erroneous opinions, and misbehaved themselves very much in language. Others are very intemperate, not to say profane, in their expressions. For instance, some of them called the crucifix in the rood-loft "block almighty." They called a chapel "an old fair milk-house," and that a "church-bell was good to hang about a cow's neck."[4] Another of them said he "threshed God Almighty out of the straw." These are strange sallies,' adds Collier, 'and very different from the modesty and discretion of the ancient Christians.

---

[1] *Life of Richard II.*, by a Monk of Evesham, edited by Hearne, p. 114. The cross of St. Paul's here alluded to was treated with every ignominy, and burnt by Thomas Cromwell.

[2] Collier, vol. iii. p. 182, ed. 1840.

[3] Flanagan's *History of Church*, vol. i.   [4] Collier, vol. iv. p. 29.

That the English clergy were careful to prevent the spreading of Lollardism we need not wonder; for the Lollards struck at the fundamentals of the Church, and had very dangerous opinions both with respect to faith and property. They had likewise been abetted by a considerable faction, and the government both in Church and State had been almost overturned by them. But then persecuting people to fire and fagot for matters of pure belief is going much too far in the other extremity.'[5]

I do not want to defend or to discuss the treatment of the Lollards under Henry V., or of their imitators under Henry VIII.; but if the opinions of the followers of Wickliffe were so far from being matters of pure belief that they were dangerous to property no less than to faith, and very nearly overturned the Church and State, the same may be said with at least equal truth of the opinions of the followers of Calvin, whether in England or in Scotland.

In 1530 Archbishop Warham collected a 'swarm of heresies and detestable opinions' out of the books of Tyndal, and forbad the reading of his books by the people. In this he had also the authority of Henry VIII., and the decree is signed, amongst others, by 'Sir Thomas More, Knight, Great Chancellor of England.' It is one of the last documents which contains a mention of the 'pontificacy of our Holy Father the Pope.' Among the strange propositions denounced in this document, I will mention only such as concern my subject. 'Saints in heaven cannot help us thither. To build a church in honour of our Lady, or of any other saint, is in vain; they cannot help thee, they be not thy friends.'[6]

Foxe gives lists[7] of articles charged against certain persons in the diocese of London in 1528-32. Among them, 'that pilgrimages be not profitable for man's soul, and should not be used;' 'that we should not offer to images in the church, nor set any lights before them;' 'that saints in heaven cannot help us, neither know any more what men do in this world than a man in the north country knoweth what is done in the south coun-

---

[5] Collier, vol. iv. p. 29.   [6] Ib. p. 141.
[7] Foxe's *Acts and Monuments*, vol. v. pp. 26-36.

try;' 'that he held against pilgrimages, and called images stocks, stones, and witches;' 'that those who go on pilgrimage to our Lady of Grace, of Walsingham and other places, were better tarry at home, and give money to succour me and my children and others of my poor neighbours than to go thither; for there they shall find but a piece of timber painted; there is neither God nor our Lady.'

Pedantry.

What has been said is sufficient to show that the seeds of momentous change were sown in many minds before Henry had contemplated any breach with the Catholic Church. But while Lollardism and Lutheranism were fostering impiety and discontent in the minds of the populace, another influence was at work which, though very different in its nature, combined to the same result in the minds of the rich and educated. I allude to the influence exercised by the new race of scholars. The revival of classic literature in the fifteenth century in Italy did not further affect devotion to our Lady than to give a certain tinge of paganism to some forms and expressions. But in Germany and England it affected a spirit of superiority and criticism of the simplicity of past ages and the barbarism of popular devotion, which predisposed many minds to indifference, doubt, or denial of our Lady's power. Trithemius, himself no despicable scholar, thus addresses these pedantic innovators: 'I caution you, O men of erudition and science, not to despise the devotion of the people, nor to reprehend as novelty their invocation of particular saints, but rather to imitate them. For there are amongst you, without offence to the good be it said, proud men, who scorn all devout exercises of the people; who count the examples and miracles of the saints as raving; who think nothing admissible which they cannot prove by the arguments of the philosophers; who refute as fables and women's dreams all revelations of God to devout persons, the legends of the saints fables, and while they preach their own erudition impugn the works of God.'[8]

* Trithemius, *De Laudibus S. Annæ*, quoted by Digby in *Compitum*, book ii. ch. ix.

I have already in a former chapter mentioned the *Colloquies* of Erasmus on pilgrimages; and there is every reason to think that he and his friend Colet, Dean of St. Paul's, had no little share in developing that spirit which ultimately brought about the overthrow of all devotion to our Lady in England. I do not forget that these men were the friends of More and of Fisher, and that they both lived and died in the communion of the Church. Yet by Erasmus's own confession they allowed themselves a liberty of doubt and of criticism which it is difficult to reconcile with a real belief in the presence of the Holy Ghost in the Church. Colet died before the days of schism came to try men's disposition, and Erasmus when he saw the frightful results of heresy somewhat retracted his early writings. But his beautiful Latin and his wit had given to his books a popularity and a power throughout Europe which has perhaps never been attained since, except by Voltaire. The young prince Henry had been one of Erasmus's patrons and admirers, and the influence of the insinuations of the Dutch priest can easily be traced in the proclamations and acts of the English king. The scoffs of Erasmus at the monks who were the guardians of our Lady's shrine prepared the minds of the upper classes, if not to approve, yet to be indifferent spectators of the outrages of the fanatics and the spoliations of kings. His sophisms about the riches of churches and about preferring alms to pilgrimages soon became commonplaces in the reforming pulpits, and were eagerly listened to by the poor. They cast a longing eye on the rich jewels that hung round our Lady's statues.

Avarice of the Poor.

The people heard gladly the advice given by men like Latimer, 'to leave pilgrimages, and do their pilgrimages to their poorer neighbours;' but when at last the shrines were pillaged, the proceeds did not go to the poor; and when pilgrimages to our Lady had ceased, and the churches were destroyed, and the monasteries were suppressed, the poor found, to their grief, that one of the great sources of piety, of tenderness of heart, and of compassion, had been dried up. To use the old apologue, they

had killed the goose that laid the golden eggs, and in attempting to get rich they had become paupers. The bitterest enemies
of the monastic system do not accuse the monks of being harsh
to the poor; the most infatuated apologist of Henry VIII. will
scarcely give him credit for almsgiving or benevolence.

Avarice of the King and Nobles.

Erasmus not only pretended that the offerings made to our
Lady should have been given to the poor, but he pointed out
that such accumulated riches must tempt the avarice of princes.
In this he spoke more truly, though not more wisely. For if the
churches must not be rich lest princes be tempted to rob them,
princes and nobles also should not build palaces and mansions,
and fill them with costly furniture and works of art, lest they
tempt the populace to insurrection and to plunder. Yet many
a worthy citizen of London who looks with pride at the splendid
services of gold and silver plate-displayed at a Lord Mayor's
banquet, plate which has been accumulated by the munificence
of centuries, will read with anger a list of the jewels in the
treasury of Canterbury, and approve of the spoliations of Henry
VIII.

There are not wanting proofs that the prophecy of Erasmus
did indeed supply a hint to Henry. Mr. Nichols has pointed
out that the instructions given to the commissioners sent to Walsingham bear evident reference to points mentioned in the *Colloquies.*

Abuses ?

It will be thought by some that whatever may have been
the violence or tyranny of Henry, yet that these must have had
a colour of justice in the eyes of contemporaries from the fla-
grant abuses to which they put an end. To be candid, had not
devotion gone to such irrational extremes, had not avarice and
imposture become so bare-faced, that the worship of the saints,
and particularly of the Blessed Virgin, crumbled as it were to
pieces by its own weight, or at least at the touch of Henry's hand
and the sound of Latimer's voice? I know this is the opinion
of many. As for myself, I have done my best to form an im-

partial judgment. I have read the documents on the suppression of monasteries, the denunciations of Foxe and Burnet, and the rest; but while I have found many vehement expressions of opinion, I have found very little trustworthy testimony to abuses.

Of course I do not mean that there were none of those occasional abuses such as the Church is ever correcting; but I can find nothing in England that can be for a moment compared to the sad state of things which existed in Milan and the surrounding country when St. Charles Borromeo took possession of his diocese. And even had there been such abuses, the example of St. Charles and similar prelates proves that the Church, to bring about a reform, required no change of doctrine, and no such acts of destruction as made up the Protestant Reformation in England.

First Ground taken by the Reformers.

One thing especially results from a careful inquiry into the words and acts of the Reformers—that at the outset they did not foresee, or had not the courage to acknowledge, the work of destruction that they were doomed to accomplish. While in reality they carried out the extremest measures which the Lollards themselves could have desired, they began by expressly repudiating any sympathy with their tenets. Years passed on, and during the whole reign of Henry they over and over again formally approved of what under Edward they renounced. I will introduce the history of Henry's sacrileges by showing what was the position of the reforming party at the time of the rupture with the Holy See.

The violent preaching of Latimer got him into trouble in 1529-1531. He was accused of maintaining certain novel doctrines, and he thus defended himself:

'*Our Lady was a sinner.*—So they did belie me to have said, when I had said nothing so, but to reprove certain, both priests and beneficed men, which do give so much to our Lady, as though she had not been saved by Christ, a whole Saviour

D D

both of her and of all that be and shall be saved.[9] I did reason after this manner: that either she was a sinner or no sinner. If a sinner, then she was delivered from sin by Christ; so that He saved her either by delivering or preserving her from sin; so that without Him neither she nor none other either be or could be saved. And, to avoid all offence, I showed how it might be answered, both to certain scriptures, which make all generally sinners, and how it might be answered unto Chrysostome and Theophylact, which make her namely and specially a sinner. But all would not serve, their malice was so great; notwithstanding that five hundred honest men can and will bear record. When they cannot reprove that thing that I do say, then they will belie me to say that thing that they can reprove; for they will needs appear to be against me.

' *Saints are not to be worshipped.*—So they lied; when I had showed divers significations of this word " saints" among the vulgar people. First, images of saints are called saints, and so they are not to be worshipped—take worshipping of them for praying to them; for they are not mediators by way of redemption, nor yet by way of intercession. And yet they may be well used, when they be applied to that use that they were ordained for, to be laymen's books for remembrance of heavenly things, &c.

' Take saints for inhabiters of heaven, and worshipping of them for praying to them—I never denied but that they might be worshipped and be our mediators, though not by way of redemption (for so Christ alone is a whole mediator both for them and for us), yet by the way of intercession.

' *Pilgrimage.*—And I never denied pilgrimage. And yet I have said that much scurf must be pared away ere ever it can be well done; superstition, idolatry, false faith and trust in the image, unjust estimation of the thing setting aside God's ordinance for doing of the thing; debts must be paid, restitutions made, wife and children be provided for, duty to our poor

---

[9] The Council of Trent affirms the belief of the Church in Mary's sinlessness. The very definition of her Immaculate Conception by Pius IX. affirms that she received this privilege ' intuitu meritorum Christi Jesu.'

neighbours discharged. And when it is at the best, before it be vowed, it need not to be done; for it is neither under the bidding of God nor of man to be done. And wives must counsel with husbands, and husbands and wives with curates, before it be vowed to be done, &c.

'*Ave Maria.*—As for the Ave Maria, who can think that I would deny it? I said it was a heavenly greeting or saluting of our Blessed Lady, wherein the angel Gabriel, sent from the Father of heaven, did annunciate and show unto her the goodwill of God towards her, what He would with her and to what He had chosen her. But I said it was not properly a prayer, as the Paternoster, which our Saviour Christ Himself made for a proper prayer, and bade us say it for a prayer, not adding that we should say ten or twenty Ave Marias withal; and I denied not but that we may well say Ave Maria also, but not so that we shall think that the Paternoster is not good, a whole and perfect prayer, nor cannot be well said without Ave Maria. So that I did not speak against well saying of it, but against superstitious saying of it, and of the Paternoster too; and yet I put a difference betwixt that and that which Christ made to be said for a prayer.'

Another specimen of Latimer's doctrine I may take from a sermon he preached at Cambridge in 1529: 'Now then, if men be so foolish of themselves that they will bestow the most part of their goods in voluntary works, which they be not bound to keep, but willingly and by their devotion, and leave the necessary works undone, which they are bound to do, they and all their voluntary works are like to go unto everlasting damnation. And I promise you, if you build a hundred churches, give as much as you can make to gilding of saints and honouring of the church, and if thou go as many pilgrimages as thy body can well suffer, and offer as great candles as oaks, if thou leave the works of mercy and commandments undone, these works shall nothing avail thee.'

There is nothing whatever in this passage that saints have not said over and over again. It was being said in Spain and Italy at that very time. There was no need to break with

Popery (as they called it) if these were the abuses they wished
to reform. If the preaching of Latimer excited opposition, it
was because, while he made a boast of imitating the zeal of men·
like St. Jerome, he had none of St. Jerome's submission to the
Church and the Holy See.

Acts of Henry.

It will not be contended that the quarrel of Henry VIII.
with the Pope was from any movement of divine grace. Until
he had conceived a guilty love for Anne Boleyn, Henry had
not detected the corruptions in the Church which he was afterwards so zealous to reform. But no sooner had he made himself 'supreme head of the Church' than his new position seems
to have awakened a sense of responsibility, and a strange zeal
for the spiritual welfare of his subjects. His first measure was
the suppression of the monasteries, which only in so far con-
cerns my subject, that many of the most famous sanctuaries of
our Lady were in the monastic churches, and that one of the
means invented for calumniating the monks previous to their
suppression was to accuse them of fostering superstition and
inventing false miracles.

Lord Herbert tells us that when the suppression of some of
the religious houses was debated in the Council, the two reasons
which most prevailed were, that the king would thereby secure
some of their riches, and that he would intimidate the men who
were most likely to be effectual supporters of the Pope's supremacy against the royal pretensions. 'But I do not deny,' says
Mr. Collier with keen irony, in answer to Burnet, 'but that
there might be sincerity at bottom, and that the courtiers might
be governed by good meaning and public regards. All that I
say is, the disinterestedness of the matter doth not lie so open
to common view; but then we are to consider that the inside
of some things is sometimes most valuable. Some people's
actions, like rich mines, are less promising upon the surface;
and when it happens thus, everybody hath not force enough to
dig down to the treasure, and reach the honesty of his neighbour's intentions.'[10]

[10] Collier, vol. v. p. 22.

But to turn from motives to facts.

The preamble to the act for the suppression of the lesser monasteries in 1535, on pretext of abuses, expressly rehearses that in 'the great and solemn monasteries of this realm, thanks be to God, religion is well kept and observed ;' but when the proceeds of the guilty monasteries had been consumed, it was found that the larger ones were no less guilty, and all were suppressed. Hence the people came to conclude, contrary to express declarations made at the outset, that the guilt, if guilt there was, lay in the monastic profession itself, and not in any accidental abuses. Exactly the same process was followed in regard to statues and devotion to our Lady. At first it was stated that prayer to our Lady was good and her images to be venerated, but that there had been abuses, and the richer shrines were pillaged on this pretence. Afterwards all prayer to our Lady was forbidden, and all images were removed. Whence the people naturally concluded that all devotion to the Blessed Virgin was in itself evil. And this has been the prevailing belief since the time of Elizabeth, though at the commencement of the Reformation such a thing had not been contemplated.

I have given already in the chapter on sanctuaries a few examples of the shameless work of plunder of our Lady's shrines which then went on. Henry had chosen for this work a suitable agent, Thomas Cromwell, a man who had served as a trooper in the army which sacked Rome in 1527, and who, as Collier remarks,[11] 'was looked on as disaffected to the monasteries and somewhat inclined to the Lutheran persuasion. This minister, to qualify him for his function, was made vicar-general of the king's supremacy. In virtue of this commission, he was constituted general visitor of all the monasteries ; not to mention his superintendency over the bishops and secular clergy.' Cromwell in his turn appointed deputies for the visitation as unscrupulous as himself. The very purpose of their commission was, as the same author observes,[12] 'to lessen the reputation of the religious houses, and make them fall unpitied. They

[11] Collier, vol. iv. p. 294.   [12] Ib. p. 309.

exerted their powers to the utmost stretch, and were far from partiality in the inquiry.'

Surely the one-sided testimony of such men as these, which was never cross-examined in a court of justice, and which we have now no means to control, since every document bearing on the sanctuaries was carefully destroyed, cannot be received as truth by any fair-minded man.

Mr. Collier, the most impartial of Protestant Church historians, writes as follows :[13] 'The king, having the dissolution of the remaining monasteries in view, thought it necessary to lessen their reputation, to lay open the superstition of their worship, and draw a charge of imposture upon some of them. And here it must be said, he was not without a colour for his proceedings; for relics had been for some time too much magnified, and many of them were counterfeited ; images ware supposed to be more significant in one place than another ; and in short, the people were drawn to tedious pilgrimages, to visionary hopes, and misapplication in their devotions.' Then after relating some particulars, which I need not quote, he adds : ' The mistaken reliance and superstitious practice with respect to images and relics is not to be denied; but whether the impostures above mentioned are matter of fact will be a question ; for William Thomas, cited by Lord Herbert, is somewhat an exceptionable authority. He wrote the book called *Il Pelerine Inglese*, in justification of King Henry's proceedings ; but, by the account which he gives of Archbishop Becket, it is plain he was either biassed or grossly mistaken.'[14]

The figures of our Lady of Worcester, Walsingham, Ipswich, Penrice, Islington, and some others, were publicly burnt.

A large image called Darvell Gatheren, or Delver Gathaernc, brought from Wales, was used to kindle the fire under Friar Forrest, who had been confessor to Queen Katharine, and who was burnt for denying the king's supremacy. Foxe tells us with glee how the following verses were set up on the gallows from which Forrest was hung in chains over the fire :

[13] Collier, vol. iv. p. 426-7.
[14] About relics of the Blessed Virgin see *antea*, p. 333 ; on William Thomas see p. 298.

> ' David Darvell Gatheren, as saith the Welchmen,
>   Brought outlaws out of hell ;
> Now is he come with spear and shield, in harness to burn in Smithfield,
>   For in Wales he may not dwell ;
> And Forrest the friar, that obstinate liar,
>   That willingly shall be dead,
> In his contumacy the gospel did deny,
>   And the king to be supreme head.'

These elegant verses were so much esteemed by their author, a certain Gray, a retainer of Thomas Cromwell, that he incorporated them in a longer poem, called the *Fantassie of Idolatry.* To write scurrilous ballads to be sung in alehouses was a means of reformation much in favour in those days, and greatly encouraged by Cromwell, who kept two or three poets for the purpose ; and Foxe, who censures the gaiety of Sir Thomas More, highly commends the wit of these gentlemen.

An account of the reformation of our Lady's cultus, and the overthrow of her Dowry in England, would be incomplete without at least one specimen of these ballads. I shall therefore give a few verses from Mr. Gray's *Fantassie.* I omit many others as too blasphemous for my pages. The curious may find the whole in Foxe.[15]

> ' To Walsingham a gadding, to Canterbury a madding,
>   As men distraught of mind ;
> With few clothes on our backs, but an image of wax
>   For the lame and for the blind.
> To Hampton, to Ipswich, to Harforth, to Shoreditch,
>   With many mo' places of price ;
> As to our Lady of Worcester, and the sweet Rood of Chester,
>   With the Blessed Lady of Penryce.
> To Lym'ster, to Kingston, to York, to Donnington,
>   To Redding, to the child of grace ;
> To Windsor, to Waltham, to Ely, to Caultam,
>   Barefooted and barelegged apace ;
> To Pomfret, to Willesden, to St. Anne of Buxton,
>   To St. Michael's Mount also.
> *   *   *   *   *
> Such was our trust, such was our lust,
>   Upon creature to call and cry ;
> As men did please, for every disease
>   To have a god peculiarly.

---

[15] Foxe's *Acts and Monuments,* vol. v. p. 404, ed. 1838.

Then ran we about to seek idols out,
    Wandering far and near,
Thinking the power of our blessed Saviour
    In other places more than there.
And now some may run, and when they have done
    The idols they shall not find ;
For the Rood of grace hath lost his place,' &c.

The public outrages done by the king himself against the images which had been held in greatest veneration gave license to many of the Lollards, Lutherans, and Calvinists, who were now flocking to the country, to denounce all devotion to the saints.   Cranmer and Cromwell would personally have been disposed to acquiesce, but the 'king's highness, our most dread sovereign lord, and supreme head of the Church of England,' was otherwise minded ; and in June 1536 the Convocation complained to the king of certain ' errors and abuses within this realm, causes of dissension, and worthy special reformation.' Among other sayings denounced are the following : ' That it was never merry in England since the Litany was brought into the service, and Sancta Maria, Sancta Catharina, &c., sung and repeated ;'[16] ' that no reverence ought to be paid to the images of the saints, and that it is downright idolatry to light lamps or tapers before an image, or to have any lights at divine service till after sunset ;' ' that it is idolatry to make any oblations ;' ' that it is a breach of God's command for Christians to make a reverence or curtsey to our Saviour's picture ;' ' that the saints are not to be honoured with invocations, that they understand nothing of our prayers ;' ' that our Lady, the Blessed Virgin, was no better than another woman, and that she can prevail with our Saviour no more than another sinful person of her sex ;' ' that it is no more purpose to pray to the saints than to throw a stone against the wind.'   The Convocation also complains, ' that some novelists are not content to preach against the excesses and irregularities in pilgrimages, fasting, invocation of saints, worshipping of images, and giving of alms, but will needs declare against the thing, and sweep off the practice ; for the reformation of abuses is not enough to satisfy these people.'

[16] Collier, vol. iv. pp. 844-8.

Of these and the rest of the propositions enumerated by the Convocation, Fuller says that they are the Protestant religion in ore ; but Collier dissents, saying that ' unless we had found a richer vein, it may very well be questioned whether the mine had been worth the working.' He omits, however, to name the richer vein. Henry, in answer to the above address, caused to be drawn up and presented to Convocation a new profession of faith, which was subscribed by himself and the majority of the bishops, and published in the king's name. This is an important document, as containing the doctrine allowed by Henry during the remainder of his reign. I extract only such parts as belong to my subject.

Of Images.

' As touching images. Truth it is, that the same hath been said in the Old Testament for the great abuses of them to have been sometime destroyed and put down ; and in the New Testament they have been also allowed, as good authors do declare ; wherefore we will, that all bishops and preachers shall instruct and teach our people committed by us unto their spiritual charge how they ought and may use them : and first, that there may be attributed unto them that they be representers of virtue and good example ; and that they also be by occasion the kindlers and stirrers of men's minds, and make men oft to remember and lament their sins and offences, especially the images of Christ and our Lady ; and that therefore it is meet they should stand in the churches, and none otherwise to be esteemed : and to the intent the rude people[17] should not from henceforth take such superstition, as in time past it is thought that the same hath used to do, we will that our bishops and preachers diligently shall teach them, and according to this doctrine reform their abuses, for else there might fortune idolatry to issue, which God forbid : and as for incensing them, and kneeling and offering unto them, with other like worshippings,—although

[17] He himself in his youth, and his father, Henry VII., and his grandmother, Lady Margaret, had not been ashamed to share the piety of the ' rude people.'

the same hath entered by devotion, and fallen into custom, yet
the people ought to be diligently taught that they in no wise
do it, nor think it meet to be done, to the same images, but
only to be done to God and His honour, although it be done
before the images, whether it be of Christ, of the cross, or of our
Lady, or of any other saint beside.'

Of Honouring of Saints.

' As touching the honouring of saints, we will that all bishops
and preachers instruct and teach our people committed by us
unto their spiritual charge, that saints now being with Christ in
heaven are to be honoured of Christian people in earth, but not
with that confidence and honour which are only due to God ;
but that they be thus to be honoured, because they be known
the elect persons of Christ, because they be passed in godly
life out of this transitory world, because they already do reign
in glory with Christ : and most specially to laud and praise
Christ in them, for their excellent virtues, which He planted in
them, for example of and by them, to such as are yet in this
world, to live in virtue and goodness ; and also not to fear to
die for Christ and His cause, as some of them did ; and finally to
take them, in that they may, to be the advancers of our prayers
and demands unto Christ. By these ways and such like be
saints to be had in reverence and honour, and by none other.'

Of Praying to Saints.

' As touching praying to saints, we will that all bishops and
preachers shall instruct and teach our people, committed by us
unto their spiritual charge, that, albeit grace, remission of sins,
and salvation cannot be obtained but of God only, by the me-
diation of our Saviour Christ, which is only sufficient Mediator
for all our sins, yet it is very laudable to pray to saints in
heaven everlastingly living, whose charity is ever permanent, to
be intercessors and to pray for us and with us to Almighty God,
after this manner :

' " All holy angels and saints in heaven, pray for us and
with us unto the Father, that for His dear Son Jesus Christ's
sake we may have grace of Him and remission of our sins, with

an earnest purpose, not wanting ghostly strength, to observe and keep His holy commandments, and never to decline from the same again unto our lives' end."

'And in this manner we may pray unto our Blessed Lady, to St. John Baptist, to all and every of the Apostles, or any other saint particularly, as our devotion doth serve us; so that it be done without any vain superstition, as to think that any saint is more merciful or will hear us sooner than Christ, or that any saint doth serve for one thing more than another, or is patron of the same: and likewise we must keep holydays unto God, in memory of Him and His saints, upon such days as the Church hath ordained their memories to be celebrated, except they be mitigated or moderated by the assent or commandment of the supreme head to the ordinaries, and then the subjects ought to obey it.'

To inculcate the above doctrines Henry had a book drawn up in 1537, called the *Institution of a Christian Man*, to serve as a guide to the bishops and preachers. It was followed in 1543 by another, called *A necessary Doctrine and Erudition for any Christian Man, set forth by the King's Majesty of England*. With regard to the Blessed Virgin the two books agree almost to a word. They both contain the Angelic Salutation or Hail Mary.

In the preface to the *Erudition* the king says:

'We have, after declaration of the commandments, expounded the seven petitions of our Paternoster, wherein be contained requests and suits for all things necessary to a Christian man in this present life; with declaration of the Ave Maria, as a prayer containing a joyful rehearsal and magnifying of God in the work of the Incarnation of Christ, which is the ground of our salvation, wherein the Blessed Virgin our Lady, for the abundance of grace wherewith God indued her, is also with this remembrance honoured and worshipped.'

The two books also contain a really very beautiful explanation of the Hail Mary, which is quite in accordance with the Catholic traditions in which the authors had been brought up.

Only at the end occurs the following admonition, which is another proof of what has been said elsewhere, that the prayer ' Holy Mary,' &c., had not yet been added in public worship to the Hail Mary :

'Fiftly we thynke it conuenient, that all bysshops and preachers shall instructe and teache the people, commytted vnto theyr spirituall charge, that this Aue Maria is not properly a prayer as the Pater noster is. For a prayer properly hath wordes of peticion, supplication, request, and suite : but this Aue Maria hath no suche. Neuerthelesse the Churche hath vsed to adioyne it to thende of the Pater noster, as an himne, laude, and prayse partly of our Lorde and Sauiour Jesu Christ for our redemption, and partly of the Blessed Virgin, for her humble consent gyuen and expressed to the aungell at this salutation. Laudes, prayses, and thākes be in this Aue Maria principally gyuen and yelded to our Lorde, as to the auctour of our sayd redemption : but herewith also the Virgin lacketh not her laudes, prayse, and thankes for her excellent and singuler vertues, and chiefely for that she humbly consented, accordynge to the sayinge of the holy matrone Saynt Elisabeth, when she said vnto this virgin, Blessed art thou, that dyddest gyve trust and credence to the aungell's wordes, for all thynges that haue been spoken to thee shal be performed.'

But instructions and injunctions and *Necessary Erudition* notwithstanding, the breach had been made in the dykes, and the waters of strife and dissension, heresy and infidelity, were pouring through and inundating the country.

Foxe has preserved for us a very lively picture of a scene which must have been of common occurrence during the reign of Henry, when the old worship was still retained, Mass and Vespers sung, the beads recited, anthems to our Lady solemnly performed; and yet at the same time the pulpits resounded with sermons against superstition and idolatry ; pious practices were called abuses and rebuked by royal proclamations; the most famous images of our Lady were publicly burnt, and jests and ballads spread far and wide, by the influence of Cromwell. There was a certain Robert Testwood, who was chorister in the

royal chapel of Windsor. He afterwards lost his life under
Henry for denying the Real Presence; but though it was death
to disbelieve any of Henry's Six Articles, people could ridicule
and insult our Lady with impunity, as is proved from the following account:

'It chanced,' says Foxe,[18] 'Testwood one day to walk in the
church at afternoon, and to behold the pilgrims, especially of
Devonshire and Cornwall, how they came in by plumps, with
candles and images of wax in their hands, to offer to good King
Henry of Windsor, as they called him' (Henry VI., who had
died in odour of sanctity). 'It pitied his heart to see such great
idolatry committed, and how vainly the people had spent their
goods in coming so far to kiss a spur, and to have an old hat
set upon their heads; insomuch that he could not refrain, but,
seeing a certain company which had done their offering and
were standing gazing about the church, he went unto them, and
with all gentleness began to exhort them to leave such false
worshipping of dumb creatures, and to learn to worship the true
living God aright; putting them in remembrance what those
things were which they worshipped, and how God many times
had plagued His people for running a-whoring to such stocks
and stones, and so would plague them and their posterity if they
would not leave it. And after this sort he admonished them
so long, till at last his words, as God would, took such place in
some of them, that they said they never would go a pilgrimage
more.

'Then he went farther, and found another sort licking and
kissing a white Lady made of alabaster, which image was mor-
ticed in a wall behind the high altar, and bordered about with
a pretty border, which was made like branches with hanging
apples and flowers. And when he saw them so superstitiously
use the image as to wipe their hands upon it, and then to
stroke them over their eyes and faces, as though there had been
great virtue in touching the picture, he up with his hand, in
which he had a key, and smote down a piece of the border about
the image, and with the glance of the stroke chanced to break

[18] Foxe's *Martyrs*, vol. v. p. 467.

off the image's nose. " Lo, good people," quoth he, " you see
what it is—nothing but earth and dust, and cannot help itself;
and how then will you have it to help you? For God's sake,
brethren, be no more deceived."   And so he gat him home to
his house, for the rumour was so great, that many came to see
the image how it was defaced.'

It appears from Foxe's account that this zealous reformer,
who was so eager for the souls of others, and who did not believe
in the Presence of our Lord in the Eucharist, or in the lawfulness of prayer to the Blessed Virgin, had yet no scruple to receive payment for singing at Holy Mass or at the Office of our
Lady.   Perhaps it was to make a compromise with his conscience that he acted as Foxe relates a little further on.   ' In
the mean time,' he writes, ' there chanced a pretty story between
one Robert Phillips, gentleman of the king's chapel, and Testwood ; which story, though it was but a merry prank of a singing-man, yet it grieved his adversary wonderfully.   The matter
was this : Robert Phillips was so notable a singing-man (wherein
he gloried), that wheresoever he came the best and longest
song, with most counter-verses in it, would be set up at his
coming.   And so, his chance being now to be at Windsor, against
his coming to the anthem a long song was set up, called " Lau-
date vivi," in which song there was one counter-verse towards
the end that began in this wise, " O Redemptrix et Salvatrix,"
which verse of all others Robert Phillips would sing, because
he knew that Testwood could not abide that ditty.   Now
Testwood, knowing his mind well enough, joined with him at
the part ; and when he heard Robert Phillips begin to fetch his
flourish with " O Redemptrix et Salvatrix," repeating the same,
one in another's neck, Testwood was as quick, on the other
side, to answer him again with " Non Redemptrix nec Salvatrix ;" and so striving there with " O" and " Non" who should
have the mastery, they made an end of the verse ; whereat was
good laughing in sleeves of some ; but Robert Phillips, with
others of Testwood's enemies, were sore offended.'

To return to public history :

In 1536, Cromwell put forth injunctions as ' visiting by the king's highness's supreme authority ecclesiastical the people and clergy.' He orders that the clergy 'should not lay out their rhetoric in flourishing upon images, relics, or miracles, upon any motive of superstition or covetousness; that they ought not to persuade their people to pilgrimages, contrary to the intentment of the late Articles, but rather exhort them to serve God and make provision for their families,' &c.[19]

But while these things were going on in the South, the parts of England more distant from the seat of government rose in arms, not to overthrow the king, but to demand the redress of their grievances, and to complain of Henry's evil councillors. The Lincolnshire insurgents complained, amongst other things, ' that they had reason to apprehend the jewels and plate of their parish churches would be seized, and fall under the same calamity with the religious houses.' They were but too good prophets. But Henry promised them justice, offered them indemnity, and persuaded them to disband. At the same time occurred the revolt in Yorkshire, called the ' Pilgrimage of grace.' When Henry found that this insurrection was no longer to be feared, he returned an answer to the petition which had been sent to him : ' We are strangely surprised to find ignorant people have the assurance to instruct us in the doctrines of the faith, especially since we have some reputation for letters.'

When the articles of religion mentioned above were sent to the North they were not well received. The clergy met at Pomfret and made a remonstrance. Among other things they say : ' We think that preaching against purgatory, worshipping of saints, pilgrimages, images, and all books set forth against the same, be worthy to be reproved or condemned by Convocation, and the pain to be executed that is devised for the doers to the contrary, . . . and that the holydays may be observed according to the laws and laudable customs ; and that the bidding of the beads and preaching may be observed as has been used by old custom.'[20]

[19] Collier, vol. iv. p. 372.
[20] Ib. p. 385. The ' bidding of beads' here referred to is not the recitation of the Rosary, but the reading of the beadroll before Mass. Henry

As the insurgents were dispersed, these remonstrances were of course unheeded. Henry, or Cromwell in his name, continued to instruct the country. ' To the intent that all superstition and hypocrisy crept into divers men's hearts may vanish away, they shall not set forth or extol any images, relics, or miracles, for any superstition or lucre, nor allure the people by any entreatment to the pilgrimages of any saints, otherwise than is permitted in the articles lately put forth, . . . as though it were proper and peculiar to that saint to give this commodity or that, seeing all goodness, health, and grace ought to be looked and asked for only of God,' &c.

In 1538 came further injunctions, 'that such feigned images as ye know, in any of your cures, to be so abused with pilgrimages or offerings of anything made thereunto, ye shall, for avoiding of that most detestable offence of idolatry, forthwith take down without delay; and shall suffer from henceforth no candles, tapers, or images of wax, to be set before any images or picture, but only the light that commonly goeth about the cross of the church by the rood-loft, the light before the sacrament of the altar, and the light about the sepulchre,' &c.

It was reserved for his son Edward VI. to quench the lights before the Blessed Sacrament, and for his daughter Elizabeth to pull down all the rood-screens. But the light of the gospel which extinguished the lights in the church shone only by degrees.

Although the Ave Maria was still said throughout England, it was now forbidden to ring the morning and evening bells, and this out of mere hatred of the Pope, who had granted an indulgence to this devotion.[21]

Processions also were still allowed; but the people were informed, that whereas in times past it had been customary in processions to sing ' Ora pro nobis' to so many saints, that they had no time to make immediate application to God Almighty in

---

had reformed this, omitting the name of the Pope, &c. The Rosary-beads were not forbidden until the next reign.

[21] See page 218.

the suffrages ' Parce nobis Domine' and ' Libera nos Domine,' it were better to omit the ' Ora pro nobis' and repeat the other.[22]

About the end of 1538, Cranmer proposed to Henry some further reformation, but without effect for the moment.[23] But a *Rationale* or explanation of ceremonies was drawn up, probably in 1541.[24] In this it is stated that ' bearing candles on Candlemas-day is a very good usage in memory of Christ, the spiritual Light, of whom Simeon did prophesy ;' so is the covering of the cross and images in Lent, with the uncovering of the same at the Resurrection. ' That upon Good Friday is renewed yearly the remembrance of the blessed Passion ; wherefore upon that day, amongst other godly ceremonies to be continued, is the creeping to the cross, where we humble ourselves to Christ before the same ; offering unto Him and kissing of the cross, in memory of our redemption ; and that day is prepared and well adorned the sepulchre (in remembrance of the sepulchre which was prophesied by the prophet Esaias to be glorious), wherein is laid the image of the cross and the most Blessed Sacrament, &c. That general processions and other particular processions, with the Litanies and other prayers, are very laudable.' We shall see presently that every one of these things will be discovered to be superstitious and unlawful before a few years have passed.

Henry VIII. having now beheaded Catherine Howard, his fifth wife, and hung and burnt Catholics and Protestants in pairs,[25] the former for adhering to the old faith, the latter for out-stripping their royal master in the new one, began, in 1542, to turn his thoughts to a little further reformation of his subjects. But I must quote the words of Foxe, his admirer :[26] ' After the death and punishment of this lady, his fifth wife, the king calling to remembrance the words of Lord Cromwell, began a little to set his foot again in the cause of religion. And although he ever bare a special favour to Thomas, Archbishop of Canterbury, yet now the more he missed the Lord Cromwell'

[22] Collier, vol. iv. p. 430.   [23] Ib. vol. v. pp. 83-5.
[24] It is given in full in Collier, vol. v. pp. 106-24.
[25] Foxe, vol. v. p. 439.   [26] Ib. p. 462.

(whom he had beheaded two years before), ' the more he inclined to the archbishop, and also to the right cause of religion.' Foxe does not care here to remind us that Cranmer had well merited his increasing influence over the king by the two divorces he had pronounced, by voting the death of Cromwell, and the rest ; but he continues : ' And therefore after the execution of this queen, the king, understanding some abuses yet to remain unreformed, namely, about pilgrimages and idolatry, and other things besides, directed his letters unto the aforesaid Archbishop of Canterbury :

" Right reverend father in God, right trusty and well-beloved, we greet you well, letting you to wit, that whereas heretofore, upon the zeal and remembrance which we had to our bounden duty towards Almighty God, perceiving sundry superstitions and abuses to be used and embraced by our people, whereby they grievously offend Him and His word, we did not only cause the images and bones of such as they resorted and offered unto, with the ornaments of the same, and all such writings and monuments of feigned miracles wherwith they were illuded, to be taken away in all places of our realm ; but also by our injunctions commanded that no offering or setting-up of lights or candles should be suffered in any church, but only to the Blessed Sacrament of the altar ; it is lately come unto our knowledge, that this our good intent and purpose notwithstanding, the shrines, coverings of shrines, and monuments of those things, do yet remain in sundry places of this realm, much to the slander of our doings, and to the great displeasure of Almighty God, the same being means to allure our subjects to their former hypocrisy and superstition ;" ' and the rest. He orders that ' if any shrine, covering of shrine, table, monument of miracles, or other pilgrimages, do continue, they be so taken away *as there remain no memory of it.*'

In Jan. 1545 those things which had been formally approved in the *Rationale* were abolished. Henry wrote to Cranmer to forbid the covering and uncovering of the cross and images in Lent, and of his own accord declares that the ' creeping to the cross' or adoration of the cross on Good Friday ' is a greater abuse than any other.'[27] Four years earlier it was called 'a godly ceremony to be continued.' But now this strange reformer's career was coming to an end. In his last speech to Parliament he drew a vivid picture of the result of his work.

After scolding his servile and apostate bishops, he turns upon the equally servile laity :

'Though the spirituality are in some fault for breaking into parties, and living upon ill terms with those of their own business, yet you of the temporality do not stand clear of envy and ill-nature; for you rail on the bishops, defame and misreport the priests, and treat the preacher with contumely and ill language. . . *Do not set up yourselves for judges of controversy, nor lay so much stress upon your vain expositions and fantastical opinions. In such sublime matters you may easily mistake.* It is true you are allowed to read the Holy Scriptures, and to have the Word of God in your mother tongue; but then this permission is only designed for private information, and the instruction of your children and family. It was never intended for mooting and dispute, nor to furnish you with reprimanding phrases and expressions of reproach against priests and preachers ; and yet this is the use a great many disorderly people make of the privilege of having the Scriptures. I am extremely sorry to find how much the Word of God is abused, with how little reverence it is mentioned, both with respect to place and occasion ; how people squabble about the sense ; how it is turned into wretched rhyme, sung, and jangled in every alehouse and tavern ; and all this in a false construction and counter-meaning to the inspired writers. I am sorry to perceive the readers of the Bible discover so little of it in their practice, for I am sure *charity was never in a more languishing condition, virtue never at a lower ebb, nor God less honoured and worse served,* in Christendom.'

After a few more judicial murders, and obtaining a grant of the lands left by the faithful as foundations for Masses for the repose of their souls, for hospitals, and confraternities, Henry also died.

[27] Collier, vol. v. p. 139.

It was a strange spectacle to see this prince robbing of his own gifts and those of his ancestors the shrines before which he had once knelt; but perhaps it is still stranger to see him in his last will invoking her whose worship in England he had wellnigh destroyed. ' In the name of God,' so runs this document,[28] ' and of the glorious and Blessed Virgin, our Lady St. Mary, and of all the holy company of heaven, we Henry, by the grace of God King of England, France and Ireland, Defender of the Faith, and in earth, immediately under God, the supreme Head of the Church of England and Ireland;' then after this profession of schism and heresy, and many protestations of humility and piety to God, he continues : ' Also we do instantly require and desire the Blessed Virgin Mary, His Mother, with all the holy company of heaven, continually to pray for us and with us while we live in this world, and in the time of passing out of the same, that we may the sooner attain everlasting life after our departure out of this transitory life, which we do both hope and claim by Christ's Passion and Word.' Then he makes arrangements for Masses at his funeral, and for two daily Masses and four solemn obits to be celebrated for his soul *for ever,* ' willing, charging, and requiring our son, Prince Edward, and all our heirs and successors which shall be kings of this realm, as they will answer before Almighty God at the dreadful day of judgment, that they do see' these dispositions carried out. But Henry's example was more powerful than his word. He had already obtained a grant of all chantries or foundations for Masses, and this grant being renewed to Edward VI. of course his royal father's foundation went with all the rest; and when the insurgents rose against the new liturgy, and asked for the Six Articles of Henry VIII., Edward reminded them that he had just the same authority to reform religion as his father. His ' heirs and successors' have had so little fear of the citation to ' answer at the dreadful day of judgment,' that they have made the renunciation of Henry's faith in the Holy Mass the test of fitness for office, and the abjuration of that in which Henry placed his hope a condition for wearing the crown.

[28] Given in Tierney's edition of *Dodd.*

Prayer-books.

It will be instructive to give as briefly as possible an account of the various changes introduced into books published by authority during the reign of Henry. Nothing can show more clearly the limping and staggering march of the Reformation. To understand what follows it must be remembered that prayer-books were of two sorts—those used in the public worship of the Church, and those intended for private devotion, generally called the Horæ, Orarium, or Prymer. I confine my remarks entirely to the subject of devotion to our Lady and the saints.

1. During the reign of Henry the old service-books continued in use, containing the lessons, antiphons, versicles, responses of our Lady, almost as in the Roman Breviary of the present day.

2. The Articles of 1536 give instructions how to honour and invoke the saints.

3. The *Instruction of a Christian Man* of 1537, and the *Erudition of a Christian Man* of 1543, both published by Henry's authority, give beautiful instruction on the Hail Mary.

4. By Cromwell's injunctions of 1536 the knolling of the Aves was abolished, and it was recommended to strike out some of the invocations of saints in the Litany.

5. As to private prayer-books, an *un*authorised Prymer was published in 1530 by Marshall, omitting the Litany, and a second edition in 1535 'cum privilegio regali,' with the Litany, but with warnings about its abuse. The book was afterwards suppressed.

6. In 1539, Hilsey, Bishop of Rochester, 'at the commandment of the right honourable lord Thomas Cromwell,' published a Prymer, in which many of the saints are omitted from the Litany.

In this Prymer, intended for children, the name of Jesus is omitted from the Hail Mary, no doubt because it had been inserted by the authority of the Pope. However, a few extracts will show that no thought had yet occurred of giving up devotion to our Lady.

The Anthem at Lauds.

'Holy Mary, most pure of virgins all,
Mother and daughter of the King celestial,
So comfort us in our desolation,
That by thy prayer and special meditation [mediation ?]
We may enjoy the reward of the heavenly reign,
And with God's elect there for to remain.'

Another Anthem.

'O glorious Mother of God, O perpetual Virgin Mary, which didst bear the Lord of all lords, and alone of all others didst give suck unto the King of angels, we beseech thee of thy pity to have us in remembrance, and to make intercession for us unto Christ, that we being supported by His help may come unto the kingdom of heaven.

'*Vers.* O holy Mother of God, perpetual Virgin Mary.

'*Resp.* Pray for us unto the Lord Jesus Christ.'

Prayer.

'Grant, we beseech Thee, O Lord God, that Thy servants may enjoy continual health of body and soul, and through the gracious intercession of Blessed Mary, perpetual Virgin, that we may be delivered from the present heaviness, and to have the fruition of the eternal gladness.   By Christ our Lord.'

The following rude verses also occur :

'O Mother of God, most gracious,
To whom Christ Johann did commend,
Saying, Mulier, ecce filius tuus,
Thy sorrows that He would amend ;
Then shortly after He said,
Lo, John, behold thy mother,
Thus in him the trust was laid,
To comfort thee above all other,—
With like pity comfort us
In this vale of misery,
And pray to thy Son Jesus
To bring us to eternal glory.

' *Vers.* Holy Mother of God, make thy petition.
' *Resp.* That we may obtain Christ's promission.'

Prayer.

'O Lord Jesus Christ, which, being among men, wert found
as man, having the experience of all our miseries, only that
Thou lackedst sin; for that exceeding charity which so far over-
cometh Thee, take pity on us, and grant us, by the intercession
of Thy glorious Mother, whom so entirely Thou didst love, to
be void of all the misery of sin and all other worldly adversities,
with Thee patiently to suffer; which livest and reignest God,
world without end. Amen.'

There is something very touching in these prayers, as they
were the last devotions to the Blessed Virgin taught by royal
authority to Christian children.   In a few years more they were
never to hear her name mentioned with reverence, gratitude,
tenderness, or compassion, and were to be taught that to invoke
her help was a sin against the majesty of God.

7. In 1542 it was proposed in Convocation to purge the
Mass-books, antiphoners, and portuises (Breviaries) from all
superstitious oraisons and versicles, and of the names and memories of all saints which be not mentioned in the Scriptures,
or other authentic doctors.   But this proposition was not carried.

8. However, in 1544 the Litany was revised by Cranmer, and
the names of the saints struck from it, though he retained three
clauses, in which the prayers of the Virgin Mary, the angels
and the patriarchs, prophets and apostles, were desired.

9. In 1545 came out the King's Prymer, abolishing all others.
This contains the Angelic Salutation, but not the other anthems
of the Prymer of 1539.

Summary.

At the death of Henry, the state of England with regard to
our Lady may perhaps be stated as follows.   No formal heresy
had as yet been taught by authority concerning her.   Prayers
were still allowed to be addressed to her; her office and antiphons were still sometimes sung; but prayer had been per-

sistently discouraged, and the fatal sophism put forth that there is a kind of opposition between the worship of God and that of our Lady, so that what is given to her is in some way taken from God, and that it is, on the whole, better to leave 'Ora pro nobis,' and keep to 'Libera nos Domine.' But, besides this, the people had seen Mary's shrines pillaged, her venerated images ignominiously burnt, her beautiful sanctuaries destroyed. They had been forced to listen to constant warnings about superstition and idolatry. They must, indeed, have been fairly puzzled. They knew full well, as Bishop Gardiner testifies, even the simplest peasant of them all, that they had never venerated images of our Lady for any intrinsic excellence, but for the sake of her who was, by means of them, brought before their minds. No wonder that we hear that the land was full of disputes as to which statues had been superstitiously abused and which not, since no real difference existed between the veneration paid to the humblest or the most famous. Besides, while they were forbidden to bow before our Lady's effigies, they were solemnly invited, until just before Henry's death, to creep to our Lord's cross and press it to their lips. They were forbidden, under pain of idolatry, to light candles before our Lady's image, while they saw a candle or lamp even burning by royal decree before the image of our Lord on the cross. They saw that their governors were ever issuing new decrees condemning what they had just before approved. Thus, while many clung to the old faith and longed for the restoration of the old worship, others became disgusted and indifferent ; many thought they could judge for themselves, and listened to the fanatical sermons which, on this subject at least, were always tolerated ; and were thus prepared to join in the scenes of violence and sacrilege which followed immediately on Henry's death.

CHAPTER II.

WERE I writing the history of a calm and rational movement, it would be necessary to treat first of deliberations, then of actions. But no one can study the history of the Reformation without seeing that action came first, deliberation afterwards. It was not a movement carried out after some preconceived plan, each step leading on to a foreseen conclusion; but a confused work of destruction, for which pretexts and justifications were sought as the work progressed. I feel therefore obliged to in-vert the natural order, and to record events before analysing professions of faith, or rather protestations of unbelief.

REIGN OF EDWARD VI.

The fanatics were waiting for Henry's death. He died on the 29th of January 1547. 'On the 10th of February the wardens and curates of St. Martin's in London, of their own authority, pulled down the images of the saints in the church. The paintings on the wall were whitewashed, and the royal arms, garnished with texts, were set in the place of the crucifix on the rood-loft. Being called before the Council to answer for themselves, the parish officers protested that they had acted with the purest horror of idolatry; but the Council, as yet unpurged of its Catholic elements, would not accept the excuses; the over-zealous curates were committed to the Tower, and the churchwardens were bound in recognisances to erect a new crucifix, within two days, in its usual place. But as soon as the Protector, and those who went along with him, had shaken off inconvenient restraints, the rising spirit was encouraged to show itself. The sermons at St. Paul's breathed of revolution.'[1]

Riots took place at Portsmouth, and there also the images

[1] Froude, vol. v. p. 88.

were destroyed. Bishop Gardiner wrote an indignant expostu-lation to the Protector, but received no redress.[2] On the con-trary, the Protector urged on the fanatics, and a body of injunc-tions was issued from ' the king's most royal majesty, by the advice of his most dear uncle . . . intending the advancement of the true honour of Almighty God, the suppression of idolatry and superstition.' All ecclesiastical persons having cure of souls were to preach at least four times a year against the Pope; they were forbidden ' to allure the people by any enticements to the pilgrimage of any saint or image ;' they were to teach ' that works devised by men's fantasies, besides [*i.e.* without authority of] Scripture, as wandering to pilgrimages, offering of money, candles, or tapers, or relics, or images, or kissing or licking of the same, praying upon beads, or suchlike superstition, have not only no promise of reward in Scripture for doing of them, but contrariwise great threats and maledictions of God, for that they be things tending to idolatry and superstition, which, of all other offences, God Almighty doth most detest and abhor, for that the same diminish most His honour and glory.

' Item, that such images as they know to have been abused with pilgrimage, offerings, censing, shall be taken down and destroyed, and that they shall suffer no torches or tapers or images of wax to be set before any image, but only two lights upon the high altar before the Sacrament, for the signification that Christ is the true light of the world;'[3] and then, after many other injunctions, returning once more to the same points, ' that they shall take away, utterly extinct and destroy, all shrines, coverings of shrines, tables, candlesticks, trindles or rolls of wax, pictures, paintings, and all other monuments of feigned miracles, pilgrimages, idolatry, and superstition, so that there remain no memory of the same on walls, glasses, windows, or elsewhere, within their churches or houses ; and they shall exhort all their parishioners to do the like within their several houses.'[4]

[2] For the very interesting correspondence see Tierney's *Dodd.*

[3] When Ridley was made Bishop of London in 1550 he would not enter the choir until these lights were extinguished.   What did that ' signify' ?

[4] Foxe, vol. v. p. 711; Wilkins, vol. iv. p. 3 ; Tierney's *Dodd*, vol. ii. app. iii.

An eye-witness writes in his journal,[5] 'In the 5th day of September began the king's visitation at Paul's, and all images pulled down ; and in the 9th day of the same month the said visitation was at St. Bride's, and after that in divers other parish churches, and so all images pulled down through all England at that time, and all churches new whitelimed, with the Commandments written on the walls.'

'On the 17th day of November at night was pulled down the Rood in Paul's with Mary and John, with all the images in the church, and two of the men that laboured at it was slain, and divers other sort hurt.

'Item, also at that time was pulled down through all the king's dominions in every church all roods with all images, and every preacher preached in their sermons against all images.'

'From wall and window,' writes Mr. Froude, 'every picture, every image, commemorative of saint, or prophet, or apostle, was to be extirpated and put away, so that there should remain no memory of the same. Painted glass survives to show that the order was imperfectly obeyed ; but, in general, spoliation became the law of the land. The statues crashed from their niches, rood and rood-loft were laid low, and the sunlight stared in white and stainless upon the whitened aisles.'[6]

If the stained glass was sometimes spared, it was simply because the churchwardens dreaded the cost of replacing it with other glass. Sometimes they merely took out the heads from the stained figures. Yet a certain White, preaching at Paul's Cross in 1577, complained that 'the churches keep their old colouring still ; though the images have lost their countenance, and though their heads be off, yet they can make somewhat of their bodies.'[7]

In February 1548 the Council writes to Cranmer, that 'albeit the king's injunctions have in many parts of the realm been quietly obeyed and executed, yet, in many other places, much

[5] *Chronicle of the Grey Friars*, published by Camden Society. The writer seems to have been a friar who kept the book of Chronicles after the suppression, and continued it till his death.

[6] Froude, vol. v. p. 37.

[7] Rev. J. Haweis, *Sketches of the Reformation*, p. 111.

strife and contention hath risen and daily riseth, and more and
more increaseth, about the execution of the same, some men
being so superstitious, or rather wilful, as they would, by their
good-will, retain all such images still, although they have been
most manifestly abused ; and in some places also the images,
which by the said injunctions were taken down, be now restored and set up again ; and almost in every place is contention for images, whether they have been abused or not ; and
while these men go on both sides contentiously to obtain their
minds, contending whether this or that image hath been offered
unto, kissed, censed, or otherwise abused, parts have, in some
places, been taken in such sort, as further inconveniences be
like to ensue if remedy be not found in time.   Considering,
therefore, that almost in no place of this realm is any sure
quietness but where all images be clean taken away and pulled
down already, to the intent that all contention in every part of
the realm, for this matter, may be clearly taken away, and that
the lively images of Christ should not contend for the dead
images, which be things not necessary, and without which
the churches of Christ continued most godly some years ; we
have thought good to signify unto you, that his highness's
pleasure, with the advice and consent of us the lord protector
and the rest of the Council, is, that immediately upon the sight
hereof, with as convenient diligence as you may, you shall not
only give order that all the images remaining in any church or
chapel within your diocese be removed and taken away, but
also, by your letters, signify unto the rest of the bishops within
your province his highness's pleasure for the like order to be
given by them,' &c.

This protector, who so unctuously declares that 'the lively
images of Christ should not contend for dead images,' is that
Duke of Somerset who pulled down so many churches to build
his new palace, and who would have added St. Margaret's,
Westminster, to the number, had not a crowd of 'lively images'
assembled with bows and clubs, and beaten off his workmen.

While the Council was so zealous for peace and charity, yet
' to show that it was not wholly inattentive to things of lesser

moment, another mandate required that all shrines should be destroyed, and that all the plate, jewels, and other valuables belonging to them, should be seized to the king's use.'[8]

When Parliament met all this was sanctioned. The outcry against pilgrimages ever alleged the avarice of the clergy as having been the source of superstition; but the Protestant Dr. Heylin[9] candidly tells us how much avarice had to do with all this work of reform. 'Though the Parliament,' he writes, 'consisted of such members as disagreed among themselves, in respect of religion, yet they agreed well enough in one common principle, which was, to serve the present time and to preserve themselves. For though a great part of the nobility, and not a few of the chief gentry in the House of Commons, were cordially affected to the Church of Rome, yet were they willing to give way to all such acts and statutes as were made against it, and of a fear of losing such church lands as they were possessed of, if that religion should prevail, and get up again. And for the rest, who either were to make or improve their fortunes, there is no question to be made, but that they came resolved to further such a reformation as should most visibly conduce to the advancement of their several ends.'

And now the Reformation proceeds rapidly. The ordinary preachers are silenced, and fanatical innovators sent through the country; a book of Homilies is drawn up; priests are allowed to marry; a new form of Communion is invented, followed by a Common Prayer-book from which the Holy Sacrifice of the Mass is abolished, as well as all prayers to the saints; all foundations for chantries, hospitals, guilds, are given to the king, and the proceeds for the greater part seized in a general scramble; altars are overthrown and wooden tables set up instead; church plate and vestments, with the exception of one or two chalices and a few old surplices,[10] are seized for the king. 'This order for undressing the churches,' says Collier, 'was, it seems, represented to the king as an inoffensive ex-

---

[8] Tierney, note to *Dodd's History*, vol. ii. p. 9.   [9] Heylin, 48.

[10] I recommend the reader to peruse a little book called *Inventory of Furniture &c. in Hertfordshire*, by J. E. Cussans. Parker, 1873.

pedient, and only calling for the superfluous plate and other goods that lay in churches, more for pomp than use. But those who called these things superfluous, and showed so slender a regard for the honour of religion, were none of the best reformers. Had these people governed in the minority of Josiah, as they did in this of Edward VI., they would, in all likelihood, have retrenched the expense of the Mosaic institution, and served God at a more frugal rate. They would have disfurnished the temple of most of the gold plate, carried off the unnecessary magnificence, and left but little plunder for Nebuchadnezzar.' And now 'these hungry zealots,' adds Dodd, 'having devoured the flesh and substance of what they called superstition, were obliged to pick the bones,' and orders were issued for the utter destruction of all the ancient church books, Latin or English. 'And be it further enacted, that if any person . . . now have, or hereafter shall have, in his custody any the books or writings of the sorts aforesaid, or any images of stone, timber, alabaster, or earth, graven, carved, or painted, which heretofore have been taken out of any church or chapel, or yet stand in any church or chapel, and do not, before the last day of June next ensuing [1550], deface and destroy . . . the said images, and deliver the said books . . . to be openly burnt, or otherwise defaced and destroyed, he shall be fined for the first and second offences, and for the third shall suffer imprisonment at the king's will.'

A few notes may here be inserted from the *Grey Friars Chronicle,* showing how all these proceedings influenced the celebration of our Lady's feasts :

'1548. This same year was put down all going abroad of processions and the serving at Paul's at Whitsuntide, and the Skinners' procession on Corpus Christi day, with all others ; and had none other but the English procession in their churches.'

'1549. The Assumption of our Lady (15th August), and that day was hanged two persons ; . . . and on that day some kept holyday and some none, as St. Steven's in Walbrook and Colechurch. Such was the division on that day as it was on Corpus Christi day.'

'1550. This year Corpus Christi was not kept holyday; and the Assumption of our Lady was such division through all London, that some holyday and some none; and also the same division was at the feast of the Nativity of our Lady' (8th Sept.).

'1552. After Allhollauday[11] was no more communion in no place but on Sundays.'

'Item, this year was neither St. Nicolas nor the Conception of our Lady kept holyday, nor yet the Assumption of our Lady before, nor the Nativity of our Lady; but put down.'

In fact, in March 1552 an act was passed restricting the feasts of our Lady to the Purification and the Annunciation, but appointing the vigils to be observed as fasts. It is almost needless to add that the last clause remained a dead letter.

From this brief review of the destruction of our Lady's *cultus* in the churches let us turn to the various changes made in the books published by the royal authority, which was now the fount of doctrine to the English people.

Books put forth under Edward.

1. The Prymer was again edited in the first year of Edward, A.D. 1547. This edition contains the 'Hail Mary.' At the end of the ' Te Deum' is the versicle, 'Pray for us, holy Mother of God,' with the response, 'That we may be made worthy to attain the promises of Christ.' At Lauds the chapter is given: 'Virgin Mary, rejoice always, which hast borne Christ, the Maker of heaven and earth; for out of thy womb thou hast brought forth the Saviour of the world.' In the Litany, too, are the words, 'Holy Virgin Mary, Mother of God our Saviour Jesus Christ, pray for us.'

But bound up with this Prymer are the injunctions given above, forbidding men to make pilgrimages, or even to use beads, under pain of God's malediction and the king's displeasure. It must have been a marvellous puzzle to the people why it was lawful to say the 'Hail Mary,' and sinful to count their prayers by means of beads.

2. But their minds were soon relieved from perplexity. In

[11] All Hallows, *i.e.* All Saints.

1549 was published the first Book of Common Prayer. In this
'the address to the Virgin Mary, which had been retained in
Henry's Litany, was omitted, together with the similar invocations of the angels and patriarchs;' the 'Hail Mary,' which till
then had been said with the 'Our Father' at the beginning
of Matins, was omitted.[12] In the Communion Service there
were words which have since been abolished : 'Here we do give
unto Thee most high praise and hearty thanks, for the wonderful
grace and virtue declared in all thy saints, from the beginning
of the world, and chiefly in the glorious and most Blessed Virgin
Mary, Mother of Thy Son Jesus Christ, our Lord and God, and
in the holy patriarchs, prophets, apostles, and martyrs, whose
examples, O Lord, and steadfastness in Thy faith and keeping
the holy commandments, grant us to follow.'[13]

It was certainly expedient amid the incessant changes of
doctrine to omit this prayer for steadfastness in faith after the
example of the saints.   Accordingly, in the revised Prayer-book
of 1552, the above thanksgiving and prayer are omitted.   Of
course these were small changes compared with those which
regarded the Holy Eucharist ; but I confine my attention to devotion to the saints.

3. While the Book of Common Prayer was being compiled
and then revised, the Primer also underwent some changes.
That of 1547, as I have said, contained several prayers to our
Lady.   But in 1549 an act was passed, allowing persons 'to
use, have, and retain any Primer in the English or Latin tongue
set forth by the late king of famous memory, King Henry VIII.,
so that the sentences of invocation or prayer to saints in the
same Primers be blotted, or clearly put out of the same.'   So
in the Primer of 1549 the three invocations of saints which had
been retained in the Litany were omitted.   'The edition of
1551 omitted the " Hail Mary," with other objectionable passages,' says Mr. Procter,[14] 'though many strong doctrinal statements still remained.   This was reprinted in 1552, with the
addition of the Catechism, and again at the commencement

---

[12] Procter, pp. 24 and 210.   [13] Ib. p. 334.
[14] *History of the Book of Common Prayer*, p. 75.

of Elizabeth's reign in 1559, and with some changes again in 1575.'

At this stage of our review I must invite attention to a statement recently put forward by the Rev. Canon Liddon. He affirms that 'the principle of restricting all prayer to God was one to which the English Reformers professed a devoted loyalty, and by means of which, so to speak, they made their way.'[15] Even were this the case, it would only prove their utter separation from the doctrine of the rest of Christendom, and from that primitive Christianity to which they so often appealed. But I here complain of this statement as contrary to the facts of history, and as giving these men credit for a consistency to which they have no claim. Canon Liddon does not indicate precisely who are the English Reformers to whom he alludes; nor how and when they either recorded or manifested loyalty to the principle he mentions. There were no two men who had so much influence on the English Reformation as Latimer and Cranmer; yet the former protested that he did *not* intend to restrict all prayer to God, and the latter merely asked to restrict invocation to certain classes of saints. The expressions of Canon Liddon would seem to imply that the Reformers had a very clear and unhesitating conviction from the beginning that prayers must be absolutely restricted to God, and that invocation of saints is unlawful; and thus, keeping their eyes fixed on this polar star, they steered safely through the various perplexities of their work of reform. If the principle of restricting prayer to God was only arrived at towards the end of many changes, then I do not understand how the Reformers can be said to 'have made their way' by its means. And yet the history I have given shows clearly that the banishment of all invocation of saints from Christian prayers was only a final result, and by no means a guiding principle, with these men.

Their first contention was that the number of invocations of the saints should be diminished, and the direct invocations of God proportionately multiplied. Afterwards many prayers were retrenched, while some were retained and approved. Gra-

[15] Bampton Lectures for 1866, note F, p. 531 (second edition).

F F

dually even these were expunged, and then only was the principle at last enunciated that it is inexpedient to invoke the saints. I say inexpedient rather than idolatrous or wicked, and because there is a strong contrast between the vehemence of language with which the Elizabethan homilies denounce the Catholics' use of images, and the kind of apology they offer for ceasing to pray to saints.

The history of the Reformation shows that the Anglican reformers stumbled on a conclusion by a series of steps which on their own principles were unjustifiable. The first of these, as I have said, was to limit the amount of invocation while allowing its lawfulness in principle. Now here I want no other reasoning than that of Canon Liddon himself. When Bishop Colenso asserts that the Church of England generally prays *through* Christ, and very seldom *to* Christ, and that therefore the whole spirit of the Anglican liturgy manifestly tends to discourage worship and prayer addressed to Christ, Canon Liddon replies that prayer to Christ is either good or bad. 'If one such ejaculation is right, then prayer to our Lord for an hour together is right also. In short, it is not a question of more or fewer prayers to Christ ; the question is, can we rightly worship Him at all? If prayer to our Lord is right, . . . then three or four hundred collects addressed to Him (supposing the use of them not to imply a lack of devotion to the Eternal Father and to the Holy Spirit) are quite as justifiable as three or four.'

This reasoning is, of course, equally applicable to the question of the invocation of saints. When, then, Cranmer published his reformed Litany (in 1547), containing only three invocations of saints, either he intended to renounce the principle of this invocation or not. If not, then what reason had he for giving so little of what he acknowledged to be good? If, however, he already recognised, as he seems to have done two years later, that there should be no invocation of saints, he must have either consciously abetted superstition, or else have been in the confused state of mind which Canon Liddon so justly criticises in Dr. Colenso. In either case it is incorrect to say that he and his fellow-compilers of the Book of Common Prayer 'professed a devoted loyalty to, and made their way by means of, the principle of restricting all prayer to God.'

On the other hand, the utter dishonesty of the proceedings of Cranmer is manifest. Theologically indeed, as Canon Liddon observes, even one invocation involves a principle; therefore while Cranmer retained even one of the invocations of the saints in the Litany, or a single antiphon of our Lady, he conceded the whole principle of prayer to saints. But practically it was otherwise. ' He was accustoming the people to the disuse of such prayer, and gradually left so little of it, that at last (in the first Common Prayer-book) even this could be quietly dropped out without notice or explanation.

This was a favourite method with the reformers, and was called 'dealing with the times.' They understood very well that what is done seldom will be soon abandoned altogether. So they were content to reduce to a minimum what they feared to contradict openly.

Hence it is that the history of the last three centuries shows us two parties opposed to each other, yet appealing with equal sincerity to the reformers. One party looks to the distinct yet only occasional words and acts of these men, and argues that such words and acts establish a principle, and that this principle must be admitted and acted on. The *principle* of confession and absolution was left; therefore they say the practice should be restored. The principle of fasting was admitted, therefore neglect of fasting is an abuse. The other party appeals with more truth to the *conduct* of the reformers. They may, it is true, have left death-bed confession, but it was only a concession to the necessities of the times; the spirit and tendency of the Reformation is against it. They may have left days of fast and abstinence in the calendar in conformity with the old habits of the people; but the foolish arguments by which this was justified,[16] and their general principles on Christian liberty, speak more powerfully against such ordinances than the formal letter of the law in their favour.

[16] I allude to the 'king's fisheries argument.'

In the mean time, while both parties now are justified in
their conclusions, the reformers stand equally condemned by
both.   If they really admitted the principles which they enunciated, they were impious in restricting their application as they
did.   If, on the contrary, they foresaw and approved the total
abolition of the practices which they restricted, they were dis-
honest to the last degree in temporising with what was evil.
If they really believed, as the Prayer-book expresses it, that
there are on this earth men endowed by God with the power to
absolve from sin, no words can express the enormity of their
crime in withdrawing the sacrament of reconciliation from a
baptised nation, with the few insignificant exceptions in which
it has (at least in form) survived their work of reformation.
If, on the other hand, they in their hearts rejected all sacerdotal
power, then nothing can be more hideous before God and man
than the public acting of what, on such a supposition, can be
nothing but a sacrilegious farce—to *pretend* to confer the Holy
Ghost with the power of forgiving or retaining sins in ordi-
nation, and to *pretend* (' by Christ's authority committed to me ')
to absolve from sin a dying man just about to appear before his
Judge !   If those things are not realities, then they are ' such
tricks played before High Heaven as make the angels weep.'
If they are realities, why are they not 'preached on the house-
tops' ?

So too, if the invocation of saints was lawful and beneficial
to men on earth, what did Cranmer mean by discountenancing
it and restricting it to so rare a use ?   ' In moral and religious,
as well as in physical and political matters, man cannot do anything well *extempore ;* he needs a sequence from which results
habit ; he cannot represent to himself what he is to love and to
perform, as a single or isolated act, and in order to repeat anything willingly, it must not have become strange to him by dis-
continuance.'[17]

But if Cranmer thought that all prayer to saints is super-

---

[17] Goethe's *Autobiography*, where he shows that Protestants have too
few sacraments, and that for the mere harmony of the spiritual life they
should either have a complete series, like Catholics, or none at all.

stitious and hurtful to the soul, and forbidden by the law of
God—and he must have thought so, since in 1549 he omitted
all such prayers from the national Prayer-book—then he must
have acted directly against his conscience in admitting such
prayers in the Litanies and Primers published by him only two
or three years before. It has been pleaded in favour of the
reformers that they did not see all truth clearly at once. But
whatever may be the value of such a plea for men; who set
themselves up against the rest of Christendom, and professed
themselves able to reform the Church of God, it cannot be
pleaded here in favour of Cranmer, unless it is shown what ray
of light descended on him so suddenly in the first years of
Edward. Besides this, I am now merely disproving the alleged
consistency and ' devoted loyalty' of these men to a principle.

REIGN OF MARY.

There is no need in this review of the overthrow of our
Lady's Dowry in England to dwell on the brief revival of
Catholic doctrines and practices in the reign of Mary. The
destruction of all shrines, statues, memorials of our Lady, had
been too complete under Henry and Edward to admit of anything but a very partial restoration during the few years that
she held the sceptre. Some statues that had been hidden
away by the piety of the faithful were again brought out and
set up in the churches. The rood was again placed on its
beam, with the statues of Mary and of John, as of old; the
Office of our Lady was once more sung in the churches, and her
beads worn in the streets, and her holydays were again observed.
But the reconciliation of the kingdom with the Sovereign
Pontiff, and the reëstablishment of the Holy Sacrifice, occupied
the public mind rather than the devotion to the saints.

The only original doctrinal treatise, or at least the most
important one, composed in this reign was that by Bishop
Bonner in his book of Homilies, and as it is little known I will
give here a few extracts.

He commences his exposition or declaration of the Ave
Maria as follows :

'It is not without great and weighty considerations that our forefathers throughout the universal or Catholic Church have next after the Paternoster set forth and commended the salutation of the Archangel Gabriel wherewith he saluted the Blessed Virgin Mary, Mother of our Saviour Jesus Christ, called the Ave Maria, the same to be frequented and devoutly used and said of all Christian people. For seeing that the high messenger of Almighty God and heavenly spirit Gabriel did most joyfully with this salutation greet the Virgin Mary, being then a mortal woman living on the earth, and not having then conceived in her undefiled and chaste womb our Saviour Christ, how much more ought we mortal, earthly, and sinful creatures with all promptness and alacrity to salute with the self-same words that Blessed Virgin now, when as not only she hath brought forth our Saviour and Redeemer Christ, but also she herself is exalted in heaven above all angels and archangels !

' Besides this, also, the matter itself contained in this salutation is of such worthiness, comfort, and spiritual fruit to the faithful rememberer and devout frequenter of the same, that all good men have always found themselves by meditation hereof greatly edified. And this thing to no man can seem strange that will duly mark the pith, effect, and weighty sense in the same salutation contained, which we will here briefly declare unto you.'

He then enters at considerable length into the explanation of the Angelic Salutation. His commentary is in most points like that put forth in the *Erudition of a Christian Man* by Henry.

Having given an exposition of the Ave Maria as it stood in his day, *i.e.* ending with the words ' Blessed is the fruit of thy womb,' Bishop Bonner continues :

'And it is here to be noted that although this salutation be not a prayer of petition, supplication, or request, or suit, yet nevertheless the Church hath used to adjoin it to the end of the Paternoster as an hymn or prayer of laud and praise, partly of our Lord and Saviour Jesus Christ, for our redemption ; and partly of the Blessed Virgin, for her humble consent given and expressed to the angel at his salutation. Indeed, lauds, praises, and thanks are in this Ave Maria principally given and yielded to our Lord, as to the author of our redemption ; but yet here withal the Virgin lacketh not her lauds, praise, and thanks for her excellent and singular virtues, and chiefly for that she believed and humbly consented, according to the saying of the holy matron St. Elizabeth, when she said to this Virgin : " Blessed art thou that didst give trust and credence to the angel's words, for all things that have been spoken unto thee shall be performed." Who is there now that hath a good Christian heart, and considereth the meaning, the effect following the author, and other the circumstances of the Ave Maria, that will not count and judge them unworthy of the name of Christian men, who, of late years, not only have in all their books and other printed papers of purpose left out this godly salutation, disdaining at the honour of the Blessed Virgin Mary herein contained, but have also to the uttermost of their power, by their inveighing against the common commendable and devout use thereof, gone about to pluck it clean out of men's hearts and minds, and so for ever to abolish the memory of her blessedness, most contrary to the determination of the Holy Ghost by the mouth of the same Virgin declared, when He said, " Ecce enim ex hoc beatam me dicent omnes generationes"? That is to say, "Behold, verily from henceforth all generations shall call me blessed ;" which thing, like as the angel of God and the godly matron Elizabeth then did, the Virgin Mary as then being in mortal estate, and neither Christ of her then born nor mankind then by Christ redeemed, so now for that the Son of this Blessed Virgin hath both redeemed us and also all mankind from eternal damnation, and she herself now is most gloriously placed in heaven, in state of immortality ; and thirdly, that such notable examples also herein set before our eyes by the angel and Elizabeth ; and finally, for that the Holy Ghost did plainly say that all generations should from thenceforth call her blessed,—for these respects, I say, the whole Catholic Church doth most joyfully use and frequent the said salutation, and so must we do, if we will be true members of the Catholic Church.

CHAPTER III.

ELIZABETH, JAMES, ETC.

SCARCELY was Mary dead when the fanatics renewed their worst excesses. Five months after the accession of Elizabeth, Feckenham reminds the Lords who are discussing a new Common Prayer-book of the daily impieties of which they are eyewitnesses : ' In Queen Mary's days, your honours do know right well how the people of this realm did live in an order. . . There was no spoiling of churches, pulling down of altars, and most blasphemous treading of sacraments under their feet, and hanging up the knave of clubs in the place thereof. There was no scotching nor cutting of the faces and legs of the crucifix and image of Christ. . . . And now, sithence the coming and reign of our most sovereign and dear lady Queen Elizabeth, by the only preachers and scaffold players of this new religion all things are turned upside down. . . Obedience is gone, humility and meekness clear abolished, virtuous chastity and strait living denied, as though they had never been heard of in this realm,' &c.

Elizabeth was herself, it is said, not altogether unfavourable to many old practices, but this did not prevent her from carrying out her father's and brother's policy. In the injunctions of 1559 she orders ' that no persons keep in their houses any abused images, tables, pictures, paintings, and other monuments of feigned miracles, pilgrimages, idolatry, and superstition ;' ' that the churchwardens of every parish shall deliver unto our visitors the inventories of vestments, copes, and other ornaments, plate, books, and specially of grayles, couchers legends, processionals, manuals, hymnals, portuesses, and suchlike pertaining to the church.'[1]

---

[1] The nature of each of these books is explained in Maskell's *Monumenta Ritualia*, and in Rock's *Church of our Fathers.*

If any one wish to see how all this was carried out he must read the returns of the churchwardens, still in existence. Those of Lincolnshire have been published by Mr. Peacocke.[2] An extract or two will suffice.

'Item, the Rood wythe Mary and John wythe all the rest off the popishe Idols bornt and mad awaie the second yeare off Quene Elizabethe.'

'Item, the tabernacles whearin the xij Apostles stode with other popish papisticall and supsticious Idolls weare brent 4° sexto Elizab'th.'

Bonfires of crucifixes and other images were made in the streets of London, and everywhere through the country the roods, before which Henry VIII. would still keep a light burning, were pulled down and cast into the fire by his daughter.

Collier admits that 'to burn the figure of the cross, and especially that of our Saviour, is, to speak softly, a horrid profanation; and, if we may reason from such indignities done to men, must be superlatively wicked;' but he adds that such disorders were done without commission, and 'were nothing but mob-execution.'[3] He is quite mistaken. The letters I am about to quote prove the sanction they received from those whom Elizabeth chose for bishops; and the words of Sandys, who was one of the visitors, are express that the crucifixes *especially* were burnt by public authority. The bishops elect eagerly warned Elizabeth when the temporalities of their sees were threatened, that she might incur the fate of the sacrilegious Belshazzar, but they had only approbation for the outrages offered to images.

That the reader may judge of the extent to which fanaticism was carried by Elizabeth's new bishops, I subjoin a few extracts from their correspondence at the beginning of her reign. The queen, while ordering the destruction of crucifixes elsewhere to carry out her policy of siding with the reformation party, on the other hand, probably to gratify her own contempt for the reformers, persisted in keeping a crucifix on the altar of her own

[2] *English Church Furniture*, by E. Peacocke, 1866.
[3] Collier, vol. vi. p. 260.

chapel, and having lights burning before it. This greatly tried the souls of the Calvinists.

Bishop Jewel, of Salisbury, writes to Peter Martyr on Nov. 16th, 1559, just a year after the queen's accession : ' That little silver cross, of ill-omened origin, still maintains its place in the queen's chapel. Wretched me ! this will soon be drawn into a precedent.'[4]

Cox, Bishop of Ely, at beginning of 1560, writes to the same : ' We are constrained, to our great distress of mind, to tolerate in our churches the image of the Cross and Him who was crucified. The Lord must be entreated that this stumbling-block may be removed.'[5]

Sampson writes (Jan. 6th, 1560) : ' O my father, what can I hope for, when the ministry of the Word is banished from court, while the crucifix is allowed with lights burning before it ? The altars indeed are removed, and images also throughout the kingdom ; the crucifix and candles are retained at court alone. And the wretched multitude are not only rejoicing at this, but will imitate it of their own accord.' (The reader will no doubt have remarked how from the outset of the Reformation, in almost every document, the Christian Catholic people are contemptuously styled the ' rude people,' the ' ignorant multitude,' the ' wretched multitude.'[6])

Sampson goes on to propose a case of conscience. ' I will propose this question : whether the image of the crucifix, placed on the table of the Lord, with lighted candles, is to be regarded as a thing indifferent ; and if it is not to be so considered, but an unlawful and wicked practice, then I ask, suppose the queen should enjoin all the bishops and clergy, either to admit this image with the candles into their churches, or to retire from the ministry of the Word, what should be our conduct in this case ? Should we not rather quit the ministry of the Word and Sacra-

---

[4] *Zurich Letters*, first series, p. 54 (Parker Society).

[5] Ibid. p. 66. Sampson, writing at the same date (see next quotation), says, ' The images are already removed.' It would seem from this and the discrepancies between Burnet and Collier, that the work was not done with equal speed in every part of the country.

[6] ' The rascal multitude.' John Knox.

ments than that these *relics of the Amorites* should be admitted ?'[7]

It was not necessary to settle this delicate point of conscience. The queen saved her bishops and ministers from such a dilemma.

Sandys, Bishop of Worcester, writes (April 1560) : 'We had, not long since, a controversy respecting images. The queen's majesty considered it not contrary to the Word of God, nay, rather for the advantage of the Church, that the image of Christ crucified, together with Mary and John, should be placed as heretofore in some conspicuous part of the church, where they might more readily be seen by all the people. Some of us thought far otherwise, and more especially as all images of every kind were, at our last visitation, not only taken down, but also burnt, and that too by public authority; and because *the ignorant and superstitious multitude* are in the habit of paying adoration to this idol above all others . . . God, in whose hands are the hearts of kings, give us tranquillity instead of a tempest, and deliver the Church of England from stumbling-blocks of this kind.'[8]

Bishop Parkhurst of Norwich writes to Bullinger (August 1562) : 'Lo! good news is brought me, namely, that the crucifix and candlesticks in the queen's chapel are broken in pieces, and, as some one has brought word, reduced to ashes. A good riddance of such a cross as that !'[9]

But, in April 1563, he writes again, that 'the cross and candles had been brought back again, to the great grief of the godly.'

The spirit of iconoclasm went to such lengths in these fanatical men, that they were not satisfied merely with removing and breaking or burning the statues; they were afraid even of the places in which they had once stood. Hence we find in churchwardens' accounts of the period entries such as these:

'1560. Paid—for pulling down the seat whereon our Lady stood in our Lady church.

'1569. Paid—for breaking down the stones in St. Margaret's chancel and our Lady chancel, that images stood on.'[10]

---

[7] *Zurich Letters*, first series, p. 64.   [8] Ib. p. 74.   [9] Ib. p. 122.
[10] *Churchwardens' Accounts of Ludlow*, published for Camden Society.

The following account of one of these scenes in the reign of
Elizabeth is from the pen of the Rev. J. Haweis, in his very
amusing and instructive book of *Sketches of the Reformation :*

'Between the chancel and the nave in every church a gal-
lery, usually of richly carved and gilded wood-work, supported
a group of statues. . . . When, however, the images were gone,
the remainder was both a symbol of the separation between
priests and people which it was the uniform tendency of the
Reformation to do away, and also a memorial of fallen idolatry.

'Peter White was minister of Eaton Soken, Bedfordshire,
but whenever he entered his church this object met him, grieved
his eye, and chafed his spirit. The rood-loft had here been
partially destroyed, but the "stump," nine whole feet in breadth,
yet remained, and the screen downward lacked nothing but the
images to make it perfect. One part of the parish, it appears,
maintained that when the idols were all cast down, the idolatrous character of the erection ceased. Another, however, urged
that " the beam whereon the idol stood" had imbibed its soul-
destroying properties, and that all the carved work should be
broken down with axes and hammers. Of this opinion was the
minister, who having, as he hoped, secured a bishop to come
and preach against it, arranged everything for its final demolition immediately after the sermon. He was disappointed, and
forced to preach himself ; but the congregation, maybe, sustained
no loss, and the loft gained no mercy. From the account of the
golden candlesticks in the Revelations, Peter White proceeded
to demonstrate the absurdity of their position who maintained
"that the part of the rood-loft yet standing is no monument of
idolatry."

" They say the rood-loft is no monument of idolatry. Tertullian telleth us that monumentum is anything that putteth in
mind the memory of things not present. Now, enter into the
consideration of your own minds, and remember with yourselves
whether, when you behold this loft, you at some time or other
think with yourselves, Some time yonder stood a crucifix, Mary,
and John ; or when your children ask you what this loft is, or
why it standeth there, and is more gay than the residue of the

church, do you not answer, It was the rood-loft—there stood the
rood, Mary, and John? And when they say, further, Where is
now the rood, and why is it now taken away, do you not answer,
They were idols, and therefore are taken away?

" Further, the laws of the realm, the judgment of our most
gracious prince (whom the Almighty ever preserve, to the utter
overthrow of idolatry), with the practice of her commissions
given unto divers learned men of this realm, teacheth us that
this rood-loft is a monument of idolatry ; for everywhere, in the
first year of her grace's reign, they gave commandment to overthrow them in every place. . . .

" Seeing, therefore, that these proofs do so clearly declare it to
be a monument of idolatry, which in truth hath and doth greatly
offend the consciences of the best sort, and disquieteth the whole
number of this congregation, let me say unto you, as Moses at
the Red Sea said unto the Israelites when Pharaoh had hemmed
them in with his army : ' Fear ye not; stand still and behold
the great works of the. Lord. Ye see the Egyptians now, but
after this day ye shall see them no more.' Be not offended ;
quiet your minds ; ye now see this monument that hath so
troubled us, but after this, in this form and fashion shall ye see
it no more." [11]

The doers of these sacrileges and the preachers of these
blasphemies were the men who invented for the opening of
Lent, instead of the blessing and sprinkling of ashes, what they
called a Commination or denunciation of curses. They began
with one which they hoped would fall on those whom they now
called papists : ' Cursed is the man that maketh any carved or
molten image, to worship it;' but they continued with words
only too applicable to those who were ever calumniating the
Church in which they had been baptised, and reviling the Sovereign Pontiff, whom all had for ages regarded as the Father of
Christendom : ' Cursed is he that curseth father or mother;'
and with the following, which might well fall on such as, to
the misleading of simple souls, abolished the ancient articles of

[11] *Sketches of the Reformation,* by Rev. J. O. W. Haweis, pp. 119-21.
White's sermon was preached in 1581.

faith and practices of devotion approved by the Church : ' Cursed
is he that removeth his neighbour's landmark : Cursed is he
that maketh the blind to go out of his way : Cursed is he that
perverteth the judgment of the stranger, fatherless, and widow.'

But I will delay no longer on the deeds of impiety that
filled this reign. They were akin to those already recorded.
We will cast a glance at the books, such at least as were published by authority, in which a pretext was sought to justify
what had been done.

Elizabeth's Calendar.

Of course during Mary's reign the old books of the Catholic
Church were restored, and the novelties of Cranmer abolished.
Elizabeth was crowned according to the Pontifical, and during
the ceremony the Litany of the Saints was sung ; but the queen
soon proved that her sentiments, or at least her political leanings, were with the reformers, and another version was made of
Edward's Book of Common Prayer, and published in 1559.
As regards the saints, nothing was left by Edward to be abolished
by his sister, and she was not inclined to restore former devotions, unless the mere insertion of some of the old saints' names
in the Calendar can be looked on as an act of devotion. ' This
was done,' says Mr. Procter,[12] ' partly no doubt that the marks
of time employed in courts of law might be understood, and
that the old dates of parochial festivities might be retained ; but
partly with the higher object of perpetuating the memory of
ancient Christian worthies, some of them connected, or supposed
to be connected, with the English Church, and thereby of
evincing how that Church was still in spirit undissevered from
the national Church of earlier years, and from the brotherhood
of Catholic Christianity.' This is no doubt a pretty interpretation in the nineteenth century, but whether it was that of the
age of Elizabeth may be judged from the following passage in
the Book of Homilies :

' Not only the unlearned and simple, but the learned and
wise; not the people only, but the bishops ; not the sheep, but

[12] *History of the Book of Common Prayer*, p. 63.

also the shepherds themselves, who should have been guides in the right way, and lights to shine in darkness, being blinded by the bewitching of images, as blind guides of the blind, fell both into the pit of damnable idolatry. In the which all the world, as it were drowned, continued until our age, by the space of above eight hundred years, unspoken against in a manner. . . . So that laity and clergy, learned and unlearned, all ages, sects, and degrees of men, women, and children of whole Christendom (an horrible and most dreadful thing to think) have been at once drowned in abominable idolatry, of all other vices most detested of God, and most damnable to man, and that by the space of eight hundred years and more.'

Such is the emphatic declaration of the Homily against Peril of Idolatry put forth by authority of Queen Elizabeth in 1562, and which the 35th Article of the Church of England declares to ' contain a godly and wholesome doctrine, and necessary for these times.' I know not what interpretation Mr. Procter puts on these Articles, or to what extent he accepts the Books of Homilies. I feel quite sure that neither he nor hundreds more of his brethren in the ministry of the Church of England at the present day hold the view so emphatically stated in the above passage by Jewel, or whoever was the author of those hideous words. But surely it is clear that the party that authorised that homily had no desire whatever to claim union of spirit with a Church sunk in the pit of damnable idolatry. It is true that during those eight hundred years that Church had produced St. Dunstan, St. William, St. Margaret, St. Swithin, St. Oswald, St. Edward, St. Hugh—names retained in the Calendar (besides thousands more of such men and women) ; but if these are saints, how did they spring from such a Church ? ' Do men gather grapes of thorns ?' Besides, each of these saints prac- tised heart and soul that very devotion which was now branded as idolatrous. Could it, then, be intended to sanction their canonisation, or to claim fellowship with them ? Their names were certainly inserted in the Calendar, and with the prefix of saint ; but I must leave it to others to find the motive, or to reconcile the act with the doctrine then expressed and still professed by the Protestant Church of England.

Professions of Faith.

In 1552 forty-two articles of religion were imposed on the nation, principally by the influence of Cranmer. It would be beside my purpose to say anything about their history or their nature. There is only one which regards the subject of my inquiry. It is the 23d, and runs as follows:

'The doctrine of the schoolmen concerning purgatory, pardons, worshipping, and adoration, as well of images as of relics, and also invocation of saints, is a fond thing, vainly invented, and grounded upon no warranty of Scripture, but rather perniciously repugnant to the Word of God.'

Ten years later, in 1562, a revision was made of these articles under Elizabeth, and they were reduced to the number of thirty-nine. The 22d is the same as that just quoted, with these exceptions. Instead of 'the doctrine of the schoolmen,' the Elizabethan article has 'the Romish doctrine;' and the word 'perniciously' is omitted.

I do not know whether the Books of Homilies should be called Professions of Faith. It is certain they were written and published as authoritative expositions of the newly-discovered Christian doctrine, and that all clergymen at least declare them to 'contain a godly and wholesome doctrine.' Yet few read them before making this declaration, and few after. Many eminent divines of the Church of England have not hesitated to profess their dissent from them on many points, and especially in their horrible language regarding the Church of the past ages.

However this may be, they were and are still put forth by authority to justify the conduct of the reformers and the position of the Anglican sect. When the second Book of Homilies was written, the work of destruction had been going on for thirty years. It had been begun from motives of avarice, and under the pretext of reforming certain abuses, but without the least thought of condemning the use and even the veneration of images. Indeed, such an idea was emphatically repudiated by the early reformers; and the opinions of the Lollards on this subject, which were adopted by Elizabeth's government, drew on them severe punishment from that of Henry.

But avarice and passion had pushed on the ruling powers from one act to another, until every shrine had been plundered, every image destroyed, every act of devotion forbidden. The plea first set up of occasional abuses was evidently insufficient to justify these measures; so the old opinions of Wickliffe and the Lollards were reproduced, and defended with a heat greater than that of former times. Indeed, the Wickliffites appear to advantage in this comparison. They adopted the theory of idolatry, and wished to put it in practice by the destruction of what they called idols; whereas the reformers of the sixteenth century began with the destruction from other motives, and then invented the theory to defend their guilty conduct.

The doctrine taught in the Homily against Peril of Idolatry is thus summed up by its author: 'Idolatry cannot possibly be separated from images set up in churches and temples, gilded and decked gloriously, and therefore our images be indeed very idols; so all the prohibitions, laws, curses, threatenings of horrible plagues, as well temporal as eternal, contained in Holy Scripture concerning idols, and the makers and maintainers and worshippers of them, appertain also to our images set up in churches and temples, and to the makers, maintainers, and worshippers of them. And all those names of abomination which God's word in the Holy Scripture giveth to the idols of the gentiles appertain to our images, being idols like to them, and having like idolatry committed unto them. Wherefore God's horrible wrath and our most dreadful danger cannot be avoided without the destruction and utter abolishing of all images and idols out of the church and temple of God, which to accomplish [may] God put in the minds of all Christian princes.'

Of course from these premises there followed inevitably what, to any but blinded fanatics, would appear a clear *reductio ad absurdum*—that the whole Christian Church had apostatised for ages, and that for ages Christianity had utterly perished out of the world. The author of the homily both saw the conclusion and admitted it in the frankest and fullest manner, as we have already seen.

And, indeed, any one who will take the trouble to look through the general index of the Parker Society's edition of the *Heroes of the Reformation* will see that this view was that of all the Elizabethan divines, whatever modification it may have received from the Caroline theologians, who, with equal bitterness against the Catholic Church, yet dreaded the consequences to their own theories of such sweeping assertions. I have no care to dwell here on the enormity of such a proposition as that of the Homilies. I adduce it merely to show the logical consequences of repudiating Catholic devotion to our Lady.

Neither shall I dwell on any impieties spoken or written of our Lady by private persons. I rejoice indeed that public professions or negations of faith went no further than they did in denying our Lady's holiness or privileges. I am glad to be able to adduce even a royal testimony to the belief of the Anglican Church in our Lady's dignity. King James I., in the epistle to Cardinal Perrone which he dictated to Isaac Casaubon, writes : ' Serenissimus Rex gloriosissimam Virginem Matrem Dei prædicat beatissimam ; neque dubitat in supremum honoris gradum esse evectam, qui humanæ creaturæ a Deo Creatore potuit tribui,—His most serene Majesty declares that the ever-glorious Virgin is indeed the most Blessed Mother of God, and has no doubt that she has been raised to the highest degree of honour that could be given by the Creator to a human creature.' And since this title of Mother of God is now so frequently refused to the Blessed Virgin by Anglicans, and indeed generally repudiated by other sects of Protestants, I am glad to bring forward a proof that an English Nonconformist minister in the time of Charles II. not only did not reject it, but considered its rejection very perilous. Thus writes John Flavel :[13] ' The proper use of words is of great importance in this doctrine' (of the Incarnation). ' We walk upon the brink of danger. The least tread awry may ingulf us in the bogs of error. Arius

[13] ' The Fountain of Life,' sermon v.

would have been content if the Council of Nice would but have gratified him in a letter—ομοουσιος and ομοιουσιος. The Nestorians also desired but a letter—θεοδοχος, θεοτοκος.[14] These seemed but small and modest requests, but, if granted, had proved no small prejudice to the truth. I am of his mind that said, "It is better not touch the bottom than not keep within the circle." '

Such utterances are unfortunately rare. Since the days of Henry the name of the Blessed Mother of God has been mentioned far more frequently in angry bursts of rage against Catholic devotion to her than in explaining her dignity or her virtues.

King James, who speaks so fairly of Mary's dignity, would not suffer that dignity to be practically recognised within the limits of his kingdom, by the invocation of her intercession with her Divine Son. In the year 1605 the following act of parliament received the royal sanction :

' And be it further enacted by the authority of this present Parliament, that no person or persons shall bring from beyond the seas, nor shall print, sell, or buy any Popish primers, lady's psalters, manuals, rosaries, Popish catechisms, missals, breviaries, portals, legends and lives of saints, containing superstitious matter, printed or written in any language whatsoever, nor any other superstitious books printed or written in the English tongue ; upon pain of forfeiture of forty shillings for every such book ; one-third part thereof to be to the king's majesty, his heirs and successors ; one other third part to him that will sue for the same ; and the other third part to the poor of the parish where such book or books shall be found, to be recovered by action of debt, bill, plaint, or information, in any of the king's majesty's courts of record, wherein no essoin, protection, or wager of law, shall be admitted or allowed, and the said books to be burned.

' And that it shall be lawful for any two justices of peace within the limits of their jurisdiction or authority, and to all mayors, bailiffs, and chief officers of cities and towns corporate

[14] ' Recipient of God,' instead of ' Mother of God.'

in their liberties, from time to time to search the houses and lodgings of every Popish recusant convict, or of every person whose wife is or shall be a Popish recusant convict, for Popish books and relics of Popery : (2) And that if any altar, pix, beads, pictures, or suchlike Popish relics, or any Popish book or books shall be found in their or any of their custody, as in the opinion of the said justices, mayor, bailiff, or chief officer as aforesaid, shall be thought unmeet for such recusant as aforesaid, to have or use the same, shall be presently defaced and burnt, if it be meet to be burned : (3) And if it be a crucifix, or any other relic of any price, the same to be defaced at the general quarter-sessions of the peace in the county where the same shall be found, and the same so defaced to be restored to the owner again.'[15]

Finally, lest any token should still linger to remind the people that England had once been called our Lady's Dowry, during the fanaticism of the Commonwealth commissions were issued for the utter destruction of even the poor remnants of statuary or painting which, by reason of their insignificance or remote position, or perhaps from some touch of Christian feeling, still remained. The journal of a wretched man, William Dowsing by name, appointed parliamentary visitor under a warrant from the Earl of Manchester, has been preserved and printed. His commission extended within the county of Suffolk, and his sacrileges were perpetrated from January 1643 until October 1644 ; at least such is the duration of this journal. I give some extracts from this curious document :

'Sudbury, Suffolk, Peter's Parish, Jan. the 9th, 1643. We brake down a picture of God the Father, 2 crucifix's, and pictures of Christ, about an hundred in all ; and gave order to take down a cross off the steeple ; and diverse angels, 20 at least, on the roof of the church.'

This is the first place mentioned in the journal.

'2. At Clane, Jan. the 6th. We brake down 1000 pictures superstitious. I brake down 200 ; 3 of God the Father, and 3 of Christ and the Holy Lamb, and 3 of the Holy Ghost like a

---

[15] *Statutes at Large,* vol. ii. p. 542.

dove with wings; and the 12 Apostles were carved in wood on the top of the roof, which we gave order to take down; and the sun and moon in the east window, by the king's arms, to be taken down.'

'10. Barham, Jan. the 22d. We brake down the 12 Apostles in the chancel, and 6 superstitious more there; and 8 in the church, one a lamb with a cross on the back; and digged down the steps, and took up 4 superstitious inscriptions of brass, one of them, "Jesu Fili Dei, miserere mei," and "O Mater Dei, memento mei,—O Mother of God, have mercy on me." [15]

'84. Helmingham, Feb. the 29th. Brake down 3 superstitious pictures, and gave order to take down 4 crosses and 9 pictures; and Adam and Eve to be beaten down.—6*s*. 8*d*.'

'99. Beccles, April the 6th. Jehovah's between church and chancel, and the sun over it; and by the altar, "My meat is flesh indeed, and My blood is drink indeed."'

'102. Benacre, April the 6th. There was 6 superstitious pictures, one crucifix, and the Virgin Mary twice, with Christ in her arms, and Christ lying in the manger, and the 3 kings coming to Christ with their presents, and St. Catherine twice pictured, and the priest of the parish . . [MS. blotted] "Materna Joannem Christi guberna,—O Christ, govern me by Thy Mother's prayers!" and 3 bishops with their mitres; and the steps to be levelled within 6 weeks; and 18 Jesus's, written in capital letters, on the roof, which we gave order to do out; and the story of Nebuchadnezzar, and "orate pro animabus," in a glass window.'

106. At Frostenden he enters the following note: 'Mr. Ellis, an high constable of the town, told me he saw an Irish man, within 2 months, bow to the cross on the steeple, and put off his hat to it.'

'121. Trembly, Aug. 21st, 1644, Martin's. There was a fryar, with a shaven crown, praying to God in these words: "Miserere mei Deus," which we brake down.'

But enough of this.

[15] Dowsing is responsible for this translation.

Scotland.

I have not deemed it necessary to relate the overthrow of devotion to our Lady in Scotland. There is here nothing to unravel. I am not writing a history of the Reformation, but have endeavoured to bring together documents bearing on a certain phase of it, illustrating these by the history of the times. In England this was necessary, because the Reformation having proceeded more slowly, more orderly, and having been managed by the craft of statesmen, the attention of the student of that history may be either distracted by the multiplicity of questions, or he may be misled by hypocritical documents. In Scotland, on the contrary, the war against the Catholic religion was open and declared, and there was little disguise attempted. How the sanctuaries of Mary were there destroyed, and from what motives, is matter of common history, and requires no illustration from my pen. With Knox and his crew there was no question of Reformation, but of cutting down root and branch, unless it may be said, with Collier, that 'they reformed like the Goths and Vandals at the sacking of Rome.'

CHAPTER IV.

DEGREES OF GUILT.

THERE are some men in whose philosophy every great religious movement is justified by the mere fact of its having taken place. Regrets they consider childish, and attempts of revival mischievous. To them the destruction of Catholic devotion to the saints seems a progress, for no other reason than because men of the sixteenth century conspired to accomplish it. It would be in vain to tell them that it was a work of violence and spoliation, or to speak to them of the character of the agents.

But those who do not hold this absurd and revolting philosophy of 'accomplished facts' will not feel it safe to accept the results of a revolution in which the work and the agents were alike unworthy. They will feel that by consenting to evil deeds they become accomplices with those who did them.

A strange defence is, indeed, not unfrequently made for the Reformation, even at the expense of the reformers. By an abuse of the scriptural maxim that 'God makes use of the base things of the world to bring to naught the things that are, that no flesh should glory in His sight' (1 Cor. i. 28), the evil intentions and wicked deeds of the reformers are admitted, while it is contended that God made use of them for a great and divine work. 'In reviewing the great events of history,' says a Protestant ecclesiastical historian,[1] 'and more especially such as have had the most direct influence on the progress of religious truth, it must occur to every reader that there is a remarkable contrast between *the instruments which have been employed by Divine Wisdom* and the results which have flowed from their operation. Whether we look to the monastery of Wittemberg [Luther], or

---

[1] *History of the Church in Scotland*, by Rev. Dr. Russell, ch. v.

to the council chamber of Henry VIII., or to the castle of St. Andrew's [Knox and the murderers of Cardinal Beaton], *nothing will be seen which can minister to human pride*, or exalt our estimate of the purity and disinterestedness of human motives. Selfish considerations are found to apply the first stimulant to the patriotic principle ; circumstances combine to strengthen its energies and give importance to its objects ; and at length an achievement is accomplished, which, so far from forming any part of the original conception, was not at first deemed either prudent or desirable.'

This is only saying in a circuitous form what Gray said epigrammatically, that ' Gospel light first shone in Bullen's eyes ;' and Horace Walpole, in the lines quoted elsewhere :

> ' From Katherine's wrongs a nation's bliss was spread,
> And Luther's light from Henry's lawless bed.'

But, with the leave of these gentlemen, it was Moses, not Pharaoh, who led Israel out of Egypt ; it was Simon Peter, not Simon Magus, who guided the Christian Church in its separation from Judaism ; and if Moses and Peter were weak instruments in the hands of God, so that all the glory belonged to the Almighty, yet they were holy instruments, worthy of God's hand—they were not blind tools, but willing coöperators with God ; they were saintly in character, pure in intention, and upright in action.

Those who reject the Reformation have no need to recur to such sophistical reasonings as those I have just quoted. The founders and upholders of our Lady's Dowry were men and women whom we may look back to with pride. Let those who reject the honours paid by the Catholic Church to Mary appeal if they will to Wickliffe and to Knox, to Latimer and Cranmer, to Cromwell and to Somerset, to Henry, Elizabeth, and James. Catholics will remember that St. Aldhelm and St. Bede, St. Dunstan and St. Edward, St. Richard and St. Hugh, St. Margaret, St. Aelred, and St. Anselm ; the Lady Margaret and Fisher, her martyred confessor ; the martyred Forrest and his spiritual daughter, good Queen Katherine ; Robert Grosstest and Thomas More—these and a host more of holy men and women, canonised and uncanonised, were our teachers in the devotion we still cherish to our Lady.

But I propose in this chapter to try to estimate the degrees of responsibility of the various classes who engaged in the overthrow of our Lady's Dowry.

The Clergy.

I have just said that Catholics, in looking back to the history of devotion to our Lady in England, have nothing of which to be ashamed. In one sense this is most true. The Dowry was the creation of saints, and its effects were sanctity; and the men who overthrew it did so only when they ceased to be Catholics, and by means the most base and unworthy. And yet I cannot forget that our Lady's Dowry in England was not destroyed by an incursion of unbaptised heathen, nor by Protestants brought up from infancy in anti-Catholic prejudice, and taught to connect the honour of the Son in some strange fashion with the dishonour or neglect of the Mother. No, alas! the enemies of our Lady had been children of the Catholic Church; they had lisped the name of Mary in infancy, and been taught by pious mothers to kneel before her statues. They were even priests of her Divine Son; and they were monks, who had made a special profession of love and veneration towards her that they might more closely and efficaciously resemble Him. The Blessed Virgin could indeed complain, as Jesus Christ had done, by the mouth of the Psalmist: 'Even the man of my peace, in whom I trusted, who ate my bread, hath greatly supplanted me' (Ps. xl. 10).

About 150 years before the destruction came, an English Dominican, Father Bromyard, writing on the sins of the clergy, had ventured to foretell the result; and he uses a comparison curiously in harmony with the subject of this work. 'The state of the modern Church,' he wrote,[2] "is well figured in the following history. A man had been long pondering over and wondering at the state of Christendom, when he fell asleep, and in a dream a statue, as of a most beautiful lady, appeared to him;

---

[2] *Summa Prædicantium*, pars ii. cap. vi. p. 143.

and while he was lost in admiration, a voice asked him whose image it was. He replied that he thought it must be the image of the most Blessed Virgin. Whereupon the statue was turned round, so that its back appeared to him, and that was all decayed and rotten. And again the voice said, "What do you now think?" "It is not the Virgin Mary," he said, "for of her it is written that she is 'all fair.'" When, then, he wished to know who it was, the voice said, "It is the image of Christendom, which in the beginning was very beautiful, but in the latter end is shamefully destroyed." All this being considered,' continued Bromyard, 'it will be no wonder if the spiritual ruin of all Christendom shall follow, first in the corruption of morals, and even perhaps in external chastisements. Even now we often see and hear of such, and we fear that more will come; for as by reason of such sins the temple and kingdom of the Jews were overthrown, as we behold them, so is it to be feared that it may happen to Christians. And we seem to have a foretaste of what will happen in what we now see, for a great part of the world which was formerly Christian is now occupied by the Saracens.'

When the calamity was still more imminent, one of those who had taken a leading part in resisting the new doctrines, Sir Thomas More, was waiting in prison the death that he knew was certain. With a piece of coal—for pen and ink were refused him—he wrote his *Dialogue of Comfort against Tribulation.* He supposes the dialogue to take place between two Hungarians; and under cover of discussing a threatened invasion of the Turks, he foretells what he sees is coming upon England from the tyranny of Henry. 'But now, cousin, this tribulation of the Turk, if he so persecute us for the faith, that those that will forsake their faith shall keep their goods, and those shall lose their goods that will not leave their faith—this manner of persecution, lo, shall like a touchstone try them, and show the feigned from the true-minded.'[3]

Alas, the Turk came, and the souls of men were tried. Among the rich and the noble, among even the priests of the

[3] Book iii. chap. xiii.

sanctuary, but few comparatively were found, with Fisher and
More, ready to sacrifice all for the faith of Christ.

The Nobles and Gentry.

Sir Thomas was a shrewd observer of the times. He did
not expect to find much heroic virtue in England in the sixteenth century.

'In the case,' says one of the speakers in his dialogue,
'where they have yet their substance untouched in their own
hands, and that the keeping or losing shall hang both in their
own hands by the Turk's' (*i.e.* Henry's) 'offer, upon the retaining or renouncing of the Christian faith ; here, uncle, I find it
that this temptation is most sore and most perilous. For I fear
me that we shall find few of such as have much to lose that
shall find in their hearts so suddenly to forsake their goods.

'*Antony.* That fear I much, cousin, too. But thereby shall
it well appear that, seemed they never so good and virtuous
before, yet were their hearts inwardly, in the deep sight of God,
not sound and sure.'

Things were even worse than Sir Thomas thought. Many
were not tried by the fear of losing their own goods, but by the
hope of gaining those of others. Mr. Froude has attempted to
vindicate the reign of Henry from the charge of having been a
reign of terror, and the conduct of Lords and Commons from
the accusation of cowardice and servility. 'What means,' he
asks triumphantly, 'had Henry VIII. at his disposal to compel
their compliance or punish their disobedience ? He had a mere
handful of men, whose number he never attempted to increase.
The complications of this reign,' he continues, 'require far
subtler and more delicate explanation. Cruel deeds were done,
but they were done by the alternating influences of the two
great parties in the State, to whom nothing was wrong which
furthered their separate objects.'[4] Without any sympathy in
Mr. Froude's attempt to justify Henry, I cannot but concur to
a great extent in his estimate of the nobility and gentry of England in the sixteenth century. They were indeed fallen from

---

[4] Preface to his edition of the *Pilgrim*, by William Thomas.

the spirit of the great warriors and statesmen, the noble gentlemen and bold citizens, in whom devotion to our Lady had been
linked with true chivalry.   Henry had subtler means at his
command than the terror of the sword.   His nobles and gentry
were men who could be bought by money ; and the plunder of
the shrines and monasteries gave him the means of buying their
allegiance.

The unblushing avarice which made them become reformers
may be seen in the following letter of Sir Thomas Elyot to
Cromwell. 'This Elyot was,' says Mr. Wright, ' a distinguished
diplomatist, a man of great learning, and had been an intimate
friend of Sir Thomas More.'   It must have been such friends
that More had in mind when he doubted their resistance of
temptation :

' My lord,' writes[5] Elyot to Cromwell two years after the
death of his friend Sir Thomas More, ' forasmuch as I suppose
that the king's most gentle communication with me, and also
his most comfortable report unto the lords of me, proceeded of
your afore-remembered recommendations, I am animate to im-
portune your good lordship, with most hearty desires, to continue my good lord, in augmenting the king's good estimation
of me ; whereof I promise you before God your lordship shall
never have cause to repent.

' And where' (*i. e.* whereas) ' I perceive that ye suspect that I
favour not truly Holy Scripture, I would God that the king and
you might see the most secret thoughts of my heart ; surely ye
should then perceive that, the order of charity saved, I have in
as much detestation as any man living all vain superstitions,
superfluous ceremonies, slanderous jugglings, counterfeit miracles, arrogant usurpations of men called spiritual and masking
religious, and all other abusions of Christ's holy doctrine and
laws.   And as much I enjoy' (rejoice) ' at the king's godly proceeding to the due reformation of the said enormities as any his
grace's poor subject living.

' I therefore beseech your good lordship now to lay apart
the remembrance of the amity between me and Sir Thomas

* *Letters on the Suppression of the Monasteries,* letter lxv.

More, which was but *usque ad aras*, as is the proverb, considering that I was never so much addict unto him as I was unto truth and fidelity toward my sovereign lord, as God is my judge.'

Having approved of the king's godly proceeding, and professed his love of pure and reformed religion according to the Gospel of Cranmer and Cromwell, and repudiated the friendship of the glorious martyr now in heaven, he comes at last to the end and purpose of his letter: 'And whereas my special trust and only expectation is to be holpen by the means of your lordship, and natural shamefastness more reigneth in me than is necessary [!], so that I would not press to the king's majesty without your lordship's assistance, with whom I have sundry times declared my indigence, and whereof it hath happened, I therefore most humbly desire you, my special good lord, so to bring me unto the king's most noble remembrance, that of his most bounteous liberality it may like his highness to reward me *with some convenient portion of his suppressed lands*, whereby I may be able to continue my life according to that honest degree whereunto his grace hath called me. . . . And whatsoever portion of land that I shall attain by the king's gift, I promise to give to your lordship the first year's fruits, with mine assured and faithful heart and service.'

Such were the men on whose word Englishmen have learnt to believe in the 'slanderous jugglings and counterfeit miracles' of the monks. These beggars for plunder, these givers and receivers of bribes, are the men who set themselves to reform 'the abusions of Christ's holy doctrines and laws.' Such were many of the Catholic gentry of that day. They fawned on Henry VIII. and renounced the authority of the Pope in order to enjoy prosperity and to increase their riches; and they were willing to be reconciled to the Pope again under Mary, provided they could still keep their sacrilegious spoils. Their plan was, as Sir Thomas More put it, 'not to be compelled utterly to forsake Christ nor all the whole Christian faith, but only some such parts thereof as may not stand with Mahomet's law.' Sir Thomas answered this theory as follows: 'Break one of Christ's commandments and break all. Forsake one point of His faith, and forsake all, as for any thank you get for the remnant. . . . Christ will not take your service to halves, but will that you should love Him with all your heart. And because that while He was living here fifteen hundred years ago, He foresaw this mind of yours that you have now, with which you would fain serve Him in some such fashion, as you might keep your worldly substance still and rather forsake His service than put all your substance from you, He telleth you plain, fifteen hundred years ago, by His own mouth, that He will no such service from you, saying, " Non potestis Deo servire et Mammonæ, —You cannot serve both God and your riches together." [6]

But men like Sir Thomas Elyot learnt their morality from other teachers[7] than Jesus Christ, and went along with Sir Thomas More, as they well said, only *usque ad aras*—to the church door, or to the door of heaven ; there they let him go in alone, since there was a chance of passing to it only through the Tower.

The People.

All the parties who actively coöperated in doing despite to our Lady were not equally guilty. I am glad to believe that many of the simple people, even of those who consented to acts of sacrilege, were deluded by sophisms into the thought that they were doing God service. I have taken Sir Thomas More as a witness to the vacillation and worldliness of the nobility, and I find in him also an explanation and a kind of apology for the frenzy of the mobs.

The device, he tells us, which was followed by the preachers of the Reformation was to invent opposition between one part of the Catholic system and another ; and then to decry doctrines and practices, not so much by argument, as by appeal to the spirit of veneration.

'I heard a religious man myself,' he writes, 'one that had

[6] *A Dialogue of Comfort against Tribulation,* book iii. ch. xiv.
[7] Sir T. Elyot compiled, from the acts and sayings of the heathen Emperor, Alexander Severus, a book called the *Image of Governance, in the Favour of Nobilitie.*

been reputed and taken for very good, and which, as far as the folk perceived, was of his own living somewhat austere and sharp; but his preaching was wonderful. Methink I hear him yet, his voice was so loud and shrill, his learning less than mean. But whereas his matter was much part against fasting, and all affliction for any penance, which he called men's inventions, he cried out ever upon them to keep well the laws of Christ. Let go their peevish penance and purpose them to mend, and seek nothing to salvation but the death of Christ. "For He is our justice and He is our Saviour, and our whole satisfaction for all our deadly sins. He did full penance for us all upon His painful Cross; He washed us there all clean with the water of His sweet side, and brought us out of the devil's danger with His dear precious Blood. Leave therefore, leave, I beseech you, these inventions of men, your foolish Lenten fasts and your peevish penance; minish never Christ's thank, nor look to save yourself. It is Christ's death, I tell you, that must save us all. Christ's death, I tell you yet again, and not your own deeds. Leave your own fasting, therefore, and lean to Christ alone, good Christian people, for Christ's dear bitter Passion."

' Now so loud and so shrill he cried Christ in their ears, and so thick he came forth with Christ's bitter Passion, and that so bitterly spoken, with the great sweat dropping down his cheeks, that I marvelled not though I saw the poor women weep, for he made my own hair stand up upon my head.

' And with such preaching were the people so brought in, that some fell to break their fasts on the fasting-days, not out of frailty or of malice first, but *almost of devotion, lest they should take from Christ the thank of His bitter Passion.* But when they were a while nuselled in that point first, they could abide and endure after many things more, with which had he then begun they would have pulled him down.

' Such one preacher much more abuseth the name of Christ and of His bitter Passion than five hundred hazarders that in their idle business swear and forswear themselves by His holy bitter Passion at dice. They carry the minds of the people from the perceiving of their craft, by the continual naming of the name of Christ.   God keep all good folk from such manner of preachers !'[8]

No words could better express the whole trick of the Reformation.   The Passion of Jesus Christ was played off against the mortifications which are its legitimate consequences, the Bible against the traditions which it presupposes and authorises, and the honour of Jesus Christ against that which is its complement, the honour of His Blessed Mother.   And to this day it is pretended that the Catholic people before the Reformation had lost sight of the Bible, the Passion, the honour of Jesus Christ ; whereas it was only the intense veneration in which these things were held which made the Reformation possible, by giving a standing-point on which to rest the sophistical levers of destruction.

All this, of course, refers to that part of the people only who welcomed the Reformation and actively furthered it.

Another and a large class of persons got their consciences involved in sacrilegious guilt, not through error of the mind or deliberate impiety, but by not refusing to share in the results of a work which they neither originated nor approved.

A writer, quoted by Sir Henry Ellis in the third series of *Original Letters*, and who was an eye-witness of the spoliation of Roche Abbey in Yorkshire, tells us :

' It would have made a heart of flint to have melted and wept to have seen the breaking-up of the house and their sorrowful departing, and the sudden spoil that fell the same day of their departure from the house.   And every person had everything good cheap, except the poor monks, friars, and nuns, that had no money to bestow of anything, as it appeared, by the suppression of an abbey hard by me, called the Roche Abbey.' After a minute description of the plundering, he continues : ' So that it seemeth that every person bent himself to filch and spoil what he could, yea, even such persons were content to spoil them that seemed not two days before to allow their religion, and do great worship and reverence at their Matins, Masses, and other service, and all other their doings ; which is

[8] *A Dialogue of Comfort against Tribulation.*

a strange thing to say, that they could this day think it to be the house of God, and the next day the house of the devil; or else they would not have been so ready to have spoiled it.

'For the better proof of this my saying, I demanded of my father, thirty years after the suppression, which had bought part of the timber of the church and all the timber in the steeple, with the bell-frame, whether he thought well of the religious persons and of the religion then used; and he told me, "Yea; for," said he, "I did see no cause to the contrary." "Well," said I, "then how came it to pass you was so ready to destroy and spoil the thing that you thought well of?" "What should I do?" said he. "Might I not, as well as others, have some profit of the spoil of the abbey? for I did see all would away, and therefore I did as others did."

'Thus you see that as well they that thought well of the religion then used, as they which thought otherwise, could agree well enough, and too well, to spoil them. Such a devil is covet-ousness and mammon!'[9]

All may not have had the candour of this old man. They may probably have snatched at their share of the spoil under the same pretext—that in any case the monks had lost it, or that it could no longer be used in the service of God and our Lady, and that they might as well have it as their neighbours; and afterwards, having a troubled conscience, they may have given a ready ear to the preachers, who told them that they had been doing a good work and rendering glory to God in the overthrow of superstition and idolatry.

But in considering as dispassionately as possible the con-duct of our ancestors, I find especially two sources of excuse for those who, to a certain degree, coöperated in the work of de-struction. First, their opinions were not asked nor their feel-ings consulted. They had merely to follow the decisions of their rulers, unless they were willing to suffer pains and penal-ties with heroic virtue. And secondly, they did not see the whole work as we see it, nor anticipate the completeness of the revolution, of which they only witnessed the beginnings.

* Ellis, vol. iii. p. 35.

H H

First, then, the people had no choice in the matter. The boasted principle of private judgment had not as yet been named by the mouth, or conceived by the brain, of an Englishman. When the people obeyed the Church they felt themselves free, for they accepted her word as the word of God, and bowed to no human authority. But when the authority of the Church was abolished, that of royal theologians was substituted. Doctrines and practices were meted out to the English at the will and caprice of their sovereigns.

As this important view of the Reformation, though incapable of serious contradiction, is frequently lost sight of, and it is the fashion to represent the overthrow of devotion to our Lady (as well as the other changes of religion) as the result of the emancipation of the individual conscience, and of the free and enlightened judgment of Englishmen, formed upon ' an open Bible,' it may be useful to give some evidence that individual judgment or conscience had simply and absolutely no share or action in the matter.

At the very outset of the Reformation, in 1535, the king and council issue an order for the regulating of the pulpits, in which they ordain, among other things, 'that from henceforth all preachers shall purely, sincerely, and justly preach the Scripture and word of Christ, and not mix them with man's institutions, nor make men believe that the force of God's law and man's law is like, or that any man is able or hath power to dispense with God's law.' But this decree gave no liberty either to preacher or hearer to determine the sense of Scripture. It was merely aimed at the Pope's authority. The same injunctions oblige all preachers to preach against the Pope's authority, and forbid them to defend it. They prohibit, during a year, any preaching for or against purgatory, for or against honouring saints, &c., and wind up with a long instruction to the preachers of the arguments by which they are to defend the king's divorce from Katherine, to be concluded as follows : ' Wherefore, good people, *I exhort you to stick to the truth and our prince,* according to our bounden duties, and despise these naughty doings of the Bishop of Rome, and charitably pray that he and all other abusers of Christ's word and works may have grace to amend.'[10]

In order to persuade the people 'to stick to the truth and our prince,' the king both suspended preachers and licensed them at his discretion; and not only so, but became himself the great preacher of his reign.

In the preamble to the Articles of Religion of 1536 he declares :[11] 'Amongst other cures appertaining to this our princely office, whereunto it has pleased Almighty God of His infinite mercy and goodness to call us, we have always esteemed and thought, like as we also yet esteem and think, that it most chiefly belongs unto our said charge diligently to foresee and cause that not only the most holy word and commandments of God should most sincerely be believed, and most reverently be observed and kept of our subjects; but also that unity and concord in opinions—namely, in such things as do concern our religion—may increase and go forward, and *all occasions of dissent* and discord touching the same be *repressed and utterly extinguished.* Wherefore,' he continues, having by his own great pains and study, and by the advice of his bishops, come to certain conclusions, 'we have caused the same to be published, willing, requiring, and commanding to accept, repute, and take them accordingly. . . . Wherefore we will and require you to accept the same, after such sort as we have here prescribed them unto you, and to conform yourselves obediently unto the same; whereby you shall not only obtain that most charitable union and loving concord, whereof shall issue your incomparable commodity, profit, and lucre, as well spiritual as other; but also you shall not a little encourage us to take farther travails, pains, and labours for your commodities in all such other matters as in time to come may happen to occur.'

The king's loving subjects were not, however, so grateful as his majesty expected. In the insurrections in Lincolnshire and Yorkshire, called the Pilgrimage of Grace, they only asked him that he would spare his pains and travails in the reformation of religion, and leave them to believe and practise as their an-

[10] Collier, vol. iv. pp. 285-9.   [11] Ib. p. 351.

cestors had done. To this the king penned an answer with
his own hand. We feel in reading it that he was more piqued
as a theologian than as a prince. ' It is,' he says, ' and always
has been, our intention to live and die in the belief and defence
of the faith of Christ. We are strangely surprised, therefore,
to find ignorant people have the assurance to instruct us in
the doctrines of the faith; especially since we have some reputation for letters, and have had the concurrence of our whole
clergy in convocation for the settling these points.'[12]

Yet Collier[13] tells us that the unsuccessful state of his
reformation, and the controversies in which he found himself
involved, made the king waver: ' His thoughts were so embar-
rassed, that he had once resolved to quit his title of head of the
Church, and return the Pope his supremacy; but being appre-
hensive his resigning in so great a point might be imputed to
fear, he stood his ground and dropped that resolution.' This
was in 1536.

It was soon found that exhortations and even commands
to believe the king's interpretations of Scripture and to avoid
disputes would not insure unanimity. So in 1539 the king had
an act of parliament passed enforcing six articles of religion
with penalties. The preamble sets forth, ' that whereas the
king's most excellent majesty is, by God's law, supreme head
immediately under Him of this whole Church and congregation
of England, intending the conservation of the same Church in
a true, sincere, and uniform doctrine of Christ's religion,' he
had set forth six articles, for contradicting one of which the
penalty of death was appointed, and for contradicting any of
the other five loss of all goods, imprisonment during the king's
pleasure, &c.[14]

The next year, by the same authority of supreme head, and
because of the spread of dangerous, erroneous, and heretical
opinions,[15] the king appointed a commission 'to draw up a form
of the principal articles of our faith, adding withal an explanation of such other points as by his grace's advice, counsel, and
consent shall be thought needful and expedient.'

[12] Collier, vol. iv. p. 381. [13] Ib. p. 396. [14] Ib. vol. v. pp. 87-9. [15] Ib. p. 66.

The thought of tolerating freedom of opinion in matters of religion had not yet occurred to any one holding office in Church or State; but many of the people, nevertheless, thought themselves free to follow the example of Henry and Cranmer rather than their counsels. To put an end to this, in 1542 another act of parliament restrained the use of the Bible. The preamble declared 'that many seditious and ignorant people had abused the liberty granted them for reading the Bible, that great diversity of opinions, animosities, tumults, and schisms have been occasioned by perverting the sense of Scripture.' Hence in future 'the reading the Bible is prohibited to all under the degrees of gentlemen and gentlewomen;' only 'it shall be lawful for all persons whatsoever to read and teach all such doctrine as is *or shall be* set forth by his majesty since the year of our Lord 1540; and if any spiritual person shall preach or maintain anything contrary to the doctrines above mentioned, he shall recant for his first offence, abjure for his second, and bear a fagot; and upon a further relapse, shall be adjudged an heretic, suffer the pains of burning, and forfeit all his goods and chattels.'

We have already seen how the king continued to the end of his reign to provide new statements of doctrine and variations of discipline for his people. In one thing only was there no variation: that the people had no choice allowed them.

Cranmer did indeed advise a certain diplomacy in dealing with men's consciences. In January 1542 he writes to the king, that 'in mine opinion, when things be altered or taken away, there should be set forth some doctrine therewith, which should declare the cause of the abolishings or alterations, *for to satisfy the consciences of your people;* . . . which, if your majesty command to be made, the people shall obey your majesty's commandments willingly, giving thanks to your majesty if they know the truth, which else they would obey with murmurations and grudgings. And it shall be a satisfaction to all other nations, when they shall see your majesty do nothing but by the authority of God's word.'[16]

[16] Collier, vol. v. p. 140.

At the death of Henry, those who seized the government wished to make many innovations on the doctrines and practices hitherto approved. Gardiner, Bishop of Winchester, foresaw the absurd appearance this would have, both to the people of England and to other nations, whom Cranmer had thought so easily to satisfy.

'Certain printers and players and preachers,' he writes to Somerset, 'make a wonderment, as though we knew not yet how to be justified, nor what sacraments we should have. And if the agreement in religion, made in the time of our late sovereign lord, be of no force in their judgment, what establishment could any new agreement have? And every incertainty is noisome to any realm; and where every man will be master there must needs be uncertainty. And one thing is marvellous, that, at the same time it is taught that all men be liars, at the selfsame time almost every man would be believed. . . . But as one asked, when he saw an old philosopher dispute with another, what they talked on, and it was answered how the old man was discussing what was virtue, it was replied, "If the old man yet dispute of virtue, when will he use it?"—so it may be said in our religion, if we be yet searching for it, when shall we begin to put it in execution?'[17]

In another letter Gardiner ventured on a certainly unwarranted prediction : ' When our sovereign lord [Edward] cometh to his perfect age (which God grant), I doubt not but God will reveal that which shall be necessary for the governing his people in religion.' He was much nearer the truth when he said, 'the Bishop of Rome wanteth not wits to beat into other princes' ears, that where his authority is abolished, there, at every change of governors, shall be change in religion, and that which hath been among us by a whole consent established shall, by the pretence of another understanding in Scripture, straight be brought in question.'

Notwithstanding the remonstrances, prophecies, and forebodings of Gardiner, Somerset and the other members of the council neither intended to leave things as they had been, nor

[17] Foxe, ii. lix. 57; Tierney's *Dodd*, vol. ii. App. pp. xix.-xxiii.

to let the people judge for themselves about the changes. Proclamations, injunctions, and acts of parliament followed one another all in the same style, as if truth had now been finally discovered, and there was no possibility of questioning whatever was determined in the king's name. In the proclamation issuing a new Communion Service, 'We would not,' says the king, 'have our subjects so much to mistake our judgment, so much to mistrust our zeal, as though we either could not discern what was to be done, or would not do all things in due time. God be praised, we know both what by His word is meet to be redressed, and have an earnest mind with all diligence and convenient speed to set forth the same.' 'Since the king was but ten years old,' says Collier, 'to suppose him a judge of controversy thus early, and make him say he knew what was fit to be done, was somewhat extraordinary.'[18] For my part I see nothing more extraordinary or absurd in it than for his father Henry, or his sister Elizabeth, to meddle with such matters. I see only the shameful degradation to which the nation had fallen. Surely, if the king was to be judge of controversies and source of spiritual light to his people, this must be on account of his office, not of his age or talents or theological learning. Edward at the age of ten, being taken for lawful king, had all the authority in this respect possessed by king or queen of England before or since.

It would be tedious to continue the subject. Enough has been said to illustrate the important fact that the overthrow of our Lady's Dowry was in no sense the work of the English people, except in so far as through fear or interest they acquiesced in it. In what proportion they resisted and refused their consent, and how far they yielded cheerfully to the innovations or lent actual coöperation, it is now perhaps impossible to discover. It would appear that the great majority disliked the changes, yet had not courage to resist them, or knew not how to make a combined opposition. They had not the courage of martyrdom. They temporised. They hoped for better times, when things would be restored once more to their former state.

[18] Collier, vol. v. p. 256.

And this brings me to the second plea I have stated in defence of our ancestors. If we would judge fairly of them we must remember that Protestantism, as we see it, was yet unknown, and could not be anticipated. Had our forefathers foreseen the utter negation of all devotion to our Lady which has now prevailed for three hundred years, they would probably have withstood the first encroachments in a very different manner. But the thing was done by degrees, and few, very few, knew whither they were tending. This is, indeed, but an insufficient apology for their disloyalty to God and to our Lady, yet it would not be just to omit so important a consideration. Besides, it is one we are most apt to forget. When we look back on a deed and its consequences, both proximate and remote, when we see that those consequences were not merely accidental, but the logical results of such a deed, we are prone to conclude at once that all those consequences were foreseen and willed. Yet this is not the case. Few men reflect deeply on what they are doing. Let, then, the multitude have the benefit of their ignorance. 'Father, forgive them, for they know not what they do' (Luke xxiii. 34). 'And now, brethren, I know that you did it through ignorance, as did also your rulers. . . . Be penitent therefore' (Acts iii. 17, 19). The rulers had indeed less excuse. It belongs to the strict duty of their office to reflect, to foresee and weigh consequences. If there is one lesson more important than another to be learnt from the history of the Reformation, it is that those who have received the. deposit of the faith and the charge of souls should not temporise, should not hope that they may yield somewhat to the bidding of the temporal ruler and go no further. Again, that they should not dream of reforming abuses, if such exist or are thought to exist, by any other action than that of the Church, or by the action of a national Church in isolation from the Catholic Church and the Rock on which it is built. As Peter of Celles said to Nicolas of St. Alban's about institutions, so must every zealous and wise ruler say of projects of reformation —though the work may be of the purest gold, it can have no legitimate currency unless it is issued from St. Peter's mint or

bears the stamp of his authority.[19] It was for this principle
that Fisher shed his blood ; and Gardiner, who thought that
the bishops of a national Church under royal supremacy could
act in defiance of the Pope, was reduced to the ignominy of
seeing a king ten years old undo his father's work, with the
boast that he had the same authority and the same divine
assistance.   Happy they who, through the study of the aberra-
tions of those times, learn like Gardiner the necessity of the
authority established by Jesus Christ, and return to their true
allegiance.

[19] See p. 82.

CHAPTER V.

CONCLUSION.

READERS who have gone through the evidence which I have presented to them in this volume will now be in a state to judge of the nature and tendency of devotion to the Blessed Virgin, as it developed itself unchecked in Catholic England. Mr. Hallam has described it as a 'monstrous superstition,' as a 'loosening of the bonds of religion,' and a 'perversion of the standard of morality.'[1] If these frightful charges are true, 'then are we found false witnesses of God,' 'our preaching is false,' and 'the faith' of Catholics 'is also false' (1 Cor. xv.). But I am without fear. Devotion to our Lady had time, space, opportunity to work out its results thoroughly in England. I have searched eagerly for those results, and described what I have found, omitting nothing that could affect the judgment of the reader.

I have endeavoured to give, not indeed a complete account, much less a minute history, of English devotion to the Virgin Mother, but at least specimens of it in its various phases. As I have looked in the writings of enemies as well as of friends, I do not think it probable that anything can have escaped my attention which is necessary that my readers may judge with full light and impartiality, as to the devotion itself, its historical origin, or its moral results.

It would be tedious to go again through the whole of the evidence, in order to rebut the charges made against this devotion, or to establish its beneficent influence. How it sprang from a lively faith in the Incarnation, and in its turn acted as the safeguard of that faith; how it was an exercise and a

[1] See Introduction to this volume, p. 5.

stimulant of Christian hope whether in the sinner or the saint, looking as they did on our Lady as the great channel of the mercies of God purchased for us by Jesus Christ; how it is one of the noblest acts of that charity which makes us love what God loves, and how it led to innumerable works of love and mercy to men; how it gave a charm and attraction to the Christian heart, without in any way substituting mere poetry and sentimentalism for solid virtue,—these are conclusions which the least attentive reader, if only moderately candid, must have drawn from the perusal of the facts and documents I have brought together.

There is one influence at least of this devotion, and in itself of no small value, to which I have not hitherto alluded, for the very reason that it has been admitted by modern writers who have the least sympathy with our faith. Mr. Lecky, in his *History of Rationalism,* has stated in the most ample terms the effect of devotion to our Lady in developing respect for women.

'The world,' he writes, 'is governed by its ideals, and seldom or never has there been one which has exercised a more profound and, on the whole, a more salutary influence than the mediæval conception of the Virgin. For the first time woman was elevated to her rightful position, and the sanctity of weakness was recognised as well as the sanctity of sorrow. No longer the slave or the toy of man, no longer associated only with ideas of degradation and of sensuality, woman rose in the person of the Virgin Mother into a new sphere, and became the object of a reverential homage of which antiquity had no conception.

'The moral charm and beauty of female excellence was, for the first time, felt. A new type of character was called into being, a new kind of admiration was fostered. Into a harsh and ignorant and benighted age this ideal type infused a conception of gentleness and of purity unknown to the proudest generations of the past. In the pages of living tenderness which many a monkish writer has left in honour of his celestial patron; in the millions who, in many lands and in many ages, have sought, with no barren desire, to mould their characters into her image ; in those holy maidens who, for the love of Mary, have separated themselves from all the glories and pleasures of the world, to seek, in fastings and vigils and humble charity, to render themselves worthy of her benediction; in the new sense of honour, in the chivalrous respect, in the softening of manners, in the refinement of tastes displayed in all the walks of society,—in these, and in many other ways, we detect its influence. All that was best in Europe clustered around it, and it is the origin of many of the purest elements of our civilisation.'[2]

This is certainly a very different appreciation from that of Mr. Hallam. My readers may judge which is the more correct.

The Rev. Mr. Brewer, in his introduction to the *Monumenta Franciscana*, edited by him for the Master of the Rolls, has dwelt with equal candour on the same theme. Even Mr. Wright, who seldom allows a word of praise to escape for anything distinctively Catholic, has written, that while ' gross attacks on the character of the ladies are common in the Middle Ages, we also frequently meet with poems written in their defence, and in these a very common argument in their favour is founded upon the worthiness of the Virgin Mary.'[3]

The following lines from a Scotch poet will serve as an example and justification of this statement :

> ' Christ to His Father He had not ane man ;
> See what worship women suld have than !
> That Son is Lord, that Son is King of kings,
> In heaven and earth His majesty aye rings.
> Sen she has berne Him in her haliness,
> And He is well and grund of all guidness,
> All women of us suld have honouring,
> Service, and love above all other thing !'[4]

The same idea is found in an old English poem given in the *Reliquiæ Antiquæ*.[5]

> ' To unpraise women it were a shame,
> For a woman was thy dame ;

---

[2] *History of Rationalism*, ch. iii. p. 44.
[3] *Poems of Walter Mapes*, p. 216, note (Camden Society, 1841).
[4] Dunbar, p. 139 (ed. Paterson).   [5] Vol. i. p. 275.

Our Blessed Lady beareth the name
Of all women where that they go.'

I may express a hope that my female readers at least will
bear these last two lines in their memory, and that if ever they
should hear words of disparagement fall from female lips against
her who is the glory of their sex, they will remind the utterers
that the present position of women in Christian society—even
in those sects which have rejected all Catholic devotion to our
Lady—is nevertheless its historical result. But as this is a
topic not unfamiliar to modern writers, I will pass on to another
and a final reflection.

In a work, which has resounded throughout England and
the world while these pages have been passing through the
press, Mr. Gladstone has stated that 'the growth of what is
often termed among Protestants "Mariolatry" was notoriously
advancing' of late years, 'but it seems not fast enough to satisfy
the dominant party' in the Catholic Church; and that the constitution on Papal Infallibility of 1870, and the decree of the
Immaculate Conception of 1854, 'were deadly blows at the old
historic, scientific, and moderate school, and an act of violence.'
On the other hand, he says that 'in days within' his own
'memory, the constant, favourite, and imposing argument of
Roman controversialists was the unbroken and absolute identity
in belief of the Roman Church from the days of our Saviour
until now.' He thinks that we have abandoned this argument
and this method to a great extent. He is mistaken; and I
hope that the present work, slight as it is, will be accepted as
some evidence that Catholics, to use his own words, are of
'those who think that against all forms, both of superstition
and of unbelief, one main preservative is to be found in maintaining the truth and authority of history, and the inestimable
value of the historic spirit.'⁶

It certainly is not true that 'Rome has substituted for the
proud boast of *semper eadem* a policy of violence and change of
faith;' and it assuredly ill befits those who accept the inheritance
of Henry, Edward, and Elizabeth, to make charges so easy of a

* *The Vatican Decrees,* by the Right Hon. W. E. Gladstone, pp. 13, 14.

crushing retort. Could our ancestors, whether Saxon or Norman, rise up at the present day, they would have to make no change of faith, and to do no violence to their own feelings, in accepting either the Vatican decrees or any dogmatic decree that has ever issued from the Apostolic Chair of St. Peter. But seeing the face of England, and the ruins of all the things they loved, they would indeed lament that England had substituted for her proud boast of being our Lady's Dowry a policy of violence and change of faith.

But I will not conclude my book with words of bitterness. It is indeed rather provoking to be accused as we are, not only by Mr. Gladstone, but by many other writers, of two contradictory tendencies—of 'change of faith,' and abandonment of old landmarks and old methods; and—of obstinate clinging to a discarded past, of 'refurbishing and parading anew every rusty tool we were fondly thought to have disused.'[7] But let these angry words cancel each other. I would ask my reader, in conclusion, to make use of one old relic of the past which I have 'refurbished.' Let him repeat the following prayer of the great Archbishop of Canterbury of the eleventh century, and he will find no difficulty in accepting the faith and devotion (which he will no longer call Mariolatry) of the Archbishop of Westminster of the nineteenth century.

Prayer of St. Anselm.

'Of a certainty, O Jesus, Son of God, and thou, O Mother Mary, you desire that whatever you love should be loved by us. Therefore, O good Son, I beg Thee, by the love Thou bearest Thy Mother, and as Thou wishest her to be loved, to grant to me that I may truly love her. And thou, O good Mother, I beg thee by the love thou bearest thy Son, as thou wishest Him to be loved, to pray for me that I may truly love Him. Behold I ask nothing that is not in accordance with your will. Since, then, this is in your power, shall my sins prevent its being done? O Jesus, lover of men, Thou wert able to love criminals even so as to die for them; canst Thou, then, refuse me, who

---

[7] *The Vatican Decrees*, p. 12.

ask only the love of Thee and Thy Mother? And thou, too, Mary, Mother of Him who loved us, who didst bear Him in thy womb, and feed Him at thy breast, art thou not able, or not willing, to obtain for one who asks it the love of thy Son and of thyself?

'O, may then my mind venerate you both as you deserve! may my heart love you, as it is right it should! may my body serve you, as it ought! in your service may my life be spent! and may my whole substance praise you in eternity! Blessed be God for ever. Amen, amen.'

APPENDIX

(To p. 313).

THE document printed by Newcourt is to be found in the Register of Bishop Gilbert, who occupied the see of London from 1436-1446. It is not dated, but the document immediately preceding is of the year 1440. It occurs quite abruptly, as a memorandum with these words: 'Nota de factur. imaginis B.M. in capella juxta Berking Church, London.' No trace of the original document is to be found in the Register. This copy would appear to have been inserted apropos of some repair; or, perhaps, at the time of the founding of the guild about this period by John Tiptoft. Newcourt has omitted a few words at the beginning, viz. the names of the legates of the Pope, besides Adrian. One is Johannes Carpentarius, the others are illegible.

I am indebted for this information to the kindness of the Rev. J. Maskell, the learned author of the *History of Berking Church*, who has carefully examined the Register.

As to the authenticity of this document:

1. In May 1291, Edward was holding his celebrated Parliament at Norham in Northumberland, as arbitrator on the succession to the Scottish throne. If we suppose, that in the words 'apud Northm. existente parliamento tam Angliæ quam Scotiæ,' Northampton has been substituted for Norham by a mere clerical error of the copyist, the place and circumstances of Edward's supposed statement agree with history.

2. Again, though I can find no record of an Adrian, Bishop of the Tartars, yet about that time many embassies were passing between Tartary and the Holy See. There is also an entry in Rymer, of the date of 1290, in which the Pope recommends to Edward the messengers whom he was sending to Tartary.

3. The Welsh certainly never held possession of the Isle of Ely. Yet in 1266, when Prince Edward was twenty-seven years old, the outlaws or the 'disinherited,' as they were called, held possession of Ely, at the same time that the Welsh were invading England.

There is no difficulty in supposing that the foreign legates, if they really heard the narrative of Edward, might have confounded these events.

4. It is beyond doubt that the heart of Richard I. was buried in Rouen ;. yet an error may be supposed on the part of the legates or of Edward ; and such a statement as that the heart was buried in Berking Chapel is not sufficient to prove the document a forgery of later times.

5. As to whether it is likely that Edward, when acting as arbitrator to the throne of Scotland, should publish a promise made to him that he and his successors should be conquerors of that country, my readers will form their own judgment. To me it does not appear to harmonise with Edward's well-known prudence and reserve, and is much more like a prediction made after the event.

Google

INDEX.

THE END.

LONDON:
ROBSON AND SONS, PRINTERS, PANCRAS ROAD, N.W.

A

Select Catalogue of Books

LATELY PUBLISHED BY

BURNS AND OATES,

17, 18 PORTMAN STREET

AND

63 PATERNOSTER ROW.

LONDON :

ROBSON AND SONS, PRINTERS, PANCRAS ROAD, N.W.

Books lately published

BY

BURNS AND OATES,

17, 18 PORTMAN STREET, W., & 63 PATERNOSTER ROW, E.C.

———0———

Sin and its Consequences. By His Grace the
ARCHBISHOP OF WESTMINSTER. 6s.

CONTENTS : I. The Nature of Sin. II. Mortal Sin.
III. Venial Sin. IV. Sins of Omission. V. The Grace
and Works of Penance. VI. Temptation. VII. The Dere-
liction on the Cross. VIII. The Joys of the Resurrection.

'We know few better books than this for spiritual reading. These lectures
are prepared with great care, and are worthy to rank with the old volumes
of sermons which are now standard works of the English tongue.'—*Weekly
Register.*

'We have had many volumes from his Grace's pen of this kind, but perhaps none more practical or more searching than the volume before us
These discourses are the clearest and simplest exposition of the theology of
the subjects they treat of that could be desired. The intellect is addressed
as well as the conscience. Both are strengthened and satisfied.'—*Tablet.*

'Of the deepest value, and of great theological and literary excellence.
More clear and lucid expositions of dogmatic and moral theology could not
be found. No one can read these very forcible, searching, and practical
sermons without being deeply stirred and greatly edified.'—*Church Herald.*

'His Grace has added to Catholic literature such a brilliant disquisition
as can hardly be equalled.'—*Catholic Times.*

'As powerful, searching, and deep as any that we have ever read. In
construction, as well as in theology and in rhetoric, they are more than remarkable, and are amongst the best from his Grace's pen.'—*Union Review.*

The Prophet of Carmel: a Series of Practical Considerations upon the History of Elias in the Old Testament ; with a Supplementary Dissertation. By the Rev. CHARLES B. GARSIDE, M.A. Dedicated to the Very Rev. JOHN HENRY NEWMAN, D.D.   5*s.*

'There is not a page in these sermons but commands our respect. They are Corban in the best sense ; they belong to the sanctuary, and are marked as divine property by a special cachet. They are simple without being trite, and poetical without being pretentious.'—*Westminster Gazette.*

' Full of spiritual wisdom uttered in pure and engaging language.'—The *Universe.*

' We see in these pages the learning of the divine, the elegance of the scholar, and the piety of the priest. Every point in the sacred narrative bearing upon the subject of his book is seized upon by the author with the greatest keenness of perception, and set forth with singular force and clearness.'—*Weekly Register.*

' Under his master-hand the marvellous career of the Prophet of Carmel displays its majestic proportions. His strong, nervous, incisive style has a beauty and a grace, a delicacy and a sensitiveness, that seizes hold of the heart and captivates the imagination. He has attained to the highest art of writing, which consists in selecting the words which express one's meaning with the greatest clearness in the least possible space.'—*Tablet.*

' The intellectual penetration, the rich imagination, the nervous eloquence which we meet with throughout the whole work, all combine to give it at once a very high place among the highest productions of our English Catholic literature.'—*Dublin Review.*

' Is at once powerful and engaging, and calculated to furnish ideas innumerable to the Christian preacher.'—*Church Review.*

' The thoughts are expressed in plain and vigorous English. The sermons are good specimens of the way in which Old Testament subjects should be treated for the instruction of a Christian congregation.'—*Church Times.*

Mary magnifying God: May Sermons. By the Rev. Fr. HUMPHREY, O.S.C.   Cloth, 2*s.* 6*d.*

' Each sermon is a complete thesis, eminent for the strength of its logic, the soundness of its theology, and the lucidness of its expression. With equal force and beauty of language the author has provided matter for the most sublime meditations.'—*Tablet.*

' Dogmatic teaching of the utmost importance is placed before us so clearly, simply, and unaffectedly, that we find ourselves acquiring invaluable lessons of theology in every page.'—*Weekly Register.*

By the same,

The Divine Teacher.   2*s.* 6*d.*

' The most excellent treatise we have ever read. It could not be clearer, and, while really deep, it is perfectly intelligible to any person of the most ordinary education.'—*Tablet.*

' We cannot speak in terms too high of the matter contained in this excellent and able pamphlet.'—*Westminster Gazette.*

Sermons by Fathers of the Society of Jesus.

Third Edition. 7s.

CONTENTS: The Latter Days: Four Sermons by the Rev. H. J. Coleridge. The Temptations of our Lord: Four Sermons by the Rev. Father Hathaway. The Angelus Bell: Five Lectures on the Remedies against Desolation by the Very Rev. Father Gallwey, Provincial of the Society. The Mysteries of the Holy Infancy: Seven Sermons by Fathers Parkinson, Coleridge, and Harper.

Also, printed separately from above,

The Angelus Bell: Five Lectures on the

Remedies against Desolation. By the Very Rev. Father GALLWEY, Provincial of the Society of Jesus. 1s. 6d.

Also Vol. II, in same series,

Discourses by the Rev. Fr. Harper, S.J. 6s.

Of Adoration in Spirit and in Truth. In

Four Books. By J. E. NIEREMBERG, S.J. With a Preface by the Rev. Father GALLWEY, S.J. 6s.

'The work is in every way a great acquisition to our English ascetical literature.'—*Weekly Register.*

'We rejoice to see this brought out, and hope it will find an extensive circulation.'—*Westminster Gazette.*

'It is more near the *Following of our Blessed Lord* than any work we have met with.'—*Catholic Opinion.*

'We hope it will be the precursor of a number of similar volumes.'—*Month.*

WORKS WRITTEN AND EDITED BY LADY GEORGIANA FULLERTON.

The Straw-cutter's Daughter, and the Por-

trait in my Uncle's Dining-room. Two Stories. Translated from the French. 2s. 6d.

Life of Luisa de Carvajal. 6s.

'Is as charming as anything she has written.'—*Month.*

'We can only thank God, who put it into the heart of the authoress to bring before us, with the learning and force which are peculiarly her own, this wonderful life of superhuman charity.'—*Tablet.*

Seven Stories.   3*s.* 6*d.*

CONTENTS: I. Rosemary: a Tale of the Fire of London. II. Reparation: a Story of the Reign of Louis XIV. III. The Blacksmith of Antwerp. IV. The Beggar of the Steps of St. Roch: a True Story. V. Trouvaille, or the Soldier's Adopted Child: a True Story. VI. Earth without Heaven: a Reminiscence. VII. Ad Majorem Dei Gloriam.

'Will well repay perusal.'—*Weekly Register.*

'Each story in this series has its own charm.'—*Tablet.*

'In this collection may be found stories sound in doctrine and intensely interesting as any which have come from the same pen.'—*Catholic Opinion.*

'As admirable for their art as they are estimable for their sound teaching.'—*Cork Examiner.*

The Gold-digger, and other Verses.   5*s.*

'Alike creditable to the heart and intellect of the authoress. We need not say that the poetry is thoroughly Catholic, and written in a spirit of the broadest and deepest humanity.'—*Catholic Times.*

'The spirit that breathes throughout is one of true Catholic devotion.'—*Weekly Register.*

'We do not know which most to admire, the genuine modesty of the preface to this volume of poems, or the Catholic tone and sweet tenderness of the verses themselves.'—*Westminster Gazette.*

Laurentia: a Tale of Japan.   Second edition.   3*s.* 6*d.*

'Has very considerable literary merit, and possesses an interest entirely its own. The dialogue is easy and natural, and the incidents are admirably grouped.'—*Weekly Register.*

'Full of romantic records of the heroism of the early Christians of Japan in the sixteenth century. Looking at its literary merits alone, it must be pronounced a really beautiful story.'—*Catholic Times.*

Life of St. Frances of Rome.   2*s.* 6*d.*; cheap edition, 1*s.* 8*d.*

Rose Leblanc: a Tale of great interest.   3*s.*

Grantley Manor: the well-known and favourite Novel.   Cloth, 3*s.* 6*d.*; cheap edition, 2*s.* 6*d.*

Germaine Cousin: a Drama.   6*d.*

Fire of London: a Drama.   6*d.*

OUR LADY'S BOOKS.
Uniformly printed in foolscap 8vo, limp cloth.
No. 1.

Memoir of the Hon. Henry E. Dormer. 2s.
No. 2.

Life of Mary Fitzgerald, a Child of the Sacred Heart. 2s.; cheap edition, 1s.

Meditations for every Day in the Year, and
for the Principal Feasts. By the Ven. Fr. NICHOLAS LANCICIUS, of the Society of Jesus. With Preface by the Rev. GEORGE PORTER, S.J. 6s. 6d.

'Most valuable, not only to religious, for whom they were originally intended, but to all those who desire to consecrate their daily life by regularly express and systematic meditation; while Father Porter's excellent little Preface contains many valuable hints on the method of meditation.'—*Dublin Review.*

'Full of Scripture, short and suggestive. The editor gives a very clear explanation of the Ignatian method of meditation. The book is a very usefu one.'—*Tablet.*

'Short and simple, and dwell almost entirely on the life of our Blessed Lord, as related in the Gospels. Well suited to the wants of Catholics living in the world.'—*Weekly Register.*

'A book of singular spirituality and great depth of piety. Nothing could be more beautiful or edifying than the thoughts set forth for reflection, clothed as they are in excellent and vigorous English.'—*Union Review.*

Meditations for the Use of the Clergy, for
every Day in the Year, on the Gospels for the Sundays. From the Italian of Mgr. SCOTTI, Archbishop of Thessalonica. Revised and edited by the Oblates of St. Charles. With a Preface by his Grace the ARCHBISHOP OF WESTMINSTER.

Vol. I. From the First Sunday in Advent to the Sixth Saturday after the Epiphany. 4s.

Vol. II. From Septuagesima Sunday to the Fourth Sunday after Easter. 4s.

Vol. III. From the Fifth Sunday after Easter to the Eleventh Sunday after Pentecost. 4s.

Vol. IV., completing the work, in preparation.

'This admirable little book will be much valued by all, but especially by the clergy, for whose use it is more immediately intended. The Archbishop states in his Preface that it is held in high esteem in Rome, and that he has himself found, by the experience of many years, its singular excellence, its practical piety, its abundance of Scripture, of the Fathers, and of ecclesiastical writers.'—*Tablet.*

'It is a sufficient recommendation to this book of meditations that our Archbishop has given them his own warm approval. . . . They are full of the language of the Scriptures, and are rich with unction of their Divine sense.'—*Weekly Register.*

'A manual of meditations for priests, to which we have seen nothing comparable.'—*Catholic World.*

'There is great beauty in the thoughts, the illustrations are striking, the learning shown in patristic quotation considerable, and the special applications to priests are very powerful. It is entirely a priest's book.'—*Church Review.*

The Question of Anglican Ordinations discussed. By the Very Rev. Canon ESTCOURT, M.A., F.A.S. With an Appendix of Original Documents and Photographic Facsimiles. One vol. 8vo, 14*s.*

'A valuable contribution to the theology of the Sacrament of Order. He treats a leading question, from a practical point of view, with great erudition, and with abundance of illustrations from the rites of various ages and countries.'—*Month.*

'Will henceforth be an indispensable portion of every priest's library, inasmuch as it contains all the information that has been collected in previous works, sifted and corrected, together with a well-digested mass of important matter which has never before been given to the public.'—*Tablet.*

'Marks a very important epoch in the history of that question, and virtually disposes of it.'—*Messenger.*

'Canon Estcourt has added valuable documents that have never appeared before, or never at full length. The result is a work of very great value.'—*Catholic Opinion.*

'Indicates conscientious and painstaking research, and will be indispensable to any student who would examine the question on which it treats.'—*Bookseller.*

'Superior, both in literary method, tone, and mode of reasoning, to the usual controversial books on this subject.'—*Church Herald.*

May Papers; or Thoughts on the Litanies of Loreto. By EDWARD IGNATIUS PURBRICK, Priest of the Society of Jesus. 3*s.* 6*d.*

'There is a brightness and vivacity in them which will make them interesting to all, old and young alike, and adds to their intrinsic value.'—*Dublin Review.*

'We very gladly welcome this volume as a valuable addition to the now happily numerous manuals of devout exercises for the month.'—*Month.*

'Written in the pure, simple, unaffected language which becomes the subject.'—*Tablet.*

'We cannot easily conceive a book more calculated to aid the cause of true religion amongst young persons of every class.'—*Weekly Register.*

'They are admirable, and expressed in chaste and beautiful language. Although compiled in the first place for boys at school, they are adapted for the spiritual reading of Catholics of every age and condition of life.'—*Catholic Opinion.*

WORKS OF THE REV. FATHER RAWES, O.S.C.

Homeward: a Tale of Redemption. Second
edition. *3s. 6d.*

'A series of beautiful word pictures.'—*Catholic Opinion.*
'A casket well worth the opening; full to the brim of gems of thought
as beautiful as they are valuable.'—*Catholic Times.*
'Full of holy thoughts and exquisite poetry, and just such a book as can
be taken up with advantage and relief in hours of sadness and depression.'—
Dublin Review.
'Is really beautiful, and will be read with profit.'—*Church Times.*

God in His Works: a Course of Five Ser-
mons. *2s. 6d.*

SUBJECTS: I. God in Creation. II. God in the Incarnation. III. God in the Holy See. IV. God in the Heart.
V. God in the Resurrection.

'Full of striking imagery, and the beauty of the language cannot fail to
make the book valuable for spiritual reading.'—*Catholic Times.*
'He has so applied science as to bring before the reader an unbroken
course of thought and argument.'—*Tablet.*

*The Beloved Disciple; or St. John the Evan-
gelist. 3s. 6d.*

'Full of research, and of tender and loving devotion.'—*Tablet.*
'This is altogether a charming book for spiritual reading.'—*Catholic
Times.*
'Through this book runs a vein of true, humble, fervent piety, which
gives a singular charm.'—*Weekly Register.*
'St. John, in his varied character, is beautifully and attractively pre-
sented to our pious contemplation.'—*Catholic Opinion.*

Septem: Seven Ways of hearing Mass. Fifth
edition. *1s.* and *2s.*; red edges, *2s. 6d.*; calf, *4s.*; French
Translation, *1s. 6d.*

'A great assistance to hearing Mass with devotion. Besides its devotional advantages it possesses a Preface, in clear and beautiful language,
well worth reading.'—*Tablet.*

Great Truths in Little Words. Third edi-
tion. Neat cloth, *3s. 6d.*

'A most valuable little work. All may learn very much about the Faith
from it.'—*Tablet.*
'At once practical in its tendency, and elegant; oftentimes poetical in its
diction.'—*Weekly Register.*
'Cannot fail to be most valuable to every Catholic; and we feel certain,
when known and appreciated, it will be a standard work in Catholic house-
holds.'—*Catholic Times.*

A2

Hymns, Original, &c.   Neat cloth, 1s.;
cheap edition, 6d.

* *The Eucharistic Month.* From the Latin of
Father LERCARI, S.J. 6d.; cloth, 1s.

* *Twelve Visits to our Lady and the Heavenly
City of God.* Second edition. 8d.

* *Nine Visits to the Blessed Sacrament.* Chiefly
from the Canticle of Canticles. Second edition. 6d.

* *Devotions for the Souls in Purgatory.* Second edition. 8d.

* Or in one vol.,
Visits and Devotions.   Neat cloth, 3s.

— — — — —

Cherubini: Memorials illustrative of his Life.
With Portrait and Catalogue of his Works. By EDWARD
BELLASIS, Barrister-at-Law. One vol., 429 pp. 10s. 6d.

'The life of a great musical composer has seldom been written with more
conscientious devotion and true love of art than in this memoir.'—*Month.*

'Gives evidence of great pains and ability in welding together all the
materials which the author has been able to collect in illustration of the life
of Cherubini. . . . The account of the different masses is exceedingly interesting, and the power displayed by Mr. Bellasis in analysing them is very
conspicuous.'—*Tablet.*

'To lovers of music we can confidently recommend this most interesting
life. Its scrupulous conscientiousness in all matters of detail evinces a care
in the compiling of the entire work which will give it a high value amongst
the records of the chief composers, and show how justly Mr. Bellasis enters
into the true spirit of his subject. . . . We sincerely hope that Cherubini
will not be the sole musician to whose memory Mr. Bellasis's rare qualifica-
tions shall be devoted.'—*Dublin Review.*

'Cherubini's career is graphically described. Mr. Bellasis appears to be
intimately versed in the higher laws and beauties of musical composition.'—
Morning Post.

'We can recommend our readers to an ample and agreeably-written
biography of one of the greatest men of the century.'—*Sunday Times.*

'Will be of great service to musical students for the numerous facts it
contains, and for the evident care which the author has taken to insure cor-
rectness.'—*Illustrated Review.*

Louise Lateau of Bois d'Haine: her Life,

her Ecstasies, and her Stigmata: a Medical Study. By
Dr. F. LEFEBVRE, Professor of General Pathology and
Therapeutics in the Catholic University of Louvain, &c.
Translated from the French. Edited by Rev. J. SPENCER
NORTHCOTE, D.D. Full and complete edition. 3s. 6d.

'The name of Dr. Lefebvre is sufficient guarantee of the importance of
any work coming from his pen. The reader will find much valuable information.'—*Tablet.*

'The whole case thoroughly entered into and fully considered. The
Appendix contains many medical notes of interest.'—*Weekly Register.*

'A full and complete answer.'—*Catholic Times.*

Twelve New Tales. By Mrs. PARSONS.

1. Bertha's Three Fingers.   2. Take Care of Yourself.
3. Don't Go In.   4. The Story of an Arm-chair.   5. Yes
and No.   6. The Red Apples under the Tree.   7. Constance
and the Water Lilies.   8. The Pair of Gold Spectacles.
9. Clara's New Shawl.   10. The Little Lodgers.   11. The
Pride and the Fall.   12. This Once.

3d. each ; in a Packet complete, 3s.; or in cloth neat, 3s. 6d.

'Sound Catholic theology and a truly religious spirit breathes from every
page, and it may be safely commended to schools and convents.'—*Tablet.*

'Full of sound instruction given in a pointed and amusing manner.'—
Weekly Register.

'Very pretty, pleasantly told, attractive to little folks, and of such a
nature that from each some moral good is inculcated. The tales are cheerful,
sound, and sweet, and should have a large sale.'—*Catholic Times.*

'A very good collection of simple tales. The teaching is Catholic
throughout.'—*Catholic Opinion.*

Marie and Paul: a Fragment. By 'Our

Little Woman.'   3s. 6d.; gilt edges, 4s.

'We heartily recommend this touching little tale, especially as a present
for children and for schools, feeling sure that none can rise from its perusal
without being touched, both at the beauty of the tale itself and by the tone
of earnest piety which runs through the whole, leaving none but holy
thoughts and pleasant impressions on the minds of both old and young.'—
Tablet.

'Well adapted to the innocent minds it is intended for. The little book
would be a suitable present for a little friend.'—*Catholic Opinion.*

'A charming tale for young and old.'—*Cork Examiner.*

'To all who read it the book will suggest thoughts for which they will be
the better, while its graceful and affecting, because simple, pictures of home
and family life will excite emotions of which none need be ashamed.'—*Month.*

'Told effectively and touchingly, with all that tenderness and pathos in
which gifted women so much excel.'—*Weekly Register.*

'A very pretty and pathetic tale.'—*Catholic World.*

'A very charming story, and may be read by both young and old.'—
Brownson's Review.

'Presents us with some deeply-touching incidents of family love and
devotion.'—*Catholic Times.*

Dame Dolores, or the Wise Nun of Easton-
mere; and other Stories. By the Author of ' Tyborne,'
&c. 4*s.*

CONTENTS : I. The Wise Nun of Eastonmere. II.ᴬ
Known Too Late. III. True to the End. IV. Olive's
Rescue.

' We have read the volume with considerable pleasure, and we trust no
small profit. The tales are decidedly clever, well worked out, and written
with a flowing and cheerful pen.'—*Catholic Times.*

' The author of *Tyborne* is too well known to need any fresh recommendation to the readers of Catholic fiction. We need only say that her present
will be as welcome to her many friends as any of her former works.'—*Month.*

.' An attractive volume ; and we know of few tales that we can more safely
or more thoroughly recommend to our young readers.'—*Weekly Register.*

Maggie's Rosary, and other Tales. By the
Author of ' Marian Howard.' Cloth extra, 3*s.*; cheap edition, 2*s.*

' We strongly recommend these stories. They are especially suited to
little girls.'—*Tablet.*

' The very thing for a gift-book for a child ; but at the same time so interesting and full of incident that it will not be contemned by children of a
larger growth.'—*Weekly Register.*

' We have seldom seen tales better adapted for children's reading.'—
Catholic Times.

' The writer possesses in an eminent degree the art of making stories for
children.'—*Catholic Opinion,*

' A charming little book, which we can heartily recommend.'—*Rosarian.*

Scenes and Incidents at Sea. A new Selec-
tion. 1*s.* 4*d.*

CONTENTS : I. Adventure on a Rock. II. A Heroic
Act of Rescue. III. Inaccessible Islands. IV. The Ship-
wreck of the Czar Alexander. V. Captain James's Adven-
tures in the North Seas. VI. Destruction of Admiral Graves's
Fleet. VII. The Wreck of the Forfarshire, and Grace Darl-
ing. VIII. The Loss of the Royal George. IX. The Irish
Sailor Boy. X. Gallant Conduct of a French Privateer.
XI. The Harpooner. XII. The Cruise of the Agamemnon.
XIII. A Nova Scotia Fog. XIV. The Mate's Story. XV.
The Shipwreck of the Æneas Transport. XVI. A Scene
in the Shrouds. XVII. A Skirmish off Bermuda. XVIII.
Charles Wager. XIX. A Man Overboard. XX. A Loss
and a Rescue. XXI. A Melancholy Adventure on the
American Seas. XXII. Dolphins and Flying Fish.

History of England, for Family Use and the

Upper Classes of Schools. By the Author of 'Christian Schools and Scholars.' Second edition. With Preface by the Very Rev. Dr. NORTHCOTE. 6s.

Tales from the Diary of a Sister of Mercy.

By C. M. BRAME. New edition. Cloth extra, 4s.

CONTENTS : The Double Marriage. The Cross and the Crown. The Novice. The Fatal Accident. The Priest's Death. The Gambler's Wife. The Apostate. The Besetting Sin.

'Written in a chaste, simple, and touching style.'—*Tablet.*

' This book is a casket, and those who open it will find the gem within.'—*Register.*

'They are well and cleverly told, and the volume is neatly got up.'—*Month.*

'Very well told ; all full of religious allusions and expressions.'—*Star.*

'Very well written, and life-like ; many very pathetic.'—*Catholic Opinion.*

By the same,

Angels' Visits: a Series of Tales. With

Frontispiece and Vignette. 3s. 6d.

'The tone of the book is excellent, and it will certainly make itself a great favourite with the young.'—*Month.*

' Beautiful collection of Angel Stories.'—*Weekly Register.*

' One of the prettiest books for children we have seen.'—*Tablet.*

' A book which excites more than ordinary praise.'—*Northern Press.*

' Touchingly written, and evidently the emanation of a refined and pious mind.'—*Church Times.*

' A charming little book, full of beautiful stories of the family of angels.'—*Church Opinion.*

ST. JOSEPH'S THEOLOGICAL LIBRARY.

Edited by Fathers of the Society of Jesus.

Vol. I.

On some Popular Errors concerning Poli-

tics and Religion. By the Right Honourable Lord ROBERT MONTAGU, M.P. 6s.

CONTENTS : Introduction. I. The Basis of Political Science. II. Religion. III. The Church. IV. Religious Orders. V. Christian Law. VI. The Mass. VII. The Principles of 1789. VIII. Liberty. IX. Fraternity. X. Equality. XI. Nationality, Non-intervention, and the Accomplished Fact. XII. Capital Punishment. XIII. Liberal Catholics.

XIV. Civil Marriage.   XV. Secularisation of Education.
XVI. Conclusion.   Additional Notes.

This book has been taken from the 'Risposte popolari
alle obiezioni piu diffuse contro la Religione; opera del P.
Secondo Franco. Torino, 1868.' It is not a translation of
that excellent Italian work, for much has been omitted,
and even the forms of expression have not been retained ;
nor yet is it an abstract, for other matter has been added
throughout. The aim of the editor has been merely to follow out the intention of P. Franco, and adapt his thoughts
to the circumstances and mind of England.

Considerations for a Three Days' Preparation for Communion. Taken chiefly from the French of
SAINT JURE, S.J. By CECILIE MARY CADDELL. 8d.

'In every respect a most excellent manual.'—*Catholic Times.*
'A simple and easy method for a devout preparation for that solemn
duty.'—*Weekly Register.*
'A beautiful compilation carefully prepared.'—*Universe.*

The Spiritual Conflict and Conquest. By
Dom J. CASTANIZA, O.S.B. Edited, with Preface and Notes,
by Canon VAUGHAN, English Monk of the Order of St. Benedict. Reprinted from the old English Translation of 1652.
With fine Original Frontispiece reproduced in Autotype.
8s. 6d.

The Letter-Books of Sir Amias Poulet,
Keeper of Mary Queen of Scots. Edited by JOHN MORRIS,
Priest of the Society of Jesus. Demy 8vo, 10s. 6d.

Sir Amias Poulet had charge of the Queen of Scots from
April 1585 to the time of her death, February 8, 1587.
His correspondence with Lord-Treasurer Burghley and Sir
Francis Walsingham enters into the details of her life in
captivity at Tutbury, Chartley, and Fotheringay. Many of
the letters now published are entirely unknown, being printed
from a recently-discovered manuscript. The others have
been taken from the originals at the Public Record Office
and the British Museum. The letters are strung together by
a running commentary, in the course of which several of
Mr. Froude's statements are examined, and the question of
Mary's complicity in the plot against Elizabeth's life is
discussed.

Sœur Eugenie: the Life and Letters of a
Sister of Charity. By the Author of 'A Sketch of the Life of St. Paula.' Second edition, enlarged. On toned paper, cloth gilt, 4*s.* 6*d.*; plain paper, cloth plain, 3*s.*

'It is impossible to read it without bearing away in one's heart some of the "odour of sweetness" which breathes forth from almost every page.'—*Tablet.*

'The most charming piece of religious biography that has appeared since the *Récits d'une Sœur.*'—*Catholic Opinion.*

'We have seldom read a more touching tale of youthful holiness.'—*Weekly Register.*

'The picture of a life of hidden piety and grace, and of active charity, which it presents is extremely beautiful.'—*Nation.*

'We strongly recommend this devout and interesting life to the careful perusal of all our readers.'—*Westminster Gazette.*

Count de Montalembert's Letters to a School-
fellow, 1827-1830. Qualis ab incepto. Translated from the French by C. F. AUDLEY. With Portrait. 5*s.*

'Simple, easy, and unaffected in a degree, these letters form a really charming volume. The observations are simply wonderful, considering that when he wrote them he was only seventeen or eighteen years of age.'—*Weekly Register.*

'A new treasure is now presented for the first time in an English casket—the letters he wrote when a schoolboy. The loftiness of the aspirations they breathe is supported by the intellectual power of which they give evidence.'—*Cork Examiner.*

'Reveal in the future ecclesiastical champion and historian a depth of feeling and insight into forthcoming events hardly to be expected from a mere schoolboy.'—*Building News.*

'Display vigour of thought and real intellectual power.'—*Church Herald.*

Ecclesiastical Antiquities of London and its
Suburbs. By ALEXANDER WOOD, M.A. Oxon., of the Somerset Archæological Society. 5*s.*

'O, who the ruins sees, whom wonder doth not fill
With our great fathers' pompe, devotion, and their skill?'

'Will prove a most useful manual to many of our readers. Stores of Catholic memories still hang about the streets of this great metropolis. For the ancient and religious associations of such places the Catholic reader can want no better cicerone than Mr. Wood.'—*Weekly Register.*

'We have indeed to thank Mr. Wood for this excellent little book.'—*Catholic Opinion.*

'Very seldom have we read a book devoted entirely to the metropolis with such pleasure.'—*Liverpool Catholic Times.*

'A very pleasing and readable book.'—*Builder.*

'Gives a plain, sensible, but learned and interesting account of the chief church antiquities of London and its suburbs. It is written by a very able and competent author—one who thoroughly appreciates his subject, and who treats it with the discrimination of a critic and the sound common sense of a practised writer.'—*Church Herald.*

LIBRARY OF RELIGIOUS BIOGRAPHY.

Edited by EDWARD HEALY THOMPSON.

Vol. I.

The Life of St. Aloysius Gonzaga, S.J.   5s.

'Contains numberless traces of a thoughtful and tender devotion to the Saint. It shows a loving penetration into his spirit, and an appreciation of the secret motives of his action, which can only be the result of a deeply affectionate study of his life and character.'—*Month.*

Vol. II.

The Life of Marie Eustelle Harpain; or the Angel of the Eucharist.   5s.

'Possesses a special value and interest apart from its extraordinay natural and supernatural beauty, from the fact that to her example and to the effect of her writings is attributed in great measure the wonderful revival of devotion to the Blessed Sacrament in France, and consequently throughout Western Christendom.'—*Dublin Review.*

'A more complete instance of that life of purity and close union with God in the world of which we have just been speaking is to be found in the history of Marie Eustelle Harpain, the sempstress of Saint-Pallais. The writer of the present volume has had the advantage of very copious materials in the French works on which his own work is founded; and Mr. Thompson has discharged his office as editor with his usual diligence and accuracy.'—*Month.*

Vol. III.

The Life of St. Stanislas Kostka.   5s.

'We strongly recommend this biography to our readers.'—*Tablet.*

'There has been no adequate biography of St. Stanislas. In rectifying this want Mr. Thompson has earned a title to the gratitude of English-speaking Catholics. The engaging Saint of Poland will now be better known among us, and we need not fear that, better known, he will not be better loved.'—*Weekly Register.*

Vol. IV.

The Life of the Baron de Renty; or Perfection in the World exemplified.   6s.

'An excellent book. The style is throughout perfectly fresh and buoyant.' —*Dublin Review.*

'This beautiful work is a compilation, not of biographical incidents, but of holy thoughts and spiritual aspirations, which we may feed on and make our own.'—*Tablet.*

'Gives full particulars of his marvellous virtue in an agreeable form.'— *Catholic Times.*

'A good book for our Catholic young men, teaching how they can sanctify the secular state.'—*Catholic Opinion.*

'Edifying and instructive, a beacon and guide to those whose walks are in the ways of the world, who toil and strive to win Christian perfection.'— *Ulster Examiner.*

Vol. V.

The Life of the Venerable Anna Maria

Taigi, the Roman Matron (1769-1837). Second edition. With Portrait. 6s.

This Biography has been written after a careful collation of previous Lives of the Servant of God with each other, and with the *Analecta Juris Pontificii,* which contain large extracts from the Processes. Various prophecies attributed to her and other holy persons have been collected in an Appendix.

'Of all the series of deeply-interesting biographies which the untiring zeal and piety of Mr. Healy Thompson has given of late years to English Catholics, none, we think, is to be compared in interest with the one before us, both from the absorbing nature of the life itself and the spiritual lessons it conveys.'—*Tablet.*

'A complete biography of the Venerable Matron in the composition of which the greatest care has been taken and the best authorities consulted. We can safely recommend the volume for the discrimination with which it has been written, and for the careful labour and completeness by which it has been distinguished.'—*Catholic Opinion.*

'We recommend this excellent and carefully-compiled biography to all our readers. The evident care exercised by the editor in collating the various lives of Anna Maria gives great value to the volume, and we hope it will meet with the support it so justly merits.'—*Westminster Gazette.*

'We thank Mr. Healy Thompson for this volume. The direct purpose of his biographies is always spiritual edification.'—*Dublin Review.*

'Contains much that is capable of nourishing pious sentiments.'—*Nation.*

'Has evidently been a labour of love.'—*Month.*

The Hidden Life of Jesus: a Lesson and

Model to Christians. Translated from the French of BOUDON, by EDWARD HEALY THOMPSON, M.A. Cloth, 3s.

'This profound and valuable work has been very carefully and ably translated by Mr. Thompson.'—*Register.*

'The more we have of such works as the *Hidden Life of Jesus* the better.'—*Westminster Gazette.*

'A book of searching power.'—*Church Review.*

'We have often regretted that this writer's works are not better known.'—*Universe.*

'We earnestly recommend its study and practice to all readers.'—*Tablet.*

'We have to thank Mr. Thompson for this translation of a valuable work which has long been popular in France.'—*Dublin Review.*

'A good translation.'—*Month.*

Also, by the same Author and Translator,

Devotion to the Nine Choirs of Holy Angels,
and especially to the Angel Guardians.   3*s.*

'We congratulate Mr. Thompson on the way in which he has accomplished his task, and we earnestly hope that an increased devotion to the Holy Angels may be the reward of his labour of love.'—*Tablet.*

'A beautiful translation.'—*Month.*

'The translation is extremely well done.'—*Weekly Register.*

New Meditations for each Day in the Year,
on the *Life of our Lord Jesus Christ.* By a Father of the Society of Jesus. With the imprimatur of his Grace the Archbishop of Westminster. New and improved edition. Two vols. Cloth, 9*s.*; also in calf, 16*s.*; morocco, 17*s.*

'We can heartily recommend this book for its style and substance ; it bears with it several strong recommendations. . . . It is solid and practical.' —*Westminster Gazette.*

'A work of great practical utility, and we give it our earnest recommendation.'—*Weekly Register.*

The Day Sanctified; being Meditations and
Spiritual Readings for Daily Use. Selected from the Works of Saints and approved Writers of the Catholic Church. Fcp. cloth, 3*s.* 6*d.*; red edges, 4*s.*

'Of the many volumes of meditations on sacred subjects which have appeared in the last few years, none has seemed to us so well adapted to its object as the one before us.'—*Tablet.*

'Deserves to be specially mentioned.'—*Month.*

'Admirable in every sense.'—*Church Times.*

'Many of the meditations are of great beauty. . . . They form, in fact, excellent little sermons, and we have no doubt will be largely used as such.' —*Literary Churchman.*

Reflections and Prayers for Holy Com-
munion. Translated from the French. With Preface by his Grace the ARCHBISHOP OF WESTMINSTER. Fcp. 8vo, cloth, 4*s.* 6*d.*; bound, red edges, 5*s.*; calf, 9*s.*; morocco, 10*s.*

'The Archbishop has marked his approval of the work by writing a preface for it, and describes it as "a valuable addition to our books of devotion."'—*Register.*

'A book rich with the choicest and most profound Catholic devotions.'— *Church Review.*

Lallemant's Doctrine of the Spiritual Life.
Edited by the late Father FABER. New edition. Cloth,
4*s*. 6*d*.

'This excellent work has a twofold value, being both a biography and a
volume of meditations. It contains an elaborate analysis of the wants, dangers, trials, and aspirations of the inner man, and supplies to the thoughtful
and devout reader the most valuable instructions for the attainment of heavenly wisdom, grace, and strength.'—*Catholic Times.*

'A treatise of the very highest value.'—*Month.*

'The treatise is preceded by a short account of the writer's life, and has
had the wonderful advantage of being edited by the late Father Faber.'—
Weekly Register.

The Rivers of Damascus and Jordan: a
Causerie. By a Tertiary of the Order of St. Dominic. 4*s*.

'Good solid reading.'—*Month.*

'Well done and in a truly charitable spirit.'—*Catholic Opinion.*

'It treats the subject in so novel and forcible a light that we are fascin-
ated in spite of ourselves, and irresistibly led on to follow its arguments and
rejoice at its conclusions.'—*Tablet.*

Legends of our Lady and the Saints; or
our Children's Book of Stories in Verse. Written for the
Recitations of the Pupils of the Schools of the Holy Child
Jesus, St. Leonard's-on-Sea. 2*s*. 6*d*.

'It is a beautiful religious idea that is realised in the *Legends of our
Lady and the Saints.* The book forms a charming present for pious children.'—*Tablet.*

'The "Legends" are so beautiful that they ought to be read by all lovers
of poetry.'—*Bookseller.*

'Graceful poems.'—*Month.*

The New Testament Narrative, in the Words
of the Sacred Writers. With Notes, Chronological Tables,
and Maps. Cloth, 2*s*.

'The compilers deserve great praise for the manner in which they have
performed their task. We commend this little volume as well and carefully
printed, and as furnishing its readers, moreover, with a great amount of useful information in the tables inserted at the end.'—*Month.*

'It is at once clear, complete, and beautiful.'—*Catholic Opinion.*

QUARTERLY SERIES.

Conducted by the Managers of the 'Month.'

———o———

VOLUMES PUBLISHED.

The Life and Letters of St. Francis Xavier.
By the Rev. H. J. COLERIDGE.   Sec. edit.   Two vols. 18*s.*

'We cordially thank Father Coleridge for a most valuable biography. . . . He has spared no pains to insure our having in good classical English a translation of all the letters which are extant. . . . A complete priest's manual might be compiled from them, entering as they do into all the details of a missioner's public and private life. . . . We trust we have stimulated our readers to examine them for themselves, and we are satisfied that they will return again and again to them as to a never-exhausted source of interest and edification.'—*Tablet.*

'A noble addition to our literature. . . . We offer our warmest thanks to Father Coleridge for this most valuable work.   The letters, we need hardly say, will be found of great spiritual use, especially for missionaries and priests.'—*Dublin Review.*

'One of the most fascinating books we have met with for a long time.'—*Catholic Opinion.*

'Would that we had many more lives of saints like this! Father Coleridge has done great service to this branch of Catholic literature, not simply by writing a charming book, but especially by setting others an example of how a saint's life should be written.'—*Westminster Gazette.*

'This valuable book is destined, we feel assured, to take a high place among what we may term our English Catholic classics. . . . The great charm lies in the letters, for in them we have, in a far more forcible manner than any biographer could give them, the feelings, experiences, and aspirations of St. Francis Xavier as pictured by his own pen.'—*Catholic Times.*

'Father Coleridge does his own part admirably, and we shall not be surprised to find his book soon take its place as the standard Life of the saintly and illustrious Francis.'—*Nation.*

'Not only an interesting but a scholarly sketch of a life remarkable alike in itself and in its attendant circumstances. We hope the author will continue to labour in a department of literature for which he has here shown his aptitude. To find a saint's life which is at once moderate, historical, and appreciative is not a common thing.'—*Saturday Review.*

'Should be studied by all missionaries, and is worthy of a place in every Christian library.'—*Church Herald.*

The Life of St. Jane Frances Fremyot de

Chantal. By EMILY BOWLES. With Preface by the Rev. H. J. COLERIDGE. Second edition. 5s. 6d.

'We venture to promise great pleasure and profit to the reader of this charming biography. It gives a complete and faithful portrait of one of the most attractive saints of the generation which followed the completion of the Council of Trent.'—*Month.*

'Sketched in a life-like manner, worthy of her well-earned reputation as a Catholic writer.'—*Weekly Register.*

'We have read it on and on with the fascination of a novel, and yet it is the life of a saint, described with a rare delicacy of touch and feeling such as is seldom met with.'—*Tablet.*

'A very readable and interesting compilation. . . . The author has done her work faithfully and conscientiously.'—*Athenæum.*

'Full of incident, and told in a style so graceful and felicitous that it wins upon the reader with every page.'—*Nation.*

'Miss Bowles has done her work in a manner which we cannot better commend than by expressing a desire that she may find many imitators. She has endued her materials with life, and clothed them with a language and a style of which we do not know what to admire most—the purity, the grace, the refinement, or the elegance. If our readers wish to know the value and the beauty of this book, they can do no better than get it and read it.'—*Westminster Gazette.*

'One of the most charming and delightful volumes which has issued from the press for many years. Miss Bowles has accomplished her task faithfully and happily, with simple grace and unpretentious language, and a winning manner which, independently of her subject, irresistibly carries us along.'—*Ulster Examiner.*

The History of the Sacred Passion. From

the Spanish of Father LUIS DE LA PALMA, of the Society of Jesus. The Translation revised and edited by the Rev. H. J. COLERIDGE. Second edition. 7s. 6d.

'A work long held in great and just repute in Spain. It opens a mine of wealth to one's soul. Though there are many works on the Passion in English, probably none will be found so generally useful both for spiritual reading and meditation. We desire to see it widely circulated.'—*Tablet.*

'A sterling work of the utmost value, proceeding from the pen of a great theologian, whose piety was as simple and tender as his learning and culture were profound and exquisite. It is a rich storehouse for contemplation on the great mystery of our Redemption, and one of those books which every Catholic ought to read for himself.'—*Weekly Register.*

'The most wonderful work upon the Passion that we have ever read. To us the charm lies in this, that it is entirely theological. It is made use of largely by those who give the Exercises of St. Ignatius; it is, as it were, the flesh upon the skeleton of the Exercises. Never has the Passion been meditated upon so before. . . . If any one wishes to understand the Passion of our Lord in its fulness, let him procure this book.'—*Dublin Review.*

'We have not read a more thoughtful work on our Blessed Lord's Passion.

It is a complete storehouse of matter for meditation, and for sermons on that divine mystery.'—*Catholic Opinion.*

'The book is—speaking comparatively of human offerings—a magnificent offering to the Crucified, and to those who wish to make a real study of the Cross will be a most precious guide.'—*Church Review.*

Ierne of Armorica: a Tale of the Time of Chlovis. By J. C. BATEMAN. 6s. 6d.

'We know of few tales of the kind that can be ranked higher than the beautiful story before us. The author has hit on the golden mean between an over-display of antiquarianism and an indolent transfer of modern modes of action and thought to a distant time. The descriptions are masterly, the characters distinct, the interest unflagging. We may add that the period is one of those which may be said to be comparatively unworked.'—*Month.*

'A volume of very great interest and very great utility. As a story it is sure to give much delight, while, as a story founded on historical fact, it will benefit all by its very able reproduction of very momentous scenes. . . . The book is excellent. If we are to have a literature of fiction at all, we hope it will include many like volumes.'—*Dublin Review.*

'Although a work of fiction, it is historically correct, and the author portrays with great skill the manners and customs of the times of which he professes to give a description. In reading this charming tale we seem to be taken by the hand by the writer, and made to assist at the scenes which he describes.'—*Tablet.*

'The author of this most interesting tale has hit the happy medium between a display of antiquarian knowledge and a mere reproduction in distant ages of commonplace modern habits of thought. The descriptions are excellent, the characters well drawn, and the subject itself is very attractive, besides having the advantage of not having been written threadbare.'—*Westminster Gazette.*

'The tale is excessively interesting, the language appropriate to the time and rank of the characters, the style flowing and easy, and the narrative leads one on and on until it becomes a very difficult matter to lay the book down until it is finished. . . . It is a valuable addition to Catholic fictional literature.'—*Catholic Times.*

'A very pretty historico-ecclesiastical novel of the times of Chlovis. It i full of incident, and is very pleasant reading.'—*Literary Churchman.*

The Life of Dona Luisa de Carvajal. By Lady GEORGIANA FULLERTON. 6s. (See p. 5.)

The Life of the Blessed John Berchmans. By the Rev. FRANCIS GOLDIE, S.J. 6s.

'A complete and life-like picture, and we are glad to be able to congratulate Father Goldie on his success.'—*Tablet.*

'Drawn up with a vigour and freedom which show great power of biographical writing.'—*Dublin Review.*

'One of the most interesting of all.'—*Weekly Register.*

. 'Unhesitatingly we say that it is the very best Life of Blessed John

Berchmans, and as such it will take rank with religious biographies of the highest merit.'—*Catholic Times.*

'Is of great literary merit, the style being marked by elegance and a complete absence of redundancy.'—*Cork Examiner.*

'This delightful and edifying volume is of the deepest interest. The perusal will afford both pleasure and profit.'—*Church Herald.*

The Life of the Blessed Peter Favre, of the

Society of Jesus, First Companion of St. Ignatius Loyola. From the Italian of Father GIUSEPPE BOERO, of the same Society. With Preface by the Rev. H. J. COLERIDGE. 6*s.* 6*d.*

This Life has been written on the occasion of the beatification of the Ven. Peter Favre, and contains the *Memoriale* or record of his private thoughts and meditations, written by himself.

'At once a book of spiritual reading, and also an interesting historical narrative. The *Memoriale, or Spiritual Diary,* is here translated at full length, and is the most precious portion of one of the most valuable biographies we know.'—*Tablet.*

'A perfect picture drawn from the life, admirably and succinctly told. The *Memoriale* will be found one of the most admirable epitomes of sound devotional reading.'—*Weekly Register.*

'The *Memoriale* is hardly excelled in interest by anything of the kind now extant.'—*Catholic Times.*

'Full of interest, instruction, and example.'—*Cork Examiner.*

'One of the most interesting to the general reader of the entire series up to this time.'—*Nation.*

'This wonderful diary, the *Memoriale,* has never been published before, and we are much mistaken if it does not become a cherished possession to thoughtful Catholics.'—*Month.*

The Dialogues of St. Gregory the Great.

An old English version. Edited, with Preface, by the Rev. H. J. COLERIDGE. 6*s.*

'The Catholic world must feel grateful to Father Coleridge for this excellent and compendious edition. The subjects treated of possess at this moment a special interest. . . . The Preface by Father Coleridge is interesting and well written, and we cordially recommend the book to the perusal of all.'—*Tablet.*

'This is a most interesting book. . . . Father Coleridge gives a very useful preface summarising the contents.'—*Weekly Register.*

'We have seldom taken up a book in which we have become at once so deeply interested. It will suit any one; it will teach all : it will confirm any who require that process; and it will last and be read when other works are quite forgotten.'—*Catholic Times.*

'Edited and published with the utmost care and the most perfect literary taste, this volume adds one more gem to the treasury of English Catholic literature.'—*New York Catholic World.*

The Life of Sister Anne Catherine Emme-
rich. Edited, with Preface, by the Rev. H. J. COLERIDGE.
5*s.*

Holywell and its Pilgrims. By the Author
of 'Tyborne.' 1*s.*

Summer Talks about Lourdes. By Miss
CADDELL. Cloth, 1*s.* 6*d.*

Blessed Margaret Mary Alacoque: a brief
and popular Account of her Life; to which are added
Selections from some of her Sayings, and the Decree of her
Beatification. By the Rev. CHARLES B. GARSIDE, M.A.
1*s.*

A Comparison between the History of the
Church and the Prophecies of the Apocalypse. Translated
from the German by EDWIN DE LISLE. 2*s.*

CATHOLIC-TRUTH TRACTS.

NEW ISSUES.

Manchester Dialogues. First Series. By the
Rev. Fr. HARPER, S.J.

    No. I. The Pilgrimage.
       II. Are Miracles going on still?
      III. Popish Miracles tested by the Bible.
      IV. Popish Miracles.
       V. Liquefaction of the Blood of St. Januarius.
     VI. 'Bleeding Nuns' and 'Winking Madonnas.'
    VII. Are Miracles physically possible?
   VIII. Are Miracles morally possible?

Price of each 3*s.* per 100, 25 for 1*s.*; also 25 of the above
assorted for 1*s.* Also the whole Series complete in neat Wrap-
per, 6*d.*

Specimen Packet of General Series, containing 100 assorted,
1*s.* 6*d.*

www.ingramcontent.com/pod-product-compliance
Lightning Source LLC
Chambersburg PA
CBHW032003110726
47901CB00004B/949